The Abinger Edition
of E. M. Forster

Edited by
ELIZABETH HEINE

Volume 2

E. M. Forster dedicated
The Longest Journey:

FRATRIBUS

The Longest Journey

E. M. Forster

Edward Arnold

© 1907, 1984 The Provost and Scholars of King's College, Cambridge
Introduction and other editorial matter copyright © 1984 Elizabeth
Heine

First published in Great Britain 1984 by
Edward Arnold (Publishers) Ltd, 41 Bedford Square, London WC1B 3DQ

Edward Arnold (Australia) Pty Ltd, 80 Waverley Road, Caulfield East,
Victoria 3145, Australia

British Library Cataloguing in Publication Data

Forster, E. M.
   The longest journey.—(The Abinger edition
of E. M. Forster; v. 2)
   I. Title   II. Series
   823'.912[F]   PR6011.O58

   ISBN 0–7131–6421–2

Text set in 11/12 pt Baskerville
Printed and bound by
Richard Clay (The Chaucer Press) Ltd, Bungay, Suffolk

Contents

Editor's Introduction

First published in April 1907, *The Longest Journey* is E. M. Forster's least known, most difficult, most personal novel, rich and adventurous in its complexity of symbolism and subtlety of structure, profound in the simplicity of its approach to the philosophical ideals of turn-of-the-century Cambridge, at once ambiguous and severe in its testing of these ideals in the realities of fiction. In *The Longest Journey* Forster borrows the patterns of Greek drama, Christian religion, and Wagnerian myth in order to question the nature of reality and the relativities of individual perceptions. "Real" and "really" become highly suspect words as they recur in the speeches of his middle-class English characters, and the revelation of at least one of the "realities" is intended to surprise both the hero and the reader, so that those approaching the novel for the first time should be warned away from all introductions, even Forster's, though it prefaces the novel here. (This is the warning!) On subsequent readings the ironies become classically fateful and the echoes more and more audible, resonating with increasing power.

Forster's introduction, which should be read before this one (and after the novel), was written in 1960 for the Oxford World's Classics edition of *The Longest Journey*. In this volume of the Abinger Edition it is supplemented by the two memoirs, printed here as Appendix B, on which he drew for his recollections. Appendix A reprints his review of Graham Greene's *The Old School*, a collection of essays by various writers which moved Forster, in 1934, to resurrect Agnes and Herbert Pembroke, the two characters from his then "forgotten" novel who are most closely associated with "the idea, or ideal, of the British Public School", as he puts it in his introductory list of the ideas that were "whirling around" him as he wrote *The Longest Journey* (p. lxvii below). Appendix C describes the manuscripts of the novel and prints the drafts which best illustrate Forster's complex restructuring of the story; these include three discarded chapters, one of them complete and one the nearly complete "fantasy" chapter he refers to in his introduction.

The appendices move backward in time from first to last; the two memoirs, editorially entitled "My Books and I" and "Uncle Willie", were read to the Bloomsbury Memoir Club sometime in the early 1920s, before the publication of *A Passage to India* in 1924, and their sardonic tone reflects the Freudian psychological awareness of their audience. Forster quarried "My Books and I" also in 1947, for his introduction to his *Collected Short Stories*, and again in 1953, for his answers to the questions asked in the interview published in the first issue of the *Paris Review*. "My Books and I" is central to any account of Forster's writing career and should be read in conjunction with *Anonymity*, published by Leonard and Virginia Woolf as a Hogarth Essay in 1925 but drafted first in 1923, when Forster was writing his still-unnamed "Indian novel".[1] In both memoirs, as in his refusal to specify the "truth" of the sexual assault (real or imagined?) in *A Passage to India*, Forster resists the idea that analytical investigations of sexual histories are necessarily helpful, either to the person analysed or to the writer who would express the full complexity of an individual like his Uncle Willie, who, he tells us, was the model for Mrs Failing, the aunt in *The Longest Journey*.

In "Uncle Willie" Forster is nonetheless relatively explicit about the oddities of his uncle's interest in young girls. In both memoirs he is also open in his references to his own homosexuality, although in "My Books and I" he insists that in his young manhood he was ignorant of the connections between his homosexual desires and his creativity. In his introduction to *The Longest Journey*, however, he leaves the particular nature of the "junction of mind with heart" that helped to inspire the book implicit, latent, as it is in the novel itself. There Forster's semi-autobiographical hero, Rickie Elliot, full of idealism and hope and gifted with an imagination of unusual symbolic intensity, misleads himself through his conventional desire for marriage and fatherhood. To most readers Rickie seems well worth saving, and the pain of his decay and death has caused the novel to be read as some kind of coming-of-age for its author, a coming to terms with a life which forgoes the possibility of

[1] In 1951 Forster reprinted *Anonymity* in *Two Cheers for Democracy* (vol. 11, Abinger Edition, 1972). He had read an early version of the essay at Cheltenham in March 1923, on a visit to his friend L. H. C. Shuttleworth; in a letter written on the flyleaf of a presentation copy of *Pharos and Pharillon* (1923), now owned by Hugh Lyon, he thanked Shuttleworth for spotting a logical fault in the essay, by then corrected for the next reading, in Cambridge. The Hogarth pamphlet was dedicated "To L.H.C.S.", in memory of Shuttleworth. Full bibliographical details of Forster's publications, including interviews, are given by B. J. Kirkpatrick, *A Bibliography of E. M. Forster*, rev. ed. (London, Rupert Hart-Davis, 1968).

procreation.[2] There is also some evidence in the manuscripts, as in the plot of the novel, that the Freudian elements in Forster's Bloomsbury memoirs need to be contrasted with the turn-of-the-century belief that homosexuality could be both innate and inheritable; it is probable that Rickie's hereditary lameness is a less obscure symbol of homosexuality than post-Freudians might think.

Written at the age of eighty-one, Forster's introduction elegantly epitomizes most of the themes of the novel and many of the autobiographical realities on which it is based. This editorial introduction deals primarily with what he omits or glances over and secondarily with matters of influence that are too complicated for explanation in the General Notes. References to Richard Strauss or Henry James or George Meredith are easily noted as part of the up-to-date intellectual equipment of 1905. Much more intricate are Forster's experiments with new techniques of narrative structure, unmentioned in his introduction. Here they are outlined first in order to establish the symbolic nature of the novel before considering the broader questions of the philosophical influence of "the Cambridge of G. E. Moore", identified so briefly in Forster's introduction, and the different sources of the mystical and Hegelian elements in the novel, apparently so incongruent with the ideas of Moore. The philosophical and ethical values of *The Longest Journey* interlink directly with Forster's most personal struggles with his homosexuality, his family and his friends; accounts of the values and "realities" of the novel often conjoin below as its evolution is described. A summary of the manuscript changes then concludes this introduction, returning also to Forster's deliberate use of a system of symbolic leitmotivs in the structure of the novel. The system creates the rhythm of "repetition plus variation", so familiar in *A Passage to India*, that Forster describes in *Aspects of the Novel* (1927). Moreover, in *The Longest Journey* as in the later novel Forster also strove to create what he terms a greater, symphonic "rhythm", a narrative structure "not rounding off but opening out".[3]

---

[2] For interesting analyses of Rickie's latent homosexuality in books written before Forster's death, see Frederick C. Crews, *E. M. Forster and the Perils of Humanism* (Princeton, Princeton Univ. Press; London, Oxford Univ. Press, 1962) and Wilfrid Stone, *The Cave and the Mountain* (Stanford, Stanford Univ. Press; London, Oxford Univ. Press, 1966). Frederick P. W. McDowell's *E. M. Forster: An Annotated Bibliography of Writings About Him* (De Kalb, Northern Illinois Univ. Press, 1977) is an excellent guide to critical writings up to 1975.

[3] *Aspects of the Novel* (vol. 12, Abinger Edition, 1973), pp. 115–16.

SYMBOLS AND ANALOGUES

Forster's characteristic method of structuring a novel by means of underlying "rhythms" comes to its first fruition in *The Longest Journey*, but the strikingly modern qualities of the novel have not been fully recognized. Here Forster's transference of musical forms to literature and his adoption of the shapes of mythic narrative foreshadow the techniques of James Joyce and T. S. Eliot. Similar too is the counterpoint of classical to modern, most comically ironic when Rickie Elliot, who believes Theocritus "to be the greatest of Greek poets" (p. 5), cannot bring himself to listen to the rudeness of the bucolic singing contest conducted in Chapter 12 by a stray soldier and Stephen Wonham, his still undiscovered illegitimate half-brother. Rickie leaves in disgust, ready to believe that Stephen is "bad inherently" (p. 192). Like T. S. Eliot in *The Waste Land*, Forster too uses his knowledge of Sir James Frazer's *Golden Bough* (1890) and, very probably, Jessie Weston's *Legends of the Wagner Drama: Studies in Mythology and Romance* (1896); the blood brothers of the novel are not only classically heroic, contrasting like Hercules and Orpheus, but also mythically twinned as Siegfried and Parsifal, and they redeem each other from the despair of misused sexuality and the dissolution of drunkenness through ritual passages of fire and water.[4] All that is lacking for full "modernity" is the break from conventional prose into something like stream-of-consciousness writing, and the discarded "fantasy" chapter shows Forster struggling to reach such a mode. But he found that "it shifted the vision too far round".[5] He chose instead to illuminate the subconscious realities of his characters through their actions and dreams, measured always against the developing symbolism of the novel, for in *The Longest Journey* whatever is at the heart of a

[4] See John Magnus, "Ritual Aspects of E. M. Forster's *The Longest Journey*" (*Modern Fiction Studies*, vol. 13, no. 2 [Summer 1967], pp. 195–210), for a suggestive account of the correspondences to the rituals analysed by the turn-of-the-century Cambridge anthropologists, and see George H. Thomson, *The Fiction of E. M. Forster* (Detroit, Wayne State Univ. Press, 1967), for further analyses of Forster's use of myth and symbol. Miss Weston considers Parsifal an English equivalent of Siegfried; her still fascinating book was then the most comprehensive explanation of Wagner's use of myths available in English. Wagner's operas were at that time very much a staple of Covent Garden seasons, the complete Ring Cycle being performed about every two years and *Siegfried* much more often, but in "Revolution at Bayreuth" (*The Listener*, 4 Nov. 1954, pp. 755–7), Forster writes that he "first heard 'The Ring' exactly fifty years ago at Dresden". The year was in fact 1905 (see p. xlvii below).

[5] Letter to E. J. Dent, April 1907, *Selected Letters of E. M. Forster: Volume One, 1879–1920*, eds. Mary Lago and P. N. Furbank (London, Collins, 1983), p. 87.

series of concentric circles, whether the circles in turn enclose or are enclosed by squares or lawns or books or turnips, is "real".

In the non-fictional world, the Figsbury Rings of Wiltshire, renamed "Cadbury Rings" in the novel, are the "real" basis for the symbol. As Forster explains, it was at the Figsbury Rings that his conversation with a club-footed shepherd boy enriched his conception of the novel, already planned as an opposition between the philosophical ideals of Cambridge and the conventional mores of "Sawston", the suburban town modelled on Tonbridge, Kent, and used in his first novel, *Where Angels Fear to Tread* (1905), and in his earlier attempt at a novel, *Nottingham Lace*.[6] Forster also tells us that in *The Longest Journey* it is Stewart Ansell who is "high-priest" of the Cambridge that "sought for reality and cared for truth", and it should be added that the dedication of the novel "to the brothers", *Fratribus*, acknowledges both the questions of blood brotherhood so fundamental to the story and the bonds of the intellectual brethren of the secret Cambridge Conversazione Society to which Forster belonged, more commonly known as the Apostles. At the end of the first chapter, which, like an overture, introduces the themes and "rhythms" of the novel as a whole, it is Ansell, Rickie's Cambridge "brother", who sketches squares within circles as he gives his extraordinary warning against "the subjective product of a diseased imagination", mistakenly invested with "the semblance of reality" (p. 17). Ansell's ideal reality appears to be wholly abstract, to be sought only in the great circular reading-room of the British Museum, where the ground-plan reflects his sketch, until Stephen Wonham presses his skull into the earth of a circular flower-bed in a squared garden and Ansell recognizes this "momentary contact with reality" (p. 222), then "joins up with Stephen and strikes" (p. lxviii).

For Rickie Elliot the circles enclose the chthonic secrets of generation, of ancestry and progeny, of life and death. He tells the history of his dead parents in the chalk-encircled dell near Madingley (in fact real, like the Figsbury Rings and the British Museum). He beholds love when he sees an engaged couple, Agnes Pembroke and Gerald Dawes, embracing in the "lover's bower" of another squared garden, and in a week Gerald is suddenly dead. Two years later Rickie becomes engaged to Agnes in the Madingley dell; then, acceding to the demands of her conventional

---

[6] The village of Sawston, south of Cambridge, provides only the name for Forster's fictional suburban town, which in *The Longest Journey* seems to be somewhat closer to London than Tonbridge actually is. *Nottingham Lace* has been published in *Arctic Summer and Other Fiction* (vol. 9, Abinger Edition, 1980).

morality, he denies the reality of Stephen, revealed to be his brother at the very centre of the Cadbury Rings. Thus Rickie's soul is corrupted and his later perception of the coming birth of his child as another step in the orderings of circles and squares (p. 183) comes to nothing when his lame little daughter dies. The illegitimate and unconventional Stephen Wonham, by contrast, lives so close to natural realities that even his room is neither square nor circle, though more encircled than conventionally squared: "no ceiling, unless you count the walls, no walls unless you count the ceiling" (p. 118). This attic room, introduced as a lapse intrinsic to such domestication of the classical Greek form, is equipped with a round window and a trap-door, is shared with the elements—the cistern and the chimney and the wind—and is guarded by a picture of the statue of the Demeter of Cnidus, the earth-goddess whose same statue silently rebukes Ansell's ignorance of procreation in the rectangular halls of the British Museum (p. 182). In the last paragraphs of the novel Stephen, out on the downs of Wiltshire, gazes over his sleeping daughter toward the Rings and knows himself to be the guardian of the "paths between" the generations. He has preserved the physical inheritance he shared with his brother, whose novel and stories are gaining intellectual immortality as well. And Stewart Ansell, to judge by the intimate use of his first name, now lives with Stephen's family; he is at least "in the house".

By such methods Forster builds *The Longest Journey*, making his realistic settings carry an increasing symbolic weight. The technique is common to all his novels, but the underlying structure of *The Longest Journey* is most similar to that of *A Passage to India*. The ease and flexibility with which Forster adapts the musical variability of leitmotivs to fiction is remarkable, but what is most unusual about his pursuit of "rhythm" is that he also finds meaning to match the interrelationships of the larger divisions of these two novels; they share a triadic structure which is at once symphonic and Hegelian, the characters advancing toward truth through a process of negation. "Cambridge", "Sawston" and "Wiltshire" identify the same testing and relearning of values as "Mosque", "Caves" and "Temple", although the values differ; "truth" or "reality" is discoverable in *The Longest Journey*, for ever unknown in *A Passage to India*. Both novels use a geometric set of leitmotivs as well. The arches of the mosques in the later novel expand into the hemispheres of caves and temple domes and overarching sky, and the most elemental substance of the leitmotivs is also similar; earth and stone, rain and water, sun and stars are homely in the earlier novel, exotic in the later. *A Passage to India* is also more subtle, for *The Longest Journey* is pointedly ornamented not only with "rhythmic" symbols but also with the classical and Wagnerian allusions that specify the analogues in characters and events. It seems incredible, especially since Forster's interest in Wagner and his use of Beethoven's Fifth Symphony in *Howards End* (1910) are well known, that no one has recognized his development of the piano chords from the "Prelude to Rhinegold" which accompany Agnes at her first entrance (see p. 5 and note). At the end of the first chapter it is Rickie's enraptured account of the coincidence of the piano-playing that provokes Ansell's warning about the "diseased imagination", but Rickie continues to idealize Agnes, and the Wagnerian association prepares the way for the description of the full orchestration of the same chords which is used to express his response to the embrace of the lovers (p. 40). Usually this description is regarded as an embarrassingly purple passage which must be carefully attributed only to Rickie, not to Forster, whose narrative voice in this novel modulates into the "tone of mind", so to speak, of the character it is presenting, and therefore often seems inseparable from the thoughts of Rickie Elliot. But Forster's presentation of Rickie's response to love is more easily perceived to be ironic when its musical correlative is recognized.[7]

The further Wagnerian analogues in *The Longest Journey* are suggestive rather than exact. Rickie is at first similar to Alberich in *Das Rheingold*, yearning for love and dazzled by its gleam. In time he becomes Parsifal, suffering because he has lost the Holy Grail (p. 153) by not asking the question that would have revealed his brother's full identity.[8] Most of the references, however, are to the Ring Cycle. Stephen, as Forster tells us (p. lxix), is Siegfried, and Forster's biographer, P. N. Furbank, points out that the discarded "fantasy" chapter which sends the Stephen character, there called "Harold", mad in the woods, was probably an analogue to

---

[7] New to Wagner studies, I am indebted to Peter Burbidge for confirming my guess and assuring me that the passage is in fact a recognizably realistic description of the music rather than, as I had long thought myself, an idealistic fancy. The ambiguities and power of Forster's narrative voice have been analysed by James McConkey in *The Novels of E. M. Forster* (Ithaca, Cornell Univ. Press, 1957; London, Oxford Univ. Press, 1958), by John Colmer in *E. M. Forster: The Personal Voice* (London and Boston, Routledge & Kegan Paul, 1975), and by Barbara Rosecrance in *Forster's Narrative Vision* (Ithaca and London, Cornell Univ. Press, 1982).

[8] See Tony Brown's essay, "E. M. Forster's *Parsifal*: A Reading of *The Longest Journey*" (*Journal of European Studies*, vol. 12, part 1, no. 45 [March 1982], pp. 30–54), to which I am indebted, for an example of how the novel as a whole can be fitted to *Parsifal* alone.

Siegfried's colloquy with the forest bird.[9] Forster in his introduction describes the chapter not quite as it is, perhaps fulfilling or recalling his earlier Wagnerian intentions by adding, even so late, that "the animals recognize" the hero. Certainly the name "Siegfried" does not survive in the manuscripts, though Forster recollects it as one of Stephen's names, and his memory may have again transformed intention into execution, or recalled some lost draft. Stephen's mythic model explains why he is conceived in Scandinavia; his mysterious birth and casual upbringing are very much those of the archetypal hero, as his guardian, Mrs Failing, tells us, likening herself to the dragon so often associated with Teutonic heroes (p. 102). Part of the fun of the novel arises when Forster introduces such a hero into conventional drawing-rooms; Agnes recognizes Forster's purpose in Rickie: "He muddles all day with poetry and old dead people, and then tries to bring it into life. It's too funny for words." (p. 50) Agnes herself, ideally, from Rickie's point of view, is Brünnhilde (p. 82), and the drafts of Chapter 31 show that Forster tried to send her into a fire after the eruption of her suppressed longing for her dead first love, brought to the surface when Stephen returns from the underworld of London, embodying Gerald almost as an avatar.

Such manuscript changes, particularly those recording Forster's efforts to "realize" the archetypal Stephen, measure his struggle to keep his symbolism in line with the practicable, believable "realities" needed in a realistic novel. For many readers he fails, losing them when realistic details become leitmotivs, and events, like the sudden deaths, "unrealistic", melodramatic; in fact Forster had his own doubts about his methods, recorded in his diary on 23 March 1906, when he had drafted at least two-thirds of the novel, perhaps more: "Doubt whether novel's any good: all ingenious symbols: little flesh and blood. Possibly I'ld better finish Lucy [*A Room with a View* (1908)] first."[10] He persevered, however, and for other readers of *The Longest Journey* the problems posed by the symbolic rhythms are precisely those at the heart of the novel, reflections of the metaphysical and ethical questions about the nature of reality and the hazards inherent in any attempts to interpret it, but particularly in attempts to create or to live by fictions which impose symbolic shape and meaning, making "real"

[9] P. N. Furbank, *E. M. Forster: A Life*, vol. 1 (London, Secker & Warburg, 1977), p. 263. Further references to this volume are noted as PNF.
[10] Forster's diary is in the King's College Library, as are all the unpublished manuscripts referred to in this introduction; quotations have been styled for clarity and consistency.

what may not exist. Forster's methods of structuring the novel—
even the many deaths, since death, like birth, argues most con-
cretely against solipsistic subjectivity—imbed the idealizations of
Rickie Elliot's "diseased imagination" in a similarly imaginative
fiction, healthy rather than diseased because it is marked throughout by its allusions and its rhythms as a consciously symbolic fictional weighing of the values of alternative approaches to reality.

APOSTOLIC QUESTIONS

Although the paradoxes of Forster's "metafiction" are themselves
intriguing, like his imaginative play with the ancient philosophical
challenge of "squaring the circle", what gives emotional and moral
power to *The Longest Journey*, saving it from bloodless abstraction,
are the issues, the questions of brotherhood and love and "personal
relations", most of them based on the biographical realities of
Forster's Apostolic experience. Rickie Elliot and Stewart Ansell
enact the moral challenges raised in turn-of-the-century Apostolic
discussions by the shift in philosophical influence from the idealism
of Hegel to the relative objectivity of G. E. Moore. Bertrand
Russell pays tribute to the liberating effect of Moore's arguments at
the metaphysical level, recalling his own sense of relief when Moore
convinced him, around 1898, "that grass is green, that the sun
and stars would exist if no one was aware of them, and also that
there is a pluralistic timeless world of Platonic ideas",[11] the last
evidenced for Russell in mathematics, for Moore in concepts like
the meaning of "good". The effect of the development of Moore's
ethical arguments on the younger Apostles is recorded not only in
The Longest Journey but in several of the Bloomsbury memoirs.
Leonard Woolf and John Maynard Keynes are characteristic in
their descriptions of the questions they debated in the early fervour
of their commitment to the ideas of Moore's *Principia Ethica*, published in October 1903. Woolf, who spent five years at Cambridge
and left in the summer of 1904 for the Civil Service exam, the
results of which sent him to Ceylon that November, writes: "But
Moore himself was continually exercised by the problems of goods
and bads as means of morality and rules of conduct and therefore
of the life of action as opposed to the life of contemplation. He and
we were fascinated by questions of what was right and wrong,

[11] "My Mental Development", *The Philosophy of Bertrand Russell*, ed. P. A. Schilpp
(Evanston & Chicago, Northwestern Univ. Press, 1944), pp. 11–12.

what one *ought* to do."[12] Keynes, who began his third year at Cambridge as Woolf left, recalls a mixture of abstract and possibly personal applications of Moore's principles of ethics:

> If A was in love with B under a misapprehension as to B's qualities, was this better or worse than A's not being in love at all? . . . How did one compare the value of a good state of mind which had bad consequences with a bad state of mind which had good consequences? . . . how much evidence as to possible consequences was it one's duty to collect before applying the calculus? Was there a separate objective standard of beauty? Was a beautiful thing, that is to say, by definition that which it was good to contemplate? Or was there an actual objective quality "beauty", just like "green" and "good"?[13]

These questions and concerns need very little adaptation to become those of *The Longest Journey*. Many passages in Moore's Apostolic essays echo in Ansell's speeches; Moore and his young Apostolic disciples, in particular Hugh Owen Meredith, Forster's closest undergraduate friend, provide a composite model for Stewart Ansell, so sure that "the cow is there" and that we misconstrue it at our peril.[14] In the opening chapter there is also an adaptation of the secret Apostolic jargon, fundamentally idealist, in which "'reality' existed solely within the Society, the rest of mankind being merely 'phenomena' living in 'the world of appearances'." (PNF, pp. 75–6.) This echo is to some extent a kind of mockery, as comic an "in-joke" as the transformation of Agnes, in the last chapter, into Mrs Keynes, mother of Bertie [Russell?], but Forster's comedy, as usual, complements his serious purpose. In *The Longest Journey* he tries out in imagination not only "real" applications of classical tragedy and religious mythology but also "real" effects of objective and subjective views, using Rickie Elliot to measure the results when the Apostolic strictures are applied not just to cows but to "real" people, invited but forgotten. Are they really there? Granted that they are, the moral questions ramify: What happens to the quality of love if the beloved is mis-

[12] *Sowing: An Autobiography of the Years 1880–1904* (London, Hogarth, 1960), pp. 148–9.

[13] "My Early Beliefs", *Two Memoirs*, ed. David Garnett (London, Rupert Hart-Davis, 1949), p. 87.

[14] Moore's Apostolic essays, for instance "Is it a duty to hate?" are quoted at length by Paul Levy in *Moore: G. E. Moore and the Cambridge Apostles* (London, Weidenfeld & Nicolson, 1979), where excellent descriptions of the Apostles of this period also appear. H. O. Meredith and Forster both came up to King's College in October 1897; Meredith was elected to the Society in May 1900 and sponsored Forster's election in February 1901.

perceived? If the beloved is in fact stupid or ugly? What ideals and desires drive us into error? If the mother is adulterous and the brother illegitimate, why do we damn, or deify? Can we base our ethics not on traditional codes but on our individual perceptions of Truth, Beauty, and Love, on our "states of mind" and "personal relations"? Is there any value in the mystic or religious state of mind if it leads to continual misinterpretations of objective realities? To what extent are we our brothers' "keepers"? Should we act in the real world, believing not in an inevitable progression toward a perfect, mystic Absolute but in a less perfect world where individual action makes a difference, hitting out "like any plough-boy" (pp. 180, 224) to save a friend?

In *The Longest Journey* Ansell's embodiment of Moorean values and Forster's support for these are obvious in the working out of the plot. Rickie Elliot, initially so like his creator that he even writes one of his short stories, "Other Kingdom" (see p. 71 and note), is sacrificed because he continually idealizes. Aestheticizing nature in his fantasies, he also, like his aunt, forgets "what other people are like" (p. 139), so that he mistakes the reality of his wife, his mother, his brother, and even himself. His death is conventionally heroic but ironic and ambiguous in its value because he dies dutifully, in a state of disillusion and despair, having "pretended again that people were real" (p. 281). Idolizing Stephen as he idolized his mother, he is "bankrupt" again when Stephen, knowing no law other than his own choice, breaks his promise and gets drunk, becoming the sodden, fallen idol whose life Rickie saves, losing his own. The ethical questions rise: Is Rickie's death made better or worse by his state of mind? Is Stephen or Rickie more worth saving? In the epilogue Forster brings the balance down on the side represented by Stewart and Stephen, in favour of life and love for those who can cut through conventional thinking to see unconventional value; he is wholly on Moore's side, or the "Bloomsbury" side, when the aesthetic concern for beauty, represented by Rickie's writings rather than his life, is preserved as well.[15]

[15] Forster explored the author's problem of creating happy or unhappy endings in "Pessimism in Literature", read at the Working Men's College in December 1906. *The Longest Journey* was by then complete; he was perhaps amused by the comments in the discussion which followed his paper, for instance: "Mr Marshall suggested for the ending of a novel, the happy and self-sacrificing death of the hero, dying whilst doing his duty. He thought that would satisfy all our desires—he hoped it would." (*Working Men's College Journal*, January-February 1907, pp. 6–10, 26–33).

PERSONAL QUESTIONS

Some of the interest of *The Longest Journey* now comes from the recognition that the moralities and personalities investing its plot are Apostolic, an interest that would seem historically adventitious were it not that the novel itself exists because of the power of those Cambridge debates for the young men and women who became the central figures of the Bloomsbury Group. Aside from *Principia Ethica* itself, *The Longest Journey* is the first published manifestation of the ethos of that group. However, both the care with which Forster sets up the balance between Rickie Elliot's imagination and Stewart Ansell's realism, and the vehemence with which he denies the viability of Rickie's way of life, are inescapably personal. Rickie Elliot's imagination is essentially Forster's own, much more strongly influenced by the mystical poets and philosophers, initially, than by the objective ones, and Rickie's ultimate failure has more to do with his inability to act in accordance with what he knows of his own nature than with that nature itself. His hereditary lameness is the key to the mystery and the power of the plot both literally, as a "reality" exactly equivalent to the facts of Stephen's ancestry, and figuratively, as a wholly conventional, static "symbol" which demands to be interpreted as something more than a limp.

In an interview with Angus Wilson in 1957 Forster qualified his acceptance of Wilson's suggestion that gentleness like Rickie Elliot's might be a defensive weapon, destructive of others, by taking it as part of his "dislike for cruelty"; he then commented, "Yes, Rickie—I could kick him for his lame leg, you know."[16] In its context the remark exemplifies paradoxical ironies; insofar as the lameness stands for Forster's own homosexuality its place in this novel about realities that "must be faced" (p. lxvi) is also an ironic reflection of the laws of the time, but regrettable only if its importance at the autobiographical level obscures its full function in the novel. To develop the dramatic ironies created by Rickie's "diseased imagination" and to make the essential link between imagination and act, theme and plot, there has to be something hereditary, relatively obvious and relatively serious and not, for instance, as hidden and ominous as the inherited syphilis of Ibsen's *Ghosts*, perhaps echoed in the early manuscript fragment in which Ansell refers to the unacknowledged Stephen as the "ghost" haunting Rickie's house (p. 366). Idealizing his mother, Rickie Elliot cannot imagine that she could have been other than the

[16] "A Conversation with E. M. Forster", *Encounter*, vol. 9, no. 5 (November 1957), p. 55.

martyr and saint he honours, and he is absolutely certain that his hated father, "as a final insult" (p. 192), must have created the healthy Stephen, so unlike the lame and gentlemanly Elliots that logic alone should have impelled Rickie to re-examine his assumptions. However, by the time Mrs Failing tells him that Stephen is his half-brother he has fallen in love and become engaged to Agnes. Even though he was once so certain that his lameness prevented marriage that he tried to give his money to Gerald and Agnes to enable them to marry, he has now become wholly unwilling to see that if Stephen is his brother and healthy, then Stephen must be his mother's son.

Granted that another hereditary defect would have done as well, Forster perhaps chose lameness as the marker because Rickie's failure to act by what he knows of himself links him to Oedipus, whose limp also signifies his ancestry and whose pride and love, one assumes, allowed him to make a mistake like Rickie's, marrying the wrong woman (one old enough to be his mother) despite all prophecy. That Forster had Greek tragedy in mind is evidenced by a relatively late draft of Mrs Failing's sibylline half-revelation, where she likens Stephen to Orestes, come to free his family from their curse (p. 341); clearly the comparison had to be dropped precisely because of Stephen's lack of relationship to the Elliots. As a "curse" the lameness is also conjoined, again at a conventionally symbolic level, with the Elliot money, unproductive and obtained by something "shady" done in past generations (p. 31). Here the influence of Samuel Butler has been recognized,[17] but such an economic inheritance, even when joined to a selfish aestheticism and a worsening limp, hardly justifies the violence informing Forster's judgement of Rickie's father and Rickie's choices. Forster's own choices do account for it, more fully if he thought that homosexuality was congenital. Since *The Longest Journey* is itself evidence that he did, a review of the ways in which Forster's experience differs from Rickie Elliot's can serve to outline both what Forster is likely to have known about homosexuality and the effects of the shift in Apostolic emphasis from theory to action, ideal to real.

Forster opens "My Books and I" by telling his audience to imagine that they have now come to this significant chapter, having already heard about his "childhood, adolescence and undergraduation" (p. 300), and his syntax suggests that perhaps there

[17] Particularly by Lee Elbert Holt, "E. M. Forster and Samuel Butler", *PMLA*, LXI (September 1946), pp. 804–19. Forster recognizes it himself in "A Book that Influenced Me", reprinted in *Two Cheers for Democracy* from "Books in General" (*New Statesman & Nation*, 15 July 1943, p. 43).

was such a memoir, now lost. Without it one is tempted to make do with *The Longest Journey*, at least so far as emotions and overall patterns are concerned. At the level of "undergraduation", always excluding Agnes, there is little point in separating Forster from Rickie, happy in his friendships and beginning to write. In his biography of his mentor and friend, *Goldsworthy Lowes Dickinson* (1934), Forster describes Dickinson's life as an undergraduate and don at King's College, Cambridge, of course the original for "Cambridge College" in the novel, in more objective but almost equally autobiographical terms; the details of Cambridge and college life in *The Longest Journey* are so accurate in those matters which can be checked that it seems safe to assume that if Rickie sees "the college cat teasing the college tortoise" (p. 4), then in Forster's student years (1897–1901) there were such animals to be seen. Rickie and Forster are also similar in their adolescence, in that each spent time in school as both a boarder and a day-boy, preferring the latter experience but emerging from public school to the freedom of Cambridge as to paradise. Forster's public school, Tonbridge, where he was a day-boy, "a Varden who never got his ears pulled" (p. lxviii), is the model for "Sawston School" in the novel, where Rickie becomes an ineffectual master and the cat's-paw of Herbert Pembroke, Agnes's older brother. With the exception of Herbert's boarding-house the details are again remarkably accurate, but the adult perspective reflects Forster's disapproval of the system, particularly of the boarding-houses. At the level of childhood, however, Rickie's and Forster's experiences diverge in detail, complicating the question of emotional congruence.

Unlike Rickie Elliot's fastidiously absent and absurdly critical father, Forster's died two months before his son's second birthday, but both author and hero were brought up by lonely, over-protective mothers and, more distantly, by fearsome elderly aunts from the moneyed, paternal side of the family. Rickie Elliot has reason to hate his father, who first neglected him and his mother and then, returning in illness to exploit the mother's care, banished the son to public school, calling him "a joke of which I have got tired" (p. 24). Nonetheless, a draft introducing Rickie's explanation of this hatred to his Cambridge friends attributes it directly and solely to the passing on of the hereditary defect:

> "Why did you hate him?"
> He replied, "I think it must be because he was lame, but I try to think it was other things."

"But you don't mind being lame," said Widdrington.
"He minds that he became it," answered Ansell.[18]

Nothing like this cause survives in the equivalent finished text (p. 20), but it seems obvious that by the time Forster wrote this deleted passage, sometime in the late summer or early autumn of 1905, he knew of the contemporary scientific view that some homosexuality was congenital, expressed in such books as Edward Carpenter's *Homogenic Love* (1894) or Havelock Ellis's *Sexual Inversion* (1897), which concludes that in some cases homosexuality is both inborn and inherited. The books were not widely available—Ellis's was suppressed in England—but Dickinson knew them, and it is most unlikely that the Apostles would not have assimilated their findings. With the possibility of such knowledge Rickie's hatred of his paternal heredity becomes something that Forster might have shared, but something to be hidden from the public eye, so that in the finished novel Rickie's hatred depends only on his experience of his father, distancing hero from author.

A genetic rather than a Freudian sense of cause, or blame, for a homosexual temperament adds poignancy to the way in which questions of inheritance and fatherhood complement the issues of brotherhood in *The Longest Journey*. To judge from his novels, Forster's desire for children was strong, and his avoidance of marriage not purely a matter of incapacity or lack of interest but perhaps also one of moral import, an unwillingness to impose his own abnormality on others. Particularly in this novel but also in *Where Angels Fear to Tread* and *Howards End* children become symbolic measures of their parents' and guardians' ability to behave honestly and unselfishly, to connect, consciously or unconsciously, the real and the ideal. Even in *A Passage to India* the union of the practical Cyril Fielding and the mystical Stella Moore is rewarded with a "son and heir" before the end of the novel.[19] But in the deleted passage Widdrington and Ansell distinguish between being and becoming, outlining a situation in which there is no self-hatred, no wish not to have been born, but an implied choice not to replicate one's abnormality. And of course in 1905 and in

18 See p. 315 for the full draft, which has here been styled for clarity.
19 The child, mentioned only in Ronnie Heaslop's peacemaking letter and often overlooked, is purely a grace note to the plot, perhaps helping to account for the two-year gap before "Temple" but yielding place to the birth of Krishna. Nonetheless, it must have arrived safely for its sex to be known and for congratulations to be offered. "Little Imber", written in 1961 and Forster's last story, is a fantasy of a future in which two men discover that they can create children from their mixed seed (see *Arctic Summer and Other Fiction*).

England congenital homosexuality could sensibly be regarded as a nearly intolerable burden, at the least a "defect", as Dickinson put it in an autobiographical manuscript of 1910, using a comparison that Forster perhaps heard earlier: "I am like a man born crippled; will and character may make more of such a life, through the very stimulus of the defect, than many normal men make of theirs."[20]

Since *The Longest Journey* focuses on just such problems of becoming, of action and responsibility, and since Rickie's lameness purely as lameness seems a relatively tolerable defect, it is worth noting the severity of the moral judgements about homosexuality expressed even by Carpenter and Ellis, who were concerned to vouch for the fact that homosexuals were not by definition insane or wilfully perverse and to argue for the revision of the law, widely publicized by the trial of Oscar Wilde in 1895, that made even private, adult homosexual acts illegal. Both Carpenter and Ellis, basing their conclusions on their own surveys and on those of European scientists like Krafft-Ebing, argue that only some homosexuality is congenital, and that, in Carpenter's words, "Too much emphasis cannot be laid on the distinction between these born lovers of their own sex, and that class of persons, with whom they are so often confused, who out of mere carnal curiosity or extravagance of desire, or from the dearth of opportunities for a more normal satisfaction (as in schools, barracks etc.) adopt some homosexual practices."[21] As hopeful as Dickinson at his most optimistic, Carpenter is of course well known for his further argument, supported by historical and anthropological studies, that true homosexual love, understood on the Greek model or in the spirit of Walt Whitman's "Calamus" poems, can be as worth while as heterosexual love and, especially with social approval, more useful

[20] *The Autobiography of G. Lowes Dickinson and Other Unpublished Writings*, ed. Dennis Proctor (London, Duckworth, 1973), p. 11. In *Goldsworthy Lowes Dickinson* (vol. 13, Abinger Edition, 1973), hereafter noted as *GLD*, Forster depended on Dickinson's autobiographical manuscripts but suppressed all overt references to homosexuality. See the *Autobiography*, p. 104, for Dickinson's quotations from letters reflecting his reading of Carpenter's pamphlet in the 1890s. Dickinson refers explicitly to Ellis's work in an unpublished dialogue on homosexuality that he wrote at the same time as most of his autobiography, shortly after World War I. The dialogue, among Dickinson's papers in the King's College Library, presents the arguments of a character like Dickinson who is explaining to an old friend, a man whom he has always loved, that the friend's son is homosexual; although Dickinson relies on Ellis's idea of congenital abnormality, he is silent about the related problem of heredity.

[21] *Homogenic Love*, reprinted in *Sexual Heretics*, ed. Brian Reade (London, Routledge & Kegan Paul, 1970), p. 332.

to the advancement of learning, art, and democracy. Ellis in his study is more interested in explaining the evidence for his finding that the sexual invert "is usually the subject of a congenital predisposing abnormality, or complexus of minor abnormalities", and his pursuit of the logical results of such a finding has more relevance to *The Longest Journey*. Ellis notes among other things that the fact that only some of those introduced to homosexual practices in schools or barracks remain homosexual in their preferences is itself evidence for an "organic predisposition"; at the same time he urges the benefits of co-education and fuller sex education in preventing "artificial homosexuality".[22] As for efforts to "cure" the truly inverted by advising and enabling marriage, common at the time, Ellis views them, logically, as a form of perversion from the natural, and he is particularly dubious about "the prospects of inverts begetting or bearing children":

> Often, no doubt, the children turn out fairly well, but for the most part they bear witness that they belong to a neurotic and failing stock. Sometimes, indeed, the tendency to sexual inversion in eccentric and neurotic families seems merely to be Nature's merciful method of winding up a concern which, from her point of view, has ceased to be profitable.[23]

Ellis's economic metaphor echoes Rickie Elliot's conscious attitude toward his family's "crookedness" as well as the advice he dreams for himself, hearing and misunderstanding his mother's voice as it repeats, "Let them die out" (p. 193). And Ellis's further description of the inverted male who undertakes marriage in a mistaken effort to be "normal"—"the mere feeble simulacrum of a normal man", given "a power of reproduction which it is undesirable he should possess"—also seems to echo in Forster's presentation of the

[22] *Sexual Inversion*, vol. 1, *Studies in the Psychology of Sex* (London, University Press, Watford, 1897), pp. 141–2. Ellis's summary of what little was known about causes of congenital anomalies includes disturbances in "early development", but it is clear that this means foetal development: "Every congenital abnormality is doubtless due to a peculiarity in the sperm or oval elements or in their mingling, or to some disturbance in their early development." (p. 135) Neither Ellis nor Carpenter considers further disturbances in early childhood in the way that Freud does. Ellis later recognized the importance of Freud's findings but kept to his opinion that when all environmental factors are accounted for there are still people, not obviously abnormal in their physiology, for whom the logic of the "organic predisposition" argument holds. See Phyllis Grosskurth, *Havelock Ellis: A Biography* (London, Allen Lane, 1980), pp. 188–9. Needless to say, the proportionate contributions of environmental experience and organic predisposition are still in question and appear to be infinitely, individually variable.

[23] Ellis, pp. 145–6.

married Rickie. Moreover, were Ellis's moral judgements not persuasive enough, there is a terrifying footnote reporting a case in which "the offspring turned out disastrously. The eldest child was an epileptic, almost an imbecile, and with strongly marked homosexual impulses; the second and third children were absolutely idiots; the youngest died of convulsions in infancy."[24] One wonders why in this case there were four children; for Rickie Elliot one, to whom "God" is "merciful" in granting death (p. 184), is more than enough.

The necessity for an obvious hereditary defect as part of the plot of *The Longest Journey* of course militates against any thought that Forster believed his own paternal inheritance to be abnormal. However, Forster for many years did, like Dickinson, believe his own homosexuality to be congenital, and if Rickie's lameness is to that extent equivalent to Forster's homosexuality then it becomes possible that in plotting the novel as he did Forster was pursuing the same Darwinian logic as Ellis, reinforcing his own celibate choices by regarding Rickie Elliot as a case of "there but for my knowledge of myself go I". Certainly Freudian reasons for Forster's conviction that his homosexuality was congenital, as for his homosexuality itself, can be suggested; the absent, unloving fathers and the ambivalent, over-protective mothers of both Rickie Elliot and Forster fit those of the Freudian stereotype of the homosexual so well that it can easily be forgotten that Forster himself learned of Freud's emphasis on early childhood development long after he wrote *The Longest Journey*, even after he first wrote *Maurice* in 1913–14. The phrasing in his letter of 13 March 1915 to Forrest Reid about that novel, which was written not for publication but to mark his increasing hope for the physical expression of "manly love" approved more by Carpenter than Ellis, shows that he still viewed Maurice's and his own homosexuality as congenital and was ready to revise Genesis to say so: "Male and Female created He not them . . . . one is left with 'perverts' (an absurd word, because it assumes they were given a choice . . .) . . . . My defence at any Last Judgement would be 'I was trying to connect up and use all the fragments I was born with' . . . ."[25]

In *Maurice* itself the hypnotist whom the hero visits in a desperate attempt to resist his abnormality tells him that he is suffering from "congenital homosexuality", and Forster again implies that this is the result of paternal heredity. Maurice, however, does not hate his father. Instead the ghost of the father regards the awakening of

[24] Ellis, p. 143n, where he adds, "No doubt this is scarcely an average case."
[25] *Maurice*, ed. P. N. Furbank (London, Edward Arnold, 1971), pp. vii–viii.

the son with envy, for he had merely passed unthinkingly "from illicit to licit love", stupidly participating only in "transient grossness" rather than developing a fully realized love for another man.[26] Now too, Maurice regards himself as incapable of begetting children without psychological change, and the hypnosis fails after he confirms his homosexual desires by "sharing" with the gamekeeper. Nonetheless he still regrets his "sterility", and in the 1913–14 version, in the scene following the conversation in the British Museum, when he and the gamekeeper define the perfection of their love by forgoing an unearned and unheroic hour in a London hotel, Maurice wishes that the emigrating gamekeeper will marry "out there", adding, "And if there's ever a child,—I shan't ever have that, so remember me."[27]

Only in the 1920s, perhaps as a result of the readings of the Bloomsbury Memoir Club, does Forster's view begin to be Freudian; sometime in 1927, considering the possibility of writing an anti-Wordsworthian novel about middle age—"there is an emotion in contemplating the shades of the prison house that *have fallen*"— he becomes explicitly, if temporarily, regretful of his choices:

> perhaps the awe with which M.A. [Middle Aged] occasionally realizes that his apparent range is really a tether of his own weaving may give me the clue I seek . . . . The occasional feeling that e.g. one's sexual outlook was not inevitable brings a gloomy reality into the cell—which cell is the proper abode of man and cannot be abandoned by him after fifty, without dissolution. How again render this readable? for either pathos or bitterness will destroy the novel at once.[28]

[26] *Maurice*, p. 139 and p. 197.

[27] Leaf 207 of the 1913–14 typescript of *Maurice*, in the King's College Library. When Forster's changing adaptations to his sexuality are mapped, however uncertainly, through his fiction, the revisions of *Maurice* need to be detailed; the hotel chapter added in the 1932 version, which seems to me very much influenced by D. H. Lawrence, is so much a reflection of Forster's later experience that from a biographical viewpoint it becomes anachronistic, a distortion of the remarkable period qualities of the pre-war *Maurice*, where the gamekeeper's abandonment of emigration is offered and accepted as a sacrifice intended to establish trust, and the two men abandon their worldly ambitions to join each other in the greenwood. Except for the added hotel chapter and the omitted epilogue, however, the published novel is for the most part identical to the early version. See Philip Gardner, "The Evolution of E. M. Forster's *Maurice*", *E. M. Forster: Centenary Revaluations*, eds. Judith Scherer Herz and Robert K. Martin (London, Macmillan, 1982), pp. 204–23.

[28] *Commonplace Book* (London, Scolar Press, 1978), p. 42. The entry is undated but falls between others of 1927. See also Virginia Woolf's diary for 31 August 1928, where Forster is recorded as definitely not wanting to be converted from his homosexuality (*The Diary of Virginia Woolf, Volume III: 1925–1930*, eds. Anne Olivier Bell and Andrew McNeillie [London, Hogarth Press, 1980], p. 193).

Perhaps after *A Passage to India* Forster wrote no more fiction for publication partly because of the Freudian dissolution of a writer's "anonymity"; he would hereafter write undisguised or not at all, and so had to keep his fictions from the eyes of the law. Certainly he is consistent throughout his adult life in his belief that homosexuality ought to be no more penalized than heterosexuality, whatever its origin, but the shift in his own sense of cause appears to have affected his later statements about *The Longest Journey*. Rickie's lameness needn't be regretted. It functions brilliantly in the novel, giving classic elegance and drama to the plot as it raises the broader moral questions about heredity and survival which have marked both Darwinian debates and racist pogroms and continue to mark even the best hopes for genetic engineering of this age. Probably Rickie's lameness is linked with homosexuality even in Forster's most vivid portrayal of the evils of the boarding-house system—the assault on Varden's ears, a kind of gang rape, is mysteriously and superstitiously perceived by Rickie as a "bitter comment" on the death of his child (p. 185)—but, primarily, it directs us to our personal responsibility for the results of our choices.

APOSTOLIC EXPERIENCE

To return to Cambridge, the divergences between Forster's experiences and Rickie Elliot's begin at about the time Forster was elected an Apostle, in February 1901, toward the end of his last year as a student. Summarizing his "youth" in his diary on 31 December 1904, the eve of his twenty-sixth birthday, he felt that it had reached its end in his then "rather sad and dull" life: "Nothing more great will come out of me: I've made my two great discoveries—the religious about four years ago, the other in the winter of 1902—and the reconstruction is practically over." P. N. Furbank explains that both discoveries—the loss of Forster's Christian faith and, apparently, his realization that he was homosexual—came about through H. O. Meredith, the first one while Forster was still at Cambridge and the "other" in the winter of 1902–03, after he had returned from a year spent abroad with his mother. In fact Furbank thinks it safe to assume that by the time Forster became an Apostle he "knew perfectly well that he was homosexual by temperament" (PNF, p. 78), but if so it becomes difficult to explain his sense of discovery and the need for "reconstruction" nearly two years later, after he and Meredith, both living in

London, "in some sense or other", as Furbank puts it, "became lovers". Furbank writes that Forster told him that the affair was by mutual agreement not a full physical relationship. Nonetheless, "for him it was immense and epoch-making; it was, he felt, as if all the 'greatness' of the world had been opened up to him" (PNF, p. 98).

If this extraordinary discovery included not merely love but full consciousness of his own homosexuality, then the date also supports what Forster tells us in "My Books and I" about his composition of "The Story of a Panic". Inspired, he wrote it in Ravello in May 1902 but was later "horrified", after it was published in August 1904, to be told that it could be interpreted in terms of buggery, or, as he discreetly writes even in a manuscript meant to be read aloud, b—— (p. 302). Looking back to his youth he remembers that he wrote the story with no such consciousness, although, still reviling the interpreter twenty years later, he can admit that the strength of his denial in 1904 must have been related to the truth in the interpretation. In contrast to "The Story of a Panic" is "Ralph and Tony", written in the summer of 1903 when Forster was again in Italy and Meredith had become engaged to be married. Instead of the first story's celebration of pubertal awakenings feared by panicky English adults but understood by a primitive Italian, there is the "decadent" Ralph, feeble and aesthetic, who would willingly marry the athletic Tony's sister if Tony would allow them all to live together, which indeed, after brutal kicking and suicidal despair and rescue and illness, is the happy ending promised. Only the first story could have been written without consciousness of homosexual desires, as Forster assures us it was, however unlikely that may seem now; the second, so full of pain and love and published only posthumously, must have been transparent even to its author.[29]

The year 1902 also saw the change in Apostolic emphasis caused by the election of Lytton Strachey and J. T. Sheppard in February, and the addition of Leonard Woolf, Saxon Sydney-Turner and L. H. Greenwood in November; in February 1903 Keynes became the newest Apostle. G. E. Moore's papers show that homosexuality

[29] "Ralph and Tony" appears in *Arctic Summer and Other Fiction*. "Ansell", another posthumously published story written in 1903 (see *The Life to Come and Other Stories* [vol. 8, Abinger Edition, 1972]), draws on Forster's childhood friendship with a garden boy named Ansell (PNF, pp. 30–31), imagining him grown up. Stewart Ansell's name is thus potent for Forster, and in *Maurice* too there is a friendship with a garden boy; Maurice, after his discovery of his homosexual temperament, looks back and "knew very well what he wanted from the garden boy" (*Maurice*, p. 191).

was a subject of Apostolic discussions long before Forster was elected in 1901, but both Bertrand Russell and Desmond Mac-Carthy, a friend first of Moore and later of the slightly younger Bloomsbury figures, insist that it was Strachey and then Keynes who put the talk into practice. Whether or not Strachey's example influenced Meredith and Forster to change or perhaps to acknowledge the nature of their undergraduate friendship, Forster's year abroad meant that he came back to Apostolic meetings that were markedly different in membership and in attitudes toward realities; the contrast to what he had known in 1901 conveniently if oversimply corresponds to the intellectual balance between Rickie and Ansell which he creates in *The Longest Journey*. In the spring of 1901 Forster attended the Saturday night meetings regularly, in company most often with the other newest Apostles—Meredith, A. R. Ainsworth, G. H. Hardy and R. G. Hawtrey—all of whom were, as P. N. Furbank puts it, "under Moore's influence".[30] At that point, however, the influence was not all Moore's. Both Moore and Dickinson attended five or six of the spring meetings, and present at two was John McTaggart Ellis McTaggart, the Hegelian idealist whose philosophy had dominated the Society. Moreover, the intellectual event among the Apostles that spring appears to have been the publication of Dickinson's philosophical dialogue, *The Meaning of Good*, which concludes with a mystically symbolic dream that he remembers was "influenced by McTaggart's idea of an eternal perfection of spirits related to one another by love" (*GLD*, p. 91), a kind of ideal extension of the bond of Apostolic brotherhood. Forster's own recollection of the book is particularly vivid:

> The dialogue came out in 1901. I remember the enthusiasm, the attractive blue cloth of the binding, the lightness of the volume, the solidity of the contents, and my great friend and fellow undergraduate,

[30] PNF, p. 76. I am indebted to the Cambridge Conversazione Society for information about Forster's attendance. In *Moore* (pp. 212–13), Paul Levy describes Strachey's moderately successful efforts to convince Moore and Ainsworth, elected an Apostle in November 1899, that their friendship was homosexual; Ainsworth married Moore's youngest sister in 1908. G. H. Hardy, the mathematician, became an Apostle in February 1898. Ralph Hawtrey, an economist and Treasury official and later Sir Ralph, was elected in March 1900. Russell was elected in February 1892, Moore in February 1894, MacCarthy in May 1896. Of those elected in 1902, Greenwood and Sheppard, both classicists, remained in Cambridge rather than moving to London and Bloomsbury. Greenwood became a Fellow of Emmanuel College, and it was he who preserved the 1913–14 typescript of *Maurice* now at King's College. John Tresidder Sheppard, later Sir John, was Provost of King's when Forster was made an Honorary Fellow in 1946.

H. O. Meredith (now [1934] Professor of Economics at Belfast), reading as he stalked along King's Parade and chanting, "You shall never take away from me my *Meaning of Good* . . ." (*GLD*, p. 92)

If in *The Longest Journey* Ansell embodies Moore's view of reality, Rickie Elliot embodies Dickinson's, a mystic and poetic variant of McTaggart's Hegelianism much influenced by Plato, Plotinus, and Shelley, and very different in style from Moore's closely reasoned linguistic analyses. In 1901, for that matter, even Leonard Woolf was a mystic, planning a collection of essays on mystic thinkers and saints to be written by himself, his sister Bella, Sydney-Turner, and Strachey, though the project was never completed, perhaps because in a year or two Moore's influence was to be the stronger.[31] Dickinson in his autobiography, however, misdates the effect of the publication of *Principia Ethica* on his own thought, writing that it appeared while he was working on *The Meaning of Good* rather than on his second dialogue, *A Modern Symposium*, published late in 1905 and, in contrast to the earlier work, a model of clarity. What is curious is that Forster accepts Dickinson's misdating, providing a description of the reception of *Principia Ethica* before his recollection of *The Meaning of Good*, whereas it ought to follow:

> It would be too much to say that Moore dethroned McTaggart, who was essentially undethronable, but he did carry the younger men by storm, and cause Lytton Strachey to exclaim, "The age of reason has come!" Dickinson, while not going so far as that, felt uneasy. Moore's steady questioning as to What *is* good? What *is* true? had already torn some large holes in the McTaggartian heaven. More care—I speak as a complete outsider here—more care had evidently to be taken as to what one said and how one said it, and intuition seemed less than ever enough. (*GLD*, p. 92)

Forster of course speaks as a "complete outsider" only so far as the more technical philosophical points are concerned, because he was in effect "there", as Henry James might say, living through the change. Probably, thirty years later, he accepted Dickinson's dating without question because for both of them the opposition was a slowly developing one, not to be pinned to particular publication dates; Forster's assertion that he never read Moore's book is probably true. In 1960, observing that "sixty years ago undergraduates all called each other by their surnames and often went

---

[31] See Leonard Woolf's letters to Saxon Sydney-Turner, at the Huntington Library, San Marino, California, and Freema Gottlieb, "A Study of the Psychological Development of Leonard Woolf", unpublished dissertation, London University, 1975.

arm-in-arm, whereas today they never go arm-in-arm but are all
on terms of Christian names", he praises Leonard Woolf's *Sowing*
and indicates more accurately his own relation to Moore:

> [*Sowing*] is beautifully written—though "beauty" is not quite the word,
> since it suggests graces and airs. And it has the distinction that comes
> from absolute honesty; no compromise: but also no arrogance. [Woolf]
> belonged up here to a group which centred in G. E. Moore and had
> its main habitat in Trinity, and although his passion for truth was
> innate there is no doubt that the company he kept confirmed it. What
> they were after was not the Truth of the mystic or the ter-uth of the
> preacher but truth with the small "t". They tried to find out more.
> They believed in the intellect rather than in intuition, and they pro-
> ceeded by argument and discussion. I hovered on the edge of the
> group myself. I seldom understood what they were saying, and was
> mainly interested in the way they said it. I did, however, grasp that
> truth isn't capturable or even eternal, but something that could and
> should be pursued.[32]

In the manuscripts of *The Longest Journey* Ansell's "lean Jewish
face" (p. 62), resembling Woolf's, replaces an indeterminate
"chubby" one, and in the revelation scene of Chapter 27 Ansell
speaks like "a Hebrew prophet passionate for satire and the truth"
(p. 225), creating the echo in Forster's late recollection. Thus
Woolf too, like Ainsworth, whose jerky movements have been
recognized in Ansell's,[33] appears to have contributed to Ansell's
uncompromising character.

Forster was present at only three meetings of the Apostles in the
academic year 1902–03, on 8 and 29 November 1902 and 31
January 1903, although he was in Cambridge more often, for instance during the controversy in February 1903 about the establishment of a King's College mission in London. These meetings
were dominated by the younger Apostles, but it was the first meeting Forster attended in the next academic year, on 24 October
1903, that could have been at once a celebration of the appearance
of *Principia Ethica* and the crystallization of the beginnings of the
Bloomsbury Group. Moore was there and so were MacCarthy,
Strachey, Woolf, Sydney-Turner, and Keynes—with Forster, all
the Apostles of this period who were central to the later group.
(Roger Eliot Fry, a friend and Apostolic contemporary of Dickinson, who called him "Podge", became part of the group at the
time of the first Post-Impressionist exhibition in 1910.) However,

[32] "Looking Back", *The Cambridge Review* (22 October 1960), p. 58.
[33] Levy, p. 210, referring in part to PNF, p. 262.

the two major elements of change that Forster recollects, the shift from the Truth of the mystic to the truth of this world, and the difference in style of argument, moving from mystical elaboration to what Keynes called "the beauty of the literalness of Moore's mind, . . . *un*fanciful and *un*dressed-up",[34] would already have been familiar to him; apparently H. O. Meredith made a stronger link between *The Meaning of Good* and *Principia Ethica* than might be expected. The ethical elements of the two books are similar, perhaps only because Dickinson and Moore shared the Apostolic commitment to the good, the beautiful, and the true. Both, like McTaggart, honoured friendship and love as the best embodiments of good, but it was a conversation with Meredith about "intrinsic goods", held one Sunday early in 1903, that Moore remembered as the one in which "the whole plan of the last chapter of *Principia*" was first formed.[35] Meredith's share in the discussions with Moore and his role as the enlightener of Forster make this winter of 1902–03, after the interim of Forster's Italian year, very much the beginning of a new life, complete with the revaluation of the old visible in *The Longest Journey*.

Through the pairing of Rickie Elliot and Stewart Ansell, Moore's influence on *The Longest Journey* is ineradicably associated with the mystical, poetic, Hegelian idealism that gave way to his disciples' painstaking analyses of the worldly realities of individual "states of mind" and "personal relationships". Moreover, Forster did not join entirely in the repudiations of the younger Apostles but continued to value those elements of Rickie Elliot's imagination which were not "diseased" by conventional assumptions, and his own early essays, published in the *Independent Review* in 1903 and 1904, bear an uncanny resemblance to Dickinson's.[36] Ansell's

---

[34] Keynes, *op. cit.*, p. 94. [35] Levy, p. 215.

[36] For example, Dickinson's "Motoring" (*Independent Review*, January 1904, pp. 575–84) reflects elements of *The Longest Journey*. On the Englishman: "He lacks imagination, and therefore he lacks greatness." On the landscape: "Such a spot, if we were a race capable of mythology, would have been peopled long ago by gracious and kindly spirits. Somewhere in the recesses would have been hidden a marble shrine; and the wanderer would have fancied, eluding him among the trunks, the gleam of a Dryad's hair, or, slipping under the wave, the silver shoulder of a nymph. Still, the place cannot be said to need such pagan denizens. And the feelings of a modern man who may be sensitive to its influences, if vaguer, are perhaps more pregnant, if less lovely, more profound, than those of the Greek he is half-inclined to envy." On country life: "Everywhere, in this older England, are the outward signs of a life traditional, stable and continuous, a life profoundly affected by generations past and to come, a life of men who laboured for posterity, and upon whose work was stamped, perhaps without their knowledge or their will, an image of the greatness, the eternity of Nature."

demand for definitions, his relentless pursuit of metaphors (p. 179), and his scorn for "Journalese" (p. 62) all reflect the Bloomsbury sensitivity to Moore's persistent, famous question: "Do you really mean exactly that?" Rickie also objects to "journalese" (p.174) but, like Forster, chooses the screening images of classical mythology, preferring their wit and beauty to analytic literalness. Forster's description above of the "beauty" of Woolf's style, invigorating the cliché of "airs and graces", is a simple example of his later balance of Ansell's and Rickie's preferences, combining literal precision and metaphor.

Forster works toward this balance in *The Longest Journey* itself, and the more mystical images that measure the health of Rickie's imagination reflect something like the change in style between Dickinson's two dialogues. Rickie's fully Wagnerian response to love, for instance, is very similar in both style and content to Dickinson's description of *Turris artis*, the tower of art in which for a moment he too seems to hear a Wagnerian "ultimate melody of things" in the dream which concludes *The Meaning of Good*. This enthusiastic idealism contrasts with the realism of the imagery that Forster associates with Ansell's cow; it also differs from Dickinson's relatively restrained use of Shelley's Platonic mysticism in *A Modern Symposium*. There he quotes the famous lines from *Adonais* as the epigraph—"Life, like a dome of many-coloured glass, Stains the white radiance of eternity"—and limits the mystic view to the speakers at the symposium who are poet and philosopher. Often associations between images and ideas persist in Forster's writings; in his biography of Dickinson he uses the Shelleyan imagery to describe the variations among the speakers and then echoes the corresponding images of *The Longest Journey*, at once realistic and poetic, as he summarizes Dickinson's night of formal talk: "When the dawn comes and they vanish into mist or sunlight they leave a strong impression of actuality behind . . . ." (*GLD*, p. 93) In *The Longest Journey* sunlight and mist are particularly associated with the realities of Agnes, who disrupts the Apostolic symposium with which the novel opens like a false sun-goddess, flicking on the electric light so that Rickie's friends "were flying from his visitor like mists before the sun" (p. 6), a simile which comments indirectly on Rickie's imagination and the Wagnerian dawn sounding in the piano chords. Listening to the debate about the reality of Ansell's cow, Rickie could imagine the true sun in its natural place, but as he becomes more and more entangled in Agnes's materialistic "realities" the clouds gather round him. He agrees to marry her on Herbert's useful terms in the twilight of fog; while she stands in the gaslight, he still lingers near the window (p. 152), but after they marry he feels that "the cloud of unreality . . . ever brooded a little more densely than before", that "the cow was not really there" (p. 176). Thus the "sunlight and mist" of the novel are at once realistic, built into the details of the settings, and idealistic, still connected to concepts of universal truths that are more "real" for being ideal.

Forster read *A Modern Symposium*—dedicated, like the novel and the biography, to the Apostles—in December 1905,[37] when *The Longest Journey* was well under way, so that the two books stand as companions rather than as leader and follower. Each uses a form of Apostolic symposium to set out differing views of reality, and each shows its author's adaptations of mystical idealism to the demands of the rationalists. Forster's development of the mystic imagery of the novel is as much a critical exercise as his use of Wagner's operas and the classics, but it is tied even more closely to questions of metaphysical realities; he draws on the poetry of Shelley and Dante not so much for narrative patterns and contrasts with modern values as for statements of unquestionable truths and their associated imagery. For instance, the interconnections between light and love in the novel, like its title, are drawn most directly from Shelley's *Epipsychidion*. Rickie quotes the lines which provide the title just before his aunt tells him that Stephen is his brother (see p. 126 and note); in Shelley's metaphor our life is our longest journey, and the problem is our choice of companions, symbolized further as a matter of main route or detour. But the lines which follow this statement on marriage and friendship give Shelley's elaboration, as Forster terms it in his Dante notebook, of the image of mirrored light which Dante uses in Canto XV of *Purgatorio* to explain the undiminishing nature of divine love. Shelley's description of a similar light of understanding and imagination influences the novel very directly; his lines appear here as Forster copied them among his notes on the canto:

> True Love in this differs from gold and clay,
> That to divide is not to take away.
> Love is like understanding that grows bright
> Gazing on many truths; 'tis like thy light
> Imagination! which from earth and sky
> And from the depths of human fantasy

[37] Letter to Dickinson, 9 December 1905, *Selected Letters*, pp. 84–5. *A Modern Symposium* is dedicated "Fratrum Societati Fratrum Minimus" (To the Society of Brothers [from] the Least of the Brothers), *GLD* "Fratrum Societati".

As from a thousand prisms and mirrors fills
The Universe with glorious beams and kills
Error, the worm, with many a sun-like arrow.

Forster's study of Dante, contemporary with the writing of *The Longest Journey*, culminated in a paper read to the Working Men's College Literary Society in November 1907, in which he again quotes Shelley's lines on "True Love".[38] This knowledge of Dante helps to account for the "mystic rose" in Rickie's recollection of the survival of Stephen's fire-boat (p. 278), and Dante's astronomical exactness may underlie Rickie's imaginative awareness of day and night, of sun and moon and stars, associated among the interlocking leitmotivs of the novel with his balanced consciousness of a conjoined good-and-evil, more complex than the familiar opposition of the Authorized Version (p. 171). The intricate gradations of saints and sinners in Dante's *Divina Commedia* may also have contributed to the sophistication of Rickie's Christianity, so much less selfish than his aunt's socially conscious variety that it is easy to forget that his faith is still not "real" enough, not sufficiently literal for him to recognize his brother's truth. However, Forster's extension of Shelley's imagery is more obvious than the possible Dantean elements of the background. After Rickie marries Agnes and takes up the conventional life of Sawston there is less and less love and light to reflect, and his imagination loses its vividness. When he concentrates only on Agnes, blinding himself to "such a real thing" as his relationship to his brother, he falls into the error that Shelley, sounding rather like Ansell, declaims against in the lines that follow those Forster copied into his Dante notebook:

Narrow
The heart that loves, the brain that contemplates,
The life that wears, the spirit that creates
One object, and one form, and builds thereby
A sepulchre for its eternity.

Forster read, respected, and emulated the poets and visionaries, Dickinson among them, a fact that helps to explain why Moore's influence came to him through his disciples rather than from his works. Moore's style is too abstract, too lacking in "poetry". Had Forster known Moore's writings directly he probably would have realized that Moore's logic works to justify intuitive perceptions,

[38] "Dante", *Working Men's College Journal* (February-April 1908), pp. 261-4, 281-6, 301-6. Forster's Dante notebook refers to the *Vita Nuova*, *De Monarchia*, and most of *Purgatorio*. Years later, perhaps in the 1940s, he added a few notes on *Inferno*.

that intuition was not less but more "than ever enough".[39] Forster absorbed the effect of the arguments, since Ansell is completely sure of his own intuitions of good, however "rational" his style of argument. But Forster, like Rickie Elliot, believed that he could not follow severely logical arguments. Like Rickie, he pursues their elements either metaphorically or pragmatically, but, unlike Rickie, not always without mockery; if Forster never studied *Principia Ethica*, he had at least flipped through the pages of *Mind*, the philosophical journal that Stewart Ansell's sister, in a wonderful incongruity, fetches out of her shopping bag at the Army and Navy Stores, first seizing the fashionably popular *Windsor* by mistake (p. 197).[40] Probably he flipped through *Principia Ethica* too, although others could have told him that the only concrete example of a beautiful work of art in its last chapter is Beethoven's Fifth Symphony; his presentation of the various reactions of the listeners in *Howards End*, some responses having perhaps a greater "good" than others, is another enactment of Moorean arguments in the "reality" of fiction. Moore's own musicianship was well-informed and passionate, like Forster's. In *The Longest Journey* Ansell is so very unmusical because a lack of an aesthetic sense in him heightens his contrast with Rickie and equalizes the balance between them. Rickie knows that his "sense of beauty" leads him astray if he isn't careful (p. 124); fatal though his errors are, they depend on the fertility of his imagination, that element in him which, when healthy, is most worth saving and is preserved through his writings.

In his fictive evaluation of the "realities" of the Cambridge

[39] See Berel Lang, "Intuition in Bloomsbury" (*Journal of the History of Ideas*, 25 [1964], pp. 295–302), for an account of how G. E. Moore, Keynes, and Roger Fry used similar ideas of intuitive knowledge.

[40] S. P. Rosenbaum, in "*The Longest Journey*: E. M. Forster's Refutation of Idealism" (*E. M. Forster: A Human Exploration*, eds. G. K. Das and John Beer [London, Macmillan, 1979], pp. 32–54), argues that Forster worked from Moore's essay, "The Refutation of Idealism", published in *Mind* in October 1903. In "The Philosophy of E. M. Forster" (*Centenary Revaluations, op. cit.* [fn. 27]), P. N. Furbank responds by noting that the question of objectivity and subjectivity with which the novel opens is a commonplace one, and that Forster's ideas on love and death move well beyond it to much broader questions of moral philosophy. It is perhaps worth noting that American readers, if unfamiliar with the British use of "stop" to mean "stay", as for a visit, may invert Ansell's objectivity to subjectivity as soon as his unnamed questioner (later implied to be Tilliard) says, "if you go, the cow stops"—but that this inversion makes no difference to, and perhaps aids, a clear perception of Ansell's role as one who can, rudely and intuitively, cut through convention-bound thought to find the good and the true. See, for instance, Frederick P. W. McDowell, *E. M. Forster* (New York, Twayne, 1969), p. 66, and its revision, published in 1982, p. 48.

philosophers Forster achieved a careful balance in what he told Bertrand Russell seemed to him "an obvious and symmetrical field" (PNF, p. 151). In his personal life he was also struggling to preserve the worth of the poetic imagination while attaining Ansell's independence of mind. At the biographical level, ironically, Meredith's experiences after the winter of 1902–03 contribute more to Rickie Elliot's than Forster's do; in fact, Ansell's final role as a kind of guardian to Stephen and his family approximates the position Forster assumed later in his life in relation to Bob Buckingham, the policeman he befriended in 1930. But when Forster returned from Italy again in October 1903, Meredith was recovering from a nervous collapse perhaps similar to the "curious breakdown" Rickie Elliot suffers after his engagement causes him to deny his brother's reality (p. 140), perhaps merely the result of overwork in writing the dissertation in economic history that won him a fellowship at King's (among Forster's Apostolic brothers it was Lytton Strachey whose dissertations, like Ansell's, twice failed to win him a fellowship at his own college, Trinity).

Apparently Meredith's illness also involved the breaking of the engagement he had entered in the spring of 1903. However, his and Forster's friend E. J. Dent, another Fellow of King's, records in his diary that Meredith became engaged again, to a different woman, in January 1904, only to break this engagement also a year later.[41] In 1905 Meredith moved to Manchester as a lecturer in economics, and in a letter to Keynes, addressed from Dunwood House, Withington, on 27 April 1906, he remarks, in an Apostolic context: "But I think I am dead really now—or perhaps I should say I realize now what was plain to others two years ago. I come to life temporarily when I meet Forster."[42] Forster's appropriation of "Dunwood House" as the name of Herbert Pembroke's boarding-house at Sawston School, where Rickie is so unlike his former self, perhaps reflects more active efforts on his part to "save" Meredith, who did finally marry in July 1906; his wife was Christabel Iles, G. E. Moore's first woman student. Forster's diary entry for 22 June 1906, the day after his return from a visit to Manchester, has a few short words or initials scratched out, but reads: "I am cut off from [?] [?]: but in recompense will [?] remain beautiful for ever? unattainable equals unchangeable? From the window I

[41] Dent's diary is in the Rowe Music Library at King's College, Cambridge, and is quoted below with the permission of the inheritors of the copyright.
[42] PNF, p. 141. The letter is among the Keynes Papers at King's College. In the manuscripts of *The Longest Journey* "Widdrington", a Northumbrian name which appears also in "Uncle Willie", for a while becomes "Withington".

see attainers: they look not happy." The next entry, for 3 July, is very brief: "Reasons against suicide: (i) selfish (ii) nature ceaselessly beautiful."

Against this background of an emotional life centred on Meredith, who could not or would not continue to return his love completely, Forster reconstructed his life and built *The Longest Journey*. Later, in *Maurice*, he reflects his experience with Meredith again through Clive Durham, whose sexual interests also shift. The relative simplicity of idea and imagery in the later novel is carefully matched to Maurice's mentality; the richness of *The Longest Journey* depends on all that Forster himself had been thinking and feeling. And his love was at this time no bar to his creativity; through 1903 and 1904 he was writing and publishing essays and short stories, based for the most part on his experiences in Italy and Greece, while also working on his two Italian novels, so that at the end of 1904, in his summary of his "youth", he noted that his "Lucy novel" was half done and that "Rescue", later *Where Angels Fear to Tread*, "only needs revising".

Meanwhile elements of *The Longest Journey* were continuing to gather, several of them becoming notable during Forster's visit to Cambridge at the end of the Michaelmas term in 1903. P. N. Furbank quotes both Dent's account of finding Forster in "high indignation"—Dent calls it a "furious state of mind", reflecting the current Cambridge parlance—because of the obscene gossip of a Stracheyan aesthete, N. F. Barwell, and also J. T. Sheppard's Apostolic paper of 5 December 1903, "King's or Trinity", in which Barwell figures as one of the more unpleasantly exclusive of Strachey's Trinity coterie (PNF, pp. 104–7). Forster is not listed among those who heard Sheppard's paper, and Dent's diary indicates that he had left Cambridge the day before, but Sheppard concludes his essay with the same quotation from *Epipsychidion* (plus the following two lines on "True Love") that appears in *The Longest Journey*, so there must have been some mutual influence, perhaps Dickinson's. The differences between Rickie and Ansell in their attitude to the "split" within their own college (p. 20) epitomize Sheppard's observations on what he terms an "old" subject. As Furbank suggests, Forster, whose "evident grief" at the "cleavage" Sheppard refers to, could have "put it in Sheppard's mind to quote those lines from Shelley". Or Sheppard could have been quoting them himself earlier in the week, defending the gentle Christianity of his own tolerant King's view; Dent's diary shows that the subjects of Apostolic discussions were by no means limited strictly to the Society. Another of Sheppard's Apostolic papers, undated, discusses definitions of vulgarity and appears to be referring to Forster as the brother "who is always so much grieved at the 'vulgarity' of those who laugh at the obscene". Sheppard adds, "even if he means simply 'bad taste' by vulgarity I think he is wrong: but probably he means something far more mysterious and more deathly."[43] In Dent's description of the Barwell incident Forster was "very much disgusted not by the subject matter but by the mind that arranged it", so that in *The Longest Journey* it appears to be Mr Failing's distinction between "coarseness" and "vulgarity", associating the latter with hypocritical discriminations (p. 207), that expresses Forster's ideas.

During this visit to Cambridge Forster also attended the triennial production of a Greek play performed in Greek. The play was Aristophanes' *The Birds*, with Sheppard in the lead role, and in Forster's diary his notes on the play inaugurate a series of thoughts on Greece and things Greek that underlie his "realizations" of Greek literature and art in *The Longest Journey*. On the play itself, notable for its coarse mortals and the lovely choruses of the birds, Forster's comment adds a further perspective to his ideas on obscenity and "vulgarity":

> The "Birds" at Cambridge: (i) People misunderstand it because they mistrust anything beautiful (ii) and we always connect beauty with solemnity; the Greeks knew that it can spring from a laugh and resolve into one: I'm sure we should understand their comedy if we admitted that, and gave up talking about "allegories". (8 December 1903)

Three months later he comments again on the humanity visible to him in the Greek sculpture at the British Museum, foreshadowing Ansell's awareness of "vanished incense and deserted temples" (p. 182):

> Each time I see those Greek things in the B. M. they are more beautiful and more hopeless. It's simple to say they are gods—down to the bulls going to sacrifice on the Parthenon frieze. But I don't believe gods would make one so unhappy. Up to Demeter and Persephone on the pediment they are human, and our perpetual rebuke.
>
> It is so curious, this desire to be simple and beautiful and strong. But our only hope lies through all these complications—not by affecting simplicity. So I'll call the Parthenon not a rebuke but a comment—which makes me feel worse. (13 March 1904)

---

[43] "May We Eat Cheese with a Knife?", Sheppard Papers, King's College Library, quoted by permission of the Trustees of the Sheppard Estate.

A week later he comments on his memories of his tour of Greece the year before, mixing sentiment, laughter, and prosaic realities again before adding a note on his choice of abstinence in his adaptation to his homosexuality:

> I look on Greece as a stronghold for sentiment—for I ragged all the time I was there, and, if anything, am more sentimental than I was before I went. And, I've just thought, I like the delicate irony with which she laid her finger on my nose and made it red, ruining my appearance, such as it is, for life: meaning either "they used to be that colour all over" or more probably "don't go talking about your affinity with the antique". But I have slept the sleep of the drunk at Troy, and [*one-word blank*] in the Castalian Spring. If I have understood the classics, this is as it should be.
>
> *Cosa farò* [*d'*]*altra?* [*What else can I do?*] I'd better eat my soul for I certainly shan't have it. I'm going to be a minority if not a solitary, and I'd best make copy out of my position. There is nothing contemptible or cynical in this: I too have sweet waters, though I shall never drink them. I can understand the draughts of the others, though they will not understand my abstinence. (21 March 1904)[44]

By this time the link between Forster's own sexual sense and his interpretations of Greek humanity is firm; it was a civilization in which he could imagine his homosexuality being accepted simply as part of the spectrum of human realities. He must have explained the reasons for his abstinence in the paper he read to the Apostles on 26 November 1904, entitled "The Bedroom, Brother?", but unfortunately it does not survive. Its date is close enough to his end-of-the-year statement that his "reconstruction" was "practically over" to make the loss a tantalizing one, particularly because, as he notes in his introduction, the "idea" of *The Longest Journey* had come to him in July and the role of Wiltshire had begun to develop in September. The "Plot" of the novel that he wrote out on 17 July 1904, transcribed below, places the illegitimate brother in Italy rather than Wiltshire and makes the Ansell-figure, Ford, a more self-sacrificing one, but Forster's sense that he had "best make copy" of his "position" was obviously contributing quite consciously to his ideas of the morality of Rickie's choices and of the relationships among the male characters.

This November meeting of the Apostles was the last Forster attended before beginning *The Longest Journey*, as well as the first at which he had given a paper since his initial effort in 1901. He

---

[44] Compare PNF, p. 111, where "draughts" has been misprinted as "drought", and, on p. 110, in the preceding quotation, "curious" as "unwise".

had also been at the meeting a week earlier, on 19 November 1904, when Lytton Strachey read "Does Absence Make the Heart Grow Fonder?", arguing that in a "marriage of true minds" the minds need absence to stay interesting to each other, whatever their sex might be.[45] The psychological rather than philosophical character of Strachey's essay and the mere fact that Forster felt confident enough to read a paper himself is evidence that the height of Apostolic enthusiasm for Moore's most stringent methods had already passed. Forster had also attended two other meetings in the previous academic year, on 13 February and 21 May 1904, but the only surviving suggestion that these visits to Cambridge contributed specific elements to the novel is Dent's note that on the night of 14 February, "Forster came in about 10:15, and made me play Wagner which was strangely unfamiliar to my awkward fingers."

LATER INFLUENCES

Although some specific expressions of the Apostolic influence on *The Longest Journey* can be dated to the winter of 1903–04, the philosophical opposition, or balance, that Forster epitomizes in the opening scene of *The Longest Journey* had been visible for some time before and of course continued to develop in his thoughts. In the 1904 "Plot" Ford is "soaked with idea of mutability", which makes him sound more like Rickie, convinced that "we are all of us bubbles on an extremely rough sea" (p. 57), than Ansell. To the Apostolic background of *The Longest Journey* must be added the influences of the following years, represented by Dante and Forster's teaching of Renaissance history in his Extension Lecturing tours, by his Latin classes at the Working Men's College and his edition of Virgil's *Aeneid*, produced for the Temple Classics series edited by Dickinson and Meredith, and by his less known work with Julia Wedgwood in her revision of *The Moral Ideal*. This history of the evolution of ethical goals, which she had first published in 1888, helps to explain both the Hegelian structure of *The Longest Journey* and some of Ansell's less Moorean characteristics, like his knowledge of Schopenhauer and the criticism that he's "read too much Hegel" (p. 197).

The record of Forster's acquaintance with "Snow" Wedgwood, an elderly friend of his Aunt Laura, also dates to the winter of

[45] *The Really Interesting Question and Other Papers*, ed. Paul Levy (London, Weidenfeld & Nicolson, 1972), pp. 101–6.

1903, when she accompanied him to the Cambridge production of *The Birds*. In April 1904 he visited Idlerocks, the Wedgwood family home near their potteries in Staffordshire; his stay probably coincided with another of Miss Wedgwood's ventures from London. His initial reading of *The Moral Ideal* must have been complete by 18 July 1904, when "Today have been working again at Miss Wedgwood's" is the sentence immediately preceding his note of the inception of *The Longest Journey* (p. lxvi). The work brackets the composition of the novel; it is next mentioned in the diary on 7 March 1907, after Forster would have finished with the proofs of the novel: "Back from long day at *Moral Ideal*. Slept at Snow's." Again, "much labour over *Moral Ideal*, to which I look back with pleasure", is his comment in his annual summary on 31 December 1907. As for the influence of the book, it is impossible to read either version of *The Moral Ideal* without becoming fully aware of an organization of thought permeated by the Hegelian zigzag of thesis-antithesis-synthesis. Miss Wedgwood advances through negation, and as she traces the evolution of ideas of good and evil from ancient India to Persia and Greece and Rome, through the rise of Christianity, her observations on the Greeks correspond to Rickie's awareness of good-and-evil, and her account of the Judaeo-Christian idea of the individual finds an echo in *Howards End* in Helen Schlegel's insistence on the importance of saying "I". The sections on India, particularly in the revision, not only provide a very early source for the knowledge of Hinduism Forster uses in *A Passage to India* but also describe the clarity of the "overarching" night sky of the sub-continent, drawing particular attention to the constellation Orion and giving a further example of the astronomical awareness that figures in the later novel as well as in *The Longest Journey*.

How much Forster contributed to the revision is unknown.[46] Perhaps he added Orion, which takes on so much symbolic significance in *The Longest Journey*; his interest in learning the constellations appears also to have originated in this 1904 period (see pp. 193 and 278 and their notes). In the revision Miss Wedgwood's problem, like Dickinson's in writing *A Modern Symposium*, was in part stylistic, a matter of moving from the idealized generalizations

---

[46] B. J. Kirkpatrick records Forster's statement that he "redrafted certain passages with the author's approval" (*op. cit.* [fn 1], p. 80 [item B2]). In *Marianne Thornton* (1956) and in "'Snow' Wedgwood", reprinted in *Two Cheers for Democracy* from "More Browning Letters" (*The Listener*, 13 October 1937, Supplement, p. xv), Forster describes something of Miss Wedgwood's character but merely mentions the book.

of late Victorian prose to the more definite statements demanded by twentieth-century rationalists. The beginning of her summing up in the first edition illustrates both the Hegelian patterning and the stylistic difficulties:

> We have seen how the evolution of the moral life of Humanity passes in throbs of antagonism from race to race, and how yet this antagonism is never a mere recoil; so that, when the Persian Dualism arose to protest against the confusion of Good and Evil in the Indian Pantheism, this dualism held some hint of an ultimate Unity, which, as the goal of all existence, must also have been in some sense its starting point. And then, again, we have seen how, when the process was reversed, and the rich variety of the artist people [the Greeks] was exchanged for the monotony of the world's lawgivers [the Romans], there was yet a sort of escape from that monotony in the influence which made of Rome the mediator of the nations, enclosing in its hard framework the variety of the Greek world. . . . When the consciousness of the race passed from that conviction which was the groundwork of all ancient morals, that the state was a unity, to the double conviction that the individual is a unity [Judaeo-Christians], it made an advance which could never again be lost, but which with the progress of the ages withers into as exclusive a doctrine as that against which it was a reaction.[47]

To a great extent the revision simply shortened sentences, but Miss Wedgwood responded to the developments of her time by adding an initial chapter on ancient Egypt and by recognizing scientific advances: "The discernment that Truth is movement is one as important for the moral world as the discernment that light is movement is for the scientific world."[48] She also became more explicit about sex, changing the title of her concluding chapter from "The Heritage of Today" to "Male and Female Created He Them". In her revised conclusion she still describes the family love that contributes to the continuing evolution of the "moral ideal" as an expression of "that law of recurrence in spiritual polarity which exhibits antagonism as the unresolved discord leading to the richest harmony",[49] using language equivalent to McTaggart's and Dickinson's most idealistic wordings of the same Hegelianism. Unlike the Cambridge philosophers, however, Miss Wedgwood finds the most complete worldly ideal not in an all-male symposium but in a heterosexual union:

> The closest bond which unites man with man is weak beside the bond which unites man with woman. That apprehension of needs and desires

[47] *The Moral Ideal* (London, Trübner, 1888), pp. 388–9.
[48] *The Moral Ideal*, rev. ed. (London; Kegan Paul, Trench, Trübner; 1907), p. 462.
[49] *Ibid.*, pp. 478–9.

not our own which elsewhere is the conquest of virtue, is here the fruit
of a satisfied instinct, and one which we share with the creatures beneath us. That emancipation from the fetters of self, which with regard
to the many seems impossible, is with regard to an individual natural
and ordinary. Surely the love of sex was given to human beings to
emphasize the lesson that the true union is between opposites. . . . An
impulse wider than humanity creates a union between two beings
whose bond is not a common set of characteristics, but one unalterably
different. The lesson of our incompleteness, the fragmentary nature of
each one of us alone, is enforced by the law which gives creative power
to the union of male with female.[50]

This argument too Forster must have considered. It was also Miss
Wedgwood who, after reading *Where Angels Fear to Tread* late in
1905, "begged him to fall in love before writing another novel"
(PNF, p. 136). Perhaps something of her concern lies behind the
"Male and Female created He not them" in Forster's letter to
Reid about *Maurice*, or behind Mrs Failing's final advice to Rickie
to follow the conventions, or even behind Rickie's novel, written
after he leaves Agnes, about "a man and a woman who meet and
are happy" (p. 277).

In the spring of 1904, family as well as friends began to gain
prominence in the background of the novel, for in April Forster
visited his Uncle Willie for the first time since 1899, inaugurating
a series of annual visits that came to an end in August 1907, perhaps partly because of the way Forster had borrowed not only his
uncle's character and house for *The Longest Journey* but also the
name of his wife, Forster's "real" Aunt Emily. In his memoir of
his uncle, Forster tells his Bloomsbury audience that he used his
uncle's character for that of Mrs Failing, the "Aunt Emily" of the
novel, and the character of his wife, Emily Forster, for that of
Charlotte Bartlett in *A Room with a View*, which, as his "Lucy
novel", was also developing throughout 1904. Surely any woman
who resembled Charlotte Bartlett, finding her house transplanted
to Wiltshire and inhabited by an aunt known to the Forster-like
hero by her name, would take offence. A draft of the contretemps
caused by Lucy's discovery that Charlotte Bartlett had given away
the secret of her lover's kiss to a novelist, who promptly used it in
a novel, exists among the early "Lucy" manuscripts.[51] Otherwise
one would suspect that the episode draws on some "reality" of
Forster's relation to his aunt. This must have been strained by *The*

[50] *Ibid.*, p. 474.
[51] *The Lucy Novels: Early Sketches for A Room with a View* (vol. 3a, Abinger Edition,
1977), pp. 92–101.

Longest Journey, perhaps particularly by the scene depicting Mrs Failing's church-going. Nor is it likely that Uncle Willie would have overlooked Agnes's comment on her floundering "Uncle Willie" (p. 141), whether or not he recognized himself or some form of his wife in Emily Failing. In his introduction Forster concludes by telling us that his uncle bought remaindered copies of the novel and sent them to the relatives they "were most likely to upset"; in the memoir he notes that the third member of the household, Miss Leo Chipman, considered him "very cynical, especially in *The Longest Journey*" (p. 297). Since Miss Chipman's position as the unexplained Canadian "daughter" bears some slight relationship to Stephen Wonham's equivocal role in Mrs Failing's establishment, her view is not surprising.

Certainly Forster's memoir is cynical, almost vicious in its portrayal of the women and at the same time rather puzzling in its lack of recognition of his novel as a contributing cause for the cessation of his visits and his omission from Aunt Emily's will. He is so sensitive about the money, in fact, sounding almost like Rickie Elliot's cousins, the hungry Silts, that it should be noted that nearly all of the money was Aunt Emily's, not Uncle Willie's. Four years younger than Edward Morgan Forster's father, William Howley Forster had been born in 1851, the last of the ten children of the Reverend Charles Forster, Rector of Stisted. The only two of the ten who survived into Forster's adulthood were William and the unmarried Laura, who, probably with her brother's knowledge, made Forster her heir in 1904; she died twenty years later. His only first cousins on the paternal side were the six children of the second oldest brother, also Reverend Charles Forster, who was Vicar of Hinxton until his death in 1891. William was thus the closest family equivalent to his father left to Forster in his adolescence. In 1877 William had married Emily Jane Nash, who was eight years older than he; just when Annie Leontine Chipman became their guest is not clear, but she was born in 1864, and was thus fifteen years older than Forster. As he explains, when William died in 1910 he left all he had—about £8,000—to his wife. When she died in 1917 she left £57,000 to her own cousins and friends, to the families of two of Forster's cousins, Mabel and Charles, and to Miss Chipman. Thus only two of William's seven nieces and nephews received anything, but these bequests were generous, as Forster says. Mabel, who had married Sir Lennox Napier, received £5,000; her five children shared another £5,000; £5,000 went to the son of Forster's cousin Charles, also Charles, and the residue of the estate, less than £5,000 after all the other bequests, also went to Charles and his son. Miss Chipman did not, as Forster says, get "almost all", but she did get about half, made up of the personal effects, all of William's money that could still be identified within the estate, and a separate bequest of £15,000, three times as much as any of the others.

Miss Chipman was one of the witnesses to William's will. She must have known that there was no formal economic tie binding her to live with Emily, only a mutual tie of trust, amply repaid. If Forster's account of William and Emily Forster is at all true, then Miss Chipman, like Stephen Wonham, "ought" to have been paid (p. 191). Sir Joseph Napier, Mabel's son, still remembers "Chip" as "great fun" both before World War I and after, on golfing holidays in Northumberland. He also recalls teasing his helpless cousin "Morgie" on earlier visits; his sisters, the eldest, Marjorie, born in 1894, were the girl cousins Forster complains "were encouraged to bait me and be rough" (p. 297). This too contributed to the cessation of Forster's journeys to Northumberland; in his diary entry of 31 December 1907, noting enjoyable visits during the year to Wiltshire and Manchester, he writes: "Less enjoyable was W.H.F., who lets Marjorie Napier and other little girls be rough to me. Go with increasing reluctance." And the diary shows that in August 1908, when he received what he considered a late and "rude" invitation from his uncle, he was glad he had made other plans and "could easily refuse". "Chip", however, kept in touch with the Napiers, sending Marjorie some family silver when she returned to Canada for good some years before her death in 1937. She also did her best to return Emily's money to Hinxton, "oddest of places" (p. 300). It came to this tiny village south of Cambridge on the death of the last of Miss Chipman's sisters, tied explicitly to the re-establishment of Hinxton as a separate parish with a resident vicar, and accepted by the Church of England on these terms. Unfortunately the money has now somehow been merged into broader-reaching accounts of the Church, so that Hinxton again lacks separate status and shares a vicar, and the grass grows high in the graveyard, obscuring the names on Uncle Willie's and Aunt Emily's cross.

How much Forster adapted his uncle's history for the sake of entertaining his Bloomsbury audience, how much his comments on the sexual jealousies of the household reflect his own awareness in 1904, are open questions. The scandals in the Cresswell family which Forster mentions were fresh that spring (p. 299), but his associated feeling that his homosexuality was outside his uncle's ken would have been present anyway, and the scandals could have reverberated for years. His next visit took place eighteen months later, in October 1905, after he had returned from a spring and summer in Germany, where he tutored the daughters of the Countess von Arnim (later Countess Russell) and began the writing of *The Longest Journey*. His memoir of his time in Nassenheide directly precedes "Uncle Willie" in manuscript, and P. N. Furbank suggests that the Countess, author of *Elizabeth and her German Garden* (1898) and a steady stream of successful novels, was also a model for the equally unconventional Mrs Failing.[52] In the 1904 "Plot" Mrs Failing's place is held by "Uncle Basil", but the Countess could easily have been amalgamated with Uncle Willie even during this October visit, since Mrs Failing does not appear until Chapter 10; in the manuscript of Chapter 1, written in Nassenheide, there is a deleted reference to her as an established author rather than as a mere widow of an essayist. Wherever she sprang from, Mrs Failing is an impressive creation, lazing toward her own loneliness despite her intelligence, so that one responds to her with an ambivalence similar to that Forster shows in his description of his uncle's virtues and vices, and in his presentation of Rickie Elliot. He visited his uncle again in August 1906, when *The Longest Journey* was nearly finished; perhaps Stephen's sentence about otter-hunting (p. 187), not in the manuscripts, draws on this visit.

The Longest Journey appears to have taken priority over Forster's half-done "Lucy" novel during the spring of 1905. *Where Angels Fear to Tread* was finished by the end of February, when Meredith and Dent read and acclaimed it. Each, according to Dent's diary, recognized something of himself in the hero, but on 9 March Dent noted that Forster told him that Philip Herriton was "drawn from himself and me, and that Hugh does not come in". In "My Books and I" Forster repeats this, using Dent for his example of how he could work from "two-thirds of a human being" in creating his fictional characters (p. 304).[53] Forster's diary entries for February show that his plans to go to Nassenheide became definite early in the month, when he was reading Samuel Butler's posthumously

[52] PNF, p. 125. Most of this memoir has been published by Leslie de Charms (pseud.) in *Elizabeth of the German Garden* (London, Heinemann, 1958), pp. 73, 101–4, and in Forster's "Recollections of Nassenheide", *The Listener*, 1 January 1959, pp. 12–14.

[53] Dent's record of his initial response to the novel reverses the viewpoint: "The book is wonderful and some chapters—especially that on the opera—moved me I think more than anything in literature. The whole work is to me an extraordinary revelation of Forster and I cursed my stupidity in not being able to understand him before." (27 February 1905; abbreviations have been spelled out.)

published novel, *The Way of All Flesh*, and criticizing it in a way that reflects his own ambitions: "so clever it is at describing character, so bad at making people: the scheme so immense, the effect so unreal because he is resolutely unconventional." On 24 February Forster noted that he was "writing 'Other Kingdom', which should make up a book of short stories". On 16 March a longer entry notes a visit to the Army and Navy Stores that morning, and records as "good for copy" a friend's story of a "boy with protruding ears whose life was a burden to him", foreshadowing Varden. The same entry notes "discoveries" of Trollope, a "real comedian who realizes that all things can have a humorous surface", and Blake, who "is always going for the Greeks". The accompanying reading list shows "some of *Barchester Towers*", Blake's "Vision of Last Judgement", Bernard Shaw's *Cashel Byron's Profession*, and *The Birth of Parsifal*, a dramatic poem by Forster's friend, R. C. Trevelyan. All of these works seem to have contributed directly or indirectly to *The Longest Journey*, Shaw's novel even more comically than Trollope's. Herbert Pembroke is a very Trollopean character, but in Chapter 12 Stephen loses his fight with the shepherd very much as Shaw's Byron, a handsome and splendidly uncultured professional boxer, loses his with the servant Bashville, who is unexpectedly skilled in Cornish wrestling. Shaw's romantic plot expresses his characteristic interest in establishing a proper balance of heredity in marriage, and it is just possible that the conversation recording the heroine's first view of a boxing ring contributes another level of significance to the earthy symbolism of the Cadbury Rings:

> "What is that?" she asked.
> "That! Oh, that's the ring."
> "It is not a ring. It is a square."
> "They call it the ring. They have succeeded in squaring the circle."[54]

By the end of March, Forster was in Dresden, visiting art galleries and, on 1 April, noting the opera: "*Siegfried* this evening. Hitherto *Rheingold* has been more wonderful, and of *Valkyrie* the first act." A few days later he was in Nassenheide, "chronicling", on 8 April, "that yesterday Blackwood offered me (bad) terms for my novel". He finished his edition of Virgil's *Aeneid* at the end of June, and the proofs of his first novel arrived early in July. On 18 August, on his way back to England, he wrote to his mother from Kiel, commenting on the final choice of the title for *Where Angels*

[54] *Cashel Byron's Profession* (London, Heron Books, 1968), p. 157.

Fear to Tread, to which he was urged by the Countess, and adding, "Should I ever write another book it will be called 'The Longest Journey', and the one after that 'Windy Corner'." "Windy Corner" is the name of Lucy's Surrey home in *A Room with a View*; he had by this time already begun *The Longest Journey*. The manuscripts of the novel are not themselves dated, but the ink of the opening chapter matches that of Forster's letters from Nassenheide and that on the surviving proofs of *Where Angels Fear to Tread*. Thereafter the evolution of the novel has to be approximately dated from the fragmentary evidence of complex revisions preserved as "scraps" and on versos. What is dated, however, and to be considered first, is the initial "Plot" of 17 July 1904. According to P. N. Furbank's working notes this was found among Forster's papers after his death "inside the early, incomplete novel", now called *Nottingham Lace*. This is the work that Forster in "My Books and I" calls "that novel about a boy named Edgar" (p. 301). Edgar resembles a younger Rickie Elliot, and Sidney Trent, the vigorous young schoolmaster who comes to Sawston and rouses Edgar from his inhibited passivity, is a forerunner of Stewart Ansell. The placing of the "Plot" perhaps reflected Forster's recognition of these affinities.[55] It reads as follows; Forster's abbreviations have been spelled out:

A "Plot" 17/7/04.

1. Renée and Mr Aldridge—a practical, unsuccessful, man—paid a visit to Humphrey [*blank*], in his second year. They are old friends: but Renée for the first time "realizes" him—that he [is] clever in the first place, and that something might be "made" of him. She disapproved of his effeminancy [*sic*], and of his friends—notably the brainy uncouth undergraduate soaked with idea of mutability, Ford, and of a don who wished to run him also.

2. Humphrey found happiness at Cambridge after a querulous childhood, and obscure life at school. Spirits and intelligence both improved. Literary powers developed.

After the departure of the visitors, he, Ford, and three or four more swore "eternal" friendship one evening by the rifle butts.

3. During the year of cramming for the Civil Service, Renée's interest in Humphrey increased. He got Home Civil, Ford taking Indian Civil Service in order that he might have it.

4. Soon after Ford's departure for India, Renée and Humphrey got engaged.

5. Uncle Basil and his household at Ponte Molino.

6. Renée and Humphrey came there for their honeymoon. Pasquale:

[55] One image from *Nottingham Lace*, a description of "bubbles" of air, recurs in *The Longest Journey*. See p. 278 and note.

whom Uncle Basil, for the sake of seeing what would happen, revealed to Humphrey as his brother. Humphrey wished to accept him. Renée naturally objects, and their dissension begins.

7. Renée gradually detached Humphrey from his friends. Her behaviour at her father's death revealed to him their dissimilarity, and the Italian brother was a constant source of discord.

8. Ford, broken down, returned to England, having stayed in Italy on the way. The first meeting with Renée and Humphrey. Humphrey giving up Home Civil to reside in Cambridge.

9. Struggle between Ford and Renée began.

10. Death of Uncle Basil, releasing Pasquale.

11. Ford and Humphrey took holiday.

12. Ford met Pasquale: who knew he was Humphrey's brother but kept silence.

13. The fire: death of Pasquale and Humphrey.

14. Epilogue: Humphrey's book successful.

To this, as Forster relates in his introduction, must be added his September meetings with the shepherds near Salisbury, where, as often before, he was visiting Maimie Aylward, a cousin by marriage and an old family friend, then in her sixties. His diary entries, for a Monday and the following Friday, are consecutive and are here given complete; the conclusion of the second describes part of the route followed by Stephen and Rickie during their morning ride in Chapter 12:

September 12. Today walked out to Figsbury Ring, to try and find the lame shepherd of last Friday: he had gone to Wilton, and I suppose I shan't again see one of the most remarkable people I've ever met. What strikes me even more than his offering me his pipe to smoke is his enormous wisdom: his head—whether he knows it or not—is out of the water: if only he isn't bowled over by the beastly money! I was: but I was simply bound to think myself unsympathetic, whether I offered that sixpence or not, and I get a comfort in the rebuff, by seeing that he's better than ever. *Vorrei cercarlo ancora—ma come si può vivere quando si domanda sempre "cosa fa?", "dove va?"* [*I would like to search for him still—but how can one live when people are always asking "what are you doing?", "where are you going?"*] This "incident" assures my opinion that the English *can* be the greatest men in the world: he was miles greater than an Italian: one cannot dare to call his simplicity naîf. The aesthetic die away attitude seems contemptible in a world which has such people.

September 16. Yesterday, seeking the son again, I found the father, whose head is out of the water too. He has shepherded for five years of Sundays, cannot read writing and has never been further than Andover. He is neatly dressed, and altogether less wonderful than the boy, though he also is free of saying "sir". I say I will look them up next year: he shows no enthusiasm, but I don't see why he should mind. The "incident" is now rounded off agreeably, and though the outline has softened I think that is only for a time.

Today train to Amesbury; and walk back through country which was sometimes fairy land, sometimes the Campagna, with a straggling row of stone pines: but not often the real Wiltshire—except a great bare skull of fields half way, surrounded by an edge of distant view.

THE MANUSCRIPTS

Wiltshire, in the person of Stephen, gave most trouble in the writing of the novel, to judge from the surviving manuscripts. They are described in detail in Appendix C; here an account of the major revisions indirectly provides a rough calendar of the writing. "Cambridge", the first section of the novel, takes up more than half of the whole and ends with Chapter 15. Stephen first appears in Chapter 10, when he and Mrs Failing are introduced before Rickie and Agnes arrive on their visit to Wiltshire. Mrs Failing has been referred to earlier, but Stephen is new. The visit runs through into the first pages of Chapter 15, and Chapters 10–14, by comparison with the first nine, have been very heavily revised. Among the earlier chapters the fifth, in which Gerald dies, is missing its first page or two and also shows evidence of much revision. Rickie's Wagnerian response to love in Chapter 3 and Ansell's circles and squares at the end of Chapter 1 are additions or revisions, and much of Chapter 2 seems to have been neatly recopied, but on the whole Forster appears to have written the first third or so of the novel, up to Chapter 10, with relative ease. How far he progressed thereafter, before he began to revise the original version of Chapters 10–14, is not clear. The abandoned "fantasy" or "Harold" chapter, still numbered XIV but associated with Chapter 12, helps to define an original Harold version of the novel which once progressed at least as far as the end of the present Chapter 14 and included what is now Chapter 29, the account of Stephen's parents that opens "Wiltshire", the final section of the novel. Chapter 29, however, has no concern with the actions of Stephen himself. It shares the distinctive rusty ink of the other Harold pages and shows "Harold", beneath the correction to "Stephen", as the name of the child (p. 239). Aside from these clues, however, there would be nothing to show what is clearly the case, that this chapter was written early and set aside for later use. Conveniently for this kind of analysis, the distinctive ink of the

1

Harold pages does not appear in the chapters of the second section of the novel, "Sawston", except on versos found in Chapters 25 and 26. Like the fantasy chapter, these versos show "Harold" only; there is no correction to "Stephen". They are preserved on earlier pages of these much-revised later chapters; their placing indicates that "Harold" had certainly been changed to "Stephen" by the time Chapters 25 and 26 were first revised, if not by the time they were initially drafted. Chapter 26 brings Stephen back "onstage" for the first time since his exit in Chapter 14, and Chapter 25 prepares for this event, so it is possible that Forster did not make the change from "Harold" to "Stephen" in Chapters 10–14 until these later chapters brought him to reconsider the Harold-Stephen character. But this would be the latest point at which the change could have been made, and Forster could in any case have discarded the fantasy chapter before the renaming. In his letter to Dent of April 1907, quoted above, he writes that he thought the "'Panic'" chapter "rather jolly" but "soon cut it out". Perhaps it survives because Forster thought it might make a separate story. In some ways the lyrically comic bathing scene of *A Room with a View* approximates Harold's adventure, but in terming Harold's experience a "panic" Forster of course demands that it be compared to "The Story of a Panic". A similar enchantment by the powers of nature also overcomes another Harold, the hero of Forster's first published story, "Albergo Empedocle".[56] Still another unintellectual and athletic Harold, associated as Stephen is with the constellation Orion, dies at a peak of physical exertion in "The Point of It", first published in 1911.

The text of the published novel differs only slightly from that of the recto pages of the main manuscript, and the surviving Harold pages among the rectos show little change beyond the correction from "Harold" to "Stephen". It is the versos and scraps that give evidence of major revision, both in the Harold version and in Chapters 20–28 of "Sawston". Even though these "Sawston" chapters may have been drafted before the renaming of the Harold-Stephen character, it is simplest to speak of the Harold version as an original draft that covered Stephen's first appearance in the novel, now limited to Chapters 10–14 but then including

---

[56] "Albergo Empedocle" (*Temple Bar*, December 1903, pp. 663–84) is the only one of Forster's published stories which was not reprinted in his lifetime; it appears in the Abinger Edition in *The Life to Come and Other Stories*. Or see *"Albergo Empedocle" and Other Writings by E. M. Forster*, ed. George H. Thomson (New York, Liveright, 1971), which reprints most of Forster's uncollected writings published before 1915, including "Pessimism in Literature" and "Dante".

both Harold's "panic" and what is now Chapter 29. The excision of the fantasy chapter is of course the major visible change, but the versos show that other visitors once joined Rickie and Agnes at tea on their arrival, and that Mrs Failing once made her half-revelation of the brothers' relationship in her garden, so that Rickie fell on gravel, not on the grassy earth of the Cadbury Rings. There was also, perhaps, a change in the character of Stephen, who may have been better spoken, more of a "gentleman", as Harold. This impression comes largely from the fantasy chapter, in which the naked Harold, recovering from his panic, thinks clearly, acts cleverly, and wins his battle with the shepherd, unlike Stephen. Harold, having stepped outside convention in his nakedness, comes to a relatively sophisticated realization of its power in society; Stephen, winning one trial of strength and losing another, muses more simply on the unpredictability of fortune. On one of the surviving rectos Harold was also capable of saying that he would teach the shepherd "gratis", a word changed to Stephen's "for nothing" (p. 107), but there are no other comparable changes still visible. There is some indication that the name "Stephen" became "Harold" and then "Stephen" again (p. 327). If the final change reflects more than a simple renaming, the Anglo-Saxon and Byronic connotations of "Harold" may have seemed to Forster at once too simple and too sophisticated for the character of Stephen. "Stephen", with its Greek meaning of "crowned" and its Christian association with martyrdom, still recalls the early kings of England even as it draws on the more ancient traditions.

To account for the number XIV on the fantasy chapter and for the events Forster describes in his introduction as leading to it, two Harold chapters must have been cut from this draft of *The Longest Journey*. Several pages now in Chapters 10 and 12, like those making up the latter half of Chapter 11, were originally Harold pages. These include the two which introduce the bucolic idyll with the soldier in Chapter 12; the original order of chapters up to this point was probably the same as the present one. But there are so many later revisions in Chapters 13 and 14 that chapter numbers which might have succeeded the XIV of the fantasy chapter have disappeared. Chapters 15–19 show less revision; descriptions of public-school life in Sawston evidently came more easily to Forster's pen than portrayals of Stephen. Even so, the opening pages of Chapters 15–17 are either late or missing, and the numbering of Chapters 20–25 shows much change; only the heading of Chapter 18 appears to be an unrevised XVIII. Thus it is not possible to say for certain whether the cutting of the fantasy chapter occurred

before or during the renaming, and even that change can be dated
only roughly. Forster's diary entry of 22 November 1905 records,
and shows, his use of "a new stylo-pen—easy but not clear". All
the pages of the Harold version show both the rusty ink and the
use of a finer nib; the original version of Chapters 10–14 and
Chapter 29 could have been written by 22 November, then revised
sometime in the next three or four months. There are no diary
entries between 3 December 1905 and 1 March 1906, but in
Chapters 19 and 20 there is a revision of the setting of Rickie's
Easter holiday which moves it from Eastbourne to Ilfracombe,
where Forster lectured in February 1906. He was then making a
lecture tour of the west, accompanied by his mother; they were in
Penzance when he wrote the diary entry of 23 March, quoted
above, in which he doubted the worth of the "ingenious symbols"
of *The Longest Journey*. Perhaps he was then in the midst of the
major revision of the early drafts of the "Sawston" chapters, or
contemplating its results. By this time the change from "Harold"
to "Stephen" must have been made, merely to allow time for the
later revisions. But it is unlikely that Forster had finished a complete first draft; the progressions of different inks throughout the
manuscripts are such that the earliest surviving drafts of the later
"Wiltshire" chapters appear to have been written after the first
and even the intermediate revisions of "Sawston".

The changes still detectible at the earliest levels of the "Sawston"
chapters have less to do with the character of Stephen than with
the plot. The calendar of events once brought Stephen and Ansell
to Sawston in the winter, soon after the November death of Rickie's
child and the illness of Varden. Varden's letter may have helped
to bring Stephen to Sawston; Ansell, perhaps in response to Widdrington's urging (which now occurs in Chapter 20 but once
followed Varden's illness and therefore, perhaps, the child's birth
and death), had at last accepted Rickie's invitation to visit and
was staying with the Elliots, not the Jacksons, when he met Stephen
in Rickie's "leafless" garden. Chapter 27 is missing from the
manuscript, but one of the versos which survive from its early
drafts shows Ansell telling Rickie that Stephen is his mother's son
very quietly, not in the midst of the schoolboys' Sunday dinner
but just before he ends his visit, at the end of the chapter. Another
verso, now found at an early level of Chapter 25, shows that at
one time a conversation between Widdrington and Ansell in the
British Museum followed this revelation; Ansell's reaction to the
Greek statuary in the museum was salvaged from this verso for use
in Chapter 20. Chapters 21 and 22, recounting the birth and death

of Rickie's child and the illness of Varden, appear originally to have been one, and there are hints that the child's death once created a more loving and sympathetic relationship between Agnes and Rickie. But very little remains that can be clearly attributed to the earliest versions of Chapters 20–27; further changes are best allotted to intermediate and final stages of revision. For instance, a discarded chapter of letters, numbered XXVIII, may have replaced rather than followed the omitted meeting in the British Museum; its two surviving typescript pages, unmarked by author or printer, are the only evidence that the manuscript was typed. Chapter 24 in its current form is particularly late, written or re-written on sheets whose versos show remnants from both earlier and later chapters. It is a very useful chapter; the meeting with Ansell's sister blackens Agnes's character as it provides further impetus for Ansell's visit to Sawston, and the dramatic unconventionality of Ansell's character is heightened when he invites himself to the Jacksons' home. A discarded sheet from the opening of Chapter 24, now a verso in Chapter 30, shows that Stephen's character was also blackened, for in the verso passage Mrs Silt, during her visit to Dunwood House, gives a graphic report of Stephen's drunken rudeness to her. Chapter 30, which brings Stephen, drunk, back to Sawston, also holds two versos drawn from the major early revision of Chapter 13; these versos and the one from Chapter 24 help to prove Forster's continuing return to earlier presentations of Stephen's character as he revised later ones.

To recapitulate, the revision of Chapters 10–14 that changed "Harold" to "Stephen" must have occurred by the time of the first major revisions of the climactic "Sawston" chapters; as the "Sawston" chapters were further revised, Forster also continued to adjust earlier ones. This process continued as the "Wiltshire" chapters reached completion. Early in October 1906 Forster and his mother took a trip to the Loire valley, and a verso showing lines from a lost or abandoned account of this journey now rests on a late page in Chapter 33. Presumably the manuscript was in a nearly final form before this trip, then prepared for the typist when Forster returned. The massive early revisions must have occurred early in the spring, or before, to leave the summer months for the further writing and rewriting. As for the "Wiltshire" chapters, the last two, Chapters 34 and 35, are relatively neat, perhaps because of recopying. Chapter 29, as indicated, was written much earlier; only its first and last pages, adjusting to its final position, are later. Like Chapter 26, Chapter 30 brings Stephen back into the action of the novel; the variants in both these chapters affect Stephen's character to a degree that requires a relatively full listing in Appendix C. On the late pages of Chapter 30 there are even some undeleted passages, absent from the published text, which suggest that Stephen, here separated from Wiltshire, might yearn for its landscape with a poet's intensity. However, it is the discarded material related to Chapter 31 which shows that Forster was still making major changes in these late chapters at the typescript stage, or even in proof.

Chapter 31 was originally, as it is now, one long chapter, but it initially presented an interview between Ansell and Stephen which led to Stephen's meeting with Rickie. Rickie and Stephen's interview then ended with thunder and lightning, with Agnes momentarily, mistakenly, in Stephen's arms, and with a fire in Dunwood House; the three men left together, Rickie being moved not merely by Stephen's voice but by his reference to Rickie's need for a greatcoat, an echo of the last words he had heard from his mother. Chapter 32 then opened with references to the rebuilding of the boarding-house in even more hygienic splendour. However, the intensity of the storm and of Agnes's response to Stephen was lessened, the fire was given up, Chapter 32 was adjusted accordingly, and the long chapter was split into two. The second of the resulting pair became the present Chapter 31, while the first presented a longer interview between Ansell and Stephen, later omitted entirely. That this Ansell-Stephen chapter was cut only in proof is an idea dependent on Forster's letter of 19 February 1907 to his mother, written on the train as he neared Manchester for a visit with the Merediths:

> Blackwood wrote tiresomely that he couldn't alter the chapters on account of expense and lack of time. I said the first reason was absurd, since I had to bear all costs over a certain per cent.; but gave in on account of the latter: they want it to be finished in ten days.

Since the manuscript offers evidence of two chapters which were omitted at the typescript stage or later, and since neither Forster's diary nor his letters record any regret about obstinacy on the publisher's part, it seems likely that the changes were made. The first of these omitted chapters, the late chapter of letters which once followed Chapter 27, appears to have been partly a balance in form to Chapter 9, partly an effort to describe events in Sawston during the ten days in which, in the published text, we follow Stephen, leaving Rickie's crisis to be indicated chiefly by the narrator's meditative comments in Chapter 28. The surviving letters show an agitated Herbert, a mysteriously abrupt Ansell, and a half-demented Rickie, "extremely ill" and unwilling to face the new reality of Stephen's ancestry. There is a similar emphasis on Rickie's illness and Herbert's embarrassment in the early drafts of Chapter 31 and in the discarded Ansell-Stephen chapter, where Agnes too is particularly ill-natured. Probably the letters could have been cut in typescript with little loss, and such timing might account for the presence of the typescript pages among Forster's scraps. Or they could have been printed and then cut as Forster wisely narrowed the focus to Stephen and Rickie. If the letters were omitted at the typescript stage, Forster's reference to altering more than one chapter in proof might also be explained by the transfer of Stephen's unromantic thoughts on marriage from the omitted Ansell-Stephen chapter to the end of Chapter 33, which is in manuscript relatively dull without them. So far as can be seen, the same rewriting of the opening pages of Chapter 31 and the end of Chapter 33 would have been required whether or not the chapter of letters was discarded at the same time as the Ansell-Stephen chapter. In comparison to some of the earlier revisions the changes would have been relatively simple to make; Forster could easily have accomplished them in ten days.

In his introduction to *The Longest Journey* Forster mentions only the omitted Harold chapter, not these late revisions, but he does tell us that in the excitement and absorption of writing the novel, "sometimes I went wrong deliberately, as if the spirit of anti-literature had jogged my elbow" (p. lxvi). By "anti-literature" he may have meant the reality of his own personal desire for an ideal homosexual love, if the omitted chapters and his recollections in "My Books and I" are a fair indication, but the major flaw that he specifies in the published novel, accepting the objections of the early reviewers, is the number of sudden deaths. These deaths, however, represent precisely the unconventional, "unrealistic" manipulation of character, act, and symbol with which Forster challenges unthinking assumptions about "reality" in *The Longest Journey*. In this case "anti-literature" takes on something of the meaning offered by an "anti-novel" like Sterne's *Tristram Shandy*, which exploits the conventions of the art-form in order to remind the reader that it is all the more "real", in terms of our limited perceptions and expectations, for being a fiction.

Forster's efforts to control both these forces of "anti-literature" are particularly well represented in the drafts of Chapter 31. There his personal desires are reflected in his use of Stephen's drunkenness and Rickie's illness as opportunities to portray men tending each other in sickness. Bedroom settings support this socially acceptable way of bringing men into close physical contact and emotional intimacy; the desire to help becomes a kind of love. At the more abstract level, the manipulation of the symbols is even more obvious in the drafts than in the finished text. In the drafts Forster gives Rickie speeches in which he tries to tell Stephen about the meanings he sees in Orion and Demeter, so that Stephen, the fictional embodiment of these meanings, can in his "reality" deny the use of the symbols. In the revisions this level of complexity is simplified and the "rhythms" recur only in Rickie's thoughts, or, perhaps, in Forster's narrative; the distinction is not always clear. Nonetheless, these drafts show very clearly the intellectual and emotional weight Forster gives to the recurring leitmotivs as he gathers them together and imposes them on the characters who here act out his hopes. He then restrains his extravagances of sentiment and artificiality as he revises, preserving his main purpose despite such elbow-joggings. Stephen's reality is the point here, and his unexpectedly articulate insistence that he is himself, in the face of Rickie's idealizing distortions, survives from the earliest drafts through successive revisions. Herbert's comment that Stephen is "the same person" whoever his parents were, present only in the published text (p. 250), makes the same point, adding depth to Herbert's character as it underlines once again Rickie's fatal dependence on an illusory ideal.

FORSTER AND THE CRITICAL RESPONSE

Familiarity with the manuscripts, like rereadings of the novel, increases respect for the control Forster exercised in shaping the final text. Few of his first readers, however, appreciated his most unconventional "realities". In his introduction Forster remembers that the reviews were "encouraging", and his diary entry of 12 June 1907 supports his memory: "Critics approve—except the *Queen* and the *World*. All say 'jerky', 'too many deaths'." *The Longest Journey* must have been a pleasing novel to review, obviously written by an ambitious and intelligent author who was equally obviously in need of advice about what his readers would stand. Their different reactions helpfully illustrate some of the same range of conventional thinking Forster holds up for inspection in the novel. Mr Pembroke perhaps wrote for *Queen*: "the lack of straightforwardness makes the interest in the book meagre". For *World* Mr Elliot, offended by the coffee grounds and gluey meringues of the first chapter and apparently arrested there, might still have bestirred himself to scribble the note, confessing his failure to follow the narrative—"it jerks and slides and slips about in a fatiguing fashion"—and judging the "group of persons" in the first chapter to be "unconventional in manner to a degree which we prefer to regard as impossible". These reviewers seem to be objecting even to the time scheme and flashbacks of the narrative, looking for events rather than conversations and revelations. At the other end of the spectrum, Mr Failing might have encouraged C. F. G. Masterman in the *Daily News*: "A book (it is to be feared) only for the few, but full of suggestion, of insight, of astonishing cleverness: the work of one who is determined to face the world of real things." In the *Morning Post* an urbane Ansell with an appreciation of black comedy, or perhaps a generous Mrs Failing, declared enjoyment: "A set of people from whom as neighbours and relations we should all pray to be delivered proves absorbing company with Mr Forster as merciless showman."[57] This is the review that Forster mentions in his introduction, notable for its calculation of a 44 per cent. death rate among the adult characters. Its statistical element may explain why Forster thought the reviewer was W. H. Beveridge (later Lord Beveridge), leader-writer for the *Morning Post* in 1906–08 and in 1942 the author of the report which laid the groundwork for the socializing legislation that reshaped Britain's economic priorities after World War II.

Beveridge, if it was he, encouraged the author despite all flaws. His brief description, which focuses on the characters and considerately omits any mention of the relationship of the brothers, moves behind manners to pick out problems of motivation and aim: Agnes's reason for marrying Rickie is "less clear" than Rickie's for marrying her, and "it is not certain that Mr Forster has not attempted the impossible in endeavouring to make intelligible and attractive the blend of pagan god and modern hooligan which goes to make Stephen Wonham". Beveridge recognizes that "the book as a whole is more provocative than satisfying", yet the author "can be tenderly imaginative as well as mordant", and "it would be altogether out of place to quarrel with a writer of Mr Forster's performance and promise about formal unities or small points", like the number of sudden deaths. But this was not the common view, and the reactions of Forster's Apostolic "brothers"

[57] These reviews and others have been collected in *E. M. Forster: The Critical Heritage*, ed. Philip Gardner (London and Boston, Routledge & Kegan Paul, 1973), pp. 65–100. All these and more are also noted in McDowell, *op. cit.* (fn. 2).

were also mixed. Strachey found the Cambridge elements "rather amusing" but the rest "dreary fandango"; Keynes read with "very great interest and a good deal of bewilderment as well as admiration" (PNF, p. 150). By the end of 1907, Forster was less aware of approval. In his diary his end-of-the-year summary shows a more regretful response:

> Shall scarcely write another *Longest Journey*, for it vexed people and I can with sincerity please them. Am anxious not to widen a gulf that must always remain wide; there is no doubt that I do not resemble other people, and even they notice it.

By this time he had finished *A Room with a View*. His next sentence suggests the themes of *Howards End*, for he notes that his scorn for "social conventions, economic trend, efficiency, etc." is lessening, so that he thinks "that others may do right to acquiesce and that I may do wrong to laugh at them, and that great art was never a conscious rebel". He adds, "A rebel, surely." In the context of *The Longest Journey* this awareness of difference and rebelliousness reflects the connection between his attack on suburban ideas of "reality" and his ambitious aim of making indirect "copy" of his homosexual temperament. But he had outdistanced his readers, and he never put so much of himself into another novel.

In later years, however, *The Longest Journey* became the novel Forster was "most glad to have written", as he tells us in his introduction, precisely because of its personal elements. He shows in "My Books and I" how highly he valued his discovery of Stephen's power to restore "to the world of experience more than he took from it" (p. 305), and he seems to have regretted the "flaws" of the novel more deeply as he realized this power. His later comments often focus, directly or indirectly, on the "reality" of Stephen. In November 1934 Peter Burra published one of the first critical analyses of the "rhythms" in Forster's novels, noticing, for instance, the increasing symbolic force of the fatal railway crossing in *The Longest Journey*. On 13 February 1935, Forster wrote to Burra, mentioning his own dissatisfaction with the novel:

> I am amazed and exasperated at the way in which I *insisted* on doing things wrong there. It wasn't incompetence; it was a perversity the origins of which I can no longer trace. But for this, it would have been my best piece of work, I am sure. . . . *The Longest Journey* has never stopped working in my mind, it is the only book which has ever given back something to the places from which I took it.[58]

[58] *Selected Letters*, vol. 2, p. 131. Forster's abbreviations, chiefly of the title of the novel, have been spelled out both here and in the letter quoted below.

Forster emphasizes the novel's power of reciprocation here as in his memoir; no doubt he could also have explained to Burra, as to Bloomsbury, something more of the "perversity" which drove him to rebel against conventions. He may have been moved to write as much as he did by Burra's very high praise for Stephen:

> He is the product of an intensely passionate imagination working upon closely recorded detail of behaviour and conduct. He is life, at the centre and at the circumference—he is the world's essential simplicity, transformed by the author's vision.[59]

Burra's stress on Stephen's reality must have been particularly welcome, since the manuscripts of the novel, like Forster's memoir, gainsay any assertion that Stephen was drawn from "closely recorded detail". Stephen is one of Forster's most "created" characters, not drawn from two-thirds of a known model or amalgamated from friends and relations but built up in revision after revision, so that Forster found himself, Pygmalion-like, aware of Stephen's presence in the landscape.

Nearly a quarter of a century later, Forster commented much more specifically on Stephen in a letter to another critic, James McConkey, like Burra a perceptive analyst of Forster's themes and rhythms. Burra admired Stephen in the light of D. H. Lawrence, introducing his praise of Stephen with the comment that "the whole novel reminds one constantly of the work which Lawrence produced a few years later". McConkey judged the same message more severely:

> If, however, Forster does not quite meet the problem he has set up in this novel, the reason is that his own concern is with the task of reconciling physical with transcendent reality; and if such a reconciliation is, as he would seem to suggest, the problem which faces Rickie and contemporary society, then Stephen Wonham, whose chief virtue lies not in reconciliation at all but in an instinctive earth-acceptance, offers a solution which is much too simple.[60]

Forster perhaps answers part of McConkey's argument a few years later, when he explains in his introduction to *The Longest Journey* that nature itself was richer in his youth, not then so imperilled

[59] Burra's essay, "The Novels of E. M. Forster", first appeared in *Nineteenth Century and After*, CXVI (November 1934), pp. 581–94. Forster approved of it so highly that in 1943 he used it for the introduction to the Everyman edition of *A Passage to India*, and it has been included in the Abinger edition of *Passage* (vol. 6, 1978), where this quotation appears on pp. 323–4.

[60] McConkey, *op. cit.* (fn. 7), p. 68.

and encroached upon. But he wrote his letter of thanks for McConkey's book on 21 September 1957, a month or so before the publication of the interview in which he expressed his wish to kick Rickie. It was a time of hardship for his characters, even for his leitmotivs:

> The one I like by far the best is *The Longest Journey*. I see it has terrible weaknesses, and was fascinated when you approached them. So much depends on Stephen. I never showed (except perhaps through his talk with Ansell) that he could understand Rickie, and scarcely that he could be fond of him. So that, in the end chapter, he lies as a somewhat empty hulk on that hillside. Who cares what he thinks, or doesn't think of? All the same I'm proud of creating him and do not consider him a minor character. . . . In *The Longest Journey* (and elsewhere) you saw connections that never occurred to me, but they seem to work very well—e.g. the teacup of experience and broken cup at the close: Ansell's "circles" and Cadbury Rings.[61]

As in the matter of Rickie's lameness, however, Forster's late defensiveness reflects the changing values of his readers; reference to the past, in this case to the manuscripts, again qualifies his comments. In alluding to Stephen's talk with Ansell, for instance, Forster seems almost to be recalling the discarded Ansell-Stephen chapter rather than Chapter 26. In the published conversation with Ansell, Stephen is dogged, simple, unimaginative, while in the unpublished one his thoughts on marriage cause Ansell to wonder whether he hasn't understood the "Elliot business" all along (p. 382). Moved to Chapter 33, these thoughts help to cement the bond between the brothers, preparing the way for Stephen's final tribute to Rickie. But perhaps the discarded conversation with Ansell, like Harold's "panic", lingered in Forster's mind, part of the "reality" of Stephen's existence for his creator if not for the readers of the novel. As for the leitmotivs, the manuscripts indicate that Forster did attempt connections between Ansell's "circles" and the Cadbury Rings, though he may have thought of them as links between Ansell and Stephen. Tiny sketches of circles and squares still decorate the opening leaf of Chapter 11, describing Cadover; at the end of Chapter 13 the "concentric circles" of

---

[61] *Selected Letters*, vol. 2, p. 267. On p. 53 of McConkey's book there is another sentence which may have influenced Forster's support of Stephen as more than a "minor character": "In *The Longest Journey*, the implication is made of man's connection, through earth, with the whole mysterious, ordered flux of the universe; yet the person who instinctively manages that connection, Stephen Wonham, is neither the major character nor of a type that gains Forster's central attention in any of the novels . . . ."

the Rings (p. 131) once reminded Stephen of "a board for some complicated game of skill", presumably a square board. And if the broken cup rose unbidden as Forster worked to concentrate his leitmotivs in the final chapters, developing one of his less conscious rhythms, the result was to make it one of the most obvious.

For Stephen's final thoughts, however, no manuscripts survive to shade Forster's late self-criticism, and in these last few paragraphs of the novel, where Stephen, now tolerant of religion in his fatherhood, seems to comprehend the symbolic meaning of the Cadbury Rings, the various "realities" of symbol and character must conjoin to create the final symphonic "rhythm". Readers who care what Stephen does or doesn't think of will in any case answer Forster's challenge for themselves. His own last word came still later, in June 1964, when he returned once more to Wiltshire and the Figsbury Rings. He was visiting William Golding: "As they walked the downs, they discussed the near-extinction of Chalk Blue butterflies, through pesticides, when one flew between them and settled on a tall grass stem, in the very entrance to the Rings. Forster, in a pantomime of the world's ruthlessness, danced after it, brandishing his walking-stick, with a cry of 'Kill, Kill!'" (PNF, II, pp. 318–19). In his diary his thoughts of death were gentler:

> I exclaimed several times that the area was marvellous, and large— larger than I recalled. I was filled with thankfulness and security and glad that I had given myself so much back. The butterfly was a moving glint, and I shall lie in Stephen's arms instead of his child. How I wish that book hadn't faults! But they do not destroy it, and the gleam, the greatness, the grass remain. I don't want any other coffin.

The autobiographical realities of *The Longest Journey* have much extended this volume of the Abinger Edition, and I am very grateful to the Provost and Scholars of King's College and to the representatives of Edward Arnold (Publishers), Ltd, for their patience and support in its preparation. My particular thanks are due to Michael Cowdy and Donald Parry of King's and to Christopher Wheeler of Arnold's. E. M. Forster expressed his own tribute to King's College in the novel, where it is the model for "the perishable home" to which Rickie Elliot returns "with a sigh of joy". Forster himself returned from the "Great World" to King's as an Honorary Fellow in 1946, and the college then became, as perhaps it had always been, his least perishable home, its reality persisting as its members come and go.

To edit *The Longest Journey* at King's College has been both a great privilege and a very practical aid. The rich resources of the King's College Library have been made constantly accessible by the staff, headed by the late Peter Croft, whose comments on the novel and the editorial process have been always perceptive and encouraging. Elizabeth Russell and her assistants, Christopher Arnold, Graham Howorth, and Clare Scanes, have been continually ingenious in finding answers to far-flung questions. Margaret Cranmer of the Rowe Music Library and Michael Halls, the Modern Archivist, have most willingly shared their knowledge of their specialties. All have been steadfast in rallying the editor's strength. Here too Frank Kermode and Donald Parry read and commented on the Editor's Introduction as it grew, and they, Michael Halls, and G. H. W. Rylands celebrated its completion with a further reading and further valued comments. The musicians of the college, particularly Peter Burbidge and Philip Radcliffe, and the philosophers and classicists, particularly T. R. Harrison, Geoffrey Lloyd, Alex Mourelatos, Robin Osborne, Samuel Scolnicov, G. C. Stead, and Patrick Wilkinson, have also been most helpful in answering queries.

In the broader environs of Cambridge, the library staff of Trinity College and of the rare books and music collections of the University Library have also generously shared their knowledge, as have the experts of the Computer Laboratory of the University, where I have been rescued from electronic folly by many helpful advisors, but most often by Simon Buck. John Dawson of the Literary and Linguistic Computing Centre of the University showed me the possibilities of the machines at the beginning of the project and, to my great delight, made the concordance at the end; a brief description of these adventures appears in the Textual Notes. Eric Chamberlain and the staff of the Fitzwilliam Museum guided my searches for Arundel prints and the paintings of G. F. Watts, quests that were aided also by Michael Trinick of the National Trust, by Wilfred Blunt of the Watts Gallery, and by T. M. Featherstone and Virginia Tandy of the Tameside Metropolitan Borough and the Astley Cheetham Art Gallery. Michael Petty, Local Studies Librarian of the Cambridgeshire Collection in the Central Library of Cambridge, not only guided me to histories of the city but also first assured me that there were other accounts of the legend of the dolls' eyes associated with the Roman Catholic church on Hills Road, and I am very grateful also to the many who have replied to my queries in the potentially endless search for the origins of the story, in particular: the Most Reverend M. N. L. Couve de

Murville, co-author of *Catholic Cambridge* (1983); P. S. Wilkins, who is rewriting the booklet on the church; Sir Edmund Paston-Bedingfeld and Sir Philip de Zulueta, who have no family recollections of the legend; Dr David Jeremy of the Business History Unit, London School of Economics; C. Wilkins-Jones, County Local Studies Librarian for Norfolk; and Caroline Goodfellow of the Bethnal Green Museum of Childhood. I am also much indebted to Joan Wildy of the Old Parsonage, Hinxton, who not only found the grave of William and Emily Forster for me, but also made the connection to Miss Chipman clear; the Master and Fellows of Jesus College, in particular Dr D. A. Blackadder, then Acting Bursar, most kindly gave me access to Miss Chipman's correspondence about the living at Hinxton. And it is a great pleasure to thank Sir Joseph Napier for his recollections of Miss Chipman and his cousin Morgan.

Further afield, I would also like to thank C. H. D. Everett, Headmaster of Tonbridge School, and Mr G. P. Hoole, retired now as librarian of the school, for showing me Tonbridge and sharing their knowledge of its history. Mrs D. Baker welcomed me to Hilden Oaks School, and Miss Rosalind Wade very kindly guided me as my trip to the south extended to Abinger Hammer and its neighbourhood. My parents most cheerfully financed and joined me in a journey to the Figsbury Rings, Old Sarum, and Stonehenge, and helped in a preliminary investigation of the differences between the English and American editions of the novel as well. My queries about Salisbury were answered by Miss Elisabeth Dimont and Mr B. M. Little, Divisional Librarian there. Donald Reiman of the Pforzheimer Library in New York and George Thomson of the University of Ottawa helped to explain the peculiarities of Forster's quotation from *Epipsychidion*. Mrs Joy Slocombe, Curator of the Ilfracombe Museum, and Michael Paxton, of Allied Biscuits, Ltd, were very helpful in describing the no longer existing Winter Gardens and Oswego biscuits. O. W. Neighbour, Music Librarian of the British Library, advised on the non-reality of Stephen's songs, and Leonard N. Beck of the Library of Congress on the non-reality of Mrs Chunk.

I am grateful too for the assurance of several other negatives. Both Dr Ian H. C. Fraser of the University of Keele and Mrs Hensleigh Wedgwood found no remnant of Forster's work on *The Moral Ideal* among the Wedgwood Papers; William A. Koshland writes that no written records of Forster's early transactions with Alfred A. Knopf, Inc., survive, although Mr Knopf retains a vivid memory of Forster's decision to take *A Passage to India* to Harcourt

Brace; and Elizabeth Wood Ellem, who sorted Forster's manuscripts when they came to King's College Library, recalls no further details of the state in which they arrived. In the search for and comparison of earlier editions of the novel B. J. Kirkpatrick very kindly made her bibliographic records available, and she too found that there is no sign that Forster made any changes to the novel after its first publication. The copy that he gave to A. R. Ainsworth in 1907, now at the Humanities Research Center in Austin, Texas, has no annotations, and the inscription reads only, "A. R. A. from E. M. F. 30/4/07." William Matheson reports that there is no inscription in the copy of the first edition in the Library of Congress, and Richard Colles Johnson writes that the unannotated "author's autograph copy" at the Newberry Library in Chicago is Morton Dauwen Zabel's copy, with an inscription reading, "For M. D. Zabel", and a note explaining that Forster signed the book in Chicago on June 6, 1947.

As for the realities of the imagination, P. N. Furbank has kept me continually aware that *The Longest Journey* is a work of art, however "realistic". The information about Forster's life which he has as always given most generously is to him a separate matter, too often liable to distract readers from the novelist's accomplishment in shaping the fiction. For me knowledge of the historical realities illumines the power of the imagined ones, but I relish discussions of such matters, and am most grateful to Nick Furbank for persisting in them. Tony Brown, Judith Herz, and Carola Kaplan have also helped to frame my perceptions of these issues, as has Evelyne Hanquart, who has helped in many other ways as well, scrutinizing both Forster's French and the Editor's Introduction with an expert eye. The transcriptions of the manuscripts in Appendix C have been proofread by Jenny Fellows, another expert familiar with the ways of the Abinger Edition. But there, as elsewhere, errors that remain are very much my own.

Forster's introduction is reprinted here with the permission of Oxford University Press, "The Old School" (from the *Spectator* of 27 July 1934) with the permission of the *Spectator*, Richard Wilbur's "Epistemology" with the permission of Faber and Faber Publishers (from Richard Wilbur, *Poems 1943–1956*) and Harcourt Brace Jovanovich Inc (from Richard Wilbur, *Ceremony and other Poems*).

ELIZABETH HEINE

Author's Introduction

The Longest Journey is the least popular of my five novels but the one I am most glad to have written. For in it I have managed to get nearer than elsewhere towards what was in my mind—or rather towards that junction of mind with heart where the creative impulse sparks. Thoughts and emotions collided if they did not always cooperate. I can remember writing it and how excited I was and how absorbed, and how sometimes I went wrong deliberately, as if the spirit of anti-literature had jogged my elbow. For all its faults, it is the only one of my books that has come upon me without my knowledge. Elsewhere I have had to look into the lumber-room of my past, and have found in it things that were useful to be sure; still I found them, they didn't find me, and the magic sense of being visited and of even returning the visit was absent.

So I am glad that the editor of the World's Classics should include it in the series, and should ask me to pen an introduction.

Where is my pen?

In an old diary, under the date of 18 July, 1904, it wrote as follows: "An idea for another novel—that of a man who discovers that he has an illegitimate brother—took place since last Saturday."[1]

That is how the novel originated—and how frigidly! But it was not published until 1907, and during the interval several other ideas intervened to confuse or enrich the original theme. There was the metaphysical idea of Reality ("the cow is there"): there was the ethical idea that reality must be faced (Rickie won't face Stephen); there was the idea, or

---

[1] The diary reads "an entire novel" rather than "another novel", and "took shape" rather than "took place". The differences are probably a typist's misreading of Forster's late hand, since the entry itself is clear.

ideal, of the British Public School; there was the title, exhorting us in the words of Shelley not to love one person only; there was Cambridge, there was Wiltshire. I did not list the above notions consciously, but they were whirling around me as I wrote, and may well have impaired my sense of direction.

Let me try to isolate Wiltshire.

The 1904 diary records that on 12 September "I walked out again to Figsbury Rings". Much lies behind this entry. It recalls an emotional thrill which set my pen going. Figsbury Rings are about five miles east of Salisbury, and are just visible from the train as it runs down towards the city. As an antiquity they are unobtrusive. There is an outer circle of embankment and an inner circle, and in the centre is one small tree. The embankments are grassed, the rest of the area is planted with rotation of crops. I was then twenty-five years old, and had begun to warm to the Wiltshire downlands which I had hitherto condemned as bare and dull, and I caught fire up on the Rings. A similar experience had already befallen me in Italy and had produced my first short story. This time it wasn't just looking at a view, it was breathing the air and smelling the fields, and there was human reinforcement from the shepherds who grazed up there. They and I talked about nothing—still one of my favourite subjects; I offered a tip of sixpence which was declined, I was offered a pull at a pipe and had to decline. The whole experience was trivial in itself but vital to the novel, for it fructified my meagre conception of the half-brothers, and gave Stephen Wonham, the bastard, his home. Figsbury Rings became Cadbury Rings. The valley of the Winterbourne below them turned into the Cad, a level crossing clanged, and that part of *The Longest Journey* was born. In a curious way it also gave birth. There was reciprocation—such as I discern in Matthew Arnold's poem of "The Scholar Gipsy". I received, I created, I restored, and for many years the Wiltshire landscape remained haunted by my fictional ghosts. Once I even tested the magic by staying with Lytton Strachey not very far from the Rings—an urbane and delightful host but not one to countenance fanciful transferences. He failed. The Rings survived, the Tree, the Tree remained, as it did for Matthew Arnold, though it was by no means his sort of tree.[2]

Cambridge is the home of Rickie, the elder brother, the legitimate, his only true home: the Cambridge of G. E. Moore which I knew at the beginning of the century: the fearless uninfluential Cambridge that sought for reality and cared for truth. Ansell is the undergraduate high-priest of that local shrine, Agnes Pembroke is its deadly debunker. Captured by her and by Sawston, Rickie goes to pieces, and cannot even be rescued when Ansell joins up with Stephen and strikes. The Cambridge chapters are still romantic and crucial for me, and I still endorse Ansell's denunciation of the Great World.

> There is no great world at all, only a little earth, for ever isolated from the rest of the little solar system. This little earth is full of tiny societies and Cambridge is one of them. All the societies are narrow, but some are good and some are bad—just as one house is beautiful inside and another is ugly. Observe the metaphor of the houses: I am coming back to it. The good societies say, "I tell you to do this because I am Cambridge." The bad ones say, "I tell you to do that because I am the great world." They lie. And fools like you listen to them, and believe that they are a thing which does not exist and never has existed, and confuse "great", which has no meaning whatever, with "good", which means salvation. Now for the other metaphor. To compare the world to Cambridge is like comparing the outsides of houses with the inside of a house. No intellectual effort is needed, no moral result is attained. You only have to say, "Oh, what a difference! Oh, what a difference!" and then go indoors again and exhibit your broadened mind.[3]

Sawston, which poses as the great world in miniature, need not detain us. It is the eternal home of Herbert and Agnes Pembroke, and owes something to my own public school. I was neither very happy nor very unhappy there—a Varden

---

[2] See "My Books and I" (p. 305 below) for Forster's longer quotation from Arnold's "Thyrsis". For the complete diary entries for 12 and 16 September 1904, see the Editor's Introduction, p. xlix.
[3] Compare pp. 62-3.

who never got his ears pulled. The best of life began when I left it, and I am always puzzled when other elderly men reminisce over their respective public schools so excitedly, and compare them as if they were works of art: it sounds as if they must have had a dullish time since.

There were changes in the book as it proceeded, as is natural in a work so dispersedly conceived. Stephen was at one time called Harold and at another Siegfried, and there was a long fantasy-chapter about him, which I cancelled and will now epitomize. (It occurs near Chapter 12 in the book.) He has made the unsuccessful expedition towards Salisbury and is riding back to Cadover alone. He comes to a pleasant place where the river is crossed by a railway bridge, dismounts, and bathes. An engine which is shunting stops on the bridge, and the engine-driver leans out and abuses him in the filthiest language for wearing no costume. The same thing once happened to my friend Lowes Dickinson in Herefordshire. Dickinson did not retaliate. Stephen does. Rushing up the embankment he storms the engine and spreads devastation with his fists. The fireman collapses, the engine moves on, and in a confused struggle he is thrown out onto the line. He is not hurt but is far from his clothes and his horse, thinks he knows a short cut home through the woods, loses his way, terrifies a picnic party, is terrified by a flock of sheep, panics, and cracks his head against a beech tree. When he comes to himself he is no longer himself but daft, fey, part of the woods, and the animals recognize him. He returns to his old life when he leaves the woods and sees Cadbury Rings and Rickie moving anxiously towards him, his arms piled high with honourable garments. (How Rickie knew he wanted them I forget.)

Only the flock of sheep survive out of this fantasy. Its work is more economically done by letting the boy fall asleep on the roof of Cadover, with the wind and the sun on him, murmuring "good oh good . . ." and unable to read a short story about getting into touch with nature.

The Longest Journey dates, and poignantly. For the England that Stephen thought so good and seemed destined to inherit is done for. The growth of the population and the applications of science have destroyed her between them. There was a freshness and an out-of-door wildness in those days which the present generation cannot imagine. I am glad to have known our countryside before its roads were too dangerous to walk on and its rivers too dirty to bathe in, before its butterflies and wild flowers were decimated by arsenical spray, before Shakespeare's Avon frothed with detergents and the fish floated belly-up in the Cam.

As for the reviews. They were encouraging. One of the reviewers—he was Will Beveridge I think—pleasantly calculated that the percentage of sudden deaths (infants excluded) amounted to over 44 per cent. of the adult population.[4] But the book did not sell, and an uncle of mine, a meddlesome tease of a man, bought a number of remainders at sixpence each and sent them to those of my relations whom they were most likely to upset. It was this same uncle who, though sedulously masculine, gave me hints for the character of Mrs Failing and whose house up in Northumberland provided the architecture and the atmosphere for Cadover.

E. M. FORSTER

---

[4] See p. lviii.

Part 1
Cambridge

Chapter 1

"The cow is there," said Ansell, lighting a match and holding it out over the carpet. No one spoke. He waited till the end of the match fell off. Then he said again, "She is there, the cow. There, now."

"You have not proved it," said a voice.

"I have proved it to myself."

"I have proved to myself that she isn't," said the voice. "The cow is *not* there." Ansell frowned and lit another match.

"She's there for me," he declared. "I don't care whether she's there for you or not. Whether I'm in Cambridge or Iceland or dead, the cow will be there."

It was philosophy. They were discussing the existence of objects. Do they exist only when there is someone to look at them? or have they a real existence of their own? It is all very interesting, but at the same time it is difficult. Hence the cow. She seemed to make things easier. She was so familiar, so solid, that surely the truths that she illustrated would in time become familiar and solid also. Is the cow there or not? This was better than deciding between objectivity and subjectivity. So at Oxford, just at the same time, one was asking, "What do our rooms look like in the vac?"

"Look here, Ansell. I'm there—in the meadow—the cow's there. You're there—the cow's there. Do you agree so far?"

"Well?"

"Well, if you go, the cow stops; but if I go, the cow goes. Then what will happen if you stop and I go?"

Several voices cried out that this was quibbling.

"I know it is," said the speaker brightly, and silence descended again, while they tried honestly to think the matter out.

Rickie, on whose carpet the matches were being dropped,

did not like to join in the discussion. It was too difficult for him. He could not even quibble. If he spoke, he should simply make himself a fool. He preferred to listen, and to watch the tobacco-smoke stealing out past the window-seat into the tranquil October air. He could see the court too, and the college cat teasing the college tortoise, and the kitchen-men with supper-trays upon their heads. Hot food for one—that must be for the geographical don, who never came in for Hall; cold food for three, apparently at half a crown a head, for someone he did not know; hot food, *à la carte*—obviously for the ladies haunting the next staircase; cold food for two, at two shillings—going to Ansell's rooms for himself and Ansell, and as it passed under the lamp he saw that it was meringues again. Then the bed-makers began to arrive, chatting to each other pleasantly, and he could hear Ansell's bed-maker say, "Oh dang!" when she found she had to lay Ansell's tablecloth; for there was not a breath stirring. The great elms were motionless, and seemed still in the glory of midsummer, for the darkness hid the yellow blotches on their leaves, and their outlines were still rounded against the tender sky. Those elms were Dryads—so Rickie believed or pretended, and the line between the two is subtler than we admit. At all events they were lady trees, and had for generations fooled the college statutes by their residence in the haunts of youth.

But what about the cow? He returned to her with a start, for this would never do. He also would try to think the matter out. Was she there or not? The cow. There or not. He strained his eyes into the night.

Either way it was attractive. If she was there, other cows were there too. The darkness of Europe was dotted with them, and in the far East their flanks were shining in the rising sun. Great herds of them stood browsing in pastures where no man came nor need ever come, or plashed knee-deep by the brink of impassable rivers. And this, moreover, was the view of Ansell. Yet Tilliard's view had a good deal in it. One might do worse than follow Tilliard, and suppose the cow not to be there unless oneself was there to see her. A cowless world, then, stretched round him on every side. Yet he had only to peep into a field, and click! it would at once become radiant with bovine life.

Suddenly he realized that this, again, would never do. As usual, he had missed the whole point, and was overlaying philosophy with gross and senseless details. For if the cow was not there, the world and the fields were not there either. And what would Ansell care about sunlit flanks or impass-able streams? Rickie rebuked his own grovelling soul, and turned his eyes away from the night, which had led him to such absurd conclusions.

The fire was dancing, and the shadow of Ansell, who stood close up to it, seemed to dominate the little room. He was still talking, or rather jerking, and he was still lighting matches and dropping their ends upon the carpet. Now and then he would make a motion with his feet as if he were running quickly backward upstairs, and would tread on the edge of the fender, so that the fire-irons went flying and the buttered-bun dishes crashed against each other in the hearth. The other philosophers were crouched in odd shapes on the sofa and table and chairs, and one, who was a little bored, had crawled to the piano and was timidly trying the "Pre-lude to Rhinegold" with his knee upon the soft pedal. The air was heavy with good tobacco-smoke and the pleasant warmth of tea, and as Rickie became more sleepy the events of the day seemed to float one by one before his acquiescent eyes. In the morning he had read Theocritus, whom he believed to be the greatest of Greek poets; he had lunched with a merry don and had tasted Zwieback biscuits; then he had walked with people he liked, and had walked just long enough; and now his room was full of other people whom he liked, and when they left he would go and have supper with Ansell, whom he liked as well as anyone. A year ago he had known none of these joys. He had crept cold and friendless and ignorant out of a great public school, preparing for a silent and solitary journey, and praying as a highest favour that he might be left alone. Cambridge had not answered his prayer. She had taken and soothed him, and warmed him, and had laughed at him a little, saying that he must not be so tragic yet awhile, for his boyhood had been but a

5

dusty corridor that led to the spacious halls of youth. In one year he had made many friends and learnt much, and he might learn even more if he could but concentrate his attention on that cow.

The fire had died down, and in the gloom the man by the piano ventured to ask what would happen if an objective cow had a subjective calf. Ansell gave an angry sigh, and at that moment there was a tap on the door.

"Come in!" said Rickie.

The door opened. A tall young woman stood framed in the light that fell from the passage.

"Ladies!" whispered everyone in great agitation.

"Yes?" he said nervously, limping towards the door (he was rather lame). "Yes? Please come in. Can I be any good—"

"Wicked boy!" exclaimed the young lady, advancing a gloved finger into the room. "Wicked, wicked boy!"

He clasped his head with his hands.

"Agnes! Oh how perfectly awful!"

"Wicked, intolerable boy!" She turned on the electric light. The philosophers were revealed with unpleasing suddenness. "My goodness, a tea-party! Oh really, Rickie, you are too bad! I say again: wicked, abominable, intolerable boy! I'll have you horsewhipped. If you please"—she turned to the symposium, which had now risen to its feet—"If you please, he asks me and my brother for the weekend. We accept. At the station, no Rickie. We drive to where his old lodgings were—Trumpery Road or some such name—and he's left them. I'm furious, and before I can stop my brother, he's paid off the cab and there we are stranded. I've walked—walked for miles. Pray can you tell me what is to be done with Rickie?"

"He must indeed be horsewhipped," said Tilliard pleasantly. Then he made a bolt for the door.

"Tilliard—do stop—let me introduce Miss Pembroke—don't all go!" For his friends were flying from his visitor like mists before the sun. "Oh, Agnes, I am so sorry; I've nothing to say. I simply forgot you were coming, and everything about you."

"Thank you, thank you! And how soon will you remember to ask where Herbert is?"

"Where is he, then?"

"I shall not tell you."

"But didn't he walk with you?"

"I shall not tell, Rickie. It's part of your punishment. You are not really sorry yet. I shall punish you again later."

She was quite right. Rickie was not as much upset as he ought to have been. He was sorry that he had forgotten, and that he had caused his visitors inconvenience. But he did not feel profoundly degraded, as a young man should who has acted discourteously to a young lady. Had he acted discourteously to his bed-maker or his gyp, he would have minded just as much, which was not polite of him.

"First, I'll go and get food. Do sit down and rest. Oh, let me introduce—"

Ansell was now the sole remnant of the discussion party. He still stood on the hearth-rug with a burnt match in his hand. Miss Pembroke's arrival had never disturbed him.

"Let me introduce Mr Ansell—Miss Pembroke."

There came an awful moment—a moment when he almost regretted that he had a clever friend. Ansell remained absolutely motionless, moving neither hand nor head. Such behaviour is so unknown that Miss Pembroke did not realize what had happened, and kept her own hand stretched out longer than is maidenly.

"Coming to supper?" asked Ansell in low, grave tones.

"I don't think so," said Rickie helplessly.

Ansell departed without another word.

"Don't mind us," said Miss Pembroke pleasantly. "Why shouldn't you keep your engagement with your friend? Herbert's finding lodgings—that's why he's not here—and they're sure to be able to give us some dinner. What jolly rooms you've got!"

"Oh no—not a bit. I say, I am sorry. I am sorry. I am most awfully sorry."

"What about?"

"Ansell—" Then he burst forth. "Ansell isn't a gentleman. His father's a draper. His uncles are farmers. He's here

7

because he's so clever—just on account of his brains. Now, sit down. He isn't a gentleman at all." And he hurried off to order some dinner.

"What a snob the boy is getting!" thought Agnes, a good deal mollified. It never struck her that those could be the words of affection—that Rickie would never have spoken them about a person whom he disliked. Nor did it strike her that Ansell's humble birth scarcely explained the quality of his rudeness. She was willing to find life full of trivialities. Six months ago and she might have minded; but now—she cared not what men might do unto her, for she had her own splendid lover, who could have knocked all these unhealthy undergraduates into a cocked hat. She dared not tell Gerald a word of what had happened: he might have come up from wherever he was and half killed Ansell. And she determined not to tell her brother either, for her nature was kindly, and it pleased her to pass things over.

She took off her gloves, and then she took off her earrings and began to admire them. These earrings were a freak of hers—her only freak. She had always wanted some, and the day Gerald asked her to marry him she went to a shop and had her ears pierced. In some wonderful way she knew that it was right. And he had given her the rings—little gold knobs, copied, the jeweller told them, from something pre-historic—and he had kissed the spots of blood on her handkerchief. Herbert, as usual, had been shocked.

"I can't help it," she cried, springing up. "I'm not like other girls." She began to pace about Rickie's room, for she hated to keep quiet. There was nothing much to see in it. The pictures were not attractive, nor did they attract her—school groups, Watts' "Sir Percival", a dog running after a rabbit, a man running after a maid, a cheap brown Madonna in a cheap green frame—in short, a collection where one mediocrity was generally cancelled by another. Over the door there hung a long photograph of a city with waterways, which Agnes, who had never been to Venice, took to be Venice, but which people who had been to Stockholm knew to be Stockholm. Rickie's mother, looking rather sweet, was standing on the mantelpiece. Some more pictures had just arrived from the framers and were leaning with their faces to the wall, but she did not bother to turn them round. On the table were dirty teacups, a flat chocolate cake, and Omar Khayyam, with an Oswego biscuit between his pages. Also a vase filled with the crimson leaves of autumn. This made her smile.

Then she saw her host's shoes: he had left them lying on the sofa. Rickie was slightly deformed, and so the shoes were not the same size, and one of them had a thick heel to help him towards an even walk. "Ugh!" she exclaimed, and removed them gingerly to the bedroom. There she saw other shoes and boots and pumps, a whole row of them, all deformed. "Ugh! Poor boy! It is too bad. Why shouldn't he be like other people? This hereditary business is too awful." She shut the door with a sigh. Then she recalled the perfect form of Gerald, his athletic walk, the poise of his shoulders, his arms stretched forward to receive her. Gradually she was comforted.

"I beg your pardon, miss, but might I ask how many to lay?" It was the bed-maker, Mrs Aberdeen.

"Three, I think," said Agnes, smiling pleasantly. "Mr Elliot'll be back in a minute. He has gone to order dinner."

"Thank you, miss."

"Plenty of teacups to wash up!"

"But teacups is easy washing, particularly Mr Elliot's."

"Why are his so easy?"

"Because no nasty corners in them to hold the dirt. Mr Anderson—he's below—has crinkly noctagons, and one wouldn't believe the difference. It was I bought these for Mr Elliot. His one thought is to save one trouble. I never seed such a thoughtful gentleman. The world, I say, will be the better for him." She took the teacups into the gyp room, and then returned with the tablecloth, and added, "if he's spared."

"I'm afraid he isn't strong," said Agnes.

"Oh, miss, his nose! I don't know what he'd say if he knew I mentioned his nose, but really I must speak to someone, and he has neither father nor mother. His nose! It poured twice with blood in the Long."

"Yes?"

"It's a thing that ought to be known. I assure you, that little room! . . . And in any case, Mr Elliot's a gentleman that can ill afford to lose it. Luckily his friends were up; and I always say they're more like brothers than anything else."

"Nice for him. He has no real brothers."

"Oh, Mr Hornblower, he is a merry gentleman, and Mr Tilliard too! And Mr Elliot himself likes his romp at times. Why, it's the merriest staircase in the buildings! Last night the bed-maker from W said to me, 'What are you doing to my gentlemen? Here's Mr Ansell come back 'ot with his collar flopping.' I said, 'And a good thing.' Some bedders keep their gentlemen just so; but surely, miss, the world being what it is, the longer one is able to laugh in it the better."

Bed-makers have to be comic and dishonest. It is expected of them. In a picture of university life it is their only function. So when we meet one who has the face of a lady, and feelings of which a lady might be proud, we pass her by.

"Yes?" said Miss Pembroke, and then their talk was stopped by the arrival of her brother.

"It is too bad!" he exclaimed. "It is really too bad."

"Now, Bertie boy, Bertie boy! I'll have no peevishness."

"I am not peevish, Agnes, but I have a full right to be. Pray, why did he not meet us? Why did he not provide rooms? And pray, why did you leave me to do all the set-tling? All the lodgings I knew are full, and our bedrooms look into a mews. I cannot help it. And then—look here! It really is too bad." He held up his foot like a wounded dog. It was dripping with water.

"Oho! This explains the peevishness. Off with it at once. It'll be another of your colds."

"I really think I had better." He sat down by the fire and daintily unlaced his boot. "I notice a great change in university tone. I can never remember swaggering three abreast along the pavement and charging inoffensive visitors into a gutter when I was an undergraduate. One of the men, too, wore an Eton tie. But the others, I should say, came from very queer schools, if they came from any schools at all."

Mr Pembroke was nearly twenty years older than his

sister, and had never been as handsome. But he was not at all the person to knock into a gutter, for though not in orders, he had the air of being on the verge of them, and his features, as well as his clothes, had the clerical cut. In his presence conversation became pure and colourless and full of under-statements, and—just as if he was a real clergyman—neither men nor boys ever forgot that he was there. He had observed this, and it pleased him very much. His conscience permitted him to enter the Church whenever his profession, which was the scholastic, should demand it.

"No gutter in the world's as wet as this," said Agnes, who had peeled off her brother's sock, and was now toasting it at the embers on a pair of tongs.

"Surely you know the running water by the edge of the Trumpington road? It's turned on occasionally to clear away the refuse—a most primitive idea. When I was up we had a joke about it, and called it the 'Pem'."

"How complimentary!"

"You foolish girl—not after me, of course. We called it the 'Pem' because it is close to Pembroke College. I re-member—" He smiled a little, and twiddled his toes. Then he remembered the bed-maker, and said, "My sock is now dry. My sock, please."

"Your sock is sopping. No, you don't!" She twitched the tongs away from him. Mrs Aberdeen, without speaking, fetched a pair of Rickie's socks and a pair of Rickie's shoes.

"Thank you; ah, thank you. I am sure Mr Elliot would allow it." Then he said in French to his sister, "Has there been the slightest sign of Frederick?"

"Now, do call him Rickie, and talk English. I found him here. He had forgotten about us, and was very sorry. Now he's gone to get some dinner, and I can't think why he isn't back."

Mrs Aberdeen left them.

"He wants pulling up sharply. There is nothing original in absent-mindedness. True originality lies elsewhere. Really, the lower classes have no *nous*. However can I wear such deformities?" For he had been madly trying to cram a right-hand foot into a left-hand shoe.

"Don't!" said Agnes hastily. "Don't touch the poor

fellow's things." The sight of the smart, stubby patent leather made her almost feel faint. She had known Rickie for many years, but it seemed so dreadful and so different now that he was a man. It was her first great contact with the abnormal, and unknown fibres of her being rose in revolt against it. She frowned when she heard his uneven tread upon the stairs.

"Agnes—before he arrives—you ought never to have left me and gone to his rooms alone. A most elementary transgression. Imagine the unpleasantness if you had found him with friends. If Gerald—"

Rickie by now had got into a fluster. At the kitchens he had lost his head, and when his turn came—he had had to wait—he had yielded his place to those behind, saying that he didn't matter. And he had wasted more precious time buying bananas, though he knew that the Pembrokes were not partial to fruit. Amid much tardy and chaotic hospitality the meal got under way. All the spoons and forks were anyhow, for Mrs Aberdeen's virtues were not practical. The fish seemed never to have been alive, the meat had no kick, and the cork of the college claret slid forth silently, as if ashamed of the contents. Agnes was particularly pleasant. But her brother could not recover himself. He still remembered their desolate arrival, and he could feel the waters of the Pem eating into his instep.

"Rickie," cried the lady, "are you aware that you haven't congratulated me on my engagement?"

Rickie laughed nervously, and said, "Why no! No more I have."

"Say something pretty, then."

"I hope you'll be very happy," he mumbled. "But I don't know anything about marriage."

"Oh, you awful boy! Herbert, isn't he just the same? But you do know something about Gerald, so don't be so chilly and cautious. I've just realized, looking at those groups, that you must have been at school together. Did you come much across him?"

"Very little," he answered, and sounded shy. He got up hastily, and began to muddle with the coffee.

"But he was in the same house. Surely that's a house group?"

"He was a prefect." He made his coffee on the simple system. One had a brown pot, into which the boiling stuff was poured. Just before serving one put in a drop of cold water, and the idea was that the grounds fell to the bottom.

"Wasn't he a kind of athletic marvel? Couldn't he knock any boy or master down?"

"Yes."

"If he had wanted to," said Mr Pembroke, who had not spoken for some time.

"If he had wanted to," echoed Rickie. "I do hope, Agnes, you'll be most awfully happy. I don't know anything about the Army, but I should think it must be most awfully interesting."

Mr Pembroke laughed faintly.

"Yes, Rickie. The Army is a most interesting profession—the profession of Wellington and Marlborough and Lord Roberts; a most interesting profession, as you observe. A profession that may mean death—death, rather than dishonour."

"That's nice," said Rickie, speaking to himself. "Any profession may mean dishonour, but one isn't allowed to die instead. The Army's different. If a soldier makes a mess, it's thought rather decent of him, isn't it, if he blows out his brains? In the other professions it somehow seems cowardly."

"I am not competent to pronounce," said Mr Pembroke, who was not accustomed to have his schoolroom satire commented on. "I merely know that the Army is the finest profession in the world. Which reminds me, Rickie—have you been thinking about yours?"

"No."

"Not at all?"

"No."

"Now, Herbert, don't bother him. Have another meringue."

"But, Rickie, my dear boy, you're twenty. It's time you thought. The Tripos is the beginning of life, not the end. In less than two years you will have got your B.A. What are you going to do with it?"

"I don't know."

"You're M.A., aren't you?" asked Agnes; but her brother proceeded—

"I have seen so many promising, brilliant lives wrecked simply on account of this—*not settling soon enough*. My dear boy, you must think. Consult your tastes if possible—but think. You have not a moment to lose. The Bar, like your father?"

"Oh, I wouldn't like that at all."

"I don't mention the Church."

"Oh, Rickie, do be a clergyman!" said Miss Pembroke. "You'd be simply killing in a wide-awake."

He looked at his guests hopelessly. Their kindness and competence overwhelmed him. "I wish I could talk to them as I talk to myself," he thought. "I'm not such an ass when I talk to myself. I don't believe, for instance, that quite all I thought about the cow was rot." Aloud he said, "I've sometimes wondered about writing."

"Writing?" said Mr Pembroke, with the tone of one who gives everything its trial. "Well, what about writing? What kind of writing?"

"I rather like"—he suppressed something in his throat— "I rather like trying to write little stories."

"Why, I made sure it was poetry!" said Agnes. "You're just the boy for poetry."

"I had no idea you wrote. Would you let me see something? Then I could judge."

The author shook his head. "I don't show it to anyone. It isn't anything. I just try because it amuses me."

"What is it about?"

"Silly nonsense."

"Are you ever going to show it to anyone?"

"I don't think so."

Mr Pembroke did not reply, firstly, because the meringue he was eating was, after all, Rickie's; secondly, because it was gluey and stuck his jaws together. Agnes observed that the writing was really a very good idea: there was Rickie's aunt—she could push him.

"Aunt Emily never pushes anyone; she says they always rebound and crush her."

"I only had the pleasure of seeing your aunt once. I should have thought her a quite uncrushable person. But she would be sure to help you."

"I couldn't show her anything. She'd think them even sillier than they are."

"Always running yourself down! There speaks the artist!"

"I'm not modest," he said anxiously. "I just know they're bad."

Mr Pembroke's teeth were clear of meringue, and he could refrain no longer. "My dear Rickie, your father and mother are dead, and you often say your aunt takes no interest in you. Therefore your life depends on yourself. Think it over carefully, but settle, and having once settled, stick. If you think that this writing is practicable, and that you could make your living by it—that you could, if needs be, support a wife—then by all means write. But you must work. Work and drudge. Begin at the bottom of the ladder and work upwards."

Rickie's head drooped. Any metaphor silenced him. He never thought of replying that art is not a ladder—with a curate, as it were, on the first rung, a rector on the second, and a bishop, still nearer heaven, at the top. He never retorted that the artist is not a bricklayer at all, but a horseman, whose business it is to catch Pegasus at once, not to practise for him by mounting tamer colts. This is hard, hot, and generally ungraceful work, but it is not drudgery. For drudgery is not art, and cannot lead to it.

"Of course I don't really think about writing," he said, as he poured the cold water into the coffee. "Even if my things ever were decent, I don't think the magazines would take them, and the magazines are one's only chance. I read somewhere, too, that Marie Corelli's about the only person who makes a thing out of literature. I'm certain it wouldn't pay me."

"I never mentioned the word 'pay'," said Mr Pembroke uneasily. "You must not consider money. There are ideals too."

"I have no ideals."

"Rickie!" she exclaimed. "Horrible boy!"

"No, Agnes, I have no ideals." Then he got very red, for it was a phrase he had caught from Ansell, and he could not remember what came next.

"The person who has no ideals," she exclaimed, "is to be pitied."

"I think so too," said Mr Pembroke, sipping his coffee. "Life without an ideal would be like the sky without the sun."

Rickie looked towards the night, wherein there now twinkled innumerable stars—gods and heroes, virgins and brides, to whom the Greeks have given their names.

"Life without an ideal—" repeated Mr Pembroke, and then stopped, for his mouth was full of coffee grounds. The same affliction had overtaken Agnes. After a little jocose laughter they departed to their lodgings, and Rickie, having seen them as far as the porter's lodge, hurried, singing as he went, to Ansell's room, burst open the door, and said, "Look here! Whatever do you mean by it?"

"By what?" Ansell was sitting alone with a piece of paper in front of him. On it was a diagram—a circle inside a square, inside which was again a square.

"By being so rude. You're no gentleman, and I told her so." He slammed him on the head with a sofa-cushion. "I'm certain one ought to be polite, even to people who aren't saved." ("Not saved" was a phrase they applied just then to those whom they did not like or intimately know.) "And I believe she is saved. I never knew anyone so always good-tempered and kind. She's been kind to me ever since I knew her. I wish you'd heard her trying to stop her brother: you'd have certainly come round. Not but what he was only being nice as well. But she is really nice. And I thought she came into the room so beautifully. Do you know—oh, of course, you despise music—but Anderson was playing Wagner, and he'd just got to the part where they sing

> '*Rheingold!*
> *Rheingold!*'

and the sun strikes into the waters, and the music, which up to then has so often been in E flat—"

"Goes into D sharp. I have not understood a single word, partly because you talk as if your mouth was full of plums, partly because I don't know whom you're talking about."

"Miss Pembroke—whom you saw."

"I saw no one."

"Who came in?"

"No one came in."

"You're an ass!" shrieked Rickie. "She came in. You saw her come in. She and her brother have been to dinner."

"You only think so. They were not really there."

"But they stop till Monday."

"You only think that they are stopping."

"But—oh, look here, shut up! The girl like an empress—"

"I saw no empress, nor any girl, nor have you seen them."

"Ansell, don't rag."

"Elliot, I never rag, and you know it. She was not really there."

There was a moment's silence. Then Rickie exclaimed, "I've got you. You say—or was it Tilliard?—no, *you* say that the cow's there. Well—there these people are, then. Got you. Yah!"

"Did it never strike you that phenomena may be of two kinds: *one*, those which have a real existence, such as the cow; *two*, those which are the subjective product of a diseased imagination, and which, to our destruction, we invest with the semblance of reality? If this never struck you, let it strike you now."

Rickie spoke again, but received no answer. He paced a little up and down the sombre room. Then he sat on the edge of the table and watched his clever friend draw within the square a circle, and within the circle a square, and inside that another circle, and inside that another square.

"Why will you do that?"

No answer.

"Are they real?"

"The inside one is—the one in the middle of everything, that there's never room enough to draw."

Chapter 2

A little this side of Madingley, to the left of the road, there is a secluded dell, paved with grass and planted with fir trees. It could not have been worth a visit twenty years ago, for then it was only a scar of chalk, and it is not worth a visit at the present day, for the trees have grown too thick and choked it. But when Rickie was up, it chanced to be the brief season of its romance, a season as brief for a chalk-pit as a man—its divine interval between the bareness of boyhood and the stuffiness of age. Rickie had discovered it in his second term, when the January snows had melted and left fiords and lagoons of clearest water between the inequalities of the floor. The place looked as big as Switzerland or Norway—as indeed for the moment it was—and he came upon it at a time when his life too was beginning to expand. Accordingly the dell became for him a kind of church—a church where indeed you could do anything you liked, but where anything you did would be transfigured. Like the ancient Greeks, he could even laugh at his holy place and leave it no less holy. He chatted gaily about it, and about the pleasant thoughts with which it inspired him; he took his friends there; he even took people whom he did not like. *"Procul este, profani!"* exclaimed a delighted aesthete on being introduced to it. But this was never to be the attitude of Rickie. He did not love the vulgar herd, but he knew that his own vulgarity would be greater if he forbade it ingress, and that it was not by preciosity that he would attain to the intimate spirit of the dell. Indeed, if he had agreed with the aesthete, he would possibly not have introduced him. If the dell was to bear any inscription, he would have liked it to be "This way to Heaven", painted on a signpost by the highroad, and he did not realize till later years that the number of visitors would not thereby have sensibly increased.

On the blessed Monday that the Pembrokes left, he walked out here with three friends. It was a day when the sky seemed enormous. One cloud, as large as a continent, was voyaging near the sun, whilst other clouds seemed anchored to the horizon, too lazy or too happy to move. The sky itself was of the palest blue, paling to white where it approached the earth; and the earth, brown, wet and odorous, was engaged beneath it on its yearly duty of decay. Rickie was open to the complexities of autumn; he felt extremely tiny—extremely tiny and extremely important; and perhaps the combination is as fair as any that exists. He hoped that all his life he would never be peevish or unkind.

"Elliot is in a dangerous state," said Ansell. They had reached the dell, and had stood for some time in silence, each leaning against a tree. It was too wet to sit down.

"How's that?" asked Rickie, who had not known he was in any state at all. He shut up Keats, whom he thought he had been reading, and slipped him back into his coat-pocket. Scarcely ever was he without a book.

"He's trying to like people."

"Then he's done for," said Widdrington. "He's dead."

"He's trying to like Hornblower."

The others gave shrill agonized cries.

"He wants to bind the college together. He wants to link us to the beefy set."

"I do like Hornblower," he protested. "I don't try."

"And Hornblower tries to like you."

"That part doesn't matter."

"But he does try to like you. He tries not to despise you. It is altogether a most public-spirited affair."

"Tilliard started them," said Widdrington. "Tilliard thinks it such a pity the college should be split into sets."

"Oh, Tilliard!" said Ansell, with much irritation. "But what can you expect from a person who's eternally beautiful? The other night we had been discussing a long time, and suddenly the light was turned on. Everyone else looked a sight, as they ought. But there was Tilliard sitting neatly on a little chair, like an undersized god, with not a curl crooked. I should say he will get into the Foreign Office."

"Why are most of us so ugly?" laughed Rickie.

"It's merely a sign of our salvation—merely another sign that the college is split."

"The college isn't split," cried Rickie, who got excited on this subject with unfailing regularity. "The college is, and has been, and always will be, one. What you call the beefy set aren't a set at all. They're just the rowing people, and naturally they chiefly see each other; but they're always nice to me or to anyone. Of course, they think us rather asses, but it's quite in a pleasant way."

"That's my whole objection," said Ansell. "What right have they to think us asses in a pleasant way? Why don't they hate us? What right has Hornblower to smack me on the back when I've been rude to him?"

"Well, what right have you to be rude to him?"

"Because I hate him. You think it is so splendid to hate no one. I tell you it is a crime. You want to love everyone equally, and that's worse than impossible—it's wrong. When you denounce sets, you're really trying to destroy friendship."

"I maintain," said Rickie—it was a verb he clung to, in the hope that it would lend stability to what followed—"I maintain that one can like many more people than one supposes."

"And I maintain that you hate many more people than you pretend."

"I hate no one," he exclaimed with extraordinary vehemence, and the dell re-echoed that it hated no one.

"We are obliged to believe you," said Widdrington, smiling a little; "but we are sorry about it."

"Not even your father?" asked Ansell.

Rickie was silent.

"Not even your father?"

The cloud above extended a great promontory across the sun. It only lay there for a moment, yet that was enough to summon the lurking coldness from the earth.

"Does he hate his father?" said Widdrington, who had not known. "Oh, good!"

"But his father's dead. He will say it doesn't count."

"Still, it's something. Do you hate yours?"

Ansell did not reply. Rickie said: "I say, I wonder whether one ought to talk like this?"

"About hating dead people?"

"Yes—"

"Did you hate your mother?" asked Widdrington.

Rickie turned crimson.

"I don't see Hornblower's such a rotter," remarked the other man, whose name was James.

"James, you are diplomatic," said Ansell. "You are trying to tide over an awkward moment. You can go."

Widdrington was crimson too. In his wish to be sprightly he had used words without thinking of their meanings. Suddenly he realized that "father" and "mother" really meant father and mother—people whom he had himself at home. He was very uncomfortable, and thought Rickie had been rather queer. He too tried to revert to Hornblower, but Ansell would not let him. The sun came out, and struck on the white ramparts of the dell. Rickie looked straight at it. Then he said abruptly—

"I think I want to talk."

"I think you do," replied Ansell.

"Shouldn't I be rather a fool if I went through Cambridge without talking? It's said never to come so easy again. All the people are dead too. I can't see why I shouldn't tell you most things about my birth and parentage and education."

"Talk away. If you bore us, we have books."

With this invitation Rickie began to relate his history. The reader who has no book will be obliged to listen to it.

*   *   *

Some people spend their lives in a suburb, and not for any urgent reason. This had been the fate of Rickie. He had opened his eyes to filmy heavens, and taken his first walk on asphalt. He had seen civilization as a row of semi-detached villas, and society as a state in which men do not know the men who live next door. He had himself become part of the gray monotony that surrounds all cities. There was no necessity for this—it was only rather convenient to his father.

Mr Elliot was a barrister. In appearance he resembled his son, being weakly and lame, with hollow little cheeks, a broad white band of forehead, and stiff impoverished hair. His voice, which he did not transmit, was very suave, with a fine command of cynical intonation. By altering it ever so little he could make people wince, especially if they were simple or poor. Nor did he transmit his eyes. Their peculiar flatness, as if the soul looked through dirty window-panes, the unkindness of them, the cowardice, the fear in them, were to trouble the world no longer.

He married a girl whose voice was beautiful. There was no caress in it, yet all who heard it were soothed, as though the world held some unexpected blessing. She called to her dogs one night over invisible waters, and he, a tourist up on the bridge, thought "that is extraordinarily adequate". In time he discovered that her figure, face, and thoughts were adequate also, and as she was not impossible socially, he married her. "I have taken a plunge," he told his family. The family, hostile at first, had not a word to say when the woman was introduced to them; and his sister declared that the plunge had been taken from the opposite bank.

Things only went right for a little time. Though beautiful without and within, Mrs Elliot had not the gift of making her home beautiful; and one day, when she bought a carpet for the dining-room that clashed, he laughed gently, said he "really couldn't", and departed. Departure is perhaps too strong a word. In Mrs Elliot's mouth it became, "My husband has to sleep more in town". He often came down to see them, nearly always unexpectedly, and occasionally they went to see him. "Father's house", as Rickie called it, only had three rooms, but these were full of books and pictures and flowers; and the flowers, instead of being squashed down into the vases as they were in mummy's house, rose gracefully from frames of lead which lay coiled at the bottom, as doubtless the sea serpent has to lie, coiled at the bottom of the sea. Once he was let to lift a frame out—only once, for he dropped some water on a creton. "I think he's going to have taste," said Mr Elliot languidly. "It is quite possible," his wife replied. She had not taken off her hat and gloves, nor even pulled up her veil. Mr Elliot laughed, and soon afterwards another lady came in, and they went away.

"Why does father always laugh?" asked Rickie in the evening when he and his mother were sitting in the nursery.

"It is a way of your father's."

"Why does he always laugh at me? Am I so funny?" Then after a pause, "You have no sense of humour, have you, mummy?"

Mrs Elliot, who was raising a thread of cotton to her lips, held it suspended in amazement.

"You told him so this afternoon. But I have seen you laugh." He nodded wisely. "I have seen you laugh ever so often. One day you were laughing alone all down in the sweet peas."

"Was I?"

"Yes. Were you laughing at me?"

"I was not thinking about you. Cotton, please—a reel of No. 50 white from my chest of drawers. Left-hand drawer. Now which is your left hand?"

"The side my pocket is."

"And if you had no pocket?"

"The side my bad foot is."

"I meant you to say, 'the side my heart is'," said Mrs Elliot, holding up the duster between them. "Most of us—I mean all of us—can feel on one side a little watch, that never stops ticking. So even if you had no bad foot you would still know which is the left. No. 50 white, please. No; I'll get it myself." For she had remembered that the dark passage frightened him.

These were the outlines. Rickie filled them in with the slowness and the accuracy of a child. He was never told anything, but he discovered for himself that his father and mother did not love each other, and that his mother was lovable. He discovered that Mr Elliot had dubbed him Rickie because he was rickety, that he took pleasure in alluding to his son's deformity, and was sorry that it was not more serious than his own. Mr Elliot had not one scrap of genius. He gathered the pictures and the books and the flower-supports mechanically, not in any impulse of love. He passed for a cultured man because he knew how to select, and he passed for an unconventional man because he did not select quite like other people. In reality he never did or said or thought one single thing that had the slightest beauty or value. And in time Rickie discovered this as well.

The boy grew up in great loneliness. He worshipped his mother, and she was fond of him. But she was dignified and reticent, and pathos, like tattle, was disgusting to her. She was afraid of intimacy, in case it led to confidences and tears, and so all her life she held her son at a little distance. Her kindness and unselfishness knew no limits, but if he tried to be dramatic and thank her, she told him not to be a little goose. And so the only person he came to know at all was himself. He would play Halma against himself. He would conduct solitary conversations, in which one part of him asked and another part answered. It was an exciting game, and concluded with the formula: "Goodbye. Thank you. I am glad to have met you. I hope before long we shall enjoy another chat." And then perhaps he would sob for loneliness, for he would see real people—real brothers, real friends—doing in warm life the things he had pretended. "Shall I ever have a friend?" he demanded at the age of twelve. "I don't see how. They walk too fast. And a brother I shall never have."

("No loss," interrupted Widdrington.

"But I shall never have one, and so I quite want one, even now.")

When he was thirteen Mr Elliot entered on his illness. The pretty rooms in town would not do for an invalid, and so he came back to his home. One of the first consequences was that Rickie was sent to a public school. Mrs Elliot did what she could, but she had no hold whatever over her husband.

"He worries me," he declared. "He's a joke of which I have got tired."

24

"Would it be possible to send him to a private tutor's?"

"No," said Mr Elliot, who had all the money. "Coddling."

"I agree that boys ought to rough it; but when a boy is lame and very delicate, he roughs it sufficiently if he leaves home. Rickie can't play games. He doesn't make friends. He isn't brilliant. Thinking it over, I feel that as it's like this, we can't ever hope to give him the ordinary education. Perhaps you could think it over too."

"No."

"I am sure that things are best for him as they are. The day-school knocks quite as many corners off him as he can stand. He hates it, but it is good for him. A public school will not be good for him. It is too rough. Instead of getting manly and hard, he will—"

"My head, please."

Rickie departed in a state of bewildered misery, which was scarcely ever to grow clearer.

Each holiday he found his father more irritable, and a little weaker. Mrs Elliot was quickly growing old. She had to manage the servants, to hush the neighbouring children, to answer the correspondence, to paper and repaper the rooms—and all for the sake of a man whom she did not like, and who did not conceal his dislike for her. One day she found Rickie tearful, and said rather crossly, "Well, what is it this time?"

He replied, "Oh, mummy, I've seen your wrinkles—your gray hair—I'm unhappy."

Sudden tenderness overcame her, and she cried, "My darling, what does it matter? Whatever does it matter now?"

He had never known her so emotional. Yet even better did he remember another incident. Hearing high voices from his father's room, he went upstairs in the hope that the sound of his tread might stop them. Mrs Elliot burst open the door, and seeing him, exclaimed, "My dear! If you please, he's hit me." She tried to laugh it off, but a few hours later he saw the bruise which the stick of the invalid had raised upon his mother's hand.

God alone knows how far we are in the grip of our bodies. He alone can judge how far the cruelty of Mr Elliot was the outcome of extenuating circumstances. But Mrs Elliot could accurately judge of its extent.

At last he died. Rickie was now fifteen, and got off a whole week's school for the funeral. His mother was rather strange. She was much happier, she looked younger, and her mourning was as unobtrusive as convention permitted. All this he had expected. But she seemed to be watching him, and to be extremely anxious for his opinion on any subject—more especially on his father. Why? At last he saw that she was trying to establish confidence between them. But confidence cannot be established in a moment. They were both shy. The habit of years was upon them, and they alluded to the death of Mr Elliot as an irreparable loss.

"Now that your father has gone, things will be very different."

"Shall we be poorer, mother?"

"No."

"Oh!"

"But naturally things will be very different."

"Yes, naturally."

"For instance, your poor father liked being near London, but I almost think we might move. Would you like that?"

"Of course, mummy." He looked down at the ground. He was not accustomed to being consulted, and it bewildered him.

"Perhaps you might like quite a different life better?"

He giggled.

"It's a little difficult for me," said Mrs Elliot, pacing vigorously up and down the room, and more and more did her black dress seem a mockery. "In some ways you ought to be consulted: nearly all the money is left to you, as you must hear sometime or other. But in other ways you're only a boy. What am I to do?"

"I don't know," he replied, appearing more helpless and unhelpful than he really was.

"For instance, would you like me to arrange things exactly as I like?"

"Oh do!" he exclaimed, thinking this a most brilliant suggestion. "The very nicest thing of all." And he added, in his half-pedantic, half-pleasing way, "I shall be as wax in your hands, mamma."

She smiled. "Very well, darling. You shall be." And she pressed him lovingly, as though she would mould him into something beautiful.

For the next few days great preparations were in the air. She went to see his father's sister, the gifted and vivacious Aunt Emily. They were to live in the country—somewhere right in the country, with grass and trees up to the door, and birds singing everywhere, and a tutor. For he was not to go back to school. Unbelievable! He was never to go back to school, and the headmaster had written saying that he regretted the step, but that possibly it was a wise one.

It was raw weather, and Mrs Elliot watched over him with ceaseless tenderness. It seemed as if she could not do too much to shield him and to draw him nearer to her.

"Put on your greatcoat, dearest," she said to him.

"I don't think I want it," answered Rickie, remembering that he was now fifteen.

"The wind is bitter. You ought to put it on."

"But it's so heavy."

"Do put it on, dear."

He was not very often irritable or rude, but he answered, "Oh, I shan't catch cold. I do wish you wouldn't keep on bothering."

He did not catch cold, but while he was out his mother died. She only survived her husband eleven days, a coincidence which was recorded on their tombstone.

*   *   *

Such, in substance, was the story which Rickie told his friends as they stood together in the shelter of the dell. The green bank at the entrance hid the road and the world, and now, as in spring, they could see nothing but snow-white ramparts and the evergreen foliage of the firs. Only from time to time would a beech leaf flutter in from the woods above, to comment on the waning year, and the warmth and radiance of the sun would vanish behind a passing cloud.

About the greatcoat he did not tell them, for he could not have spoken of it without tears.

Chapter 3

Mr Ansell, a provincial draper of moderate prosperity, ought by rights to have been classed not with the cow, but with those phenomena that are not really there. But his son, with pardonable illogicality, excepted him. He never suspected that his father might be the subjective product of a diseased imagination. From his earliest years he had taken him for granted, as a most undeniable and lovable fact. To be born one thing and grow up another—Ansell had accomplished this without weakening one of the ties that bound him to his home. The rooms above the shop still seemed as comfortable, the garden behind it as gracious, as they had seemed fifteen years before, when he would sit behind Miss Appleblossom's central throne, and she, like some allegorical figure, would send the change and receipted bills spinning away from her in little boxwood balls. At first the young man had attributed these happy relations to his own tact. But in time he perceived that the tact was all on the side of his father. Mr Ansell was not merely a man of some education; he had what no education can bring—the power of detecting what is important. Like many fathers, he had spared no expense over his boy—he had borrowed money to start him at a rapacious and fashionable private school; he had sent him to tutors; he had sent him to Cambridge. But he knew that all this was not the important thing. The important thing was freedom. The boy must use his education as he chose, and if he paid his father back it would certainly not be in his own coin. So when Stewart said, "At Cambridge, can I read for the Moral Science Tripos?" Mr Ansell had only replied, "This philosophy—do you say that it lies behind everything?"

"Yes, I think so. It tries to discover what is good and true."

"Then, my boy, you had better read as much of it as you can."

And a year later: "I'd like to take up this philosophy seriously, but I don't feel justified."

"Why not?"

"Because it brings in no return. I think I'm a great philosopher, but then all philosophers think that, though they don't dare to say so. But, however great I am, I shan't earn money. Perhaps I shan't ever be able to keep myself. I shan't even get a good social position. You've only to say one word, and I'll work for the Civil Service. I'm good enough to get in high."

Mr Ansell liked money and social position. But he knew that there is a more important thing, and replied, "You must take up this philosophy seriously, I think."

"Another thing—there are the girls."

"There is enough money now to get Mary and Maud as good husbands as they deserve." And Mary and Maud took the same view.

It was in this plebeian household that Rickie spent part of the Christmas vacation. His own home, such as it was, was with the Silts, needy cousins of his father's, and combined to a peculiar degree the restrictions of hospitality with the discomforts of a boarding-house. Such pleasure as he had outside Cambridge was in the homes of his friends, and it was a particular joy and honour to visit Ansell, who, though as free from social snobbishness as most of us will ever manage to be, was rather careful whom he drove up to the façade of his shop.

"I like our new lettering," he said thoughtfully. The words "Stewart Ansell" were repeated again and again along the High Street—curly gold letters that seemed to float in tanks of glazed chocolate.

"Rather!" said Rickie. But he wondered whether one of the bonds that kept the Ansell family united might not be their complete absence of taste—a surer bond by far than the identity of it. And he wondered this again when he sat at tea opposite a long row of crayons—Stewart as a baby, Stewart as a small boy with large feet, Stewart as a larger boy with smaller feet, Mary reading a book whose leaves were as thick as eiderdowns. And yet again did he wonder it when he woke with a gasp in the night to find a harp in luminous paint throbbing and glowering at him from the adjacent wall. "Watch and Pray" was written on the harp, and until Rickie hung a towel over it the exhortation was partially successful.

It was a very happy visit. Miss Appleblossom—who now acted as housekeeper—had met him before, during her never-forgotten expedition to Cambridge, and her admiration of University life was as shrill and as genuine now as it had been then. The girls at first were a little aggressive, for on his arrival he had been tired, and Maud had taken it for haughtiness, and said he was looking down on them. But this passed. They did not fall in love with him, nor he with them, but a morning was spent very pleasantly in snowballing in the back garden. Ansell was rather different to what he was in Cambridge, but to Rickie not less attractive. And there was a curious charm in the hum of the shop, which swelled into a roar if one opened the partition door on a market-day.

"Listen to your money!" said Rickie. "I wish I could hear mine. I wish my money was alive."

"I don't understand."

"Mine's dead money. It's come to me through about six dead people—silently."

"Getting a little smaller and a little more respectable each time, on account of the death-duties."

"It needed to get respectable."

"Why? Did your people, too, once keep a shop?"

"Oh, not as bad as that! They only swindled. About a hundred years ago an Elliot did something shady and founded the fortunes of our house."

"I never knew anyone so relentless to his ancestors. You make up for your soapiness towards the living."

"You'd be relentless if you'd heard the Silts, as I have, talk about 'a fortune, small perhaps, but unsoiled by trade'! Of course Aunt Emily is rather different. Oh, goodness me! I've forgotten my aunt. She lives not so far. I shall have to call on her."

Accordingly he wrote to Mrs Failing, and said he should like to pay his respects. He told her about the Ansells, and so worded the letter that she might reasonably have sent an invitation to his friend.

She replied that she was looking forward to their *tête-à-tête*.

"You mustn't go round by the trains," said Mr Ansell. "It means changing at Salisbury. By the road it's no great way. Stewart shall drive you over Salisbury Plain, and fetch you too."

"There's too much snow," said Ansell.

"Then the girls shall take you in their sledge."

"That I will," said Maud, who was not unwilling to see the inside of Cadover. But Rickie went round by the trains.

"We have all missed you," said Ansell, when he returned. "There is a general feeling that you are no nuisance, and had better stop till the end of the vac."

This he could not do. He was bound for Christmas to the Silts—"as a *real* guest", Mrs Silt had written, underlining the word "real" twice. And after Christmas he must go to the Pembrokes.

"These are no reasons. The only real reason for doing a thing is because you want to do it. I think the talk about 'engagements' is cant."

"I think perhaps it is," said Rickie. But he went. Never had the turkey been so athletic, or the plum-pudding tied into its cloth so tightly. Yet he knew that both these symbols of hilarity had cost money, and it went to his heart when Mr Silt said in a hungry voice, "Have you thought at all of what you want to be? No? Well, why should you? You have no need to be anything." And at dessert: "I wonder who Cadover goes to? I expect money will follow money. It always does." It was with a guilty feeling of relief that he left for the Pembrokes.

The Pembrokes lived in an adjacent suburb, or rather "sububurb"—the tract called Sawston, celebrated for its public school. Their style of life, however, was not particularly suburban. Their house was small and its name was

Shelthorpe, but it had an air about it which suggested a certain amount of money and a certain amount of taste. There were decent water-colours in the drawing-room. Madonnas of acknowledged merit hung upon the stairs. A replica of the Hermes of Praxiteles—of course only the bust—stood in the hall with a real palm behind it. Agnes, in her slapdash way, was a good housekeeper, and kept the pretty things well dusted. It was she who insisted on the strip of brown holland that led diagonally from the front door to the door of Herbert's study: boys' grubby feet should not go treading on her Indian square. It was she who always cleaned the picture frames and washed the bust and the leaves of the palm. In short, if a house could speak—and sometimes it does speak more clearly than the people who live in it—the house of the Pembrokes would have said, "I am not quite like other houses, yet I am perfectly comfortable. I contain works of art and a micro-scope and books. But I do not live for any of these things or suffer them to disarrange me. I live for myself and for the greater houses that shall come after me. Yet in me neither the cry of money nor the cry for money shall ever be heard."

Mr Pembroke was at the station. He did better as a host than as a guest, and welcomed the young man with real friendliness.

"We were all coming, but Gerald has strained his ankle slightly, and wants to keep quiet, as he is playing next week in a match. And, needless to say, that explains the absence of my sister."

"Gerald Dawes?"

"Yes; he's with us. I'm so glad you'll meet again."

"So am I," said Rickie, with extreme awkwardness. "Does he remember me?"

"Vividly."

Vivid also was Rickie's remembrance of him.

"A splendid fellow," asserted Mr Pembroke.

"I hope that Agnes is well."

"Thank you, yes; she is well. And I think you're looking more like other people yourself."

"I've been having a very good time with a friend."

"Indeed. That's right. Who was that?"

Rickie had a young man's reticence. He generally spoke of "a friend", "a person I know", "a place I was at". When the book of life is opening, our readings are secret, and we are unwilling to give chapter and verse. Mr Pembroke, who was halfway through the volume, and had skipped or forgotten the earlier pages, could not understand Rickie's hesitation, nor why with such awkwardness he should pronounce the harmless dissyllable "Ansell".

"Ansell? Wasn't that the pleasant fellow who asked us to lunch?"

"No. That was Anderson, who keeps below. You didn't see Ansell. The ones who came to breakfast were Tilliard and Hornblower."

"Of course. And since then you have been with the Silts. How are they?"

"Very well, thank you. They want to be remembered to you."

The Pembrokes had formerly lived near the Elliots, and had shown great kindness to Rickie when his parents died. They were thus rather in the position of family friends.

"Please remember us when you write." He added, almost roguishly, "The Silts are kindness itself. All the same, it must be just a little—dull, we thought, and we thought that you might like a change. And of course we are delighted to have you besides. That goes without saying."

"It's very good of you," said Rickie, who had accepted the invitation because he felt he ought to.

"Not a bit. And you mustn't expect us to be otherwise than quiet in the holidays. There is a library of a sort, as you know, and you will find Gerald a splendid fellow."

"Will they be married soon?"

"Oh no!" whispered Mr Pembroke, shutting his eyes, as if Rickie had made some terrible *faux pas*. "It will be a very long engagement. He must make his way first. I have seen such endless misery result from people marrying before they have made their way."

"Yes. That is so," said Rickie despondently, thinking of the Silts.

"It's a sad unpalatable truth," said Mr Pembroke, thinking that the despondency might be personal, "but one must accept it. My sister and Gerald, I am thankful to say, have accepted it, though naturally it has been a bitter pill."

Their cab lurched round the corner as he spoke, and the two patients came in sight. Agnes was leaning over the creosoted garden gate, and behind her there stood a young man who had the figure of a Greek athlete and the face of an English one. He was fair and clean-shaven, and his colourless hair was cut rather short. The sun was in his eyes, and they, like his mouth, seemed scarcely more than slits in his healthy skin. Just where he began to be beautiful the clothes started. Round his neck went an up-and-down collar and a mauve-and-gold tie, and the rest of his limbs were hidden by a gray lounge suit, carefully creased in the right places.

"Lovely! lovely!" cried Agnes, banging on the gate. "Your train must have been to the minute."

"Hullo!" said the athlete, and vomited with the greeting a cloud of tobacco-smoke. It must have been imprisoned in his mouth some time, for no pipe was visible.

"Hullo!" returned Rickie, laughing violently. They shook hands.

"Where are you going, Rickie?" asked Agnes. "You aren't grubby. Why don't you stop? Gerald, get the large wicker chair. Herbert has letters, but we can sit here till lunch. It's like spring."

The garden of Shelthorpe was nearly all in front—an unusual and pleasant arrangement. The front gate and the servants' entrance were both at the side, and in the remaining space the gardener had contrived a little lawn where one could sit concealed from the road by a fence, from the neighbour by a fence, from the house by a tree, and from the path by a bush.

"This is the lovers' bower," observed Agnes, sitting down on the bench. Rickie stood by her till the chair arrived.

"Are you smoking before lunch?" asked Mr Dawes.

"No, thank you. I hardly ever smoke."

"No vices. Aren't you at Cambridge now?"

"Yes."

"What's your college?"

Rickie told him.

"Do you know Carruthers?"

"Rather!"

"I mean A. P. Carruthers, who got his soccer blue."

"Rather! He's secretary to the college musical society."

"A. P. Carruthers?"

"Yes."

Mr Dawes seemed offended. He tapped on his teeth, and remarked that the weather had no business to be so warm in winter.

"But it was fiendish before Christmas," said Agnes.

He frowned, and asked, "Do you know a man called Gerrish?"

"No."

"Ah."

"Do you know James?"

"Never heard of him."

"He's my year too. He got a blue for hockey his second term."

"I know nothing about the 'Varsity."

Rickie winced at the abbreviation "'Varsity". It was at that time the proper thing to speak of "the University".

"I haven't the time," pursued Mr Dawes.

"No, no," said Rickie politely.

"I had the chance of being an Undergrad myself, and, by Jove, I'm thankful I didn't!"

"Why?" asked Agnes, for there was a pause.

"Puts you back in your profession. Men who go there first, before the Army, start hopelessly behind. The same with the Stock Exchange or Painting. I know men in both, and they've never caught up the time they lost in the 'Varsity—unless, of course, you turn parson."

"I love Cambridge," said she. "All those glorious buildings, and everyone so happy and running in and out of each other's rooms all day long."

"That might make an Undergrad happy, but I beg leave to state it wouldn't me. I haven't four years to throw away for the sake of being called a 'Varsity man and hobnobbing with lords."

Rickie was prepared to find his old schoolfellow ungrammatical and bumptious, but he was not prepared to find him peevish. Athletes, he believed, were simple, straightforward people, cruel and brutal if you like, but never petty. They knocked you down and hurt you, and then went on their way rejoicing. For this, Rickie thought, there is something to be said: he had escaped the sin of despising the physically strong—a sin against which the physically weak must guard. But here was Dawes returning again and again to the subject of the University, full of transparent jealousy and petty spite, nagging, nagging, nagging, like a maiden lady who has not been invited to a tea-party. Rickie wondered whether, after all, Ansell and the extremists might not be right, and bodily beauty and strength be signs of the soul's damnation.

He glanced at Agnes. She was writing down some orderings for the tradespeople on a piece of paper. Her handsome face was intent on the work. The bench on which she and Gerald were sitting had no back, but she sat as straight as a dart. He, though strong enough to sit straight, did not take the trouble.

"Why don't they talk to each other?" thought Rickie.

"Gerald, give this paper to the cook."

"I can give it to the other slavey, can't I?"

"She'll be dressing."

"Well, there's Herbert."

"He's busy. Oh, you know where the kitchen is. Take it to the cook."

He disappeared slowly behind the tree.

"What do you think of him?" she immediately asked.

He murmured civilly.

"Has he changed since he was a schoolboy?"

"In a way."

"Do tell me all about him. Why won't you?"

She might have seen a flash of horror pass over Rickie's

face. The horror disappeared, for, thank God, he was now a man, whom civilization protects. But he and Gerald had met, as it were, behind the scenes, before our decorous drama opens, and there the elder boy had done things to him— absurd things, not worth chronicling separately. An apple-pie bed is nothing; pinches, kicks, boxed ears, twisted arms, pulled hair, ghosts at night, inky books, befouled photographs, amount to very little by themselves. But let them be united and continuous, and you have a hell that no grown-up devil can devise. Between Rickie and Gerald there lay a shadow that darkens life more often than we suppose. The bully and his victim never quite forget their first relations. They meet in clubs and country houses, and clap one another on the back; but in both the memory is green of a more strenuous day, when they were boys together.

He tried to say, "He was the right kind of boy, and I was the wrong kind." But Cambridge would not let him smooth the situation over by self-belittlement. If he had been the wrong kind of boy, Gerald had been a worse kind. He murmured, "We are different, very," and Miss Pembroke, perhaps suspecting something, asked no more. But she kept to the subject of Mr Dawes, humorously depreciating her lover and discussing him without reverence. Rickie laughed, but felt uncomfortable. When people were engaged, he felt that they should be outside criticism. Yet here he was criticizing. He could not help it. He was dragged in.

"I hope his ankle is better."

"Never was bad. He's always fussing over something."

"He plays next week in a match, I think Herbert says."

"I dare say he does."

"Shall we be going?"

"Pray go if you like. I shall stop at home. I've had enough of cold feet."

It was all very colourless and odd.

Gerald returned, saying, "I can't stand your cook. What's she want to ask me questions for? I can't stand talking to servants. I say, 'If I speak to you, well and good'—and it's another thing besides if she were pretty."

"Well, I hope our ugly cook will have lunch ready in a

minute," said Agnes. "We're frightfully unpunctual this morning, and I daren't say anything, because it was the same yesterday, and if I complain again they might leave. Poor Rickie must be starved."

"Why, the Silts gave me all these sandwiches and I've never eaten them. They always stuff one."

"And you thought you'd better, eh?" said Mr Dawes, "in case you weren't stuffed here."

Miss Pembroke, who house-kept somewhat economically, looked annoyed.

The voice of Mr Pembroke was now heard calling from the house, "Frederick! Frederick! My dear boy, pardon me. It was an important letter about the Church Defence, other-wise—Come in and see your room."

He was glad to quit the little lawn. He had learnt too much there. It was dreadful: they did not love each other. More dreadful even than the case of his father and mother, for they, until they married, had got on pretty well. But this man was already rude and brutal and cold: he was still the school bully who twisted up the arms of little boys, and ran pins into them at chapel, and struck them in the stomach when they were swinging on the horizontal bar. Poor Agnes; why ever had she done it? Ought not somebody to interfere?

He had forgotten his sandwiches, and went back to get them.

Gerald and Agnes were locked in each other's arms.

He only looked for a moment, but the sight burnt into his brain. The man's grip was the stronger. He had drawn the woman onto his knee, was pressing her, with all his strength, against him. Already her hands slipped off him, and she whispered, "Don't—you hurt—" Her face had no expression. It stared at the intruder and never saw him. Then her lover kissed it, and immediately it shone with mysterious beauty, like some star.

Rickie limped away without the sandwiches, crimson and afraid. He thought, "Do such things actually happen?" and he seemed to be looking down coloured valleys. Brighter they glowed, till gods of pure flame were born in them, and then he was looking at pinnacles of virgin snow. While Mr

Pembroke talked, the riot of fair images increased. They invaded his being and lit lamps at unsuspected shrines. Their orchestra commenced in that suburban house, where he had to stand aside for the maid to carry in the luncheon. Music flowed past him like a river. He stood at the springs of creation and heard the primeval monotony. Then an obscure instrument gave out a little phrase. The river continued unheeding. The phrase was repeated, and a listener might know it was a fragment of the Tune of tunes. Nobler instruments accepted it, the clarionet protected, the brass encouraged, and it rose to the surface to the whisper of violins. In full unison was Love born, flame of the flame, flushing the dark river beneath him and the virgin snows above. His wings were infinite, his youth eternal; the sun was a jewel on his finger as he passed it in benediction over the world. Creation, no longer monotonous, acclaimed him, in widening melody, in brighter radiances. Was Love a column of fire? Was he a torrent of song? Was he greater than either— the touch of a man on a woman?

It was the merest accident that Rickie had not been disgusted. But this he could not know.

Mr Pembroke, when he called the two dawdlers into lunch, was aware of a hand on his arm and a voice that murmured, "Don't—they may be happy."

He stared, and struck the gong. To its music they approached, priest and high priestess.

"Rickie, can I give these sandwiches to the boot boy?" said the one. "He would love them."

"The gong! Be quick! The gong!"

"Are you smoking before lunch?" said the other.

But they had got into heaven, and nothing could get them out of it. Others might think them surly or prosaic. He knew. He would remember every word they spoke. He would treasure every motion, every glance of either, and so in time to come, when the gates of heaven had shut, some faint radiance, some echo of wisdom might remain with him outside.

As a matter of fact, he saw them very little during his visit. He checked himself because he was unworthy. What right had he to pry, even in the spirit, upon their bliss? It was no crime to have seen them on the lawn. It would be a crime to go to it again. He tried to keep himself and his thoughts away, not because he was ascetic, but because they would not like it if they knew. This behaviour of his suited them admirably. And when any gracious little thing occurred to them—any little thing that his sympathy had contrived and allowed—they put it down to chance or to each other.

So the lovers fall into the background. They are part of the distant sunrise, and only the mountains speak to them. Rickie talks to Mr Pembroke, amidst the unlit valleys of our over-habitable world.

Chapter 4

Sawston School had been founded by a tradesman in the seventeenth century. It was then a tiny grammar school in a tiny town, and the City Company who governed it had to drive half a day through woods and heather on the occasion of their annual visit. In the twentieth century they still drove, but only from the railway station; and found themselves not in a tiny town, nor yet in a large one, but amongst innumerable residences, detached and semi-detached, which had gathered round the school. For the intentions of the founder had been altered, or at all events amplified, and instead of educating the "poore of my home", he now educated the upper middle classes of England. The change had taken place not so very far back. Till the nineteenth century the grammar school was still composed of day scholars from the neighbourhood. Then two things happened. Firstly, the school's property rose in value, and it became rich. Secondly, for no obvious reason, it suddenly emitted a quantity of bishops. The bishops, like the stars from a Roman candle, were of all colours, and flew in all directions, some high, some low, some to distant colonies, one into the Church of Rome. But many a father traced their course in the papers; many a mother wondered whether her son, if properly ignited, might not burn as bright; many a family moved to the place where living and education were so cheap, where day-boys were not looked down upon, and where the orthodox and the up-to-date were said to be combined. The school doubled its numbers. It built new classrooms, laboratories, and a gymnasium. It dropped the prefix "Grammar". It coaxed the sons of the local tradesmen into a new foundation, the "Commercial School", built a couple of miles away. And it started boarding-houses. It had not the gracious antiquity of Eton or Winchester, nor, on the other hand, had it a conscious policy like Lancing, Wellington, and other purely modern foundations. Where traditions served, it clung to them. Where new departures seemed desirable, they were made. It aimed at producing the average Englishman, and, to a very great extent, it succeeded.

Here Mr Pembroke passed his happy and industrious life. His technical position was that of master to a form low down on the Modern Side. But his work lay elsewhere. He organized. If no organization existed, he would create one. If one did exist, he would modify it. "An organization," he would say, "is after all not an end in itself. It must contribute to a movement." When one good custom seemed likely to corrupt the school, he was ready with another; he believed that without innumerable customs there was no safety, either for boys or men. Perhaps he is right, and always will be right. Perhaps each of us would go to ruin if for one short hour we acted as we thought fit, and attempted the service of perfect freedom. The school caps, with their elaborate symbolism, were his; his the many-tinted bathing-drawers, that showed how far a boy could swim; his the hierarchy of jerseys and blazers. It was he who instituted Bounds, and Call, and the two sorts of exercise-paper, and the three sorts of caning, and "The Sawstonian", a bi-terminal magazine. His plump finger was in every pie. The dome of his skull, mild but impressive, shone at every masters' meeting. He was generally acknowledged to be the coming man.

His last achievement had been the organization of the day-boys. They had been left too much to themselves, and were weak in *esprit de corps*; they were apt to regard home, not school, as the most important thing in their lives. Moreover, they got out of their parents' hands; they did their preparation any time and sometimes anyhow. They shirked games, they were out at all hours, they ate what they should not, they smoked, they bicycled on the asphalt. Now all was over. Like the boarders, they were to be in at 7.15 p.m., and were not allowed out after unless with a written order from their parent or guardian; they, too, must work at fixed hours in the evening, and before breakfast next morning from 7 to 8. Games were compulsory. They must not go to parties in term time. They must keep to bounds. Of course the reform was not complete. It was impossible to control the dieting, though, on a printed circular, day-parents were implored to provide simple food. And it is also believed that some mothers disobeyed the rule about preparation, and allowed their sons to do all the work overnight and have a longer sleep in the morning. But the gulf between day-boys and boarders was considerably lessened, and grew still narrower when the day-boys too were organized into a House with housemaster and colours of their own. "Through the House," said Mr Pembroke, "one learns patriotism for the school, just as through the school one learns patriotism for the country. Our only course, therefore, is to organize the day-boys into a House." The headmaster agreed, as he often did, and the new community was formed. Mr Pembroke, to avoid the tongues of malice, had refused the post of house-master for himself, saying to Mr Jackson, who taught the sixth, "You keep too much in the background. Here is a chance for you." But this was a failure. Mr Jackson, a scholar and a student, neither felt nor conveyed any enthusiasm, and when confronted with his House, would say, "Well, I don't know what we're all here for. Now I should think you'd better go home to your mothers." He returned to his background, and next term Mr Pembroke was to take his place.

Such were the themes on which Mr Pembroke discoursed to Rickie's civil ear. He showed him the school, and the library, and the subterranean hall where the day-boys might leave their coats and caps, and where, on festal occasions, they supped. He showed him Mr Jackson's pretty house, and whispered, "Were it not for his brilliant intellect, it would be a case of Quick-march!" He showed him the rac-quet-court, happily completed, and the chapel, unhappily still in need of funds. Rickie was impressed, but then he was impressed by everything. Of course a House of day-boys seemed a little shadowy after Agnes and Gerald, but he imparted some reality even to that.

"The racquet-court," said Mr Pembroke, "is most grati-fying. We never expected to manage it this year. But before the Easter holidays every boy received a subscription card, and was given to understand that he must collect thirty shillings. You will scarcely believe me, but they nearly all responded. Next term there was a dinner in the great school, and all who had collected, not thirty shillings, but as much as a pound, were invited to it—for naturally one was not precise for a few shillings, the response being the really valuable thing. Practically the whole school had to come."

"They must enjoy the court tremendously."

"Ah, it isn't used very much. Racquets, as I daresay you know, is rather an expensive game. Only the wealthier boys play—and I'm sorry to say that it is not of our wealthier boys that we are always proudest. But the point is that no public school can be called first-class until it has one. They are building them right and left."

"And now you must finish the chapel?"

"Now we must complete the chapel." He paused reverently, and said, "And here is a fragment of the original building."

Rickie at once had a rush of sympathy. He, too, looked with reverence at the morsel of Jacobean brickwork, ruddy and beautiful amidst the machine-squared stones of the modern apse. The two men, who had so little in common, were thrilled with patriotism. They rejoiced that their country was great, noble, and old.

"Thank God I'm English," said Rickie suddenly.

"Thank Him indeed," said Mr Pembroke, laying a hand on his back.

"We've been nearly as great as the Greeks, I do believe. Greater, I'm sure, than the Italians, though they did get closer to beauty. Greater than the French, though we do take all their ideas. I can't help thinking that England is immense. English literature certainly."

Mr Pembroke removed his hand. He found such patriotism somewhat craven. Genuine patriotism comes only from the heart. It knows no parleying with reason. English ladies will declare abroad that there are no fogs in London, and Mr Pembroke, though he would not go to this, was only restrained by the certainty of being found out. On this occasion he remarked that the Greeks lacked spiritual insight, and had a low conception of woman.

"As to women—oh! there they were dreadful," said Rickie, leaning his hand on the chapel. "I realize that more and more. But as to spiritual insight, I don't quite like to say; and I find Plato too difficult, but I know men who don't, and I fancy they mightn't agree with you."

"Far be it from me to disparage Plato. And for philosophy as a whole I have the greatest respect. But it is the crown of a man's education, not the foundation. Myself, I read it with the utmost profit, but I have known endless trouble result from boys who attempted it too soon, before they were set."

"But if those boys had died first," cried Rickie with sudden vehemence, "without knowing what there is to know—"

"Or isn't to know!" said Mr Pembroke sarcastically.

"Or what there isn't to know. Exactly. That's it."

"My dear Rickie, what do you mean? If an old friend may be frank, you are talking great rubbish." And, with a few well-worn formulae, he propped up the young man's orthodoxy. The props were unnecessary. Rickie had his own equilibrium. Neither the Revivalism that assails a boy at about the age of fifteen, nor the scepticism that meets him five years later, could sway him from his allegiance to the church into which he had been born. But his equilibrium was personal, and the secret of it useless to others. He desired that each man should find his own.

"What does philosophy do?" the propper continued. "Does it make a man happier in life? Does it make him die more peacefully? I fancy that in the long run Herbert Spencer will get no further than the rest of us. Ah, Rickie! I wish you could move among schoolboys, and see their healthy contempt for all that they cannot touch!" Here he was going too far, and had to add, "Their spiritual capacities, of course, are another matter." Then he remembered the Greeks, and said, "Which proves my original statement."

Submissive signs, as of one propped, appeared in Rickie's face. Mr Pembroke then questioned him about the men who found Plato not difficult. But here he kept silence, patting the school chapel gently, and presently the conversation turned to topics with which they were both more competent to deal.

"Does Agnes take much interest in the school?"

"Not as much as she did. It is the result of her engagement. If our naughty soldier had not carried her off, she might have made an ideal schoolmaster's wife. I often chaff him about it, for he a little despises the intellectual professions. Natural, perfectly natural. How can a man who faces death feel as we do towards *mensa* or *tupto?*"

"Perfectly true. Absolutely true."

Mr Pembroke remarked to himself that Frederick was improving.

"If a man shoots straight and hits straight and speaks straight, if his heart is in the right place, if he has the instincts of a Christian and a gentleman—then I, at all events, ask no better husband for my sister."

"How could you get a better?" he cried. "Do you remember the thing in *The Clouds?*" And he quoted, as well as he could, from the invitation of the Dikaios Logos, the description of the young Athenian, perfect in body, placid in mind, who neglects his work at the Bar and trains all day among the woods and meadows, with a garland on his head and a friend to set the pace; the scent of new leaves is upon them; they rejoice in the freshness of spring; over their heads the plane-tree whispers to the elm—perhaps the most glorious invitation to the brainless life that has ever been given.

"Yes, yes," said Mr Pembroke, who did not want a brother-in-law out of Aristophanes. Nor had he got one, for Mr Dawes would not have bothered over the garland or noticed the spring, and would have complained that the friend ran too slowly or too fast.

"And as for her—!" But he could think of no classical parallel for Agnes. She slipped between examples. A kindly Medea, a Cleopatra with a sense of duty—these suggested her a little. She was not born in Greece, but came overseas to it—a dark, intelligent princess. With all her splendour, there were hints of splendour still hidden—hints of an older, richer, and more mysterious land. He smiled at the idea of her being "not there". Ansell, clever as he was, had made a bad blunder. She had more reality than any other woman in the world.

Mr Pembroke looked pleased at this boyish enthusiasm. He was fond of his sister, though he knew her to be full of faults. "Yes, I envy her," he said. "She has found a worthy helpmeet for life's journey, I do believe. And though they chafe at the long engagement, it is a blessing in disguise. They learn to know each other thoroughly before contracting more intimate ties."

Rickie did not assent. The length of the engagement seemed to him unspeakably cruel. Here were two people who loved each other, and they could not marry for years because they had no beastly money. Not all Herbert's pious skill could make this out a blessing. It was bad enough being "so rich" at the Silts; here he was more ashamed of it than ever. In a few weeks he would come of age and his money be his own. What a pity things were so crookedly arranged. He did not want money, or at all events he did not want so much.

"Suppose," he meditated, for he became much worried over this—"suppose I had a hundred pounds a year less than I shall have. Well, I should still have enough. I don't want anything but food, lodging, clothes, and now and then a railway fare. I haven't any tastes. I don't collect anything or play games. Books are nice to have, but after all there is Mudie's, or if it comes to that, the Free Library. Oh, my profession! I forgot I shall have a profession. Well, that will leave me with more to spare than ever." And he supposed away till he lost touch with the world and with what it permits, and committed an unpardonable sin.

It happened towards the end of his visit—another airless day of that mild January. Mr Dawes was playing against a scratch team of cads, and had to go down to the ground in the morning to settle something. Rickie proposed to come too.

Hitherto he had been no nuisance. "You will be frightfully bored," said Agnes, observing the cloud on her lover's face. "And Gerald walks like a maniac."

48

"I had a little thought of the Museum this morning," said Mr Pembroke. "It is very strong in flint arrowheads."

"Ah, that's your line, Rickie. I do envy you and Herbert the way you enjoy the past."

"I almost think I'll go with Dawes, if he'll have me. I can walk quite fast just to the ground and back. Arrowheads are wonderful, but I don't really enjoy them yet, though I hope I shall in time."

Mr Pembroke was offended, but Rickie held firm.

In a quarter of an hour he was back at the house alone, nearly crying.

"Oh, did the wretch go too fast?" called Miss Pembroke from her bedroom window.

"I went too fast for him." He spoke quite sharply, and before he had time to say he was sorry and didn't mean exactly that, the window had shut.

"They've quarrelled," she thought. "Whatever about?"

She soon heard. Gerald returned in a cold stormy temper. Rickie had offered him money.

"My dear fellow, don't be so cross. The child's mad."

"If it was, I'd forgive that. But I can't stand un-healthiness."

"Now, Gerald, that's where I hate you. You don't know what it is to pity the weak."

"Woman's job. So you wish I'd taken a hundred pounds a year from him. Did you ever hear such blasted cheek? Marry us—he, you, and me—a hundred pounds down and as much annual—he, of course, to pry into all we did, and we to kowtow and eat dirt-pie to him. If that's Mr Rickety Elliot's idea of a soldier and an Englishman, it isn't mine, and I wish I'd had a horsewhip."

She was roaring with laughter. "You're babies, a pair of you, and you're the worst. Why couldn't you let the little silly down gently? There he was puffing and sniffing under my window, and I thought he'd insulted you. Why didn't you accept?"

"Accept?" he thundered.

"It would have taken the nonsense out of him for ever. Why, he was only talking out of a book."

"More fool he."

"Well, don't be angry with a fool. He means no harm. He muddles all day with poetry and old dead people, and then tries to bring it into life. It's too funny for words."

Gerald repeated that he could not stand unhealthiness.

"I don't call that exactly unhealthy."

"I do. And why he could give the money's worse."

"What do you mean?"

He became shy. "I hadn't meant to tell you. It's not quite for a lady." For, like most men who are rather animal, he was intellectually a prude. "He says he can't ever marry, owing to his foot. It wouldn't be fair to posterity. His grandfather was crocked, his father too, and he's as bad. He thinks that it's hereditary, and may get worse next generation. He's discussed it all over with other Undergrads. A bright lot they must be. He daren't risk having any children. Hence the hundred quid."

She stopped laughing. "Oh, little beast, if he said all that!"

He was encouraged to proceed. Hitherto he had not talked about their schooldays. Now he told her everything—the "barley-sugar", as he called it, the pins in chapel, and how one afternoon he had tied him head downward onto a tree-trunk and then run away—of course only for a moment.

For this she scolded him well. But she had a thrill of joy when she thought of the weak boy in the clutches of the strong one.

Chapter 5

Gerald died that afternoon. He was broken up in the football match. Rickie and Mr Pembroke were on the ground when the accident took place. It was no good torturing him by a drive to the hospital, and he was merely carried to the little pavilion and laid upon the floor. A doctor came, and so did a clergyman, but it seemed better to leave him for the last few minutes with Agnes, who had ridden down on her bicycle.

It was a strange lamentable interview. The girl was so accustomed to health, that for a time she could not understand. It must be a joke that he chose to lie there in the dust, with a rug over him and his knees bent up towards his chin. His arms were as she knew them, and their admirable muscles showed clear and clean beneath the jersey. The face, too, though a little flushed, was uninjured: it must be some curious joke.

"Gerald, what have you been doing?"

He replied, "I can't see you. It's too dark."

"Oh, I'll soon alter that," she said in her old brisk way. She opened the pavilion door. The people who were standing by it moved aside. She saw a deserted meadow, steaming and gray, and beyond it slate-roofed cottages, row beside row, climbing a shapeless hill. Towards London the sky was yellow. "There. That's better." She sat down by him again, and drew his hand into her own. "Now we are all right, aren't we?"

"Where are you?"

This time she could not reply.

"What is it? Where am I going?"

"Wasn't the rector here?" said she after a silence.

"He explained heaven, and thinks that I—but—I couldn't tell a parson; but I don't seem to have any use for any of the things there."

51

"We are Christians," said Agnes shyly. "Dear love, we don't talk about these things, but we believe them. I think that you will get well and be as strong again as ever; but, in any case, there is a spiritual life, and we know that some day you and I—"

"I shan't do as a spirit," he interrupted, sighing pitifully. "I want you as I am, and it cannot be managed. The rector had to say so. I want—I don't want to talk. I can't see you. Shut that door."

She obeyed, and crept into his arms. Only this time her grasp was the stronger. Her heart beat louder and louder as the sound of his grew more faint. He was crying like a little frightened child, and her lips were wet with his tears. "Bear it bravely," she told him.

"I can't," he whispered. "It isn't to be done. I can't see you," and passed from her trembling, with open eyes.

She rode home on her bicycle, leaving the others to follow. Some ladies who did not know what had happened bowed and smiled as she passed, and she returned their salute.

"Oh, miss, is it true?" cried the cook, her face streaming with tears.

Agnes nodded. Presumably it was true. Letters had just arrived: one was for Gerald from his mother. Life, which had given them no warning, seemed to make no comment now. The incident was outside nature, and would surely pass away like a dream. She felt slightly irritable, and the grief of the servants annoyed her.

They sobbed. "Ah, look at his marks! Ah, little he thought—little he thought!" In the brown holland strip by the front door a heavy football boot had left its impress. They had not liked Gerald, but he was a man, they were women, he had died. Their mistress ordered them to leave her.

For many minutes she sat at the foot of the stairs, rubbing her eyes. An obscure spiritual crisis was going on. Should she weep like the servants? or should she bear up and trust in the consoler Time? Was the death of a man so terrible after all? As she invited herself to apathy there were steps on the gravel, and Rickie Elliot burst in. He was splashed with mud, his breath was gone, and his hair fell wildly over his meagre face. She thought, "These are the people who are left alive!" From the bottom of her soul she hated him.

"I came to see what you're doing," he cried.

"Resting."

He knelt beside her, and she said, "Would you please go away?"

"Yes, dear Agnes, of course; but I must see first that you mind."

Her breath caught. Her eyes moved to the treads, going outwards, so firmly, so irretrievably.

He panted, "It's the worst thing that can ever happen to you in all your life, and you've got to mind it—you've got to mind it. They'll come saying, 'Bear up—trust to time.' No, no; they're wrong. Mind it."

Through all her misery she knew that this boy was greater than they supposed. He rose to his feet, and with intense conviction cried: "But I know—I understand. It's your death as well as his. He's gone, Agnes, and his arms will never hold you again. In God's name, mind such a thing, and don't sit fencing with your soul. Don't stop being great; that's the one crime he'll never forgive you."

She faltered, "Who—who forgives?"

"Gerald."

At the sound of his name she slid forward, and all her dishonesty left her. She acknowledged that life's meaning had vanished. Bending down, she kissed the footprint. "How can he forgive me?" she sobbed. "Where has he gone to? You never could dream such an awful thing. He couldn't see me though I opened the door—wide—plenty of light; and then he could not remember the things that should comfort him. He wasn't a—he wasn't ever a great reader, and he couldn't remember the things. The rector tried, and he couldn't—I came, and I couldn't—" She could not speak for tears. Rickie did not check her. He let her accuse herself, and fate, and Herbert, who had postponed their marriage. She might have been a wife six months; but Herbert had spoken of self-control and of all life before them. He let her kiss the footprints till their marks gave way to the marks of her lips. She moaned, "He is gone—where is he?" and then he replied quite quietly, "He is in heaven."

She begged him not to comfort her; she could not bear it.

"I did not come to comfort you. I came to see that you mind. He is in heaven, Agnes. The greatest thing is over."

Her hatred was lulled. She murmured, "Dear Rickie!" and held up her hand to him. Through her tears his meagre face showed as a seraph's who spoke the truth and forbade her to juggle with her soul. "Dear Rickie—but for the rest of my life what am I to do?"

"Anything—if you remember that the greatest thing is over."

"I don't know you," she said tremulously. "You have grown up in a moment. You never talked to us, and yet you understand it all. Tell me again—I can only trust you—where he is."

"He is in heaven."

"You are sure?"

It puzzled her that Rickie, who could scarcely tell you the time without a saving clause, should be so certain about immortality.

Chapter 6

He did not stop for the funeral. Mr Pembroke thought that he had a bad effect on Agnes, and prevented her from acquiescing in the tragedy as rapidly as she might have done. As he expressed it, "one must not court sorrow", and he hinted to the young man that they desired to be alone. Rickie went back to the Silts.

He was only there a few days. As soon as term opened he returned to Cambridge, for which he longed passionately. The journey thither was now familiar to him, and he took pleasure in each landmark. The fair valley of Tewin Water, the cutting into Hitchin where the train traverses the chalk, Baldock Church, Royston with its promise of downs, were nothing in themselves, but dear as stages in his pilgrimage towards the abode of peace. On the platform he met friends. They had all had pleasant vacations: it was a happy world. The atmosphere alters.

Cambridge, according to her custom, welcomed her sons with open drains. Petty Cury was up, so was Trinity Street, and navvies peeped out of King's Parade. Here it was gas, there electric light, but everywhere something, and always a smell. It was also the day that the wheels fell off the station tram, and Rickie, who was naturally inside, was among the passengers who "sustained no injury but a shock, and had as hearty a laugh over the mishap afterwards as anyone".

Tilliard fled into a hansom, cursing himself for having tried to do the thing cheaply. Hornblower also swept past yelling derisively, with his luggage neatly piled above his head. "Let's get out and walk," muttered Ansell. But Rickie was succouring a distressed female—Mrs Aberdeen. "Oh, Mrs Aberdeen, I never saw you; I am so glad to see you—I am so very glad." Mrs Aberdeen was cold. She did not like being spoken to outside the college, and was also distrait about her basket. Hitherto no genteel eye had ever seen inside it, but in the collision its little calico veil fell off, and there was revealed—nothing. The basket was empty, and never would hold anything illegal. All the same she was distrait, and "We shall meet later, sir, I dessy," was all the greeting Rickie got from her.

"Now what kind of life has Mrs Aberdeen?" he exclaimed, as he and Ansell pursued the Station Road. "Here these bedders come and make us comfortable. We owe an enormous amount to them, their wages are absurd, and we know nothing about them. Off they go to Barnwell, and then their lives are hidden. I just know that Mrs Aberdeen has a husband, but that's all. She never will talk about him. Now I do so want to fill in her life. I see one half of it. What's the other half? She may have a real jolly house, in good taste, with a little garden, and books, and pictures. Or, again, she mayn't. But in any case one ought to know. I know she'd dislike it, but she oughtn't to dislike. After all, bedders are to blame for the present lamentable state of things, just as much as gentlefolk. She ought to want me to come. She ought to introduce me to her husband."

They had reached the corner of Hills Road. Ansell spoke for the first time. He said, "Ugh!"

"Drains?"

"Yes. A spiritual cesspool."

Rickie laughed.

"I expected it from your letter."

"The one you never answered?"

"I answer none of your letters. You are quite hopeless by now. You can go to the bad. But I refuse to accompany you. I refuse to believe that every human being is a moving wonder of supreme interest and tragedy and beauty—which was what the letter in question amounted to. You'll find plenty who will believe it. It's a very popular view among people who are too idle to think; it saves them the trouble of detecting the beautiful from the ugly, the interesting from the dull, the tragic from the melodramatic. You had just come from Sawston, and were apparently carried away by the fact that Miss Pembroke had the usual amount of arms and legs."

Rickie was silent. He had told his friend how he felt, but not what had happened. Ansell could discuss love and death admirably, but somehow he would not understand lovers or a dying man, and in the letter there had been scant allusion to these concrete facts. Would Cambridge understand them either? He watched some dons who were peeping into an excavation, and throwing up their hands with humorous gestures of despair. These men would lecture next week on Catiline's conspiracy, on Luther, on Evolution, on Catullus. They dealt with so much and they had experienced so little. Was it possible he would ever come to think Cambridge narrow? In his short life Rickie had known two sudden deaths, and that is enough to disarrange any placid outlook on the world. He knew once for all that we are all of us bubbles on an extremely rough sea. Into this sea humanity has built, as it were, some little breakwaters—scientific knowledge, civilized restraint—so that the bubbles do not break so frequently or so soon. But the sea has not altered, and it was only a chance that he, Ansell, Tilliard, and Mrs Aberdeen had not all been killed in the tram.

They waited for the other tram by the Roman Catholic Church, whose florid bulk was already receding into twilight. It is the first big building that the incoming visitor sees. "Oh, here come the colleges!" cries the Protestant parent, and then learns that it was built by a Papist who made a fortune out of movable eyes for dolls. "Built out of dolls' eyes to contain idols"—that, at all events, is the legend and the joke. It watches over the apostate city, taller by many a yard than anything within, and asserting, however wildly, that here is eternity, stability, and bubbles unbreakable upon a windless sea.

A costly hymn tune announced five o'clock, and in the distance the more lovable note of St Mary's could be heard, speaking from the heart of the town. Then the tram arrived—the slow stuffy tram that plies every twenty minutes between the unknown and the market-place—and took them past the desecrated grounds of Downing, past Addenbrooke's

Hospital, girt like any Venetian palace with a mantling canal, past the Fitzwilliam, towering upon immense substructures like any Roman temple, right up to the gates of one's own college, which looked like nothing else in the world. The porters were glad to see them, but wished it had been a hansom. "Our luggage," explained Rickie, "comes in the hotel omnibus, if you would kindly pay a shilling for mine." Ansell turned aside to some large lighted windows, the abode of a hospitable don, and from other windows there floated familiar voices and the familiar mistakes in a Beethoven sonata. The college, though small, was civilized, and proud of its civilization. It was not sufficient glory to be a Blue there, nor an additional glory to get drunk. Many a maiden lady, who had read that Cambridge men were sad dogs, was surprised and perhaps a little disappointed at the reasonable life which greeted her. Miss Appleblossom in particular had had a tremendous shock. The sight of young fellows making tea and drinking water had made her wonder whether this was Cambridge College at all. "It is so," she exclaimed afterwards. "It is just as I say; and what's more, I wouldn't have it otherwise. Stewart says it's as easy as easy to get into the swim, and not at all expensive." The direction of the swim was determined a little by the genius of the place—for places have a genius, though the less we talk about it the better—and a good deal by the tutors and resident fellows, who treated with rare dexterity the products that came up yearly from the public schools. They taught the perky boy that he was not everything, and the limp boy that he might be something. They even welcomed those boys who were neither limp nor perky, but odd—those boys who had never been at a public school at all, and such do not find a welcome everywhere. And they did everything with ease—one might almost say with nonchalance—so that the boys noticed nothing, and received education, often for the first time in their lives.

But Rickie turned to none of these friends, for just then he loved his rooms better than any person. They were all he really possessed in the world, the only place he could call his own. Over the door was his name, and through the paint,

like a gray ghost, he could still read the name of his predecessor. With a sigh of joy he entered the perishable home
that was his for a couple of years. There was a beautiful fire,
and the kettle boiled at once. He made tea on the hearth-
rug and ate the biscuits which Mrs Aberdeen had brought
for him up from Anderson's. "Gentlemen," she said, "must
learn to give and take." He sighed again and again, like one
who has escaped from danger. With his head on the fender
and all his limbs relaxed, he felt almost as safe as he felt
once when his mother killed a ghost in the passage by carrying him through it in her arms. There was no ghost now; he
was frightened at reality; he was frightened at the splendours
and horrors of the world.

A letter from Miss Pembroke was on the table. He did not
hurry to open it, for she, and all that she did, was over-
whelming. She wrote like the Sibyl; her sorrowful face moved
over the stars and shattered their harmonies; last night he
saw her with the eyes of Blake, a virgin widow, tall, veiled,
consecrated, with her hands stretched out against an everlasting wind. Why would she write? Her letters were not for
the likes of him, nor to be read in rooms like his.

"We are not leaving Sawston," she wrote. "I saw how
selfish it was of me to risk spoiling Herbert's career. I shall
get used to any place. Now that he is gone, nothing of that
sort can matter. Everyone has been most kind, but you have
comforted me most, though you did not mean to. I cannot
think how you did it, or understood so much. I still think of
you as a little boy with a lame leg—I know you will let me
say this—and yet when it came to the point you knew more
than people who have been all their lives with sorrow and
death."

Rickie burnt this letter, which he ought not to have done,
for it was one of the few tributes Miss Pembroke ever paid to
imagination. But he felt that it did not belong to him: words
so sincere should be for Gerald alone. The smoke rushed up
the chimney, and he indulged in a vision. He saw it reach
the outer air and beat against the low ceiling of clouds. The
clouds were too strong for it; but in them was one chink,
revealing one star, and through this the smoke escaped into

the light of stars innumerable. Then—but then the vision failed, and the voice of science whispered that all smoke remains on earth in the form of smuts, and is troublesome to Mrs Aberdeen.

"I am jolly unpractical," he mused. "And what is the point of it when real things are so wonderful? Who wants visions in a world that has Agnes and Gerald?" He turned on the electric light and pulled open the table-drawer. There, among spoons and corks and string, he found a fragment of a little story that he had tried to write last term. It was called "The Bay of the Fifteen Islets", and the action took place on St John's Eve off the coast of Sicily. A party of tourists land on one of the islands. Suddenly the boatmen become uneasy, and say that the island is not generally there. It is an extra one, and they had better have tea on one of the ordinaries. "Pooh, volcanic!" says the leading tourist, and the ladies say how interesting. The island begins to rock, and so do the minds of its visitors. They start and quarrel and jabber. Fingers burst up through the sand—black fingers of sea devils. The island tilts. The tourists go mad. But just before the catastrophe one man, *integer vitæ scelerisque purus*, sees the truth. Here are no devils. Other muscles, other minds, are pulling the island to its subterranean home. Through the advancing wall of waters he sees no grisly faces, no ghastly medieval limbs, but—But what nonsense! When real things are so wonderful, what is the point of pretending?

And so Rickie deflected his enthusiasms. Hitherto they had played on gods and heroes, on the infinite and the impossible, on virtue and beauty and strength. Now, with a steadier radiance, they transfigured a man who was dead and a woman who was still alive.

Chapter 7

Love, say orderly people, can be fallen into by two methods: (1) through the desires; (2) through the imagination. And if the orderly people are English, they add that (1) is the inferior method, and characteristic of the South. It is inferior. Yet those who pursue it at all events know what they want; they are not puzzling to themselves or ludicrous to others; they do not take the wings of the morning and fly into the uttermost parts of the sea before walking to the registry office; they cannot breed a tragedy quite like Rickie's.

He is, of course, absurdly young—not twenty-one—and he will be engaged to be married at twenty-three. He has no knowledge of the world; for example, he thinks that if you do not want money you can give it to friends who do. He believes in humanity because he knows a dozen decent people. He believes in women because he has loved his mother. And his friends are as young and as ignorant as himself. They are full of the wine of life. But they have not tasted the cup—let us call it the teacup—of experience, which has made men of Mr Pembroke's type what they are. Oh, that teacup! To be taken at prayers, at friendship, at love, till we are quite sane, quite efficient, quite experienced, and quite useless to God or man. We must drink it, or we shall die. But we need not drink it always. Here is our problem and our salvation. There comes a moment—God knows when—at which we can say, "I will experience no longer. I will create. I will be an experience." But to do this we must be both acute and heroic. For it is not easy, after accepting six cups of tea, to throw the seventh in the face of the hostess. And to Rickie this moment has not, as yet, been offered.

Ansell, at the end of his third year, got a first in the Moral Science Tripos. Being a scholar, he kept his rooms in college, and at once began to work for a fellowship. Rickie got a creditable second in the Classical Tripos, Part I, and retired to sallow lodgings in Mill Lane, carrying with him the degree of B.A. and a small exhibition, which was quite as much as he deserved. For Part II he read Greek Archaeology, and got a second. All this means that Ansell was much cleverer than Rickie. As for the cow, she was still going strong, though turning a little academic as the years passed over her.

"We are bound to get narrow," sighed Rickie. He and his friend were lying in a meadow during their last summer term. In his incurable love for flowers he had plaited two garlands of buttercups and cow-parsley, and Ansell's lean Jewish face was framed in one of them. "Cambridge is wonderful, but—but it's so tiny. You have no idea—at least, I think you have no idea—how the great world looks down on it."

"I read the letters in the papers."

"It's a bad lookout."

"How?"

"Cambridge has lost touch with the times."

"Was she ever intended to touch them?"

"She satisfies," said Rickie mysteriously, "neither the professions, nor the public schools, nor the great thinking mass of men and women. There is a general feeling that her day is over, and naturally one feels pretty sick."

"Do you still write short stories?"

"Why?"

"Because your English has gone to the devil. You think and talk in Journalese. Define a great thinking mass."

Rickie sat up and adjusted his floral crown.

"Estimate the worth of a general feeling."

Silence.

"And thirdly, where is the great world?"

"Oh, that—!"

"Yes. That," exclaimed Ansell, rising from his couch in violent excitement. "Where is it? How do you set about finding it? How long does it take to get there? What does it think? What does it do? What does it want? Oblige me with specimens of its art and literature." Silence. "Till you do, my opinions will be as follows: There is no great world at

62

all, only a little earth, for ever isolated from the rest of the little solar system. The little earth is full of tiny societies, and Cambridge is one of them. All the societies are narrow, but some are good and some are bad—just as one house is beautiful inside and another ugly. Observe the metaphor of the houses: I am coming back to it. The good societies say, 'I tell you to do this because I am Cambridge'. The bad ones say, 'I tell you to do that because I am the great world'—not because I am 'Peckham', or 'Billingsgate', or 'Park Lane', but 'because I am the great world'. They lie. And fools like you listen to them, and believe that they are a thing which does not exist and never has existed, and confuse 'great', which has no meaning whatever, with 'good', which means salvation. Look at this great wreath: it'll be dead tomorrow. Look at that good flower: it'll come up again next year. Now for the other metaphor. To compare the world to Cambridge is like comparing the outsides of houses with the inside of a house. No intellectual effort is needed, no moral result is attained. You only have to say, 'Oh, what a difference! Oh, what a difference!' and then come indoors again and exhibit your broadened mind."

"I never shall come indoors again," said Rickie. "That's the whole point." And his voice began to quiver. "It's well enough for those who'll get a fellowship, but in a few weeks I shall go down. In a few years it'll be as if I've never been up. It matters very much to me what the world is like. I can't answer your questions about it; and that's no loss to you, but so much the worse for me. And then you've got a house—not a metaphorical one, but a house with father and sisters. I haven't, and never shall have. There'll never again be a home for me like Cambridge. I shall only look at the outsides of homes. According to your metaphor, I shall live in the street, and it matters very much to me what I find there."

"You'll live in another house right enough," said Ansell, rather uneasily. "Only take care you pick out a decent one. I can't think why you flop about so helplessly, like a bit of seaweed. In four years you've taken as much root as anyone."

63

"Where?"

"I should say you've been fortunate in your friends."

"Oh—that!" But he was not cynical—or cynical in a very tender way. He was thinking of the irony of friendship—so strong it is, and so fragile. We fly together, like straws in an eddy, to part in the open stream. Nature has no use for us: she has cut her stuff differently. Dutiful sons, loving husbands, responsible fathers—these are what she wants, and if we are friends it must be in our spare time. Abram and Sarai were sorrowful, yet their seed became as sand of the sea, and distracts the politics of Europe at this moment. But a few verses of poetry is all that survives of David and Jonathan.

"I wish we were labelled," said Rickie. He wished that all the confidence and mutual knowledge that is born in such a place as Cambridge could be organized. People went down into the world saying, "We know and like each other; we shan't forget." But they did forget, for man is so made that he cannot remember long without a symbol; he wished there was a society, a kind of friendship office, where the marriage of true minds could be registered.

"Why labels?"

"To know each other again."

"I have taught you pessimism splendidly." He looked at his watch.

"What time?"

"Not twelve."

Rickie got up.

"Why go?" He stretched out his hand and caught hold of Rickie's ankle.

"I've got that Miss Pembroke to lunch—that girl whom you say never's there."

"Then why go? All this week you have pretended Miss Pembroke awaited you. Wednesday—Miss Pembroke to lunch. Thursday—Miss Pembroke to tea. Now again—and you didn't even invite her."

"To Cambridge, no. But the Hall man they're stopping with has so many engagements that she and her friend can often come to me, I'm glad to say. I don't think I ever told you much, but over two years ago the man she was going to marry was killed at football. She nearly died of grief. This visit to Cambridge is almost the first amusement she has felt up to taking. Oh, they go back tomorrow! Give me breakfast tomorrow."

"All right."

"But I shall see you this evening. I shall be round at your paper on Schopenhauer. Lemme go."

"Don't go," he said idly. "It's much better for you to talk to me."

"Lemme go, Stewart."

"It's amusing that you're so feeble. You—simply—can't—get—away. I wish I wanted to bully you."

Rickie laughed, and suddenly overbalanced into the grass. Ansell, with unusual playfulness, held him prisoner. They lay there for a few minutes, talking and ragging aimlessly. Then Rickie seized his opportunity and jerked away.

"Go, go!" yawned the other. But he was a little vexed, for he was a young man with great capacity for pleasure, and it pleased him that morning to be with his friend. The thought of two ladies waiting lunch did not deter him; stupid women, why shouldn't they wait? Why should they interfere with their betters? With his ear on the ground he listened to Rickie's departing steps, and thought, "He wastes a lot of time keeping engagements. Why will he be pleasant to fools?" And then he thought, "Why has he turned so unhappy? It isn't as if he's a philosopher, or tries to solve the riddle of existence. And he's got money of his own." Thus thinking, he fell asleep.

Meanwhile Rickie hurried away from him, and slackened and stopped, and hurried again. He was due at the Union in ten minutes, but he could not bring himself there. He dared not meet Miss Pembroke: he loved her.

The devil must have planned it. They had started so gloriously; she had been a goddess both in joy and sorrow. She was a goddess still. But he had dethroned the god whom once he had glorified equally. Slowly, slowly, the image of Gerald had faded. That was the first step. Rickie had thought, "No matter. He will be bright again. Just now all the radiance chances to be in her." And on her he had fixed his eyes. He thought of her awake. He entertained her willingly in dreams. He found her in poetry and music and in the sunset. She made him kind and strong. She made him clever. Through her he kept Cambridge in its proper place, and lived as a citizen of the great world. But one night he dreamt that she lay in his arms. This displeased him. He determined to think a little about Gerald instead. Then the fabric collapsed.

It was hard on Rickie thus to meet the devil. He did not deserve it, for he was comparatively civilized, and knew that there was nothing shameful in love. But to love this woman! If only it had been anyone else! Love in return—that he could expect from no one, being too ugly and too unattractive. But the love he offered would not then have been vile. The insult to Miss Pembroke, who was consecrated, and whom he had consecrated, who could still see Gerald, and always would see him, shining on his everlasting throne—this was the crime from the devil, the crime that no penance would ever purge. She knew nothing. She never would know. But the crime was registered in heaven.

He had been tempted to confide in Ansell. But to what purpose? He would say, "I love Miss Pembroke," and Stewart would reply, "You ass." And then, "I'm never going to tell her." "You ass," again. After all, it was not a practical question; Agnes would never hear of his fall. If his friend had been, as he expressed it, "labelled"; if he had been a father, or still better a brother, one might tell him of the discreditable passion. But why irritate him for no reason? Thinking "I am always angling for sympathy; I must stop myself," he hurried onward to the Union.

He found his guests halfway up the stairs, reading the advertisements of coaches for the Long Vacation. He heard Mrs Lewin say, "I wonder what he'll end by doing." A little overacting his part, he apologized nonchalantly for his lateness.

"It's always the same," cried Agnes. "Last time he forgot I was coming altogether." She wore a flowered muslin—something indescribably liquid and cool. It reminded him a little of those swift piercing streams, neither blue nor green, that gush out of the Dolomites. Her face was clear and brown, like the face of a mountaineer; her hair was so plentiful that it seemed banked up above it; and her little toque, though it answered the note of the dress, was almost ludicrous, poised on so much natural glory. When she moved, the sunlight flashed on her earrings.

He led them up to the luncheon-room. By now he was conscious of his limitations as a host, and never attempted to entertain ladies in his lodgings. Moreover, the Union seemed less intimate. It had a faint flavour of a London club; it marked the undergraduate's nearest approach to the great world. Amid its waiters and serviettes one felt impersonal, and able to conceal the private emotions. Rickie felt that if Miss Pembroke knew one thing about him, she would know everything. During this visit he took her to no place that he greatly loved.

"Sit down, ladies. Fall to. I'm sorry. I was out towards Coton with a dreadful friend."

Mrs Lewin pushed up her veil. She was a typical Mayterm chaperon, always pleasant, always hungry, and always tired. Year after year she came up to Cambridge in a tight silk dress, and year after year she nearly died of it. Her feet hurt, her limbs were cramped in a canoe, black spots danced before her eyes from eating too much mayonnaise. But still she came, if not as a mother as an aunt, if not as an aunt as a friend. Still she ascended the roof of King's, still she counted the balls of Clare, still she was on the point of grasping the organization of the May races. "And who is your friend?" she asked.

"His name is Ansell."

"Well, now, did I see him two years ago—as a bed-maker in something they did at the Footlights? Oh, how I roared."

"You didn't see Mr Ansell at the Footlights," said Agnes, smiling.

"How do you know?" asked Rickie.

"He'd scarcely be so frivolous."

"Do you remember seeing him?"

"For a moment."

What a memory she had! And how splendidly during that moment she had behaved!

"Isn't he marvellously clever?"

"I believe so."

"Oh, give me clever people!" cried Mrs Lewin. "They are kindness itself at the Hall, but I assure you I am depressed at times. One cannot talk bump-rowing for ever."

"I never hear about him, Rickie; but isn't he really your greatest friend?"

"I don't go in for greatest friends."

"Do you mean you like us all equally?"

"All differently, those of you I like."

"Ah, you've caught it!" cried Mrs Lewin. "Mr Elliot gave it you there well."

Agnes laughed, and, her elbows on the table, regarded them both through her fingers—a habit of hers. Then she said, "Can't we see the great Mr Ansell?"

"Oh, let's. Or would he frighten me?"

"He would frighten you," said Rickie. "He's a trifle weird."

"My good Rickie, if you knew the deathly dullness of Sawston—everyone saying the proper thing at the proper time, I so proper, Herbert so proper! Why, weirdness is the one thing I long for! Do arrange something."

"I'm afraid there's no opportunity. Ansell goes some vast bicycle ride this afternoon; this evening you're tied up at the Hall; and tomorrow you go."

"But there's breakfast tomorrow," said Agnes. "Look here, Rickie, bring Mr Ansell to breakfast with us at Buol's."

Mrs Lewin seconded the invitation.

"Bad luck again," said Rickie boldly; "I'm already fixed up for breakfast. I'll tell him of your very kind intention."

"Let's have him alone," murmured Agnes.

"My dear girl, I should die through the floor! Oh, it'll be all right about breakfast. I rather think we shall get asked this evening by that shy man who has the pretty rooms in Trinity."

"Oh, very well. Where is it you breakfast, Rickie?"

He faltered. "To Ansell's, it is—" It seemed as if he was

making some great admission. So self-conscious was he, that he thought the two women exchanged glances. Had Agnes already explored that part of him that did not belong to her? Would another chance step reveal the part that did? He asked them abruptly what they would like to do after lunch.

"Anything," said Mrs Lewin—"anything in the world."

A walk? A boat? Ely? A drive? Some objection was raised to each. "To tell the truth," she said at last, "I do feel a wee bit tired, and what occurs to me is this. You and Agnes shall leave me here and have no more bother. I shall be perfectly happy snoozling in one of these delightful drawing-room chairs. Do what you like, and then pick me up after it."

"Alas! it's against regulations," said Rickie. "The Union won't trust lady visitors on its premises alone."

"But who's to know I'm alone? With a lot of men in the drawing-room, how's each to know that I'm not with the others?"

"That would shock Rickie," said Agnes, laughing. "He's frightfully high-principled."

"No, I'm not," said Rickie, thinking of his recent shiftiness over breakfast.

"Then come for a walk with me. I want exercise. Some connection of ours was once rector of Madingley. I shall walk out and see the church."

Mrs Lewin was accordingly left in the Union.

"This is jolly!" Agnes exclaimed as she strode along the somewhat depressing road that leads out of Cambridge past the observatory. "Do I go too fast?"

"No, thank you. I get stronger every year. If it wasn't for the look of the thing, I should be quite happy."

"But you don't care for the look of the thing. It's only ignorant people who do that, surely."

"Perhaps, I care. I like people who are well-made and beautiful. They are of some use in the world. I understand why they are there. I cannot understand why the ugly and crippled are there, however healthy they may feel inside. Don't you know how Turner spoils his pictures by introducing a man like a bolster in the foreground? Well, in actual life every landscape is spoilt by men of worse shapes still."

"You sound like a bolster with the stuffing out." They laughed. She always blew his cobwebs away like this, with a puff of humorous mountain air. Just now—the associations he attached to her were various—she reminded him of a heroine of Meredith's—but a heroine at the end of the book. All had been written about her. She had played her mighty part, and knew that it was over. He and he alone was not content, and wrote for her daily a trivial and impossible sequel.

Last time they had talked about Gerald. But that was some six months ago, when things felt easier. Today Gerald was the faintest blur. Fortunately the conversation turned to Mr Pembroke and to education. Did women lose a lot by not knowing Greek? "A heap," said Rickie, roughly. But modern languages? Thus they got to Germany, which he had visited last Easter with Ansell; and thence to the German Emperor, and what a to-do he made; and from him to our own king (still Prince of Wales), who had lived while an undergraduate at Madingley Hall. Here it was. And all the time he thought, "It is hard on her. She has no right to be walking with me. She would be ill with disgust if she knew. It is hard on her to be loved."

They looked at the Hall, and went inside the pretty little church. Some Arundel prints hung upon the pillars, and Agnes expressed the opinion that pictures inside a place of worship were a pity. Rickie did not agree with this. He said again that nothing beautiful was ever to be regretted.

"You're cracked on beauty," she whispered—they were still inside the church. "Do hurry up and write something."

"Something beautiful?"

"I believe you can. I'm going to lecture you seriously all the way home. Take care that you don't waste your life."

They continued the conversation outside. "But I've got to hate my own writing. I believe that most people come to that stage—not so early though. What I write is too silly. It can't happen. For instance, a stupid vulgar man is engaged to a lovely young lady. He wants her to live in the towns, but she only cares for woods. She shocks him this way and that, but gradually he tames her, and makes her nearly as dull as he is. One day she has a last explosion—over the snobby wedding presents—and flies out of the drawing-room window, shouting, 'Freedom and Truth!' Near the house is a little dell full of fir trees, and she runs into it. He comes there the next moment. But she's gone."

"Awfully exciting. Where?"

"Oh Lord, she's a Dryad!" cried Rickie, in great disgust. "She's turned into a tree."

"Rickie, it's very good indeed. That kind of thing has something in it. Of course you get it all through Greek and Latin. How upset the man must be when he sees the girl turn."

"He doesn't see her. He never guesses. Such a man could never see a Dryad."

"So you describe how she turns just before he comes up?"

"No. Indeed I don't ever say that she does turn. I don't use the word 'Dryad' once."

"I think you ought to put that part plainly. Otherwise, with such an original story, people might miss the point. Have you had any luck with it?"

"Magazines? I haven't tried. I know what the stuff's worth. You see, a year or two ago I had a great idea of getting into touch with Nature, just as the Greeks were in touch; and seeing England so beautiful, I used to pretend that her trees and coppices and summer fields of parsley were alive. It's funny enough now, but it wasn't funny then, for I got in such a state that I believed, actually believed, that Fauns lived in a certain double hedgerow near the Gog Magogs, and one evening I walked round a mile sooner than go through it alone."

"Good gracious!" She laid her hand on his shoulder.

He moved to the other side of the road. "It's all right now. I've changed those follies for others. But while I had them I began to write, and even now I keep on writing, though I know better. I've got quite a pile of little stories, all harping on this ridiculous idea of getting into touch with Nature."

"I wish you weren't so modest. It's simply splendid as an

idea. Though—but tell me about the Dryad who was engaged to be married. What was she like?"

"I can show you the dell in which the young person disappeared. We pass it on the right in a moment."

"It does seem a pity that you don't make something of your talents. It seems such a waste to write little stories and never publish them. You must have enough for a book. Life is so full in our days that short stories are the very thing; they get read by people who'd never tackle a novel. For example, at our Dorcas we tried to read out a long affair by Henry James—Herbert saw it recommended in *The Times*. There was no doubt it was very good, but one simply couldn't remember from one week to another what had happened. So now our aim is to get something that just lasts the hour. I take you seriously, Rickie, and that is why I am so offensive. You are too modest. People who think they can do nothing so often do nothing. I want you to plunge."

It thrilled him like a trumpet-blast. She took him seriously. Could he but thank her for her divine affability! But the words would stick in his throat, or worse still, would bring other words along with them. His breath came quickly, for he seldom spoke of his writing, and no one, not even Ansell, had advised him to plunge.

"But do you really think that I could take up literature?"

"Why not? You can try. Even if you fail, you can try. Of course we think you tremendously clever; and I met one of your dons at tea, and he said that your degree was not in the least a proof of your abilities: he said that you knocked up and got flurried in examinations. Oh!"—her cheek flushed—"I wish I was a man. The whole world lies before them. They can do anything. They aren't cooped up with servants and tea-parties and twaddle. But where's this dell where the Dryad disappeared?"

"We've passed it." He had meant to pass it. It was too beautiful. All he had read, all he had hoped, all he had loved, seemed to quiver in its enchanted air. It was perilous. He dared not enter it with such a woman.

"How long ago?" She turned back. "I don't want to miss the dell. Here it must be," she added after a few moments, and sprang up the green bank that hid the entrance from the road. "Oh, what a jolly place!"

"Go right in if you want to see it," said Rickie, and did not offer to go with her. She stood for a moment looking at the view, for a few steps will increase a view in Cambridgeshire. The wind blew her dress against her. Then, like a cataract again, she vanished pure and cool into the dell.

The young man thought of her feelings no longer. His heart throbbed louder and louder, and seemed to shake him to pieces.

"Rickie!"

She was calling from the dell. For an answer he sat down where he was, on the dust-bespattered margin. She could call as loud as she liked. The devil had done much, but he should not take him to her.

"Rickie!"—and it came with the tones of an angel. He drove his fingers into his ears, and invoked the name of Gerald. But there was no sign, neither angry motion in the air nor hint of January mist. June—fields of June, sky of June, songs of June. Grass of June beneath him, grass of June over the tragedy he had deemed immortal. A bird called out of the dell: "Rickie!"

A bird flew into the dell.

*　　*　　*

"Did you take me for the Dryad?" she asked. She was sitting down with his head on her lap. He had laid it there for a moment before he went out to die, and she had not let him take it away.

"I prayed you might not be a woman," he whispered.

"Darling, I am very much a woman. I do not vanish into groves and trees. I thought you would never come to me."

"Did you expect—?"

"I hoped. I called hoping."

Inside the dell it was neither June nor January. The chalk walls barred out the seasons, and the fir trees did not seem to feel their passage. Only from time to time the odours of summer slipped in from the wood above, to comment on the waxing year. She bent down to touch him with her lips.

He started, and cried passionately, "Never forget that your greatest thing is over. I have forgotten: I am too weak. You shall never forget. What I said to you then is greater than what I say to you now. What he gave you then is greater than anything you will get from me."

She was frightened. Again she had the sense of something abnormal. Then she said, "What is all this nonsense?" and folded him in her arms.

Chapter 8

Ansell stood looking at his breakfast-table, which was laid for four instead of for two. His bed-maker, equally peevish, explained how it had happened. Last night, at one in the morning, the porter had been awoke with a note for the kitchens, and in that note Mr Elliot said that all these things were to be sent to Mr Ansell's.

"The fools have sent the original order as well. Here's the lemon sole for two. I can't move for food."

"The note being ambigerous, the Kitchens judged best to send it all." She spoke of the kitchens in a half-respectful, half-pitying way, much as one speaks of Parliament.

"Who's to pay for it?" He peeped into the new dishes. Kidneys entombed in an omelette, hot roast chicken in watery gravy, a glazed but pallid pie.

"And who's to wash it up?" said the bed-maker to her help outside.

Ansell had disputed late last night concerning Schopenhauer, and was a little cross and tired. He bounced over to Tilliard, who kept opposite. Tilliard was eating gooseberry jam.

"Did Elliot ask you to breakfast with me?"

"No," said Tilliard mildly.

"Well, you'd better come, and bring everyone you know."

So Tilliard came, bearing himself a little formally, for he was not very intimate with his neighbour. Out of the window they called to Widdrington. But he laid his hand on his stomach, thus indicating it was too late.

"Who's to pay for it?" repeated Ansell, as a man appeared from the Buttery carrying coffee on a bright tin tray.

"College coffee! How nice!" remarked Tilliard, who was cutting the pie. "But before term ends you must come and

75

try my new machine. My sister gave it me. There is a bulb at the top, and as the water boils—"

"He might have counter-ordered the lemon sole. That's Rickie all over. Violently economical, and then loses his head, and all the things go bad."

"Give them to the bedder while they're hot." This was done. She accepted them dispassionately, with the air of one who lives without nourishment. Tilliard continued to describe his sister's coffee machine.

"What's that?" They could hear panting and rustling on the stairs.

"It sounds like a lady," said Tilliard fearfully. He slipped the piece of pie back. It fell into position like a brick.

"Is it here? Am I right? Is it here?" The door opened and in came Mrs Lewin. "Oh horrors! I've made a mistake."

"That's all right," said Ansell awkwardly.

"I wanted Mr Elliot. Where are they?"

"We expect Mr Elliot every moment," said Tilliard.

"Don't tell me I'm right," cried Mrs Lewin, "and that you're the terrifying Mr Ansell." And, with obvious relief, she wrung Tilliard warmly by the hand.

"I'm Ansell," said Ansell, looking very uncouth and grim.

"How stupid of me not to know it," she gasped, and would have gone on to I know not what, but the door opened again. It was Rickie.

"Here's Miss Pembroke," he said. "I am going to marry her."

There was a profound silence.

"We oughtn't to have done things like this," said Agnes, turning to Mrs Lewin. "We have no right to take Mr Ansell by surprise. It is Rickie's fault. He was that obstinate. He would bring us. He ought to be horsewhipped."

"He ought indeed," said Tilliard pleasantly, and bolted. Not till he gained his room did he realize that he had been less apt than usual. As for Ansell, the first thing he said was, "Why didn't you counter-order the lemon sole?"

In such a situation Mrs Lewin was of priceless value. She led the way to the table, observing, "I quite agree with Miss Pembroke. I loathe surprises. Never shall I forget my horror when the knife-boy painted the dove's cage with the dove inside. He did it as a surprise. Poor Parsival nearly died. His feathers were bright green!"

"Well, give me the lemon soles," said Rickie. "I like them."

"The bedder's got them."

"Well, there you are! What's there to be annoyed about?"

"And while the cage was drying we put him among the bantams. They had been the greatest allies. But I suppose they took him for a parrot or a hawk, or something that bantams hate; for while his cage was drying they picked out his feathers, and *picked* out his feathers, and *Picked* out his feathers, till he was perfectly bald. 'Hugo, look,' said I. 'This is the end of Parsival. Let me have no more surprises.' He burst into tears."

Thus did Mrs Lewin create an atmosphere. At first it seemed unreal, but gradually they got used to it, and breathed scarcely anything else throughout the meal. In such an atmosphere everything seemed of small and equal value, and the engagement of Rickie and Agnes, like the feathers of Parsival, fluttered lightly to the ground. Ansell was generally silent. He was no match for these two quite clever women. Only once was there a hitch.

They had been talking gaily enough about the betrothal when Ansell suddenly interrupted with, "When is the marriage?"

"Mr Ansell," said Agnes, blushing, "I wish you hadn't asked that. That part's dreadful. Not for years, as far as we can see."

But Rickie had not seen as far. He had not talked to her of this at all. Last night they had spoken only of love. He exclaimed, "Oh, Agnes—don't!" Mrs Lewin laughed roguishly.

"Why this delay?" asked Ansell.

Agnes looked at Rickie, who replied, "I must get money, worse luck."

"I thought you'd got money."

He hesitated, and then said, "I must get my foot on the ladder, then."

77

Ansell began with, "On which ladder?" but Mrs Lewin, using the privilege of her sex, exclaimed, "Not another word. If there's a thing I abominate, it is plans. My head goes whirling at once." What she really abominated was questions, and she saw that Ansell was turning serious. To appease him, she put on her clever manner and asked him about Germany. How had it impressed him? Were we so totally unfitted to repel invasion? Was not German scholarship overestimated? He replied discourteously, but he did reply; and if she could have stopped him thinking, her triumph would have been complete.

When they rose to go, Agnes held Ansell's hand for a moment in her own.

"Goodbye," she said. "It was very unconventional of us to come as we did, but I don't think any of us are conventional people."

He only replied, "Goodbye." The ladies started off. Rickie lingered behind to whisper, "I would have it so. I would have you begin square together. I can't talk yet—I've loved her for years—I can't think what she's done it for. I'm going to write short stories. I shall start this afternoon. She declares there may be something in me."

As soon as he had left, Tilliard burst in, white with agitation, and crying, "Did you see my awful *faux pas*—about the horsewhip? What shall I do? I must call on Elliot. Or had I better write?"

"Miss Pembroke will not mind," said Ansell gravely. "She is unconventional." He knelt in an armchair and hid his face in the back.

"It was like a bomb," said Tilliard.

"It was meant to be."

"I do feel a fool. What must she think?"

"Never mind, Tilliard. You've not been as big a fool as myself. At all events, you told her he must be horsewhipped."

Tilliard hummed a little tune. He hated anything nasty, and there was nastiness in Ansell. "What did *you* tell her?" he asked.

"Nothing."

"What do you think of it?"

"I think: Damn those women."

"Ah, yes. One hates one's friends to get engaged. It makes one feel so old: I think that is one of the reasons. The brother just above me has lately married, and my sister was quite sick about it, though the thing was suitable in every way."

"Damn *these* women, then," said Ansell, bouncing round in the chair. "Damn these particular women."

"They looked and spoke like ladies."

"Exactly. Their diplomacy was ladylike. Their lies were ladylike. They've caught Elliot in a most ladylike way. I saw it all during the one moment we were natural. Generally we were clattering after the married one, whom—like a fool—I took for a fool. But for one moment we were natural, and during that moment Miss Pembroke told a lie, and made Rickie believe it was the truth."

"What did she say?"

"She said 'we see' instead of 'I see'."

Tilliard burst into laughter. This jaundiced young philosopher, with his kinky view of life, was too much for him.

"She said 'we see'," repeated Ansell, "instead of 'I see', and she made him believe that it was the truth. She caught him and makes him believe that he caught her. She came to see me and makes him think that it is his idea. That is what I mean when I say that she is a lady."

"You are too subtle for me. My dull eyes could only see two happy people."

"I never said they weren't happy."

"Then, my dear Ansell, why are you so cut up? It's beastly when a friend marries—and I grant he's rather young—but I should say it's the best thing for him. A decent woman— and you have proved not one thing against her—a decent woman will keep him up to the mark and stop him getting slack. She'll make him responsible and manly, for much as I like Rickie, I always think him a little effeminate. And, really"—his voice grew sharper, for he was irritated by Ansell's conceit—"and, really, you talk as if you were mixed up in the affair. They pay a civil visit to your rooms, and you see nothing but dark plots and challenges to war."

"War!" cried Ansell, crashing his fists together. "It's war, then!"

"Oh, what a lot of tommyrot," said Tilliard. "Can't a man and woman get engaged? My dear boy—excuse me talking like this—what on earth is it to do with us? We're his friends, and I hope we always shall be, but we shan't keep his friendship by fighting. We're bound to fall into the background. Wife first, friends some way after. You may resent the order, but it is ordained by nature."

"The point is, not what's ordained by nature or any other fool, but what's right."

"You are hopelessly unpractical," said Tilliard, turning away. "And let me remind you that you've already given away your case by acknowledging that they're happy."

"She is happy because she has conquered; he is happy because he has at last hung all the world's beauty onto a single peg. He was always trying to do it. He used to call the peg humanity. Will either of these happinesses last? His can't. Hers only for a time. I fight this woman not only because she fights me, but because I foresee the most appalling catastrophe. She wants Rickie partly to replace another man whom she lost two years ago, partly to make something out of him. He is to write. In time she will get sick of this. He won't get famous. She will only see how thin he is and how lame. She will long for a jollier husband, and I don't blame her. And, having made him thoroughly miserable and degraded, she will bolt—if she can do it like a lady."

Such were the opinions of Stewart Ansell.

Chapter 9

Seven letters written in June:

Cambridge.

Dear Rickie,

I would rather write, and you can guess what kind of letter this is when I say it is a fair copy: I have been making rough drafts all the morning. When I talk I get angry, and also at times try to be clever—two reasons why I fail to get attention paid to me. This is a letter of the prudent sort. If it makes you break off the engagement, its work is done. You are not a person who ought to marry at all. You are unfitted in body: that we once discussed. You are also unfitted in soul: you want and you need to like many people, and a man of that sort ought not to marry. "You never were attached to that great sect" who can like one person only, and if you try to enter it you will find destruction. I have read in books—and I cannot afford to despise books, they are all that I have to go by—that men and women desire different things. Man wants to love mankind; woman wants to love one man. When she has him her work is over. She is the emissary of Nature, and Nature's bidding has been fulfilled. But man does not care a damn for Nature—or at least only a very little damn. He cares for a hundred things besides, and the more civilized he is the more he will care for these other hundred things, and demand not only a wife and children, but also friends, and work, and spiritual freedom.

I believe you to be extraordinarily civilized.

Yours ever,
S.A.

Shelthorpe, 9 Sawston Park Road,
Sawston.

Dear Ansell,

But I'm in love—a detail you've forgotten. I can't listen to English Essays. The wretched Agnes may be an "emissary of Nature", but I only grinned when I read it. I may be extraordinarily civilized, but I don't feel so; I'm in love, and I've found a woman to love me, and I mean to have the hundred other things as well. She wants me to have them—friends, and work, and spiritual freedom, and everything. You and your books miss this, because your books are too sedate. Read poetry—not only Shelley. Understand Beatrice, and Clara Middleton, and Brünnhilde in the first scene of *Götterdämmerung*. Understand Goethe when he says "the eternal feminine leads us on", and don't write another English Essay.

Yours ever affectionately,
R.E.

Cambridge.

Dear Rickie,

What am I to say? "Understand Xanthippe and Mrs Bennet, and Elsa in the question scene of *Lohengrin*"? "Understand Euripides when he says the eternal feminine leads us a pretty dance"? I shall say nothing of the sort. The allusions in this English Essay shall not be literary. My personal objections to Miss Pembroke are as follows:

(1) She is not serious.
(2) She is not truthful.

Shelthorpe, 9 Sawston Park Road,
Sawston.

My dear Stewart,

You couldn't know. I didn't know for a moment. But this letter of yours is the most wonderful thing that has ever happened to me yet—more wonderful (I don't exaggerate) than the moment when Agnes promised to marry me. I always knew you liked me, but I never knew how much until this letter. Up to now I think we have been too much like the strong heroes in books who feel so much and say so little, and feel all the more for saying so little. Now that's over and we shall never be that kind of an ass again. We've hit—by accident—upon something permanent. You've writen to me,"I hate the woman who will be your wife, and I write back, "Hate her. Can't I love you both?" She will never come between us, Stewart (she wouldn't wish to, but that's by the way), because our friendship has now passed beyond intervention. No third person could break it. We couldn't ourselves, I fancy. We may quarrel and argue till one of us dies, but the thing is registered. I only wish, dear man, you could be happier. For me, it's as if a light was suddenly held behind the world.

R.E.

Shelthorpe, 9 Sawston Park Road,
Sawston.

Dear Mrs Lewin,

The time goes flying, but I am getting to learn my wonderful boy. We speak a great deal about his work. He has just finished a curious thing called "Nemi"—about a Roman ship that is actually sunk in some lake. I cannot think how he describes the things, when he has never seen them. If, as I hope, he goes to Italy next year, he should turn out something really good. Meanwhile, we are hunting for a publisher. Herbert believes that a collection of short stories is hard to get published. It is, after all, better to write one long one.

But you must not think we only talk books. What we say on other topics cannot so easily be repeated! Oh, Mrs Lewin, he is a dear, and dearer than ever now that we have him at Sawston. Herbert, in a quiet way, has been making inquiries about those Cambridge friends of his. Nothing against them, but they seem to be terribly eccentric. None of them are good at games, and they spend all their spare time thinking and discussing. They discuss what one knows and what one never will know and what one had much better not know. Herbert says it is because they have not got enough to do.

Ever your grateful and affectionate friend,
Agnes Pembroke.

Shelthorpe, 9 Sawston Park Road,
Sawston.

Dear Mr Silt,
Thank you for the congratulations, which I have handed over to the delighted Rickie.[1] I am sorry that the rumour reached you that I was not pleased. Anything pleases me that promises my sister's happiness, and I have known your cousin nearly as long as you have. It will be a very long engagement, for he must make his way first. The dear boy is not nearly as wealthy as he supposed; having no tastes, and hardly any expenses, he used to talk as if he was a millionaire. He must at least double his income before they can dream of more intimate ties. This has been a bitter pill, but I am glad to say that they have accepted it bravely.
Hoping that you and Mrs Silt will profit by your week at Margate,

I remain, yours very sincerely,
Herbert Pembroke.

Cadover, Wilts.

Dear { Miss Pembroke,
       Agnes,
I hear that you are going to marry my nephew. I have no idea what he is like, and wonder whether you would bring him that I may find out. Isn't September rather a nice month? You might have to go to Stonehenge, but with that exception would be left unmolested. I do hope you will manage the visit. We met once at Mrs Lewin's, and I have a very clear recollection of you.
Believe me,

Yours sincerely,
Emily Failing.

[1] The congratulations were really addressed to Agnes—a social blunder which Mr Pembroke deftly corrects.

Chapter 10

The rain tilted a little from the south-west. For the most part it fell from a gray cloud silently, but now and then the tilt increased, and a kind of sigh passed over the country as the drops lashed the walls, trees, shepherds, and other motionless objects that stood in their slanting career. At times the cloud would descend and visibly embrace the earth, to which it had only sent messages; and the earth itself would bring forth clouds—clouds of a whiter breed—which formed in the shallow valleys and followed the courses of the streams. It seemed the beginning of life. Again God said, "Shall we divide the waters from the land or not? Was not the firmament labour and glory sufficient?" At all events it was the beginning of life pastoral, behind which imagination cannot travel.

Yet complicated people were getting wet—not only the shepherds. For instance, the piano-tuner was sopping. So was the vicar's wife. So were the lieutenant and the peevish damsels in his Battlesden car. Gallantry, charity, and art pursued their various missions, perspiring and muddy, while out on the slopes beyond them stood the eternal man and the eternal dog, guarding eternal sheep until the world is vegetarian.

Inside an arbour—which faced east, and thus avoided the bad weather—there sat a complicated person who was dry. She looked at the drenched world with a pleased expression, and would smile when a cloud lay down on the village, or when the rain sighed louder than usual against her solid shelter. Ink, paper-clips, and foolscap paper were on a table before her, and she could also reach an umbrella, a waterproof, a walking-stick, and an electric bell. Her age was between elderly and old, and her forehead was wrinkled with an expression of slight but perpetual pain. But the lines round her mouth indicated that she had laughed a great deal during her life, just as the clean tight skin round her eyes perhaps indicated that she had not often cried. She was dressed in brown silk. A brown silk shawl lay most becomingly over her beautiful hair.

After long thought she wrote on the paper in front of her, "The subject of this memoir first saw the light at Wolverhampton on May the 14th, 1842." She laid down her pen and said "Ugh!" A robin hopped in and she welcomed him. A sparrow followed and she stamped her foot. She watched some thick white water which was sliding like a snake down the gutter of the gravel path. It had just appeared. It must have escaped from a hollow in the chalk up behind. The earth could absorb no longer. The lady did not think of all this, for she hated questions of whence and wherefore, and the ways of the earth ("our dull stepmother") bored her unspeakably. But the water, just the snake of water, was amusing, and she flung her golosh at it to dam it up. Then she wrote feverishly, "The subject of this memoir first saw the light in the middle of the night. It was twenty to eleven. His pa was a parson, but he was not his pa's son, and never went to heaven." There was the sound of a train, and presently white smoke appeared, rising laboriously through the heavy air. It distracted her, and for about a quarter of an hour she sat perfectly still, doing nothing. At last she pushed the spoilt paper aside, took a fresh piece, and was beginning to write, "On May the 14th, 1842," when there was a crunch on the gravel, and a furious voice said, "I am sorry for Flea Thompson."

"I daresay I am sorry for him too," said the lady: her voice was languid and pleasant. "Who is he?"

"Flea's a liar, and next time we meet he'll be a football." Off slipped a sodden ulster. He hung it up angrily upon a peg: the arbour provided several.

"But who is he, and why has he that disastrous name?"

"Flea? Fleance. All the Thompsons are named out of Shakespeare. He grazes the Rings."

"Ah, I see. A pet lamb."

"Lamb! Shepherd!"

"One of my shepherds?"

"The last time I go with his sheep. But not the last time he sees me. I am sorry for him. He dodged me today."

"Do you mean to say"—she became animated—"that you have been out in the wet keeping the sheep of Flea Thompson?"

"I had to." He blew on his fingers and took off his cap. Water trickled over his unshaven cheeks. His hair was so wet that it seemed worked upon his scalp in bronze.

"Get away, bad dog!" screamed the lady, for he had given himself a shake and spattered her dress with water. He was a powerful boy of twenty, admirably muscular, but rather too broad for his height. People called him "Podge" until they were dissuaded. Then they called him "Stephen" or "Mr Wonham". Then he said, "You can call me Podge if you like."

"As for Flea—!" he began tempestuously. He sat down by her, and with much heavy breathing told the story—"Flea has a girl at Wintersbridge, and I had to go with his sheep while he went to see her. Two hours. We agreed. Half an hour to go, an hour to kiss his girl, and half an hour back—and he had my bike. Four hours! Four hours and seven minutes I was on the Rings, with a fool of a dog, and sheep doing all they knew to the turnips."

"My farm is a mystery to me," said the lady, stroking her fingers. "Some day you must really take me to see it. It must be like a Gilbert and Sullivan opera, with a chorus of agitated employers. How is it that I have escaped? Why have I never been summoned to milk the cows, or flay the pigs, or drive the young bullocks to the pasture?"

He looked at her with astonishingly blue eyes—the only dry things he had about him. He could not see into her: she would have puzzled an older and a cleverer man. He may have seen round her.

"A thing of beauty you are not. But I sometimes think you are a joy for ever."

"I beg your pardon?"

"Oh, you understand right enough," she exclaimed irritably, and then smiled, for he was conceited, and did not like being told that he was not a thing of beauty. "Large and steady feet," she continued, "have this disadvantage—you can knock down a man, but you will never knock down a woman."

"I don't know what you mean. I'm not likely—"

"Oh, never mind—never, never mind. I was being funny. I repent. Tell me about the sheep. Why did you go with them?"

"I did tell you. I had to."

"But why?"

"He had to see his girl."

"But why?"

His eyes shot past her again. It was so obvious that the man had to see his girl. For two hours though—not for four hours seven minutes.

"Did you have any lunch?"

"I don't hold with regular meals."

"Did you have a book?"

"I don't hold with books in the open. None of the older men read."

"Did you commune with yourself, or don't you hold with that?"

"Oh Lord, don't ask me!"

"You distress me. You rob the Pastoral of its lingering romance. Is there no poetry and no thought in England? Is there no one, in all these downs, who warbles with eager thought the Doric lay?"

"Chaps sing to themselves at times, if you mean that."

"I dream of Arcady: I open my eyes: Wiltshire. Of Amaryllis: Flea Thompson's girl. Of the pensive shepherd, twitching his mantle blue: you in an ulster. Aren't you sorry for me?"

"May I put in a pipe?"

"By all means put a pipe in. In return, tell me of what you were thinking for the four hours and the seven minutes."

He laughed shyly. "You do ask a man such questions."

"Did you simply waste the time?"

"I suppose so."

"I thought that Colonel Robert Ingersoll says you must be strenuous."

At the sound of this name he whisked open a little cupboard, and declaring, "I haven't a moment to spare," took out of it a pile of *Clarion* and other reprints, adorned as to their covers with bald or bearded apostles of humanity. Selecting a bald one, he began at once to read, occasionally exclaiming, "That's got them," "That's knocked Genesis," with similar ejaculations of an aspiring mind. She glanced at the pile. Renan, minus the style. Darwin, minus the modesty. A comic edition of the book of Job, by "Excelsior", Pittsburgh, Pa. *The Beginning of Life*, with diagrams. *Angel or Ape?* by Mrs Julia P. Chunk. She was amused, and wondered idly what was passing within his narrow but not uninteresting brain. Did he suppose that he was going to "find out"? She had tried once herself, but had since subsided into a sprightly orthodoxy. Why didn't he read poetry, instead of wasting his time between books like these and country like that?

The cloud parted, and the increase of light made her look up. Over the valley she saw a grave sullen down, and on its flanks a little brown smudge—her sheep, together with her shepherd, Fleance Thompson, returned to his duties at last. A trickle of water came through the arbour roof. She shrieked in dismay.

"That's all right," said her companion, moving her chair, but still keeping his place in his book.

She dried up the spot on the manuscript. Then she wrote: "Anthony Eustace Failing, the subject of this memoir, was born at Wolverhampton." But she wrote no more. She was fidgety. Another drop fell from the roof. Likewise an earwig. She wished she had not been so playful in flinging her golosh into the path. The boy who was overthrowing religion breathed somewhat heavily as he did so. Another earwig. She touched the electric bell.

"I'm going in," she observed. "It's far too wet." Again the cloud parted and caused her to add, "Weren't you rather kind to Flea?" But he was deep in the book. He read like a poor person, with lips apart and a finger that followed the print. At times he scratched his ear, or ran his tongue along

a straggling blond moustache. His face had after all a certain
beauty: at all events the colouring was regal—a steady crimson from throat to forehead: the sun and the winds had
worked on him daily ever since he was born. "The face of a
strong man," thought the lady. "Let him thank his stars he
isn't a silent strong man, or I'd turn him into the gutter."
Suddenly it struck her that he was like an Irish terrier. He
worried infinity as if it was a bone. Gnashing his teeth, he
tried to carry the eternal subtleties by violence. As a man he
often bored her, for he was always saying and doing the
same things. But as a philosopher he really was a joy for
ever, an inexhaustible buffoon. Taking up her pen, she began
to caricature him. She drew a rabbit-warren where rabbits
were at play in four dimensions. Before she had introduced
the principal figure, she was interrupted by the footman. He
had come up from the house to answer the bell. On seeing
her he uttered a respectful cry.

"Madam! Are you here? I am very sorry. I looked for you
everywhere. Mr Elliot and Miss Pembroke arrived nearly an
hour ago."

"Oh dear, oh dear!" exclaimed Mrs Failing. "Take these
papers. Where's the umbrella? Mr Stephen will hold it over
me. You hurry back and apologize. Are they happy?"

"Miss Pembroke inquired after you, madam."

"Have they had tea?"

"Yes, madam."

"Leighton!"

"Yes, sir."

"I believe you knew she was here all the time. You didn't
want to wet your pretty skin."

"You must not call me 'she' to the servants," said Mrs
Failing as they walked away, she limping with a stick, he
holding a great umbrella over her. "I will not have it." Then
more pleasantly, "And don't tell him he lies. We all lie. I knew
quite well they were coming by the four-six train. I saw it pass."

"That reminds me. Another child run over at the Roman
crossing. Whish—bang—dead."

"Oh my foot! Oh my foot, my foot!" said Mrs Failing,
and paused to take breath.

"Bad?" he asked callously.

Leighton, with bowed head, passed them with the manuscript and disappeared among the laurels. The twinge of pain, which had been slight, passed away, and they proceeded, descending a green airless corridor which opened into the gravel drive.

"Isn't it odd," said Mrs Failing, "that the Greeks should be enthusiastic about laurels—that Apollo should pursue anyone who could possibly turn into such a frightful plant? What do you make of Rickie?"

"Oh, I don't know."

"Shall I lend you his story to read?"

He made no reply.

"Don't you think, Stephen, that a person in your precarious position ought to be civil to my relatives?"

"Sorry, Mrs Failing. I meant to be civil. I only hadn't anything to say."

She laughed. "Are you a dear boy? I sometimes wonder; or are you a brute?"

Again he had nothing to say. Then she laughed more mischievously, and said—

"How can you be either, when you are a philosopher? Would you mind telling me—I am so anxious to learn— what happens to people when they die?"

"Don't ask *me*." He knew by bitter experience that she was making fun of him.

"Oh, but I do ask you. Those paper books of yours are so up-to-date. For instance, what has happened to the child you say was killed on the line?"

The rain increased. The drops pattered hard on the leaves, and outside the corridor men and women were struggling, however stupidly, with the facts of life. Inside it they wrangled. She teased the boy, and laughed at his theories, and proved that no man can be an agnostic who has a sense of humour. Suddenly she stopped, not through any skill of his, but because she had remembered some words of Bacon: "The true atheist is he whose hands are cauterized by holy things." She thought of her distant youth. The world was not so humorous then, but it had been more important. For a moment she respected her companion, and determined to vex him no more.

They left the shelter of the laurels, crossed the broad drive, and were inside the house at last. She had got quite wet, for the weather would not let her play the simple life with impunity. As for him, he seemed a piece of the wet.

"Look here," she cried, as he hurried up to his attic, "don't shave!"

He was delighted with the permission.

"I have an idea that Miss Pembroke is of the type that pretends to be unconventional and really isn't. I want to see how she takes it. Don't shave."

In the drawing-room she could hear the guests conversing in the subdued tones of those who have not been welcomed. Having changed her dress and glanced at the poems of Milton, she went to them, with uplifted hands of apology and horror.

"But I must have tea," she announced, when they had assured her that they understood. "Otherwise I shall start by being cross. Agnes, stop me. Give me tea."

Agnes, looking pleased, moved to the table and served her hostess. Rickie followed with a pagoda of sandwiches and little cakes.

"I feel twenty-seven years younger. Rickie, you are so like your father. I feel it is twenty-seven years ago, and that he is bringing your mother to see me for the first time. It is curious—almost terrible—to see history repeating itself."

The remark was not tactful.

"I remember that visit well," she continued thoughtfully. "I suppose it was a wonderful visit, though we none of us knew it at the time. We all fell in love with your mother. I wish she would have fallen in love with us. She couldn't bear me, could she?"

"I never heard her say so, Aunt Emily."

"No; she wouldn't. I am sure your father said so, though. My dear boy, don't look so shocked. Your father and I hated each other. He said so, I said so, I say so; say so too. Then we shall start fair.—Just a cocoanut cake.—Agnes, don't you agree that it's always best to speak out?"

"Oh, rather, Mrs Failing. But I'm shockingly straightforward."

"So am I," said the lady. "I like to get down to the bedrock.—Hullo! Slippers? Slippers in the drawing-room?"

A young man had come in silently. Agnes observed with a feeling of regret that he had not shaved. Rickie, after a moment's hesitation, remembered who it was, and shook hands with him.

"You've grown since I saw you last."

He showed his teeth amiably.

"How long ago was that?" asked Mrs Failing.

"Three years, wasn't it? Came over from the Ansells—friends."

"How disgraceful, Rickie! Why don't you come and see me oftener?"

He could not retort that she never asked him.

"Agnes will make you come. Oh, let me introduce—Mr Wonham—Miss Pembroke."

"I am deputy hostess," said Agnes. "May I give you some tea?"

"Thank you, but I have had a little beer."

"It is one of the shepherds," said Mrs Failing, in low tones. Agnes smiled rather wildly. Mrs Lewin had warned her that Cadover was an extraordinary place, and that one must never be astonished at anything. A shepherd in the drawing-room! No harm. Still one ought to know whether it was a shepherd or not. At all events he was in gentleman's clothing. She was anxious not to start with a blunder, and therefore did not talk to the young fellow, but tried to gather what he was from the demeanour of Rickie.

"I am sure, Mrs Failing, that you need not talk of 'making' people come to Cadover. There will be no difficulty, I should say."

"Thank you, my dear. Do you know who once said those exact words to me?"

"Who?"

"Rickie's mother."

"Did she really?"

"My sister-in-law was a dear. You will have heard Rickie's

praises, but now you must hear mine. I never knew a woman who was so unselfish and yet had such capacities for life."

"Does one generally exclude the other?" asked Rickie.

"Unselfish people, as a rule, are deathly dull. They have no colour. They think of other people because it is easier. They give money because they are too stupid or too idle to spend it properly on themselves. That was the beauty of your mother—she gave away, but she also spent on herself, or tried to."

The light faded out of the drawing-room, in spite of it being September and only half past six. From her low chair Agnes could see the trees by the drive, black against a blackening sky. That drive was half a mile. long, and she was praising its gravelled surface when Rickie called in a voice of alarm, "I say, when did our train arrive?"

"Four-six."

"I said so."

"It arrived at four-six on the timetable," said Mr Wonham. "I want to know when it got to the station?"

"I tell you again it was punctual. I tell you I looked at my watch. I can do no more."

Agnes was amazed. Was Rickie mad? A minute ago and they were boring each other over dogs. What had happened?

"Now, now! Quarrelling already?" asked Mrs Failing. The footman, bringing a lamp, lit up two angry faces.

"He says—"

"He says—"

"He says we ran over a child."

"So you did. You ran over a child in the village at four-seven by my watch. Your train was late. You couldn't have got to the station till four-ten."

"I don't believe it. We had passed the village by four-seven. Agnes, hadn't we passed the village? It must have been an express that ran over the child."

"Now is it likely"—he appealed to the practical world—"is it likely that the company would run a stopping train and then an express three minutes after it?"

"A child—" said Rickie. "I can't believe that the train

killed a child." He thought of their journey. They were alone in the carriage. As the train slackened speed he had caught her for a moment in his arms. The rain beat on the windows, but they were in heaven.

"You've got to believe it," said the other, and proceeded to "rub it in". His healthy, irritable face drew close to Rickie's. "Two children were kicking and screaming on the Roman crossing. Your train, being late, came down on them. One of them was pulled off the line, but the other was caught. How will you get out of that?"

"And how will you get out of it?" cried Mrs Failing, turning the tables on him. "Where's the child now? What has happened to its soul? You must know, Agnes, that this young gentleman is a philosopher."

"Oh, drop all that," said Mr Wonham, suddenly collapsing.

"Drop it? Where? On my nice carpet?"

"I hate philosophy," remarked Agnes, trying to turn the subject, for she saw that it made Rickie unhappy.

"So do I. But I daren't say so before Stephen. He despises us women."

"No, I don't," said the victim, swaying to and fro on the window-sill, whither he had retreated.

"Yes, he does. He won't even trouble to answer us. Stephen! Podge! Answer me. What has happened to the child's soul?"

He flung open the window and leant from them into the dusk. They heard him mutter something about a bridge.

"What did I tell you? He won't answer my question." The delightful moment was approaching when the boy would lose his temper: she knew it by a certain tremor in his heels.

"There wants a bridge," he exploded. "A bridge instead of all this rotten talk and the level-crossing. It wouldn't break you to build a two-arch bridge. Then the child's soul, as you call it—well, nothing would have happened to the child at all."

A gust of night air entered, accompanied by rain. The flowers in the vases rustled, and the flame of the lamp shot up and smoked the glass. Slightly irritated, she ordered him to close the window.

Chapter 11

Cadover was not a large house. But it is the largest house with which this story has dealings, and must always be thought of with a certain respect. It was built about the year 1800, and favoured the architecture of ancient Rome—chiefly by means of five lank pilasters, which stretched from the top of it to the bottom. Between the pilasters was the glass front door, to the right of them the drawing-room windows, to the left of them the windows of the dining-room, above them a triangular area, which the better-class servants knew as a "pendiment", and which had in its middle a small round hole, according to the usage of Palladio. The classical note was also sustained by eight gray steps which led from the building down into the drive, and by an attempt at a formal garden on the adjoining lawn. The lawn ended in a ha-ha ("Ha! ha! who shall regard it?"), and thence the bare land sloped down into the village. The main garden (walled) was to the left as one faced the house, while to the right was that laurel avenue, leading up to Mrs Failing's arbour.

It was a comfortable but not very attractive place, and, to a certain type of mind, its situation was not attractive either. From the distance it showed as a gray box, huddled against evergreens. There was no mystery about it. You saw it for miles. Its hill had none of the beetling romance of Devonshire, none of the subtle contours that prelude a cottage in Kent, but proffered its burden crudely, on a huge bare palm. "There's Cadover," visitors would say. "How small it still looks. We shall be late for lunch." And the view from the windows, though extensive, would not have been accepted by the Royal Academy. A valley, containing a stream, a road, a railway; over the valley fields of barley and wurzel, divided by no pretty hedges, and passing into a great and formless down—this was the outlook, desolate at all times, and almost terrifying beneath a cloudy sky. The down was called "Cadbury Rings" ("Cocoa Squares" if you were young and funny), because high upon it—one cannot say "on the top", there being scarcely any tops in Wiltshire—because high upon it there stood a double circle of entrenchments. A bank of grass enclosed a ring of turnips, which enclosed a second bank of grass, which enclosed more turnips, and in the middle of the pattern grew one small tree. British? Roman? Saxon? Danish? The competent reader will decide. The Thompson family knew it to be far older than the Franco-German war. It was the property of Government. It was full of gold and dead soldiers who had fought with the soldiers on Castle Rings and been beaten. The road to Londinium, having forded the stream and crossed the valley road and the railway, passed up by these entrenchments. The road to London lay half a mile to the right of them.

To complete this survey one must mention the church and the farm, both of which lay over the stream, in Cadford. Between them they ruled the village, one claiming the souls of the labourers, the other their bodies. If a man desired other religion or other employment he must leave. The church lay up by the railway, the farm was down by the water meadows. The vicar, a gentle charitable man, scarcely realized his power, and never tried to abuse it. Mr Wilbraham, the agent, was of another mould. He knew his place, and kept others to theirs: all society seemed spread before him like a map. The line between the county and the local, the line between the labourer and the artisan—he knew them all, and strengthened them with no uncertain touch. Everything with him was graduated—carefully graduated civility towards his superiors, towards his inferiors carefully graduated incivility. So—for he was a thoughtful person—so alone, declared he, could things be kept together.

Perhaps the Comic Muse, to whom so much is now attributed, had caused this estate to be left to Mr Failing. Mr Failing was the author of some brilliant books on socialism— that was why his wife married him—and for twenty-five years he reigned up at Cadover and tried to put his theories

97

into practice. He believed that things could be kept together by accenting the similarities, not the differences of men. "We are all much more alike than we confess" was one of his favourite speeches. As a speech it sounded very well, and his wife had applauded; but when it resulted in hard work, evenings in the reading-room, mixed parties, and long unobtrusive talks with dull people, she got bored. In her piquant way she declared that she was not going to love her husband, and succeeded. He took it quietly, but his brilliancy decreased. His health grew worse, and he knew that when he died there was no one to carry on his work. He felt, besides, that he had done very little. Toil as he would, he had not a practical mind, and could never dispense with Mr Wilbraham. For all his tact, he would often stretch out the hand of brotherhood too soon, or withhold it when it would have been accepted. Most people misunderstood him, or only understood him when he was dead. In after years his reign became a golden age; but he counted a few disciples in his lifetime, a few young labourers and tenant farmers, who swore tempestuously that he was not really a fool. This, he told himself, was as much as he deserved.

Cadover was inherited by his widow. She tried to sell it; she tried to let it; but she asked too much, and as it was neither a pretty place nor fertile, it was left on her hands. With many a groan she settled down to banishment. Wiltshire people, she declared, were the stupidest in England. She told them so to their faces, which made them no brighter. And their county was worthy of them: no distinction in ·it—no style—simply land.

But her wrath passed, or remained only as a graceful fretfulness. She made the house comfortable, and abandoned the farm to Mr Wilbraham. With a good deal of care she selected a small circle of acquaintances, and had them to stop in the summer months. In the winter she would go to town and frequent the salons of the literary. As her lameness increased she moved about less, and at the time of her nephew's visit seldom left the place that had been forced upon her as a home. Just now she was busy. A prominent politician had quoted her husband. The young generation asked, "Who is this Mr Failing?" and the publishers wrote, "Now is the time." She was collecting some essays and penning an introductory memoir.

Rickie admired his aunt, but did not care for her. She reminded him too much of his father. She had the same affliction, the same heartlessness, the same habit of taking life with a laugh—as if life is a pill! He also felt that she had neglected him. He would not have asked much: as for "prospects", they never entered his head; but she was his only near relative, and a little kindness and hospitality during the lonely years would have made incalculable difference. Now that he was happier and could bring her Agnes, she had asked him to stop at once. The sun as it rose next morning spoke to him of a new life. He too had a purpose and a value in the world at last. Leaning out of the window, he gazed at the earth washed clean and heard through the pure air the distant noises of the farm.

But that day nothing was to remain divine but the weather. His aunt, for reasons of her own, decreed that he should go for a ride with the Wonham boy. They were to look at Old Sarum, proceed thence to Salisbury, lunch there, see the sights, call on a certain canon for tea, and return to Cadover in the evening. The arrangement suited no one. He did not want to ride, but to be with Agnes; nor did Agnes want to be parted from him, nor Stephen to go with him. But the clearer the wishes of her guests became, the more determined was Mrs Failing to disregard them. She smoothed away every difficulty, she converted every objection into a reason, and she ordered the horses for half past nine.

"It is a bore," he grumbled as he sat in their little private sitting-room, breaking his fingernails upon the coachman's gaiters. "I can't ride. I shall fall off. We should have been so happy here. It's just like Aunt Emily. Can't you imagine her saying afterwards, 'Lovers are absurd. I made a point of keeping them apart,' and then everybody laughing."

With a pretty foretaste of the future, Agnes knelt before him and did the gaiters up. "Who is this Mr Wonham, by the bye?"

"I don't know. Some connection of Mr Failing's, I think."

"Does he live here?"

"He used to be at school or something. He seems to have grown into a tiresome person."

"I suppose that Mrs Failing has adopted him."

"I suppose so. I believe that she has been quite kind. I do hope that she'll be kind to you this morning. I hate leaving you with her."

"Why, you say she likes me."

"Yes, but that wouldn't prevent—you see she doesn't mind what she says or what she repeats if it amuses her. If she thought it really funny, for instance, to break off our engagement, she'd try."

"Dear boy, what a frightful remark! But it would be funnier for us to see her trying. Whatever could she do?"

He kissed the hands that were still busy with the fastenings. "Nothing. I can't see one thing. We simply lie open to each other, you and I. There isn't one new corner in either of us that she could reveal. It's only that I always have in this house the most awful feeling of insecurity."

"Why?"

"If anyone says or does a foolish thing it's always here. All the family breezes have started here. It's a kind of focus for aimed and aimless scandal. You know, when my father and mother had their special quarrel, my aunt was mixed up in it—I never knew how or how much—but you may be sure that she didn't calm things down, unless she found things more entertaining calm."

"Rickie! Rickie!" cried the lady from the garden, "your riding-master's impatient."

"We really oughtn't to talk of her like this here," whispered Agnes. "It's a horrible habit."

"The habit of the country, Agnes. Ugh, this gossip!" Suddenly he flung his arms over her. "Dear—dear—let's beware of I don't know what—of nothing at all perhaps."

"Oh, buck up!" yelled the irritable Stephen. "Which am I to shorten—left stirrup or right?"

"Left!" shouted Agnes.

"How many holes?"

They hurried down. On the way she said: "I'm glad of the warning. Now I'm prepared. Your aunt will get nothing out of me."

Her betrothed tried to mount with the wrong foot, according to his invariable custom. She also had to pick up his whip. At last they started, the boy showing off pretty consistently, and she was left alone with her hostess.

"Dido is quiet as a lamb," said Mrs Failing, "and Stephen is a good fielder. What a blessing it is to have cleared out the men. What shall you and I do this heavenly morning?"

"I'm game for anything."

"Have you quite unpacked?"

"Yes."

"Any letters to write?"

"No."

"Then let's go to my arbour. No, we won't. It gets the morning sun, and it'll be too hot today." Already she regretted clearing out the men. On such a morning she would have liked to drive, but her third animal had gone lame. She feared, too, that Miss Pembroke was going to bore her. However, they did go to the arbour. In languid tones she pointed out the various objects of interest.

"There's the Cad, which goes into the something, which goes into the Avon. Cadbury Rings opposite, Cadchurch to the extreme left: you can't see it. You were there last night. It is famous for the drunken parson and the railway station. Then Cad Dauntsey. Then Cadford, that side of the stream, connected with Cadover, this. Observe the fertility of the Wiltshire mind."

"A terrible lot of Cads," said Agnes brightly.

Mrs Failing divided her guests into those who made this joke and those who did not. The latter class was very small.

"The vicar of Cadford—not the nice drunkard—declares the name is really 'Chadford', and he worried on till I put up a window to St Chad in our church. His wife pronounces it 'Hyadford'. I could smack them both. How do you like Podge? Ah! you jump; I meant you to. How do you like Podge Wonham?"

"Very nice," said Agnes, laughing.

"Nice! He is a hero."

There was a long interval of silence. Each lady looked, without much interest, at the view. Mrs Failing's attitude towards Nature was severely aesthetic—an attitude more sterile than the severely practical. She applied the test of beauty to shadow and odour and sound; they never filled her with reverence or excitement; she never knew them as a resistless trinity that may intoxicate the worshipper with joy. If she liked a ploughed field, it was only as a spot of colour—not also as a hint of the endless strength of the earth. And today she could approve of one cloud, but object to its fellow. As for Miss Pembroke, she was not approving or objecting at all. "A hero?" she questioned, when the interval had passed. Her voice was indifferent, as if she had been thinking of other things.

"A hero? Yes. Didn't you notice how heroic he was?"

"I don't think I did."

"Not at dinner? Ah, Agnes, always look out for heroism at dinner. It is their great time. They live up to the stiffness of their shirt-fronts. Do you mean to say that you never noticed how he set down Rickie?"

"Oh, that about poetry!" said Agnes, laughing. "Rickie would not mind it for a moment. But why do you single out that as heroic?"

"To snub people! to set them down! to be rude to them! to make them feel small! Surely that's the life-work of a hero?"

"I shouldn't have said that. And as a matter of fact Mr Wonham was wrong over the poetry. I made Rickie look it up afterwards."

"But of course. A hero always is wrong."

"To me," she persisted, rather gently, "a hero has always been a strong wonderful being, who champions—"

"Ah, wait till you are the dragon! I have been a dragon most of my life, I think. A dragon that wants nothing but a peaceful cave. Then in comes the strong, wonderful, delightful being, and gains a princess by piercing my hide. No, seriously, my dear Agnes, the chief characteristics of a hero are infinite disregard for the feelings of others, plus general inability to understand them."

"But surely Mr Wonham—"

"Yes; aren't we being unkind to the poor boy. Ought we to go on talking?"

Agnes waited, remembering the warnings of Rickie, and thinking that anything she said might perhaps be repeated.

"Though even if he was here he wouldn't understand what we are saying."

"Wouldn't understand?"

Mrs Failing gave the least flicker of an eye towards her companion. "Did you take him for clever?"

"I don't think I took him for anything." She smiled. "I have been thinking of other things, and of another boy."

"But do think for a moment of Stephen. I will describe how he spent yesterday. He rose at eight. From eight to eleven he sang. The song was called 'Father's boots will soon fit Willie'. He stopped once to say to the footman, 'She'll never finish her book. She idles.' 'She' being I. At eleven he went out, and stood in the rain till four, but had the luck to see a child run over at the level-crossing. By half past four he had knocked the bottom out of Christianity."

Agnes looked bewildered.

"Aren't you impressed? I was. I told him that he was on no account to unsettle the vicar. Open that cupboard. One of those sixpenny books tells Podge that he's made of hard little black things, another that he's made of brown things, larger and squashy. There seems a discrepancy, but anything is better for a thoughtful youth than to be made in the Garden of Eden. Let us eliminate the poetic, at whatever cost to the probable." Then for a moment she spoke more gravely. "Here he is at twenty, with nothing to hold on by. I don't know what's to be done. I suppose it's my fault. But I've never had any bother over the Church of England; have you?"

"Of course I go with my Church," said Miss Pembroke, who hated this style of conversation. "I don't know, I'm sure. I think you should consult a man."

"Would Rickie help me?"

"Rickie would do anything he can." And Mrs Failing noted the half official way in which she vouched for her lover. "But of course Rickie is a little—complicated. I doubt whether Mr Wonham would understand him. He wants—doesn't he?—someone who's a little more assertive and more accustomed to boys. Someone more like my brother."

"Agnes!" she seized her by the arm. "Do you suppose that Mr Pembroke would undertake my Podge?"

She shook her head. "His time is so filled up. He gets a boarding-house next term. Besides—after all I don't know what Herbert would do."

"Morality. He would teach him morality. The Thirty-Nine Articles may come of themselves, but if you have no morals you come to grief. Morality is all I demand from Mr Herbert Pembroke. He shall be excused the use of the globes. You know, of course, that Stephen was expelled from a public school? He stole."

The school was not a public one, and the expulsion, or rather request for removal, had taken place when Stephen was fourteen. A violent spasm of dishonesty—such as often heralds the approach of manhood—had overcome him. He stole everything, especially what was difficult to steal, and hid the plunder beneath a loose plank in the passage. He was betrayed by the inclusion of a ham. This was the crisis of his career. His benefactress was just then rather bored with him. He had stopped being a pretty boy, and she rather doubted whether she would see him through. But she was so enraged with the letters of the schoolmaster, and so delighted with those of the criminal, that she had him back and gave him a prize.

"No," said Agnes, "I didn't know. I should be happy to speak to Herbert, but, as I said, his time will be very full. But I know he has friends who make a speciality of weakly or—or unusual boys."

"My dear, I've tried it. Stephen kicked the weakly boys and robbed apples with the unusual ones. He was expelled again."

Agnes began to find Mrs Failing rather tiresome. Wherever you trod on her, she seemed to slip away from beneath your feet. Agnes liked to know where she was and where other people were as well. She said: "My brother thinks a great deal of home life. I daresay he'd think that Mr Wonham is best where he is—with you. You have been so kind to him. You"—she paused—"have been to him both father and mother."

"I'm too hot," was Mrs Failing's reply. It seemed that Miss Pembroke had at last touched a topic on which she was reticent. She rang the electric bell—it was only to tell the footman to take the reprints to Mr Wonham's room—and then murmuring something about work, proceeded herself to the house.

"Mrs Failing—" said Agnes, who had not expected such a speedy end to their chat.

"Call me Aunt Emily. My dear?"

"Aunt Emily, what did you think of that story Rickie sent you?"

"It is bad," said Mrs Failing. "But. But. But." Then she escaped, having told the truth, and yet leaving a pleasurable impression behind her.

Chapter 12

The excursion to Salisbury was but a poor business—in fact, Rickie never got there. They were not out of the drive before Mr Wonham began doing acrobatics. He showed Rickie how very quickly he could turn round in his saddle and sit with his face to Aeneas's tail. "I see," said Rickie coldly, and became almost cross when they arrived in this condition at the gate behind the house, for he had to open it, and was afraid of falling. As usual, he anchored just beyond the fastenings, and then had to turn Dido, who seemed as long as a battleship. To his relief a man came forward, and murmuring, "Worst gate in the parish," pushed it wide and held it respectfully. "Thank you," cried Rickie; "many thanks." But Stephen, who was riding into the world back first, said majestically, "No, no; it doesn't count. You needn't think it. You make it worse by touching your hat. Four hours and seven minutes! You'll see me again." The man answered nothing.

"Eh, but I'll hurt him," he chanted, as he swung into position. "That was Flea. Eh, but he's forgotten my fists; eh, but I'll hurt him."

"Why?" ventured Rickie. Last night, over cigarettes, he had been bored to death by the story of Flea. The boy had a little reminded him of Gerald—the Gerald of history, not the Gerald of romance. He was more genial, but there was the same brutality, the same peevish insistence on the pound of flesh.

"Hurt him till he learns."

"Learns what?"

"Learns, of course," retorted Stephen. Neither of them was very civil. They did not dislike each other, but they each wanted to be somewhere else—exactly the situation that Mrs Failing had expected.

"He behaved badly," said Rickie, "because he is poorer than we are, and more ignorant. Less money has been spent on teaching him to behave."

"Well, I'll teach him for nothing."

"Perhaps his fists are stronger than yours!"

"They aren't. I looked."

After this conversation flagged. Rickie glanced back at Cadover, and thought of the insipid day that lay before him. Generally he was attracted by fresh people, and Stephen was almost fresh: they had been to him symbols of the unknown, and all that they did was interesting. But now he cared for the unknown no longer. He knew.

Mr Wilbraham passed them in his dogcart, and lifted his hat to his employer's nephew. Stephen he ignored: he could not find him on the map.

"Good morning," said Rickie. "What a lovely morning!"

"I say," called the other, "another child dead!" Mr Wilbraham, who had seemed inclined to chat, whipped up his horse and left them.

"There goes an out and outer," said Stephen; and then, as if introducing an entirely new subject—"Don't you think Flea Thompson treated me disgracefully?"

"I suppose he did. But I'm scarcely the person to sympathize." The allusion fell flat, and he had to explain it. "I should have done the same myself—promised to be away two hours, and stopped four."

"Stopped—oh—oh, I understand. You being in love, you mean?"

He smiled and nodded.

"Oh, I've no objection to Flea loving. He says he can't help it. But as long as my fists are stronger, he's got to keep it in line."

"In line?"

"A man like that, when he's got a girl, thinks the rest can go to the devil. He goes cutting his work and breaking his word. Wilbraham ought to sack him. I promise you when I've a girl I'll keep her in line, and if she turns nasty, I'll get another."

Rickie smiled and said no more. But he was sorry that

anyone should start life with such a creed—all the more sorry because the creed caricatured his own. He too believed that life should be in a line—a line of enormous length, full of countless interests and countless figures, all well beloved. But woman was not to be "kept" to this line. Rather did she advance it continually, like some triumphant general, making each unit still more interesting, still more lovable, than it had been before. He loved Agnes, not only for herself, but because she was lighting up the human world. But he could scarcely explain this to an inexperienced animal, nor did he make the attempt.

For a long time they proceeded in silence. The hill behind Cadover was in harvest, and the horses moved regretfully between the sheaves. Stephen had picked a grass leaf, and was blowing catcalls upon it. He blew very well, and this morning all his soul went into the wail. For he was ill. He was tortured with the feeling that he could not get away and do—do something, instead of being civil to this anaemic prig. Four hours in the rain was better than this: he had not wanted to fidget in the rain. But now the air was like wine, and the stubble was smelling of wet, and over his head white clouds trundled more slowly and more seldom through broadening tracts of blue. There never had been such a morning, and he shut up his eyes and called to it. And whenever he called, Rickie shut up his eyes and winced.

At last the blade broke. "We don't go quick, do we?" he remarked, and looked on the weedy track for another.

"I wish you wouldn't let me keep you. If you were alone you would be galloping or something of that sort."

"I was told I must go your pace," he said mournfully. "And you promised Miss Pembroke not to hurry."

"Well, I'll disobey." But he could not rise above a gentle trot, and even that nearly jerked him out of the saddle.

"Sit like *this*," said Stephen. "Can't you see—like *this*?" Rickie lurched forward, and broke his thumb-nail on the horse's neck. It bled a little, and had to be bound up.

"Thank you—awfully kind—no tighter, please—I'm simply spoiling your day."

"I can't think how a man can help riding. You've only to

leave it to the horse so!—so!—just as you leave it to the water in swimming."

Rickie left it to Dido, who stopped immediately.

"I said *leave* it." His voice rose irritably. "I didn't say 'die'. Of course she stops if you die. First you sit her as if you're Sandow exercising, and then you sit like a corpse. Can't you tell her you're alive? That's all she wants."

In trying to convey the information, Rickie dropped his whip. Stephen picked it up and rammed it into the belt of his own Norfolk jacket. He was scarcely a fashionable horseman. He was not even graceful. But he rode as a living man, though Rickie was too much bored to notice it. Not a muscle in him was idle, not a muscle working hard. When he returned from a gallop his limbs were still unsatisfied and his manners still irritable. He did not know that he was ill: he knew nothing about himself at all.

"Like a howdah in the Zoo," he grumbled. "Mother Failing will buy elephants." And he proceeded to criticize his benefactress. Rickie, keenly alive to bad taste, tried to stop him, and gained instead a criticism of religion. Stephen overthrew the Mosaic cosmogony. He pointed out the discrepancies in the Gospels. He levelled his wit against the most beautiful spire in the world, now rising against the southern sky. Between whiles he went for a gallop. After a time Rickie stopped listening, and simply went his way. For Dido was a perfect mount, and as indifferent to the motions of Aeneas as if she was strolling in the Elysian fields. He had had a bad night, and the strong air made him sleepy. The wind blew from the Plain. Cadover and its valley had disappeared, and though they had not climbed much and could not see far, there was a sense of infinite space. The fields were enormous, like fields on the Continent, and the brilliant sun showed up their colours well. The green of the turnips, the gold of the harvest, and the brown of the newly turned clods, were each contrasted with morsels of gray down. But the general effect was pale, or rather silvery, for Wiltshire is not a county of heavy tints. Beneath these colours lurked the unconquerable chalk, and wherever the soil was poor it emerged. The grassy track, so gay with scabious and bedstraw, was snow-white at the bottom of its ruts. A dazzling amphitheatre gleamed in the flank of a distant hill, cut for some Olympian audience. And here and there, whatever the surface crop, the earth broke into little embankments, little ditches, little mounds: there had been no lack of drama to solace the gods.

In Cadover, the perilous house, Agnes had already parted from Mrs Failing. His thoughts returned to her. Was she, the soul of truth, in safety? Was her purity vexed by the lies and selfishness? Would she elude the caprice which had, he vaguely knew, caused suffering before? Ah, the frailty of joy! Ah, the myriads of longings that pass without fruition, and the turf grows over them! Better men, women as noble— they had died up here and their dust had been mingled, but only their dust. These are morbid thoughts, but who dare contradict them? There is much good luck in the world, but it is luck. We are none of us safe. We are children, playing or quarrelling on the line, and some of us have Rickie's temperament, or his experiences, and admit it.

So he mused, that anxious little speck, and all the land seemed to comment on his fears and on his love.

Their path lay upward, over a great bald skull, half grass, half stubble. It seemed each moment there would be a splendid view. The view never came, for none of the inclines were sharp enough, and they moved over the skull for many minutes, scarcely shifting a landmark or altering the blue fringe of the distance. The spire of Salisbury did alter, but very slightly, rising and falling like the mercury in a thermometer. At the most it would be half hidden; at the least the tip would show behind the swelling barrier of earth. They passed two elder trees—a great event. The bare patch, said Stephen, was owing to the gallows. Rickie nodded. He had lost all sense of incident. In this great solitude—more solitary than any Alpine range—he and Agnes were floating alone and for ever, between the shapeless earth and the shapeless clouds. An immense silence seemed to move towards them. A lark stopped singing, and they were glad of it. They were approaching the Throne of God. The silence touched them; the earth and all danger dissolved, but ere they quite vanished Rickie heard himself saying, "Is it exactly what we intended?"

"Yes," said a man's voice; "it's the old plan." They were in another valley. Its sides were thick with trees. Down it ran another stream and another road: it, too, sheltered a string of villages. But all was richer, larger, and more beautiful—the valley of the Avon below Amesbury.

"I've been asleep!" said Rickie, in awestruck tones.

"Never!" said the other facetiously. "Pleasant dreams?"

"Perhaps—I'm really tired of apologizing to you. How long have you been holding me on?"

"All in the day's work." He gave him back the reins.

"Where's that round hill?"

"Gone where the good niggers go. I want a drink."

This is Nature's joke in Wiltshire—her one joke. You toil on windy slopes, and feel very primeval. You are miles from your fellows, and lo! a little valley full of elms and cottages. Before Rickie had waked up to it, they had stopped by a thatched public-house, and Stephen was yelling like a maniac for beer.

There was no occasion to yell. He was not very thirsty, and they were quite ready to serve him. Nor need he have drunk in the saddle, with the air of a warrior who carries important dispatches and has not the time to dismount. A real soldier, bound on a similar errand, rode up to the inn, and Stephen at first feared that he would yell louder, and was hostile. But they made friends and treated each other, and slanged the proprietor and ragged the pretty girls; while Rickie, as each wave of vulgarity burst over him, sunk his head lower and lower, and wished that the earth would swallow him up. He was only used to Cambridge, and to a very small corner of that. He and his friends there believed in free speech. But they spoke freely about generalities. They were scientific and philosophic. They would have shrunk from the empirical freedom that results from a little beer.

That was what annoyed him as he rode down the new valley with two chattering companions. He was more skilled than they were in the principles of human existence, but he was not so indecently familiar with the examples. A sordid

village scandal—such as Stephen described as a huge joke—
sprang from certain defects in human nature, with which he
was theoretically acquainted. But the example! He blushed
at it like a maiden lady, in spite of its having a parallel in a
beautiful idyll of Theocritus. Was experience going to be
such a splendid thing after all? Was the outside of houses so
very beautiful?

"That's spicy!" the soldier was saying. "Got any more
like that?"

"I'se got a pome," said Stephen, and drew a piece of
paper from his pocket. The valley had broadened. Old
Sarum rose before them, ugly and majestic.

"Write this yourself?" he asked, chuckling.

"Rather," said Stephen, lowering his head and kissing
Aeneas between the ears.

"But who's old Em'ly?" Rickie winced and frowned.

"Now you're asking."

> "Old Em'ly she limps,
> And as—"

"I am so tired," said Rickie. Why should he stand it any
longer? He would go home to the woman he loved. "Do you
mind if I give up Salisbury?"

"But we've seen nothing!" cried Stephen.

"I shouldn't enjoy anything, I am so absurdly tired."

"Left turn, then—all in the day's work." He bit at his
moustache angrily.

"Good gracious me, man!—of course I'm going back
alone. I'm not going to spoil your day. How could you think
it of me?"

Stephen gave a loud sigh of relief. "If you do want to go
home, here's your whip. Don't fall off. Say to her *you* wanted
it, or there might be ructions."

"Certainly. Thank you for your kind care of me."

> "Old Em'ly she limps,
> And as—"

Soon he was out of earshot. Soon they were lost to view. Soon they were out of his thoughts. He forgot the coarseness and the drinking and the ingratitude. A few months ago he would not have forgotten so quickly, and he might also have detected something else. But a lover is dogmatic. To him the world shall be beautiful and pure. When it is not, he ignores it.

"He's not tired," said Stephen to the soldier; "he wants his girl." And they winked at each other, and cracked jokes over the eternal comedy of love. They asked each other if they'd let a girl spoil a morning's ride. They both exhibited a profound cynicism. Stephen, who was quite without ballast, described the household at Cadover: he should say that Rickie would find Miss Pembroke kissing the footman.

"I say the footman's kissing old Em'ly."

"Jolly day," said Stephen. His voice was suddenly constrained. He was not sure whether he liked the soldier after all, nor whether he had been wise in showing him his compositions.

> "Old Em'ly she limps,
> And as I—"

"All right, Thomas. That'll do."

> "Old Em'ly—"

"I wish you'd dry up, like a good fellow. This is the lady's horse, you know, hang it, after all."

"In-deed!"

"Don't you see—when a fellow's on a horse, he can't let another fellow—kind of—don't you know?"

The man did know. "There's sense in that," he said approvingly. Peace was restored, and they would have reached Salisbury if they had not had some more beer. It unloosed the soldier's fancies, and again he spoke of old Em'ly, and recited the poem, with Aristophanic variations.

"Jolly day," repeated Stephen, with a straightening of the eyebrows and a quick glance at the other's body. He then warned him against the variations. In consequence he was accused of being a member of the Y.M.C.A. His blood boiled at this. He refuted the charge, and became great friends with the soldier, for the third time.

"Any objection to 'Sorcy Mr and Mrs Tackleton'?"

"Rather not."

The soldier sang "Saucy Mr and Mrs Tackleton". It is really a work for two voices, most of the sauciness disappearing when taken as a solo. Nor is Mrs Tackleton's name Em'ly.

"I call it a jolly rotten song," said Stephen crossly. "I won't stand being got at."

"P'r'aps y'like therold songs. Lishen.

> "Of all the gulls that arsshmart,
>   There's none like pretty—Em'ly;
> For she's the darling of merart—"

"Now, that's wrong." He rode up close to the singer.

"Shright."

"'Tisn't."

"It's as my mother taught me."

"I don't care."

"I'll not alter from mother's way."

Stephen was baffled. Then he said, "How does your mother make it rhyme?"

"Wot?"

"Squat. You're an ass, and I'm not. Poems want rhymes. 'Alley' comes next line."

He said "alley" was —— welcome to come if it liked.

"It can't. You want Sally. Sally—alley. Em'ly—alley doesn't do."

"Emily—femily!" cried the soldier, with an inspiration that was not his when sober. "My mother taught me femily.

> "For she's the darling of merart,
>   And she lives in my femily."

"Well, you'd best be careful, Thomas, and your mother too."

"*Your* mother's no better than she should be," said Thomas vaguely.

"Do you think I haven't heard that before?" retorted the boy.

The other concluded he might now say anything. So he might—the name of old Emily excepted. Stephen cared little about his benefactress's honour, but a great deal about his own. He had made Mrs Failing into a test. For the moment he would die for her, as a knight would die for a glove. He is not to be distinguished from a hero.

Old Sarum was passed. They approached the most beautiful spire in the world. "Lord! another of these large churches!" said the soldier. Unfriendly to Gothic, he lifted both hands to his nose, and declared that old Em'ly was buried there. He lay in the mud. His horse trotted back towards Amesbury. Stephen had twisted him out of the saddle.

"I've done him!" he yelled, though no one was there to hear. He rose up in his stirrups and shouted with joy. He flung his arms round Aeneas's neck. The elderly horse understood, capered, and bolted. It was a centaur that dashed into Salisbury and scattered the people. In the stable he would not dismount. "I've done him!" he yelled to the ostlers—apathetic men. Stretching upwards, he clung to a beam. Aeneas moved on and he was left hanging. Greatly did he incommode them by his exercises. He pulled up, he circled, he kicked the other customers. At last he fell to the earth, deliciously fatigued. His body worried him no longer.

He went, like the baby he was, to buy a white linen hat. There were soldiers about, and he thought it would disguise him. Then he had a little lunch to steady the beer. This day had turned out admirably. All the money that should have fed Rickie he could spend on himself. Instead of toiling over the Cathedral and seeing the stuffed penguins, he could stop the whole time in the cattle market. There he met and made some friends. He watched the cheap-jacks, and saw how necessary it was to have a confident manner. He spoke confidently himself about lambs, and people listened. He spoke confidently about pigs, and they roared with laughter. He must learn more about pigs. He witnessed a performance—not too namby-pamby—of Punch and Judy. "Hullo, Podge!" cried a naughty little girl. He tried to catch her, and failed. She was one of the Cadford children. For Salisbury on market day, though it is not picturesque, is certainly representative, and you read the names of half the Wiltshire villages upon the carriers' carts. He found, in Penny Farthing Street, the cart from Wintersbridge. It would not start for several hours, but the passengers always used it as a club, and sat in it every now and then during the day. No less than three ladies were there now, staring at the shafts. One of them was Flea Thompson's girl. He asked her, quite politely, why her lover had broken faith with him in the rain. She was silent. He warned her of approaching vengeance. She was still silent, but another woman hoped that a gentleman would not be hard on a poor person. Something in this annoyed him; it wasn't a question of gentility and poverty—it was a question of two men. He determined to go back by Cadbury Rings, where the shepherd would now be.

He did. But this part must be treated lightly. He rode up to the culprit with the air of a Saint George, spoke a few stern words from the saddle, tethered his steed to a hurdle, and took off his coat. "Are you ready?" he asked.

"Yes, sir," said Flea, and flung him on his back.

"That's not fair," he protested.

The other did not reply, but flung him on his head.

"How on earth did you learn that?"

"By trying often," said Flea.

Stephen sat on the ground, picking mud out of his forehead. "I meant it to be fists," he said gloomily.

"I know, sir."

"It's jolly smart though, and—and I beg your pardon all round." It cost him a great deal to say this, but he was sure that it was the right thing to say. He must acknowledge the better man. Whereas most people, if they provoke a fight and are flung, say, "You cannot rob me of my moral victory."

There was nothing further to be done. He mounted again, not exactly depressed, but feeling that this delightful world is extraordinarily unreliable. He had never expected to fling the soldier, or to be flung by Flea. "One nips or is nipped," he thought, "and never knows beforehand. I should not be surprised if many people had more in them than I suppose, while others were just the other way round. I haven't seen that sort of thing in Ingersoll, but it's quite important." Then his thoughts turned to a curious incident of long ago, when he had been "nipped"—as a little boy. He was trespassing in those woods, when he met in a narrow glade a flock of sheep. They had neither dog nor shepherd, and advanced towards him silently. He was accustomed to sheep, but had never happened to meet them in a wood before, and disliked it. He retired, slowly at first, then fast; and the flock, in a dense mass, pressed after him. His terror increased. He turned and screamed at their long white faces; and still they came on, all stuck together, like some horrible jelly. If once he got into them! Bellowing and screeching, he rushed into the undergrowth, tore himself all over, and reached home in convulsions. Mr Failing, his only grown-up friend, was sympathetic, but quite stupid. "Pan ovium custos," he remarked as he pulled out the thorns. "Why not?" "Pan ovium custos." Stephen learnt the meaning of the phrase at school. "A pan of eggs for custard." He still remembered how the other boys looked as he peeped at them between his legs, awaiting the descending cane.

So he returned, full of pleasant disconnected thoughts. He had had a rare good time. He liked everyone—even that poor little Elliot—and yet no one mattered. They were all out. On the landing he saw the new housemaid. He felt skittish and irresistible. Should he slip his arm round her waist? Perhaps better not; she might box his ears. And he wanted to smoke on the roof before dinner. So he only said, "Please will you stop the boy blacking my brown boots," and she, with downcast eyes, answered, "Yes, sir; I will indeed."

His room was in the pediment. Classical architecture, like all things in this world that attempt serenity, is bound to have its lapses into the undignified, and Cadover lapsed hopelessly when it came to Stephen's room. It gave him one round window, to see through which he must lie upon his stomach, one trapdoor opening upon the leads, three iron girders, three beams, six buttresses, no ceiling, unless you count the walls, no walls unless you count the ceiling, and in its embarrassment presented him with the gurgly cistern that supplied the bath water. Here he lived, absolutely happy, and unaware that Mrs Failing had poked him up here on purpose, to prevent him from growing too bumptious. Here he worked and sang and practised on the ocharoon. Here, in the crannies, he had constructed shelves and cupboards and useless little drawers. He had only one picture—the Demeter of Cnidus—and she hung straight from the roof like a joint of meat. Once she was in the drawing-room; but Mrs Failing had got tired of her, and decreed her removal and this degradation. Now she faced the sunrise; and when the moon rose its light also fell on her, and trembled, like light upon the sea. For she was never still, and if the draught increased she would twist on her string, and would sway and tap upon the rafters until Stephen woke up and said what he thought of her. "Want your nose?" he would murmur. "Don't you wish you may get it." Then he drew the clothes over his ears, while above him, in the wind and the darkness, the goddess continued her motions.

Today, as he entered, he trod on the pile of sixpenny reprints. Leighton had brought them up. He looked at the portraits on their covers, and began to think that these people were not everything. What a fate, to look like Colonel Ingersoll, or to marry Mrs Julia P. Chunk! The Demeter turned towards him as he bathed, and in the cold water he sang—

> "They aren't beautiful, they aren't modest;
> I'd just as soon follow an old stone goddess"—

and sprang upward through the skylight onto the roof.

Years ago, when a nurse was washing him, he had slipped from her soapy hands and got up here. She implored him to remember that he was a little gentleman; but he forgot the fact—if it was a fact—and not even the butler could get him down. Mr Failing, who was sitting alone in the garden too ill to read, heard a shout, "Am I an acro-ter-ium?" He looked up and saw a naked child poised on the summit of Cadover. "Yes," he replied; "but they are unfashionable. Go in," and the vision had remained with him as something peculiarly gracious. He felt that nonsense and beauty have close connections—closer connections than Art will allow—and that both would remain when his own heaviness and his own ugliness had perished. Mrs Failing found in his remains a sentence that puzzled her. "I see the respectable mansion. I see the smug fortress of culture. The doors are shut. The windows are shut. But on the roof the children go dancing for ever."

Stephen was a child no longer. He never stood on the pediment now, except for a bet. He never, or scarcely ever, poured water down the chimneys. When he caught the cat, he seldom dropped her into the housekeeper's bedroom. But still, when the weather was fair, he liked to come up after bathing, and get dry in the sun. Today he brought with him a towel, a pipe of tobacco, and Rickie's story. He must get it done sometime, and he was tired of the sixpenny reprints. The sloping gable was warm, and he lay back on it with closed eyes, gasping for pleasure. Starlings criticized him, soots fell on his clean body, and over him a little cloud was tinged with the colours of evening. "Good! good!" he whispered. "Good, oh good!" and opened the manuscript reluctantly.

What a production! Who was this girl? Where did she go to? Why so much talk about trees? "I take it he wrote it when feeling bad," he murmured, and let it fall into the gutter. It fell face downwards, and on the back he saw a neat little resumé in Miss Pembroke's handwriting, intended for such as him. "Allegory. Man = modern civilization (in bad sense). Girl = getting into touch with Nature."

In touch with Nature! The girl was a tree! He lit his pipe and gazed at the radiant earth. The foreground was hidden, but there was the village with its elms, and the Roman Road, and Cadbury Rings. There, too, were those woods, and little beech copses, crowning a waste of down. Not to mention the air, or the sun, or water. Good, oh good!

In touch with Nature! What cant would the books think of next? His eyes closed. He was sleepy. Good, oh good! Sighing into his pipe, he fell asleep.

Chapter 13

Glad as Agnes was when her lover returned for lunch, she was at the same time rather dismayed: she knew that Mrs Failing would not like her plans altered. And her dismay was justified. Their hostess was a little stiff, and asked whether Stephen had been obnoxious.

"Indeed he hasn't. He spent the whole time looking after me."

"From which I conclude he was more obnoxious than usual."

Rickie praised him diligently. But his candid nature showed everything through. His aunt soon saw that they had not got on. She had expected this—almost planned it. Nevertheless she resented it, and her resentment was to fall on him.

The storm gathered slowly, and many other things went to swell it. Weakly people, if they are not careful, hate one another, and when the weakness is hereditary the temptation increases. Elliots had never got on among themselves. They talked of "The Family", but they always turned outwards to the health and beauty that lie so promiscuously about the world. Rickie's father had turned, for a time at all events, to his mother. Rickie himself was turning to Agnes. And Mrs Failing now was irritable, and unfair to the nephew who was lame like her horrible brother and like herself. She thought him invertebrate and conventional. She was envious of his happiness. She did not trouble to understand his art. She longed to shatter him, but knowing as she did that the human thunderbolt often rebounds and strikes the wielder, she held her hand.

Agnes watched the approaching clouds. Rickie had warned her; now she began to warn him. As the visit wore away she urged him to be pleasant to his aunt, and so convert it into a success.

He replied, "Why need it be a success?"—a reply in the manner of Ansell.

She laughed. "Oh, that's so like you men—all theory! What about your great theory of hating no one? As soon as it comes in useful you drop it."

"I don't hate Aunt Emily. Honestly. But certainly I don't want to be near her or think about her. Don't you think there are two great things in life that we ought to aim at— truth and kindness? Let's have both if we can, but let's be sure of having one or the other. My aunt gives up both for the sake of being funny."

"And Stephen Wonham," pursued Agnes. "There's another person you hate—or don't think about, if you prefer it put like that."

"The truth is, I'm changing. I'm beginning to see that the world has many people in it who don't matter. I had time for them once. Not now." There was only one gate to the kingdom of heaven now.

Agnes surprised him by saying, "But the Wonham boy is evidently a part of your aunt's life. She laughs at him, but she is fond of him."

"What's that to do with it?"

"You ought to be pleasant to him on account of it."

"Why on earth?"

She flushed a little. "I'm old-fashioned. One ought to consider one's hostess, and fall in with her life. After we leave it's another thing. But while we take her hospitality I think it's our duty."

Her good sense triumphed. Henceforth he tried to fall in with Aunt Emily's life. Aunt Emily watched him trying. The storm broke, as storms sometimes do, on Sunday.

Sunday church was a function at Cadover, though a strange one. The pompous landau rolled up to the house at a quarter to eleven. Then Mrs Failing said, "Why am I being hurried?" and after an interval descended the steps in her ordinary clothes. She regarded the church as a sort of sitting-room, and refused even to wear a bonnet there. The village was shocked, but at the same time a little proud; it would point out the carriage to strangers and gossip about the pale smiling lady who sat in it, always alone, always late, her hair always draped in an expensive shawl.

This Sunday, though late as usual, she was not alone. Miss Pembroke, *en grande toilette*, sat by her side. Rickie, looking plain and devout, perched opposite. And Stephen actually came too, murmuring that it would be the Benedicite, which he had never minded. There was also the Litany, which drove him into the air again, much to Mrs Failing's delight. She enjoyed this sort of thing. It amused her when her protégé left the pew, looking bored, athletic, and dishevelled, and groping most obviously for his pipe. She liked to keep a thoroughbred pagan to shock people. "He's gone to worship Nature," she whispered. Rickie did not look up. "Don't you think he's charming?" He made no reply. "Charming," whispered Agnes over his head.

During the sermon she analysed her guests. Miss Pembroke—undistinguished, unimaginative, tolerable. Rickie—intolerable. "And how pedantic!" she mused. "He smells of the University library. If he was stupid in the right way he would be a don." She looked round the tiny church; at the whitewashed pillars, the humble pavement, the window full of magenta saints. There was the vicar's wife. And Mrs Wilbraham's bonnet. Ugh! The rest of the congregation were poor women, with flat, hopeless faces—she saw them Sunday after Sunday, but did not know their names—diversified with a few reluctant ploughboys, and the vile little school children, row upon row. "Ugh! what a hole," thought Mrs Failing, whose Christianity was of the type best described as "cathedral". "What a hole for a cultured woman! I don't think it has blunted my sensations, though; I still see its squalor as clearly as ever. And my nephew pretends he is worshipping. Pah! the hypocrite." Above her the vicar spoke of the danger of hurrying from one dissipation to another. She treasured his words, and continued: "I cannot stand smugness. It is the one, the unpardonable sin. Fresh air! The fresh air that has made Stephen Wonham fresh and companionable and strong. Even if it kills, I will let in the fresh air."

Thus reasoned Mrs Failing, in the facile vein of Ibsenism.

She imagined herself to be a cold-eyed Scandinavian heroine. Really she was an English old lady, who did not mind giving other people a chill provided it was not infectious.

Agnes, on the way back, noted that her hostess was a little snappish. But one is so hungry after morning service, and either so hot or so cold, that he would be a saint indeed who becomes a saint at once. Mrs Failing, after asserting vindictively that it was impossible to make a living out of literature, was courteously left alone. Roast beef and moselle might yet work miracles, and Agnes still hoped for the introductions— the introductions to certain editors and publishers—on which her whole diplomacy was bent. Rickie would not push himself. It was his besetting sin. Well for him that he would have a wife, and a loving wife, who knew the value of enterprise.

Unfortunately lunch was a quarter of an hour late, and during that quarter of an hour the aunt and the nephew quarrelled. She had been inveighing against the morning service, and he quietly and deliberately replied, "If organized religion is anything—and it is something to me—it will not be wrecked by a harmonium and a dull sermon."

Mrs Failing frowned. "I envy you. It is a great thing to have no sense of beauty."

"I think I have a sense of beauty, which leads me astray if I am not careful."

"But this is a great relief to me. I thought the present-day young man was an agnostic! Isn't agnosticism all the thing at Cambridge?"

"Nothing is the 'thing' at Cambridge. If a few men are agnostic there, it is for some grave reason, not because they are irritated with the way the parson says his vowels."

Agnes intervened. "Well, I side with Aunt Emily. I believe in ritual."

"Don't, my dear, side with me. He will only say you have no sense of religion either."

"Excuse me," said Rickie—perhaps he too was a little hungry—"I never suggested such a thing. I never would suggest such a thing. Why cannot you understand my position? I almost feel it is that you won't."

"I try to understand your position night and day, dear—what you mean, what you like, why you came to Cadover, and why you stop here when my presence is so obviously unpleasing to you."

"Luncheon is served," said Leighton, but he said it too late. They discussed the beef and the moselle in silence. The air was heavy and ominous. Even the Wonham boy was affected by it, shivered at times, choked once, and hastened anew into the sun. He could not understand clever people.

Agnes, in a brief anxious interview, advised the culprit to take a solitary walk. She would stop near Aunt Emily, and pave the way for an apology.

"Don't worry too much. It doesn't really matter."

"I suppose not, dear. But it seems a pity, considering we are so near the end of our visit."

"Rudeness and crossness matter, and I've shown both, and already I'm sorry, and hope she'll let me apologize. But from the selfish point of view it doesn't matter a straw. She's no more to us than the Wonham boy or the boot boy."

"Which way will you walk?"

"I think to that entrenchment. Look at it." They were sitting on the steps. He stretched out his hand to Cadbury Rings, and then let it rest for a moment on her shoulder. "You're changing me," he said gently. "God bless you for it."

He enjoyed his walk. Cadford was a charming village, and for a time he hung over the bridge by the mill. So clear was the stream that it seemed not water at all, but some invisible quintessence in which the happy minnows and the weeds were vibrating. And he paused again at the Roman crossing, and thought for a moment of the unknown child. The line curved suddenly: certainly it was dangerous. Then he lifted his eyes to the down. The entrenchment showed like the rim of a saucer, and over its narrow line peeped the summit of the central tree. It looked interesting. He hurried forward, with the wind behind him.

The Rings were curious rather than impressive. Neither embankment was over twelve feet high, and the grass on them had not the exquisite green of Old Sarum, but was gray and wiry. But Nature (if she arranges anything) had arranged that from them, at all events, there should be a view. The whole system of the country lay spread before Rickie, and he gained an idea of it that he never got in his elaborate ride. He saw how all the water converges at Salisbury; how Salisbury lies in a shallow basin, just at the change of the soil. He saw to the north the Plain, and the stream of the Cad flowing down from it, with a tributary that broke out suddenly, as the chalk streams do: one village had clustered round the source and clothed itself with trees. He saw Old Sarum, and hints of the Avon valley, and the land above Stonehenge. And behind him he saw the great wood beginning unobtrusively, as if the down too needed shaving; and into it the road to London slipped, covering the bushes with white dust. Chalk made the dust white, chalk made the water clear, chalk made the clean rolling outlines of the land, and favoured the grass and the distant coronals of trees. Here is the heart of our island: the Chilterns, the North Downs, the South Downs radiate hence. The fibres of England unite in Wiltshire, and did we condescend to worship her, here we should erect our national shrine.

People at that time were trying to think imperially. Rickie wondered how they did it, for he could not imagine a place larger than England. And other people talked of Italy, the spiritual fatherland of us all. Perhaps Italy would prove marvellous. But at present he conceived it as something exotic, to be admired and reverenced, but not to be loved like these unostentatious fields. He drew out a book—it was natural for him to read when he was happy, and to read out loud—and for a little time his voice disturbed the silence of that glorious afternoon. The book was Shelley, and it opened at a passage that he had cherished greatly two years before, and marked as "very good".

> I never was attached to that great sect
> Whose doctrine is that each one should select
> Out of the world a mistress or a friend,
> And all the rest, though fair and wise, commend
> To cold oblivion—though it is the code
> Of modern morals, and the beaten road

Which those poor slaves with weary footsteps tread
Who travel to their home among the dead
By the broad highway of the world—and so
With one sad friend, perhaps a jealous foe,
The dreariest and the longest journey go.

It was "very good"—fine poetry, and, in a sense, true. Yet he was surprised that he had ever selected it so vehemently. This afternoon it seemed a little inhuman. Half a mile off two lovers were keeping company where all the villagers could see them. They cared for no one else; they felt only the pressure of each other, and so progressed, silent and oblivious, across the land. He felt them to be nearer the truth than Shelley. Even if they suffered or quarrelled, they would have been nearer the truth. He wondered whether they were Henry Adams and Jessica Thompson, both of this parish, whose banns had been asked, for the second time, in the church this morning. Why could he not marry on fifteen shillings a week? And he looked at them with respect, and wished that he was not a cumbersome gentleman.

Presently he saw something less pleasant—his aunt's pony carriage. It had crossed the railway, and was advancing up the Roman road along by the straw stacks. His impulse was to retreat, but someone waved to him. It was Agnes. She waved continually, as much as to say, "Wait for us." Mrs Failing herself raised the whip in a nonchalant way. Stephen Wonham was following on foot, some way behind. He put the Shelley back into his pocket and waited for them. When the carriage stopped by some hurdles he went down from the embankment and helped them to dismount. He felt rather nervous.

His aunt gave him one of her disquieting smiles, but said pleasantly enough, "Aren't the Rings a little immense? Agnes and I came here because we wanted an antidote to the morning service."

"Pang!" said the church bell suddenly; "pang! pang!" It sounded petty and ludicrous. They all laughed. Rickie blushed, and Agnes, with a glance that said "apologize", darted away to the entrenchment, as though unable to restrain her curiosity.

"The pony won't move," said Mrs Failing. "Leave him for Stephen to tie up. Will you walk me to the tree in the middle? Booh! I'm tired. Give me your arm—unless you're tired as well."

"No. I came out partly in the hope of helping you."

"How sweet of you." She contrasted his blatant unselfishness with the hardness of Stephen. Stephen never came out to help you. But if you got hold of him he was some good. He didn't wobble and bend at the critical moment. Her fancy compared Rickie to the cracked church bell sending forth its message of "Pang! pang!" to the countryside, and Stephen to the young pagans who were said to lie under this field guarding their pagan gold.

"This place is full of ghosties," she remarked; "have you seen any yet?"

"I've kept on the outer rim so far."

"Let's go to the tree in the centre."

"Here's the path." The bank of grass where he had sat was broken by a gap, through which chariots had entered, and farm carts entered now. The track, following the ancient track, led straight through turnips to a similar gap in the second circle, and thence continued, through more turnips, to the central tree.

"Pang!" said the bell, as they paused at the entrance.

"You needn't unharness," shouted Mrs Failing, for Stephen was approaching the carriage.

"Yes, I will," he retorted.

"You will, will you?" she murmured with a smile. "I wish your brother wasn't quite so uppish. Let's get on. Doesn't that church distract you?"

"It's so faint here," said Rickie. And it sounded fainter inside, though the earthwork was neither thick nor tall; and the view, though not hidden, was greatly diminished. He was reminded for a moment of that chalk pit near Madingley, whose ramparts excluded the familiar world. Agnes was here, as she had once been there. She stood on the farther barrier, waiting to receive them when they had traversed the heart of the camp.

"Admire my mangel-wurzels," said Mrs Failing. "They are said to grow so splendidly on account of the dead soldiers. Isn't it a sweet thought? Need I say it is your brother's?"

"Wonham's—?" he suggested. It was the second time that she had made the little slip. She nodded, and he asked her what kind of ghosties haunted this curious field.

"The D.," was her prompt reply. "He leans against the tree in the middle, especially on Sunday afternoons, and all his worshippers rise through the turnips and dance round him."

"Oh, these were decent people," he replied, looking downwards—"soldiers and shepherds. They have no ghosts. They worshipped Mars or Pan—Erda perhaps; not the devil."

"Pang!" went the church, and was silent, for the afternoon service had begun. They entered the second entrenchment, which was in height, breadth, and composition similar to the first, and excluded still more of the view. His aunt continued friendly. Agnes stood watching them.

"Soldiers may seem decent in the past," she continued, "but wait till they turn into Tommies from Bulford Camp, who rob the chickens."

"I don't mind Bulford Camp," said Rickie, looking, though in vain, for signs of its snowy tents. "The men there are the sons of the men here, and have come back to the old country. War's horrible, yet one loves all continuity. And no one could mind a shepherd."

"Indeed! What about your brother—a shepherd if ever there was? Look how he bores you! Don't be so sentimental."

"But—oh, you mean—"

"Your brother Stephen."

He glanced at her nervously. He had never known her so queer before. Perhaps it was some literary allusion that he had not caught; but her face did not at that moment suggest literature. In the deferential tones that one uses to an old and infirm person he said, "Stephen Wonham isn't my brother, Aunt Emily."

"My dear, you're that precise. One can't say 'half-brother' every time."

They approached the central tree.

"How you do puzzle me," he said, dropping her arm and beginning to laugh. "How could I have a half-brother?"

She made no answer.

Then a horror leapt straight at him, and he beat it back and said, "I will not be frightened." The tree in the centre revolved, the tree disappeared, and he saw a room—the room where his father had lived in town. "Gently," he told himself, "gently."

Still laughing, he said, "I, with a brother—younger—it's not possible." The horror leapt again, and he exclaimed, "It's a foul lie!"

"My dear, my dear!"

"It's a foul lie! He wasn't—I won't stand—"

"My dear, before you say several noble things remember that it's worse for him than for you—worse for your brother, for your half-brother, for your younger brother."

But he heard her no longer. He was gazing at the past, which he had praised so recently, which gaped ever wider, like an unhallowed grave. Turn where he would, it encircled him. It took visible form: it was this double entrenchment of the Rings. His mouth went cold, and he knew that he was going to faint among the dead. He started running, missed the exit, stumbled on the inner barrier, fell into darkness—

"Get his head down," said a voice. "Get the blood back into him. That's all he wants. Leave him to me. Elliot!"— the blood was returning—"Elliot, wake up!"

He woke up. The earth he had dreaded lay close to his eyes, and seemed beautiful. He saw the structure of the clods. A tiny beetle swung on a grass blade. On his own neck a human hand pressed, guiding the blood back to his brain.

There broke from him a cry, not of horror but of acceptance. For one short moment he understood. "Stephen—" he began, and then he heard his own name called: "Rickie! Rickie!" Agnes had hurried from her post on the margin, and, as if understanding also, caught him to her breast.

Stephen offered to help them further, but finding that he

made things worse, he stepped aside to let them pass and then sauntered inwards. The whole field, with its concentric circles, was visible, and the broad leaves of the turnips rustled in the gathering wind. Miss Pembroke and Elliot were moving towards the Cadover entrance. Mrs Failing stood watching in her turn on the opposite bank. He was not an inquisitive boy; but as he leant against the tree he wondered what it was all about, and whether he would ever know.

Chapter 14

On the way back—at that very level-crossing where he had
paused on his upward route—Rickie stopped suddenly and
told the girl why he had fainted. Hitherto she had asked
him in vain. His tone had gone from him, and he told her
harshly and brutally, so that she started away with a horrified cry. Then his manner altered, and he exclaimed: "Will
you mind? Are you going to mind?"

"Of course I mind," she whispered. She turned from him,
and saw up on the skyline two figures that seemed to be of
enormous size.

"They're watching us. They stand on the edge watching
us. This country's so open—you—you can't—they watch us
wherever we go. Of course you mind."

They heard the rumble of the train, and she pulled herself
together. "Come, dearest, we shall be run over next. We're
saying things that have no sense." But on the way back he
repeated: "They can still see us. They can see every inch of
this road. They watch us for ever." And when they arrived
at the steps, there, sure enough, were still the two figures
gazing from the outer circle of the Rings.

She made him go to his room at once: he was almost
hysterical. Leighton brought out some tea for her, and she
sat drinking it on the little terrace. Of course she minded.
Again she was menaced by the abnormal. All had seemed so
fair and so simple, so in accordance with her ideas; and
then, like a corpse, this horror rose up to the surface. She
saw the two figures descend and pause while one of them
harnessed the pony; she saw them drive downward, and
knew that before long she must face them and the world.
She glanced at her engagement-ring.

When the carriage drove up Mrs Failing dismounted, but
did not speak. It was Stephen who inquired after Rickie.

She, scarcely knowing the sound of her own voice, replied that he was a little tired.

"Go and put up the pony," said Mrs Failing rather sharply. "Agnes, give me some tea."

"It is rather strong," said Agnes as the carriage drove off and left them alone. Then she noticed that Mrs Failing herself was agitated. Her lips were trembling, and she saw the boy depart with manifest relief.

"Do you know," she said hurriedly, as if talking against time—"do you know what upset Rickie?"

"I do indeed know."

"Has he told anyone else?"

"I believe not."

"Agnes—have I been a fool?"

"You have been very unkind," said the girl, and her eyes filled with tears.

For a moment Mrs Failing was annoyed. "Unkind? I do not see that at all. I believe in looking facts in the face. Rickie must know his ghosts sometime. Why not this afternoon?"

She rose with quiet dignity, but her tears came faster. "That is not so. You told him to hurt him. I cannot think what you did it for. I suppose because he was rude to you after church. It is a mean, cowardly revenge."

"What—what if it's a lie?"

"Then, Mrs Failing, it is sickening of you. There is no other word. Sickening. I am sorry—a nobody like myself— to speak like this. How *could* you, oh, how could you demean yourself? Why, not even a poor person—" Her indignation was fine and genuine. But her tears fell no longer. Nothing menaced her if they were not really brothers.

"It is not a lie, my dear; sit down. I will swear so much solemnly. It is not a lie, but—"

Agnes waited.

"—we can call it a lie if we choose."

"I am not so childish. You have said it, and we must all suffer. You have had your fun: I conclude you did it for fun. You cannot go back. He—" She pointed towards the stables, and could not finish her sentence.

"I have not been a fool twice."

Agnes did not understand.

"My dense lady, can't you follow? I have not told Stephen one single word, neither before nor now."

There was a long silence.

Indeed, Mrs Failing was in an awkward position. Rickie had irritated her, and, in her desire to shock him, she had imperilled her own peace. She had felt so unconventional up on the hillside, when she loosed the horror against him; but now it was darting at her as well. Suppose the scandal out. Stephen, who was absolutely without delicacy, would tell it to people as soon as tell them the time. His paganism would be too assertive; it might even be in bad taste. After all, she held a prominent position in the neighbourhood; she was talked about, respected, looked up to. After all, she was growing old. And therefore, though she had no true regard for Rickie, nor for Agnes, nor for Stephen, nor for Stephen's parents, in whose tragedy she had assisted, yet she did feel that if the scandal revived it would disturb the harmony of Cadover, and therefore tried to retrace her steps. It is easy to say shocking things: it is so different to be connected with anything shocking. Life and death were not involved, but comfort and discomfort were.

The silence was broken by the sound of feet on the gravel. Agnes said hastily, "Is that really true—that he knows nothing?"

"You, Rickie, and I are the only people alive that know. He realizes what he is—with a precision that is sometimes alarming. Who he is, he doesn't know and doesn't care. I suppose he would know when I'm dead. There are papers."

"Aunt Emily, before he comes, may I say to you I'm sorry I was so rude?"

Mrs Failing had not disliked her courage. "My dear, you may. We're all off our hinges this Sunday. Sit down by me again."

Agnes obeyed, and they awaited the arrival of Stephen. They were clever enough to understand each other. The thing must be hushed up. The matron must repair the consequences of her petulance. The girl must hide the stain in her future husband's family. Why not? Who was injured? What does a grown-up man want with a grown-up brother? Rickie upstairs, how grateful he would be to them for saving him.

"Stephen!"

"Yes."

"I'm tired of you. Go and bathe in the sea."

"All right."

And the whole thing was settled. She liked no fuss, and so did he. He sat down on the step to tighten his bootlaces. Then he would be ready. Mrs Failing laid two or three sovereigns on the step above him. Agnes tried to make conversation, and said, with averted eyes, that the sea was a long way off.

"The sea's downhill. That's all I know about it." He swept up the money with a word of pleasure: he was kept like a baby in such things. Then he started off, but slowly, for he meant to walk till the morning.

"He will be gone days," said Mrs Failing. "The comedy is finished. Let us come in."

She went to her room. The storm that she had raised had shattered her. Yet, because it was stilled for a moment, she resumed her old emancipated manner, and spoke of it as a comedy.

As for Miss Pembroke, she pretended to be emancipated no longer. People like "Stephen Wonham" were social thunderbolts, to be shunned at all costs, or at almost all costs. Her joy was now unfeigned, and she hurried upstairs to impart it to Rickie.

"I don't think we are rewarded if we do right, but we are punished if we lie. It's the fashion to laugh at poetic justice, but I do believe in half of it. Cast bitter bread upon the waters, and after many days it really will come back to you." These were the words of Mr Failing. They were also the opinions of Stewart Ansell, another unpractical person. Rickie was trying to write to him when she entered with the good news.

"Dear, we're saved! He doesn't know, and he never is to know. I can't tell you how glad I am. All the time we saw

135

them standing together up there, she wasn't telling him at all. She was keeping him out of the way, in case you let it out. Oh, I like her! She may be unwise, but she is nice, really. She said, 'I've been a fool, but I haven't been a fool twice.' You must forgive her, Rickie. I've forgiven her, and she me; for at first I was so angry with her. Oh, my darling boy, I am so glad!"

He was shivering all over, and could not reply. At last he said, "Why hasn't she told him?"

"Because she has come to her senses."

"But she can't behave to people like that. She must tell him."

"Why?"

"Because he must be told such a real thing."

"Such a real thing?" the girl echoed, screwing up her forehead. "But—but you don't mean you're glad about it?"

His head bowed over the letter. "My God—no! But it's a real thing. She must tell him. I nearly told him myself—up there—when he made me look at the ground, but you happened to prevent me."

How Providence had watched over them!

"She won't tell him. I know that much."

"Then, Agnes, darling"—he drew her to the table—"we must talk together a little. If she won't, then we ought to."

"*We* tell him?" cried the girl, white with horror. "Tell him now, when everything has been comfortably arranged?"

"You see, darling"—he took hold of her hand—"what one must do is to think the thing out and settle what's right. I'm still all trembling and stupid. I see it mixed up with other things. I want you to help me. It seems to me that here and there in life we meet with a person or incident that is symbolical. It's nothing in itself, yet for the moment it stands for some eternal principle. We accept it, at whatever cost, and we have accepted life. But if we are frightened and reject it, the moment, so to speak, passes; the symbol is never offered again. Is this nonsense? Once before a symbol was offered to me—I shall not tell you how; but I did accept it, and cherished it through much anxiety and repulsion, and in the end I am rewarded. There will be no reward this time, I think, from such a man—the son of such a man. But I want to do what is right."

"Because doing right is its own reward," said Agnes anxiously.

"I do not think that. I have seen few examples of it. Doing right is simply doing right."

"I think that all you say is wonderfully clever; but since you ask me, it *is* nonsense, dear Rickie, absolutely."

"Thank you," he said humbly, and began to stroke her hand. "But all my disgust; my indignation with my father, my love for—" He broke off; he could not bear to mention the name of his mother. "I was trying to say, I oughtn't to follow these impulses too much. There are other things. Truth. Our duty to acknowledge each man accurately, however vile he is. And apart from ideals" (here she had won the battle)—"and leaving ideals aside, I couldn't meet him and keep silent. It isn't in me. I should blurt it out."

"But you won't meet him!" she cried. "It's all been arranged. We've sent him to the sea. Isn't it splendid? He's gone. My own boy won't be fantastic, will he?" Then she fought the fantasy on its own ground. "And, by the bye, what you call the 'symbolic moment' is over. You had it up by the Rings. You tried to tell him. I interrupted you. It's not your fault. You did all you could."

She thought this excellent logic, and was surprised that he looked so gloomy. "So he's gone to the sea. For the present that does settle it. Has Aunt Emily talked about him yet?"

"No. Ask her tomorrow if you wish to know. Ask her kindly. It would be so dreadful if you did not part friends, and—"

"What's that?"

It was Stephen calling up from the drive. He had come back. Agnes threw out her hand in despair.

"Elliot!" the voice called.

They were facing each other, silent and motionless. Then Rickie advanced to the window. The girl darted in front of him. He thought he had never seen her so beautiful. She was stopping his advance quite frankly, with widespread arms.

"Elliot!"

He moved forward—into what? He pretended to himself he would rather see his brother before he answered; that it was easier to acknowledge him thus. But at the back of his soul he knew that the woman had conquered, and that he was moving forward to acknowledge her. "If he calls me again—" he thought.

"Elliot!"

"Well, if he calls me once again, I will answer him, vile as he is."

He did not call again.

Stephen had really come back for some tobacco, but as he passed under the windows he thought of the poor fellow who had been "nipped" (nothing serious, said Mrs Failing), and determined to shout goodbye to him. And once or twice, as he followed the river into darkness, he wondered what it was like to be so weak—not to ride, not to swim, not to care for anything but books and a girl.

They embraced passionately. The danger had brought them very near to each other. They both needed a home to confront the menacing tumultuous world. And what weary years of work, of waiting, lay between them and that home! Still holding her fast, he said, "I was writing to Ansell when you came in."

"Do you owe him a letter?"

"No." He paused. "I was writing to tell him about this. He would help us. He always picks out the important point."

"Darling, I don't like to say anything, and I know that Mr Ansell would keep a secret, but haven't we picked out the important point for ourselves?"

He released her and tore the letter up.

Chapter 15

The sense of purity is a puzzling, and at times a fearful thing. It seems so noble, and it starts at one with morality. But it is a dangerous guide, and can lead us away not only from what is gracious, but also from what is good. Agnes, in this tangle, had followed it blindly, partly because she was a woman, and it meant more to her than it can ever mean to a man; partly because, though dangerous, it is also obvious, and makes no demand upon the intellect. She could not feel that Stephen had full human rights. He was illicit, abnormal, worse than a man diseased. And Rickie, remembering whose son he was, gradually adopted her opinion. He, too, came to be glad that his brother had passed from him untried, that the symbolic moment had been rejected. Stephen was the fruit of sin; therefore he was sinful. He, too, became a sexual snob.

And now he must hear the unsavoury details. That evening they sat in the walled garden. Agnes, according to arrangement, left him alone with his aunt. He asked her, and was not answered.

"You are shocked," she said in a hard, mocking voice. "It is very nice of you to be shocked, and I do not wish to grieve you further. We will not allude to it again. Let us all go on just as we are. The comedy is finished."

He could not tolerate this. His nerves were shattered, and all that was good in him revolted as well. To the horror of Agnes, who was within earshot, he replied, "You used to puzzle me, Aunt Emily, but I understand you at last. You have forgotten what other people are like. Continual selfishness leads to that. I am sure of it. I see now how you look at the world. 'Nice of me to be shocked!' I want to go tomorrow, if I may."

"Certainly, dear. The morning trains are the best." And so the disastrous visit ended.

As he walked back to the house he met a certain poor woman, whose child Stephen had rescued at the level-crossing, and who had decided, after some delay, that she must thank the kind gentleman in person. "He has got some brute courage," thought Rickie, "and it was decent of him not to boast about it." But he had labelled the boy as "Bad", and it was convenient to revert to his good qualities as seldom as possible. He preferred to brood over his coarseness, his caddish ingratitude, his irreligion. Out of these he constructed a repulsive figure, forgetting how slovenly his own perceptions had been during the past week, how dogmatic and intolerant his attitude to all that was not Love.

During the packing he was obliged to go up to the attic to find the Dryad manuscript, which had never been returned. Leighton came too, and for about half an hour they hunted in the flickering light of a candle. It was a strange, ghostly place, and Rickie was quite startled when a picture swung towards him, and he saw the Demeter of Cnidus, shimmering and gray. Leighton suggested the roof: Mr Stephen sometimes left things on the roof. So they climbed out of the skylight—the night was perfectly still—and continued the search among the gables. Enormous stars hung overhead, and the roof was bounded by chasms, impenetrable and black. "It doesn't matter," said Rickie, suddenly convinced of the futility of all that he did. "Oh, let us look properly," said Leighton, a kindly, pliable man, who had tried to shirk coming, but who was genuinely sympathetic now that he had come. They were rewarded: the manuscript lay in a gutter, charred and smudged.

The rest of the year was spent by Rickie partly in bed—he had a curious breakdown—partly in the attempt to get his little stories published. He had written eight or nine, and hoped they would make up a book, and that the book might be called *Pan Pipes*. He was very energetic over this; he liked to work, for some imperceptible bloom had passed from the world, and he no longer found such acute pleasure in people. Mr Failing's old publishers, to whom the book was submitted, replied that, greatly as they found themselves interested, they did not see their way to making an offer at present. They were very polite, and singled out for special praise "Andante Pastorale", which Rickie had thought too sentimental, but which Agnes had persuaded him to include. The stories were sent to another publisher, who considered them for six weeks, and then returned them. A fragment of red cotton, placed by Agnes between the leaves, had not shifted its position.

"Can't you try something longer, Rickie?" she said; "I believe we're on the wrong track. Try an out-and-out love-story."

"My notion just now," he replied, "is to leave the passions on the fringe." She nodded, and tapped for the waiter: they had met in a London restaurant. "I can't soar; I can only indicate. That's where the musicians have the pull, for music has wings, and when she says 'Tristan' and he says 'Isolde', you are on the heights at once. What do people mean when they call love music artificial?"

"I know what they mean, though I can't exactly explain. Or couldn't you make your stories more obvious? I don't see any harm in that. Uncle Willie floundered hopelessly. He doesn't read much, and he got muddled. I had to explain, and then he was delighted. Of course, to write down to the public would be quite another thing and horrible. You have certain ideas, and you must express them. But couldn't you express them more clearly?"

"You see—" He got no further than "you see".

"The soul and the body. The soul's what matters," said Agnes, and tapped for the waiter again. He looked at her admiringly, but felt that she was not a perfect critic. Perhaps she was too perfect to be a critic. Actual life might seem to her so real that she could not detect the union of shadow and adamant that men call poetry. He would even go further and acknowledge that she was not as clever as himself—and he was stupid enough! She did not like discussing anything or reading solid books, and she was a little angry with such women as did. It pleased him to make these concessions, for they touched nothing in her that he valued. He looked round the restaurant, which was in Soho, and decided that she was incomparable.

"At half past two I call on the editor of the *Holborn*. He's got a stray story to look at, and he's written about it."

"Oh, Rickie! Rickie! Why didn't you put on a boiled shirt!"

He laughed, and teased her. "The soul's what matters. We literary people don't care about dress."

"Well, you ought to care. And I believe you do. Can't you change?"

"Too far." He had rooms in South Kensington. "And I've forgot my card-case. There's for you!"

She shook her head. "Naughty, naughty boy! Whatever will you do?"

"Send in my name, or ask for a bit of paper and write it. Hullo! that's Tilliard!"

Tilliard blushed, partly on account of the *faux pas* he had made last June, partly on account of the restaurant. He explained how he came to be pigging in Soho: it was so frightfully convenient and so frightfully cheap.

"Just why Rickie brings me," said Miss Pembroke.

"And I suppose you're here to study life?" said Tilliard, sitting down.

"I don't know," said Rickie, gazing round at the waiters and the guests.

"Doesn't one want to see a good deal of life for writing? There's life of a sort in Soho—*Un peu de faisan, s'il vous plait.*"

Agnes also grabbed at the waiter, and paid. She always did the paying, Rickie muddled so with his purse.

"I'm cramming," pursued Tilliard, "and so naturally I come into contact with very little at present. But later on I hope to see things." He blushed a little, for he was talking for Rickie's edification. "It is most frightfully important not to get a narrow or academic outlook, don't you think? A person like Ansell, who goes from Cambridge, home—home, Cambridge—it must tell on him in time."

"But Mr Ansell is a philosopher."

"A very kinky one," said Tilliard abruptly. "Not my idea of a philosopher. How goes his dissertation?"

"He never answers my letters," replied Rickie. "He never would. I've heard nothing since June."

"It's a pity he sends in this year. There are so many good people in. He'd have a far better chance if he waited."

"So I said, but he wouldn't wait. He's so keen about this particular subject."

"What is it?" asked Agnes.

"About things being real, wasn't it, Tilliard?"

"That's near enough."

"Well, good luck to him!" said the girl. "And good luck to you, Mr Tilliard! Later on, I hope, we'll meet again."

They parted. Tilliard liked her, though he did not feel that she was quite in his *couche sociale*. His sister, for instance, would never have been lured into a Soho restaurant—except for the experience of the thing. Tilliard's *couche sociale* permitted experiences. Provided his heart did not go out to the poor and the unorthodox, he might stare at them as much as he liked. It was seeing life.

Agnes put her lover safely into an omnibus at Cambridge Circus. She shouted after him that his tie was rising over his collar, but he did not hear her. For a moment she felt depressed, and pictured quite accurately the effect that his appearance would have on the editor. The editor was a tall neat man of forty, slow of speech, slow of soul, and extraordinarily kind. He and Rickie sat over a fire, with an enormous table behind them, whereon stood many books waiting to be reviewed.

"I'm sorry," he said, and paused.

Rickie smiled feebly.

"Your story does not convince." He tapped it. "I have read it—with very great pleasure. It convinces in parts, but it does not convince as a whole; and stories, don't you think, ought to convince as a whole?"

"They ought indeed," said Rickie, and plunged into self-depreciation. But the editor checked him.

"No—no. Please don't talk like that. I can't bear to hear anyone talk against imagination. There are countless openings for imagination—for the mysterious, for the supernatural, for all the things you are trying to do, and which, I hope, you will succeed in doing. I'm not *objecting* to imagination; on the contrary, I'd advise you to cultivate it, to accent it. Write a really good ghost story and we'd take it at once. Or"—he suggested it as an alternative to imagination—"or you might get inside life. It's worth doing."

"Life?" echoed Rickie anxiously. He looked round the pleasant room, as if life might be fluttering there, like an imprisoned bird. Then he looked at the editor; perhaps he was sitting inside life at this very moment.

"See life, Mr Elliot, and then send us another story." He held out his hand. "I am sorry I have had to say 'No, thank you'; it's so much nicer to say, 'Yes, please'." He laid his hand on the young man's sleeve, and added, "Well, the interview's not been so alarming after all, has it?"

"I don't think that either of us is a very alarming person," was not Rickie's reply. It was what he thought out afterwards in the omnibus. His reply was "Ow," delivered with a slight giggle.

As he rumbled westward, his face was drawn, and his eyes moved quickly to the right and left, as if he would discover something in the squalid fashionable streets—some bird on the wing, some radiant archway, the face of some god beneath a beaver hat. He loved, he was loved, he had seen death and other things; but the heart of all things was hidden. There was a password and he could not learn it, nor could the kind editor of the *Holborn* teach him. He sighed, and then sighed more piteously. For had he not known the password once—known it and forgotten it already?

But at this point his fortunes become intimately connected with those of Mr Pembroke.

Part 2

Sawston

Chapter 16

In three years Mr Pembroke had done much to solidify the day-boys at Sawston School. If they were not solid, they were at all events curdling, and his activities might reasonably turn elsewhere. He had served the school for many years, and it was really time he should be entrusted with a boarding-house. The headmaster, an impulsive man who darted about like a minnow and gave his mother a great deal of trouble, agreed with him, and also agreed with Mrs Jackson when she said that Mr Jackson had served the school for many years and that it was really time he should be entrusted with a boarding-house. Consequently, when Dunwood House fell vacant, the headmaster found himself in rather a difficult position.

Dunwood House was the largest and most lucrative of the boarding-houses. It stood almost opposite the school buildings. Originally it had been a villa residence—a red-brick villa, covered with creepers and crowned with terracotta dragons. Mr Annison, founder of its glory, had lived here, and had had one or two boys to live with him. Times changed. The fame of the bishops blazed brighter, the school increased, the one or two boys became a dozen, and an addition was made to Dunwood House that more than doubled its size. A huge new building, replete with every convenience, was stuck onto its right flank. Dormitories, cubicles, studies, a preparation-room, a dining-room, parquet floors, hot-air pipes—no expense was spared, and the twelve boys roamed over it like princes. Baize doors communicated on every floor with Mr Annison's part, and he, an anxious gentle man, would stroll backwards and forwards, a little depressed at the hygienic splendours, and conscious of some vanished intimacy. Somehow he had known his boys better when they had all muddled together as one family, and algebras lay strewn upon the drawing-room chairs. As the house filled, his interest in it decreased. When he retired—which he did the same summer that Rickie left Cambridge—it had already passed the summit of excellence and was beginning to decline. Its numbers were still satisfactory, and for a little time it would subsist on its past reputation. But that mysterious asset the tone had lowered, and it was therefore of great importance that Mr Annison's successor should be a first-class man. Mr Coates, who came next in seniority, was passed over, and rightly. The choice lay between Mr Pembroke and Mr Jackson, the one an organizer, the other a humanist. Mr Jackson was master of the Sixth, and—with the exception of the headmaster, who was too busy to impart knowledge—the only first-class intellect in the school. But he could not, or rather would not, keep order. He told his form that if it chose to listen to him it would learn; if it didn't, it wouldn't. One half listened. The other half made paper frogs, and bored holes in the raised map of Italy with their penknives. When the penknives gritted he punished them with undue severity, and then forgot to make them show the punishments up. Yet out of this chaos two facts emerged. Half the boys got scholarships at the University, and some of them—including several of the paper-frog sort—remained friends with him throughout their lives. Moreover, he was rich, and had a competent wife. His claim to Dunwood House was stronger than one would have supposed.

The qualifications of Mr Pembroke have already been indicated. They prevailed—but under conditions. If things went wrong, he must promise to resign.

"In the first place," said the headmaster, "you are doing so splendidly with the day-boys. Your attitude towards the parents is magnificent. I don't know how to replace you there. Whereas, of course, the parents of a boarder—"

"Of course," said Mr Pembroke.

The parent of a boarder, who only had to remove his son if he was discontented with the school, was naturally in a more independent position than the parent who had brought all his goods and chattels to Sawston, and was renting a house there.

"Now the parents of boarders—this is my second point—practically demand that the housemaster should have a wife."

"A most unreasonable demand," said Mr Pembroke.

"To my mind also a bright motherly matron is quite sufficient. But that is what they demand. And that is why—do you see?—we *have* to regard your appointment as experimental. Possibly Miss Pembroke will be able to help you. Or I don't know whether if ever—" He left the sentence unfinished. Two days later Mr Pembroke proposed to Mrs Orr.

He had always intended to marry when he could afford it; and once he had been in love, violently in love, but had laid the passion aside, and told it to wait till a more convenient season. This was, of course, the proper thing to do, and prudence should have been rewarded. But when, after the lapse of fifteen years, he went, as it were, to his spiritual larder and took down Love from the top shelf to offer him to Mrs Orr, he was rather dismayed. Something had happened. Perhaps the god had flown; perhaps he had been eaten by the rats. At all events, he was not there.

Mr Pembroke was conscientious and romantic, and knew that marriage without love is intolerable. On the other hand, he could not admit that love had vanished from him. To admit this, would argue that he had deteriorated. Whereas he knew for a fact that he improved, year by year. Each year he grew more moral, more efficient, more learned, more genial. So how could he fail to be more loving? He did not speak to himself as follows, because he never spoke to himself; but the following notions moved in the recesses of his mind: "It is not the fire of youth. But I am not sure that I approve of the fire of youth. Look at my sister! Once she has suffered, twice she has been most imprudent, and put me to great inconvenience besides, for if she was stopping with me she would have done the housekeeping. I rather suspect that it is a nobler, riper emotion that I am laying at the feet of Mrs

Orr." It never took him long to get muddled, or to reverse cause and effect. In a short time he believed that he had been pining for years, and only waiting for this good fortune to ask the lady to share it with him.

Mrs Orr was quiet, clever, kindly, capable, and amusing, and they were old acquaintances. Altogether it was not surprising that he should ask her to be his wife, nor very surprising that she should refuse. But she refused with a violence that alarmed them both. He left her house declaring that he had been insulted, and she, as soon as he left, passed from disgust into tears.

He was much annoyed. There was a certain Miss Herriton who, though far inferior to Mrs Orr, would have done instead of her. But now it was impossible. He could not go offering himself about Sawston. Having engaged a matron who had a reputation for being bright and motherly, he moved into Dunwood House and opened the Michaelmas term. Everything went wrong. The cook left; the boys had a disease called roseola; Agnes, who was still drunk with her engagement, was of no assistance, but kept flying up to London to push Rickie's fortunes; and, to crown everything, the matron was too bright and not motherly enough: she neglected the little boys and was over-attentive to the big ones. She left abruptly, and the voice of Mrs Jackson arose, prophesying disaster.

Should he avert it by taking orders? Parents do not demand that a housemaster should be a clergyman, yet it reassures them when he is. And he would have to take orders sometime, if he hoped for a school of his own. His religious convictions were ready to hand, but he spent several uncomfortable days hunting up his religious enthusiasms. It was not unlike his attempt to marry Mrs Orr. But his piety was more genuine, and this time he never came to the point. His sense of decency forbade him hurrying into a Church that he reverenced. Moreover, he thought of another solution: Agnes must marry Rickie in the Christmas holidays, and they must come, both of them, to Sawston, she as housekeeper, he as assistant-master. The girl was a good worker when once she was settled down; and as for Rickie, he could easily be fitted in somewhere in the school. He was not a good classic, but good enough to take the Lower Fifth. He was no athlete, but boys might profitably note that he was a perfect gentleman all the same. He had no experience, but he would gain it. He had no decision, but he could simulate it. "Above all," thought Mr Pembroke, "it will be something regular for him to do." Of course this was not "above all". Dunwood House held that position. But Mr Pembroke soon came to think that it was, and believed that he was planning for Rickie, just as he had believed that he was pining for Mrs Orr.

Agnes, when she got back from the lunch in Soho, was told of the plan. She refused to give any opinion until she had seen her lover. A telegram was sent to him, and next morning he arrived. He was very susceptible to the weather, and perhaps it was unfortunate that the morning was foggy. His train had been stopped outside Sawston Station, and there he had sat for half an hour, listening to the unreal noises that came from the line, and watching the shadowy figures that worked there. The gas was alight in the great drawing-room, and in its depressing rays he and Agnes greeted each other, and discussed the most momentous question of their lives. They wanted to be married: there was no doubt of that. They wanted it, both of them, dreadfully. But should they marry on these terms?

"I'd never thought of such a thing, you see. When the scholastic agencies sent me circulars after the Tripos, I tore them up at once."

"There are the holidays," said Agnes. "You would have three months in the year to yourself, and could do your writing then."

"But who'll read what I've written?" and he told her about the editor of the *Holborn*.

She became extremely grave. At the bottom of her heart she had always mistrusted the little stories, and now people who knew agreed with her. How could Rickie, or anyone, make a living by pretending that Greek gods were alive, or that young ladies could vanish into trees? A sparkling society tale, full of verve and pathos, would have been another thing, and the editor might have been convinced by it.

"But what does he *mean*?" Rickie was saying. "What does he *mean* by life?"

"I know what he means, but I can't exactly explain. You ought to see life, Rickie. I think he's right there. And Mr Tilliard was right when he said one oughtn't to be academic."

He stood in the twilight that fell from the window, she in the twilight of the gas. "I wonder what Ansell would say," he murmured.

"Oh, poor Mr Ansell!"

He was somewhat surprised. Why was Ansell poor? It was the first time the epithet had been applied to him.

"But to change the conversation," said Agnes. "If we did marry, we might get to Italy at Easter and escape this horrible fog."

"Yes. Perhaps there—" Perhaps life would be there. He thought of Renan, who declares that on the Acropolis at Athens beauty and wisdom do exist, really exist, as external powers. He did not aspire to beauty or wisdom, but he prayed to be delivered from the shadow of unreality that had begun to darken the world. For it was as if some power had pronounced against him—as if, by some heedless action, he had offended an Olympian god. Like many another, he wondered whether the god might be appeased by work—hard uncongenial work. Perhaps he had not worked hard enough, or had enjoyed his work too much, and for that reason the shadow was falling.

"—And above all, a schoolmaster has wonderful opportunities of doing good; one mustn't forget that."

To do good! For what other reason are we here? Let us give up our refined sensations, and our comforts, and our art, if thereby we can make other people happier and better. The woman he loved had urged him to do good! With a vehemence that surprised her, he exclaimed, "I'll do it."

"Think it over," she cautioned, though she was greatly pleased.

"No; I think over things too much."

The room grew brighter. A boy's laughter floated in, and it seemed to him that people were as important and vivid as they had been six months before. Then he was at Cambridge, idling in the parsley meadows, and weaving perishable garlands out of flowers. Now he was at Sawston, preparing to work a beneficent machine. No man works for nothing, and Rickie trusted that to him also benefits might accrue; that his wound might heal as he laboured, and his eyes recapture the Holy Grail.

Chapter 17

In practical matters Mr Pembroke was often a generous man. He offered Rickie a good salary, and insisted on paying Agnes as well. And as he housed them for nothing, and as Rickie would also have a salary from the school, the money question disappeared—if not for ever, at all events for the present.

"I can work you in," he said. "Leave all that to me, and in a few days you shall hear from the headmaster. He shall create a vacancy. And once in, we stand or fall together. I am resolved on that."

Rickie did not like the idea of being "worked in", but he was determined to raise no difficulties. It is so easy to be refined and high-minded when we have nothing to do. But the active, useful man cannot be equally particular. Rickie's programme involved a change in values as well as a change of occupation.

"Adopt a frankly intellectual attitude," Mr Pembroke continued. "I do not advise you at present even to profess any interest in athletics or organization. When the headmaster writes, he will probably ask whether you are an all-round man. Boldly say no. A bold 'no' is at times the best. Take your stand upon classics and general culture."

Classics! A second in the Tripos. General culture! A smattering of English Literature, and less than a smattering of French.

"That is how we begin. Then we get you a little post—say that of librarian. And so on, until you are indispensable."

Rickie laughed; the headmaster wrote, the reply was satisfactory, and in due course the new life began.

Sawston was already familiar to him. But he knew it as an amateur, and under an official gaze it grouped itself afresh.

The school, a bland Gothic building, now showed as a fortress of learning, whose outworks were the boarding-houses.
Those straggling roads were full of the houses of the parents
of the day-boys. These shops were in bounds, those out. How
often had he passed Dunwood House! He had once confused
it with its rival, Cedar View. Now he was to live there—
perhaps for many years. On the left of the entrance a large
saffron drawing-room, full of cosy corners and dumpy chairs:
here the parents would be received. On the right of the entrance a study, which he shared with Herbert: here the boys
would be caned—he hoped not often. In the hall a framed
certificate praising the drains, the bust of Hermes, and a
carved teak monkey holding out a salver. Some of the furniture had come from Shelthorpe, some had been bought from
Mr Annison, some of it was new. But throughout he recognized a certain decision of arrangement. Nothing in the
house was accidental, or there merely for its own sake. He
contrasted it with his room at Cambridge, which had been a
jumble of things that he loved dearly and of things that he
did not love at all. Now these also had come to Dunwood
House, and had been distributed where each was seemly—
Sir Percival to the drawing-room, the photograph of Stockholm to the passage, his chair, his inkpot, and the portrait of
his mother to the study. And then he contrasted it with the
Ansells' house, to which their resolute ill-taste had given
unity. He was extremely sensitive to the inside of a house,
holding it an organism that expressed the thoughts, conscious
and subconscious, of its inmates. He was equally sensitive to
places. He would compare Cambridge with Sawston, and
either with a third type of existence, to which, for want of a
better name, he gave the name of "Wiltshire".

It must not be thought that he is going to waste his time.
These contrasts and comparisons never took him long, and
he never indulged in them until the serious business of the
day was over. And, as time passed, he never indulged in
them at all.

The school returned at the end of January, before he had
been settled in a week. His health had improved, but not
greatly, and he was nervous at the prospect of confronting

the assembled house. All day long cabs had been driving up, full of boys in bowler hats too big for them; and Agnes had been superintending the numbering of the said hats, and the placing of them in cupboards, since they would not be wanted till the end of the term. Each boy had, or should have had, a bag, so that he need not unpack his box till the morrow. One boy had only a brown-paper parcel, tied with hairy string, and Rickie heard the firm pleasant voice say, "But you'll bring a bag next term," and the submissive, "Yes, Mrs Elliot," of the reply. In the passage he ran against the head boy, who was alarmingly like an undergraduate. They looked at each other suspiciously, and parted. Two minutes later he ran into another boy, and then into another, and began to wonder whether they were doing it on purpose, and if so, whether he ought to mind. As the day wore on, the noises grew louder—trampings of feet, breakdowns, jolly little squawks—and the cubicles were assigned, and the bags unpacked, and the bathing arrangements posted up, and Herbert kept on saying, "All this is informal—all this is informal. We shall meet the house at eight-fifteen."

And so, at eight-ten, Rickie put on his cap and gown—hitherto symbols of pupilage, now to be symbols of dignity—the very cap and gown that Widdrington had so recently hung upon the college fountain. Herbert, similarly attired, was waiting for him in their private dining-room, where also sat Agnes, ravenously devouring scrambled eggs. "But you'll wear your hoods," she cried. Herbert considered, and then said she was quite right. He fetched his white silk, Rickie the fragment of rabbits' wool that marks the degree of B.A. Thus attired, they proceeded through the baize door. They were a little late, and the boys, who were marshalled in the preparation-room, were getting uproarious. One, forgetting how far his voice carried, shouted, "Cave! Here comes the Whelk." And another young devil yelled, "The Whelk's brought a limpet with him!"

"You mustn't mind," said Herbert kindly. "We masters make a point of never minding nicknames—unless, of course, they are applied openly, in which case a thousand lines is not too much." Rickie assented, and they entered the preparation-room just as the prefects had established order.

Here Herbert took his seat on a high-legged chair, while Rickie, like a queen-consort, sat near him on a chair with somewhat shorter legs. Each chair had a desk attached to it, and Herbert flung up the lid of his, and then looked round the preparation-room with a quick frown, as if the contents had surprised him. So impressed was Rickie that he peeped sideways, but could only see a little blotting-paper in the desk. Then he noticed that the boys were impressed too. Their chatter ceased. They attended.

The room was almost full. The prefects, instead of lolling disdainfully in the back row, were ranged like councillors beneath the central throne. This was an innovation of Mr Pembroke's. Carruthers, the head boy, sat in the middle, with his arm round Lloyd. It was Lloyd who had made the matron too bright: he nearly lost his colours in consequence. These two were very grown-up. Beside them sat Tewson, a saintly child in spectacles, who had risen to this height by reason of his immense learning. He, like the others, was a school prefect. The house prefects, an inferior brand, were beyond, and behind came the indistinguishable many. The faces all looked alike as yet—except the face of one boy, who was inclined to cry.

"School," said Mr Pembroke, slowly closing the lid of the desk—"school is the world in miniature." Then he paused, as a man well may who has made such a remark. It is not, however, the intention of this work to quote an opening address. Rickie, at all events, refused to be critical: Herbert's experience was far greater than his, and he must take his tone from him. Nor could anyone criticize the exhortations to be patriotic, athletic, learned, and religious, that flowed like a four-part fugue from Mr Pembroke's mouth. He was a practised speaker—that is to say, he held his audience's attention. He told them that this term, the second of his reign, was *the* term for Dunwood House; that it behoved every boy to labour during it for his house's honour, and, through the house, for the honour of the school. Taking a wider range, he spoke of England, or rather of Great Britain, and of her continental foes. Portraits of empire-builders hung on the wall, and he pointed to them. He quoted imperial poets. He showed how patriotism has broadened since the days of Shakespeare, who, for all his genius, could only write of his country as—

> This fortress built by Nature for herself
> Against infection and the hand of war;
> This happy breed of men, this little world;
> This precious stone set in the silver sea.

And it seemed that only a short ladder lay between the preparation-room and the Anglo-Saxon hegemony of the globe. Then he paused, and in the silence came "sob, sob, sob", from a little boy, who was regretting a villa in Guildford and his mother's half acre of garden.

The proceeding terminated with the broader patriotism of the school anthem, recently composed by the organist. Words and tune were still a matter for taste, and it was Mr Pembroke (and he only because he had the music) who gave the right intonation to

> "Perish each laggard! Let it not be said
> That Sawston such within her walls hath bred."

"Come, come," he said pleasantly, as they ended with harmonies in the style of Richard Strauss. "This will never do. We must grapple with the anthem this term. You're as tuneful as—as day-boys!" Hearty laughter, and then the whole house filed past them and shook hands.

"But how did it impress you?" Herbert asked, as soon as they were back in their own part. Agnes had provided them with a tray of food: the meals were still anyhow, and she had to fly at once to see after the boys.

"I liked the look of them."

"I meant rather, how did the house impress you as a house?"

"I don't think I thought," said Rickie rather nervously. "It is not easy to catch the spirit of a thing at once. I only saw a room full of boys."

"My dear Rickie, don't be so diffident. You are perfectly right. You only did see a roomful of boys. As yet there's nothing else to see. The house, like the school, lacks tradition. Look at Winchester. Look at the traditional rivalry between Eton and Harrow. Tradition is of incalculable importance, if a school is to have any status. Why should Sawston be without?"

"Yes. Tradition is of incalculable value. And I envy those schools that have a natural connection with the past. Of course Sawston has a past, though not of the kind that you quite want. The sons of poor tradesmen went to it at first. So wouldn't its traditions be more likely to linger in the Commercial School?" he concluded nervously.

"You have a great deal to learn—a very great deal. Listen to me. Why has Sawston no traditions?" His round, rather foolish, face assumed the expression of a conspirator. Bending over the mutton, he whispered, "I can tell you why. Owing to the day-boys. How can traditions flourish in such soil? Picture the day-boy's life—at home for meals, at home for preparation, at home for sleep, running home with every fancied wrong. There are day-boys in your class, and, mark my words, they will give you ten times as much trouble as the boarders—late, slovenly, stopping away at the slightest pretext. And then the letters from the parents! 'Why has my boy not been moved this term?' 'Why has my boy been moved this term?' 'I am a dissenter, and do not wish my boy to subscribe to the school mission.' 'Can you let my boy off early to water the garden?' Remember that I have been a day-boy housemaster, and tried to infuse some *esprit de corps* into them. It is practically impossible. They come as units, and units they remain. Worse. They infect the boarders. Their pestilential, critical, discontented attitude is spreading over the school. If I had my own way—"

He stopped somewhat abruptly.

"Was that why you laughed at their singing?"

"Not at all. Not at all. It is not my habit to set one section of the school against the other."

After a little they went the rounds. The boys were in bed now. "Good night!" called Herbert, standing in the corridor of the cubicles, and from behind each of the green curtains came the sound of a voice replying, "Good night, sir!" "Good night," he observed into each dormitory. Then he went to the switch in the passage and plunged the whole house into darkness. Rickie lingered behind him, strangely impressed. In the morning those boys had been scattered over England, leading their own lives. Now, for three months, they must change everything—see new faces, accept new ideals. They, like himself, must enter a beneficent machine, and learn the value of *esprit de corps*. Good luck attend them—good luck and a happy release. For his heart would have them not in these cubicles and dormitories, but each in his own dear home, amongst faces and things that he knew.

Next morning, after chapel, he made the acquaintance of his class. Towards that he felt very differently. *Esprit de corps* was not expected of it. It was simply two dozen boys who were gathered together for the purpose of learning Latin. His duties and difficulties would not lie here. He was not required to provide it with an atmosphere. The scheme of work was already mapped out, and he started gaily upon familiar words—

> *"Pan, ovium custos, tua si tibi Mænala curæ,*
> *Adsis, O Tegeæe, favens."*

"Do you think that beautiful?" he asked, and received the honest answer, "No, sir; I don't think I do." He met Herbert in high spirits in the quadrangle during the interval. But Herbert thought his enthusiasm rather amateurish, and cautioned him.

"You must take care they don't get out of hand. I approve of a lively teacher, but discipline must be established first."

"I felt myself a learner, not a teacher. If I'm wrong over a point, or don't know, I mean to tell them at once."

Herbert shook his head.

"It's different if I was really a scholar. But I can't pose as one, can I? I know much more than the boys, but I know very little. Surely the honest thing is to be myself to them.

Let them accept or refuse me as that. That's the only attitude we shall any of us profit by in the end."

Mr Pembroke was silent. Then he observed, "There is, as you say, a higher attitude and a lower attitude. Yet here, as so often, cannot we find a golden mean between them?"

"What's that?" said a dreamy voice. They turned and saw a tall, spectacled man, who greeted the newcomer kindly, and took hold of his arm. "What's that about the golden mean?"

"Mr Jackson—Mr Elliot: Mr Elliot—Mr Jackson," said Herbert, who did not seem quite pleased. "Rickie, have you a moment to spare me?"

But the humanist spoke to the young man about the golden mean and the pinchbeck mean, adding, "You know the Greeks aren't broad church clergymen. They really aren't, in spite of much conflicting evidence. Boys will regard Sophocles as a kind of enlightened bishop, and something tells me that they are wrong."

"Mr Jackson is a classical enthusiast," said Herbert. "He makes the past live. I want to talk to you about the humdrum present."

"And I am warning him against the humdrum past. That's another point, Mr Elliot. Impress on your class that many Greeks and most Romans were frightfully stupid, and if they disbelieve you, read Ctesiphon with them, or Valerius Flaccus. Whatever is that noise?"

"It comes from your classroom, I think," snapped the other master.

"So it does. Ah, yes. I expect they are putting your little Tewson into the waste-paper basket."

"I always lock my classroom in the interval—"

"Yes?"

"—and carry the key in my pocket."

"Ah. But, Mr Elliot, I am a cousin of Widdrington's. He wrote to me about you. I am so glad. Will you, first of all, come to supper next Sunday?"

"I am afraid," put in Herbert, "that we poor housemasters must deny ourselves festivities in term time."

"But mayn't he come once, just once?"

"May, my dear Jackson! My brother-in-law is not a baby. He decides for himself."

Rickie naturally refused. As soon as they were out of hearing, Herbert said, "This is a little unfortunate. Who is Mr Widdrington?"

"I knew him at Cambridge."

"Let me explain how we stand," he continued, after a pause. "Jackson is the worst of the reactionaries here, while I—why should I conceal it?—have thrown in my lot with the party of progress. You will see how we suffer from him at the masters' meetings. He has no talent for organization, and yet he is always inflicting his ideas on others. It was like his impertinence to dictate to you what authors you should read, and meanwhile the sixth-form room like a bear-garden, and a school prefect being put into the waste-paper basket. My good Rickie, there's nothing to smile at. How is the school to go on with a man like that? It would be a case of 'quick march', if it was not for his brilliant intellect. That's why I say it's a little unfortunate. You will have very little in common, you and he."

Rickie did not answer. He was very fond of Widdrington, who was a quaint, sensitive person. And he could not help being attracted by Mr Jackson, whose welcome contrasted pleasantly with the official breeziness of his other colleagues. He wondered, too, whether it is so very reactionary to contemplate the antique.

"It is true that I vote Conservative," pursued Mr Pembroke, apparently confronting some objector. "But why? Because the Conservatives, rather than the Liberals, stand for progress. One must not be misled by catchwords."

"Didn't you want to ask me something?"

"Ah, yes. You found a boy in your form called Varden?"

"Varden? Yes; there is."

"Drop on him heavily. He has broken the statutes of the school. He is attending as a day-boy. The statutes provide that a boy must reside with his parents or guardians. He does neither. It must be stopped. You must tell the headmaster."

"Where does the boy live?"

"At a certain Mrs Orr's, who has no connection with the school of any kind. It must be stopped. He must either enter a boarding-house or go."

"But why should I tell?" said Rickie. He remembered the boy, an unattractive person with protruding ears. "It is the business of his housemaster."

"Housemaster—exactly. Here we come back again. Who is now the day-boys' housemaster? Jackson once again—as if anything was Jackson's business! I handed the house back last term in a most flourishing condition. It has already gone to rack and ruin for the second time. To return to Varden. I have unearthed a put-up job. Mrs Jackson and Mrs Orr are friends. Do you see? It all works round."

"I see. It does—or might."

"The headmaster will never sanction it when it's put to him plainly."

"But why should I put it?" said Rickie, twisting the ribbons of his gown round his fingers.

"Because you're the boy's form-master."

"Is that a reason?"

"Of course it is."

"I only wondered whether—" He did not like to say that he wondered whether he need do it his first morning.

"By some means or other you must find out—of course you know already, but you must find out from the boy. I know—I have it! Where's his health certificate?"

"He had forgotten it."

"Just like them. Well, when he brings it, it will be signed by Mrs Orr, and you must look at it and say, 'Orr—Orr— Mrs Orr?' or something to that effect, and then the whole thing will come naturally out."

The bell rang, and they went in for the hour of school that concluded the morning. Varden brought his health certificate—a pompous document asserting that he had not suffered from roseola or kindred ailments in the holidays— and for a long time Rickie sat with it before him, spread open upon his desk. He did not quite like the job. It suggested intrigue, and he had come to Sawston not to intrigue but to labour. Doubtless Herbert was right, and Mr Jackson and Mrs Orr were wrong. But why could they not have it out among themselves? Then he thought, "I am a coward, and that's why I'm raising these objections," called the boy up to him, and it did all come out naturally, more or less. Hitherto Varden had lived with his mother; but she had left Sawston at Christmas, and now he would live with Mrs Orr. "Mr Jackson, sir, said it would be all right."

"Yes, yes," said Rickie; "quite so." He remembered Herbert's dictum: "Masters must present a united front. If they do not—the deluge." He sent the boy back to his seat, and after school took the compromising health certificate to the headmaster. The headmaster was at that time easily excited by a breach of the constitution. "Parents or guardians," he repeated—"parents or guardians," and flew with those words on his lips to Mr Jackson.

To say that Rickie was a cat's-paw is to put it too strongly. Herbert was strictly honourable, and never pushed him into an illegal or really dangerous position; but there is no doubt that on this and on many other occasions he had to do things that he would not otherwise have done. There was always some diplomatic corner that had to be turned, always something that he had to say or not to say. As the term wore on he lost his independence—almost without knowing it. He had much to learn about boys, and he learnt not by direct observation—for which he believed he was unfitted—but by sedulous imitation of the more experienced masters. Originally he had intended to be friends with his pupils, and Mr Pembroke commended the intention highly; but you cannot be friends either with boy or man unless you give yourself away in the process, and Mr Pembroke did not commend this. He, for "personal intercourse", substituted the safer "personal influence", and gave his junior hints on the setting of kindly traps, in which the boy does give himself away and reveals his shy delicate thoughts, while the master, intact, commends or corrects them. Originally Rickie had meant to help boys in the anxieties that they undergo when changing into men: at Cambridge he had numbered this among life's duties. But here is a subject in which we must inevitably speak as one human being to another, not as one who has authority or the shadow of authority, and for this reason the elder schoolmaster could suggest nothing but a few formulae. Formulae, like kindly traps, were not in Rickie's line, so he abandoned these subjects altogether and confined himself to working hard at what was easy. In the house he did as Herbert did, and referred all doubtful subjects to him. In his form, oddly enough, he became a martinet. It is so much simpler to be severe. He grasped the school regulations, and insisted on prompt obedience to them. He adopted the doctrine of collective responsibility. When one boy was late, he punished the whole form. "I can't help it," he would say, as if he was a power of nature. As a teacher he was rather dull. He curbed his own enthusiasms, finding that they distracted his attention, and that while he throbbed to the music of Virgil the boys in the back row were getting unruly. But on the whole he liked his form work: he knew why he was there, and Herbert did not overshadow him so completely.

What was amiss with Herbert? He had known that something was amiss, and had entered into partnership with open eyes. The man was kind and unselfish; more than that, he was truly charitable, and it was a real pleasure to him to give pleasure to others. Certainly he might talk too much about it afterwards; but it was the doing, not the talking, that he really valued, and benefactors of this sort are not too common. He was, moreover, diligent and conscientious: his heart was in his work, and his adherence to the Church of England no mere matter of form. He was capable of affection: he was usually courteous and tolerant. Then what was amiss? Why, in spite of all these qualities, should Rickie feel that there was something wrong with him—nay, that he was wrong as a whole, and that if the Spirit of Humanity should ever hold a judgement he would assuredly be classed among the goats? The answer at first sight appeared a graceless one—it was that Herbert was stupid. Not stupid in the ordinary sense—he had a business-like brain, and acquired knowledge easily—but stupid in the important sense: his whole life was coloured by a contempt of the intellect. That he had a tolerable intellect of his own was not the point: it is in what we value, not in what we have, that the test of us resides. Now, Rickie's intellect was not remarkable. He came to his worthier results rather by imagination and instinct than by logic. An argument confused him, and he could with difficulty follow it even on paper. But he saw in this no reason for satisfaction, and tried to make such use of his brain as he could, just as a weak athlete might lovingly exercise his body. Like a weak athlete, too, he loved to watch the exploits, or rather the efforts, of others—their efforts not so much to acquire knowledge as to dispel a little of the darkness by which we and all our acquisitions are surrounded. Cambridge had taught him this, and he knew, if for no other reason, that his time there had not been vain. And Herbert's contempt for such efforts revolted him. He saw that for all his fine talk about a spiritual life he had but one test for things—success: success for the body in this life or for the soul in the life to come. And for this reason Humanity, and perhaps such other tribunals as there may be, would assuredly reject him.

Chapter 18

Meanwhile he was a husband. Perhaps his union should have been emphasized before. The crown of life had been attained, the vague yearnings, the misread impulses, had found accomplishment at last. Never again must he feel lonely, or as one who stands out of the broad highway of the world and fears, like poor Shelley, to undertake the longest journey. So he reasoned, and at first took the accomplishment for granted. But as the term passed he knew that behind the yearning there remained a yearning, behind the drawn veil a veil that he could not draw. His wedding had been no mighty landmark: he would often wonder whether such and such a speech or incident came after it or before. Since that meeting in the Soho restaurant there had been so much to do—clothes to buy, presents to thank for, a brief visit to a Training College, a honeymoon as brief. In such a bustle, what spiritual union could take place? Surely the dust would settle soon: in Italy, at Easter, he might perceive the infinities of love. But love had shown him its infinities already. Neither by marriage nor by any other device can men ensure themselves a vision; and Rickie's had been granted him three years before, when he had seen his wife and a dead man clasped in each other's arms. She was never to be so real to him again.

She ran about the house looking handsomer than ever. Her cheerful voice gave orders to the servants. As he sat in the study correcting compositions, she would dart in and give him a kiss. "Dear girl—" he would murmur, with a glance at the rings on her hand. The tone of their married life was soon set. It was to be a frank good-fellowship, and before long he found it difficult to speak in a deeper key.

One evening he made the effort. There had been more beauty than was usual at Sawston. The air was pure and quiet. Tomorrow the fog might be here, but today one said, "It is like the country." Arm in arm they strolled in the side-garden, stopping at times to notice the crocuses, or to wonder when the daffodils would flower. Suddenly he tightened his pressure, and said, "Darling, why don't you still wear earrings?"

"Earrings?" She laughed. "My taste has improved, perhaps."

So after all they never mentioned Gerald's name. But he hoped it was still dear to her. He did not want her to forget the greatest moment in her life. His love desired not ownership but confidence, and to a love so pure it does not seem terrible to come second.

He valued emotion—not for itself, but because it is the only final path to intimacy. She, ever robust and practical, always discouraged him. She was not cold; she would willingly embrace him. But she hated being upset, and would laugh or thrust him off when his voice grew serious. In this she reminded him of his mother. But his mother—he had never concealed it from himself—had glories to which his wife would never attain; glories that had unfolded against a life of horror—a life even more horrible than he had guessed. He thought of her often during these earlier months. Did she bless his union, so different to her own? Did she love his wife? He tried to speak of her to Agnes, but again she was reluctant. And perhaps it was this aversion to acknowledge the dead, whose images alone have immortality, that made her own image somewhat transient, so that when he left her no mystic influence remained, and only by an effort could he realize that God had united them for ever.

They conversed and differed healthily upon other topics. A rifle corps was to be formed: she hoped that the boys would have proper uniforms, instead of shooting in their old clothes, as Mr Jackson had suggested. There was Tewson; could nothing be done about him? He would slink away from the other prefects and go with boys of his own age. There was Lloyd: he would not learn the school anthem, saying that it hurt his throat. And above all there was

Varden, who, to Rickie's bewilderment, was now a member of Dunwood House.

"He had to go somewhere," said Agnes. "Lucky for his mother that we had a vacancy."

"Yes—but when I meet Mrs Orr—I can't help feeling ashamed."

"Oh, Mrs Orr! Who cares for her? Her teeth are drawn. If she chooses to insinuate that we planned it, let her. Hers was rank dishonesty. She attempted to set up a boarding-house."

Mrs Orr, who was quite rich, had attempted no such thing. She had taken the boy out of charity, and without a thought of being unconstitutional. But in had come this offi-cious "Limpet" and upset the headmaster, and she was scolded, and Mrs Varden was scolded, and Mr Jackson was scolded, and the boy was scolded and placed with Mr Pem-broke, whom she revered less than any man in the world. Naturally enough, she considered it a further attempt of the authorities to snub the day-boys, for whose advantage the school had been founded. She and Mrs Jackson discussed the subject at their tea-parties, and the latter lady was sure that no good, no good of any kind, would come to Dunwood House from such ill-gotten plunder.

"We say, 'Let them talk'," persisted Rickie, "but I never did like letting people talk. We are right and they are wrong, but I wish the thing could have been done more quietly. The headmaster does get so excited. He has given a gang of foolish people their opportunity. I don't like being branded as the 'day-boy's foe', when I think how much I would have given to be a day-boy myself. My father found me a nuis-ance, and put me through the mill, and I can never forget it—particularly the evenings."

"There's very little bullying here," said Agnes.

"There was very little bullying at my school. There was simply the atmosphere of unkindness, which no discipline can dispel. It's not what people do to you, but what they mean, that hurts."

"I don't understand."

"Physical pain doesn't hurt—at least not what I call

hurt—if a man hits you by accident or in play. But just a little tap, when you know it comes from hatred, is too terrible. Boys do hate each other: I remember it, and see it again. They can make strong isolated friendships, but of general good-fellowship they haven't a notion."

"All I know is there's very little bullying here."

"You see, the notion of good-fellowship develops late: you can just see its beginning here among the prefects: up at Cambridge it flourishes amazingly. That's why I pity people who don't go up to Cambridge: not because a University is smart, but because those are the magic years, and—with luck—you see up there what you couldn't see before and mayn't ever see again."

"Aren't these the magic years?" the lady demanded.

He laughed and hit at her. "I'm getting somewhat involved. But hear me, O Agnes, for I am practical. I approve of our public schools. Long may they flourish. But I do not approve of the boarding-house system. It isn't an inevitable adjunct—"

"Good gracious me!" she shrieked. "Have you gone mad?"

"Silence, madam. Don't betray me to Herbert, or he'll give us the sack. But seriously, what is the good of throwing boys so much together? Isn't it building their lives on a wrong basis? They don't understand each other. I wish they did, but they don't. They don't realize that human beings are simply marvellous. When they do, the whole of life changes, and you get the true thing. But don't pretend you've got it before you have. Patriotism and *esprit de corps* are all very well, but masters a little forget that they must grow from a sentiment. They cannot create one. Cannot—cannot—cannot. I never cared a straw for England until I cared for Englishmen, and boys can't love the school when they hate each other. Ladies and gentlemen, I will now conclude my address. And most of it is copied out of Mr Ansell."

The truth is, he was suddenly ashamed. He had been carried away on a flood of his old emotions. Cambridge and all that it meant had stood before him passionately clear, and beside it stood his mother and the sweet family life which nurses up a boy until he can salute his equals. He was ashamed, for he remembered his new resolution—to work without criticizing, to throw himself vigorously into the machine, not to mind if he was pinched now and then by the elaborate wheels.

"Mr Ansell!" cried his wife, laughing somewhat shrilly. "Aha! Now I understand. It's just the kind of thing poor Mr Ansell would say. Well, I'm brutal. I believe it *does* Varden *good* to have his ears pulled now and then, and I don't care whether they pull them in play or not. Boys ought to rough it, or they never grow up into men, and your mother would have agreed with me. Oh yes; and you're all wrong about patriotism. It can, can, can create a sentiment."

She was unusually precise, and had followed his thoughts with an attention that was also unusual. He wondered whether she was not right, and regretted that she proceeded to say, "My dear boy, you mustn't talk these heresies inside Dunwood House! You sound just like one of that reactionary Jackson set, who want to fling the school back a hundred years and have nothing but day-boys all dressed anyhow."

"The Jackson set have their points."

"You'd better join it."

"The Dunwood House set has its points." For Rickie suffered from the Primal Curse, which is not—as the Authorized Version suggests—the knowledge of good and evil, but the knowledge of good-and-evil.

"Then stick to the Dunwood House set."

"I do, and shall." Again he was ashamed. Why would he see the other side of things? He rebuked his soul, not unsuccessfully, and then they returned to the subject of Varden.

"I'm certain he suffers," said he, for she would do nothing but laugh. "Each boy who passes pulls his ears—very funny, no doubt; but every day they stick out more and get redder, and this afternoon, when he didn't know he was being watched, he was holding his head and moaning. I hate the look about his eyes."

"I hate the whole boy. Nasty weedy thing."

"Well, I'm a nasty weedy thing, if it comes to that."

"No, you aren't," she cried, kissing him. But he led her back to the subject. Could nothing be suggested? He drew up some new rules—alterations in the times of going to bed, and so on—the effect of which would be to provide fewer opportunities for the pulling of Varden's ears. The rules were submitted to Herbert, who sympathized with weakliness more than did his sister, and gave them his careful consideration. But unfortunately they collided with other rules, and on a closer examination he found that they also ran contrary to the fundamentals on which the government of Dunwood House was based. So nothing was done. Agnes was rather pleased, and took to teasing her husband about Varden. At last he asked her to stop. He felt uneasy about the boy—almost superstitious. His first morning's work had brought sixty pounds a year to their hotel.

Chapter 19

They did not get to Italy at Easter. Herbert had the offer of
some private pupils, and needed Rickie's help. It seemed
unreasonable to leave England when money was to be made
in it, so they went to Ilfracombe instead. They spent three
weeks among the natural advantages and unnatural disadvantages of that resort. It was out of the season, and they
encamped in a huge hotel, which took them at a reduction.
By a disastrous chance the Jacksons were down there too,
and a good deal of constrained civility had to pass between
the two families. Constrained it was not in Mr Jackson's
case. At all times he was ready to talk, and as long as they
kept off the school it was pleasant enough. But he was very
indiscreet, and feminine tact had often to intervene. "Go
away, dear ladies," he would then observe. "You think you
see life because you see the chasms in it. Yet all the chasms
are full of female skeletons." The ladies smiled anxiously. To
Rickie he was friendly and even intimate. They had long
talks on the deserted Capstone, while their wives sat reading
in the Winter Garden and Mr Pembroke kept an eye upon
the tutored youths. "Once I had tutored youths," said Mr
Jackson, "but I lost them all by letting them paddle with
my nieces. It is so impossible to remember what is proper."
And sooner or later their talk gravitated towards his central
passion—the Fragments of Sophocles. Some day ("never,"
said Herbert) he would edit them. At present they were
merely in his blood. With the zeal of a scholar and the
imagination of a poet he reconstructed lost dramas—Niobe,
Phaedra, Philoctetes against Troy, whose names, but for an
accident, would have thrilled the world. "Is it worth it?" he
cried. "Had we better be planting potatoes?" And then: "We
had; but this is the second best."

Agnes did not approve of these colloquies. Mr Jackson

was not a buffoon, but he behaved like one, which is what matters; and from the Winter Garden she could see people laughing at him, and at her husband, who got excited too. She hinted once or twice, but no notice was taken, and at last she said rather sharply, "Now, you're not to, Rickie. I won't have it."

"He's a type that suits me. He knows people I know, or would like to have known. He was a friend of Tony Failing's. It is so hard to realize that a man connected with one was great. Uncle Tony seems to have been. He loved poetry and music and pictures, and everything tempted him to live in a kind of cultured paradise, with the door shut upon squalor. But to have more decent people in the world—he sacrificed everything to that. He would have 'smashed the whole beauty-shop' if it would help him. I really couldn't go as far as that. I don't think one need go as far—pictures might have to be smashed, but not music or poetry; surely they help—and Jackson doesn't think so either."

"Well, I won't have it, and that's enough." She laughed, for her voice had a little been that of the professional scold. "You see we must hang together. He's in the reactionary camp."

"He doesn't know it. He doesn't know that he is in any camp at all."

"His wife is, which comes to the same."

"Still, it's the holidays—" He and Mr Jackson had drifted apart in the term, chiefly owing to the affair of Varden. "We were to have the holidays to ourselves, you know." And following some line of thought, he continued, "He cheers one up. He does believe in poetry. Smart, sentimental books do seem absolutely absurd to him, and gods and fairies far nearer to reality. He tries to express all modern life in the terms of Greek mythology, because the Greeks looked very straight at things, and Demeter or Aphrodite are thinner veils than 'The survival of the fittest', or 'A marriage has been arranged', and other draperies of modern journalese."

"And do you know what that means?"

"It means that poetry, not prose, lies at the core."

"No. I can tell you what it means—balderdash."

His mouth fell. She was sweeping away the cobwebs with a vengeance. "I hope you're wrong," he replied, "for those are the lines on which I've been writing, however badly, for the last two years."

"But you write stories, not poems."

He looked at his watch. "Lessons again. One never has a moment's peace."

"Poor Rickie! You shall have a real holiday in the summer." And she called after him to say, "Remember, dear, about Mr Jackson. Don't go talking so much to him."

Rather arbitrary. Her tone had been a little arbitrary of late. But what did it matter? Mr Jackson was not a friend, and he must risk the chance of offending Widdrington. After the lesson he wrote to Ansell, whom he had not seen since June, asking him to come down to Ilfracombe, if only for a day. On reading the letter over, its tone displeased him. It was quite pathetic: it sounded like a cry from prison. "I can't send him such nonsense," he thought, and wrote again. But phrase it as he would, the letter always suggested that he was unhappy. "What's wrong?" he wondered. "I could write anything I wanted to him once." So he scrawled "Come!" on a postcard. But even this seemed too serious. The postcard followed the letters, and Agnes found them all in the waste-paper basket.

Then she said, "I've been thinking—oughtn't you to ask Mr Ansell over? A breath of sea air would do the poor thing good."

There was no difficulty now. He wrote at once, "My dear Stewart,—We both so much wish you could come over." But the invitation was refused. A little uneasy, he wrote again, using the dialect of their past intimacy. The effect of this letter was not pathetic but jaunty, and he felt a keen regret as soon as it slipped into the box. It was a relief to receive no reply.

He brooded a good deal over this painful yet intangible episode. Was the pain all of his own creating? or had it been produced by something external? And he got the answer that brooding always gives—it was both. He was morbid, and had been so since his visit to Cadover—quicker to register discomfort than joy. But, none the less, Ansell was definitely brutal, and Agnes definitely jealous. Brutality he could understand, alien as it was to himself. Jealousy, equally alien, was a harder matter. Let husband and wife be as sun and moon, or as moon and sun. Shall they therefore not give greeting to the stars? He was willing to grant that the love that inspired her might be higher than his own. Yet did it not exclude them both from much that is gracious? That dream of his when he rode on the Wiltshire expanses—a curious dream: the lark silent, the earth dissolving. And he awoke from it into a valley full of men.

She was jealous in many ways—sometimes in an open humorous fashion, sometimes more subtly, never content till "we" had extended our patronage and, if possible, our pity. She began to patronize and pity Ansell, and most sincerely trusted that he would get his fellowship. Otherwise what was the poor fellow to do? Ridiculous as it may seem, she was even jealous of Nature. One day her husband escaped from Ilfracombe to Morthoe, and came back ecstatic over its fangs of slate, piercing an oily sea. "Sounds like an hippopotamus," she said peevishly. And when they returned to Sawston through the Virgilian counties, she disliked him looking out of the window, for all the world as if Nature was some dangerous woman.

He resumed his duties with a feeling that he had never left them. Again he confronted the assembled house. This term was again *the* term; school still the world in miniature. The music of the four-part fugue entered into him more deeply, and he began to hum its little phrases. The same routine, the same diplomacies, the same old sense of only half knowing boys or men—he returned to it all; and all that changed was the cloud of unreality, which ever brooded a little more densely than before. He spoke to his wife about this—he spoke to her about everything—and she was alarmed, and wanted him to see a doctor. But he explained that it was nothing of any practical importance, nothing that interfered with his work or his appetite, nothing more than a feeling that the cow was not really there. She laughed, and "How is the cow today?" soon passed into a domestic joke.

Chapter 20

Ansell was in his favourite haunt—the reading-room of the British Museum. In that book-encircled space he always could find peace. He loved to see the volumes rising tier above tier into the misty dome. He loved the chairs that glide so noiselessly, and the radiating desks, and the central area, where the catalogue shelves curve round the super-intendent's throne. There he knew that his life was not ignoble. It was worth while to grow old and dusty seeking for truth though truth is unattainable, restating questions that have been stated at the beginning of the world. Failure would await him, but not disillusionment. It was worth while reading books, and writing a book or two which few would read, and no one, perhaps, endorse. He was not a hero, and he knew it. His father and sisters, by their steady goodness, had made this life possible. But, all the same, it was not the life of a spoilt child.

In the next chair to him sat Widdrington, engaged in his historical research. His desk was edged with enormous volumes, and every few moments an assistant brought him more. They rose like a wall against Ansell. Towards the end of the morning a gap was made, and through it they held the following conversation.

"I've been stopping with my cousin at Sawston."

"M'm."

"It was quite exciting. The air rang with battle. About two-thirds of the masters have lost their heads, and are trying to produce a gimcrack copy of Eton. Last term, you know, with a great deal of puffing and blowing, they fixed the numbers of the school. This term they want to create a new boarding-house."

"They are very welcome."

"But the more boarding-houses they create, the less room

they leave for day-boys. The local mothers are frantic, and so is my queer cousin. I never knew him so excited over sub-Hellenic things. There was an indignation meeting at his house. He is supposed to look after the day-boys' interests, but no one thought he would—least of all the people who gave him the post. The speeches were most eloquent. They argued that the school was founded for day-boys, and that it's intolerable to handicap them. One poor lady cried, 'Here's my Harold in the school, and my Toddie coming on. As likely as not I shall be told there is no vacancy for him. Then what am I to do? If I go, what's to become of Harold; and if I stop, what's to become of Toddie?' I must say I was touched. Family life is more real than national life—at least I've ordered all these books to prove it is—and I fancy that the bust of Euripides agreed with me, and was sorry for the hot-faced mothers. Jackson will do what he can. He didn't quite like to state the naked truth—which is, that boarding-houses pay. He explained it to me afterwards: they are the only future open to a stupid master. It's easy enough to be a beak when you're young and athletic, and can offer the latest University smattering. The difficulty is to keep your place when you get old and stiff, and younger smatterers are pushing up behind you. Crawl into a boarding-house and you're safe. A master's life is frightfully tragic. Jackson's fairly right himself, because he has got a first-class intellect. But I met a poor brute who was hired as an athlete. He has missed his shot at a boarding-house, and there's nothing in the world for him to do but to trundle down the hill."

Ansell yawned.

"I saw Rickie too. Once I dined there."

Another yawn.

"My cousin thinks Mrs Elliot one of the most horrible women he has ever seen. He calls her 'Medusa in Arcady'. She's so pleasant, too. But certainly it was a very stony meal."

"What kind of stoniness?"

"No one stopped talking for a moment."

"That's the real kind," said Ansell moodily. "The only kind."

"Well, I," he continued, "am inclined to compare her to an electric light. Click! she's on. Click! she's off. No waste. No flicker."

"I wish she'd fuse."

"She'll never fuse—unless anything was to happen at the main."

"What do you mean by the main?" said Ansell, who always pursued a metaphor relentlessly.

Widdrington did not know what he meant, and suggested that Ansell should visit Sawston to see whether one could know.

"It is no good me going. I should not find Mrs Elliot: she has no real existence."

"Rickie has."

"I very much doubt it. I had two letters from Ilfracombe last April, and I very much doubt that the man who wrote them can exist." Bending downwards, he began to adorn the manuscript of his dissertation with a square, and inside that a circle, and inside that another square. It was his second dissertation: the first had failed.

"I think he exists: he is so unhappy."

Ansell nodded. "How did you know he was unhappy?"

"Because he was always talking." After a pause he added, "What clever young men we are!"

"Aren't we? I expect we shall get asked in marriage soon. I say, Widdrington, shall we—?"

"Accept? Of course. It is not young-manly to say no."

"I meant shall we ever do a more tremendous thing—fuse Mrs Elliot."

"No," said Widdrington promptly. "We shall never do that all our lives." He added, "I think you might go down to Sawston, though."

"I have already refused or ignored three invitations."

"So I gathered."

"What's the good of it?" said Ansell through his teeth. "I will not put up with little things. I would rather be rude than listen to twaddle from a man I've known."

"You might go down to Sawston, just for a night, to see him."

"I saw him last month—at least, so Tilliard informs me. He says that we all three lunched together, that Rickie paid, and that the conversation was most interesting."

"Well, I contend that he does exist, and that if you go—oh, I can't be clever any longer. You really must go, man. I'm certain he's miserable and lonely. Dunwood House reeks of commerce and snobbery and all the things he hated most. He doesn't do any writing. He doesn't make any friends. He is so odd, too. In this day-boy row that has just started he's gone for my cousin. Would you believe it? Quite spitefully. It made quite a difficulty when I wanted to dine. It isn't like him—either the sentiments or the behaviour. I'm sure he's not himself. Pembroke used to look after the day-boys, and so he can't very well take the lead against them, and perhaps Rickie's doing his dirty work—and has overdone it, as decent people generally do. He's even altering to talk to. Yet he's not been married a year. Pembroke and that wife simply run him. I don't see why they should, and no more do you; and that's why I want you to go to Sawston, if only for one night."

Ansell shook his head, and looked up at the dome as other men look at the sky. In it the great arc lamps sputtered and flared, for the month was again November. Then he lowered his eyes from the cold violet radiance to the books.

"No, Widdrington; no. We don't go to see people because they are happy or unhappy. We go when we can talk to them. I cannot talk to Rickie, therefore I will not waste my time at Sawston."

"I think you're right," said Widdrington softly. "But we are bloodless brutes. I wonder whether—if we were different people—something might be done to save him. That is the curse of being a little intellectual. You and our sort have always seen too clearly. We stand aside—and meanwhile he turns into stone. Two philosophic youths repining in the British Museum! What have we done? What shall we ever do? Just drift and criticize, while people who know what they want snatch it away from us and laugh."

"Perhaps you are that sort. I'm not. When the moment comes I shall hit out like any ploughboy. Don't believe those lies about intellectual people. They're only written to soothe the majority. Do you suppose, with the world as it is, that it's an easy matter to keep quiet? Do you suppose that I didn't want to rescue him from that ghastly woman? Action! Nothing's easier than action; as fools testify. But I want to act rightly."

"The superintendent is looking at us. I must get back to my work."

"You think this all nonsense," said Ansell, detaining him. "Please remember that if I do act, you are bound to help me."

Widdrington looked a little grave. He was no anarchist. A few plaintive cries against Mrs Elliot were all that he was prepared to emit.

"There's no mystery," continued Ansell. "I haven't the shadow of a plan in my head. I know not only Rickie but the whole of his history: you remember the day near Madingley. Nothing in either helps me: I'm just watching."

"But what for?"

"For the Spirit of Life."

Widdrington was surprised. It was a phrase unknown to their philosophy. They had trespassed into poetry.

"You can't fight Medusa with anything else. If you ask me what the Spirit of Life is, or to what it is attached, I can't tell you. I only tell you, watch for it. Myself I've found it in books. Some people find it out of doors or in each other. Never mind. It's the same spirit, and I trust myself to know it anywhere, and to use it rightly."

But at this point the superintendent sent a message.

Widdrington then suggested a stroll in the galleries. It was foggy: they needed fresh air. He loved and admired his friend, but today he could not grasp him. The world as Ansell saw it seemed such a fantastic place, governed by brand-new laws. What more could one do than to see Rickie as often as possible, to invite his confidence, to offer him spiritual support? And Mrs Elliot—what power could "fuse" a respectable woman?

Ansell consented to the stroll, but, as usual, only breathed depression. The comfort of books deserted him among those marble goddesses and gods. The eye of an artist finds pleasure in texture and poise, but he could only think of the vanished incense and deserted temples beside an unfurrowed sea.

"Let us go," he said. "I do not like carved stones."

"You are too particular," said Widdrington. "You are always expecting to meet living people. One never does. I am content with the Parthenon frieze." And he moved along a few yards of it, while Ansell followed, conscious only of its pathos.

"There's Tilliard," he observed. "Shall we kill him?"

"Please," said Widdrington, and as he spoke Tilliard joined them. He brought them news. That morning he had heard from Rickie: Mrs Elliot was expecting a child.

"A child?" said Ansell, suddenly bewildered.

"Oh, I forgot," interposed Widdrington. "My cousin did tell me."

"You forgot! Well, after all, I forgot that it might be. We are indeed young men." He leant against the pedestal of Ilissus and remembered their talk about the Spirit of Life. In his ignorance of what a child means, he wondered whether the opportunity he sought lay here.

"I am very glad," said Tilliard, not without intention. "A child will draw them even closer together. I like to see young people wrapped up in their child."

"I suppose I must be getting back to my dissertation," said Ansell. He left the Parthenon to pass by the monuments of our more reticent beliefs—the temple of the Ephesian Artemis, the statue of the Cnidian Demeter. Honest, he knew that here were powers he could not cope with, nor, as yet, understand.

Chapter 21

The mists that had gathered round Rickie seemed to be breaking. He had found light neither in work for which he was unfitted nor in a woman who had ceased to respect him, and whom he was ceasing to love. Though he called himself fickle and took all the blame of their marriage on his own shoulders, there remained in Agnes certain terrible faults of heart and head, and no self-reproach would diminish them. The glamour of wedlock had faded; indeed, he saw now that it had faded even before wedlock, and that during the final months he had shut his eyes and pretended it was still there. But now the mists were breaking.

That November the supreme event approached. He saw it with Nature's eyes. It dawned on him, as on Ansell, that personal love and marriage only cover one side of the shield, and that on the other is graven the epic of birth. In the midst of lessons he would grow dreamy, as one who spies a new symbol for the universe, a fresh circle within the square. Within the square shall be a circle, within the circle another square, until the visual eye is baffled. Here is meaning of a kind. His mother had forgotten herself in him. He would forget himself in his son.

He was at his duties when the news arrived—taking preparation. Boys are marvellous creatures. Perhaps they will sink below the brutes; perhaps they will attain to a woman's tenderness. Though they despised Rickie, and had suffered under Agnes's meanness, their one thought this term was to be gentle and to give no trouble.

"Rickie—one moment—"

His face grew ashen. He followed Herbert into the passage, closing the door of the preparation-room behind him. "Oh, is she safe?" he whispered.

"Yes, yes," said Herbert; but there sounded in his answer a sombre hostile note.

"Our boy?"

"Girl—a girl, dear Rickie; a little daughter. She—she is in many ways a healthy child. She will live—oh yes." A flash of horror passed over his face. He hurried into the preparation-room, lifted the lid of his desk, glanced mechanically at the boys, and came out again.

Mrs Lewin appeared through the door that led into their own part of the house.

"Both going on well!" she cried; but her voice also was grave, exasperated.

"What is it?" he gasped. "It's something you daren't tell me."

"Only this—" stuttered Herbert. "You mustn't mind when you see—she's lame."

Mrs Lewin disappeared.

"Lame! but not as lame as I am?"

"Oh, my dear boy, worse. Don't—oh, be a man in this. Come away from the preparation-room. Remember she'll live—in many ways healthy—only just this one defect."

The horror of that week never passed away from him. To the end of his life he remembered the excuses—the consolations that the child would live; suffered very little, if at all; would walk with crutches; would certainly live. God was more merciful. A window was opened too wide on a draughty day. After a short, painless illness his daughter died. But the lesson he had learnt so glibly at Cambridge should be heeded now; no child should ever be born to him again.

Chapter 22

That same term there took place at Dunwood House another
event. With their private tragedy it seemed to have no connection; but in time Rickie perceived it as a bitter comment.
Its developments were unforeseen and lasting. It was perhaps
the most terrible thing he had to bear.

Varden had now been a boarder for ten months. His
health had broken in the previous term—partly, it is to be
feared, as the result of the indifferent food—and during the
summer holidays he was attacked by a series of agonizing
earaches. His mother, a feeble person, wished to keep him at
home, but Herbert dissuaded her. Soon after the death of
the child there arose at Dunwood House one of those waves
of hostility of which no boy knows the origin nor any master
can calculate the course. Varden had never been popular—
there was no reason why he should be—but he had never
been seriously bullied hitherto. One evening nearly the
whole house set on him. The prefects absented themselves,
the bigger boys stood round, and the lesser boys, to whom
power was delegated, flung him down, and rubbed his face
under the desks, and wrenched at his ears. The noise penetrated the baize doors, and Herbert swept through and
punished the whole house, including Varden, whom it would
not do to leave out. The poor man was horrified. He
approved of a little healthy roughness, but this was pure
brutality. What had come over his boys? Were they not
gentlemen's sons? He would not admit that if you herd together human beings before they can understand each other
the great god Pan is angry, and will in the end evade your
regulations and drive them mad. That night the victim was
screaming with pain, and the doctor next day spoke of an
operation. The suspense lasted a whole week. Comment was
made in the local papers, and the reputation not only of the

house but of the school was imperilled. "If only I had known," repeated Herbert—"if only I had known I would have arranged it all differently. He should have had a cubicle." The boy did not die, but he left Sawston, never to return.

The day before his departure Rickie sat with him some time, and tried to talk in a way that was not pedantic. In his own sorrow, which he could share with no one, least of all with his wife, he was still alive to the sorrows of others. He still fought against apathy, though he was losing the battle.

"Don't lose heart," he told him. "The world isn't all going to be like this. There are temptations and trials, of course, but nothing at all of the kind you have had here."

"But school is the world in miniature, is it not, sir?" asked the boy, hoping to please one master by echoing what had been told him by another. He was always on the lookout for sympathy: it was one of the things that had contributed to his downfall.

"I never noticed that myself. I was unhappy at school, and in the world people can be very happy."

Varden sighed and rolled about his eyes. "Are the fellows sorry for what they did to me?" he asked in an affected voice. "I am sure I forgive them from the bottom of my heart. We ought to forgive our enemies, oughtn't we, sir?"

"But they aren't your enemies. If you meet in five years' time you may find each other splendid fellows."

The boy would not admit this. He had been reading some revivalistic literature. "We ought to forgive our enemies," he repeated; "and however wicked they are, we ought not to wish them evil. When I was ill, and death seemed nearest, I had many kind letters on this subject."

Rickie knew about these "many kind letters". Varden had induced the silly nurse to write to people—people of all sorts, people that he scarcely knew or did not know at all—detailing his misfortune, and asking for spiritual aid and sympathy.

"I am sorry for them," he pursued. "I would not like to be like them."

Rickie sighed. He saw that a year at Dunwood House had

produced a sanctimonious prig. "Don't think about them, Varden. Think about anything beautiful—say, music. You like music. Be happy. It's your duty. You can't be good until you've had a little happiness. Then perhaps you will think less about forgiving people and more about loving them."

"I love them already, sir." And Rickie, in desperation, asked if he might look at the many kind letters.

Permission was gladly given. A neat bundle was produced, and for about twenty minutes the master perused it, while the invalid kept watch on his face. Rooks cawed out in the playing-fields, and close under the window there was the sound of delightful, good-tempered laughter. A boy is no devil, whatever boys may be. The letters were chilly productions, somewhat clerical in tone, by whomsoever written. Varden, because he was ill at the time, had been taken seriously. The writers declared that his illness was fulfilling some mysterious purpose: suffering engendered spiritual growth: he was showing signs of this already. They consented to pray for him, some majestically, others shyly. But they all consented with one exception, who worded his refusal as follows:

Dear A. C. Varden,

I ought to say that I never remember seeing you. I am sorry that you are ill, and hope you are wrong about it. Why did you not write before, for I could have helped you then. When they pulled your ear, you ought to have gone like this (here was a rough sketch). I could not undertake praying, but would think of you instead, if that would do. I am twenty-two in April, built rather heavy, ordinary broad face, with eyes, &c. I write all this because you have mixed me with someone else, for I am not married, and do not want to be. I cannot think of you always, but will promise a quarter of an hour daily (say 7.0— 7.15 a.m.), and might come to see you when you are better— that is, if you are a kid, and you read like one. I have been otter-hunting.

Yours sincerely,
Stephen Wonham.

Chapter 23

Rickie went straight from Varden to his wife, who lay on the sofa in her bedroom. There was now a wide gulf between them. She, like the world she had created for him, was unreal.

"Agnes, darling," he began, stroking her hand, "such an awkward little thing has happened."

"What is it, dear? Just wait till I've added up this book."

She had got over the tragedy: she got over everything.

When she was at leisure he told her. Hitherto they had seldom mentioned Stephen. He was classed among the unprofitable dead.

She was more sympathetic than he expected. "Dear Rickie," she murmured with averted eyes. "How tiresome for you."

"I wish that Varden had stopped with Mrs Orr."

"Well, he leaves us for good tomorrow."

"Yes, yes. And I made him answer the letter and apologize. They had never met. It was some confusion with a man in the Church Army, living at a place called Codford. I asked the nurse. It is all explained."

"There the matter ends."

"I suppose so—if matters ever end."

"If, by ill-luck, the person does call, I will just see him and say that the boy has gone."

"You, or I. I have got over all nonsense by this time. He's absolutely nothing to me now." He took up the tradesman's book and played with it idly. On its crimson cover was stamped a grotesque sheep. How stale and stupid their life had become!

"Don't talk like that, though," she said uneasily. "Think how disastrous it would be if you made a slip in speaking to him."

"Would it? It would have been disastrous once. But I expect, as a matter of fact, that Aunt Emily has made the slip already."

His wife was displeased. "You need not talk in that cynical way. I credit Aunt Emily with better feeling. When I was there she did mention the matter, but only once. She, and I, and all who have any sense of decency, know better than to make slips, or to think of making them."

Agnes kept up what she called "the family connection". She had been once alone to Cadover, and also corresponded with Mrs Failing. She had never told Rickie anything about her visit, nor had he ever asked her. But, from this moment, the whole subject was reopened.

"Most certainly he knows nothing," she continued. "Why, he does not even realize that Varden lives in our house! We are perfectly safe—unless Aunt Emily were to die. Perhaps then—but we are perfectly safe for the present."

"When she did mention the matter, what did she say?"

"We had a long talk," said Agnes quietly. "She told me nothing new—nothing new about the past, I mean. But we had a long talk about the present. I think"—and her voice grew displeased again—"that you have been both wrong and foolish in refusing to make up your quarrel with Aunt Emily."

"Wrong and wise, I should say."

"It isn't to be expected that she—so much older and so sensitive—can make the first step. But I know she'd be glad to see you."

"As far as I can remember that final scene in the garden, I accused her of 'forgetting what other people were like'. She'll never pardon me for saying that."

Agnes was silent. To her the phrase was meaningless. Yet Rickie was correct: Mrs Failing had resented it more than anything.

"At all events," she suggested, "you might go and see her."

"No, dear. Thank you, no."

"She is, after all—" She was going to say "your father's sister", but the expression was scarcely a happy one, and she turned it into, "She is, after all, growing old and lonely."

"So are we all!" he cried, with a lapse of tone that was now characteristic in him.

"She oughtn't to be so isolated from her proper relatives."

There was a moment's silence. Still playing with the book, he remarked, "You forget, she's got her favourite nephew."

A bright red flush spread over her cheeks. "What is the matter with you this afternoon?" she asked. "I should think you'd better go for a walk."

"Before I go, tell me what is the matter with you." He also flushed. "Why do you want me to make it up with my aunt?"

"Because it's right and proper."

"So? Or because she is old?"

"I don't understand," she retorted. But her eyes dropped. His sudden suspicion was true: she was legacy-hunting.

"Agnes, dear Agnes," he began with passing tenderness, "how can you think of such things? You behave like a poor person. We don't want any money from Aunt Emily, or from anyone else. It isn't virtue that makes me say it: we are not tempted in that way: we have as much as we want already."

"For the present," she answered, still looking aside.

"There isn't any future," he cried in a gust of despair.

"Rickie, what do you mean?"

What did he mean? He meant that the relations between them were fixed—that there would never be an influx of interest, nor even of passion. To the end of life they would go on beating time, and this was enough for her. She was content with the daily round, the common task, performed indifferently. But he had dreamt of another helpmate, and of other things.

"We don't want money—why, we don't even spend any on travelling. I've invested all my salary and more. As far as human foresight goes, we shall never want money." And his thoughts went out to the tiny grave. "You spoke of 'right and proper', but the right and proper thing for my aunt to do is to leave every penny she's got to Stephen."

Her lip quivered, and for one moment he thought that she was going to cry. "What am I to do with you?" she said. "You talk like a person in poetry."

"I'll put it in prose. He's lived with her for twenty years, and he ought to be paid for it."

Poor Agnes! Indeed, what was she to do? The first moment she set foot in Cadover she had thought, "Oh, here is money. We must try and get it." Being a lady, she never mentioned the thought to her husband, but she concluded that it would occur to him too. And now, though it had occurred to him at last, he would not even write his aunt a little note.

He was to try her yet further. While they argued this point he flashed out with, "I ought to have told him that day when he called up to our room. There's where I went wrong first."

"Rickie!"

"In those days I was sentimental. I minded. For two pins I'd write to him this afternoon. Why shouldn't he know he's my brother? What's all this ridiculous mystery?"

She became incoherent.

"But *why* not? A reason why he shouldn't know."

"A reason why he *should* know," she retorted. "I never heard such rubbish! Give me a reason why he should know."

"Because the lie we acted has ruined our lives."

She looked in bewilderment at the well-appointed room.

"It's been like a poison we won't acknowledge. How many times have you thought of my brother? I've thought of him every day—not in love; don't misunderstand; only as a medicine I shirked. Down in what they call the subconscious self he has been hurting me." His voice broke. "Oh, my darling, we acted a lie then, and this letter reminds us of it and gives us one more chance. I have to say 'we' lied. I should be lying again if I took quite all the blame. Let us ask God's forgiveness together. Then let us write, as coldly as you please, to Stephen, and tell him he is my father's son."

Her reply need not be quoted. It was the last time he attempted intimacy. And the remainder of their conversation, though long and stormy, is also best forgotten.

191

Thus the first effect of Varden's letter was to make them quarrel. They had not openly disagreed before. In the evening he kissed her and said, "How absurd I was to get angry about things that happened last year. I will certainly not write to the person." She returned the kiss. But he knew that they had destroyed the habit of reverence, and would quarrel again.

On his rounds he looked in at Varden and asked nonchalantly for the letter. He carried it off to his room. It was unwise of him, for his nerves were already unstrung, and the man he had tried to bury was stirring ominously. In the silence he examined the handwriting till he felt that a living creature was with him, whereas he, because his child had died, was dead. He perceived more clearly the cruelty of Nature, to whom our refinement and piety are but as bubbles, hurrying downwards on the turbid waters. They break, and the stream continues. His father, as a final insult, had brought into the world a man unlike all the rest of them—a man dowered with coarse kindliness and rustic strength, a kind of cynical ploughboy, against whom their own misery and weakness might stand more vividly relieved. "Born an Elliot—born a gentleman." So the vile phrase ran. But here was an Elliot whose badness was not even gentlemanly. For that Stephen was bad inherently he never doubted for a moment. And he would have children: he, not Rickie, would contribute to the stream; he, through his remote posterity, might be mingled with the unknown sea.

Thus musing he lay down to sleep, feeling diseased in body and soul. It was no wonder that the night was the most terrible he had ever known. He revisited Cambridge, and his name was a gray ghost over the door. Then there recurred the voice of a gentle shadowy woman, Mrs Aberdeen. "It doesn't seem hardly right." Those had been her words, her only complaint against the mysteries of change and death. She bowed her head and laboured to make her "gentlemen" comfortable. She was labouring still. As he lay in bed he asked God to grant him her wisdom; that he might keep sorrow within due bounds; that he might abstain from extreme hatred and envy of Stephen. It was seldom that he prayed so definitely, or ventured to obtrude his private wishes. Religion was to him a service, a mystic communion with good; not a means of getting what he wanted on the earth. But tonight, through suffering, he was humbled, and became like Mrs Aberdeen.

Hour after hour he awaited sleep and tried to endure the faces that frothed in the gloom—his aunt's, his father's, and, worst of all, the triumphant face of his brother. Once he struck at it, and awoke, having hurt his hand on the wall. Then he prayed hysterically for pardon and rest.

Yet again did he awake, and from a more mysterious dream. He heard his mother crying. She was crying quite distinctly in the darkened room. He whispered, "Never mind, my darling, never mind," and a voice echoed, "Never mind—come away—let them die out—let them die out." He lit a candle, and the room was empty. Then, hurrying to the window, he saw above mean houses the frosty glories of Orion.

Henceforward he deteriorates. Let those who censure him suggest what he should do. He has lost the work that he loved, his friends, and his child. He remained conscientious and decent, but the spiritual part of him proceeded towards ruin.

Chapter 24

The coming months, though full of degradation and anxiety, were to bring him nothing so terrible as that night. It was the crisis of his agony. He was an outcast and a failure. But he was not again forced to contemplate these facts so clearly. Varden left in the morning, carrying the fatal letter with him. The whole house was relieved. The good angel was with the boys again, or else (as Herbert preferred to think) they had learnt a lesson, and were more humane in consequence. At all events, the disastrous term concluded quietly.

In the Christmas holidays the two masters made an abortive attempt to visit Italy, and at Easter there was talk of a cruise in the Aegean. Herbert actually went, and enjoyed Athens and Delphi. The Elliots paid a few visits together in England. They returned to Sawston about ten days before school opened, to find that Widdrington was again stopping with the Jacksons. Intercourse was painful, for the two families were scarcely on speaking terms; nor did the triumphant scaffoldings of the new boarding-house make things easier. (The party of progress had carried the day.) Widdrington was by nature touchy, but on this occasion he refused to take offence, and often dropped in to see them. His manner was friendly but critical. They agreed he was a nuisance. Then Agnes left, very abruptly, to see Mrs Failing, and while she was away Rickie had a little stealthy intercourse.

Her absence, convenient as it was, puzzled him. Mrs Silt, half goose, half stormy-petrel, had recently paid a flying visit to Cadover, and thence had flown, without an invitation, to Sawston. Generally she was not a welcome guest. On this occasion Agnes had welcomed her, and—so Rickie thought—had made her promise not to tell him something that she knew. The ladies had talked mysteriously. "Mr Silt would be one with you there," said Mrs Silt. Could there be any connection between the two visits?

Agnes's letters told him nothing: they never did. She was too clumsy or too cautious to express herself on paper. A drive to Stonehenge; an anthem in the Cathedral; Aunt Emily's love. And when he met her at Waterloo he learnt nothing (if there was anything to learn) from her face.

"How did you enjoy yourself?"

"Thoroughly."

"Were you and she alone?"

"Sometimes. Sometimes other people."

"Will Uncle Tony's *Essays* be published?"

Here she was more communicative. The book was at last in proof. Aunt Emily had written a charming introduction; but she was so idle, she never finished things off.

They got into an omnibus for the Army and Navy Stores: she wanted to do some shopping before going down to Sawston.

"Did you read any of the *Essays?*"

"Every one. Delightful. Couldn't put them down. Now and then he spoilt them by statistics—but you should read his descriptions of Nature. He agrees with you: says the hills and trees are alive! Aunt Emily called you his spiritual heir, which I thought nice of her. We both so lamented that you have stopped writing." She quoted fragments of the *Essays* as they went up in the Stores' lift.

"What else did you talk about?"

"I've told you all my news. Now for yours. Let's have tea first."

They sat down in the corridor amid ladies in every stage of fatigue—haggard ladies, scarlet ladies, ladies with parcels that twisted from every finger like joints of meat. Gentlemen were scarcer, but all were of the sub-fashionable type, to which Rickie himself now belonged.

"I haven't done anything," he said feebly. "Ate, read, been rude to tradespeople, talked to Widdrington. Herbert arrived this morning. He has brought a most beautiful photograph of the Parthenon."

"Mr Widdrington?"

"Yes."

"What did you talk about?"

She might have heard every word. It was only the feeling of pleasure that he wished to conceal. Even when we love people, we desire to keep some corner secret from them, however small: it is a human right: it is personality. She began to cross-question him, but they were interrupted. A young lady at an adjacent table suddenly rose and cried, "Yes, it is you. I thought so from your walk." It was Maud Ansell.

"Oh, do come and join us!" he cried. "Let me introduce my wife."

Maud bowed quite stiffly, but Agnes, taking it for ill-breeding, was not offended.

"That I will come!" she continued in shrill, pleasant tones, adroitly poising her tea things on either hand, and transferring them to the Elliots' table. "Why haven't you ever come to us, pray?"

"I think you didn't ask me!"

"You weren't to be asked." She sprawled forward with a wagging finger. But her eyes had the honesty of her brother's. "Don't you remember the day you left us? Father said, 'Now, Mr Elliot—' Or did he call you 'Elliot'? How one does forget. Anyhow, father said you weren't to wait for an invitation, and you said, 'No; I won't.' Ours is a fair-sized house"—she turned somewhat haughtily to Agnes—"and the second spare room, which we call the 'harp room' on account of a harp that hangs on the wall, is always reserved for Stewart's friends."

"How is Mr Ansell, your brother?"

Maud's face fell. "Hadn't you heard?" she said in awe-struck tones.

"No."

"He hasn't got his fellowship. It's the second time he's failed. That means he will never get one. He will never be a don, nor live in Cambridge and that, as we had hoped."

"Oh, poor, poor fellow!" said Mrs Elliot with a remorse that was sincere, though her congratulations would not have been. "I am so very sorry."

But Maud turned to Rickie. "Mr Elliot, you might know. Tell me. What is wrong with Stewart's philosophy? What ought he to put in, or to alter, so as to succeed?"

Agnes, who knew better than this, smiled.

"I don't know," said Rickie sadly. They were none of them so clever, after all.

"Hegel," she continued vindictively. "They say he's read too much Hegel. But they never tell him what to read instead. Their own stuffy books, I suppose. Look here—no, that's the *Windsor*." After a little groping she produced a copy of *Mind*, and handed it round as if it was a geological specimen. "Inside that there's a paragraph written about something Stewart's written about before, and there it says he's read too much Hegel, and it seems now that that's been the trouble all along." Her voice trembled. "I call it most unfair, and the fellowship's gone to a man who has counted the petals on an anemone."

Rickie had no inclination to smile.

"I wish Stewart had tried Oxford instead."

"I don't wish it!"

"You say that," she continued hotly, "and then you never come to see him, though you knew you were not to wait for an invitation."

"If it comes to that, Miss Ansell," retorted Rickie, in the laughing tones that one adopts on such occasions, "Stewart won't come to me, though he *has* had an invitation."

"Yes," chimed in Agnes, "we ask Mr Ansell again and again, and he will have none of us."

Maud looked at her with a flashing eye. "My brother is a very peculiar person, and we ladies can't understand him. But I know one thing, and that's that he has a reason all round for what he does. Look here, I must be getting on. Waiter! Wai-ai-aiter! Bill, please. Separately, of course. Call the Army and Navy cheap! I know better!"

"How does the drapery department compare?" said Agnes sweetly.

The girl gave a sharp choking sound, gathered up her parcels, and left them. Rickie was too much disgusted with his wife to speak.

"Appalling person!" she gasped. "It was naughty of me, but I couldn't help it. What a dreadful fate for a clever man! To fail in life completely, and then to be thrown back on a family like that!"

"Maud is a snob and a Philistine. But, in her case, something emerges."

She glanced at him, but proceeded in her suavest tones, "Do let us make one great united attempt to get Mr Ansell to Sawston."

"No."

"What a changeable friend you are! When we were engaged you were always talking about him."

"Would you finish your tea, and then we will buy the linoleum for the cubicles."

But she returned to the subject again, not only on that day but throughout the term. Could nothing be done for poor Mr Ansell? It seemed that she could not rest until all that he had once held dear was humiliated. In this she strayed outside her nature: she was unpractical. And those who stray outside their nature invite disaster. Rickie, goaded by her, wrote to his friend again. The letter was in all ways unlike his old self. Ansell did not answer it. But he did write to Mr Jackson, with whom he was not acquainted.

Dear Mr Jackson,
  I understand from Widdrington that you have a large house. I would like to tell you how convenient it would be for me to come and stop in it. June suits me best.

Yours truly,
Stewart Ansell.

To which Mr Jackson replied that not only in June but during the whole year his house was at the disposal of Mr Ansell and of anyone who resembled him.

But Agnes continued her life, cheerfully beating time. She, too, knew that her marriage was a failure, and in her spare moments regretted it. She wished that her husband was handsomer, more successful, more dictatorial. But she would think, "No, no; one mustn't grumble. It can't be helped."

Ansell was wrong in supposing she might ever leave Rickie. Spiritual apathy prevented her. Nor would she ever be tempted by a jollier man. Here criticism would willingly alter its tone. For Agnes also has her tragedy. She belonged to the type—not necessarily an elevated one—that loves once and once only. Her love for Gerald had not been a noble passion: no imagination transfigured it. But such as it was, it sprang to embrace him, and he carried it away with him when he died. *Les amours qui suivent sont moins involontaires:* by an effort of the will she had warmed herself for Rickie.

She is not conscious of her tragedy, and therefore only the gods need weep at it. But it is fair to remember that hitherto she moves as one from whom the inner life has been withdrawn.

Chapter 25

"I am afraid," said Agnes, unfolding a letter that she had received in the morning, "that things go far from satisfactorily at Cadover."

The three were alone at supper. It was the June of Rickie's second year at Sawston.

"Indeed?" said Herbert, who took a friendly interest. "In what way?"

"Do you remember us talking of Stephen—Stephen Wonham, who by an odd coincidence—"

"Yes. Who wrote last year to that miserable failure Varden. I do."

"It is about him."

"I did not like the tone of his letter."

Agnes had made her first move. She waited for her husband to reply to it. But he, though full of a painful curiosity, would not speak. She moved again.

"I don't think, Herbert, that Aunt Emily, much as I like her, is the kind of person to bring a young man up. At all events the results have been disastrous this time."

"What has happened?"

"A tangle of things." She lowered her voice. "Drink."

"Dear! Really! Was Mrs Failing fond of him?"

"She used to be. She let him live at Cadover ever since he was a little boy. Naturally that cannot continue."

Rickie never spoke.

"And now he has taken to be violent and rude," she went on.

"In short, a beggar on horseback. Who is he? Has he no relatives?"

"She has always been both father and mother to him. Now it must all come to an end. I blame her—and she blames herself—for not being severe enough. He has grown up without fixed principles. He has always followed his inclinations, and one knows the result of that."

Herbert assented. "To me Mrs Failing's course is perfectly plain. She has a certain responsibility. She must pay the youth's passage to one of the colonies, start him handsomely in some business, and then break off all communications."

"How funny! It is exactly what she is going to do."

"I shall then consider that she has behaved in a thoroughly honourable manner." He held out his plate for gooseberries. "His letter to Varden was neither helpful nor sympathetic, and, if written at all, it ought to have been both. I am not in the least surprised to learn that he has turned out badly. When you write next, would you tell her how sorry I am?"

"Indeed I will. Two years ago, when she was already a little anxious, she did so wish you could undertake him."

"I could not alter a grown man." But in his heart he thought he could, and smiled at his sister amiably. "Terrible, isn't it?" he remarked to Rickie. Rickie, who was trying not to mind anything, assented. And an onlooker would have supposed them a dispassionate trio, who were sorry both for Mrs Failing and for the beggar who would bestride her horses' backs no longer. A new topic was introduced by the arrival of the evening post.

Herbert took up all the letters, as he often did.

"Jackson?" he exclaimed. "What does the fellow want?" He read, and his tone was mollified, "'Dear Mr Pembroke—Could you, Mrs Elliot, and Mr Elliot come to supper with us on Saturday next? I should not merely be pleased, I should be grateful. My wife is writing formally to Mrs Elliot'—(Here, Agnes, take your letter)—'but I venture to write as well, and to add my more uncouth entreaties.'—An olive-branch. It is time! But (ridiculous person!) does he think that we can leave the House deserted and all go out pleasuring in term time?—Rickie, a letter for you."

"Mine's the formal invitation," said Agnes. "How very odd! Mr Ansell will be there. Surely we asked him here! Did you know he knew the Jacksons?"

"This makes refusal very difficult," said Herbert, who was anxious to accept. "At all events, Rickie ought to go."

"I do not want to go," said Rickie, slowly opening his own letter. "As Agnes says, Ansell has refused to come to us. I cannot put myself out for him."

"Who's yours from?" she demanded.

"Mrs Silt," replied Herbert, who had seen the handwriting. "I trust she does not want to pay us a visit this term, with the examinations impending and all the machinery at full pressure. Though, Rickie, you will have to accept the Jacksons' invitation."

"I cannot possibly go. I have been too rude; with Widdrington we always meet here. I'll stop with the boys—" His voice caught suddenly. He had opened Mrs Silt's letter.

"The Silts are not ill, I hope?"

"No. But, I say"—he looked at his wife—"I do think this is going too far. Really, Agnes—"

"What has happened?"

"It is going too far," he repeated. He was nerving himself for another battle. "I cannot stand this sort of thing. There are limits."

He laid the letter down. It was Herbert who picked it up, and read: "'Aunt Emily has just written to us. We are so glad that her troubles are over, in spite of the expense. It never does to live apart from one's own relatives so much as she has done up to now. He goes next Saturday to Canada. What you told her about him just turned the scale. She has asked us—'"

"No, it's too much," he interrupted. "What I told her—told her about him—no, I will have it out at last. Agnes!"

"Yes?" said his wife, raising her eyes from Mrs Jackson's formal invitation.

"It's you—it's you. I never mentioned him to her. Why, I've never seen her or written to her since. I accuse you."

Then Herbert overbore him, and he collapsed. He was asked what he meant. Why was he so excited? Of what did he accuse his wife. Each time he spoke more feebly, and before long the brother and sister were laughing at him. He felt bewildered, like a boy who knows that he is right but cannot put his case correctly. He repeated, "I've never mentioned him to her. It's a libel. Never in my life." And they cried, "My dear Rickie, what an absurd fuss!" Then his brain cleared. His eye fell on the letter that his wife had received from his aunt, and he reopened the battle.

"Agnes, give me that letter, if you please."

"Mrs Jackson's?"

"My aunt's."

She put her hand on it, and looked at him doubtfully. She saw that she had failed to bully him.

"My aunt's letter," he repeated, rising to his feet and bending over the table towards her.

"Why, dear?"

"Yes, why indeed?" echoed Herbert. He too had bullied Rickie, but from a purer motive: he had tried to stamp out a dissension between husband and wife. It was not the first time he had intervened.

"The letter. For this reason: it will show me what you have done. I believe you have ruined Stephen. You have worked at it for two years. You have put words into my mouth to 'turn the scale' against him. He goes to Canada—and all the world thinks it is owing to me. As I said before—I advise you to stop smiling—you have gone a little too far."

They were all on their feet now, standing round the little table. Agnes said nothing, but the fingers of her delicate hand tightened upon the letter. When her husband snatched at it she resisted, and with the effect of a harlequinade everything went on the floor—lamb, mint sauce, gooseberries, lemonade, whiskey. At once they were swamped in domesticities. She rang the bell for the servant, cries arose, dusters were brought, broken crockery (a wedding present) picked up from the carpet; while he stood wrathfully at the window, regarding the obscured sun's decline.

"I *must* see her letter," he repeated, when the agitation was over. He was too angry to be diverted from his purpose. Only slight emotions are thwarted by an interlude of farce.

"I've had enough of this quarrelling," she retorted. "You know that the Silts are inaccurate. I think you might have given me the benefit of the doubt. If you will know—have you forgotten that ride you took with him?"

"I—" he was again bewildered. "The ride where I dreamt—?"

"The ride where you turned back because you could not listen to a disgraceful poem."

"I don't understand."

"The poem was about Aunt Emily. He read it to you and a stray soldier. Afterwards you told me. You said, 'Really it is shocking, his ingratitude. She ought to know about it.' She does know, and I should be glad of an apology."

He had said something of the sort in a fit of irritation. Mrs Silt was right—he had helped to turn the scale.

"Whatever I said, you knew what I meant. You knew I'd sooner cut my tongue out than have it used against him. Even then." He sighed. Had he ruined his brother? A curious tenderness came over him, and passed when he remembered his own dead child. "*We* have ruined him, then. Have you any objection to 'we'? *We* have disinherited him."

"I decide against you," interposed Herbert. "I have now heard both sides of this deplorable affair. You are talking most criminal nonsense. 'Disinherit!' Sentimental twaddle. It's been clear to me from the first that Mrs Failing has been imposed upon by the Wonham man, a person with no legal claim on her, and anyone who exposes him performs a public duty—"

"—And gets money."

"Money?" He was always uneasy at the word. "Who mentioned money?"

"Just understand me, Herbert, and of what it is that I accuse my wife." Tears came into his eyes. "It is not that I like the Wonham man, or think that he isn't a drunkard and worse. He's too awful in every way. But he ought to have my aunt's money, because he's lived all his life with her, and is her nephew as much as I am. You see, my father went wrong." He stopped, amazed at himself. How easy it had been to say! He was withering up: the power to care about this stupid secret had died.

When Herbert understood, his first thought was for Dunwood House. "Why have I never been told?" was his first remark.

"We settled to tell no one," said Agnes. "Rickie, in his anxiety to prove me a liar, has broken his promise."

"I ought to have been told," said Herbert, his anger increasing. "Had I known, I could have averted this deplorable scene."

"Let me conclude it," said Rickie, again collapsing and leaving the dining-room. His impulse was to go straight to Cadover and make a business-like statement of the position to Stephen. Then the man would be armed, and perhaps fight the two women successfully. But he resisted the impulse. Why should he help one power of evil against another? Let them go intertwined to destruction. To enrich his brother would be as bad as enriching himself. If their aunt's money ever did come to him, he would refuse to accept it. That was the easiest and most dignified course. He troubled himself no longer with justice or pity, and the next day he asked his wife's pardon for his behaviour.

In the dining-room the conversation continued. Agnes, without much difficulty, gained her brother as an ally. She acknowledged that she had been wrong in not telling him, and he then declared that she had been right on every other point. She slurred a little over the incident of her treachery, for Herbert was sometimes clear-sighted over details, though easily muddled in a general survey. Mrs Failing had had plenty of direct causes of complaint, and she dwelt on these. She dwelt, too, on the very handsome way in which the young man, "though he knew nothing, and had never asked to know," was being treated by his aunt.

"'Handsome' is the word," said Herbert. "I hope not indulgently. He does not deserve indulgence."

And she knew that he, like herself, could remember money, and that it lent an unacknowledged halo to her cause.

"It is not a savoury subject," he continued, with sudden stiffness. "I understand why Rickie is so hysterical. My impulse"—he laid his hand on her shoulder—"is to abandon it at once. But if I am to be of any use to you, I must hear it all. There are moments when we must look facts in the face."

She did not shrink from the subject as much as he thought, as much as she herself could have wished. Two years before, it had filled her with a physical loathing. But by now she had accustomed herself to it.

"I am afraid, Bertie boy, there is nothing else to hear. I have tried to find out again and again, but Aunt Emily will not tell me. I suppose it is natural. She wants to shield the Elliot name. She only told us in a fit of temper; then we all agreed to keep it to ourselves; then Rickie again mismanaged her, and ever since she has refused to let us know any details."

"A most unsatisfactory position."

"So I feel." She sat down again with a sigh. Mrs Failing had been a great trial to her orderly mind. "She is an odd woman. She is always laughing. She actually finds it amusing that we know no more."

"They are an odd family."

"They are indeed."

Herbert, with unusual sweetness, bent down and kissed her.

She thanked him.

Their tenderness soon passed. They exchanged it with averted eyes. It embarrassed them. There are moments for all of us when we seem obliged to speak in a new unprofitable tongue. One might fancy a seraph, vexed with our normal language, who touches the pious to blasphemy, the blasphemous to piety. The seraph passes, and we proceed unaltered—conscious, however, that we have not been ourselves, and that we may fail in this function yet again. So Agnes and Herbert, as they proceeded to discuss the Jacksons' supper-party, had an uneasy memory of spiritual deserts, spiritual streams.

Chapter 26

Poor Mr Ansell was actually sitting in the garden of Dunwood House. It was Sunday morning. The air was full of roasting beef. The sound of a manly hymn, taken very fast, floated over the road from the school chapel. He frowned, for he was reading a book, the *Essays* of Anthony Eustace Failing.

He was here on account of this book—at least so he told himself. It had just been published, and the Jacksons were sure that Mr Elliot would have a copy. For a book one may go anywhere. It would not have been logical to enter Dunwood House for the purpose of seeing Rickie, when Rickie had not come to supper yesterday to see him. He was at Sawston to assure himself of his friend's grave. With quiet eyes he had intended to view the sods, with unfaltering fingers to inscribe the epitaph. Love remained. But in high matters he was practical. He knew that it would be useless to reveal it.

"Morning!" said a voice behind him.

He saw no reason to reply to this superfluous statement, and went on with his reading.

"Morning!" said the voice again.

As for the *Essays*, the thought was somewhat old-fashioned, and he picked many holes in it; nor was he anything but bored by the prospect of the brotherhood of man. However, Mr Failing stuck to his guns, such as they were, and fired from them several good remarks. Very notable was his distinction between coarseness and vulgarity (coarseness, revealing something; vulgarity, concealing something), and his avowed preference for coarseness. Vulgarity, to him, had been the primal curse, the shoddy reticence that prevents man opening his heart to man, the power that makes against equality. From it sprang all the things that he hated—class shibboleths, ladies, lidies, the game laws, the Conservative party—all the things that accent the divergencies rather than the similarities in human nature. Whereas coarseness—But at this point Herbert Pembroke had scrawled with a blue pencil: "Childish. One reads no further."

"Morning!" repeated the voice.

Ansell read further, for here was the book of a man who had tried, however unsuccessfully, to practise what he preached. Mrs Failing, in her Introduction, described with delicate irony his difficulties as a landlord; but she did not record the love in which his name was held. Nor could her irony touch him when he cried: "Attain the practical through the unpractical. There is no other road." Ansell was inclined to think that the unpractical is its own reward, but he respected those who attempted to journey beyond it. We must all of us go over the mountains. There is certainly no other road.

"Nice morning!" said the voice.

It was not a nice morning, so Ansell felt bound to speak. He answered: "No. Why?" A clod of earth immediately struck him on the back. He turned round indignantly, for he hated physical rudeness. A square man of ruddy aspect was pacing the gravel path, his hands deep in his pockets. He was very angry. Then he saw that the clod of earth nourished a blue lobelia, and that a wound of corresponding size appeared on the pie-shaped bed. He was not so angry. "I expect they will mind it," he reflected. Last night, at the Jacksons', Agnes had displayed a brisk pity that made him wish to wring her neck. Maud had not exaggerated. Mr Pembroke had patronized through a sorrowful voice and large round eyes. Till he met these people he had never been told that his career was a failure. Apparently it was. They would never have been civil to him if it had been a success, if they or theirs had anything to fear from him.

In many ways Ansell was a conceited man; but he was never proud of being right. He had foreseen Rickie's catastrophe from the first, but derived from this no consolation. In many ways he was pedantic; but his pedantry lay close to the vineyards of life—far closer than that fetish Experience of the innumerable teacups. He had a great many facts to learn, and before he died he learnt a suitable quantity. But he never forgot that the holiness of the heart's imagination can alone classify these facts—can alone decide which is an exception, which an example. "How unpractical it all is!" That was his comment on Dunwood House. "How un-business-like! They live together without love. They work without conviction. They seek money without requiring it. They die, and nothing will have happened, either for them-selves or for others." It is a comment that the academic mind will often make when first confronted with the world.

But he was becoming illogical. The clod of earth had dis-turbed him. Brushing the dirt off his back, he returned to the book. What a curious affair was the essay on "Gaps"! Solitude, star-crowned, pacing the fields of England, has a dialogue with Seclusion. He, poor little man, lives in the choicest scenery—among rocks, forests, emerald lawns, azure lakes. To keep people out he has built round his domain a high wall, on which is graven his motto—"*Procul este, pro-fani*". But he cannot enjoy himself. His only pleasure is in mocking the absent Profane. They are in his mind night and day. Their blemishes and stupidities form the subject of his great poem, "In the Heart of Nature". Then Solitude tells him that so it always will be until he makes a gap in the wall, and permits his seclusion to be the sport of circum-stance. He obeys. The Profane invade him; but for short intervals they wander elsewhere, and during those intervals the heart of Nature is revealed to him.

This dialogue had really been suggested to Mr Failing by a talk with his brother-in-law. It also touched Ansell. He looked at the man who had thrown the clod, and was now pacing with obvious youth and impudence upon the lawn. "Shall I improve my soul at his expense?" he thought. "I suppose I had better." In friendly tones he remarked, "Were you waiting for Mr Pembroke?"

"No," said the young man. "Why?"

Ansell, after a moment's admiration, flung the *Essays* at him. They hit him in the back. The next moment he lay on his own back in the lobelia pie.

"But it hurts!" he gasped, in the tones of a puzzled civilization. "What you do hurts!" For the young man was nicking him over the shins with the rim of the book cover. "Little brute—*ee—ow!*"

"Then say Pax!"

Something revolted in Ansell. Why should he say Pax? Freeing his hand, he caught the little brute under the chin, and was again knocked into the lobelias by a blow on the mouth.

"Say Pax!" he repeated, pressing the philosopher's skull into the mould; and he added, with an anxiety that was somehow not offensive, "I do advise you. You'd really better."

Ansell swallowed a little blood. He tried to move, and he could not. He looked carefully into the young man's eyes and into the palm of his right hand, which at present swung unclenched, and he said "Pax!"

"Shake hands!" said the other, helping him up. There was nothing Ansell loathed so much as the hearty Britisher; but he shook hands, and they stared at each other awkwardly. With civil murmurs they picked the little blue flowers off each other's clothes. Ansell was trying to remember why they had quarrelled, and the young man was wondering why he had not guarded his chin properly. In the distance a hymn swung off—

"Fight the good . Fight with . All thy . Might."

They would be across from chapel soon.

"Your book, sir?"

"Thank you, sir—yes."

"Why!" cried the young man—"why, it's *What We Want*! At least the binding's exactly the same."

"It's called *Essays*," said Ansell.

"Then that's it. Mrs Failing, you see, she wouldn't call it that, because three W's, you see, in a row, she said, are vulgar, and sound like Tolstoy, if you've heard of him."

Ansell confessed to an acquaintance, and then said, "Do you think *What We Want* vulgar?" He was not at all interested, but he desired to escape from the atmosphere of pugilistic courtesy, more painful to him than blows themselves.

"It *is* the same book," said the other—"same title, same binding." He weighed it like a brick in his muddy hands.

"Open it to see if the inside corresponds," said Ansell, swallowing a laugh and a little more blood with it.

With a liberal allowance of thumbmarks, he turned the pages over and read, "'—the rural silence that is not a poet's luxury but a practical need for all men.' Yes, it *is* the same book." Smiling pleasantly over the discovery, he handed it back to the owner.

"And is it true?"

"I beg your pardon?"

"Is it true that rural silence is a practical need?"

"Don't ask me!"

"Have you ever tried it?"

"What?"

"Rural silence."

"A field with no noise in it, I suppose you mean. I don't understand."

Ansell smiled, but a slight fire in the man's eye checked him. After all, this was a person who could knock one down. Moreover, there was no reason why he should be teased. He had it in him to retort "No. Why?" He was not stupid in essentials. He was irritable—in Ansell's eyes a frequent sign of grace. Sitting down on the upturned seat, he remarked, "I like the book in many ways. I don't think *What We Want* would have been a vulgar title. But I don't intend to spoil myself on the chance of mending the world, which is what the creed amounts to. Nor am I keen on rural silences."

"Curse!" he said thoughtfully, sucking at an empty pipe.

"Tobacco?"

"Please."

"Rickie's is invariably filthy."

"Who says I know Rickie?"

"Well, you know his aunt. It's a possible link. Be gentle with Rickie. Don't knock him down if he doesn't think it's a nice morning."

The other was silent.

"Do you know him well?"

"Kind of." He was not inclined to talk. The wish to smoke was very violent in him, and Ansell noticed how he gazed at the wreaths that ascended from bowl and stem, and how, when the stem was in his mouth, he bit it. He gave the idea of an animal with just enough soul to contemplate its own bliss. United with refinement, such a type was common in Greece. It is not common today, and Ansell was surprised to find it in a friend of Rickie's. Rickie, if he could even "kind of know" such a creature, must be stirring in his grave.

"Do you know his wife too?"

"Oh yes. In a way I know Agnes. But thank you for this tobacco. Last night I nearly died. I have no money."

"Take the whole pouch—do."

After a moment's hesitation he did. "Fight the good" had scarcely ended, so quickly had their intimacy grown.

"I suppose you're a friend of Rickie's?"

Ansell was tempted to reply, "I don't know him at all." But it seemed no moment for the severer truths, so he said, "I knew him well at Cambridge, but I have seen very little of him since."

"Is it true that his baby was lame?"

"I believe so."

His teeth closed on his pipe. Chapel was over. The organist was prancing through the voluntary, and the first ripple of boys had already reached Dunwood House. In a few minutes the masters would be here too, and Ansell, who was becoming interested, hurried the conversation forward.

"Have you come far?"

"From Wiltshire. Do you know Wiltshire?" And for the first time there came into his face the shadow of a sentiment, the passing tribute to some mystery. "It's a good county. I live in one of the finest valleys out of Salisbury Plain. I mean, I lived."

"Have you been dismissed from Cadover, without a penny in your pocket?"

He was alarmed at this. Such knowledge seemed simply diabolical. Ansell explained that if his boots were chalky, if his clothes had obviously been slept in, if he knew Mrs

Failing, if he knew Wiltshire, and if he could buy no tobacco—then the deduction was possible. "You do just attend," he murmured.

The house was filling with boys, and Ansell saw, to his regret, the head of Agnes over the thuya hedge that separated the small front garden from the side lawn where he was sitting. After a few minutes it was followed by the heads of Rickie and Mr Pembroke. All the heads were turned the other way. But they would find his card in the hall, and if the man had left any message they would find that too. "What are you?" he demanded. "Who you are—your name—I don't care about that. But it interests me to class people, and up to now I have failed with you."

"I—" He stopped. Ansell reflected that there are worse answers. "I really don't know what I am. Used to think I was something special, but strikes me now I feel much like other chaps. Used to look down on the labourers. Used to take for granted I was a gentleman, but really I don't know where I do belong."

"One belongs to the place one sleeps in and to the people one eats with."

"As often as not I sleep out of doors and eat by myself, so that doesn't get you any further."

A silence, akin to poetry, invaded Ansell. Was it only a pose to like this man, or was he really wonderful? He was not romantic, for Romance is a figure with outstretched hands, yearning for the unattainable. Certain figures of the Greeks, to whom we continually return, suggested him a little. One expected nothing of him—no purity of phrase nor swift edged thought. Yet the conviction grew that he had been back somewhere—back to some table of the gods, spread in a field where there is no noise, and that he belonged for ever to the guests with whom he had eaten.

Meanwhile he was simple and frank, and what he could tell he would tell to anyone. He had not the suburban reticence. Ansell asked him, "Why did Mrs Failing turn you out of Cadover? I should like to hear that too."

"Because she was tired of me. Because, again, I couldn't keep quiet over the farm hands. I ask you, is it right?" He became incoherent. Ansell caught, "And they grow old—they don't play games—it ends they can't play." An illustration emerged. "Take a kitten—if you fool about with her, she goes on playing well into a cat."

"But Mrs Failing minded no mice being caught."

"Mice?" said the young man blankly. "What I was going to say is, that someone was jealous of my being at Cadover. I'll mention no names, but I fancy it was Mrs Silt. I'm sorry for her if it was. Anyhow, she set Mrs Failing against me. It came on the top of other things—and out I went."

"What did Mrs Silt, whose name I don't mention, say?"

He looked guilty. "I don't know. Easy enough to find something to say. The point is that she said something. You know, Mr—I don't know your name, mine's Wonham, but I'm more grateful than I can put it over this tobacco. I mean, you ought to know there *is* another side to this quarrel. It's wrong, but it's there."

Ansell told him not to be uneasy: he had already guessed that there might be another side. But he could not make out why Mr Wonham should have come straight from the aunt to the nephew. They were now sitting on the upturned seat. *What We Want*, a good deal shattered, lay between them.

"On account of above-mentioned reasons, there was a row. I don't know—you can guess the style of thing. She wanted to treat me to the colonies, and had up the parson to talk soft-sawder and make out that a boundless continent was the place for a lad like me. I said, 'I can't run up to the Rings without getting tired, nor gallop a horse out of this view without tiring it, so what is the point of a boundless continent?' Then I saw that she was frightened of me, and bluffed a bit more, and in the end I was nipped. She caught me—just like her—when I had nothing on but flannels, and was coming into the house, having licked the Cadchurch team. She stood up in the doorway between those stone pilasters and said, 'No! Never again!' and behind her was Wilbraham, whom I tried to turn out, and the gardener, and poor old Leighton, who hates being hurt. She said, 'There's a hundred pounds for you at the London bank, and as much more in December. Go!' I said, 'Keep your ——

money, and tell me whose son I am.' I didn't care really. I only said it on the off-chance of hurting her. Sure enough, she caught onto the door-handle (being lame) and said, 'I can't—I promised—I don't really want to,' and Wilbraham did stare. Then—she's very queer—she burst out laughing, and went for the packet after all, and we heard her laugh through the window as she got it. She rolled it at me down the steps, and she says, 'A leaf out of the eternal comedy for you, Stephen,' or something of that sort. I opened it as I walked down the drive, she laughing always and catching onto the handle of the front door. Of course it wasn't comic at all. But down in the village there were both cricket teams, already a little tight, and the mad plumber shouting 'Rights of Man!' They knew I was turned out. We did have a row, and kept it up too. They daren't touch Wilbraham's windows, but there isn't much glass left up at Cadover. When you start, it's worth going on, but in the end I had to cut. They subscribed a bob here and a bob there, and these are Flea Thompson's Sundays. I sent a line to Leighton not to forward my own things: I don't fancy them. They aren't really mine." He did not mention his great symbolic act, performed, it is to be feared, when he was rather drunk and the friendly policeman was looking the other way. He had cast all his flannels into the little millpond, and then waded himself through the dark cold water to the new clothes on the other side. Someone had flung his pipe and his packet after him. The packet had fallen short. For this reason it was wet when he handed it to Ansell, and ink that had been dry for twenty-three years had begun to run again.

"I wonder if you're right about the hundred pounds," said Ansell gravely. "It is pleasant to be proud, but it is unpleasant to die in the night through not having any tobacco."

"But I'm not proud. Look how I've taken your pouch! The hundred pounds was—well, can't you see yourself, it was quite different? It was, so to speak, *inconvenient* for me to take the hundred pounds. Or look again how I took a shilling from a boy who earns nine bob a week! Proves pretty conclusively I'm not proud."

Ansell saw it was useless to argue. He perceived, beneath the slatternly use of words, the man—buttoned up in them, just as his body was buttoned up in a shoddy suit—and he wondered more than ever that such a man should know the Elliots. He looked at the face, which was frank, proud, and beautiful, if truth is beauty. Of mercy or tact such a face knew little. It might be coarse, but it had in it nothing vulgar or wantonly cruel. "May I read these papers?" he said.

"Of course. Oh yes; didn't I say? I'm Rickie's half-brother, come here to tell him the news. He doesn't know. There it is, put shortly for you. I was saying, though, that I bolted in the dark, slept in the rifle-butts above Salisbury—the sheds where they keep the cardboard men, you know, never locked up as they ought to be. I turned the whole place upside down to teach them."

"Here is your packet again," said Ansell. "Thank you. How interesting!" He rose from the seat and turned towards Dunwood House. He looked at the bow-windows, the cheap picturesque gables, the terracotta dragons clawing a dirty sky. He listened to the clink of plates and to the voice of Mr Pembroke taking one of his innumerable roll-calls. He looked at the bed of lobelias. How interesting! What else was there to say?

"One must be the son of someone," remarked Stephen. And that was all he had to say. To him those names on the moistened paper were mere antiquities. He was neither proud of them nor ashamed. A man must have parents, or he cannot enter the delightful world. A man, if he has a brother, may reasonably visit him, for they may have interests in common. He continued his narrative—how in the night he had heard the clocks, how at daybreak, instead of entering the city, he had struck eastward to save money—while Ansell still looked at the house and found that all his imagination and knowledge could lead him no farther than this: how interesting!

"—And what do you think of that for a holy horror?"

"For a what?" said Ansell, his thoughts far away.

"This man I am telling you about, who gave me a lift towards Andover, who said I was a blot on God's earth."

One o'clock struck. It was strange that neither of them had had any summons from the house.

"He said I ought to be ashamed of myself. He said, '*I'll not be the means of bringing shame to an honest gentleman and lady.*' I told him not to be a fool. I said I knew what I was about. Rickie and Agnes are properly educated, which leads people to look at things straight, and not go screaming about blots. A man like me, with just a little reading at odd hours—I've got so far, and Rickie has been through Cambridge."

"And Mrs Elliot?"

"Oh, she won't mind, and I told the man so; but he kept on saying, '*I'll* not be the means of bringing shame to an honest gentleman and lady,' until I got out of his rotten cart." His eye watched the man, a Nonconformist, driving away over God's earth. "I caught the train by running. I got to Waterloo at—"

Here the parlourmaid fluttered towards them. Would Mr Wonham come in? Mrs Elliot would be glad to see him now.

"Mrs Elliot?" cried Ansell. "Not Mr Elliot?"

"It's all the same," said Stephen, and moved towards the house. "You see, I only left my name. They don't know why I've come."

"Perhaps Mr Elliot sees me meanwhile?"

The parlourmaid looked blank. Mr Elliot had not said so. He had been with Mrs Elliot and Mr Pembroke in the study. Now the gentlemen had gone upstairs.

"All right, I can wait." After all, Rickie was treating him as he had treated Rickie, as one in the grave, to whom it is futile to make any loving motion. Gone upstairs—to brush his hair for dinner! The irony of the situation appealed to him strongly. It reminded him of the Greek Drama, where the actors know so little and the spectators so much.

"But, by the bye," he called after Stephen, "I think I ought to tell you—don't—"

"What is it?"

"Don't—" Then he was silent. He had been tempted to explain everything, to tell the fellow how things stood—that he must avoid this if he wanted to attain that; that he must break the news to Rickie gently; that he must have at least one battle royal with Agnes. But it was contrary to his own spirit to coach people: he held the human soul to be a very delicate thing, which can receive eternal damage from a little patronage. Stephen must go into the house simply as himself, for thus alone would he remain there.

"I ought to knock my pipe out? Was that it?"

"By no means. Go in, your pipe and you."

He hesitated, torn between propriety and desire. Then he followed the parlourmaid into the house smoking. As he entered the dinner-bell rang, and there was the sound of rushing feet, which died away into shuffling and silence. Through the window of the boys' dining-hall came the colourless voice of Rickie—

"Benedictus benedicat."

Ansell prepared himself to witness the second act of the drama; forgetting that all this world, and not part of it, is a stage.

Chapter 27

The parlourmaid took Mr Wonham to the study. He had been in the drawing-room before, but had got bored, and so had strolled out into the garden. Now he was in better spirits, as a man ought to be who has knocked down a man. As he passed through the hall he sparred at the teak monkey, and hung his cap on the bust of Hermes. And he greeted Mrs Elliot with a pleasant clap of laughter. "Oh, I've come with the most tremendous news!" he cried.

She bowed, but did not shake hands, which rather surprised him. But he never troubled over "details". He seldom watched people, and never thought that they were watching him. Nor could he guess how much it meant to her that he should enter her presence smoking. Had she not said once at Cadover, "Oh, *please* smoke; I love the smell of a pipe"?

"Would you sit down? Exactly there, please." She placed him at a large table, opposite an inkpot and a pad of blotting-paper. "Will you tell your 'tremendous news' to me? My brother and my husband are giving the boys their dinner."

"Ah!" said Stephen, who had had neither time nor money for breakfast in London.

"I told them not to wait for me."

So he came to the point at once. He trusted this handsome woman. His strength and his youth called to hers, expecting no prudish response. "It's very odd. It is that I'm Rickie's brother. I've just found out. I've come to tell you all."

"Yes?"

He felt in his pocket for the papers. "Half-brother I ought to have said."

"Yes?"

"I'm illegitimate. Legally speaking, that is. I've been turned out of Cadover. I haven't a penny. I—"

"There is no occasion to inflict the details." Her face, which had been an even brown, began to flush slowly in the centre of the cheeks. The colour spread till all that he saw of her was suffused, and she turned away. He thought he had shocked her, and so did she. Neither knew that the body can be insincere and express not the emotions we feel but those that we should like to feel. In reality she was quite calm, and her dislike of him had nothing emotional in it as yet.

"You see—" he began. He was determined to tell the fidgety story, for the sooner it was over the sooner they would have something to eat. Delicacy he lacked, and his sympathies were limited. But such as they were, they rang true: he put no decorous phantom between him and his desires.

"I do see. I have seen for two years." She sat down at the head of the table, where there was another inkpot. Into this she dipped a pen. "I have seen everything, Mr Wonham—who you are, how you have behaved at Cadover, how you must have treated Mrs Failing yesterday; and now"—her voice became very grave—"I see why you have come here, penniless. Before you speak, we know what you will say."

His mouth fell open, and he laughed so merrily that it might have given her a warning. But she was thinking how to follow up her first success. "And I thought I was bringing tremendous news!" he cried. "I only twisted it out of Mrs Failing last night. And Rickie knows too?"

"We have known for two years."

"But come, by the bye, if you've known for two years, how is it you didn't—" The laugh died out of his eyes. "You aren't ashamed?" he asked, half rising from his chair. "You aren't like the man towards Andover?"

"Please, please sit down," said Agnes, in the even tones she used when speaking to the servants; "let us not discuss side issues. I am a horribly direct person, Mr Wonham. I go always straight to the point." She opened a cheque-book. "I am afraid I shall shock you. For how much?"

He was not attending.

"There is the paper we suggest you shall sign." She pushed towards him a pseudo-legal document, just composed by Herbert.

"In consideration of the sum of ...., I agree to perpetual silence—to restrain from libellous . . . never to molest the said Frederick Elliot by intruding—"

His brain was not quick. He read the document over twice, and he could still say, "But what's that cheque for?"

"It is my husband's. He signed for you as soon as we heard you were here. We guessed you had come to be silenced. Here is his signature. But he has left the filling in for me. For how much? I will cross it, shall I? You will just have started a banking account, if I understand Mrs Failing rightly. It is not quite accurate to say you are penniless: I heard from her just before you returned from your cricket. She allows you two hundred a year, I think. But this additional sum—shall I date the cheque Saturday or for tomorrow?"

At last he found words. Knocking his pipe out on the table, he said slowly, "Here's a very bad mistake."

"It is quite possible," retorted Agnes. She was glad she had taken the offensive, instead of waiting till he began his blackmailing, as had been the advice of Rickie. Aunt Emily had said that very spring, "One's only hope with Stephen is to start bullying first." Here he was, quite bewildered, smearing the pipe-ashes with his thumb. He asked to read the document again. "A stamp and all!" he remarked.

They had anticipated that his claim would exceed two pounds.

"I see. All right. It takes a fool a minute. Never mind. I've made a bad mistake."

"You refuse?" she exclaimed, for he was standing at the door. "Then do your worst! We defy you!"

"That's all right, Mrs Elliot," he said roughly. "I don't want a scene with you, nor yet with your husband. We'll say no more about it. It's all right. I meant no harm."

"But your signature then! You must sign—you—"

He pushed past her, and said as he reached for his cap, "There, that's all right. It's my mistake. I'm sorry." He spoke like a farmer who has failed to sell a sheep. His manner was utterly prosaic, and up to the last she thought he had not understood her. "But it's money we offer you," she informed him, and then darted back to the study, believing for one terrible moment that he had picked up the blank cheque. When she returned to the hall he had gone. He was walking down the road rather quickly. At the corner he cleared his throat, spat into the gutter, and disappeared.

"There's an odd finish," she thought. She was puzzled, and determined to recast the interview a little when she related it to Rickie. She had not succeeded, for the paper was still unsigned. But she had so cowed Stephen that he would probably rest content with his two hundred a year, and never come troubling them again. Clever management, for one knew him to be rapacious: she had heard tales of him lending to the poor and exacting repayment to the uttermost farthing. He had also stolen at school. Moderately triumphant, she hurried into the side-garden: she had just remembered Ansell: she, not Rickie, had received his card.

"Oh, Mr Ansell!" she exclaimed, awaking him from some day-dream. "Haven't either Rickie or Herbert been out to you? Now, do come into dinner, to show you aren't offended. You will find all of us assembled in the boys' dining-hall."

To her annoyance he accepted.

"That is, if the Jacksons are not expecting you."

The Jacksons did not matter. If he might brush his clothes and bathe his lip, he would like to come.

"Oh, what has happened to you? And oh, my pretty lobelias!"

He replied, "A momentary contact with reality," and she, who did not look for sense in his remarks, hurried away to the dining-hall to announce him.

The dining-hall was not unlike the preparation-room. There was the same parquet floor, and dado of shiny pitch-pine. On its walls also were imperial portraits, and over the harmonium to which they sang the evening hymns was spread the Union Jack. Sunday dinner, the most pompous meal of the week, was in progress. Her brother sat at the head of the high table, her husband at the head of the second. To each she gave a reassuring nod and went to her

222

own seat, which was among the junior boys. The beef was being carried out; she stopped it. "Mr Ansell is coming," she called. "Herbert, there is more room by you; sit up straight, boys." The boys sat up straight, and a respectful hush spread over the room.

"Here he is!" called Rickie cheerfully, taking his cue from his wife. "Oh, this is splendid!" Ansell came in. "I'm so glad you managed this. I couldn't leave these wretches last night!" The boys tittered suitably. The atmosphere seemed normal. Even Herbert, though longing to hear what had happened to the blackmailer, gave adequate greeting to their guest: "Come in, Mr Ansell; come here. Take us as you find us!"

"I understood," said Stewart, "that I should find you all. Mrs Elliot told me I should. On that understanding I came."

It was at once evident that something had gone wrong.

Ansell looked round the room carefully. Then clearing his throat and ruffling his hair, he began—

"I cannot see the man with whom I have talked, intimately, for an hour, in your garden."

The worst of it was they were all so far from him and from each other, each at the end of a tableful of inquisitive boys. The two masters looked at Agnes for information, for her reassuring nod had not told them much. She looked hopelessly back.

"I cannot see this man," repeated Ansell, who remained by the harmonium in the midst of astonished waitresses. "Is he to be given no lunch?"

Herbert broke the silence by fresh greetings. Rickie knew that the contest was lost, and that his friend had sided with the enemy. It was the kind of thing he would do. One must face the catastrophe quietly and with dignity. Perhaps Ansell would have turned on his heel, and left behind him only vague suspicions, if Mrs Elliot had not tried to talk him down. "Man," she cried—"what man? Oh, I know—terrible bore! Did he get hold of you?"—thus committing their first blunder, and causing Ansell to say to Rickie, "Have you seen your brother?"

"I have not."

"Have you been told he was here?"

Rickie's answer was inaudible.

"Have you been told you have a brother?"

"Let us continue this conversation later."

"Continue it? My dear man, how can we until you know what I'm talking about? You must think me mad; but I tell you solemnly that you have a brother of whom you've never heard, and that he was in this house ten minutes ago." He paused impressively. "Your wife has happened to see him first. Being neither serious nor truthful, she is keeping you apart, telling him some lie and not telling you a word."

There was a murmur of alarm. One of the prefects rose, and Ansell set his back to the wall, quite ready for a battle. For two years he had waited for his opportunity. He would hit out at Mrs Elliot like any ploughboy now that it had come. Rickie said: "There is a slight misunderstanding. I, like my wife, have known what there is to know for two years"—a dignified rebuff, but their second blunder.

"Exactly," said Agnes. "Now I think Mr Ansell had better go."

"Go?" exploded Ansell. "I've everything to say yet. I beg your pardon, Mrs Elliot, I am concerned with you no longer. This man"—he turned to the avenue of faces—"this man who teaches you has a brother. He has known of him two years and been ashamed. He has—oh—oh—how it fits together! Rickie, it's you, not Mrs Silt, who must have sent tales of him to your aunt. It's you who've turned him out of Cadover. It's you who've ordered him to be ruined today. Mrs Elliot, I beg your pardon."

Now Herbert arose. "Out of my sight, sir! But have it from me first that Rickie and his aunt have both behaved most generously. No, no, Agnes, I will not be interrupted. Garbled versions must not get about. If the Wonham man is not satisfied now, he must be insatiable. He cannot levy blackmail on us for ever. Sir, I give you two minutes; then you will be expelled by force."

"Two minutes!" sang Ansell. "I can say a great deal in that." He put one foot on a chair and held his arms over the

quivering room. He seemed transfigured into a Hebrew prophet passionate for satire and the truth. "Oh, keep quiet for
two minutes," he cried, "and I'll tell you something you'll
be glad to hear. You're a little afraid Stephen may come
back. Don't be afraid. I bring good news. You'll never see
him nor anyone like him again. I must speak very plainly,
for you are all three fools. I don't want you to say afterwards,
'Poor Mr Ansell tried to be clever'. Generally I don't mind,
but I should mind today. Please listen. Stephen is a bully;
he drinks; he knocks one down; but he would sooner die
than take money from people he did not love. Perhaps he
will die, for he has nothing but a few pence that the poor
gave him and some tobacco which, to my eternal glory, he
accepted from me. Please listen again. Why did he come
here? Because he thought you would love him, and was ready
to love you. But I tell you, don't be afraid. He would sooner
die now than say you were his brother. Perhaps he will die,
for he has nothing but a few pence that the poor gave him
and some tobacco which, to my eternal glory, he accepted
from me. Please listen again—"

"Now, Stewart, don't go on like that," said Rickie bitterly.
"It's easy enough to preach when you are an outsider. You
would be more charitable if such a thing had happened to
yourself. Easy enough to be unconventional when you
haven't suffered and know nothing of the facts. You love
anything out of the way, anything queer, that doesn't often
happen, and so you get excited over this. It's useless, my
dear man; you have hurt me, but you will never upset me.
As soon as you stop this ridiculous scene we will finish our
dinner. Spread this scandal; add to it. I'm too old to mind
such nonsense. I cannot help my father's disgrace, on the
one hand; nor, on the other, will I have anything to do with
his blackguard of a son."

So the secret was given to the world. Agnes might colour
at his speech; Herbert might calculate the effect of it on the
entries for Dunwood House; but he cared for none of these
things. Thank God! he was withered up at last.

"Please listen again," resumed Ansell. "Please correct two
slight mistakes: firstly, Stephen is one of the greatest people

I have ever met; secondly, he's not your father's son. He's the son of your mother."

It was Rickie, not Ansell, who was carried from the hall, and it was Herbert who pronounced the blessing—

"Benedicto benedicatur."

A profound stillness succeeded the storm, and the boys, slipping away from their meal, told the news to the rest of the school, or put it in the letters they were writing home.

Chapter 28

The soul has her own currency. She mints her spiritual coinage and stamps it with the image of some beloved face. With it she pays her debts, with it she reckons, saying, "This man has worth, this man is worthless." And in time she forgets its origin; it seems to her to be a thing unalterable, divine. But the soul can also have her bankruptcies.

Perhaps she will be the richer in the end. In her agony she learns to reckon clearly. Fair as the coin may have been, it was not accurate; and though she knew it not, there were treasures that it could not buy. The face, however beloved, was mortal, and as liable as the soul herself to err. We do but shift responsibility by making a standard of the dead.

There is, indeed, another coinage that bears on it not man's image but God's. It is incorruptible, and the soul may trust it safely; it will serve her beyond the stars. But it cannot give us friends, or the embrace of a lover, or the touch of children, for with our fellow mortals it has no concern. It cannot even give the joys we call trivial—fine weather, the pleasures of meat and drink, bathing and the hot sand afterwards, running, dreamless sleep. Have we learnt the true discipline of a bankruptcy if we turn to such coinage as this? Will it really profit us so much if we save our souls and lose the whole world?

Part 3

Wiltshire

Chapter 29

Robert—there is no occasion to mention his surname: he was a young farmer of some education who tried to coax the aged soil of Wiltshire scientifically—came to Cadover on business and fell in love with Mrs Elliot. She was there on her bridal visit, and he, an obscure nobody, was received by Mrs Failing into the house and treated as her social equal. He was good-looking in a bucolic way, and people sometimes mistook him for a gentleman until they saw his hands. He discovered this, and one of the slow, gentle jokes he played on society was to talk upon some cultured subject with his hands behind his back and then suddenly reveal them. "Do you go in for boating?" the lady would ask; and then he explained that those particular weals are made by the handles of the plough. Upon which she became extremely interested, but found an early opportunity of talking to some one else.

He played this joke on Mrs Elliot the first evening, not knowing that she observed him as he entered the room. He walked heavily, lifting his feet as if the carpet was furrowed, and he had no evening clothes. Everyone tried to put him at his ease, but she rather suspected that he was there already, and envied him. They were introduced, and spoke of Byron, who was still fashionable. Out came his hands—the only rough hands in the drawing-room, the only hands that had ever worked. She was filled with some strange approval, and liked him.

After dinner they met again, to speak not of Byron but of manure. The other people were so clever and so amusing that it relieved her to listen to a man who told her three times not to buy artificial manure ready made, but, if she would use it, to make it herself at the last moment. Because the ammonia evaporated. Here were two packets of powder.

Did they smell? No. Mix them together and pour some coffee—An appalling smell at once burst forth, and everyone began to cough and cry. This was good for the earth when she felt sour, for he knew when the earth was ill. He knew, too, when she was hungry: he spoke of her tantrums—the strange unscientific element in her that will baffle the scientist to the end of time. "Study away, Mrs Elliot," he told her; "read all the books you can get hold of; but when it comes to the point, stroll out with a pipe in your mouth and do a bit of guessing." As he talked, the earth became a living being—or rather a being with a living skin—and manure no longer dirty stuff, but a symbol of regeneration and of the birth of life from life. "So it goes on for ever!" she cried excitedly. He replied: "Not for ever. In time the fire at the centre will cool, and nothing can go on then."

He advanced into love with open eyes, slowly, heavily, just as he had advanced across the drawing-room carpet. But this time the bride did not observe his tread. She was listening to her husband, and trying not to be so stupid. When he was close to her—so close that it was difficult not to take her in his arms—he spoke to Mr Failing, and was at once turned out of Cadover.

"I'm sorry," said Mr Failing, as he walked down the drive with his hand on his guest's shoulder. "I had no notion you were that sort. Anyone who behaves like that has to stop at the farm."

"Anyone?"

"Anyone." He sighed heavily, not for any personal grievance, but because he saw how unruly, how barbaric, is the soul of man. After all, this man was more civilized than most.

"Are you angry with me, sir?" He called him "sir", not because he was richer or cleverer or smarter, not because he had helped to educate him and had lent him money, but for a reason more profound—for the reason that there are gradations in heaven.

"I did think you—that a man like you wouldn't risk making people unhappy. My sister-in-law—I don't say this to stop you loving her; something else must do that—my sister-in-law, as far as I know, doesn't care for you one little bit. If you had said anything, if she had guessed that a chance person was in this fearful state, you would simply have opened hell. A woman of her sort would have lost all—"

"I knew that."

Mr Failing removed his hand. He was displeased.

"But something here," said Robert incoherently. "This here." He struck himself heavily on the heart. "This here, doing something so unusual, makes it not matter what she loses—I—" After a silence he asked, "Have I quite followed you, sir, in that business of the brotherhood of man?"

"How do you mean?"

"I thought love was to bring it about."

"Love of another man's wife? Sensual love? You have understood nothing—nothing." Then he was ashamed, and cried, "I understand nothing myself." For he remembered that sensual and spiritual are not easy words to use; that there are, perhaps, not two Aphrodites, but one Aphrodite with a Janus face. "I only understand that you must try to forget her."

"I will not try."

"Promise me just this, then—not to do anything crooked."

"I'm straight. No boasting, but I couldn't do a crooked thing—no, not if I tried."

And so appallingly straight was he in after years, that Mr Failing wished that he had phrased the promise differently.

Robert simply waited. He told himself that it was hopeless; but something deeper than himself declared that there was hope. He gave up drink, and kept himself in all ways clean, for he wanted to be worthy of her when the time came. Women seemed fond of him, and caused him to reflect with pleasure, "They do run after me. There must be something in me. Good. I'd be done for if there wasn't." For six years he turned up the earth of Wiltshire, and read books for the sake of his mind, and talked to gentlemen for the sake of their patois, and each year he rode to Cadover to take off his hat to Mrs Elliot, and, perhaps, to speak to her about the crops. Mr Failing was generally present, and it struck neither man that those dull little visits were so many words out of which a lonely woman might build sentences. Then Robert went to London on business. He chanced to see Mr Elliot with a strange lady. The time had come.

He became diplomatic, and called at Mr Elliot's rooms to find things out. For if Mrs Elliot was happier than he could ever make her, he would withdraw, and love her in renunciation. But if he could make her happier, he would love her in fulfilment. Mr Elliot admitted him as a friend of his brother-in-law's, and felt very broadminded as he did so. Robert, however, was a success. The youngish men there found him interesting, and liked to shock him with tales of naughty London and naughtier Paris. They spoke of "experience" and "sensations" and "seeing life", and when a smile ploughed over his face, concluded that his prudery was vanquished. He saw that they were much less vicious than they supposed: one boy had obviously read his sensations in a book. But he could pardon vice. What he could not pardon was triviality, and he hoped that no decent woman would pardon it either. There grew up in him a cold, steady anger against these silly people who thought it advanced to be shocking, and who described, as something particularly choice and educational, things that he had understood and fought against for years. He inquired after Mrs Elliot, and a boy tittered. It seemed that she "did not know", that she lived in a remote suburb, taking care of a skinny baby. "I shall call some time or other," said Robert. "Do," said Mr Elliot, smiling. And next time he saw his wife he congratulated her on her rustic admirer.

She had suffered terribly. She had asked for bread, and had been given not even a stone. People talk of hungering for the ideal, but there is another hunger, quite as divine, for facts. She had asked for facts and had been given "views", "emotional standpoints", "attitudes towards life". To a woman who believed that facts are beautiful, that the living world is beautiful beyond the laws of beauty, that manure is neither gross nor ludicrous, that a fire, not eternal, glows at the heart of the earth, it was intolerable to be put off with what the Elliots called "philosophy", and, if she refused, to be told that she had no sense of humour. "Marrying into the Elliot family." It had sounded so splendid, for she was a penniless child with nothing to offer, and the Elliots held their heads high. For what reason? What had they ever done, except say sarcastic things, and limp, and be refined? Mr Failing suffered too, but she suffered more, inasmuch as Frederick was more impossible than Emily. He did not like her, he practically lived apart, he was not even faithful or polite. These were grave faults, but they were human ones: she could even imagine them in a man she loved. What she could never love was a dilettante.

Robert brought her an armful of sweet-peas. He laid it on the table, put his hands behind his back, and kept them there till the end of the visit. She knew quite well why he had come, and though she also knew that he would fail, she loved him too much to snub him or to stare in virtuous indignation. "Why have you come?" she asked gravely, "and why have you brought me so many flowers?"

"My garden is full of them," he answered. "Sweet-peas need picking down. And, generally speaking, flowers are plentiful in July."

She broke his present into bunches—so much for the drawing-room, so much for the nursery, so much for the kitchen and her husband's room: he would be down for the night. The most beautiful she would keep for herself. Presently he said, "Your husband is no good. I've watched him for a week. I'm thirty, and not what you call hasty, as I used to be, or thinking that nothing matters like the French. No. I'm a plain Britisher, yet—I—I've begun wrong end, Mrs Elliot; I should have said that I've thought chiefly of you for six years, and that though I talk here so respectfully, if I once unhooked my hands—"

There was a pause. Then she said with great sweetness, "Thank you; I am glad you love me," and rang the bell.

"What have you done that for?" he cried.

"Because you must now leave the house, and never enter it again."

"I don't go alone," and he began to get furious.

Her voice was still sweet, but strength lay in it too, as she said, "You either go now with my thanks and my blessing, or else you go with the police. I am Mrs Elliot. We need not discuss Mr Elliot. I am Mrs Elliot, and if you make one step towards me I give you in charge."

But the maid answered the bell not of the drawing-room, but of the front door. They were joined by Mr Elliot, who held out his hand with much urbanity. It was not taken. He looked quickly at his wife, and said, "Am I *de trop?*" There was a long silence. At last she said, "Frederick, turn this man out."

"My love, why?"

Robert said that he loved her.

"Then I am *de trop*," said Mr Elliot, smoothing out his gloves. He would give these sodden barbarians a lesson. "My hansom is waiting at the door. Pray make use of it."

"Don't!" she cried, almost affectionately. "Dear Frederick, it isn't a play. Just tell this man to go, or send for the police."

"On the contrary; it is French comedy of the best type. Don't you agree, sir, that the police would be an inartistic error?" He was perfectly calm and collected, whereas they were in a pitiable state.

"Turn him out at once!" she cried. "He has insulted your wife. Save me, save me!" She clung to her husband and wept. "He was going—I had managed him—he would never have known—" Mr Elliot repulsed her.

"If you don't feel inclined to start at once," he said with easy civility, "let us have a little tea. My dear sir, do forgive me for not shooting you. *Nous avons changé tout cela.* Please don't look so nervous. Please do unclasp your hands—"

He was alone.

"That's all right," he exclaimed, and strolled to the door. The hansom was disappearing round the corner. "That's all right," he repeated in more quavering tones as he returned to the drawing-room and saw that it was littered with sweet-peas. Their colour got on his nerves—magenta, crimson; magenta, crimson. He tried to pick them up, and they

236

escaped. He trod them underfoot, and they multiplied and danced in the triumph of summer like a thousand butterflies. The train had left when he got to the station. He followed on to London, and there he lost all traces. At midnight he began to realize that his wife could never belong to him again.

Mr Failing had a letter from Stockholm. It was never known what impulse sent them there. "I am sorry about it all, but it was the only way." The letter censured the law of England, "which obliges us to behave like this, or else we should never get married. I shall come back to face things: she will not come back till she is my wife. He must bring an action soon, or else we shall try one against him. It seems all very unconventional, but it is not really. It is only a difficult start. We are not like you or your wife: we want to be just ordinary people, and make the farm pay, and not be noticed all our lives."

And they were capable of living as they wanted. The class difference, which so intrigued Mrs Failing, meant very little to them. It was there, but so were other things. They both cared for work and living in the open, and for not speaking unless they had got something to say. Their love of beauty, like their love for each other, was not dependent on detail: it grew not from the nerves but from the soul.

> I believe a leaf of grass is no less than the journey work of the stars,
> And the pismire is equally perfect, and a grain of sand, and the egg of the wren,
> And the tree toad is a chef-d'œuvre for the highest,
> And the running blackberry would adorn the parlours of heaven.

They had never read these lines, and would have thought them nonsense if they had. They did not dissect—indeed they could not. But she, at all events, divined that more than perfect health and perfect weather, more than personal love, had gone to the making of those seventeen days.

"Ordinary people!" cried Mrs Failing on hearing the

letter. At that time she was young and daring. "Why, they're divine! They're forces of Nature! They're as ordinary as volcanoes. We all knew my brother was disgusting, and wanted him to be blown to pieces, but we never thought it would happen. Do look at the thing bravely, and say, as I do, that they are guiltless in the sight of God."

"I think they are," replied her husband. "But they are not guiltless in the sight of man."

"You conventional!" she exclaimed in disgust.

"What they have done means misery not only for themselves but for others. For your brother, though you will not think of him. For the little boy—did you think of him? And perhaps for another child, who will have the whole world against him if it knows. They have sinned against society, and you do not diminish the misery by proving that society is bad or foolish. It is the saddest truth I have yet perceived that the Beloved Republic"—here she took up a book—"of which Swinburne speaks"—she put the book down—"will not be brought about by love alone. It will approach with no flourish of trumpets, and have no declaration of independence. Self-sacrifice and—worse still—self-mutilation are the things that sometimes help it most, and that is why we should start for Stockholm this evening." He waited for her indignation to subside, and then continued. "I don't know whether it can be hushed up. I don't yet know whether it ought to be hushed up. But we ought to provide the opportunity. There is no scandal yet. If we go, it is just possible there never will be any. We must talk over the whole thing and—"

"—And lie!" interrupted Mrs Failing, who hated travel.

"—And see how to avoid the greatest unhappiness."

There was to be no scandal. By the time they arrived Robert had been drowned. Mrs Elliot described how they had gone swimming, and how, "since he always lived inland," the great waves had tired him. They had raced for the open sea.

"What are your plans?" he asked. "I bring you a message from Frederick."

"I heard him call," she continued, "but I thought he was laughing. When I turned, it was too late. He put his hands behind his back and sank. For he would only have drowned me with him. I should have done the same."

Mrs Failing was thrilled, and kissed her. But Mr Failing knew that life does not continue heroic for long, and he gave her the message from her husband: Would she come back to him?

To his intense astonishment—at first to his regret—she replied, "I will think about it. If I loved him the very least bit I should say no. If I had anything to do with my life I should say no. But it is simply a question of beating time till I die. Nothing that is coming matters. I may as well sit in his drawing-room and dust his furniture, since he has suggested it."

And Mr Elliot, though he made certain stipulations, was positively glad to see her. People had begun to laugh at him, and to say that his wife had run away. She had not. She had been with his sister in Sweden. In a half-miraculous way the matter was hushed up. Even the Silts only scented "something strange". When Stephen was born, it was abroad. When he came to England, it was as the child of a friend of Mr Failing's. Mrs Elliot returned unsuspected to her husband.

But though things can be hushed up, there is no such thing as beating time; and as the years passed she realized her terrible mistake. When her lover sank, eluding her last embrace, she thought, as Agnes was to think after her, that her soul had sunk with him, and that never again should she be capable of earthly love. Nothing mattered. She might as well go and be useful to her husband and to the little boy who looked exactly like him, and who, she thought, was exactly like him in disposition. Then Stephen was born, and altered her life. She could still love people passionately; she still drew strength from the heroic past. Yet, to keep to her bond, she must see this son only as a stranger. She was protected by the conventions, and must pay them their fee. And a curious thing happened. Her second child drew her towards her first. She began to love Rickie also, and to be more than useful to him. And as her love revived, so did her capacity for suffering. Life, more important, grew more bitter. She minded her husband more, not less; and when at last he died, and she saw a glorious autumn, beautiful with the voices of boys who should call her mother, the end came for her as well, before she could remember the grave in the alien north and the dust that would never return to the dear fields that had given it.

Chapter 30

Stephen, the son of these people, had one instinct that troubled him. At night—especially out of doors—it seemed rather strange that he was alive. The dry grass pricked his cheek, the fields were invisible and mute, and here was he, throwing stones at the darkness or smoking a pipe. The stones vanished, the pipe would burn out. But he would be here in the morning when the sun rose, and he would bathe, and run in the mist. He was proud of his good circulation, and in the morning it seemed quite natural. But at night, why should there be this difference between him and the acres of land that cooled all round him until the sun returned? What lucky chance had heated him up, and sent him, warm and lovable, into a passive world? He had other instincts, but these gave him no trouble. He simply gratified each as it occurred, provided he could do so without grave injury to his fellows. But the instinct to wonder at the night was not to be thus appeased.

At first he had lived under the care of Mr Failing—the only person to whom his mother spoke freely, the only person who had treated her neither as a criminal nor as a pioneer. In their rare but intimate conversations she had asked him to educate her son. "I will teach him Latin," he answered. "The rest such a boy must remember." Latin, at all events, was a failure: who could attend to Virgil when the sound of the thresher arose, and you knew that the stack was decreasing and that rats rushed more plentifully each moment to their doom? But he was fond of Mr Failing, and cried when he died. Mrs Elliot, a pleasant woman, died soon after.

There was something fatal in the order of these deaths. Mr Failing had made no provision for the boy in his will: his wife had promised to see to this. Then came Mr Elliot's death, and, before the new home was created, the sudden death of Mrs Elliot. She also left Stephen no money: she had none to leave. Chance threw him into the power of Mrs Failing. "Let things go on as they are," she thought. "I will take care of this pretty little boy, and the ugly little boy can live with the Silts. After my death—well, the papers will be found after my death, and they can meet then. I like the idea of their mutual ignorance. It is amusing."

He was then twelve. With a few brief intervals of school, he lived in Wiltshire until he was driven out. Life had two distinct sides—the drawing-room and the other. In the drawing-room people talked a good deal, laughing as they talked. Being clever, they did not care for animals: one man had never seen a hedgehog. In the other life people talked and laughed separately, or even did neither. On the whole, in spite of the wet and gamekeepers, this life was preferable. He knew where he was. He glanced at the boy, or later at the man, and behaved accordingly. There was no law—the policeman was negligible. Nothing bound him but his own word, and he gave that sparingly.

It is impossible to be romantic when you have your heart's desire, and such a boy disappointed Mrs Failing greatly. His parents had met for one brief embrace, had found one little interval between the power of the rulers of this world and the power of death. He was the child of poetry and of rebellion, and poetry should run in his veins. But he lived too near to the things he loved to seem poetical. Parted from them, he might yet satisfy her, and stretch out his hands with a pagan's yearning. As it was, he only rode her horses, and trespassed, and bathed, and worked, for no obvious reason, upon her fields. Affection she did not believe in, and made no attempt to mould him; and he, for his part, was very content to harden untouched into a man. His parents had given him excellent gifts—health, sturdy limbs, and a face not ugly—gifts that his habits confirmed. They had also given him a cloudless spirit—the spirit of the seventeen days in which he was created. But they had not given him the spirit of their six years of waiting, and love for one person was never to be the greatest thing he knew.

"Philosophy" had postponed the quarrel between them.

Incurious about his personal origin, he had a certain interest in our eternal problems. The interest never became a passion: it sprang out of his physical growth, and was soon merged in it again. Or, as he put it himself, "I must get fixed up before starting." He was soon fixed up as a materialist. Then he tore up the sixpenny reprints, and never amused Mrs Failing so much again.

About the time he fixed himself up, he took to drink. He knew of no reason against it. The instinct was in him, and it hurt nobody. Here, as elsewhere, his motions were decided, and he passed at once from roaring jollity to silence. For those who live on the fuddled borderland, who crawl home by the railings and maunder repentance in the morning, he had a biting contempt. A man must take his tumble and his headache. He was, in fact, as little disgusting as is conceivable; and hitherto he had not strained his constitution or his will. Nor did he get drunk as often as Agnes suggested. The real quarrel gathered elsewhere.

Presentable people have run wild in their youth. But the hour comes when they turn from their boorish company to higher things. This hour never came for Stephen. Somewhat a bully by nature, he kept where his powers would tell, and continued to quarrel and play with the men he had known as boys. He prolonged their youth unduly. "They won't settle down," said Mr Wilbraham to his wife. "They're wanting things. It's the germ of a Trades Union. I shall get rid of a few of the worst." Then Stephen rushed up to Mrs Failing and worried her. "It wasn't fair. So-and-so was a good sort. He did his work. Keen about it? No. Why should he be? Why should he be keen about somebody else's land? But keen enough. And very keen on football." She laughed, and said a word about So-and-so to Mr Wilbraham. Mr Wilbraham blazed up. "How could the farm go on without discipline? How could there be discipline if Mr Stephen interfered? Mr Stephen liked power. He spoke to the men like one of themselves, and pretended it was all equality, but he took care to come out top. Natural, of course, that, being a gentleman, he should. But not natural for a gentleman to loiter all day with poor people and learn their work, and

put wrong notions into their heads, and carry their newfang-
led grievances to Mrs Failing. Which partly accounted for
the deficit on the past year." She rebuked Stephen. Then he
lost his temper, was rude to her, and insulted Mr Wilbraham.

The worst days of Mr Failing's rule seemed to be returning. And Stephen had a practical experience, and also a
taste for battle, that her husband had never possessed. He
drew up a list of grievances, some absurd, others fundamental. No newspapers in the reading-room, you could put
a plate under the Thompsons' door, no level cricket pitch,
no allotments and no time to work in them, Mrs Wilbraham's knife-boy underpaid. "Aren't you a little unwise?"
she asked coldly. "I am more bored than you think over the
farm." She was wanting to correct the proofs of the book
and rewrite the prefatory memoir. In her irritation she wrote
to Agnes. Agnes replied sympathetically, and Mrs Failing,
clever as she was, fell into the power of the younger woman.
They discussed him at first as a wretch of a boy; then he got
drunk and somehow it seemed more criminal. All that she
needed now was a personal grievance, which Agnes casually
supplied. Though vindictive, she was determined to treat
him well, and thought with satisfaction of our distant
colonies. But he burst into an odd passion: he would sooner
starve than leave England. "Why?" she asked. "Are you in
love?" He picked up a lump of the chalk—they were by the
arbour—and made no answer. The vicar murmured, "It is
not like going abroad—Greater Britain—blood is thicker
than water—" A lump of chalk broke her drawing-room
window on the Saturday.

Thus Stephen left Wiltshire, half blackguard, half martyr.
Do not brand him as a socialist. He had no quarrel with
society, nor any particular belief in people because they are
poor. He only held the creed of "here am I and there are
you", and therefore class distinctions were trivial things to
him, and life no decorous scheme, but a personal combat or
a personal truce. For the same reason ancestry also was trivial, and a man not the dearer because the same woman
was mother to them both. Yet it seemed worth while to go

to Sawston with the news. Perhaps nothing would come of it; perhaps friendly intercourse, and a home while he looked around.

When they wronged him he walked quietly away. He never thought of allotting the blame, nor of appealing to Ansell, who still sat brooding in the side-garden. He only knew that educated people could be horrible, and that a clean liver must never enter Dunwood House again. The air seemed stuffy. He spat in the gutter. Was it yesterday he had lain in the rifle-butts over Salisbury? Slightly aggrieved, he wondered why he was not back there now. "I ought to have written first," he reflected. "Here is my money gone. I cannot move. The Elliots have, as it were, practically robbed me." That was the only grudge he retained against them. Their suspicions and insults were to him as the curses of a tramp whom he passed by the wayside. They were dirty people, not his sort. He summed up the complicated tragedy as a "take in".

While Rickie was being carried upstairs, and while Ansell (had he known it) was dashing about the streets for him, he lay under a railway arch trying to settle his plans. He must pay back the friends who had given him shillings and clothes. He thought of Flea, whose Sundays he was spoiling—poor Flea, who ought to be in them now, shining before his girl. "I daresay he'll be ashamed and not go to see her, and then she'll take the other man." He was also very hungry. That worm Mrs Elliot would be through her lunch by now. Tying his braces round him, and tearing up those old wet documents, he stepped forth to make money. A villainous young brute he looked: his clothes were dirty, and he had lost the spring of the morning. Touching the walls, frowning, talking to himself at times, he slouched disconsolately northwards; no wonder that some tawdry girls screamed at him, or that matrons averted their eyes as they hurried to afternoon church. He wandered from one suburb to another, till he was among people more villainous than himself, who bought his tobacco from him and sold him food. Again the neighbourhood "went up", and families, instead of sitting on their doorsteps, would sit behind thick muslin curtains. Again it would "go down" into a more avowed despair. Far into the night he wandered, until he came to a solemn river majestic as a stream in hell. Therein were gathered the waters of Central England—those that flow off Hindhead, off the Chilterns, off Wiltshire north of the Plain. Therein they were made intolerable ere they reached the sea. But the waters he had known escaped. Their course lay southward into the Avon by forests and beautiful fields, ever swift, ever pure, until they mirrored the tower of Christchurch and greeted the ramparts of the Isle of Wight. Of these he thought for a moment as he crossed the black river and entered the heart of the modern world.

Here he found employment. He was not hampered by genteel traditions, and, as it was near quarter-day, managed to get taken on at a furniture warehouse. He moved people from the suburbs to London, from London to the suburbs, from one suburb to another. His companions were hurried and querulous. In particular, he loathed the foreman, a pious humbug who allowed no swearing, but indulged in something far more degraded—the Cockney repartee. The London intellect, so pert and shallow, like a stream that never reaches the ocean, disgusted him almost as much as the London physique, which for all its dexterity is not permanent, and seldom continues into the third generation. His father, had he known it, had felt the same; for between Mr Elliot and the foreman the gulf was social, not spiritual: both spent their lives in trying to be clever. And Tony Failing had once put the thing into words: "There's no such thing as a Londoner. He's only a country man on the road to sterility."

At the end of ten days he had saved scarcely anything. Once he passed the bank where a hundred pounds lay ready for him, but it was still inconvenient for him to take them. Then duty sent him to a suburb not very far from Sawston. In the evening a man who was driving a trap asked him to hold it, and by mistake tipped him a sovereign. Stephen called after him; but the man had a woman with him and wanted to show off, and though he had meant to tip a shilling, and could not afford that, he shouted back that his sovereign was as good as anyone's, and that if Stephen did not think so he could do various things and go to various places. On the action of this man much depends. Stephen changed the sovereign into a postal order, and sent it off to the people at Cadford. It did not pay them back, but it paid them something, and he felt that his soul was free.

A few shillings remained in his pocket. They would have paid his fare towards Wiltshire, a good county; but what should he do there? Who would employ him? Today the journey did not seem worth while. "Tomorrow, perhaps," he thought, and determined to spend the money on pleasure of another kind. Twopence went for a ride on an electric tram. From the top he saw the sun descend—a disc with a dark red edge. The same sun was descending over Salisbury intolerably bright. Out of the golden haze the spire would be piercing, like a purple needle; then mists arose from the Avon and the other streams. Lamps flickered, but in the outer purity the villages were already slumbering. Salisbury is only a Gothic upstart beside these. For generations they have come down to her to buy or to worship, and have found in her the reasonable crisis of their lives; but generations before she was built they were clinging to the soil, and renewing it with sheep and dogs and men, who found the crisis of their lives upon Stonehenge. The blood of these men ran in Stephen; the vigour they had won for him was as yet untarnished; out on those downs they had united with rough women to make the thing he spoke of as "himself"; the last of them had rescued a woman of a different kind from streets and houses such as these. As the sun descended he got off the tram with a smile of expectation. A public-house lay opposite, and a boy in a dirty uniform was already lighting its enormous lamp. His lips parted, and he went in.

Two hours later, when Rickie and Herbert were going the rounds, a brick came crashing at the study window. Herbert peered into the garden, and a hooligan slipped by him into the house, wrecked the hall, lurched up the stairs, fell against the banisters, balanced for a moment on his spine, and slid over. Herbert called for the police. Rickie, who was upon the landing, caught the man by the knees and saved his life.

"What is it?" cried Agnes, emerging.

"It's Stephen come back," was the answer. "Hullo, Stephen!"

Chapter 31

Hither had Rickie moved in ten days—from disgust to penitence, from penitence to longing, from a life of horror to a new life, in which he still surprised himself by unexpected words. Hullo, Stephen! For the son of his mother had come back, to forgive him, as she would have done, to live with him, as she had planned.

"He's drunk this time," said Agnes wearily. She too had altered: the scandal was ageing her, and Ansell came to the house daily.

"Hullo, Stephen!"

But Stephen was now insensible.

"Stephen, you live here—"

"Good gracious me!" interposed Herbert. "My advice is, that we all go to bed. The less said the better while our nerves are in this state. Very well, Rickie. Of course, Wonham sleeps the night if you wish." They carried the drunken mass into the spare room. A mass of scandal it seemed to one of them, a symbol of redemption to the other. Neither acknowledged it a man, who would answer them back after a few hours' rest.

"Ansell thought he would never forgive me," said Rickie. "For once he's wrong."

"Come to bed now, I think." And as Rickie laid his hand on the sleeper's hair, he added, "You won't do anything foolish, will you? You are still in a morbid state. Your poor mother—Pardon me, dear boy; it is my turn to speak out. You thought it was your father, and minded. It is your mother. Surely you ought to mind more?"

"I have been too far back," said Rickie gently. "Ansell took me a journey that was even new to him. We got behind right and wrong, to a place where only one thing matters—that the Beloved should rise from the dead."

"But you won't do anything rash?"

"Why should I?"

"Remember poor Agnes," he stammered. "I—I am the first to acknowledge that we might have pursued a different policy. But we are committed to it now. It makes no difference whose son he is. I mean, he is the same person. You and I and my sister stand or fall together. It was our agreement from the first. I hope—No more of these distressing scenes with her, there's a dear fellow. I assure you they make my heart bleed."

"Things will quiet down now."

"To bed now; I insist upon that much."

"Very well," said Rickie, and when they were in the passage, locked the door from the outside. "We want no more muddles," he explained.

Mr Pembroke was left examining the hall. The bust of Hermes was broken. So was the pot of the palm. He could not go to bed without once more sounding Rickie. "You'll do nothing rash," he called. "The notion of him living here was, of course, a passing impulse. We three have adopted a common policy."

"Now, you go away!" called a voice that was almost flippant. "I never did belong to that great sect whose doctrine is that each one should select—at least, I'm not going to belong to it any longer. Go away to bed."

"A good night's rest is what you need," threatened Herbert, and retired, not to find one for himself.

But Rickie slept. The guilt of months and the remorse of the last ten days had alike departed. He had thought that his life was poisoned, and lo! it was purified. He had cursed his mother, and Ansell had replied, "You may be right, but you stand too near to settle. Step backwards. Pretend that it happened to me. Do you want me to curse my mother? Now, step forward and see whether anything has changed." Something had changed. He had journeyed—as on rare occasions a man must—till he stood behind right and wrong. On the banks of the gray torrent of life, love is the only flower. A little way up the stream and a little way down had Rickie glanced, and he knew that she whom he loved had risen from the dead, and might rise again. "Come away—let them die out—let them die out." Surely that dream was a vision! Tonight also he hurried to the window—to remember, with a smile, that Orion is not among the stars of June.

"Let me die out. She will continue," he murmured, and in making plans for Stephen's happiness, fell asleep.

Next morning after breakfast he announced that his brother must live at Dunwood House. They were awed by the very moderation of his tone. "There's nothing else to be done. Cadover's hopeless, and a boy of those tendencies can't go drifting. There is also the question of a profession for him, and his allowance."

"We have to thank Mr Ansell for this," was all that Agnes could say; and "I foresee disaster," was the contribution of Herbert.

"There's plenty of money about," Rickie continued. "Quite a man's-worth too much. It has been one of our absurdities. Don't look so sad, Herbert. I'm sorry for you people, but he's sure to let us down easy." For his experience of drunkards and of Stephen was small. He supposed that he had come without malice to renew the offer of ten days ago.

"It is the end of Dunwood House."

Rickie nodded, and hoped not. Agnes, who was not looking well, began to cry. "Oh, it is too bad," she complained, "when I've saved you from him all these years." But he could not pity her, nor even sympathize with her wounded delicacy. The time for such nonsense was over. He would take his share of the blame: it was cant to assume it all.

Perhaps he was over-hard. He did not realize how large his share was, nor how his very virtues were to blame for her deterioration. "If I had a girl, I'd keep her in line," is not the remark of a fool nor of a cad. Rickie had not kept his wife in line. He had shown her all the workings of his soul, mistaking this for love; and in consequence she was the worse woman after two years of marriage, and he, on this morning of freedom, was harder upon her than he need have been.

The spare room bell rang. Herbert had a painful struggle between curiosity and duty, for the bell for chapel was ringing also, and he must go through the drizzle to school. He promised to come up in the interval. Rickie, who had rapped his head that Sunday on the edge of the table, was still forbidden to work. Before him a quiet morning lay. Secure of his victory, he took the portrait of their mother in his hand and walked leisurely upstairs. The bell continued to ring.

"See about his breakfast," he called to Agnes, who replied, "Very well." The handle of the spare room door was moving slowly. "I'm coming," he cried. The handle was still. He unlocked and entered, his heart full of charity. But within stood a man who probably owned the world.

Rickie scarcely knew him; last night he had seemed so colourless, so negligible. In a few hours he had recaptured motion and passion and the imprint of the sunlight and the wind. He stood, not consciously heroic, with arms that dangled from broad stooping shoulders, and feet that played with a hassock on the carpet. But his hair was beautiful against the gray sky, and his eyes, recalling the sky unclouded, shot past the intruder as if to some worthier vision. So intent was their gaze that Rickie himself glanced backwards, only to see the neat passage and the banisters at the top of the stairs. Then the lips beat together twice, and out burst a torrent of amazing words.

"Add it all up, and let me know how much. I'd sooner have died. It never took me that way before. I must have broken pounds' worth. If you'll not tell the police, I promise you shan't lose, Mr Elliot, I swear. But it may be months before I send it. Everything is to be new. You've not to be a penny out of pocket, do you see? Do let me go, this once again."

"What's the trouble?" asked Rickie, as if they had been friends for years. "My dear man, we've other things to talk about. Gracious me, what a fuss! If you'd smashed the whole house I wouldn't mind, so long as you came back."

"I'd sooner have died," gulped Stephen.

"You did nearly! It was I who caught you. Never mind yesterday's rag. What can you manage for breakfast?"

The face grew more angry and more puzzled. "Yesterday wasn't a rag," he said without focusing his eyes. "I was drunk, but naturally meant it."

"Meant what?"

"To smash you. Bad liquor did what Mrs Elliot couldn't. I've put myself in the wrong. You've got me."

It was a poor beginning.

"As I have got you," said Rickie, controlling himself, "I want to have a talk with you. There has been a ghastly mistake."

But Stephen, with a countryman's persistency, continued on his own line. He meant to be civil, but Rickie went cold round the mouth. For he had not even been angry with them. Until he was drunk, they had been dirty people—not his sort. Then the trivial injury recurred, and he had reeled to smash them as he passed. "And I will pay for everything," was his refrain, with which the sighing of raindrops mingled. "You shan't lose a penny, if only you let me free."

"You'll pay for my coffin if you talk like that any longer! Will you, one, forgive my frightful behaviour; two, live with me?" For his only hope was in a cheerful precision.

Stephen grew more agitated. He thought it was some trick.

"I was saying I made an unspeakable mistake. Ansell put me right, but it was too late to find you. Don't think I got off easily. Ansell doesn't spare one. And you've got to forgive me, to share my life, to share my money.—I've brought you this photograph—I want it to be the first thing you accept from me—you have the greater right—I know all the story now. You know who it is?"

"Oh yes; but I don't want to drag all that in."

"It is only her wish if we live together. She was planning it when she died."

"I can't follow—because—to share your life? Did you know I called here last Sunday week?"

"Yes. But then I only knew half. I thought you were my father's son."

Stephen's anger and bewilderment were increasing. He stuttered. "What—what's the odds if you did?"

"I hated my father," said Rickie. "I loved my mother." And never had the phrases seemed so destitute of meaning.

"Last Sunday week," interrupted Stephen, his voice suddenly rising, "I came to call on you. Not as this or that's son. Not to fall on your neck. Nor to live here. Nor—damn your dirty little mind! I meant to say I didn't come for money. Sorry. Sorry. I simply came as I was, and I haven't altered since."

"Yes—yet our mother—for me she has risen from the dead since then—I know I was wrong—"

"And where do I come in?" He kicked the hassock. "*I* haven't risen from the dead. *I* haven't altered since last Sunday week. I'm—" He stuttered again. He could not quite explain what he was. "The man towards Andover—after all, he was having principles. But you've—" His voice broke. "I mind it—I'm—*I* don't alter—blackguard one week—live here the next—I keep to one or the other—you've hurt something most badly in me that I didn't know was there."

"Don't let us talk," said Rickie. "It gets worse every minute. Simply say you forgive me; shake hands, and have done with it."

"That I won't. That I couldn't. In fact, I don't know what you mean."

Then Rickie began a new appeal—not to pity, for now he was in no mood to whimper. For all its pathos, there was something heroic in this meeting. "I warn you to stop here with me, Stephen. No one else in the world will look after you. As far as I know, you have never been really unhappy yet or suffered, as you should do, from your faults. Last night you nearly killed yourself with drink. Never mind why I'm willing to cure you. I am willing, and I warn you to give me the chance. Forgive me or not, as you choose. I care for other things more."

Stephen looked at him at last, faintly approving. The offer was ridiculous, but it did treat him as a man.

"Let me tell you of a fault of mine, and how I was punished for it," continued Rickie. "Two years ago I behaved badly to you, up at the Rings. No, even a few days before that. We went for a ride, and I thought too much of other matters, and did not try to understand you. Then came the Rings, and in the evening, when you called up to me most kindly, I never answered. But the ride was the beginning. Ever since then I have taken the world at secondhand. I have bothered less and less to look it in the face—until not only you, but everyone else has turned unreal. Never Ansell: he kept away, and somehow saved himself. But everyone else. Do you remember in one of Tony Failing's books, 'Cast bitter bread upon the waters, and after many days it really does come back to you'? This has been true of my life; it will be equally true of a drunkard's, and I warn you to stop with me."

"I can't stop after that cheque," said Stephen more gently. "But I do remember the ride. I was a bit bored myself."

Agnes, who had not been seeing to the breakfast, chose this moment to call from the passage. "Of course he can't stop," she exclaimed. "For better or worse, it's settled. We've none of us altered since last Sunday week."

"There you're right, Mrs Elliot!" he shouted, starting out of the temperate past. "We haven't altered." With a rare flash of insight he turned on Rickie. "I see your game. You don't care about *me* drinking, or to shake *my* hand. It's some one else you want to cure—as it were, that old photograph. You talk to me, but all the time you look at the photograph." He snatched it up. "I've my own idea of good manners, and to look friends between the eyes is one of them; and this"— he tore the photograph across—"and this"—he tore it again—"and these—" He flung the pieces at the man, who had sunk into a chair. "For my part, I'm off."

Then Rickie was heroic no longer. Turning round in his chair, he covered his face. The man was right. He did not love him, even as he had never hated him. In either passion he had degraded him to be a symbol for the vanished past. The man was right, and would have been lovable. He longed to be back riding over those windy fields, to be back in those mystic circles, beneath pure sky. Then they could have watched and helped and taught each other, until the word was a reality, and the past not a torn photograph, but Demeter the goddess rejoicing in the spring. Ah, if he had seized those high opportunities! For they led to the highest of all, the symbolic moment, which, if a man accepts, he has accepted life.

The voice of Agnes, which had lured him then ("For my sake," she had whispered), pealed over him now in triumph. Abruptly it broke into sobs that had the effect of rain. He started up. The anger had died out of Stephen's face, not for a subtle reason but because here was a woman, near him, and unhappy.

She tried to apologize, and brought on a fresh burst of tears. Something had upset her. They heard her locking the door of her room. From that moment their intercourse was changed.

"Why does she keep crying today?" mused Rickie, as if he spoke to some mutual friend.

"I can make a guess," said Stephen, and his heavy face flushed.

"Did you insult her?" he asked feebly.

"But who's Gerald?"

Rickie raised his hand to his mouth.

"She looked at me as if she knew me, and then gasps 'Gerald', and started crying."

"Gerald is the name of some one she once knew."

"So I thought." There was a long silence, in which they could hear a piteous gulping cough. "Where is he now?" asked Stephen.

"Dead."

"And then you—?"

Rickie nodded.

"Bad, this sort of thing."

"I didn't know of this particular thing. She acted as if she had forgotten him. Perhaps she had, and you woke him up. There are queer tricks in the world. She is overstrained. She has probably been plotting ever since you burst in last night."

"Against me?"

"Yes."

Stephen stood irresolute. "I suppose you and she pulled together?" he said at last.

"Get away from us, man! I mind losing you. Yet it's as well you don't stop."

"Oh, *that's* out of the question," said Stephen, brushing his cap.

"If you've guessed anything, I'd be obliged if you didn't mention it. I've no right to ask, but I'd be obliged."

He nodded, and walked slowly along the landing and down the stairs. Rickie accompanied him, and even opened the front door. It was as if Agnes had absorbed the passion out of both of them. The suburb was now wrapped in a cloud, not of its own making. Sigh after sigh passed along its streets to break against dripping walls. The school, the houses were hidden, and all civilization seemed in abeyance. Only the simplest sounds, the simplest desires emerged. They agreed that this weather was strange after such a sunset.

"That's a collie," said Stephen, listening.

"I wish you'd have some breakfast before starting."

"No food, thanks. But you know——" He paused. "It's all been a muddle, and I've no objection to your coming along with me."

The cloud descended lower.

"Come with me as a man," said Stephen, already out in the mist. "Not as a brother; who cares what people did years back? We're alive together, and the rest is cant. Here am I, Rickie, and there are you, a fair wreck. They've no use for you here—never had any, if the truth was known—and they've only made you beastly. This house, so to speak, has the rot. It's common sense that you should come."

"Stephen, wait a minute. What do you mean?"

"Wait's what we won't do," said Stephen at the gate.

"I must ask——"

He did wait for a minute, and sobs were heard, faint, hopeless, vindictive. Then he trudged away, and Rickie soon lost his colour and his form. But a voice persisted, saying, "Come, I do mean it. Come; I will take care of you, I can manage you."

The words were kind; yet it was not for their sake that Rickie plunged into the impalpable cloud. In the voice he had found a surer guarantee. Habits and sex may change with the new generation, features may alter with the play of a private passion, but a voice is apart from these. It lies nearer to the racial essence and perhaps to the divine; it can, at all events, overleap one grave.

Chapter 32

Mr Pembroke did not receive a clear account of what had happened when he returned for the interval. His sister—he told her frankly—was concealing something from him. She could make no reply. Had she gone mad, she wondered. Hitherto she had pretended to love her husband. Why choose such a moment for the truth?

"But I understand Rickie's position," he told her. "It is an unbalanced position, yet I understand it; I noted its approach while he was ill. He imagines himself his brother's keeper. Therefore we must make concessions. We must negotiate." The negotiations were still progressing in November, the month during which this story draws to its close.

"I understand his position," he then told her. "It is both weak and defiant. He is still with those Ansells. Read this letter, which thanks me for his little stories. We sent them last month, you remember—such of them as we could find. It seems that he fills up his time by writing: he has already written a book."

She only gave him half her attention, for a beautiful wreath had just arrived from the florist's. She was taking it up to the cemetery: today her child had been dead a year.

"On the other hand, he has altered his will. Fortunately, he cannot alter much. But I fear that what is not settled on you, will go. Should I read what I wrote on this point, and also my minutes of the interview with old Mr Ansell, and the copy of my correspondence with Stephen Wonham?"

But her fly was announced. While he put the wreath in for her, she ran for a moment upstairs. A few tears had come to her eyes. A scandalous divorce would have been more bearable than this withdrawal. People asked, "Why did her husband leave her?" and the answer came, "Oh, nothing particular; he only couldn't stand her; she lied and taught him to lie; she kept him from the work that suited him, from his friends, from his brother—in a word, she tried to run him, which a man won't pardon." A few tears; not many. To her, life never showed itself as a classic drama, in which, by trying to advance our fortunes, we shatter them. She had turned Stephen out of Wiltshire, and he fell like a thunderbolt on Sawston and on herself. In trying to gain Mrs Failing's money she had probably lost money which would have been her own. But irony is a subtle teacher, and she was not the woman to learn from such lessons as these. Her suffering was more direct. Three men had wronged her; therefore she hated them, and, if she could, would do them harm.

"These negotiations are quite useless," she told Herbert when she came downstairs. "We had much better bide our time. Tell me just about Stephen Wonham, though."

He drew her into the study again. "Wonham is or was in Scotland, learning to farm with connections of the Ansells: I believe the money is to go towards setting him up. Apparently he is a hard worker. He also drinks!"

She nodded and smiled. "More than he did?"

"My informant, Mr Tilliard—oh, I ought not to have mentioned his name. He is one of the better sort of Rickie's Cambridge friends, and has been dreadfully grieved at the collapse, but he does not want to be mixed up in it. This autumn he was up in the Lowlands, close by, and very kindly made a few unobtrusive inquiries for me. The man is becoming an habitual drunkard."

She smiled again. Stephen had evoked her secret, and she hated him more for that than for anything else that he had done. The poise of his shoulders that morning—it was no more—had recalled Gerald. If only she had not been so tired! He had reminded her of the greatest thing she had known, and to her cloudy mind this seemed degradation. She had turned to him as to her lover; with a look, which a man of his type understood, she had asked for his pity; for one terrible moment she had desired to be held in his arms. Even Herbert was surprised when she said, "I'm glad he drinks. I hope he'll kill himself. A man like that ought never to have been born."

"Perhaps the sins of the parents are visited on the children," said Herbert, taking her to the carriage. "Yet it is not for us to decide."

"I feel sure he will be punished. What right has he—" She broke off. What right had he to our common humanity? It was a hard lesson for anyone to learn. For Agnes it was impossible. Stephen was illicit, abnormal, worse than a man diseased. Yet she had turned to him: he had drawn out the truth.

"My dear, don't cry," said her brother, drawing up the windows. "I have great hopes of Mr Tilliard—the Silts have written—Mrs Failing will do what she can—"

As she drove to the cemetery, her bitterness turned against Ansell, who had kept her husband alive in the days after Stephen's expulsion. If he had not been there, Rickie would have renounced his mother and his brother and all the outer world, troubling no one. The mystic, inherent in him, would have prevailed. So Ansell himself had told her. And Ansell, too, had sheltered the fugitives and given them money, and saved them from the ludicrous checks that so often stop young men. But when she reached the cemetery, and stood beside the tiny grave, all her bitterness, all her hatred were turned against Rickie.

"But he'll come back in the end," she thought. "A wife has only to wait. What are his friends beside me? They too will marry. I have only to wait. His book, like all that he has done, will fail. His brother is drinking himself away. Poor aimless Rickie! I have only to keep civil. He will come back in the end."

She had moved, and found herself close to the grave of Gerald. The flowers she had planted after his death were dead, and she had not liked to renew them. There lay the athlete, and his dust was as the little child's whom she had brought into the world with such hope, with such pain.

Chapter 33

That same day Rickie, feeling neither poor nor aimless, left the Ansells' for a night's visit to Cadover. His aunt had invited him—why, he could not think, nor could he think why he should refuse the invitation. She could not annoy him now, and he was not vindictive. In the dell near Madingley he had cried, "I hate no one," in his ignorance. Now, with full knowledge, he hated no one again. The weather was pleasant, the country attractive, and he was ready for a little change.

Maud and Stewart saw him off. Stephen, who was down for a holiday, had been left with his chin on the luncheon-table. He had wanted to come to Cadover also. Rickie pointed out that you cannot visit where you have broken the windows. There was an argument—there generally was—and now the young man had turned sulky.

"Let him do what he likes," said Ansell. "He knows more than we do. He knows everything."

"Is he to get drunk?" Rickie asked.

"Most certainly."

"And to go where he isn't asked?"

Maud, though liking a little spirit in a man, declared this to be impossible.

"Well, I wish you joy!" Rickie called, as the train moved away. "He means mischief this evening. He told me piously that he felt it beating up. Goodbye!"

"But we'll wait for you to pass," they cried. For the Salisbury train always backed out of the station and then returned, and the Ansell family, including Stewart, took an incredible pleasure in seeing it do this.

The carriage was empty. Rickie settled himself down for his little journey. First he looked at the coloured photographs. Then he read the directions for obtaining luncheon-baskets, and felt the texture of the cushions. Through the windows a signal-box interested him. Then he saw the ugly little town that was now his home, and up its chief street the Ansells' memorable façade. The spirit of a genial comedy dwelt there. It was so absurd, so kindly. The house was divided against itself and yet stood. Metaphysics, commerce, social aspirations—all lived together in harmony. Mr Ansell had done much, but one was tempted to believe in a more capricious power—the power that abstains from "nipping". "One nips or is nipped, and never knows beforehand," quoted Rickie, and opened the poems of Shelley, a man less foolish than you supposed. How pleasant it was to read! If business worried him, if Stephen was noisy or Ansell perverse, there still remained this paradise of books. It seemed as if he had read nothing for two years.

Then the train stopped for the shunting, and he heard protests from minor officials who were working on the line. They complained that someone who didn't ought to, had mounted on the footboard of the carriage. Stephen's face appeared, convulsed with laughter. With the action of a swimmer he dived in through the open window, and fell comfortably on Rickie's luggage and Rickie. He declared it was the finest joke ever known. Rickie was not so sure. "You'll be run over next," he said. "What did you do that for?"

"I'm coming with you," he giggled, rolling all that he could onto the dusty floor.

"Now, Stephen, this is too bad. Get up. We went into the whole question yesterday."

"I know; and I settled we wouldn't go into it again, spoiling my holiday."

"Well, it's execrable taste."

Now he was waving to the Ansells, and showing them a piece of soap: it was all his luggage, and even that he abandoned, for he flung it at Stewart's lofty brow.

"I can't think what you've done it for. You know how strongly I felt."

Stephen replied that he should stop in the village; meet Rickie at the lodge gates; that kind of thing.

"It's execrable taste," he repeated, trying to keep grave.

"Well, you did all you could," he exclaimed with sudden sympathy. "Leaving me talking to old Ansell, you might have thought you'd got your way. I've as much taste as most chaps, but, hang it! your aunt isn't the German Emperor. She doesn't own Wiltshire."

"You ass!" sputtered Rickie, who had taken to laugh at nonsense again.

"No, she isn't," he repeated, blowing a kiss out of the window to maidens. "Why, we started for Wiltshire on the wet morning!"

"When Stewart found us at Sawston railway station?" He smiled happily. "I never thought we should pull through."

"Well, we *didn't*. We never did what we meant. It's nonsense that I couldn't have managed you alone. I've a notion. Slip out after your dinner this evening, and we'll get thundering tight together."

"I've a notion I won't."

"It'd do you no end of good. You'll get to know people— shepherds, carters—" He waved his arms vaguely, indicating democracy. "Then you'll sing."

"And then?"

"Plop."

"Precisely."

"But I'll catch you," promised Stephen. "We shall carry you up the hill to bed. In the morning you wake, have your row with old Em'ly, she kicks you out, we meet—we'll meet at the Rings!" He danced up and down the carriage. Someone in the next carriage punched at the partition, and when this happens, all lads of mettle know that they must punch the partition back.

"Thank you. I've a notion I won't," said Rickie when the noise subsided—subsided for a moment only, for the following conversation took place to an accompaniment of dust and bangs. "Except as regards the Rings. We will meet there."

"Then I'll get tight by myself."

"No, you won't."

"Yes, I will. I swore to do something special this evening. I feel like it."

"In that case, I get out at the next station." He was laughing, but quite determined. Stephen had grown too dictatorial of late. The Ansells spoilt him. "It's bad enough having you there at all. Having you there drunk is impossible. I'd sooner not visit my aunt than think, when I sat with her, that you're down in the village teaching her labourers to be as beastly as yourself. Go if you will. But not with me."

"Why shouldn't I have a good time while I'm young, if I don't harm anyone?" said Stephen defiantly.

"Need we discuss it again? Because you harm yourself."

"Oh, I can stop myself any minute I choose. I just say 'I won't' to you or any other fool, and I don't."

Rickie knew that the boast was true. He continued, "There is also a thing called Morality. You may learn in the Bible, and also from the Greeks, that your body is a temple."

"So you said in your longest letter."

"Probably I wrote like a prig, for the reason that I have never been tempted in this way; but surely it is wrong that your body should escape you."

"I don't follow," he retorted, punching.

"It isn't right, even for a little time, to forget that you exist."

"I suppose you've never been tempted to go to sleep?"

Just then the train passed through a coppice in which the gray undergrowth looked no more alive than firewood. Yet every twig in it was waiting for the spring. Rickie knew that the analogy was false, but argument confused him, and he gave up this line of attack also.

"Do be more careful over life. If your body escapes you in one thing, why not in more? A man will have other temptations."

"You mean women," said Stephen quietly, pausing for a moment in his game. "But that's absolutely different. That would be harming someone else."

"Is that the only thing that keeps you straight?"

"What else should?" And he looked not into Rickie, but past him, with the wondering eyes of a child. Rickie nodded, and referred himself to the window.·

He observed that the country was smoother and more plastic. The woods had gone, and under a pale-blue sky long contours of earth were flowing, merging, rising a little to bear some coronal of beeches, parting a little to disclose some green valley, where cottages stood under elms or beside translucent waters. It was Wiltshire at last. The train had entered the chalk. At last it slackened at a wayside platform. Without speaking he opened the door.

"What's that for?"

"To go back."

Stephen had forgotten the threat. He said that this was not playing the game.

"Surely!"

"I can't have you going back."

"Promise to behave decently then."

He was seized and pulled away from the door.

"We change at Salisbury," he remarked. "There is an hour to wait. You will find me troublesome."

"It isn't fair," exploded Stephen. "It's a low-down trick. How can I let you go back?"

"Promise, then."

"Oh, yes, yes, yes. Y.M.C.A. But for this occasion only."

"No, no. For the rest of your holiday."

"Yes, yes. Very well. I promise."

"For the rest of your life?"

Somehow it pleased him that Stephen should bang him crossly with his elbow and say, "No. Get out. You've gone too far." So had the train. The porter at the end of the wayside platform slammed the door, and they proceeded towards Salisbury through the slowly modulating downs. Rickie pretended to read. Over the book he watched his brother's face, and wondered how bad temper could be consistent with a mind so radiant. In spite of his obstinacy and conceit, Stephen was an easy person to live with. He never fidgeted or nursed hidden grievances, or indulged in a shoddy pride. Though he spent Rickie's money as slowly as he could, he asked for it without apology: "You must put it down against me," he would say. In time—it was still very vague—he would rent or purchase a farm. There is no formula in which we may sum up decent people. So Ansell had preached, and had of course proceeded to offer a formula: "They must be serious, they must be truthful." Serious not in the sense of glum; but they must be convinced that our life is a state of some importance, and our earth not a place to beat time on. Of so much Stephen was convinced: he showed it in his work, in his play, in his self-respect, and above all—though the fact is hard to face—in his sacred passion for alcohol. Drink, today, is an unlovely thing. Between us and the heights of Cithaeron the river of sin now flows. Yet the cries still call from the mountain, and granted a man has responded to them, it is better he respond with the candour of the Greek.

"I shall stop at the Thompsons' now," said the disappointed reveller. "Prayers."

Rickie did not press his triumph, but it was a happy moment, partly because of the triumph, partly because he was sure that his brother must care for him. Stephen was too selfish to give up any pleasure without grave reasons. He was certain that he had been right to disentangle himself from Sawston, and to ignore the threats and tears that still tempted him to return. Here there was real work for him to do. Moreover, though he sought no reward, it had come. His health was better, his brain sound, his life washed clean, not by the waters of sentiment, but by the efforts of a fellow man. Stephen was man first, brother afterwards. Herein lay his brutality and also his virtue. "Look me in the face. Don't hang on me clothes that don't belong—as you did on your wife, giving her saints' robes, whereas she was simply a woman of her own sort, who needed careful watching. Tear up the photographs. Here am I, and there are you. The rest is cant." The rest was not cant, and perhaps Stephen would confess as much in time. But Rickie needed a tonic, and a man, not a brother, must hold it to his lips.

"I see the old spire," he called, and then added, "I don't mind seeing it again."

"No one does, as far as I know. People have come from the other side of the world to see it again."

"Pious people. But I don't hold with bishops." He was young enough to be uneasy. The cathedral, a fount of superstition, must find no place in his life. At the age of twenty he had settled things. "I've got my own philosophy," he once told Ansell, "and I don't care a straw about yours." Ansell's mirth had annoyed him not a little. And it was strange that one so settled should feel his heart leap up at the sight of an old spire. "I regard it as a public building," he told Rickie, who agreed. "It's useful, too, as a landmark." His attitude today was defensive. It was part of a subtle change that Rickie had noted in him since his return from Scotland. His face gave hints of a new maturity. "You can see the old spire from the Ridgeway," he said, suddenly laying a hand on Rickie's knee, "before rain as clearly as any telegraph post."

"How far is the Ridgeway?"

"Seventeen miles."

"Which direction?"

"North, naturally. North again from that you see Devizes, the vale of Pewsey, and the other downs. Also towards Bath. It is something of a view. You ought to get on the Ridgeway."

"I shouldn't have time for that."

"Or Beacon Hill. Or let's do Stonehenge."

"If it's fine, I suggest the Rings."

"It will be fine." Then he murmured the names of villages.

"I wish you could live here," said Rickie kindly. "I believe you love these particular acres more than the whole world."

Stephen replied that this was not the case: he was only used to them. He wished they were driving out, instead of waiting for the Cadchurch train.

They had advanced into Salisbury, and the cathedral, a public building, was gray against a tender sky. Rickie suggested that, while waiting for the train, they should visit it. He spoke of the incomparable north porch.

"I've never been inside it, and I never will. Sorry to shock

you, Rickie, but I must tell you plainly. I'm an atheist. I
don't believe in anything."

"I do," said Rickie.

"When a man dies, it's as if he's never been," he asserted.
The train drew up in Salisbury station. Here a little incident
took place which caused them to alter their plans.

They found outside the station a trap driven by a small
boy, who had come in from Cadford to fetch some wire-
netting. "That'll do us," said Stephen, and called to the
boy, "If I pay your railway ticket back, and if I give you
sixpence as well, will you let us drive back in the trap?" The
boy said no. "It will be all right," said Rickie. "I am Mrs
Failing's nephew." The boy shook his head. "And you know
Mr Wonham?" The boy couldn't say he didn't. "Then
what's your objection? Why? What is it? Why not?" But
Stephen leant against the timetables and spoke of other
matters.

Presently the boy said, "Did you say you'd pay my railway
ticket back, Mr Wonham?"

"Yes," said a bystander. "Didn't you hear him?"

"I heard him right enough."

Now Stephen laid his hand on the splash-board, saying,
"What I want, though, is this trap here of yours, see, to
drive in back myself"; and as he spoke the bystander followed
him in canon, "What he wants, though, is that there trap of
yours, see, to drive hisself back in."

"*I've* no objection," said the boy, as if deeply offended.
For a time he sat motionless, and then got down, remarking,
"I won't rob you of your sixpence."

"Silly little fool," snapped Rickie, as they drove through
the town.

Stephen looked surprised. "What's wrong with the boy?
He had to think it over. No one had asked him to do such a
thing before. Next time he'd let us have the trap quick
enough."

"Not if he had driven in for a cabbage instead of wire-
netting."

"He never would drive in for a cabbage."

Rickie shuffled his feet. But his irritation passed. He saw

that the little incident had been a quiet challenge to the civilization that he had known. "Organize", "Systematize", "Fill up every moment", "Induce *esprit de corps*". He reviewed the watchwords of the last two years, and found that they ignored personal contest, personal truces, personal love. By following them Sawston School had lost its quiet usefulness and become a frothy sea, wherein plunged Dunwood House, that unnecessary ship. Humbled, he turned to Stephen and said, "No, you're right. Nothing is wrong with the boy. He was honestly thinking it out." But Stephen had forgotten the incident, or else he was not inclined to talk about it. His assertive fit was over.

The direct road from Salisbury to Cadover is extremely dull. The city—which God intended to keep by the river; did she not move there, being thirsty, in the reign of William Rufus?—the city has strayed out of her own plain, climbed up her slopes, and tumbled over them in ugly cataracts of brick. The cataracts are still short, and doubtless they meet or create some commercial need. But instead of looking towards the cathedral, as all the city should, they look outwards at a pagan entrenchment, as the city should not. They neglect the poise of the earth, and the sentiments she has decreed. They are the modern spirit.

Through them the road descends into an unobtrusive country where, nevertheless, the power of the earth grows stronger. Streams do divide. Distances do still exist. It is easier to know the men in your valley than those who live in the next, across a waste of down. It is easier to know men well. The country is not paradise, and can show the vices that grieve a good man everywhere. But there is room in it, and leisure.

"I suppose," said Rickie as the twilight fell, "this kind of thing is going on all over England." Perhaps he meant that towns are after all excrescences, gray fluxions, where men, hurrying to find one another, have lost themselves. But he got no response, and expected none. Turning round in his seat, he watched the winter sun slide out of a quiet sky. The horizon was primrose, and the earth against it gave momentary hints of purple. All faded: no pageant would conclude the gracious day, and when he turned eastward the night was already established.

"Those verlands—" said Stephen, scarcely above his breath.

"What are verlands?"

He pointed at the dusk, and said, "Our name for a kind of field." Then he drove his whip into its socket, and seemed to swallow something. Rickie, straining his eyes for verlands, could only see a tumbling wilderness of brown.

"Are there many local words?"

"There have been."

"I suppose they die out."

The conversation turned curiously. In the tone of one who replies, he said, "I expect that sometime or other I shall marry."

"I expect you will," said Rickie, and wondered a little why the reply seemed not abrupt. "Would we see the Rings in the daytime from here?"

"(We do see them.) But Mrs Failing once said no decent woman would have me."

"Did you agree to that?"

"Drive a little, will you?"

The horse went slowly forward into the wilderness, that turned from brown to black. Then a luminous glimmer surrounded them, and the air grew cooler: the road was descending between parapets of chalk.

"But, Rickie, mightn't I find a girl—naturally not refined—and be happy with her in my own way? I would tell her straight I was nothing much—faithful, of course, but that she should never have all my thoughts. Out of no disrespect to her, but because all one's thoughts can't belong to any single person."

While he spoke even the road vanished, and invisible water came gurgling through the wheel-spokes. The horse had chosen the ford.

"You can't own people. At least a fellow can't. It may be different for a poet. (Let the horse drink.) And I want to marry someone, and don't yet know who she is, which a poet again will tell you is disgusting. Does it disgust you?

Being nothing much, surely I'd better go gently. For it's something rather outside that makes one marry, if you follow me: not exactly oneself. (Don't hurry the horse.) We want to marry, and yet—I can't explain. I fancy I'll go wading: this is our stream."

Romantic love is greater than this. There are men and women—we know it from history—who have been born into the world for each other, and for no one else, who have accomplished the longest journey locked in each other's arms. But romantic love is also the code of modern morals, and, for this reason, popular. Eternal union, eternal ownership—these are tempting baits for the average man. He swallows them, will not confess his mistake, and—perhaps to cover it—cries "dirty cynic" at such a man as Stephen.

Rickie watched the black earth unite to the black sky. But the sky overhead grew clearer, and in it twinkled the Plough and the central stars. He thought of his brother's future and of his own past, and of how much truth might lie in that antithesis of Ansell's: "A man wants to love mankind, a woman wants to love one man." At all events, he and his wife had illustrated it, and perhaps the conflict, so tragic in their own case, was elsewhere the salt of the world. Meanwhile Stephen called from the water for matches: there was some trick with paper which Mr Failing had showed him, and which he would show Rickie now, instead of talking nonsense. Bending down, he illumined the dimpled surface of the ford. "Quite a current," he said, and his face flickered out in the darkness. "Yes, give me the loose paper, quick! Crumple it into a ball."

Rickie obeyed, though intent on the transfigured face. He believed that a new spirit dwelt there, expelling the crudities of youth. He saw steadier eyes, and the sign of manhood set like a bar of gold upon steadier lips. Some faces are knit by beauty, or by intellect, or by a great passion: had Stephen's waited for the touch of the years?

But they played as boys who continued the nonsense of the railway carriage. The paper caught fire from the match, and spread into a rose of flame. "Now gently with me," said Stephen, and they laid it flower-like on the stream. Gravel and tremulous weeds leapt into sight, and then the flower sailed into deep water, and up leapt the two arches of a bridge. "It'll strike!" they cried; "no, it won't; it's chosen the left," and one arch became a fairy tunnel, dropping diamonds. Then it vanished for Rickie; but Stephen, who knelt in the water, declared that it was still afloat, far through the arch, burning as if it would burn for ever.

Chapter 34

The carriage that Mrs Failing had sent to meet her nephew returned from Cadchurch Station empty. She was preparing for a solitary dinner when he somehow arrived, full of apologies, but more sedate than she had expected. She cut his explanations short. "Never mind how you got here. You are here, and I am quite pleased to see you." He changed his clothes and they proceeded to the dining-room.

There was a bright fire, but the curtains were not drawn. Mr Failing had believed that windows with the night behind are more beautiful than any pictures, and his widow had kept to the custom. It was brave of her to persevere, lumps of chalk having come out of the night last June. For some obscure reason—not so obscure to Rickie—she had preserved them as mementoes of an episode. Seeing them in a row on the mantelpiece, he expected that their first topic would be Stephen. But they never mentioned him, though he was latent in all that they said.

It was of Mr Failing that they spoke. The *Essays* had been a success. She was really pleased. The book was brought in at her request, and between the courses she read it aloud to her nephew, in her soft yet unsympathetic voice. Then she sent for the press notices—after all no one despises them— and read their comments on her introduction. She wielded a graceful pen, was apt, adequate, suggestive, indispensable, unnecessary. So the meal passed pleasantly away, for no one could so well combine the formal with the unconventional, and it only seemed charming when papers littered her stately table.

"My man wrote very nicely," she observed. "Now, you read me something out of him that you like. Read 'The True Patriot'."

He took the book and found: "Let us love one another.

274

Let our children, physical and spiritual, love one another. It is all that we can do. Perhaps the earth will neglect our love. Perhaps she will confirm it, and suffer some rallying-point, spire, mound, for the new generations to cherish."

"He wrote that when he was young. Later on he doubted whether we had better love one another, or whether the earth will confirm anything. He died a most unhappy man."

He could not help saying, "Not knowing that the earth had confirmed him."

"Has she? It is quite possible. We meet so seldom in these days, she and I. Do you see much of the earth?"

"A little."

"Do you expect that she will confirm you?"

"It is quite possible."

"Beware of her, Rickie, I think."

"I think not."

"Beware of her, surely. Going back to her really is going back—throwing away the artificiality which (though you young people won't confess it) is the only good thing in life. Don't pretend you are simple. Once I pretended. Don't pretend that you care for anything but for clever talk such as this, and for books."

"The talk," said Leighton afterwards, "certainly was clever. But it meant something all the same." He heard no more, for his mistress told him to retire.

"And my nephew, this being so, make up your quarrel with your wife." She stretched out her hand to him with real feeling. "It is easier now than it will be later. Poor lady, she has written to me foolishly and often, but, on the whole, I side with her against you. She would grant you all that you fought for—all the people, all the theories. I have it, in her writing, that she will never interfere with your life again."

"She cannot help interfering," said Rickie, with his eyes on the black windows. "She despises me. Besides, I do not love her."

"I know, my dear. Nor she you. I am not being senti-mental. I say once more, beware of the earth. We are

275

conventional people, and conventions—if you will but see it—are majestic in their way, and will claim us in the end. We do not live for great passions or for great memories, or for anything great."

He threw up his head. "We do."

"Now listen to me. I am serious and friendly tonight, as you must have observed. I have asked you here partly to amuse myself—you belong to my March Past—but also to give you good advice. There has been a volcano—a phenomenon which I too once greatly admired. The eruption is over. Let the conventions do their work now, and clear the rubbish away. My age is fifty-nine, and I tell you solemnly that the important things in life are little things, and that people are not important at all. Go back to your wife."

He looked at her, and was filled with pity. He knew that he would never be frightened of her again. Only because she was serious and friendly did he trouble himself to reply. "There is one little fact I should like to tell you, as confuting your theory. The idea of a story—a long story—had been in my head for a year. As a dream to amuse myself—the kind of amusement you would recommend for the future. I should have had time to write it, but the people round me coloured my life, and so it never seemed worth while. For the story is not likely to pay. Then came the volcano. A few days after it was over I lay in bed looking out upon a world of rubbish. Two men I know—one intellectual, the other very much the reverse—burst into the room. They said, 'What happened to your short stories? They weren't good, but where are they? Why have you stopped writing? Why haven't you been to Italy? You *must* write. You *must* go. Because to write, to go, is you.' Well, I have written, and yesterday we sent the long story out on its rounds. The men do not like it, for different reasons. But it mattered very much to them that I should write it, and so it got written. As I told you, this is only one fact; other facts, I trust, have happened in the last five months. But I mention it to prove that people are important, and therefore, however much it inconveniences my wife, I will not go back to her."

"And Italy?" asked Mrs Failing.

This question he avoided. Italy must wait. Now that he had the time, he had not the money.

"Or what is the long story about, then?"

"About a man and a woman who meet and are happy."

"Somewhat of a *tour de force*, I conclude."

He frowned. "In literature we needn't intrude our own limitations. I'm not so silly as to think that all marriages turn out like mine. My character is to blame for our catastrophe, not marriage."

"My dear, I too have married; marriage is to blame."

But here again he seemed to know better.

"Well," she said, leaving the table and moving with her dessert to the mantelpiece, "so you are abandoning marriage and taking to literature. And are happy."

"Yes."

"Why?"

"Because, as we used to say at Cambridge, the cow is there. The world is real again. This is a room, that a window, outside is the night—"

"Go on."

He pointed to the floor. "The day is straight below, shining through other windows into other rooms."

"You are very odd," she said after a pause, "and I do not like you at all. There you sit, eating my biscuits, and all the time you know that the earth is round. Who taught you? I am going to bed now, and all the night, you tell me, you and I and the biscuits go plunging eastwards, until we reach the sun. But breakfast will be at nine as usual. Good night."

She rang the bell twice, and her maid came with her candle and her walking-stick: it was her habit of late to go to her room as soon as dinner was over, for she had no one to sit up with. Rickie was impressed by her loneliness, and also by the mixture in her of insight and obtuseness. She was so quick, so clear-headed, so imaginative even. But all the same, she had forgotten what people were like. Finding life dull, she had dropped lies into it, as a chemist drops a new element into a solution, hoping that life would thereby sparkle or turn some beautiful colour. She loved to mislead others, and in the end her private view of false and true was obscured, and she misled herself. How she must have enjoyed their errors over Stephen! But her own error had been greater, inasmuch as it was spiritual entirely.

Leighton came in with some coffee. Feeling it unnecessary to light the drawing-room lamp for one small young man, he persuaded Rickie to say he preferred the dining-room. So Rickie sat down by the fire playing with one of the lumps of chalk. His thoughts went back to the ford, from which they had scarcely wandered. Still he heard the horse in the dark drinking, still he saw the mystic rose, and the tunnel dropping diamonds. He had driven away alone, believing the earth had confirmed him. He stood behind things at last, and knew that conventions are not majestic, and that they will not claim us in the end.

As he mused, the chalk slipped from his fingers, and fell on the coffee-cup, which broke. The china, said Leighton, was expensive. He believed it was impossible to match it now. Each cup was different. It was a harlequin set. The saucer, without the cup, was therefore useless. Would Mr Elliot please explain to Mrs Failing how it happened.

Rickie promised he would explain.

He had left Stephen preparing to bathe, and had heard him working upstream like an animal, splashing in the shallows, breathing heavily as he swam the pools; at times reeds snapped, or clods of earth were pulled in. By the fire he remembered it was again November. "Should you like a walk?" he asked Leighton, and told him who stopped in the village tonight. Leighton was pleased. At nine o'clock the two young men left the house, under a sky that was still only bright in the zenith. "It will rain tomorrow," Leighton said.

"My brother says, fine tomorrow."

"Fine tomorrow," Leighton echoed.

"Now which do you mean?" asked Rickie, laughing.

Since the plumes of the fir trees touched over the drive, only a very little light penetrated. It was clearer outside the lodge gate, and bubbles of air, which seemed to have travelled from an immense distance, broke gently and separately on his face. They paused on the bridge. He asked whether the little fish and the bright green weeds were here now as well as in the summer. The footman had not noticed. Over the bridge they came to the crossroads, of which one led to Salisbury and the other up through the string of villages to the railway station. The road in front was only the Roman road, the one that went onto the downs. Turning to the left, they were in Cadford.

"He will be with the Thompsons," said Rickie, looking up at dark eaves. "Perhaps he's in bed already."

"Perhaps he will be at The Antelope."

"No. Tonight he is with the Thompsons."

"With the Thompsons." After a dozen paces he said, "The Thompsons have gone away."

"Where? Why?"

"They were turned out by Mr Wilbraham on account of our broken windows."

"Are you sure?"

"Five families were turned out."

"That's bad for Stephen," said Rickie, after a pause. "He was looking forward—oh, it's monstrous in any case!"

"But the Thompsons have gone to London," said Leighton. "Why, that family—they say it's been in the valley hundreds of years, and never got beyond shepherding. To various parts of London."

"Let us try The Antelope, then."

"Let us try The Antelope."

The inn lay up in the village. Rickie hastened his pace. This tyranny was monstrous. Some men of the age of undergraduates had broken windows, and therefore they and their families were to be ruined. The fools who govern us find it easier to be severe. It saves them trouble to say, "The innocent must suffer with the guilty." It even gives them a thrill of pride. Against all this wicked nonsense, against the Wilbrahams and Pembrokes who try to rule our world Stephen would fight till he died. Stephen was a hero. He was a law to himself, and rightly. He was great enough to despise our small moralities. He was attaining love. This evening Rickie caught Ansell's enthusiasm, and felt it worth while to sacrifice everything for such a man.

"The Antelope," said Leighton. "Those lights under the greatest elm."

"Would you please ask if he's there, and if he'd come for a turn with me. I don't think I'll go in."

Leighton opened the door. They saw a little room, blue with tobacco-smoke. Flanking the fire were deep settles, hiding all but the legs of the men who lounged in them. Between the settles stood a table, covered with mugs and glasses. The scene was picturesque—fairer than the cut-glass palaces of the town.

"Oh yes, he's there," he called, and after a moment's hesitation came out.

"Would he come?"

"No. I shouldn't say so," replied Leighton, with a furtive glance. He knew that Rickie was a milksop. "First night, you know, sir, among old friends."

"Yes, I know," said Rickie. "But he might like a turn down the village. It looks stuffy inside there, and poor fun probably to watch others drinking."

Leighton shut the door.

"What was that he called after you?"

"Oh, nothing. A man when he's drunk—he says the worst he's ever heard. At least, so they say."

"A man when he's drunk?"

"Yes, sir."

"But Stephen isn't drinking?"

"No, no."

"He couldn't be. If he broke a promise—I don't pretend he's a saint. I don't want him one. But it isn't in him to break a promise."

"Yes, sir; I understand."

"In the train he promised me not to drink—nothing theatrical: just a promise for these few days."

"No, sir."

"'No, sir,'" stamped Rickie. "'Yes! no! yes!' Can't you speak out? Is he drunk or isn't he?"

Leighton, justly exasperated, cried, "He can't stand, and I've told you so again and again."

"Stephen!" shouted Rickie, darting up the steps. Heat and

the smell of beer awaited him, and he spoke more furiously than he had intended. "Is there anyone here who's sober?" he cried. The landlord looked over the bar angrily, and asked him what he meant. He pointed to the deep settles. "Inside there he's drunk. Tell him he's broken his word, and I will not go with him to the Rings."

"Very well. You won't go with him to the Rings," said the landlord, stepping forward and slamming the door in his face.

In the room he was only angry, but out in the cool air he remembered that Stephen was a law to himself. He had chosen to break his word, and would break it again. Nothing else bound him. To yield to temptation is not fatal for most of us. But it was the end of everything for a hero.

"He's suddenly ruined!" he cried, not yet remembering himself. For a little he stood by the elm tree, clutching the ridges of its bark. Even so would he wrestle tomorrow, and Stephen, imperturbable, reply, "My body is my own." Or worse still, he might wrestle with a pliant Stephen who promised him glibly again. While he prayed for a miracle to convert his brother, it struck him that he must pray for himself. For he, too, was ruined.

"Why, what's the matter?" asked Leighton. "Stephen's only being with friends. Mr Elliot, sir, don't break down. Nothing's happened bad. No one's died yet, or even hurt themselves." Ever kind, he took hold of Rickie's arm, and, pitying such a nervous fellow, set out with him for home. The shoulders of Orion rose behind them over the topmost boughs of the elm. From the bridge the whole constellation was visible, and Rickie said, "May God receive me and pardon me for trusting the earth."

"But, Mr Elliot, what have you done that's wrong?"

"Gone bankrupt, Leighton, for the second time. Pretended again that people were real. May God have mercy on me!"

Leighton dropped his arm. Though he did not understand, a chill of disgust passed over him, and he said, "I will go back to The Antelope. I will help them put Stephen to bed."

"Do. I will wait for you here." Then he leant against the

parapet and prayed passionately, for he knew that the conventions would claim him soon. God was beyond them, but ah, how far beyond, and to be reached after what degradation! At the end of this childish detour his wife awaited him, not less surely because she was only his wife in name. He was too weak. Books and friends were not enough. Little by little she would claim him and corrupt him and make him what he had been; and the woman he loved would die out, in drunkenness, in debauchery, and her strength would be dissipated by a man, her beauty defiled in a man. She would not continue. That mystic rose and the face it illumined meant nothing. The stream—he was above it now—meant nothing, though it burst from the pure turf and ran for ever to the sea. The bather, the shoulders of Orion—they all meant nothing, and were going nowhere. The whole affair was a ridiculous dream.

Leighton returned, saying, "Haven't you seen Stephen? They say he followed us: he can still walk: I told you he wasn't so bad."

"I don't think he passed me. Ought we to look?" He wandered a little along the Roman road. Again nothing mattered. At the level-crossing he leant on the gate to watch a slow goods train pass. In the glare of the engine he saw that his brother had come this way, perhaps through some sodden memory of the Rings, and now lay drunk over the rails. Wearily he did a man's duty. There was time to raise him up and push him into safety. It is also a man's duty to save his own life, and therefore he tried. The train went over his knees. He died up in Cadover, whispering, "You have been right," to Mrs Failing.

She wrote of him to Mrs Lewin afterwards as "one who has failed in all he undertook; one of the thousands whose dust returns to the dust, accomplishing nothing in the interval. Agnes and I buried him to the sound of our cracked bell, and pretended that he had once been alive. The other, who was always honest, kept away."

Chapter 35

From the window they looked over a sober valley, whose sides were not too sloping to be ploughed, and whose trend was followed by a grass-grown track. It was late on Sunday afternoon, and the valley was deserted except for one labourer, who was coasting slowly downward on a rusty bicycle. The air was very quiet. A jay screamed up in the woods behind, but the ringdoves, who roost early, were already silent. Since the window opened westward, the room was flooded with light, and Stephen, finding it hot, was working in his shirt-sleeves.

"You guarantee they'll sell?" he asked, with a pen between his teeth. He was tidying up a pile of manuscripts.

"I guarantee that the world will be the gainer," said Mr Pembroke, now a clergyman, who sat beside him at the table with an expression of refined disapproval on his face.

"I'd got the idea that the long story had its points, but that these shorter things didn't—what's the word?"

"'Convince' is probably the word you want. But that type of criticism is quite a thing of the past. Have you seen the illustrated American edition?"

"I don't remember."

"Might I send you a copy? I think you ought to possess one."

"Thank you." His eye wandered. The bicycle had disappeared into some trees, and thither, through a cloudless sky, the sun was also descending.

"Is all quite plain?" said Mr Pembroke. "Submit these ten stories to the magazines, and make your own terms with the editors. Then—I have your word for it—you will join forces with me; and the four stories in my possession, together with yours, should make up a volume, which we might well call *Pan Pipes*."

"Are you sure *Pan Pipes* haven't been used up already?"

Mr Pembroke clenched his teeth. He had been bearing with this sort of thing for nearly an hour. "If that is the case, we can select another. A title is easy to come by. But that is the idea it must suggest. The stories, as I have twice explained to you, all centre round a Nature theme. Pan, being the god of—"

"I know that," said Stephen impatiently.

"—Being the god of—"

"All right. Let's get furrard. I've learnt that."

It was years since the schoolmaster had been interrupted, and he could not stand it. "Very well," he said. "I bow to your superior knowledge of the classics. Let us proceed."

"Oh yes—the introduction. There must be one. It was the introduction with all those wrong details that sold the other book."

"You overwhelm me. I never penned the memoir with that intention."

"If you won't do one, Mrs Keynes must!"

"My sister leads a busy life. I could not ask her. I will do it myself since you insist."

"And the binding?"

"The binding," said Mr Pembroke coldly, "must really be left to the discretion of the publisher. We cannot be concerned with such details. Our task is purely literary." His attention wandered. He began to fidget, and finally bent down and looked under the table. "What have we here?" he asked.

Stephen looked also, and for a moment they smiled at each other over the prostrate figure of a child, who was cuddling Mr Pembroke's boots. "She's after the blacking," he explained. "If we left her there, she'd lick them brown."

"Indeed. Is that so very safe?"

"It never did me any harm. Come up! Your tongue's dirty."

"Can I—" She was understood to ask whether she could clean her tongue on a lollie.

"No, no!" said Mr Pembroke. "Lollipops don't clean little girls' tongues."

"Yes, they do," he retorted. "But she won't get one." He lifted her onto his knee, and rasped her tongue with his handkerchief.

"Dear little thing," said the visitor perfunctorily. The child began to squall, and kicked her father in the stomach. Stephen regarded her quietly. "You tried to hurt me," he said. "Hurting doesn't count. Trying to hurt counts. Go and clean your tongue yourself. Get off my knee." Tears of another sort came into her eyes, but she obeyed him. "How's the great Bertie?" he asked.

"Thank you. My nephew is perfectly well. How came you to hear of his existence?"

"Through the Silts, of course. It isn't five miles to Cadover."

Mr Pembroke raised his eyes mournfully. "I cannot conceive how the poor Silts go on in that great house. Whatever she intended, it could not have been that. The house, the farm, the money—everything down to the personal articles that belonged to Mr Failing, and should have reverted to his family!—"

"It's legal. Intestate succession."

"I do not dispute it. But it is a lesson to one to make a will. Mrs Keynes and myself were electrified."

"They'll do there. They offered me the agency, but—" He looked down the cultivated slopes. His manners were growing rough, for he saw few gentlemen now, and he was either incoherent or else alarmingly direct. "However, if Lawrie Silt's a Cockney like his father, and if my next is a boy and like me—" A shy beautiful look came into his eyes, and passed unnoticed. "They'll do," he repeated. "They've turned out Wilbraham and built new cottages, and bridged the railway, and made other necessary alterations." There was a moment's silence.

Mr Pembroke took out his watch. "I wonder if I might have the trap? I mustn't miss my train, must I? It is good of you to have granted me an interview. It is all quite plain?"

"Yes."

"A case of half and half—division of profits."

"Half and half?" said the young farmer slowly. "What do

you take me for? Half and half, when I provide ten of the stories and you only four?"

"I—I—" stammered Mr Pembroke.

"I consider you did me over the long story, and I'm damned if you do me over the short ones!"

"Hush! if you please, hush!—if only for your little girl's sake." He lifted a clerical palm.

"You did me," his voice drove, "and all the Thirty-Nine Articles won't stop me saying so. That long story was meant to be mine. I got it written. You've done me out of every penny it fetched. It's dedicated to me—flat out—and you even crossed out the dedication and tidied me out of the introduction. Listen to me, Pembroke. You've done people all your life—I think without knowing it, but that won't comfort us. A wretched devil at your school once wrote to me, and he'd been done. Sham food, sham religion, sham straight talks—and when he broke down, you said it was the world in miniature." He snatched at him roughly. "But I'll show you the world." He twisted him round like a baby, and through the open door they saw only the quiet valley, but in it a rivulet that would in time bring its waters to the sea. "Look even at that—and up behind where the Plain begins and you get on the solid chalk—think of us riding some night when you're ordering your hot bottle—that's the world, and there's no miniature world. There's one world, Pembroke, and you can't tidy men out of it. They answer you back—do you hear?—they answer back if you do them. If you tell a man this way that four sheep equal ten, he answers back you're a liar."

Mr Pembroke was speechless, and—such is human nature—he chiefly resented the allusion to the hot bottle; an unmanly luxury in which he never indulged; contenting himself with night-socks. "Enough—there is no witness present—as you had doubtless observed." But there was. For a little voice cried, "Oh, mummy, they're fighting—such fun—" and feet went pattering up the stairs. "Enough. You talk of 'doing', but what about the money out of which you 'did' my sister? What about this picture"—he pointed to a faded photograph of Stockholm—"which you caused to be filched from the walls of my house? What about—enough! Let us conclude this disheartening scene. You object to my terms. Name yours. I shall accept them. It is futile to reason with one who is the worse for drink."

Stephen was quiet at once. "Steady on!" he said gently. "Steady on in that direction. Take one-third for your four stories and the introduction, and I will keep two-thirds for myself." Then he went to harness the horse, while Mr Pembroke, watching his broad back, desired to bury a knife in it. The desire passed, partly because it was unclerical, partly because he had no knife, and partly because he soon blurred over what had happened. To him all criticism was "rudeness": he never heeded it, for he never needed it: he was never wrong. All his life he had ordered little human beings about, and now he was equally magisterial to big ones: Stephen was a fifth-form lout whom, owing to some flaw in the regulations, he could not send up to the headmaster to be caned.

This attitude makes for tranquillity. Before long he felt merely an injured martyr. His brain cleared. He stood deep in thought before the only other picture that the bare room boasted—the Demeter of Cnidus. Outside the sun was sinking, and its last rays fell upon the immortal features and the shattered knees. Sweet-peas offered their fragrance, and with it there entered those more mysterious scents that come from no one flower or clod of earth, but from the whole bosom of evening. He tried not to be cynical. But in his heart he could not regret that tragedy, already half forgotten, conventionalized, indistinct. Of course death is a terrible thing. Yet death is merciful when it weeds out a failure. If we look deep enough, it is all for the best. He stared at the picture and nodded.

Stephen, who had met his visitor at the station, had intended to drive him back there. But after their spurt of temper he sent him with the boy. He remained in the doorway, glad that he was going to make money, glad that he had been angry; while the glow of the clear sky deepened, and the silence was perfected, and the scents of the night grew stronger. Old vagrancies awoke, and he resolved that, dearly as he loved his house, he would not enter it again till dawn. "Good night!" he called, and then the child came running, and he whispered, "Quick, then! Bring me a rug." "Good night," he repeated, and a pleasant voice called through an upper window, "Why good night?" He did not answer till the child was wrapped up in his arms.

"It is time that she learnt to sleep out," he cried. "If you want me, we're out on the hillside, where I used to be."

The voice protested, saying this and that.

"Stewart's in the house," said the man, "and it cannot matter, and I am going anyway."

"Stephen, I wish you wouldn't. I wish you wouldn't take her. Promise you won't say foolish things to her. Don't—I wish you'd come up for a minute—"

The child, whose face was laid against his, felt the muscles in it harden.

"Don't tell her foolish things about yourself—things that aren't any longer true. Don't worry her with old dead dreadfulnesses. To please me—don't."

"Just tonight I won't, then."

"Stevie, dear, please me more—don't take her with you."

At this he laughed impertinently. "I suppose I'm being kept in line," she called, and, though he could not see her, she stretched her arms towards him. For a time he stood motionless, under her window, musing on his happy tangible life. Then his breath quickened, and he wondered why he was here, and why he should hold a warm child in his arms. "It's time we were starting," he whispered, and showed the sky, whose orange was already fading into green. "Wish everything good night."

"Good night, dear mummy," she said sleepily. "Good night, dear house. Good night, you pictures—long picture—stone lady. I see you through the window—your faces are pink."

The twilight descended. He rested his lips on her hair, and carried her, without speaking, until he reached the open down. He had often slept here himself alone, and on his wedding-night, and he knew that the turf was dry, and that if you laid your face to it you would smell the thyme. For a moment the earth aroused her, and she began to chatter. "My prayers—" she said anxiously. He gave her one hand, and she was asleep before her fingers had nestled in its palm. Their touch made him pensive, and again he marvelled why he, the accident, was here. He was alive and had created life. By whose authority? Though he could not phrase it, he believed that he guided the future of our race, and that, century after century, his thoughts and his passions would triumph in England. The dead who had evoked him, the unborn whom he would evoke—he governed the paths between them. By whose authority?

Out in the west lay Cadover and the fields of his earlier youth, and over them descended the crescent moon. His eyes followed her decline, and against her final radiance he saw, or thought he saw, the outline of the Rings. He had always been grateful, as people who understood him knew. But this evening his gratitude seemed a gift of small account. The ear was deaf, and what thanks of his could reach it? The body was dust, and in what ecstasy of his could it share? The spirit had fled, in agony and loneliness, never to know that it bequeathed him salvation.

He filled his pipe, and then sat pressing the unlit tobacco with his thumb. "What am I to do?" he thought. "Can he notice the things he gave me? A parson would know. But what's a man like me to do, who works all his life out of doors?" As he wondered, the silence of the night was broken. The whistle of Mr Pembroke's train came faintly, and a lurid spot passed over the land—passed, and the silence returned. One thing remained that a man of his sort might do. He bent down reverently and saluted the child; to whom he had given the name of their mother.

The Old School

A review of The Old School: Essays by Divers Hands, *ed. Graham Greene* [*London, Jonathan Cape, 1934*], *reprinted from* The Spectator, *27 July 1934, p. 136.*

Suppose me a schoolmaster, called (say) Mr Herbert Pembroke, and I have a boarding-house in the imaginary public school of Sawston. My day's work is over, my boys (whom I call bies) are safe in their cubicles and I take up a new book, as I still sometimes do, entitled *The Old School*. The title placates. It suggests caps with tassels, and photogravures in oak, and the words of the school anthem which I myself have composed flit pleasantly through my mind:

> Perish each sluggard! Let it not be said
> That Sawston such within her walls hath bred!

But as I read I turn purple in the face, then pale, then petrified, and finally open the study door and burst out to my sister, who does the matroning for me: "Agnes! Agnes! Pray what is the meaning of this?"

Agnes is used to being asked what things mean and she does not immediately come. When she does I exclaim that here is the most disgraceful, ill-conditioned, unnecessary book ever published, and I cannot trust myself to speak about it.

She composes herself to listen.

"Here is a collection of reminiscences by boys who seem recently to have left their schools, and one would like to know under what circumstances. Here is the sorriest set of sluggards ever collected. Here are fine nincompoops. Come! They shirk games and the O.T.C., they have no notion of *esprit de corps*, they do not even work. And their names! E. Arnot Robertson! What a name for a boy! And Seán O'Faoláin! Scarcely a name at all! This personage writes of Cork, if you please, and pray whoever heard of Cork as a school?"

"Well, if the boys do not come from proper schools it is naturally not a proper book," says Agnes, who is adding up the washing under the rim of the study table where she thinks I cannot see it. "I don't think you ought to worry—(one pound three and two)—over that, Herbert."

"I am far from worrying, but I really must observe that Winchester, Malvern and Rugby are among the national institutions vilified."

"Does Sawston come in?"

"Sawston! Certainly not. How could it? I should be very mortified indeed if any of our old—"

"Thirty-seven pillow cases. Might I look at this queer book now for a moment?"

"Yes, but omit the chapter on St Paul's."

My sister glances about, opines that though E. Arnot Robertson went to Sherborne he was a girl, and then hands the volume back with that bright smile of hers which both sustains and irritates me.[1] "Oh, there's nothing to take any notice of," she says. "They turn out to be only authors—not people who matter—they are just writing to one another about how they didn't get on at their schools. We must remind the library to choose more sensibly for us next time. And talking of choosing—what, Herbert, oh, what about a fresh laundry? Do you agree to us trying the Snow White at Michaelmas?"

"I am far from supposing that the Snow White . . . ."

And far from supposing, far from imagining, Mr Herbert Pembroke and his sister fade away into ghosts. They have been evoked for a moment from a forgotten novel in which, nearly thirty years back, I tried to write about this same topic of one's old school. I did not like mine. I felt towards it what most of the contributors to this volume feel towards theirs, and the Pembrokes were what is now called a compensation-device. I invented them in order to get back a bit of my own.

> So shall Sawston flourish, so shall manhood be
> Serving God and Country, ruling land and sea.

I actually had to sing that. It seems incredible.

All the same, this book is not easy to review. It is rather scrappy. Here are eighteen men and women who have mostly been educated on public-school lines and have mostly disliked it, but not all of them have disliked it nor have they all been to public schools. Nor do they approach their immaturities in the same spirit. Some of them gossip sedately, others are charming, others do a raspberry, others use personal experience as a basis for some theory of education. The editor, Mr Graham Greene (Berkhamsted), shovels everything together as well as he can, but the book could, I think, have cohered better if he had either kept his selection strictly to public schools or else had worked to a much bigger plan and included a great many other educational models instead of merely a few—thus giving a real cross-section of adolescent England.

The contribution I have enjoyed most is Mr O'Faoláin's. He was educated by some gentle muddled monks at Cork, who taught him that there are twelve minerals, that combustion is due to phlogiston, and that

---

[1] E. Arnot Robertson (later Lady Turner), listed in *Who Was Who* but not now as well known as the other writers Forster mentions, attended the girls' school in Sherborne, Somerset, which is separate from Sherborne School itself. O.T.C., above, stands for Officer Training Corps; many of the essayists were students during World War I.

circumcision is a small circle cut out on the forehead of Jewish children. He acquired this knowledge with an open book balanced upon his head, in order to protect it from the showers of broken glass which fell on occasion from the roof. The protection was adequate, and out of the cold and the smells of that huge crumbling room in that vanished school he has constructed a faery world of affection and beauty. The point of Cork is that there was *esprit de corps*, though it was never mentioned and could not have been pronounced. The monks and the boys worked together as a family, and conspired to defeat the Board of Education. One of the inspectors urged scholars to clean their teeth and supervise their hair, etc., and when he had gone, Brother Josephus "swept us together into his bosom for ever and ever in one wave of indignation by saying in contempt of all inspectors, 'Boys! He thinks ye're filth.'" That *was* education, and if one thinks of the washing and washing and washing at Winchester—which as far as my information goes is the most bleached of our Big Five—one realizes the humanizing power of a little dirt, and the limitations of laundries, even when they are snow-white. There was superstition and ignorance at Cork, but these are evils which can be rectified. They have not the paralysing permanency of good form.

Except for Mr O'Faoláin, and Miss Elizabeth Bowen, who gives a calming and charming account of Downe House, and Mr Stephen Spender, who liked his time as a day-boy at University College School, and Mr William Plomer, who, though he did not like Rugby finely eulogizes his late headmaster—except for these and for some scattered praises and happinesses, the general tone of the collection is vinegary. My own tone. If it seems a little monotonous, a little too much like Mrs Gamp's salad, it is surely a needful change after so much oil.[2] The amount of praise lavished on our public schools both by themselves and by sentimental foreign visitors has been preposterous and has led to unendurable complacency. So as for "Honour", read Mr W. H. Auden's devastating analysis of its workings at Holt. As for Imperial training see Mr Derek Verschoyle on Malvern. The boarding-house system, fagging, the uneasy attitude of the authorities towards sex, the snobbery—see *passim*. No longer can Mr Pembroke and his sister lead the massed choirs in:

> Lo the flag of Sawston lifted high appears.
> Bravely hath it waved for twice two hundred years.

For the flag is getting torn, and according to Mr Greene, the entire system is doomed for economic reasons.

[2] Mrs Gamp, better known for her umbrella, takes vinegar with her salad in Chapters 25 and 49 of Dickens's *Martin Chuzzlewit*. In the Valhalla of Forster's story, "The Celestial Omnibus", the boy-hero meets both Mrs Gamp and Mrs Harris, her imaginary alter ego.

appendix b
Memoirs

Edward Morgan Forster wrote his memoirs of his Uncle Willie and of his writing career on pages at the back of the notebook he used as a diary from December 1903 to August 1909, but both the handwriting and the substance of the memoirs indicate that they were written in the early 1920s to be read to the Bloomsbury Memoir Club, as noted in the Editor's Introduction (p. viii). Unlike the diary entries, which Forster wrote on recto pages only, reserving the versos for reading lists or later comments, the memoirs are closely written on both sides of the leaves. These pages (c. 6″ x 8″) were numbered consecutively with those of the diary before being separately archived: "Uncle Willie" runs from 120, a verso, to the bottom of 125; "My Books and I", less closely written and more heavily revised, from 126 to the bottom of 132. Both memoirs have been editorially titled and styled for clarity. That is, abbreviations have been spelled out, ordinary misspellings and miswritings regularized, and omitted punctuation supplied, particularly in dialogues, but oddities like Forster's "neither–or" and his emphatic capitals have not been changed. The more interesting revisions have been described in the footnotes, where deletions are set off not by quotation marks but by the angle brackets explained on p. 311.

Much of the background for "Uncle Willie" is described in the Editor's Introduction (pp. xliii–xlvi). Other relatives whom Forster mentions in this memoir include Aunt Monie, the great-aunt he later memorialized in Marianne Thornton, 1797–1887: A Domestic Biography *(1956). Aunt Sophie, who married John Leven and became Countess of Leven and Melville, was one of Marianne's younger sisters. Another, Laura, brought Thornton money into her marriage with the impecunious Rev. Charles Forster; she became Uncle Willie's mother and Forster's grandmother. It was Forster's father, Edward Morgan Llewellyn Forster, who was allowed by the scholarly Rector of Stisted to become an architect. In the younger generation, Brian Southey was probably the grandson of Watson Thornton, one of Marianne's brothers, whose daughter Marian married Reginald Southey. Ethel Owen was one of Forster's first cousins, a daughter of the Rev. Charles Forster who was Vicar of Hinxton; her husband Fred was a Fellow of Jesus College, Cambridge. A family tree appears in P. N. Furbank's biography,* E. M. Forster: A Life, *noted here, as in the Editor's Introduction, as P.NF. Brief biographical sketches of William Howley Forster and his more important neighbours appear in James Jamieson's* Northumberland *(vol. 14 of Pike's New Century Series; Brighton, W. T. Pike, 1905), accompanied by photographs. There is a strong family resemblance between the uncle and the novelist, who was called "Morgan" by his relatives and friends.*

293

UNCLE WILLIE

Forty years ago Miss Emily Nash of Hinxton Hall, Cambridgeshire, sat alone there in the pouring rain. She was an orphan now and rich in a quiet way, but her long ugly face was already parchmenty, her hair a smeary yellowy-white, and she was lonely as she was always to be. "It was as if the walls spoke." They did not speak to any purpose, for when my Uncle Willie asked her to marry him she said yes. What impelled him to this step is more obscure. He was handsome, amusing, intelligent, athletic, and much her junior. Youngest son of the Rev. Charles Forster, Rector of Stisted, Chancellor of Ardfert, Chaplain to the Bishop of Limerick and author of *Mohammedanism Unveiled, A Commentary on the Rosetta Stone, One Primeval Language, A Historical Geography of Arabia, The Life and Letters of Bishop Jebb*, and *The Apocalypse its own Interpreter*: son of the Rev. Charles Forster, I say, he was unlikely to marry for money. Had he been jilted by someone else? This is more likely, for he was excessively proud, as it used to be called, and was always anxious to announce to the world that it had no power to harm him. He had no profession. He wanted to be a soldier, but the Rev. Charles Forster had forbidden it: he permitted his sons to be either clergymen or barristers or—by a strange concession—architects. So Willie, who always was the boy for tricks, hesitated between the three until the old man died, and then chose nothing. Anyhow they were married, and scarcely was the ring on before he bolted with her round the world. She raised no objection: whatever Willie did was right on her lips: what it was in her clotted and shifty eyes no one knows. She was passionately fond of sport she said, in after years she said, "Ah those were happy days." They went to American Rocky Mountains, where he deserted her to shoot wapiti: he was great at game and had been there before. Then on to Japan, where he bought shopsful of rubbish—cabinets, bad china, tinted photographs of rickshaws and waterfalls, boxes that waggled like a chicken's neck, knives with little knives on their backs, a monkey in teak, a samisen[?], and cranes in a blue silk pond. Some of the packing cases broke in transit, but enough reached England to litter their houses in later years and permanently to embitter me against the further east. On their return they went to Northumberland, in which county they were permanently to reside. "I belong to dear, dear Cambridgeshire," Aunt Emily would say. "But Northumberland suits the Uncle." He established himself with horses [and] fishing rods in a remote valley of the Cheviots, and there Canada gradually joined them, and was fully installed by the time I was old enough to pay my first visit.

There have always been aunts in my family, and Uncle Willie also had his aunts, whose opinions on the subject of Canada still faintly resound down the years. His Aunt Monie spoke her mind, and as she had a formidable tongue they quarrelled—one of his earliest quarrels. His Aunt Sophie, who had quarrelled with Aunt Monie, took his side. Canada was so called from the land of her origin. She was the daughter of a Colonial

Colonel whom he had met while shooting the wapiti, and she had come to England to school. He began by inviting her out on her half-holidays, which as Aunt Emily observed was nice for Canada and nice for Willie, then he made Emily invite her to Northumberland, and her visits grew longer and longer until they were not to Northumberland but from it. An adopted "daughter". That was the suggestion. But Aunt Monie did not accept it. For my own part I neither accept it or reject it. Uncle Willie held his head high. He was acutely resentful of criticism and interference— a quality I share with him, different though we are in other respects. And he let it be known he wouldn't be spoken to, which I don't do. And he never never never forgave. His queer judgements about people, the fantastic legends he wove about them in later years, all arose from the irritant of revenge, though the corrosive acid of unemployment fomented them. As for Canada she was *très petite*, intelligent, hard, and a first-class horsewoman. She made the house pleasant and the county side liked her. Her name was changed in after years, partly perhaps because Aunt Monie made malicious confusion between it and the other colonies. "How is Willie and his Australia?" she would inquire. Or, "When next does Nova Zembla come to town?" She was called Leo, a diminutive of Leontine, her baptismal name. Leo Chipman. She is still alive.

My own experiences—if I omit a childish visit where Uncle Willie disliked me because I "lagged"—my experiences begin when I was about seventeen and the trio had moved into a new house, Acton, on the Coquet. Architecturally, though not in other respects, Acton is the model for Cadover in *The Longest Journey*, a bare classical block, with a big dining-room on the right of the Hall and a big drawing-room on the left, where the cranes hung in their blue silk pond. Much light, and views over agriculture and trees down to the sea and Warkworth Castle. A jolly and rather a noble house. There was lavish hospitality—the trio welcomed visitors, though for different reasons—and at first visitors enjoyed coming. But a sinister spirit brooded. Sooner or later everyone who went there got into trouble. There was Arthur, to whom Miss Chipman said, "Call me Leo," and of whom she then complained to Uncle Willie. There was Adela who said to Aunt Emily, "But Emily do you think Leo Chipman is quite truthful," and Aunt Emily told Uncle Willie this. You see, both of the women were trying to amuse their man, Leo because it was her job, he had trained her to it, Emily because it gave a momentary importance. This, or something like it, brought about the downfall of Brian Southey, Sir Lennox Napier, and Fred and Ethel Owen, most of them relatives of mine and the subject of immense apologias and pronunciamentos from Uncle Willie to their successors. Soon after one arrived he would take one apart, and pour forth his grievances, and I would say, "You and Miss Chipman seem the only people who have behaved properly," for I was ever deferential. "Er-er," he would reply with rather an attractive stammer, while he gave himself time to make up the next lie. How he lied! When he gave up hunting and fishing he had little else to do, and when possible he hooked the lies onto a little truth, so that when the victim was enmeshed he could not even roll away. Watching the ruins of my kinsmen, I sometimes thought: "Someday I shall offend him myself. I wonder how." He was nice to talk to, and his badly cut loose country clothes suited him. He was generally in gray flannel or light brown; he had a ruddy complexion, plausible blue eyes, and a brown moustache. To the end of his life he looked young. Courteous to his guests though he abused them when they left, more than courteous to his servants—charming to them—he broke down badly when he came to his wife. He was abominably rude to her. I shouldn't think he said anything decent to her during the final fifteen years. Obviously they never met at night and by day only at meals where it would be, "Is this salmon or is it bull-trout?" She clears her throat and says, "It is what Leo got in the net." "Would you kindly answer my question please. Everyone is waiting to be served." "I would only point out that—" "I ask you to point out nothing, only to say whether this is salmon or bull-trout." She rises, peeps at the dish and quavers, "Salmon." "Bull-trout," says Leo gruffly, having not intervened till now. "Exactly. Take it away. It makes me sick and it makes Morgan sick. No explanations please." And Morgan would think "poor Aunt Emily" and Aunt Emily would see what he was thinking, and would say, "How about a little prowl in the kitchen garden?" which if wise he avoids, for some trap is imminent. Poor Aunt Emily! On the face of it her life was Hell—insults from her husband, impertinence from Miss Chipman, who really ran the house. New visitors tried to be polite to her, but in the prevailing atmosphere it was difficult. Besides, she was a ghastly bore, and a treacherous sneak. Except for an occasional visit from her brother, Poppy Nash, she had no friends of her own, and then Poppy died. She loved society and pension life—which is why I have remodelled her as Miss Bartlett in *A Room with a View*, hoping to give her a happier immortality in art. But she could scarcely ever come South, because the proprieties were strictly observed at Acton, and Uncle Willie and Leo could never be left in the house alone. He never went away, Leo not often, so year by year Aunt Emily's plan for a little jaunt to The Empire Club, Dover Street, had to be curtailed. There were futile plans, girls were invited to keep dear Leontine company, then fell through, so that Uncle Willie was left alone with her during the hours when copulation is possible in Northumberland. This drove him half out of his mind. He sent furious telegrams after his wife and she had to come back, to resume her duties. A hell of a life, yet did she think it so? I shall advance reasons to the contrary before I close. It was purgatory however for such visitors who were both sensitive and adult, and such dropped off in time. I was young and liked eating salmon and bull-trout, the difference between which is imperceptible except to experts. I enjoyed myself a little less each time, but continued to go.

About a mile away the river Coquet curved through overhanging woods. It was a black and sombre water and fell over a weir into a pool where drowning was said to be inevitable, because when you cast you could feel the depths plucking at your line with the strength of a great fish. We would go above the weir and net salmon—not very sporting I gather, but Uncle Willie was no pedant and felt he had done his bit with the wapiti and elk. Excessively considerate of his neighbours, he was anxious that we should not net too far over the stream and so impinge on the Northumbrian Anglers' Federation who fished the opposite bank. "Leo," shouting, "turn the boat." Leo would shout back from the boat, and with an expression of mark on her face, help the man to toss the coiled nets into the water. Uncle Willie from his pony: "You've done it again—you've got the curve too wide—the fish are escaping." She:—"Shut up." Meanwhile the keepers and hangers on grew also excited and I, not liking to be, was miserable. I had the idea that everyone was cross and that if I had so much as an emotion I should make things worse. So I mooned on the bank, to be annexed as likely as not by Aunt Emily who had toiled down, unsuitably dressed and at no one's invitation, to see the fun. When the net was drawn in the fish, eight or nine of them sometimes, were seen floundering and knocked on the head with soda-water bottles. Now and then I went fishing alone, yes, or rabbit shooting, but always in a fluster, because I couldn't fit it onto my normal activities, and each time that the gun went off and the rabbit ran away I felt that Northumberland knew. Otter-hunting was better. I liked the dogs and the scrambling, and was in at the kill. The otter, flayed and crimson, I took calmly enough, for my attitude towards animals is the normal English.[1] I don't mean by this that I could follow the subtleties of Miss Chipman, who didn't mind how much animals suffered if it was according to rule, but was wrung to her heart by irregularity. She was out once with a man, and they met a dying sheep. She commanded him to put it out of its agony, and when he failed, slew it herself and blasted the man's reputation in the neighbourhood. She wouldn't have been angry with me in like circumstances, for she scarcely considered me as a man. I was quaint, pleasant and cynical—very cynical, especially in *The Longest Journey*—. That was my ticket. In later years I sometimes clashed with a younger generation of cousins and the little girls were encouraged to bait me and be rough.

There is a tradition of mild scholarliness in our family, and my uncle did not resent my continuing it. His own reading was narrow but not inconsiderable. He had read Parkman's History of Canada, *Fire Fountains* and the other travel books of Gordon Cumming, all the novels of Fielding, Smollett, Lever, and Lover, Valentine Vox, Sylvester Sound, Casanova's *Memoirs*, Sir George Trevelyan's life of Macaulay, and he liked one poem: it was by Byron, but I have forgotten the words.[2] Outside these limits, he

[1] A clause following "English" and referring to Virginia Woolf has been deleted in pencil: ⟨, though Virginia thinks otherwise⟩.

[2] The lesser novelists in this list are the Irish ones, Charles James Lever (1806–72) and Samuel Lover (1797–1868). One work by the pseudonymous Valentine Vox, *The Cabinet of Irish and Yankee Wit and Humour* (1864), is listed in the catalogue of the British Library, but nothing appears for Sylvester Sound. Constance Frederica Gordon Cumming's *Fire Fountains* (1883) is about Hawaii; the formal title of Francis Parkman's multi-volume history is *France and England in the New World*.

rallied one agreeably, though with music he took up a firmer line. Many men dislike music, he had a genuine hatred of it, comparable to a dog's. "They tell me a piano's like a gun," he said. "It hurts less when you let it off yourself." So that when Aunt Emily and I played duets upon her dear old grand from Hinxton he would open the drawing-room door, scowl, and mutter, "Lord." Aunt Emily loved music, just as she loved sport. She could never have too much. But one must not disturb the uncle, alas. Religion partook of the general emotional fare. "I believe in doing as your host does," said Uncle Willie. "If you're in a religious house, wear your trousers out and pray like blazes." He did not wear out his, but he stood no nonsense either, keeping in with both parson and priest and remarking that during the hour for compulsory religious instruction those little boys who were atheists ought to do the goose step. Aunt Emily went to church of course—she valued her privileges. Miss Chipman went too, but separately, and in the trap: her Sunday clothes were peculiar, very smartly decorated, but of sporting cut in their fundamentals—a shooting skirt and jacket dabbed over with fluffiness and blobliness, while a veil depended from her trim hat and blew into her mouth. She was specially downright on Sundays. Having left the trap in the pub, she joined Aunt Emily in the Acton pew: Aunt Emily did not think it right to have the trap out on Sundays, on account of the work it gave the servants. Both ladies received the Holy Communion when it was available. Then came the walk (or drive) and some big rag party in the afternoon, when Uncle Willie would emerge from his sanctum and get merry among a lot of girls.

For it will not have escaped such an audience as this that Sex played a large part in my uncle's life. The morbid marriage, the flight round the world, the coming of Canada, the increasing tendency to seclusion in irritability in a life that promised so fair—you can work it out, can't you? I can't so well. For one thing, he was never an ass. He satisfied one's aesthetic requirements and thus lulled one's critical faculty. What I rake up now will make him sound like an ass, perhaps, but if you want to get a picture of him you mustn't let it get ridiculous. Give him his due, he wasn't that. Well, Canada like Aunt Emily got old, and gradually one began to suspect he wouldn't marry her when Aunt Emily died; she had refused several offers, but, loyal to her trainer, she never revealed her intentions or hopes. She may have been awfully deep. Anyhow she made no objection to the youthful feminine trash that thronged the house as years went on, and of course Aunt Emily did not object. May and Nellie Lambert were the silliest, but Norey Riddell and her sister ran them close and lived closer. Then there were the Miss Piddocks to whom he gave false teeth. Little girls he took an interest in too, and would pay for their school: indeed in the end he was interested in nothing but little girls, and the last great row of his life was about Hyacinth, aged twelve, the daughter of some prominent people in the county. He heard, I don't know how, that Hyacinth wet her sheets at night, and he concluded, I don't know why, that her mother ill-treated her in consequence. The usual methods

were employed. Aunt Emily was made to call and brought back information that was rejected as fatuous. Miss Chipman went, as spy in chief.
Then a girl whom I know outside Northumberland was sent, and she has
told me that the whole thing was illusion. Hyacinth was not ill-treated
at all. How it used to bore me! And how circumspectly one had to
walk. For if you tried to play up and rollick among his nymphs he
would suddenly be shocked and scent impropriety. So one sat while
May and Nellie Lambert were encouraged to tell stories against their
mother and the Piddocks against their step-mother who drank and was
called Bomby[?], and Norey and Lal Riddell sprawled or sulked: and
Uncle Willie having been quite witty with *vers d'occasion* and the like—
none of which the girls understood—would suddenly bolt as if he was
going to vomit and not be seen again. Next morning he would say: "I
say aren't they awful they *are* stupid. Oh Lor!" and then fall to talking
scandal. All the houses in the county are fantastic with drink or divorce
in my recollection. Lady Ravenshaw proposed to her footman. The
stories about Ida Widdrington, whom I think Roger knew, are awful,
and those of Eric Creswell her husband worse.[3] Some establishments
took methylated spirit only. Of course he had his limitations. I [*one-word
blank*] was outside his vision and though he once referred to "the worst
thing in creation" he was not illuminating about it. It never struck him
as it did me that the groom was alone during hours that are possible in
Northumberland. If the servants' lodge redressed the balance of the
drawing-room, it needed redressing. No male but my uncle had a
chance, and he grew particularly down on young men. He would greet
them with his old generosity, offer a horse or fishing, but a hitch
occurred almost at once: the young man was discredited for insolence,
apathy or incompetence. Their normal life was three days.

How or why I stopped going north, I do not remember: I think there
was a difficulty one summer about the plans, so that I dropped out of it.
Letters between my uncle and myself grew less frequent, and presently it
was dropped across one that he was ill. He changed houses too for some
queer reason. Moved from Acton a couple of miles to an immense place,
Felton Park, which the Riddles had vacated, and camped out in one of

---

[3] Roger Fry regarded Ida Widdrington as his first love; she refused his offer of
marriage in the winter of 1891–2. A few years later her mother became the "older
woman" in his life (see Frances Spalding, *Roger Fry: Art and Life* [London, Granada,
1980], pp. 38–41, 48). In 1899 Ida married Addison Cresswell (not Eric Creswell),
whose mother had become the second wife of Lord Ravensworth (not Ravenshaw),
who died in 1903. A letter of May 1904 from Mrs Widdrington to Roger Fry, now
among the Fry papers at King's College Library, reports that "Addy's mother"
had married her coachman, to the King's fury, and that Addy himself had returned
to Ida after running away with a married woman. Jamieson's *Northumberland* places
the Cresswells at Cresswell Hall, Morpeth, the Widdringtons at Newton Hall,
Felton, and the Riddells at Felton Park, Felton, but shows no children for the
Riddells (not Riddles, as Forster spells it below). Nor are there Lamberts or Piddocks listed; the names may be wrong.

the wings. His disease was said to be jaundice, but I think it was cancer. The conclusion is very shadowy to me, but you must picture Aunt Emily torn between her sense of duty and her feelings of obedience, and yielding to the latter. He couldn't bear her near him and she didn't go near him. Nonchalant and efficient, Canada saw him through. His body was carried to Hinxton oddest of places—Hinxton near Cambridge, the home of his wife, and that wife and Leo were free from their harness at last. The will was a surprise, but not a great surprise. He left everything to Emily, absolutely, together with a paper of wishes. In this direction she was trustworthy. "Leo," she wrote, "has been amply provided for . . . Leo is kindly helping me with the things." But the next bit of news staggers me still. Aunt Emily and Miss Chipman took a house together at Alnmouth. Habit was too strong for them. They couldn't think of anything to do. I never went there, but Aunt Emily was happy it is said, and cosier than at Acton, and Miss Chipman took up a career of public usefulness to which she had long been disposed but which Uncle Willie had suppressed. She rescued girls and promoted the Empire, and even paid a flying visit to her father the colonel of Canada, who was still alive. Then came the Great War, so clearly foreseen by Mr Chamberlain, and she felt alive at last, and rushed about snapping orders. Aunt Emily was equally moved, and tried to learn to cook. But she had become very old and slow and could not get the dishes done, so she had to stand about in the canteen instead and hinder the people who were cooking. Next year she died, and I will only trouble you with her will, which is thought faithfully to express the last wishes of my uncle. Miss Chipman got almost all—is from my point of view a very rich woman and had most of the furniture. There are generous legacies, allowances, etc., to my cousins. And I got nothing at all. Isn't it odd! Is there some endless fantasy about me, crawling away like a tapeworm? Or was I merely the wrong sex and age? Anyhow no one seems to have quarrelled with Uncle Willie as completely as I have. Not a message, not a letter, not even a box with a neck like a chicken. Silence absolute. But this evening I have broken it.

MY BOOKS AND I

Every Memoir contains a chapter entitled "My books and I". Please imagine that you have come to it. You have listened to my childhood, adolescence and undergraduation. Now we stand in the smaller of the two sitting rooms of Wedd, my tutor at King's, saying goodbye to him. Wedd has already helped me by remarking in a lecture that we all know more than we think. A cry of relief and endorsement arose from my mind, tortured so long by being told that it knew less than it pretended. And now he helps me again, for he tells me that I might write, could write, might be a writer. I was amazed yet not overawed. Like other great teachers of the young, Wedd always pointed to something already existing. He brought not only help but happiness, because what he said was demonstrably true. Of course I could write—not that anyone would read me, but that didn't signify. I had no subject in my mind, but that didn't signify. I had a special and unusual apparatus, to which Wedd called my attention—something which philosophy and scholarship and athletics all despised, still I had it and they hadn't. I had already contributed some fanciful freakish stuff to the University Magazines, and I think I must have begun that novel about a boy named Edgar who lived in a suburb with a Mr and Mrs Manchett who were unsympathetic towards him, and who made friends (Edgar did I mean) with a young man opposite who was also suburban but had something blowy about him and they all went up a hill for a picnic, at which point the manuscript broke off. This wasn't writing, though. The apparatus was working, not inaccurately, but feebly, and dreamily because I wasn't sure it was there. Wedd told me. He said the great good word. The great evil word was not said for many years afterwards. I will tell you what it was later on if I have time and inclination.[1]

Having left Wedd, I travelled abroad for ten months, reached Ravello about May and took a walk. I sit down at the edge of a valley, a few miles above the town, and the first chapter of "The Story of a Panic" rushes into my mind as if it had waited for me there. The first chapter deals with a party of tourists who are frightened, all except a boy, named Eustace. I conceived this as an entire story, and wrote it out when I returned to the hotel, but a few days later I added some more until it was three times as long. Of these two processes the first—that of sitting down on a theme as if it was an ant-hill—has been rare. I did it again next year in Greece where in a hollow tree not far from Olympia the whole of "The Road from Colonus" hung ready for me. And I did it, or rather tried it on, a third time in Cornwall, at the Gurnard's Head. Here, just in the same way, a story met me, and since the "Panic" and "Colonus" had both been published and admired, I hailed it as a masterpiece. It was about a man who was saved from drowning by some fishermen, and knew not how to reward them. What is your life worth? £5? £5,000? He ended by giving nothing, he lived among them, hated and despised. As the theme swarmed over me, I put my hand into my purse, drew out a golden sovereign and inserted it into a collecting box of the Royal Lifeboat Institution which had been erected for this very purpose upon the Gurnard's Head. I could well afford it. I was bound to make the money over and over again. Calm sea, flat submerged rock whereon my hero was to cling and stagger, village whence his rescuers should sally—I carried off the lot, and only had to improvise an inland residence where the hero's wife, a very understanding woman, should retire. I have forgotten the name of

[1] No record of this "evil word" is known. Nathaniel Wedd (1864–1940) taught classics; another Apostle, he too resembled Ansell in his iconoclasm (see PNF, pp. 55, 58–9). The novel "about a boy named Edgar" is *Nottingham Lace*; see the Editor's Introduction, pp. xi, xlviii.

this story. "The Rock" I think. Not an editor would look at it.[2] And I have never sat down in a theme since. *The Longest Journey*—that indeed depends from an encounter, but indirectly, complicatedly, not yet to be considered. The *genius loci* has only inspired me thrice, and on the third occasion did me out of £1. As a rule I am set going by my own arguments or memories, or by the motion of my pen, and the various methods don't necessarily produce different results. Compare the first chapter of the "Panic", caught straight off the spot which it describes, with the two subsequent chapters, in which I set myself to wonder what would happen to Eustace and his party after they returned to the hotel and night fell. As far as the reader's concerned, it's all of a piece, I think. He doesn't notice that a fresh hemisphere has swung into action. All a writer's faculties—including that very valuable faculty, faking—do conspire together thus and do contrive an even surface, one putting some words here, another there.

"Oh dear," says Mr Charles Sayle at this point—for we must back to Cambridge for a moment. "Oh dear," he says, to Maynard Keynes, preparatory to discussing "The Story of a Panic"; "Oh dear, oh dear, is this Young King's?" Then he showed Maynard what the Story was about. B—— by a waiter at the Hotel, Eustace commits bestiality with a goat on that valley where I had sat. In the subsequent chapters, he tells the waiter how nice it has been and they try to b—— each other again. While alive to the power of my writing, to its colour, its beauty, its Hellenic grace, Charles Sayle could not believe his eyes. He was horrified, he longed to meet me. Of course Maynard flew chirrupping with the news. It seemed to him great fun, to me disgusting. I was horrified and did not want to meet Charles Sayle. In after years I realized that in a stupid and unprofitable way he was right and that this was the cause of my indignation. I knew, as their creator, that Eustace and the footmarks and the waiter, had none of the conjunctions he visualized, I had no thought of sex for them, no thought of sex was in my mind. All the same I had been excited as I wrote and the passages where Sayle thought something was up had excited me most. Similarly in the scene in *Where Angels Fear to Tread* where Gino tortures Philip by pinching his broken arm, my nearest approach to a strong scene. This too stirred me, I neither knew nor wondered why, and even if I had heard of Masochism I should have denied the connection. And there are other passages in my books, becoming less frequent and less intense as I grew older and more sophisticated and the clouds lift from that enchanted valley where beauty is lust, lust beauty, and neither has

[2] "The Rock" has been published in *The Life to Come and Other Stories* (vol. 8, Abinger Edition, 1972). It was probably written during Forster's trip to the west early in 1906. The story, very short for its burden, takes the form of an interview with the understanding wife. A beautiful sunset "was flaming under the wych-elm" when her husband realized that he must leave her and go to the village. Deleted in the memoir after "retire" is an echo of this: ⟨and a row of wych elms through which she should contemplate the sunsets⟩.

nor needs to have a name. When Eustace escaped that night over the terrace-wall, where did he go? Ladies have sometimes asked me. I don't know. But in my happier moments I can follow him and I have never to this day forgiven the author of *Erotidia*, because he thinks he knows and slips out after twilight in his strongest spectacles, year after year, for a peep of a nightshirt.[3]

My dislike to explaining my work or hearing it explained runs both wide and deep, and if you had invited me to read this chapter I should certainly have made some excuse. So make the most of the treat. The process of writing is, saving your presence, something sacred and mysterious, and I imagine painting to be the same and that painters only talk so much because they know that their explanations are unintelligible. Me, whose every word tells, must show greater care, and I confess to reticence, to secrecy. I would like books to be anonymous. I believe in inspiration. Matthew Arnold, in one of his letters, says: "I have ripened and am ripening so slowly that I should be glad of as much time as possible, yet I can feel, I rejoice to say, an inward spring which seems more and more to gather strength, and to promise to resist outward shocks, if they must come, however rough. But of this inward spring one must not talk, for it does not like being talked about and threatens to depart if one will not leave it in mystery."[4] I like these sentiments of Matthew Arnold. They suit both my present and my past, and I shall cling to them until everyone comes back feeling quite well from Vienna. They tend to veil one's failures, it's true, but why shouldn't failures be veiled? If one saw them naked one couldn't get on. Character drawing—to take one of my own; in no book have I got down more than the person I like, the person whom I think I am, and the people who irritate me; no more, and the population of the earth is 1700 million. With such defects, with such capacity for being wounded in his most private parts, I find it natural that a writer should

[3] Charles Sayle (1864–1924) was a friend and contemporary of Ernest Dowson and Lionel Johnson at Oxford before he came to Cambridge as Assistant Librarian at the University Library; *Erotidia* was published in 1889. In "My Books and I" this paragraph is the most heavily corrected. "B——" replaces "Corrupted"; "valley" replaces "very spot"; "b—— each other again" replaces "commit sodomy together"; "Hellenic" replaces "Classic"; "believe his eyes" replaces "ignore its vicious tendencies. An awful story. 'A notable story,' he repeated, a remarkable story, he wondered how the Independent Review dare publish it." Before "In after years" a sentence has been deleted: ⟨I said Sayle was absolutely wrong, and Maynard agreed.⟩ Thereafter, "indignation" replaces "revulsion"; "excited as I wrote" replaces "physically excited about them"; and after "where did he go?" a further question which does not match the text of the story has been deleted: ⟨⟨and why in after years did his ⟨face⟩ \portrait/ appear in the Illustrated Papers?⟩⟩ Another deletion follows *Erotidia*: ⟨and other Poems', or entered his rooms⟩.

[4] Arnold wrote this letter to his mother on 24 December 1863, his forty-first birthday, reporting the sudden death of Thackeray that morning and considering the recent sudden death of his father-in-law. In the letter Arnold wrote "gain strength" rather than "gather strength" (*Letters of Matthew Arnold: 1848–1888*, ed. George W. E. Russell, vol. 1 [London and New York, Macmillan, 1895], p. 213).

act the mystery man, and I approve of the devices of Conrad, for example, though Conrad finds it easier than I because he despises his fellow creatures. So far as I tell you anything this evening it is because I respect and love you—and this although I know that I can hold the lot of you for a second in the hollow of my hand. Before you slip through my fingers, realize this.

The transformation of material isn't quite interesting enough to be related, I think. If Forster has been to Italy, signs will appear in his Italian novels of course. Similarly with people whom he has met. A useful trick is to look back upon such a person with half-closed eyes, wilfully observing certain characteristics. I am then left with about two-thirds of a human being and can get to work. This is what I did with E. J. Dent, who became Philip in *Where Angels*, with Uncle Willie who became Mrs Failing in *The Longest Journey* and with the three Miss Dickinsons who condensed into two Miss Schlegels.[5] A likeness isn't aimed at and couldn't be obtained, because a man is only himself amid the particular circumstances of his life and not amid other circumstances, and consequently to refer back to Dent when Philip was in difficulties with Gino, or to ask one and a half Miss Dickinsons how Helen should comport herself with an illegitimate baby ruined the atmosphere and the book. When all goes well, the original material soon disappears, and a character who belongs to the book and nowhere else emerges. All this is obvious and well known, and I needn't go into the various tricks and processes—many of them disingenuous—by which Life is transmuted into a Forster novel. This isn't a craftsman's guild. It's more worth while to relate an experience which I had in Wiltshire and which influenced my whole literary emotion.

I have been in Wiltshire all my life but everything dates from September 1904, when I walked out to Figsbury Rings. They are a double embankment, not conspicuous, but visible from the main line, on the left, halfway between Porton Station and Salisbury. In the centre of their circle stands one small tree, and the spaces between their earthworks are planted with rotation of crops, the earthworks themselves remaining grassed. Why is the place important to me? Because in the September of 1904 I met there a person whom I forgot in about a month, but who set the place going, and the place set Wiltshire going. He was a shepherd boy. Charles Sayle wipes his glasses, but our interview was of no interest to any type of

---

[5] In this sentence "condensed into" replaces "originated the"; deleted after "Schlegels" is: ⟨in H.E. Dent recognized himself.⟩ For Dent, see also p. xlvi. In *Howards End* the two Miss Schlegels and their brother Tibby may also have reflected something of the two Miss Stephens and their brother Adrian, all perhaps among Forster's audience. Vanessa and Virginia Stephen were introduced to their husbands at Cambridge by their brother Thoby, who died in 1906. Vanessa married the worldly Clive Bell in 1907; Virginia, who might be said to have shown something like Helen Schlegel's "tense, wounding excitement" in her youth, married Leonard Woolf in 1912.

observer.[6] I tried to find him on subsequent occasions, but failed, and my romantic feeling died off. But in other directions it spread, and I began to look at Wiltshire—not for the shepherd boy or anyone. I just looked until it began to look back at me. A relation sprang up which will never cease. I have tested it by staying in Wiltshire with Lytton and Sydney who would elsewhere have modified my outlook, just as Uncle Willie and George Hodgkin and the Rev. Howard MacMunn and Lady Low and Lady Morison have all modified my outlook on Northumberland until I couldn't tell you what Northumberland is.[7] Wiltshire I know. And *The Longest Journey* is not only the result of that knowledge, it is also the reinforcing cause. I had planned the book before I took that walk to Figsbury Rings; its meagre theme (a man learns he has an illegitimate brother) and its meagre moral (we oughtn't to like one person specially) had both been noted. Then the emotion welled up, spoiling it as a novel but giving it its quality. Stephen Wonham—that theoretic figure—is in a sense so dead, because he is constructed from without,[8] in a sense so alive because the material out of which he was constructed is living. Although vague and stagy, he is the only character who exists for me outside his book, and restores to the world of experience more than he took from it. Now when I revisit Figsbury, he lies behind it, as once it lay behind him, and as once again—thrice removed from my present wealth—a jejune shepherd lay behind a Figsbury still jejune.

> Quick! let me fly, and cross
> Into yon farther field!—'Tis done; and see,
> Back'd by the sunset, which doth glorify
> The orange and pale violet evening-sky,
> Bare on its lonely ridge, the Tree! the Tree![9]

The tree in the middle of Figsbury is different, the sky in Wiltshire cannot be those colours, yet I fancy that Matthew Arnold had a similar

[6] A deleted sentence follows: ⟨We talked about nothing for a quarter of an hour.⟩
[7] Lytton Strachey was perhaps part of Forster's audience; by all accounts Sydney Waterlow (1878–1944), later Sir Sydney, would have liked to be. As a nephew of Countess von Arnim he made Forster known to her, and he introduced Forster to Henry James, but he was always a difficult friend (see PNF, pp. 122–3). On his trips to Northumberland Forster would also visit acquaintances in the area; Howard MacMunn was a contemporary of his at Tonbridge and Cambridge and was ordained in Durham, and George Hodgkin, a cousin of Roger Fry who took his B.A. at Trinity in 1903, lived in Newcastle-upon-Tyne. Lady Low was the mother-in-law of Malcolm Darling, to whom Forster dedicated *The Hill of Devi* in 1953; the Lows were Scottish. Lady Morison was the wife of the guardian of Syed Ross Masood, to whom Forster dedicated *A Passage to India*; her husband was Principal of Armstrong College, Newcastle-upon-Tyne, in the 1920s. For both friendships see *The Hill of Devi and Other Indian Writings* (vol. 14, Abinger Edition, 1983).
[8] A few words are deleted here: ⟨⟨not created ⟨with in⟩ from within⟩⟩.
[9] Lines from Arnold's "Thyrsis", but see also his related poem, "The Scholar Gypsy"; Forster has conjoined the two in his introduction (p. lxvii). In the quotation here Forster omitted only a comma or two, so they have been restored.

intercourse with the Oxford-trodden coppices of Oxfordshire. The original experience—of the kind called human, but really fatuous and shallow—is of no importance and may take any form.[10] Soon it dies, and the continual births and deaths of such are part of the disillusionment and tiringness of this our mortal state. We do constantly invest strangers and strange objects with a glamour they cannot retain. But now and then, before the experience dies it turns a key and bequeaths us something which philosophically may be also a glamour but which actually's tough. From this a book may spring. From the book, with the violence and persistency that only art possesses, a stream of emotion may beat back against and into the world. Thus much the prim uxorious Arnold knew. Thus much the tedious scholar-gypsy took. And though I don't care for the scenery or sentiment of the poems, they excite by the sense of give-and-take, of creation from scarcely anything of something, until a whole landscape is charged with an emotion, permanent as its origins were transitory. Years later, close to Figsbury, I met the shepherd again. I recognized him because he would have been, and was, a middle-aged mangy farm labourer with a club foot. I felt no pleasure, no sadness, nothing at all except a passing fancy that everyone and everything I encountered was equally unreal.[11] I did not speak to him nor hand him over his share in the royalties of *The Longest Journey*. He didn't see me, wouldn't have spoken if he had, and stumped past.

Figsbury is thus more complicated than Ravello or the Gurnard's Head. I used the scenery afterwards, but at the time it was too flimsy and pale, and a long period of reinforcement, such as preceded *Howards End*, had to follow. Yet indirectly the *genius loci* did address me, and *The Longest Journey* is the last of my books that has come upon me without my knowledge. Elsewhere I have had to look into the lumber-room of my past, and have found in it things that were mine and useful, to be sure: still I found them, they didn't find me, and that wonderful sense of being visited, and even returning the visit, was absent.[12] We write in order to do good work, but our reward is the extraordinary experiences that have accompanied it.

---

[10] In this sentence "fatuous and" replaces "accidental or".

[11] In this sentence "fancy" replaces "fear".

[12] Two deleted sentences originally followed "find me": ⟨And it is the only book that has come near to describing England. I was turning from Italy, I hadn't yet turned to the East.⟩ Also, "being visited" was originally followed by: ⟨⟨ ⟨is not there⟩ was absent. I slip into the language of ⟨supern⟩ the supernatural⟩⟩.

The Manuscripts of *The Longest Journey*

The major elements of Forster's complex restructuring of *The Longest Journey* are described in the Editor's Introduction (pp. l–lvii). The manuscripts themselves consist of 636 variously sized leaves, now mounted and bound into four large guard-books in a way that frames verso passages for inspection. Sixty-five of the leaves, preserving all that survives of the Harold chapter, the omitted chapter of letters, and the drafts of Chapter 31, have been gathered in an appendix at the end of the fourth volume and numbered *A1* to *A65* (numbers on manuscript leaves have been italicized throughout these descriptions, a *v* indicating the verso page of a leaf). All the passages on these sixty-five sheets, whether recto or verso, are transcribed below, together with those variants, usually on verso pages in the main manuscript, which best illustrate the evolution of the novel as a whole. Because the main manuscript of *The Longest Journey* is a nearly complete "final draft", meant to be legible to a typist unfamiliar with the material, its recto pages usually show relatively minor stylistic differences from the published text, and these changes are recorded below only when they are of particular interest, affecting characterization or the development of a leitmotiv. Some further differences between the manuscript and the book are shown because it is possible that a mistyping may have escaped Forster's eye in proofreading; several did, and are listed in the Textual Notes, but on the whole it has been assumed that in his proofreading Forster accepted most of the changes initiated by others. It was probably Blackwood's editor or typesetter who occasionally objected to Forster's use of "was" rather than "were" in conditions contrary to fact, "as if he was running", for instance, being the manuscript reading for the phrase at 5:15 (page and line references to the text of the Abinger edition are given in this manner throughout). It may have been Forster who spelled out contractions or inserted "that"; it was probably not he who changed many sentences beginning "And" or "But" to clauses following semi-colons. The longer transcriptions below, given with Forster's original spelling and punctuation, show the characteristics of his unedited writing. If lax or unorthodox about some matters, he was very careful about "quites" and "rathers" and "things", singular and plural forms of the last being changed either in manuscript or later (a dagger indicates later) to words and phrases like "joys" (5:33†, *6*), "bonds" (30:35, *43*), "affair" (72:10, *138*), "scandal" (134:10, *272*), "this stupid secret" (204:36†, *435*), and, on *543*, "theories" (275:32†) and "in their way" (276:2). But such minor changes are rarely shown below except as part of more complex revisions.

The present position of the sixty-five leaves in the appendix to the main manuscript reflects the fact that the archivist who sorted the manuscripts, Elizabeth Ellem, had them bound in accordance with their resemblance to the published text, not with Forster's major division. The "Preliminary Checklist" of his papers, compiled in September 1970, some three months after his death, records that the manuscripts of *The Longest Journey* came to the King's College Library in two sections, a main bulk of 589 sheets, "unsorted, the pages being neither numbered nor consecutive", and a group of forty-three further sheets held in an envelope "inscribed in EMF's hand: '*The Longest Journey* / scraps / including scrapped chapter'". Forster's envelope does not survive and the forty-three sheets were not listed or marked to indicate their provenance; the final total of 636 leaves, initialled by Elizabeth Ellem in December 1970, presumably includes four unmarked and unnoted sheets that turned up in other caches of Forster's papers. Nonetheless, the descriptions of the "scraps" given in the Checklist do show that the twenty-two leaves added to make up the sixty-five now in the appendix must have included the most finished drafts of the two-chapter version of Chapter 31. Moved from the main manuscript to the appendix in the archival sorting and binding, this two-chapter version was apparently cut to the published chapter only in proof (see p. lv).

Interpretation of the descriptions below and of those in the Checklist depends to some extent on a knowledge of Forster's writing habits. For *The Longest Journey* he used unruled quarto sheets (c. 8″ x 10″), often tearing them neatly across in order to remove unwanted matter or to insert new material; a consecutive series of untorn pages, neither decapitated nor depeditated, can indicate a section that was rewritten or one that was relatively easy to draft. His chapter headings are roman numerals centred at the top of the opening page, and he usually left the last page of a chapter blank after the final sentence. The two-chapter version of Chapter 31 opens with an unmistakably complete chapter of thirteen sheets, now numbered *A23–A35*; the first six are consecutive full quartos in the same ink as the seventh, *A29*, which is obviously part of the same sequence, depeditated only to remove unnecessary blank space. *A30* is decapitated, probably to remove unwanted matter, because *A30–A32* form another consecutive series, ending like the first in a depeditation that removes blank space before the decapitated *A33* and the depeditated *A34*; these two are consecutive earlier sheets which can be patched back into their original places in the earlier draft. *A35* is a sheet decapitated before use, losing no text and long enough to hold the last five lines of the chapter and several blank inches as a sign of the chapter ending. The succeeding chapter opens with two full quartos in an ink similar to that of *A35* but then, except for the full quarto of *A42*, becomes a series of torn sheets and breaks off with *A46*. Both chapter headings, originally XXXII and XXXIII, have been reduced by the deletion of their final numerals to XXXI and XXXII. What is important is that the chapters make an obvious pair and contain within their fifteen most orderly sheets several clearly consecutive series of pages. However scrambled the "scraps" may have been, the descriptions in the Checklist show that these chapters would have been recognized as chapters had they been found in Forster's envelope.

The descriptions in the Checklist read as follows:

a) AMS of Harold version, headed XIV and beginning "He never got to Salisbury . . ." (16 quarto pp. and 1 torn p.);
b) TS of letters in early Stephen version, headed XIX [*sic*] (2 quarto pp.);
c) AMS fragment of Stephen version, headed XXXII (3 quarto pp. and 2 torn pp.);
d) AMS fragment of Stephen version, headed XXXIII (1 quarto p. and 1 torn p.);
e) AMS of Stephen version (fragments consisting of 11 quarto pp. and 6 torn pp.).

None of the four divisions of autograph manuscript (AMS) corresponds to the obviously consecutive leaves of the two-chapter version of Chapter 31. Division *a* describes the Harold chapter, Forster's "scrapped chapter"; incomplete but consecutive as far as it goes and written in a distinctive rusty ink, it is now bound in the appendix as *A1–A17*. *A18* is a battered sheet naming Harold in deleted passages on both recto and verso; it is the only obvious candidate for a position as one of the four leaves that turned up elsewhere. The two typescript sheets (TS) of *b* are the only two that have survived. Headed XXIX, not XIX, they are bound as *A21–A22* and are preceded by two matching manuscript leaves, *A19–A20*, which, having reached the typist, probably came from the main manuscript rather than elsewhere; distinctive in their letter forms, they would surely have been described had they been among Forster's "scraps". Apparently this chapter of letters never reached the printer, for the typescript is unmarked by author or printer even though it shows an obvious inversion. Its number, XXIX, accounts for the headings of the published Chapters 29–35 in the manuscript, where they are XXX–XXXVI, although some untraceable renumbering of Chapters 29 and 30 seems also to have affected the numbers of the two-chapter version of Chapter 31. Another imperfect and puzzling number sequence occurs at Chapters 21–24, and authorial oversight cannot be discounted, but Chapter 29, written in rusty ink when Stephen was Harold, apparently went unnumbered for a long time, gaining the number XXX in a late revision of its opening. Chapter 30 is headed XXXI but still bears a cryptic "n - 2" at the top left of its opening page, suggesting that it too was numbered after it was written. Even the earliest drafts of Chapter 31 are headed XXXII, but no explanation emerges for the change in the numbering of the divided chapter, from XXXII and XXXIII to XXXI and XXXII. (In the descriptions below, only the first twenty chapters are identified either by the roman number of their manuscript heading or by "Chapter" and the arabic number of their published order, since there is no difference. Beyond XX, or Chapter 20, the published chapters are identified in the arabic form. The unpublished chapters are referred to descriptively rather than by number, e.g. the "Harold chapter".)

If so little typescript survives because Forster had no carbon and Blackwood sent him proofs only, without his typescript, the lack would help to explain most of the larger gaps in the main manuscript. The end of Chapter 26 and all of Chapter 27 are missing, as are the openings of Chapters 5 and 17 and the last few pages of the last chapter. All these passages, like the final version of Chapter 31, might have been much changed in proof; reference to the manuscript could have been necessary and those pages lost after their separation from the main bulk. Probably too neat an explanation, especially for the loss of random odd-sized leaves, such use of the manuscript would help to account for the disappearance of most of the second chapter in the two-chapter version of Chapter 31. Of the three further divisions described in the Checklist, *c* and *d* correspond to sheets related to the earlier, long, one-chapter version of Chapter 31; assuming that none of Forster's "scraps" made their way back into the main manuscript, most of the miscellaneous sheets in *e* must also have belonged to the earlier draft. Section *c* corresponds roughly to the five sheets numbered *A48–A52*, although the depeditated *A51* was obviously written at a different time and is in fact a draft of *A27*, and *A52* is a full quarto which is not fully consecutive with its present partners. But *A48* is a full quarto unambiguously headed XXXII and written at the same time as the following full quarto, *A49*, and its depeditated successor, *A50*; these three pages preserve the opening of the earlier, long, one-chapter version of Chapter 31 which now runs, with gaps, from *A48* to *A63*. Several of the gaps can be filled by sheets now in the two-chapter version, and they are so filled in the chronological reconstruction printed below. The two pages described in section *d* above are now *A64* and *A65*; they opened Chapter 32 when the preceding chapter closed with a fire at Dunwood House. They were replaced by *506* and *507*, *506* being at first headed XXXIII; this number was overwritten to XXXIV and then replaced by XXXIII again, a sequence which suggests that the episode of fire might have been changed even before the long chapter was split into two.

Chapter 31 as it was published corresponds only roughly to what remains of the second of the two chapters in the revision, resembling it and the end of the earlier, long chapter chiefly in outline. Unfortunately the miscellaneous group of Forster's "scraps", section *e* above, is described too generally to allow identification of the fragments it included, although some must have been sorted into the series of eleven leaves (*A36-A46*) now composing the incomplete second chapter. *A47*, not consecutive and torn across at both top and bottom, is a related fragment that preserves imagery foreshadowing both *Howards End* and *A Passage to India*; it might have made its way into another cache of papers before being retrieved and bound. Discounting *A47*, however, there are now twenty-four leaves in the two-chapter draft, which is a minimum of two too many to have come from the main manuscript. Forster's "scraps" must have included some of the messier fragments now reposing between *A37* and *A47*. Fortunately this makes no difference to the chronological presentation given below, though it would have been interesting to know just which sheets were among Forster's miscellaneous "scraps".

Although not every chapter of *The Longest Journey* was as much rewritten as Chapter 31, in most the interspersing of torn sheets indicates at least three and sometimes four or more levels of revision. Forster wrote on one side of his quarto sheets only, to begin with, but when saving paper would use the free side of discarded sheets. Occasionally these discarded verso passages are contemporary with their immediate rectos; more often they are widely separated by space or time from their origins. The second leaf of the main manuscript, for instance, bearing the part-title "Cambridge", has on its verso, *2v*, a version of Rickie's second letter to Ansell and the beginning of Agnes's letter to Mrs Lewin, from Chapter 9. (The first sheet, *1*, carries the title alone.) Now crossed through and inverted, *2v* once followed *155*; it was replaced by *156* and *157*, which was depeditated to remove the extra space remaining even after the beginning of Agnes's letter was recopied. The ink of *2v* matches that of the earlier pages in Chapter 9; *156* and *157* show a similar black ink, slightly darker *in situ* but not otherwise distinguishable within the range of gray-black inks that dominate the manuscript. Usually it is the interspersing of torn sheets rather than different inks that is the chief evidence of complex revision.

The major conclusions to be drawn about the timing of Forster's revisions appear in the Editor's Introduction. Details of the more widely variant passages are given separately below for each of the published chapters, and the discernible levels of revision are summarized. The omitted chapters, like the scattered versos, are grouped with the published chapters which are closest to their original placing. The Harold chapter appears with Chapter 12, while the omitted letters follow Chapter 28. The descriptions above may be taken as guides to Forster's habits of revision; it should be remembered that an inserted page is not necessarily altogether new but may recopy passages as part of the linking process. Similarly, when a passage is keyed to the Abinger text, e.g. *506-7* (259:1–29 in), words given within the parentheses, like "in", mark the inclusive limits of the published passage, usually but not necessarily the first or last words of the manuscript page. The published limits of manuscript passages uninterrupted by tearing or by an obvious change in ink have been given in this parenthetical fashion; the extent of Forster's revisions can be roughly estimated by marking the given passage limits in the Abinger text. Inks which are distinctive are mentioned in the summaries, and ink and pen are often described as a unit, for instance, "fine-pointed blue". The most obviously different inks are the initial scratchy black of Chapter 1, so similar to that of Forster's letters from Nassenheide; the gray-green which succeeds it and runs through into the earliest pages of Chapters 5 and 6, growing increasingly black; and the rusty black of the Harold version, which is particularly distinguishable when out of context, as on the verso pages related to Chapter 13. Changes in names are also noted in the descriptions of each chapter rather than listed separately among the variants.

The following symbols are used to mark Forster's additions and deletions; in each case the three dots represent one or more words.

(1) . . . ← . . .	the arrow always points to the later version, most often to the Abinger text to which the variants are keyed.
(2) \. . ./	words between oboli inserted by Forster.
(3) ⟨. . .⟩	words within angle brackets deleted by Forster.
(4) {. . .}	words within brace brackets inserted, then deleted, by Forster.
(5) ⟨. . .⟩\. . ./	(*a*) words deleted, then reinserted, by Forster; or (*b*) words between oboli substituted by Forster for words within angle brackets.
(6) *⟨. . .⟩*	words enclosed within square brackets by Forster, as though for possible deletion or revision, but not deleted and usually not revised.
(7) ⟨⟨. . .⟨. . .⟩. . .⟩⟩	deleted passage (within double angle brackets) within which a deletion (single angle brackets) has already occurred. If doubly bracketed deletions fall within a longer deletion single brackets have been used again; triple angle brackets have been reserved for verso passages inserted in the extra chapters.
(8) \\. . .\. . ./. . .//	inserted passage (between double oboli) within which a further insertion (between single oboli) has been made.
(9) [. . .]	words (or letters) clearly intended by Forster and supplied by the editor; or—*if italicized*—interpolated editorial comments; words whose illegibility makes their reading doubtful are followed by an editorial question mark.

The starred angle brackets of (6) are used to avoid confusion with the square brackets of (9). Forster's occasional ampersands have been spelled out and his occasional series of dashes have been transcribed as single long dashes. His characteristic misspellings, like "vigourous" and "ancle", have been silently reproduced, but peculiar miswritings are marked *sic*. His punctuation is reproduced within all quoted passages, but opening and closing punctuation marks in the briefer listings are usually included only to aid in locating the text. Editorially bracketed suspension points mark the edges of fragments that break off in mid-sentence, but suspension points in the Abinger texts given to locate variants merely indicate repetition. When the Abinger page and line numbers are marked by a dagger (†), it means that the change occurred not in the manuscript but in typescript or proof. At the daggered level the first arrow encountered usually marks the change to the manuscript level, but manuscript changes, particularly series of deletions, can be shown before the arrow. In complicated cases a further dagger marks the end of revisions made in typescript or proof and the beginning of changes which are visible in the manuscript. This ordering is easier to follow in practice than it may sound, since common sense underlies the identification of changes "visible in the manuscript". Oboli mark simple insertions at the daggered level for clarity, since no arrow is involved. Usually the need first to locate the Abinger text determines whether the order of a change is shown by arrows or by a succession of brackets and oboli; at the manuscript level oboli marking the final text show that Forster inserted the change rather than making it *currente calamo*, "with running pen", in the course of the same line. In some cases, for instance 3:20, there will be an "undaggered" but obvious difference between the Abinger text and the first text shown, which in these cases is the final manuscript reading. In the lists of variants the numbers of the manuscript leaves are given in brackets after the first of the variants transcribed from the given leaf; the numbers usually precede longer manuscript passages or that part of a passage which continues on a different leaf. Paragraph openings are marked ¶ when an inset opening would be awkward.

CHAPTER I

Twenty-one leaves (*3–23*), nineteen of them full quartos in scratchy black ink or pencil, make up this chapter, which appears to have undergone very little change. There are two versos, the first, *13v*, unrelated to the novel; it shows a few experiments in creating a foolishly pretentious visitor to Greece, e.g.: "I drove to Sparta in a cumbersome but ⟨comforta⟩ not ostentatious carriage" or "⟨Taygetus⟩ \The gigantic mountain/ was \vaguely/ covered with \opaque and/ diaphanous clouds." The second, *21v*, originally the first of the series of pencilled quartos, *17–19* (13:15 interesting–15:27), must have been discarded quite soon, for it was replaced by *15* (11:34–12:23 But) and *16*, written in the black ink also used to revise *17–19*. Forster wrote *Where Angels Fear to Tread* in pencil, but here seems to have been temporarily short of ink rather than recopying from a full pencil draft; a similar unexplained shift to pencil marks his letter to his mother of 8 July 1905. *21v* is shown below as an illustration of the kind of improvements Forster made not only in expansion, as in the first paragraph, but also in the process of recopying.

Only the last two leaves were shortened, when *23* was decapitated to allow the insertion of *22* (17:10 been–18), a half-sheet which carries only a few more lines than could have been written on the top it replaced. The brownish ink of *23* matches a few changes in the earlier pages, most obviously those to "meringues" (4:14) from "Macedoine"; to "bovine" (5:2) from "animal"; to "little room" (5:12) from "whole room"; to "walked" twice (5:29), from "played fives" and "played"; to "quite pleasantly" (7:30, the "quite" omitted from the book) from "not un-pleasantly"; to "a good deal mollified" (8:4) from "and sat down"; and to "frowned" (12:6) from "started nervously". The grayish ink of the latest sheet, *22*, matches still fewer changes, one of them the return to Rickie's spontaneous "Agnes!" at her first entrance (6:19). The more formal "Miss Pembroke" had taken over in his direct addresses to her but was changed back in every instance by the time of publication (not always in MS). The other clearly grayish changes are those to "slightly deformed" (9:8) from "club footed" and to "her brother's sock" (11:12) from "his sock". Changes from the manuscript to the book are again minor, most occurring in Rickie and Ansell's concluding conversation, the same exchange that took the insertion of *22*.

The naming of characters also suggests that most of this chapter was easily drafted rather than recopied: "Rickie" replaces "Gustav" in the first six pages (*until* 7:28); Herbert was first called "Jack", but only once (7:2); for a moment "the geographical don" (4:8) was "Mr Stokoe", sharing the name of Forster's predecessor as tutor in Nassenheide. "Tilliard" replaces "Tillyard" not only in this chapter but in all its appearances before the revision of Chapter 20.

3   3   off⟨⟨, and burnt a little ⟨round⟩ \brown/ hole⟩⟩. [*3*]

      5   said ⟨⟨someone⟨.⟩ ⟨sullenly.⟩ on the sofa.⟩⟩ a voice.

      8   there." ⟨There was a faint hooray.⟩ Ansell frowned ⟨irritably,⟩ and

   10   declared {in a faint weary voice}.

   20   subjectivity and objectivity ⟨and similar tiresome words⟩.

   25   \Well?/ ← I agree for the sake of argument.

   27   \Then what'll . . . I go?/ ← How'll that be if we both leave the meadow together?

   32   \Rickie, . . . dropped/ ← Gustav, in whose rooms the discussion was being held [*4*]

5 21   \the Prelude to Rhinegold/ ← a few ⟨cord⟩ chords [*6*]

6 14† \rather/ lame [*7*]

   20   She ⟨shook hands with him and⟩ turned

   25   \Symposium . . . feet/ ← philosophers, who had risen to their feet and were giggling nervously

   33   \indeed be horsewhipped/ ← be drawn and quartered

7 17   party. {He was a little hollow eyed man \squarely built, and/ dressed in a lemon-coloured Norfolk.} He [*8*]

   26   maidenly. ⟨⟨Then she dropped it⟨, flushed crimson, and turned away, with her face to the wall⟩ \and flushed, very slightly/.⟩⟩

8 8† \the quality of/ [*9*]

   21   \asked her to marry him/ ← kissed her

   31   \Percival/ ← Galahad [*10; see also* 155:22]

9 15   sigh⟨, believing herself to be overcome with pity⟩. [*11*]

   27† Because ⟨there's⟩ no

   28† he's ⟨the gentleman⟩ below

10 2   known. ⟨Mr Elliot puts it down to nay, he having stumbled while walking in a flowery meadow. But would nay start it again in the night?⟩ I [*12*]

   12† flopping ← flapping

   21† is really ← really is [*13*]

11 7   \observed/ ← noticed [*14*]

   8   \His conscience . . . demand it/ ← By profession he was a schoolmaster

   12   had ⟨calmly⟩ peeled

   13   \embers/ ← blaze

   24   \sopping/ ← not dry

   36   \such deformities/ ← his things [*15*]

12 16† were not partial to ← did not care for

   20   \kick/ ← soul

   27† \on my engagement/ [*16*]

   38† \he . . . shy./ He got up ⟨rather⟩ hastily†

[*See* 12:12 *for comparison to the beginning of 21v; the end is identical with* 13:15. *21v:*] ¶He had to wait his turn ⟨in⟩ \at/ the kitchens and when his turn came he had lost his head and yielded it to those behind, saying that it didn't matter. Afterwards he had wasted much precious time struggling for bananas, and the shop was full, it being Market Day, and neither Agnes or Herbert ate bananas. Amid ⟨much⟩

tardy and chaotic hospitality the meal got under way. Mr Pembroke was worried over his foot and his sister had all she could do to keep him pleasant.

"Rickie! Pray condole with Herbert."

⟨"Why?"⟩ \"What about?"/

"Oh the rudeness!" She struck the table with her hand. "He's losing me."

"Then I congratulate you," mumbled Rickie. "I hope you'll be very happy, but I don't know anything about marriage."

She laughed. "Oh you are a cure! Just the same. But you do know something about Gerald, so don't be so cautious. I've just ⟨found out⟩ \realized/ you must have been at school together.⟨"⟩ ⟨He just remembers you, but only just.⟩ Of course he was older. Do you remember him?"

"Yes" said Rickie, with more than his usual nervousness.

"Then tell me every scrap you remember.⟨"⟩ I wonder whether he remembers you."

"He was a great deal older, as you say. In the eleven and the fifteen, captain of his house, a prefect of course—"

"⟨He says he developed awfully quickly.⟩ Wasn't he a kind of athletic prodigy— I mean he could knock any boy or master down?"

"Yes."

"If he had wanted to" corrected Mr Pembroke.

"If he had wanted to" echoed Rickie. "Well I hope you'll be very happy. I don't know anything about the army, but I should think it must be most awfully interesting."

```
13  21   \, speaking to himself/ ← dreamily [17]
      †  Any profession ← Other professions
     26   \am . . . pronounce/ ← don't know, I'm sure
14   2†  Agnes . . . proceeded— ← ⟨his sister.⟩ Agnes.
     7†  \, like your father/
      9   church. ⟨It is too serious even to suggest.⟩"
     11   \be simply killing/ ← look simply ripping [18]
     21   \suppressed/ ← ⟨swallowed so⟩ kept down
          throat⟨—no less a thing than his virginity⟩—
     27   author ⟨blushed and⟩ shook
     37   push him. ⟨It was, so to speak, in the family.⟩"
15   1   once⟨, though I love her books⟩. [19]
      3   help you. ⟨The same name! Oh do try!⟩"
      4   "I ← "No. And I
      †  anything ← my things
     36†  not ⟨only⟩ consider† ← \not/ only consider [20]
16   6†  \, sipping his coffee/
     10†  \their/ names⟨, once and for ever⟩.
     19†  a circle inside a square ← a square inside a circle [21]
     37†  \so often/
17   7†  in? ← in.
      9†  \She came in. You saw her come in./
     11†  really there ← there really [22]
     14†  shut up ← shut it
     17†  \She was not really there./
     20†  you ← you \do/ [23]
     21†  these people ← they
     31†  \clever/
```

CHAPTER 2

The three versos (*32v, 36v, 38v*) among the seventeen leaves (*24–40*) of II show
that an early draft in black ink, running at least through Rickie's memory of his
mother's second request for "No. 50 white" (23:31), was almost completely recopied in gray-green ink which was then used, on full quartos neat enough to
suggest further recopying, until the end of the chapter. The main draft includes
two early sheets, *28* (20:5 with–*28*) and the preceding half-sheet, *27* (*begins* 19:33),
which was originally inserted between *32v* and *28*. A finer black ink marks the
two late sheets, *30–1* (21:30 Some–22:29 said he), which begin Rickie's recollections and obviously replace at least one leaf, gray-green or earlier. The
gray-green sheet which must have followed *29* (*ends* 21:13 he) is missing, but *36v*
is its discarded draft.

"Widdrington" has been changed to "Withington" throughout the chapter, perhaps in the late fine black ink, and the "aesthete" of the first paragraph is in
manuscript merely a "don".

19 1   On the . . . [*25*] ← [*32v:*] ¶In those days it was worth while bringing out
the right book to read there, even if it was the wrong shape. First of all
Rickie had brought Omar Khayyam: then, as his instincts grew truer, he
brought Keats⟨.⟩ instead. He brought Keats the blessed Monday the
Pembrokes departed, and Ansell came too, and brought Spinoza. As they
reached the dell two more of their set met them on bicycles⟨.⟩\,/ and
joined them.

"Elliot is ⟨an⟩\in/ a dangerous state" said Ansell, after they had sat in
silence a little time, their backs against fir trees, their bodies protected
from the autumn ground by mackintosh squares.

"How's [*then like the text, without the two sentences about the book, to* "I don't try",
followed by:]

"Adieu⟨."⟩\, then."/

"Tillyard's another" said Widdrington. "Tillyard thinks it such a pity the
college should be split.⟨"⟩ ⟨That's why he rows and occasionly gets
drunk. Out of a sense of duty.⟩\"/

⟨"The college isn't split" cried Rickie, who got excited on this⟩ [*end 32v,
see* 20:4]

28   \That . . . matter./ ← Oh I don't know or care about that! [*26*]

31†   "Tilliard . . . thinks ← "And ⟨Tillyard's⟩\Tilliard's/ caught it of them"
said ⟨Widdrington⟩\Withington/. He's started trying as well. He thinks

38   chair, . . . laughed Rickie. ← chair, with not a god-like curl crooked.⟨"
¶"Most of us are dreadfully plain," laughed Rickie "I wonder why."⟩\I
should . . . Foreign Office."/ ¶"Most of us are dreadfully ugly" laughed
Rickie. "I wonder why." [*27*]

20 6   one⟨, if only people won't talk about it⟩. [*28*]

28†   and . . . one. ← so that the dell re-echoed. "I hate no one."

38   "Oh, good!" [*29*] ← [*Except for the paragraph about the cloud, added on 29, 36v
is like the text from* "We are obliged" *to* "Oh, good!" *It then reads:*] ¶⟨My⟩
\But my/ father is dead," said Rickie. He would not have admitted hostile
feeling towards the living. So long as his father had lived he had hidden
from himself the truth.

"Why did you hate him?"

He replied⟨, almost in a whisper.⟩ "I think it must be because he was
⟨tame⟩ \lame/, but I try to think it was other things."

"But you don't mind being lame." said Widdrington.

"He minds that he became it" answered Ansell.

3¹5

"I ought to mind talking about these things" said Rickie thoughtfully, "but I don't."

"Talk about them⟨."⟩ then."

"Now?"

"Yes. If you bore us we have books." And with this invitation Rickie began to relate his history⟨, not exactly as follows⟩. The reader, who has no book, will be obliged to listen to it.

21   5   "Yes—" ⟨¶"If I loved live people" said Ansell "I'd be careful what I said. But how can it matter when it's all the other way round?⟩ [*29*]

22 22 \family/. ← relatives. "But that's ⟨my way⟩ \quite like me/. I always meant to marry a nobody." [*31*]

     25 \from the opposite bank/ ← on the other side

23   6 \another lady came in and/ [*32*]

     9 "It is ← [*This speech is reached differently in the first paragraph of 38v:*] ¶Rickie must have been six years old when he asked his mother "Why does Mrs Hamm always come dancing down the steps when Mr Hamm comes home?" His mother replied "It is a way of Mrs Hamm's" And about the same date he asked "Why does father always laugh at me? Am I so funny?" Mrs Elliot replied "It is [*From this point 38v is similar to the text; Mrs Elliot's second* "No. 50 white" *ends both her speech and the page.*]

    32 \that the . . . him/ ← the steps in the passage [*33*]

    38 \dubbed/ ← named [*34*]

24   1 \sorry that it was not/ ← glad that it was

    7† In reality he never ← \In reality he was sterile—too sterile to find himself out./ ⟨⟨It is not necessary to create, but it is necessary to ⟨be creative⟩ \have creative power/.⟩⟩ ⟨Mr Elliot⟩ \He/ never

26 32† mockery. "⟨It is a little difficult for me.⟩ In [*38*]

27 10 Emily. ⟨⟨(Aunt Emily had not come to ⟨f⟩ the funeral.)⟩⟩ They [*39*]

    32 dell. ⟨The outer world seemed far removed, and so did⟩ The [*40*]

    34 \snow white ramparts and/

CHAPTER 3

The first five sheets of the twenty-seven in III (*41–67*) are full quartos written in a black ink, with pencil variations, resembling that of I. The gray-green of II, used for the rest of III as well, begins with *46* (32:32 to be–33:15 people), which recopies with little difference a pencilled verso, *49v*. Later fine gray-black insertions among the greener sheets give Rickie's reactions to the news of Gerald's presence (*48*, 33:30–34:10 harmless), to Agnes's query about Gerald (*59–60*, 37:38–38:24 uncomfortable), and to his sight of their embrace (the *Rheingold* passage, *64–5*, 39:36 and–40:29). But from *52* (*begins* 35:34 where) to *67* the gray-green sheets are themselves so fragmented, only *57* (37:11 had–30) and *63* (*begins* 39:15) being whole, that the ink was probably being used for the first draft. One gray-green verso, *75v*, transcribed below as the last of the variants in this chapter, survives on the back of a later insertion in IV.

Gerald's initial rank of "Captain", consistent through the gray-green stage, is deleted or changed to "Mr" in the later black ink. "Failing" in its one appearance here, as in IX, replaces "Hatchard" (*45*, 32:1); both Mrs Failing's name and that of the Pembrokes' house, Shelthorpe (33:1), added to *46* in black ink, must have been decided after the initial drafting of Chapter 9.

29 31 good ⟨and beautiful⟩ and true [*42*]

30 19† view. ⟨⟨¶"I shall never be able to thank ⟨you⟩ \them/" ⟨said⟩ \thought/ Stewart⟨, with tears in his eyes⟩. "All I can hope, is never to disgrace ⟨you⟩ \them/."⟩⟩

31 33 \You . . . living./ [*44*]

37 \Of . . . different./ ← And even Aunt Emily—

32 8† "It means . . . too." ← "By road it's not ten miles. Stewart shall drive you." [*45*]

22 Pembrokes⟨⟨, to renew his acquaintance with ⟨Captain⟩ Gerald Dawes⟩⟩.

25 cant." ⟨¶"I wish you would keep yours. You drive me wild."⟩

37† the tract ← the ⟨low-lyin⟩ healthy tract [*46*]

39 \its name was Shelthorpe/ ← semi-detached [*46, 49v*]

34 10† dissyllable ← \word/ [*49*]

23 friends⟨, though their knowledge of his relatives was not as extensive as they supposed⟩.

35 4 \one must accept it/ ← you cannot realize it too fully [*50*]

6 \accepted/ ← realized

19 places. ⟨⟨Such was the ⟨appearance⟩ present appearance of the boy who had tortured Rickie at school.⟩⟩ [*51*]

26 hands ⟨⟨with great success, considering that ⟨the last time their hands had been in⟩ \\hitherto ⟨they⟩ \their hands/ had only met for// the process known as 'barley sugar'⟩⟩.

38 \observed . . . bench/ ← said Agnes, sinking onto a seat [*52*]

36 3† No vices. ← Much better not.

36 parson. ⟨⟨Are you smoking?" [*54/56:*] ¶⟨"No thank you. I hardly ever smoke.⟩ \Rickie did not answer./ He felt bewildered. He⟩⟩ \Rickie/ [*55 inserts the two paragraphs after* parson.]

37 26 Rickie. ⟨⟨"I ⟨suppose I ought⟩ \want/ to go, but she will keep me."⟩⟩ [*57*]

37 "In a way." [*Placed just above the depeditation of 58, this was originally followed by* "Isn't he a lump?" ¶ *They laughed, but he felt uneasy. He had no experience now torn through and deleted at the top of 61; 59–60 replaces the question.*]

38 2 protects. ⟨Never again would Gerald torture his flesh: the conventions would not permit it.⟩ But [*59, not permit it not actually deleted.*]

3† our ← the

11 \suppose/ ← confess

13 \country houses/ ← on platforms

24† uncomfortable. ⟨He had no experience [*60/61:*] of lovers, and hated gaining it.⟩

34 odd. ⟨And they had not been engaged a year.⟩

39 8† \weren't stuffed/ ← didn't get enough [*62*]

23† Ought ← Sacred as an engagement is, ought [*63*]

27 but ⟨till the end of his life⟩ the ⟨group⟩ \sight/ ⟨stayed⟩ {was} ⟨photographed upon⟩ \burnt into/

35† crimson⟨, trembling⟩ and afraid.† [*The next sentence was added in the black ink of 64–5; the original last line of 63, now deleted, was* ¶"Church Defence" *began Mr Pembroke* "makes a sad inroad]

40 6 \and heard . . . monotony/ [*64*]

10† clarionet ← brass

† brass ← clarinet

13 \river/ ← waters

15 world. ⟨The eye \alone/ could not reach him, nor the ear \nor could the touch alone/; yet was he not super sensual, and the more of a man invokes him the swifter his response⟩ Creation

18 \greater . . . woman?/ ← simply the touch of a man on a woman, and his ⟨dwelling a⟩ temple a little lawn ⟨bounded⟩ \girt/ by small bushes and a fragile fence? Greater than anything, if Love was this. [*65*]

25† stared ← gave a genial laugh
28† \said the one/
30† \said the other/ [*66*]

41 6 \his sympathy . . . allowed/ ← ⟨means⟩ his love \had/ contrived and ⟨his tact⟩ allowed [*67*]

    7 \put it down/ ← attributed it

[*The chapter may once have ended on 66, at* outside (40:36), *since the last two paragraphs are written in the thinner ink of the later greenish pages, like 55 and 63, and became the final paragraphs when 67 was depeditated through a line about the school. 66 is an earlier sheet, decapitated but still showing a deleted end-of-paragraph sentence:* A china stall. *No closing quotations marks are visible; the sentence originally preceded Gerald's repetitive question about smoking. The china stall perhaps concluded Rickie's non-Wagnerian response to Love, preserved in part in the early greenish ink of 75v:*] ¶⟨Nothing is like a book.⟩ That bench in the prim little garden, those creosoted fences, that white winter sky—who had celebrated these things, who had set them as scenery for the ⟨divine⟩ Divine? What ⟨artists⟩ \artist/ had ever painted ⟨lovers?⟩ \Agnes and Gerald?/ What poet had ever written about ⟨love?⟩ \their kiss?/ Pretty pictures, pretty poems: and lo! the ⟨Divine⟩ \Actual/, ⟨the Immortal, the Unspeakable,⟩ and at ⟨one⟩ \a/ glimpse of it they perished, even as handsome mortals once perished at a glimpse of goddess or god. Poems? \Pictures?/ Why the whole world perished as well—all of it that was not, like ⟨this⟩ \their/ Love, sincere. Navy Leagues, defended Churches, University degrees, ⟨bazaars⟩:—they too should perish, they should perish utterly, for in none of them was the breath of eternal [. . .]

CHAPTER 4
The twenty-one sheets of IV (*68–88*) begin with the later gray-green ink of III; the first is a short insert, ending at "semi-" (42:8), and indicates again that the position of the chapter break was an afterthought. Finer black additions among the variable gray-green pages provide the comparisons to other public schools (*70*, 42:30 of–43:5); the details of Herbert's customs (*72*, 43:16 we acted–28 and); the account of Herbert's planned advancement (*74-5*, 44:10 the–44:30 him); and the discussion of philosophy (*79–80*, 46:3–47:4). For *75v* see above. After the decapitated, relatively greenish *81* (*ends* 47:14 speaks), there are no further insertions and the ink of the remaining seven sheets, all full quartos, becomes increasingly black. One further verso, *84v*, described below, is a draft of its own recto; the draft does not fill its page and *84* (48:10 intimate–29 And) appears to have been written without concern for recopying. On the greenish sheets "Mr" Dawes is still being demoted from "Captain".

43 7 \master . . . Side/ ← adviser to the Army class and form master to the Remove [*71*]

   10 it. ⟨⟨For if there was a thing he ⟨had⟩ hated more than independence it was stagnation.⟩⟩ "An

   13 \believed . . . men./ ← did not believe that either ⟨men or boys could⟩ the school or the world could live decently without one.

   29 \weak in esprit de corps/ ← lacking in patriotism [*73*]

   34† asphalt. ← asphalt, and ⟨generally speaking,⟩ had a high old time \generally/.

44 23† \to your mothers/ [*75*]

   35 \a house of Day Boys seemed/ ← Day boys I to P seemed [*76*]

45 27 \laying . . . back./ ← patting him on the back. "Ah Rickie, that's the finest thing you've said since you've been here." [*77*]

   32† ideas. I ← ideas. Of course ⟨I don't know, and⟩ I've got all this criticism out of books. But I [*78*]

   35 comes ⟨not from the head, but⟩ \only/
   37 \there are . . . London/ ← the climate of London is delightful
46 2 conception of Woman. ⟨(Then he reverted) to his school)⟩
47 4 \Does Agnes . . . school?/ [*80*] ← [*81:*] ⟨What an interest she takes⟩ \She
         seems to take a great interest/ in the school.
       5 \Not . . . soldier/ ← Keen. If our naughty captain
      29 Aristophanes⟨, and had also not followed the Greek⟩. [*82*]
48 1 \made a bad blunder/ ← \come a cropper/ ← gone wrong for once [*83*]
       6 faults⟨, and he liked her to be praised⟩.
      10 intimate ties . . . years [*84 and 84v are identical from* intimate *to* years, *but
         then the deleted verso moves directly to Rickie's lameness. From 84v:*] years, because
         they ⟨were poor⟩ had no money. How monstrous that he could not give
         them any! He had a little, and could do with a little less, for he⟨, he,⟩
         \himself/ could never marry: ⟨he had a duty to posterity:⟩ he was ⟨phy-
         sically unfit and had no right to⟩ tainted with the Elliot lameness, and
         had no right to transmit it further. ⟨All this he⟩ \He/ had talked \this/
         over one evening with Ansell. Money, and he might not give any. If he
         even mentioned it they and everyone would be shocked or offended. And
         this in a world that ⟨de⟩ says it is practical. [*84v ends here, with space
         remaining; 84 is very neat.*]
      22 this ⟨trivial fortune⟩— [*84*]
      35 something. ⟨⟨To his ⟨intense⟩ \gr/ disgust⟩⟩ Rickie [*85*]
49 9 offended\, but . . . firm/. ← offended. He went to the sacred diary [*86:*]
         wherein he recorded his own more intimate experiences and the more
         heinous crimes of others. There, with a beating heart he wrote 'F. E.
         hsippu', which may be deciphered by ⟨anyone who wishes⟩ \those who
         will/. [*uppish!*] At once he felt better.
      10 In a ← Meanwhile Rickie had done for himself. In a
50 1 he. ⟨And beast." ¶"No he isn't a beast. Only a fool. He muddles all day
         with poetry,⟩" [*87*]
       2† \He means no harm./
         \He/ muddles ← The dear thing muddles
       4 \bring it into/ ← find it all and act the same in
      11 prude⟨⟨, and ⟨had strong⟩ was reticent in mentioning anything to the
         opposite sex⟩⟩. [*88*]
      13 was ⟨only a bit⟩ crocked, his father ⟨worse,⟩ \too, and/ he's ⟨worse still⟩
         \as bad/.
      25 well⟨⟨, and made him see that he was really ⟨more beastly⟩ \worse/
         than Rickie⟩⟩. But she ⟨\had/ thrilled with excitement at the⟩ \had a
         wild thrill of joy when she/

CHAPTER 5
There are nine leaves (*89–97*) in this chapter, but no leaf headed V and no manuscript equivalent to the first paragraph of the published chapter, which would have
filled at least one-third of a quarto. There was much revision. The earliest sheets,
in greenish black, are *91* (52:6–19 returned), decapitated and depeditated, and the
last two, the decapitated *96* (54:11–15 trust) and the depeditated *97*, which still
shows the quotation mark for a new paragraph at its tear. *89–90* (*begins* 51:8) are
later; the latest are the four central full quartos, *92–5*, written as a series in a
scratchy gray-black ink. One full, undeleted verso, *95v*, transcribed below as the
last of the variants in this chapter, survives from the intermediate level; a similarly

inked half-sentence appears at a tear on a verso in the next chapter, *105v:* "and then he couldn't remember The things ⟨we're[?]⟩" [*see* 53:31].

51 24   own. ⟨He gripped with all his force, and she nearly cried.⟩ ⟨"There. There"⟩ "Now [*89*]

28† going? ⟨What happens next?⟩"

52 9   door.⟨"⟩ {It's darker than ever with it open."}\"/ [*91*]

12 faint. ⟨ ⟨⟨In the gloom ⟨they⟩ \she/ could \see/ the rows of pegs that were screwed into the walls, and from these were suspended coats, knee guards, ear protectors, and other unfamiliar things.⟩⟩ \\The fog ⟨crept⟩ \came/ into the pavilion, and through the thick air the great coats and knee protectors and ear guards loomed in strange menacing fashion from their pegs on the boarded wall.// ⟩ He

13† "Bear . . . him. ← "Courage," she told him. "Go bravely."

17 She rode [*This and the following three paragraphs, to* leave her. *are in manuscript one paragraph.*]

26 dream. ⟨She told the servant to go back to her work.⟩ She [*92*]

29 thought!" In ← thought", ⟨pointing to the \strip of/ brown holland that stretched to the front door⟩ \and pointed to the dints that a football boot leaves/. [*Then the final two sentences in the paragraph, deleted here and recopied below.*] In

34 \rubbing her eyes/ ← her soul in suspense

38† invited herself to apathy ← mused,

53 2† She . . . alive!" ← He thrilled her with disgust. [*93*]

4 he cried ⟨in a strange voice⟩.

11† \so firmly, so irretrievably/

19 \as well as his./ ← too. Then suffer for he was your life. [*94*]

20 \hold/ ← hurt

† again⟨, and the footprints we look at—they will never point inwards⟩.

23 Who—\Who forgives?"/ ← Who—Whose forgiveness?" Her hatred was lulled⟨.⟩,

26 \dishonesty/ ← ⟨petty⟩ subterfuges

27 footprint⟨, and knew that she embraced reality⟩.

35 \let/ ← watched [*95, twice:* her accuse; her kiss]

39 their ⟨outline was blurred⟩ marks

    \marks/ of ← prints of

54 11† "Anything—if you ← "What⟨ever⟩ you like. But always [*96*]

[*Inverted and undeleted, 95v could have followed 91 before its depeditation, but Herbert's presence makes the passage difficult to place. 95v:*] What was immortal? Not Gerald. He was impossible without a body, just as he was impossible with⟨out⟩ a body maimed, crouched on the dusty floor⟨, knees towards⟩. It was another curious joke.

"How well I am bearing it." she thought. "I am bearing it splendidly." She stared at herself in the glass again till she was half mesmerised.

Herbert's voice awoke her, and for a moment she was shattered. His fault! If it had not been for him, for six—eight months she might have been a wife. Gerald had said 'Hang the money. Let's get married and face things after', and she, while she was with him, had agreed. Then came Herbert and talked of prudence and making one's way and self control repaid a thousand times, and of all life before them. All life! Eight months had been before them. Exactly eight months.

But she ⟨calmed herself⟩ \did not break down/. All life, like eight months, would have come to an end at last. We must all die ⟨some⟩. We must all die sometime. There was comfort in the reflection, and ⟨again⟩ she thought "I am bearing it quite well."

CHAPTER 6

The first of the twelve leaves in VI (*98–109*) is an addition, written in the ink of the latest pages in V and shortened to remove blank space; the second sheet, *99*, bears a deleted VI and once opened the chapter at the present third paragraph (55:17). Only one further page, *105* (58:24 genius–35), was shortened; for its verso see the description of Chapter 5 above. The intermediate ink of V, more black than green, here runs from *99* to the middle of *102* (57:14 narrow), where Forster shifted to a pen with a much narrower nib, used for many chapters thereafter. Probably this neat chapter was easy to write rather than recopied. The last leaf shows an undeleted verso draft of its recto, evidently soon abandoned, and only a few rewordings show the late ink of *98*: "with the eyes of Blake" (59:18) for "as Blake must ⟨have⟩ see her", on *106*; "one of the few tributes" (59:33) for "the only tribute", and "indulged in a vision" (59:36) for "had a pagan vision", both on *107*; and "turned" for "clicked" (60:7), on *108*.

55 19 peeped ⟨roguishly⟩ out [*99*]
    28 out ⟨⟨of the damned ⟨thing⟩ \tram/⟩⟩ and
56 8 Road. ⟨⟨It was not exactly raining, nor ⟨wh⟩ ⟨were the streets⟩ \was the pavement/exactly wet, but both the air and the earth seemed slimy.⟩⟩ "Here [*100*]
57 6† scant allusion to ← no mention of [*102*]
    7 \concrete/ ← \underlying/ ← simple
58 5 world. ⟨All for a penny.⟩ The [*103*]
    8† mine." ← the two."† ⟨Then he went to his rooms—the only place in the world that was really his own, and they only for two years.⟩ [*104*]
    16 \reasonable life/ ← decorous playfulness, the literary conversation, the music and the tea
    21† easy to ← anything to
    27 \that came up yearly from/ ← forced upon them by [*105*]
59 6† for him up ← up \for him/ [*106*]
    22 "We ← ⟨The letter, when he opened it, was an honest and sincere performance, and also remarkable⟩ "We [*107*]
    23† to ⟨suggest it, and⟩ risk
    24 any place⟨⟨, even to the ⟨place⟩ \pavilion/ where he died⟩⟩.
60 3† is ⟨extremely⟩ troublesome [*108*]
    8 the ⟨electric⟩ light
    12 \on St John's Eve/ ← in midsummer
    17 interesting. ⟨There is no water and two men, one old, one young, go to find some⟩ The
    21 one man, ⟨one young man,⟩ *integer*
    24 Through the ← [*108* ends with a deleted azure *which once led to the shorter chapter ending on 109v:*] onslaught of the sea gleams no grisly form, but— But what awful nonsense! When real things are so wonderful, what is the point?

CHAPTER 7

There are seven shortened inserts among the thirty-three leaves of VII (*110–142*), variously torn to admit the additions, all of which intensify Rickie's relation to Agnes by developing his unwillingness to allow her to know him more intimately. One of the matching later changes on an earlier page provides the evidence that lunch did not at first occur at the Union (69:9); also later are the change in Ansell's physiognomy (62:11), the reordering of Billingsgate (63:9), and the shifts to cow-parsley from hemlock (62:11, 71:26). As in VI, the overall impression is one of neat and relatively minor adjustments rather than much recopying. The seven inserted sheets are *118, 121, 122, 124, 128, 130,* and *132.* One leaf was torn to provide both *118* (65:30–33) and *121* (66:22–31), and both paragraphs appear to have replaced passages giving some reference to a metaphor about Ansell asleep, for *117* ends with "asleep ⟨and so did⟩.", while *120* is torn through at a deleted "Why should he wake him up? To". *121* was in its turn depeditated through a draft of the opening of the next paragraph: "his guests in the hall reading the telegrams." *122* (*ends* 66:38 muslin) carries the revision, presumably because space ran out on the pre-shortened *121*. The other four inserts show a slightly scratchier ink. *124* (67:8–17) is purely an addition, lying between two once-joined leaves and replacing nothing. *128* (68:19 a–30) replaces half of one quarto and a line or two of another; torn through on *127* is Mrs Lewin's unused response to the idea of the "frightening" Ansell: "'Oh bosh![?] Mr Elliot, perhaps I'm not such a coward [. . .]". This was replaced by a "He" which leads to "is a trifle weird", the first of the lines on *128.* Like *124, 130* (68:38–69:5) lies between two once-joined leaves, but its two paragraphs replace one torn-through line: "Rickie asked them what they would like to do after lunch." *132* (69:15–25) settles Mrs Lewin for her nap at the Union.

61 28 tea, to ⟨⟨shout "Damn you, I'ld sooner ⟨hall⟩ have a stomach ache", and⟩⟩ throw [*111*]

62 11 \cow-parsley/ ← white hemlock [*112*]
\Ansell's . . . them/ ← Ansell was wearing one round his ⟨chin⟩ \chubby/ face, as if he had the mumps

13 \it's so tiny/ ← there's no space here

63 9 \"Billingsgate" . . . Lane"/ ← "Birmingham" or "Billingsgate" [*113*]

19 \Oh what a difference! [*twice*]/ ← Oh how small! [*thrice, 114*]

24 fellowship⟨, or at all events have a Cambridge connection⟩.

64 2 \"I . . . friends/ [*114*] ← "In the hearts of your friends" said Ansell, pretending to speak bombastically. [*115*]

10† as ⟨the⟩ sand

33 week⟨—the one idle week you and I could have had together—⟩ you [*116*]

34† Wednesday ⟨I was taking you in a trailer⟩—Miss

35† Thursday ⟨drowning you in a canoe⟩—Miss

65 1† \much/

36† \whom . . . equally/ [*119*]

67 13 felt ⟨more competent,⟩ impersonal [*124*]

68 19 Rickie ⟨desperately⟩. \"He/ [*127*]

69 9 \Agnes . . . bother/ ← Miss Pembroke shall drop me at ⟨Union⟩ the Union and ⟨be bothered with me no mo⟩ have no more bother [*131*]

21† \over breakfast/ [*132*]

70 12 blur⟨⟨—presumably in heaven, but he could not have stated his spiritual where⟨upo⟩abouts with any conviction.⟩⟩⟨, and he⟩. [*135*]

71 11† the girl ← his bride [*136*]

26 \parsley/ ← hemlock [*137*]

32 shoulder ⟨in the greatest alarm⟩.

72 6 talents. ⟨You know how rude I am: it⟩ It seems ⟨to me⟩ such [*138*]

34 \too/ beautiful. ← so beautiful, ⟨so⟩ \and/ full of high memories. [*139*]

73 10 pieces. ⟨⟨Sweat oozed ⟨on⟩ \from/ his forehead. He hoped that he was dying.⟩⟩ [*140*]

30† and trees ← of trees [*141*]

CHAPTER 8

The ten full quartos of VIII (*143–152*) again give the impression of an easily composed chapter, revised in manuscript even less than VII. A few changes are clearly in a different ink, including that which spells Tilliard's name in its later form as it revises his repeated description of the coffee machine (76:8); others in the same ink appear at 79:13 and 80:1 below.

75 2† \instead of for two/ [*143*]

7 Here's the ⟨scrambled eggs and⟩ lemon sole

10 half pitiful, half respectful

29† man ⟨in a fairly white robe⟩ appeared [*144*]

31† coffee! How nice!" ← coffee is ⟨too filthy⟩ \very nice/ "

76 8 \Tilliard continued his account of the coffee machine./ ← ¶"My sister gave me this \coffee/ machine. She says it makes the best coffee she ever tasted. The only objection is the noise. For there is a bulb at the top, and when the water boils—"

26† "Here's ← "This is [*145*]

36 counterorder ⟨the scrambed [*146:*] eggs and⟩ the lemon sole?"

77 2 died. ⟨We call the dove Parsival because that suggests the Bible without⟩ His [*146*]

13 \was perfectly bald/ ← looked like a beefsteak

22 silent⟨, and did little more than fill the plates of the talkers with food⟩. [*147*]

36† \worse luck/

78 4 questions⟨. Even if unanswered they disturbed her peace⟩,

9 \discourteously/ ← sulkily [*148*]

12 Agnes⟨, (who had spoken little, but with taste,)⟩ held

17† He only replied "Good bye⟨," much to Rickie's relief⟩."† ← "Good bye" he replied, ← "I am glad you came," he replied, "but I hope that next time you will find me better prepared."

 † off⟨, arm in arm, and he⟩\. Rickie/

21† \short stories/

79 5 married ⟨a daughter of Lord Addlestone's⟩ and ⟨we were⟩ \my sister was/ [*149*]

12† during \the/ one ⟨moment—the⟩ moment [*150*]

13 \like a fool I/ ← —fool that I was—I at first

80 1 "It is war⟨. I'll fight her for my friend.⟩ \then/." [*151*]

19 \not only because she fights me but/ [*152*]

21 \to replace . . . lost/ ← because she lost ⟨ano⟩ her other man

22 partly ⟨because she hopes⟩ to make something ⟨of him⟩ \out of/.

24 \He won't get famous./

27 degraded ⟨and friendless⟩, she

28 \Stewart Ansell./ ← Ansell. Most of them were wrong.

CHAPTER 9

The eight sheets of IX (*153–160*) were originally seven, all written in the narrow-nibbed gray-black ink of the two preceding chapters, before *156* and *157* replaced what is now *2v* (see 82:30 below and p. 310). The blacker ink of *156–7* also changes Ansell's address from "31, High Street, Andover" to "Cambridge". "Shelthorpe", in a softer gray ink, had earlier replaced "Calabria", and the same gray marks the changes from "Ortrud" to "Elsa", shown below, from "August" to "September" (84:24), and from "Hatchard" to "Failing" (84:32).

323

81 1† Seven . . . June: ← \Seven letters./ ← A week of correspondance. [*153*]

    9 work⟨—I might almost say my work—⟩is done

   17 to ⟨know men⟩ love mankind

82 9† them⟨⟨: I may say she is inspiring me⟨.⟩—to⟩⟩\—/friends [*154*]

   17 R.E. ← F.M.E. [*155, consider E.M.F.*]

   21† Elsa \in the question scene/ ← ⟨Ortrud⟩ \Elsa/ in the second act

   26 \serious/ ← saved

   27 truthful. ⟨⟨ ⟨¶She has no idea what work is. To her it is something⟩ \Yours ever, S.A./⟩⟩

   30 My dear Stewart [*Rickie's original reply to Ansell's unsigned letter, opening* My dear Stewart *and signed* F.E., *survives on 2v:*] ¶That's the letter I wanted. You didn't mean to make me happy, but you have, for you've given yourself away. You've shown how much you love me. Up till now, I think, we've been too much like the strong heroes in books, who feel so much and say so little and feel all the more for saying so little. Now that's over, and we shall never be that kind of an ass again. You taught me. You were kind to me. You made other people be kind, and never seemed to do anything. And now, \at the crisis of my life/ when you think I'm going wrong, you stick to me, and tell me exactly what you think. You won't slur it over. No more will I. You hate Agnes. Well, hate her. My dear man——can't I love you both?

   31† for a moment ← till I read it \twice/ [*156*]

83 10 \dear man, you could with honesty be happier/ ← you were happier, dear man. [*157*]

   23 for ⟨publishers, or rather editors⟩ a publisher [*158*]

      \Herbert/ ← Mr Jackson

   30† Nothing . . . eccentric. ← They are ⟨very⟩ well spoken of, but seem to be terribly ⟨exclusive and⟩ eccentric.

84 12† more intimate ties ← marriage [*159; see also 48:10*]

   24 \that I may find out/ ← to see me [*160*]

CHAPTER 10

Twelve torn sheets, six verso passages and at least four inks differentiate levels of composition among the twenty-five pages of the much-revised X (*161–185*). The narrow-nibbed gray-black of the preceding chapters, increasingly rusty, continues at the earliest level and survives at *161–2* (*ends* 86:6 of), *164* (86:28 the–87:11 a), *176–7* (92:4 were–26 curious), their versos, *176v* and *177v*, and *180–2* (93:19–94:36 world). These pages are the first of the "Harold version" proper, since on *182* a blacker "Mr Wonham" (94:18) replaces "Stephen⟨.⟩ Lodge". In the next chapter, on *197*, the shift is from "Stephen" to "Harold" to "Stephen" again, suggesting that the progression was "Stephen Lodge", then "Harold Lodge", then "Harold Wonham" and only then "Stephen Wonham"; the distinctive ink is a good indication of an early page even when it is not reinforced by evidence of names.

At the second and later levels of X Stephen's name is unchanged. The blotchier gray-black ink of the second level appears chiefly in the first part of the chapter, on *163*, *165–7* (*ends* 88:9), and *170–1* (89:3–37 a), with one similar fragment as the next-to-last sheet, *184* (95:15–25). A lighter gray marks a third level of revision through the middle and later sections, on *168–9*, *173–5* (*begins* 90:15 by), *178–9*, and *183*. The latest sheets are the last, *185*, and *172*, both loosely written in a narrow-nibbed gray. The second and third levels encompass massive revisions; the related versos give some idea of the timing of the changes. One depeditated early page in the next chapter, *192*, preserves on its inverted verso a half-sentence at the tear, "valleys and followed the courses of the streams", indicating that a draft of the first paragraph of X was soon abandoned. *176v* and *177v*, described below at 92:15, show that for a short time Rickie and Agnes shared their arrival and tea with other guests. At the second level an undeleted and evidently soon-abandoned draft of *165*, shown below at 87:11, survives on *186v*, the verso of the opening sheet of XI, which is a second-level revision in its own setting. *184v* holds undeleted lines completely unrelated to *The Longest Journey* but reminiscent of the early fragments of Forster's fiction printed in *Arctic Summer*, particularly "At the National Gallery":

⟨sister's horses,⟩ panthers they become at my command, panthers of Titian, Io Titian, ⟨Itali⟩ Venetian School, National Gallery, Trafalgar Square.

The third stage shows no useful verso; two words on *178v*, "to say", are simply a wrong beginning of *175*, "-thing to say" (91:17). But at the latest level *172v*, inverted, shows two deleted lines: ⟨to a person." He meant that he had a right to visit any land that he loved.⟩. Not exact to any particular late passage, they still link *172* and *185* to the revised pages of Chapter 33, written in a similar loose form. Apparently Forster returned to Stephen's first chapter as his last approached, providing among other things, on *172*, earlier notice of the moustache observed by Rickie on p. 272; "blond" (90:1) was added even later, in typescript or proof.

Throughout Chapters 10–14 the vicar has been demoted from "rector", either in manuscript or later.

86 27 \crunch/on ← splosh on [*end 163; 164, an earlier page, shows a deleted top line:* as chapter n - 1 would prove)—when there was a splosh on]

39 \Lamb! Shepherd!/ ← Flea a lamb! He's an under shepherd. [*164*]

87 3† \He dodged me today./

11 shake . . . like." ← [*165, complete, revising 186v. Both were written to replace the top of 166, where a torn-through* Podge, *until they were dissuaded is half visible. Identical to 165 until* was, *186v then reads:*] powerfully but not splendidly built, being rather too short for his width, and the immense stores of life in him had not made him graceful or romantic—unless Life itself is a romance. People called him 'Fatty', but only once: he could knock ⟨most men⟩ \a man/ down, ⟨but⟩ \though/ not ⟨most women⟩ a woman. Large steady feet have at times their disadvantages, and, though he ⟨⟨would ⟨lik⟩ have liked to be⟩⟩ \thought he was/ irresistable, he was not. [*see* 88:1]

88 23 me!" ⟨he said ruefully.⟩ [*168*]

25 there ⟨noth⟩ no poetry ⟨of any kind⟩ \and no thought/

39 so. ⟨⟨We—I mean they—don't go worrying ⟨ahead⟩ \when we're alone/ like house people do. We just sit \tight/. Of course I'm different, because I'm educated.⟩⟩ \"/ [*169*]

89 16 \a sprightly/ ← cultured [*171*]

18 time \between ⟨these⟩ books like these and ⟨the open air.⟩ country like that?/ ← time? He had no experience and no culture. He had ⟨talked⟩ been nowhere, he understood nothing, and yet he tried.

32 \who . . . so/ ← kicked the table leg

90 1† \blond/ [*172*]

10 \saying . . . things/ ← repeating himself, always relating some prowess that he had performed or some wrong that he had sustained

15 \the principal figure/ ← their assailant

325

15 \by the footman./ [*173, where the passage replaced by 172 (89:38 poor–90:15 interrupted) is deleted:*] poor person, with ⟨his lips parted⟩ \lips apart/, and ⟨⟨following the print with ⟨his⟩ a finger⟩⟩ \a finger that followed the print/. She compared him to an Irish terrier⟨, worrying the infinite⟩\; he worried infinity/ as if it was a bone⟨, and tried and tried⟩\. He tried/ to carry \the/ eternal subtleties by violence. Before she had finished a ⟨sketch⟩ \caricature/ of him, the footman arrived in a mackintosh.

25 \"Have they had tea?"/ ← \"Are they ⟨stopp⟩ stuffed⟨?"⟩ fed?" [*173*]

30 skin. ⟨You wouldn't look."⟩\"/

91   1 callously. ⟨"The damp's very searching." He looked at an enormous cloud, black and shapeless, which had fallen suddenly on to the earth, and now swept up the hill towards them.⟩ Leighton [*174*]

26 \making fun of him/ ← \teasin/ ← getting at him [*175*]

39 \humourous/ ← ludicrous

92   4 \⟨and⟩ were inside the house/ ← [*176; a deleted version of lines now on 174 (91:10) appears at the decapitated top of 176 and leads to this change:*] ⟨¶"What⟩ \What/ do you make of Rickie?" ¶He said nothing. ¶"I will lend you his story to read." ¶They were inside

7 \as he . . . attic/ ← after him in excited tones [*176*]

12 shave.⟨"⟩ {And be sure you are ⟨very⟩ hospitable.}"

15 and glanced . . . Milton [*added in the recopying of 177v, which is otherwise like the uncorrected 176 from* "Look (92:7) *to* hands (92:16). *176v then followed:*] of apology and horror. They begged her not to be disturbed. Carriage at the station. Not to say carriages. All ⟨made⟩ friends at once. Delicious tea awaiting them. Time to unpack. No wonder she worked out of doors. Yet who would think it August? And Mr. Strike affirmed "never never has there been such displacement of the seasons since the mild weather of January two year back."

"I must have tea" she announced, "or I shall be unpleasant. "Miss Pembroke, stop me. Give me tea."

Agnes, after a little hesitation, moved to the table and served her hostess. Miss Harmer, a kind little lady with a snow white face, handed the cream and sugar. Rickie followed with sandwiches, while Mr Strike revolved in the background crying "Allow me! I can't let everybody work like this.

"Thank you. Now I am pleasant. Oh Rickie how like you are to your father! I feel it is twenty six years ago, and that he is bringing your mother to see me for the first time? [*torn*] here last?"

24 \twenty seven/ ← twenty six [*177, twice*]

26 \It is curious—/ [*end 177; added in the gray ink of 178*]

28† not tactful⟨, and he winced⟩. ← ⟨far from⟩\not/ . . . winced. [*178*]

34 ¶⟨He laughed nervously.⟩ "I never

37† \I say so/ . . . too ← \Say so too./ ← and you must say so too.

38 fair ⟨and square⟩.

93   6† regret ← resentment

10 \He . . . aimiably./ ← ⟨"How⟩ ⟨to[?]⟩ He made no reply.⟨"⟩

12† \Came . . . friends./ [*179*]

19 "I am . . . said [*deleted as the last line of 179, extraneous there because the same words open 180, where they are preceded by a deleted and inexplicable end-of-paragraph* "Badly?"]

23† Mrs Lewin . . . her ← She had heard [*180*]

26 \No harm/. ← Delightful.

28 She was ⟨extremely⟩ anxious not to ⟨make blunders,⟩ \start with a
blunder,/

37 "⟨Lucy—⟩Rickie's mother⟨—my brother Frederick's wife⟩."

38 \Did she really!/ ← Ah—!

94 5 easier ⟨than thinking of themselves⟩. [*181*]

10 The light ← ⟨⟨His ⟨father⟩ \mother/ and Aunt Emily had ⟨not been
friends⟩\been fairly friendly. His father and Aunt Emily had not./ Agnes
knew this⟨, and, though⟩\. Though/ she liked being compared to Mrs
Elliot, \she/ changed the conversation, or rather ⟨reverted to the subject
of⟩ \went back to/ Cadover.⟩⟩ The light

19 \I . . . ⟨arrived⟩ got to/ ← The point is when did it arrive in [*182*]

22 \amazed/ ← transfixed with horror

95 6 \healthy/ ← honest [*183*]
\irritable/ ← prosaic

14 \philosopher/ ← metaphysician [*183 is depeditated below the next, deleted
statement:*] "Then I'm frightened of him

15 \suddenly collapsing/ ← gruffly [*184*]

16 \Where? . . . carpet?"/ ← Why?" Heedless of the general discomfort, she
continued to tease him.

CHAPTER 11

The first nine of the twenty sheets of XI (*186–205*) show the first three layers of
composition visible in X, but the remaining eleven, from the decapitated *195* (*begins
99:31*) onward, are all of the earliest level, written in the now distinctive narrow-
nibbed, rusty ink and showing shifts from "Harold" to "Stephen" or "Podge", and
from "Lodge" to "Wonham", and once, on *197*, from "Stephen" to "Harold" to
"Stephen" again (101:9). Two depeditated leaves among the first nine, *188* (97:4
the–12 dead) and *192* (98:22–29), also show the early ink; the blotchier gray-black
of the second level of X marks only *186* (*ends* 96:12 sustained) and *193* (*ends* 99:12
happier), both depeditated. *187*, *189–91*, and *194* are in the lighter gray of the third
level; the depeditations of *191* and *194* remove blank space, not unwanted passages.
There are no versos except *186v* and *192v*, both related to X. *186* shows a few
sketches to the right of the chapter number; three are squares or circles between vertical
parallel lines, another is a circle within a square, and there are two sets of vertical
parallels, one beneath a triangular pedimental outline and the other below a qua-
drangular roof form. Together they indicate that Forster wanted to draw likenesses
between the architecture of Cadover and the recurring motiv of circle and square.

96 11 \The classical . . . sustained/ [*186, added there in the ink of 187 and replacing a
torn-through opening of the next paragraph, recopied on 187.*]

15† bare land ← ⟨meadow⟩ land [*187*]

28† would . . . Academy ← was not of the kind that goes into a picture

97 6 \grass/ ← earth [*188, twice*]

98 10 \decreased/ ← deserted him [*190*]

12 done ⟨but⟩ \very/ little. ⟨The Holy Roman Empire⟩ Toil

20 \really/ [*191; after* deserved. *an undeleted paragraph follows:*] ¶The night
before his death, the nurse, a cultured person, opined that he would
never see another sun. He overheard her and asked if he might see the
stars instead. ⟨There was⟩ \The/ ⟨request was easily granted⟩ \blind
was drawn up/, and again he noted that the stars are innumerable and
differ in brilliancy, but that they do not differ greatly, and that they do
not converge on any one point of the sky. "It is not impossible" he whispered.

"Not impossible." The nurse, to please him further, pointed out the moon, which, in the full glory of her borrowed light, was rising over Cadbury Rings. But this was a failure. He mistook the moon for his wife, and the blind was lowered. [*192 opens with a deleted version of the conclusion:*] He mistook the moon for his wife, and had to be ⟨c[?]\taken/⟩ taken back to bed again. ¶Mrs Failing determined to leave Cadover at once.

22† was . . . widow ← now belonged to Mrs Failing [*192*]

31 \\and ⟨left⟩ \abandoned/ the farm to Mr Wilbraham// ← and gave up bothering about the farm [*193*]

99 4 \admired/ ← disliked
\but did not care for her/

37 With ← "Would she really?" With [*195*]

100 1 \Some . . . think/ ← My aunt has been very kind over that, I believe

4 "He used ← "⟨Yes. She brought him up.⟩ \I think so./ I always forget about him, though. He used
\something/ ← else out all day

7 ¶"⟨I don't know.⟩ I suppose ⟨she must have.⟩ \so./ I know that ⟨as regards him⟩ she has [*196*]

16† for us ← for me

22 \Why?/ ← I believe I understand.

101 3 \nothing/ ← no change [*197*]

19 \clearing out/ ← packing off [*198*]

20† third animal ← \the third horse/ ← one of the other pair

25 Avon. ⟨⟨So if ⟨Harold Lodge⟩ \Mr Wonham/ spits over the bridge, as he sometimes does, the tribute falls into the sea at Christchurch.⟩⟩ \\Cadbury ⟨down⟩ \Ring/ opposite.//

102 7 sound: ⟨she appreciated them separately.⟩ they [*199*]

12 she could approve \of one cloud/, but object to \its fellow/. ← she ⟨should admire⟩ \could approve/ the clouds, but ⟨criticise⟩ \object to/ the shadows that fell from them.

13 \approving or objecting/ ← criticising or admiring

23 laughing. "⟨⟨Mr ⟨Lodge⟩ \Wonham/ is such a boy.⟩⟩ Rickie [*200*]

103 6 \, and thinking . . . repeated/ [*201*]

13 \took him for anything/ ← considered him

20 four⟨. A dog bit him, but he⟩, but had

29† thoughtful youth ← young man [*202*]

† in . . . Eden. ← by God.

30† \Let us . . . probable./

104 8 \my Podge?/ ← Harold?

9† \He gets . . . term./

17 \stole/ ← broke open a desk and stole [*203*]

105 16 \that story . . . you?/ ← Rickie's story? [*205*]

CHAPTER 12

Twenty-two of the thirty-seven pages of XII (*206–242*) are torn, while eight are early, seven of them showing the change from "Harold" to "Stephen" as well as the distinctive rusty ink. The eight provide the following passages: the chapter opening, *206–7* (*ends* 107:6); the idea of keeping people "in line", *209–10* (107:30–108:11); the summary of Stephen's "wit", *213* (109:17–27 fields); Rickie's dream of the "Throne of God", *218* (110:31 trees–111:2); and the meeting with the soldier, *220–1* (111:15–112:7). The later inks are less distinguishable, but the latest pages, in a more loosely written scratchy black, are *214* (109:32 continent-110:6); *226* (114:1 consequence-6), and *229-30* (115:1-33 lunch). *216* (109:27 He-32 on the), wrongly numbered, leads to *214* and is corrected in the late ink; the last paragraph of the chapter, rewritten as a whole in an intermediate gray-black ink, then had its last line added in the late scratchy black. Although there was much revision only four versos survive; three are noted below at 106:22 and 110:5. The fourth, *245v*, now in the next chapter, shows an inverted half-sentence which probably reflects an early version of Stephen's remembered encounter with the sheep (p. 117): "fellow—destruction! a large flock of sheep." No fragment gives any hint of the bathing scene Forster describes in his introduction as the prelude to the Harold chapter, printed below as the last variant of Chapter 12.

106 1† \The . . . there./ [*206*]

  7† gate . . . anchored ← \upper/ gate, \for . . . he/ anchored ← gate, so that he was obliged to open it. He never could manage gates. He always anchored

  19 \"That was . . . him."/ ← and swaggered past Mr Wilbraham and over the bridge. Mr Wilbraham looked blank—not out of rudeness, but [*207:*] because ⟨Harold⟩ \Stephen/ was an exception: he could not find him on the map. "Eh but I'll hurt him."

  22 death ⟨over⟩ by the story of Flea. [*Except for* ⟨over⟩ *220v is identical to 207 until this point, but then reads:*]
     "Hurt him till he learns."
     He reminded Rickie of Gerald—the Gerald of history, not the Gerald of romance. Kinder than Gerald, and more interesting; but there was the same brutality, the same peevish insistence on the pound of flesh. Were all healthy men so? Is it only the healthy woman who can join ⟨health⟩ \healthiness/ to a soul? Harold was an appalling animal
     "It was kind of you to go with his sheep. There aren't many men in England who'ld do it. And it was shocking of him to keep you longer than he said. But if I were you, I'ld pardon him."
     "Why?"
     "Because—because of the reason ⟨of⟩ that kept him."
     "Love!" said Harold with appalling contempt. The sacred word reechoed down the streets of Cadford. "Love!"
     Rickie blushed but insisted ⟨it⟩. "Yes. Love. You ought to forgive Flea Thompson."
     "Look here, Mr Elliot, you don't understand. I've no [. . .]

  24 \He was . . . there/ ← There [*207*]

107 3 \teaching him to behave/ ← ⟨his education⟩ him. If you played him false, he'd have a right to be angry with you. But you havn't an equal right to be angry with him.

  4 \"Well . . . nothing."/ ← "I teach him to behave gratis" was the cultured response.

  13 Mr ← "Good morning" said a voice. Mr [*208*]

  18 \seemed/ ← been

  29 nodded. ⟨⟨¶"But you haven't caught on (⟨seven⟩ four hours seven minutes by the bye⟩⟩ [*209:*] \"Oh/

  34 \the rest/ ← I

  39 \But/ ← What was ⟨Harold⟩ \Stephen/ to him? Yet [*210*]

108 1 a ⟨joyless⟩ creed

  9 \lighting up/ ← transfiguring
     he could scarcely explain this to a young animal⟨.⟩\, nor did he make

the attempt./ ← ⟨to⟩ \he could scarcely/ explain this to a young animal⟨⟨
⟨was indeed a⟩ \would be a/ hopeless task⟩⟩.

14† between the sheaves ← \up the aisles/ ← between the corn cocks [211]
16† ill⟨—ill with vitality⟩.
26 \We don't . . . we?/ ← It's pretty slow here, isn't it
30 \go your pace/ ← keep with you
109 8 \\⟨Rickie, in⟩ \In/ . . . he// ← On this he grew agitated and [212]
17 \Mother Failing/ ← Mrs Elliot [213]
18 elephants. ⟨She won't listen to me.⟩"
23† most beautiful . . . world ← spire of Salisbury
39 emerged⟨, showing like a veil of white⟩ ⟨and⟩. [214]
110 5 drama ⟨for the gods to witness⟩ to solace the gods. [*An undeleted paragraph follows:*] ¶Fashion changes. The desire to live up in this country has gone. It is not beautiful enough. It is not wild enough. Nature does not smile neither does she frown, and today we demand one or the other. Her impassive countenance is more than we can stand. But the soldier was here at the [215:] beginning and has come again, and the shepherd who was here at the beginning, is here still. [*Both 214v and 215v show a few undeleted words, each group abandoned as a wrong start for a new page. On 214v unconquerable chalk appears, matching no extant page. On 215v, inverted, is a variant of the opening of 215: beginning and is here still, as*]
15 dust⟨!⟩ ⟨He was haunted by Pagan terrors.⟩ These [215]
39 \\all \its/ danger// ← the clouds [218]
111 7† \below Amesbury/ [219]
17† elms ← mills [220]
\cottages/ ← railway stations
34† philosophic ← philosophical
35† empirical ← personal
39 \indecently/ ← beastly [221]
112 11 The valley had broadened. ← They were ⟨leaving⟩ \still descending/ the valley. [222]
14 Stephen, ⟨modestly⟩ lowering his ⟨eyes⟩ \head/
16† \Rickie winced and frowned./
20 \Why should . . . give up?"/ ← He could stand them no longer: he must go home. [223]
22† \Salisbury/
28 day ⟨any more. What an idea!"⟩ \How . . . me?"/
31 home ⟨now's the time. There's the short cut. Here's⟩ \here's/
33† \Certainly. . . . me./
113 3 \drinking/ ← \sensuality/ ← vulgarity and slang
4 \so quickly . . . also/ ← ⟨them,⟩ \these things,/ and beneath them he might
5 dogmatic. ⟨His verdicts are few.⟩ To
6 \ignores it/ ← forgets it ← shuts his eyes
114 1† against the variations. ← \against singing/ old Em'ly \with variations/. ← off old Em'ly for the second time. [225]
3 charge, ⟨both by theory and by practice,⟩ and [226]
11 \crossly./ ← \, who saw that he had unloosed the devil./ [227]
† \"I won't . . . at."/
22† from ⟨my⟩ mother's [228]
115 8 Stephen ⟨had made it into a test. He⟩ cared [229]
9† his benefactress's ← Mrs Failing's

11† a ⟨leather⟩ glove

16 \declared that old Em'ly lived there./ ← said "Old Em'ly's house." [*230*]

31† white linen hat. ← new cap.

116 12 sat in it ⟨⟨between their shopping, ⟨cont⟩ staring at the horseless shafts.⟩⟩ every [*233*]

15† him ⟨and left him⟩ in the rain.

19 \\it wasn't . . . to ⟨ride⟩ \go/ back by Cadbury Rings⟨.⟩\, where . . . be.//// ← and he flung a stone at the tarpaulin. The carrier came out, and he had to run for it again.

27 protested. ⟨"It's boxing."⟩ The [*234*]

36 He ⟨acknowledged the better man⟩ ⟨had tried force, and⟩ must [*235*]

37 \most/ ← \complicated/ ← cultivated

117 3 \unreliable/ ← chancy

16 \pressed/ ← ran [*236*]

23 not?" ⟨⟨He had never been nipped that way again, and did not expect that he ever would be. Looking back, he ⟨attributed it to⟩ \put it down to/ indigestion.⟩⟩ 'Pan

31 out. ⟨⟨Leighton did not think that Mrs Failing had minded his desertion. She had laughed⟨.⟩: for Mr Elliot had come in⟩⟩ \On/

38† was ⟨up⟩ in [*238*]

pediment. ⟨⟨Its one window, round and curtainless, showed from without like a Cyclops' eye, and ⟨a⟩ \its/ little skylight opened out upon the roof.⟩⟩ Classical

118 1† its ⟨little⟩ lapses

7† gurgly ← enormous

8 \bath . . . lived,/ ← house with {cold} \bath/ water, and gurgled from time to time like an uneasy cow. Here he lived—he and his bed and his bath—

37 \soapy/ ← scandalised [*240*]

\and got . . . a fact{—once and for all}/ ← She had implored him not to forget himself, but he had insisted on ⟨so⟩ doing so

119 2† and ⟨no one,⟩ not even

7 him⟨. He never forgot⟩ \as . . . gracious/

11 \in his remains/ ← \as she tried to edit his 'remains'/ ← , when she went through his papers,

23 \tired of/ ← rather off [*241*]

28 \reluctantly/ ← with a little sigh. It read like the work of a tom-fool.

30 girl? ⟨Was she a tree? Was the tree a⟩ Where [*242*]

37 tree! ⟨Lord bless us and save us!⟩ He

39† \with its elms,/

120 3† \Good, oh good!/

4† \cant/

would . . . next? ← a rotten affected idea! How could one be in touch?

5† sleepy. \Good, oh good!/† Sighing . . . asleep. ← sleepy. He was asleep. ← sleepy. He slept. ← tired. He was asleep.

[*The characteristic rusty ink of the Harold pages is the only one used on the eighteen leaves of the Harold version now bound into the appendix. In fact the seventeen consecutive pages of the nearly complete Harold chapter, subdivided into three parts, are so neat that wholesale recopying may be suspected. Only one sheet in the group, A4, was truncated, but four verso passages survive within the chapter. One, on A8v, is a variant of the passages on recto and verso of A18 and appears with them below, after the consecutive text. The other three, A5v, A7v, and A14v, are all quite similar to their revisions. They have been inserted in the text below, which shows all variants, but have been marked by triple angle brackets for easy skipping. Only A5v was not crossed through; only A7v shows a full quarto page of text.*

On A5, "far darting" is a Homeric epithet for Apollo, while the allusion on A15 to Virgil's use of "poured" probably refers to the shepherd's posture in the Georgics ("fususque per herbam", 2.527), although some association to the fallen warrior in the Aeneid ("effundit harena", 12.276) may also have operated.)

[*A1:*]

⟨XIV.⟩ \XIV/

1.

He never ⟨got to⟩ got to Salisbury. His captors began to quarrel over him at once. The stoker wanted justice—for the railway company, for the proprieties, and for his eye. The police should see to it. These —— —— gentlemen should be taught. But the driver objected. He was a haggard elderly man, who seemed stoker pecked, and rather weary of theocracy generally. Police, he said, were more trouble than they were worth. As to the company, they need never know. As to the proprieties, was the stoker a dancing mistress? As to the eye, it would get well. Let him give the boy one back, or two back if he could, and then they would chuck him on to the line.

"And get nothing out of him?" he grumbled.

"Only a lock of my hair" said Harold, "and that you'll have to come for."

"None more of this⟨" s⟩\!"/ screamed the driver, as they banged against the machinery. "Murder in a minute, and me had up for your broken necks, and She all broken besides." He shut off steam, and as soon as he could, booted his visitor out of the engine.

Harold fell on his knees and cut them. But there was time to sling a flint ⟨after⟩ \at/ his prison, and star the green paint on its side. He even ran after it a little way, hooting victoriously. Then he stopped ⟨suddenly, scratched his head⟩ and said '⟨my⟩ \My/ hat!' His hat [*A2:*] was exactly ⟨four⟩ \two/ miles away.

It was a trying situation, but ⟨at first Harold believed⟩ \he believed at first/ that he was equal to it. He started to walk back. The railway had left the valley and he was screened from the ⟨public view⟩ \British Public/ by a cutting. On either side of him rose chalky cliffs, topped with a brown layer of earth. ⟨Fir trees⟩ \Trees/ lined the summits, and completed the sense of seclusion. He was even more secluded than he supposed. An angel, poised in the air, would have seen him as a little white spot, moving cheerfully through ⟨an⟩ \the precincts of an/ enormous wood—the largest wood in the county—which extended from ⟨the⟩ \this: railway on to the down ⟨above⟩ \against/ Cadover. Noting his courage under misfortunes, the angel would pay a compliment to the dauntless spirit of man; but noting the simultaneous departure of Rickie in an opposite direction the angel would drop a tear at man's incompetence and say: "⟨Ye⟩ \O/ nymphs and woodland Fauns⟨,"⟩\!/ O dryads and satyrs⟨,⟩\!/ O all ye hosts of earth whose deity I am ⟨obliged⟩ \compelled/ to ⟨recognise!⟩ \greet!/ whom the Greeks have detected and honoured, whom the Church has exorcised, whom the scientific spirit has denied! but who ⟨nevertheless⟩ \still/ remain, wherever \there/ still remains much grass, much water, or many trees! Guard, O guard, this ⟨ignorant,⟩ inefficient [*A3:*] and most bumptious youth who advances without a talisman against your unsuspected powers." Thus would the angel express himself, supposing there to be Fauns and dryads, and supposing there to be an angel.

When the railway entered the valley, Harold felt annoyed. He had to walk not in a cutting but along an embankment. There was a village in the distance, and he was afraid of being seen, for his courage, like the water from the river, was evaporating. He felt unsafe and dry. Still—one more curve, and all would be over: he would regain his companion and his pool.

All was over.

His second misfortune followed closely. ⟨He stepped aside as if⟩ \Stepping aside/ to let the up train \pass/, ⟨and⟩ \he/ fell as if a giant had smitten him. Someone had knocked him over with an empty soda water bottle.

Whether intentionally, he never knew. Nor was the bottle a heavy one. But the speed of the train had lent ⟨im⟩ \it/ impetus, and it bruised ⟨it b⟩ him badly. A fit of childish passion seized him and he smashed it to pieces. After that he was equal to the situation no longer ⟨and he⟩\. He/ entered the woods thinking "They want to kill me. But I'm safe here. Trains can't come through the trees. I hope they kill Elliot. I hate him. Hallo!" ⟨he⟩ \He/ turned round in his tracks and ⟨⟨⟨[A7v:] said nervously "Hallo man! I see you." There was no reply. He continued to penetrate the wood⟨⟨, which consisted entirely ⟨for⟩ of pines⟩⟩. "Mother Failing will be sick if he's late. I believe she hates him. Not a bad sort, Mother Failing, but I wish she'ld shave.—⟨H⟩ Hallo!" He stopped. "I say, don't walk behind. It gives me the jumps." No one was behind. He continued to penetrate the wood. The trees were small and far apart, so that he could see or be seen for a considerable distance. He walked upon pine needles and fir cones. A jay squawked, and \he/ flung himself face downwards. "Fact is" he observed after a pause "I'm getting nervous. No. Doesn't do. Must just go ahead. Walk back to Cadover. What's clothes? Nothing to be ashamed of. A man's a man and so on. I'ld call on Mrs Wilbraham. Or at the rectory. If they don't like it they can—Damn you!" He spun round. "I won't be looked at." But he only saw the thin trunks of the firs, and heard nothing, not even the jay. Yet someone had been there. He advanced stealthily. In a few minutes he was mad.

⟨⟨Put a man in a ⟨bad⟩ \strange/ position.⟩⟩ Rob ⟨him [*not actually deleted*]⟩ \any man/ of his money, of his reputation, or, better still, of his clothes. Then ⟨place him⟩ let him ⟨have⟩ \be alone with/ nothing to lean against⟨—nothing as broad as his⟩\. Let his back have nothing to/⟩⟩⟩ [A4:] said nervously "Hallo man! I see you." There was no reply. He continued to penetrate the wood. "Mother Failing hates him too. I hope he's late for lunch. She's a good sort, but I wish she'ld shave.—Hallo!" He stopped. "I say, don't walk behind. It gives me the jumps." No one was behind. He continued to penetrate the wood. The ⟨trees⟩ \trunks/ were ⟨small and⟩ far apart, so that he could see or be seen for a long distance. To the angel he is invisible, by reason of the interlacing boughs. A jay squawked, and he flung himself face downwards, driving his head into the fallen leaves. "Fact is," he observed on getting up "I'm a little nervous. It doesn't do. It isn't my way. It isn't the way of Harold Wonham to be ⟨⟨[*line torn through, first five words conjectural:*] nervous." He next bounced over the crackling leaves. The wood⟩ \continued to penetrate the wood, which here/⟩⟩ [A5:] nervous." He continued to ⟨suggest⟩ penetrate the wood, which here suggested a cathedral, with russet pavement and columns of grey. It had no altar or central dome, but in the aisles stood chantreys of brushwood—dark growths of holly ⟨an⟩ bryony and yew, tangles, small but solemn, for ever unpierced by the far darting shafts of the sun. Leaves over head were sometimes opaque, sometimes sprays of fairyland, straining the light through transparent flakes of green. ⟨⟨⟨[A5v:] flakes was greener: they slid apart and the light was paler—paler—till for a moment a path was blown, and there appeared, infinitely distant, scraps of the forgotten sky. "At all events the train ⟨catch⟩ can't catch him in these beeches. He is quite safe. He has only to walk—walk back t⟩⟩⟩ In the wind—they alone could feel it—they slid together, three or four or twenty thick, and the light was subdued: they slid apart and it came brighter—brighter—brighter—till for a moment a path was blown, and there appeared, infinitely distant, scraps of the forgotten sky. "The railway train can't go among these beeches. Harold is quite safe. He has only to walk to Cadover. How strange he looks without his clothes. I should not quite like it, but that man does anything. He is going to call on Mrs Wilbraham. ⟨O⟩ And at the rectory. ⟨If⟩ They won't really mind. If they do, they can—⟨"⟩ Damn you!" He [*A6:*] spun round. "I won't be looked at." But he only saw the leaf strewn floor, the lowly chantreys, the vaults of shimmering green, and he heard nothing, not even the voice of the jay. Yet some one had been there. He continued to penetrate the wood. Some one looked at him again. Again. He could feel ⟨them⟩ \the glances/ pass over him, and still saw nothing. They grew bolder and spattered his face like rain drops. They filled his mouth and ears and blinded him. They were ancle deep—they swept him off his legs. He spread out his arms crying "Harold, be a man! Conquer them! Swim to land! Be a man—be Harold—be Harold—Harold—" A huge grey thing rose out of the earth and kicked \him/ between the eyes. The whole wood burst into flame, and as the thunder followed he fell senseless.

[*A7:*]

2.

He sat up, leaning ⟨against the tree⟩ \his back against it/. The roots extended either side of him, and interlaced like polished snakes in front, so that he was severed on all sides from the world. His brain had been wiped clean, and he was as a little child. ⟨⟨Pleased ⟨by⟩ \at/ ⟩⟩ \Liking/ the smooth bark, he laid his cheek ⟨against⟩ to it and kissed the ⟨wood⟩ living wood, again and again. Then he stood up, smiling, but full of reverence. The sun delighted him, and he stepped from his ⟨nursery⟩ \nursery/ to salute it. But he turned again to bow to the huge grey column ⟨of the tree,⟩\,/ which had—which had done something for him, he could not remember what. Far away in the wood he still kept sight of it, and when at last it disappeared, he felt sorry, and, because he felt sorry, cried.

Soon he recovered. Another ⟨tree⟩ tempted him to climb, and for twenty minutes he swung about in the branches. Then he slipped to the ⟨grownd⟩ ground, and shuffled forward through the leaves. The beeches gave place to oak and ash, the dry leaves to turf, which sprang beneath him delightfully. On either side grew bracken, as high as his shoulders. Much sky was visible and his flesh began to tingle in the sun. ⟨He [*A8:*] felt uneasy—he could not think why.⟩ Then he stopped, with a little sob. He had met his first human being.

It was walking slowly towards him up a narrow glade, rolling its head suspiciously from right to left. In one hand it held a basket, in the other a branch of elder to torment the flies. He and a rabbit saw it together. They flattened down in the bracken and awaited their doom

*⟨"It has come for you."

"It has come for you."

"I am so small: perhaps It did not see."

"I am so large: perhaps It will not dare."⟩*

The human being had come for blackberries. It walked unevenly and panted. Presently it was joined by a second example. ⟨Harold could hear them communicating.⟩ \They communicated./ One said "Had you thought at all of letting out the tucks?" The other answered "The false hem brings it to her ancles, and that must do." They passed on.

That glade had more surprises. It ended in a grassy semicircle, which was littered all over with human remains[$A9$:]—⟨papers⟩ \paper/, bicycles, bottles, and two more examples, snoring on their backs. This time he did not fly. He came slowly forward, sniffing. ⟨⟨Even ⟨in his madness⟩ \then/ he⟩⟩ \He/ knew it was wrong to steal those sandwiches. The food of a man, even when he cannot eat it, is a sacred thing⟨,⟩ \—/unlike the nuts of the squirrel or the honey of the bee or the eggs of the bird, which we may devour unchallenged. Harold, when he stretched out his hand, parted with another great tradition.

Voices awoke him. He had eaten and slept among the bracken, charmed even ⟨though⟩ through dreams by the pattern of fronds against the sky and by the strengthening ⟨warmth⟩ \\ ⟨carr[?]⟩ \caress/ // of the sun. But these voices—how unmelodious, how unlike the voice of nature, who never speaks unless she has something to say. The patter of rain, the crack of the seed vessel, the cry of the bitten rabbit—these have meaning. But what was the meaning of "Agatha keep off! Agatha don't look! Warn Mrs Hamilton. It is most unpleasant.⟨"⟩ \"?/ And then: "Well sir! Have you any explanation?"

[$A10$:] "⟨It's just a young fellow having his joke"⟩ \It may be all a joke"/ said the other man, who was podgy, fair and mild, but who likewise carried a stick.

"This is no joke. Well sir—have you any explanation?"

Harold, who could \not/ get away, began to whimper.

"Are you aware that I am a ⟨magistrate?"⟩ \J.P.?"/

⟨"⟩He buried his face in the ground, and sobbed.

"Where are your clothes?"

More tears.

"He's sorry" said the fair man. "He is really sorry."

"This is no sorrow.⟨"⟩ Come ⟨here⟩ \up/—!" And with much courage the ⟨magistrate⟩ \J.P/ wrenched the head ⟨of⟩ out of the ground and so discovered that the eyes, though brown and intelligent, had not the peculiar ⟨intelligence of civilised man⟩ \\⟨looks⟩ \look/ that ⟨denotes⟩ \stamps/ a modern man//. "Mad" he observed curtly. "We can't leave him to die. We must wrap him up in the rug and drive him back. You watch him. He's quite harmless."

The fair man did not like the task. "There now!" he said nodding and smiling at Harold. "That's all right. There now! ⟨⟨⟨[$A14v$:] There now! There now!"⟩ He said it so often that Harold got angry. Could he not spring up like a ⟨leopard⟩ \squirrel/, trip the ⟨fair man⟩ \there-now/ backwards, and jump on him? He could. The magistrate, returning, ⟨received himself⟩ \himself received/ pang! pang! a box on either ear. Shrieks of agitation ⟨of⟩ \and/ dismay, ⟨recedin⟩ and the silly people were far behind, a little ⟨chattering⟩ scandalised ⟨whispered⟩ \whisper/ in ⟨a silent world⟩ \the forests/ of purity and truth.

He ran because he had started running.⟩⟩⟩ [$A11$:] There now! There now!" He said it so often that Harold got angry. Could he not spring up like a squirrel, trip the there-now backwards and jump on him? He could. The J.P., returning, himself received pang! pang! a box on either ear. Shrieks of horror and dismay died to a little scandalised whisper, ⟨t⟩ and that into silence. He had escaped from the ⟨pollution⟩ snare.

He ran because he had started running—at first in terror, then in simple joy. He chased the sunset ⟨thro⟩ down golden clearings, through ⟨peril⟩ darkening woods, over roads—actually over smooth perilous roads. He entered the water to reach it, and for a long time splashed and waded, for the pool was swollen by the rains. Then came the central depth and he ⟨rose⟩ sank, and rose ⟨delighted⟩ into glory,

335

while the ripples took mysterious hues and struck, with the noise of sipping, against the distant reeds. But the evening caught ⟨him. Even⟩ hold of him and made his joy frenzy. He could not stay quiet, even in the water. He made the rats dive and the moor hens plough glistening furrows. Breast high, he hooted [*A12:*] and splashed till all the wood heard him, and the stock doves—who go to bed early and hate being disturbed—came tumbling out of the beech trees and whirred over the ⟨pool.⟩ shattered pool. Mud after water—black mud to roll in,—and after that more glades and more woods and more cathedrals and more there-nows, together with a there-nowlet, whom they left in their flight. It laughed and he gave it a ⟨flower⟩ fir cone to vex them. And always before him the ⟨coloured⟩ \⟨evening⟩ western sky/, golden ⟨an⟩\ at/first, then orange, then crimson and green. Onward he rushed into colour, to bathe in it, to possess it, to be joined to it, to free it from the trees that still lay black across its bosom. The sun should be his—why not, when the earth was his already? He had seen her secrets⟨.⟩\,/⟨and tasted her Therefore⟩ and tasted her bitterness. Therefore he trod her down and she yielded. He frightened her, even as she had frightened him. Her trees dwindled at his bidding, her bushes ⟨⟨obscured ⟨heaven⟩ the sun⟩⟩ no longer obscured the ⟨sun⟩ light. Down she rushed, to make room for vast horizons, for chasms of purple, for included seas, for rocks and continents of gold, for ⟨the sun⟩ \her bridegroom/, father of colour, father of life, the sun, naked, unattainable, ⟨glorious⟩ \immortal/. Naked and ⟨glorious⟩ \mortal/, he [*A13:*] did for one instant attain \to/ it, being himself a god, ⟨and outside⟩ \\⟨who knew not⟩ ⟨untroubled⟩ \unvexed/ by// good or evil. Heaven did open⟨.⟩\, and he had the vision/ Then he saw a ⟨b⟩ circle of earth enclosing a ring of turnips, which enclosed another circle of earth, which enclosed more turnips, and in the centre of the pattern one small tree.

He shivered and whispered his own name.

3.

⟨Cadover⟩ \Cadbury/ Rings were about half a mile beyond him, lying like a great plate on the slope of the down. Over its rim rose the plantations of Cadover and the smoke of the allied villages, the valley itself being hidden. On the rim itself stood animals, who slowly moved inwards, one after the other, in a thick brown stream, nibbling as they moved and causing Harold to observe "If the sheep aren't getting at the turnips!" But he had more to occupy him. How was he to cross that pestilential belt of civilisation, and be in time for dinner? Seven o'clock struck. He looked at himself humourously, and peeled off a little mud. He was scratched and blistered all over, his feet and his nose were bleeding, and on his forehead [*A14:*] there had arisen a mighty bump. He fondled it, murmuring "This explains", and looked humourously back at the wood. Then he shook his head and laughed, and feeling abnormally fit but in other ways normal, lay down in the grass to think out his return.

He had a perfect right to go as he was, and any fool had a perfect right to be shocked at him. But unfortunately fools never keep within their rights. They call in the police. Harold saw the whole ⟨tyranny⟩ \tangle/ of convention, to which most men are unconscious slaves. He too must ⟨enter it again.⟩ \re enter it./ But his ⟨ens⟩ slavery should be conscious. Never again would he pretend that he enjoyed it, or that it was universal, like the light or the air. It was an arrangement—a temporary device to keep things goings [*sic*]. Behind it lay no immortal sanction. No halo surrounded its clumsy head, no living grass supported its feet of clay. Ninety nine times must a man bow before it \for the sake of mankind/. But the hundredth time comes, when the evil exceeds the good too greatly, and the man, with luck and courage, shall be a slave no longer. And ⟨even⟩ now, in this little matter of the clothes, Harold sought to satisfy not himself, but the police.

[*A15:*] He watched the sheep carefully. The whole flock had spread over the turnips, unrebuked by shepherd or dog. He reconnoitred the down, and then sprinted at full speed, till he was hidden in the outer ditch of The Rings. After that he was cautious, advancing on his hands and knees, and holding his breath.

Just as he expected. Flea Thompson was "poured"—as Virgil calls it—on the grass, utterly slack and listless, his head on his arms and close below his eyes the carte-de-visite photograph of a female. ⟨The⟩ \His/ dog, equally descœuvré, was sleeping a dozen yards away⟨, by a little tree⟩. Was it for this that Mrs Failing gave him nine shillings a week, and his father a cottage for nothing? Harold nodded, and commenced operations with the dog.

Friendship was hopeless. Dogs are arrant snobs, and this one had bitten him even in his three guinea suit. Now that he looked like a black devil it was war to the knife. Could he kill it? Scarcely, and before it was strangled Flea would have taken alarm. He observed its collar. The ring was large and rusty and stood up at right angles to the leather. On the ground [*A16:*] lay a long piece of ⟨string⟩ \cord/. The dog was sleeping near a black thorn.

Harold tied one end of the ⟨string⟩ cord to the ⟨bush⟩ \black thorn/. Then he crept to the dog, holding the other end in his hand. He threaded it through the ring. There was a piercing yell, and the dog was twitched backwards and left roosting like a bird. Flea ⟨sat up, saying⟩ \,/ who was soft and ⟨slow⟩ \weakly/, sat up saying "Well Rough, what is it then?" ⟨And before⟩ \Before/ he understood the cord was secure, and Fate fell on him also, and robbed him of his boots.

In the dying light of the sunset, amid the harmonies of evening, the two fought and kicked and bit each other ⟨on the rampart⟩ where men had fought two thousand years before. But those fought for life, these for respectability, than which is life less dear. Flea, a sensible fellow of thirty, wanted peace. As soon as he saw that Hell had not opened, he called Harold by his name. He was sorry: he would take any message to Cadover: he would lend—anything in moderation. Then, as things got worse: he would lend almost everything—this and that and that but he must keep so-[*A17:*]-and-so. He must: one died without it. Shoddy cloth tore, buttons flew. He disappeared, a gibbering phantom, and Harold dressed himself⟨.⟩ \,/ and cried "Four hours, seven minutes."

So the day ended. He strode down the slope in his unaccustomed finery, at times even wearing the hat. He crossed the bridge and was never detected. Then came a final joy. A cart came furiously down the Cadover drive, and in it sat Rickie, his arms piled with honourable garments, crying continually "Oh poor fellow! I saw him through the opera glass! Oh poor fellow."

He ⟨led⟩ \let/ them go. The things would come in useful. On the sweep he saw Miss Pembroke and heard her call ⟨"Leighton—⟩ \"Aunt Emily!/ Here's an odd dirty man." But he slipped up to his room, drunk with victory, and youth, and happiness ⟨"I have done the whole thing!" he cried.⟩ \,/ and with something that is greater than all three put together. "I have done the whole thing fine!" he cried. ⟨"I have—I have got there!"⟩ His eye fell on the sixpenny reprints—the abridgement of Darwin, the translation of Renan, the maxims of Ingersoll and Mrs Chunk. He flung them all into the grate, ⟨—a sight⟩ \—a sight/ [. . .]

[*The last page or pages of the Harold chapter appear to have been lost long ago. The existing seventeen leaves show signs of having been pinned together and folded top to bottom as a group;*

337

on the lower half of the verso of the last [A17v] are three identifications, each in a different ink but all in Forster's late handwriting:

> Longest Journey—omission.
> From L.J.
> Harold = Stephen.

One further leaf, differently perforated and folded (top to bottom and then side to side), and looking rather battered, has been bound as A18, with the perforation in the customary upper left corner; the direction of the folding would have preserved A18 rather than its verso, used inverted. Both passages were crossed through; both could have begun new stages of the narrative but are not set off or otherwise marked as beginnings. Since each fills only half its page both could as easily be regarded as deleted conclusions of a chapter following or even preceding the Harold chapter, or perhaps of an early form of the Harold chapter itself. A related deletion survives on A8v. The order of the three passages is conjectural, although the earliest appears to be that on A18, not only because of the name Lodge but also by reason of the handwriting and the heavier deletion:]

[*A18:*] "It's funny about Mr Lodge" said Agnes, when Rickie was out of the room. "That engine must have gone to Salisbury. It had nowhere else to go to. Why hasn't he got back here, or, if he was really taken up, why hasn't he wired? Surely they'ld lend him sixpence."

"They have" said Mrs Failing, for Rickie came in with a telegram. She read "Riding on engines illegal. No case reported today.—Station Master."

Even she was a little uneasy at last. Harold the materialist, the semi-bounder, the foe to poetry and wonder, had been snatched into a world which could ⟨co⟩ not be measured or touched.

[*A8v:*] any station in between. You may be sure we shall hear."

Rickie came in. There was a telegram at last. The station master had condescended to answer on the reply-paid.

Mrs Failing read out: "Riding on companies [*sic*] engines illegal. No case reported to day."

Even she was a little uneasy at last. Harold the materialist, the nascent bounder, the foe to poetry and wonder, had been snatched into a world which could not be touched or measured.

[*A18v:*] Slowly the afternoon wore away, getting hotter and more brilliant as it proceeded. The drawing room at tea time was no longer dark and the tree tops in the avenue rose in ⟨clear glory,⟩ delicate sun lit spires. The silence of nature was ⟨at times⟩ broken by squawks from the kitchen, for the men and the great coats had returned. Nor had the Salisbury station master answered. Even Mrs Failing was slightly uneasy. Harold, the materialist, the bounder, the foe of poetry and wonder, had been snatched in a fiery chariot ⟨into⟩ \to/ a world that could not be touched or measured.

CHAPTER 13

Of the twenty-four leaves in XIII (*243–266*) only two, *248–9* (123:23 The–124:15) show the distinctive early ink of the preceding chapters. Five fragments, however, all preserved on verso pages in Chapters 25 and 26, come from the same early draft. Two of the rectos of these versos (*423, 427*) are among the earliest pages in Chapter 25 and show a wider-nibbed, gray-brown, rather uneven ink similar to that of the third level of composition in XIII. Interleaving and a darker ink identifying the second level at *247* (*begins* 123:10 protegé), *250–1* (*ends* 125:6 late), *256*

(126:34–127:18 fifteen), and *258–60* (128:3–129:13 down-). Two further versos now in Chapter 30, *487v* and *495v*, come from the second level of XIII; their placement again indicates Forster's continuing return to earlier chapters as he created and recreated Stephen. Most of the pages of XIII are of the third level of composition and resemble many pages in XII; two others, *264–5* (130:12–33), share the latest scratchy black of XII.

The five fragmented earliest verso survivals are so different from the completed chapter that they precede the later variants given below. None of the five was crossed through, and all were decapitated or depedditated, so far as can be seen, not in their original positions but as their recto pages were revised. The recto passages, in numerical order, are: *423* (200:1–7); *427* (201:27–33 my); *444* (208:39 the vineyards–209:6 comment on); *445* (209:6 Dunwood–11); *447* (209:15 star-crowned–26 short intervals). In probable narrative order, the fragments read as follows:

[*427v:*] -ion. Running into a tree. Unless a sensation raises a bump as big as a pigeon's egg you ⟨think⟩ are oblivious to it. You came through the wood. You ran into a tree. Is that the whole adventure?"

"Yes."

Rickie and Agnes, who were sitting further down the walk, could hear scraps of the conversation. Agnes was a little gloomy. It was most unfortunate that their hostess was ⟨no⟩ so taken up with Mr Wonham. She and Rickie were [*end of page*]

[*444v:*] appeared, could in no wise be put forward. It must e'en take its time, which meant a wait of fifty minutes.

From the upstairs sitting room Agnes saw Harold go off to the stables. "Rickie!" she called "There's aunt Emily left all alone in the herbaceous border." [*Only the last few words of the first line of the next paragraph are visible:*] Rickie [. . .] was tussling with *The Woods* [*Perhaps Rickie was reading "The Woods of Westermain", the poem by George Meredith which begins, "Enter these enchanted woods, You who dare."*]

[*423v:*] arm. Unless you're too [tired?"]

"No indeed. I came out partly in the hope of helping you."

"How sweet of you." She contrasted his blatant unselfishness with the ⟨sane⟩ refreshing hardness of Harold. Harold never came out to help you. But if you got hold of him he was some good. He didn't wobble and bend at the critical moment. "The lame leading the lame" she said sharply. "How's your foot?" [*end of paragraph and page; compare p.* 128]

[*447v:*] -al documents are in her bedroom—not, I'm afraid, in a black box—"

He could not see or hear her, or even think. He only knew that he was in a mire of shame and that never, all his life, would he be cleansed. The sun turned—or was he himself turning, staggering, falling on to hard gravel?

"Father's—Hullo!"

Mrs Failing had disappeared, and he was alone with his brother.

"Get out!" he cried. "Don't touch me! Don't look at me."

"What the—" His voice dropped. "Elliot, have you been frightened?"

"I can't bear it—I can't bear to see you." Then ⟨he⟩ a ray of truth came to him. He saw that there was nothing splendid about his disgust, and, with the help of God, he would crush it down. "Man, I'm sorry" he whispered, getting up, but still averting his eyes. [*end of paragraph and page*]

[*445v, opening with two deleted half-lines:*] ⟨for whom he [. . .]⟩ ⟨⟨for whom ⟨he had still⟩ \as a lover, he still had/ love to spare, [. . .]⟩⟩ had come at last, and he would accept him, ⟨though⟩ ⟨if he came⟩ \although [he]/ might come from the devil. Yes: although he might be the devil himself

"Harold—" And raising his eyes for the first ⟨times⟩ time, he met two eyes that

339

were at all events attentive. Then he heard his own name called. "Rickie! Rickie!" and Agnes came swiftly [*end of page; compare* p. 130]

121 8 \From which I conclude/ ← I asked whether [*243*]

      † \more/ obnoxious \than usual/

122 11 funny. ⟨In the end she won't even be funny.⟩" [*244*]

    15 "The truth ← "Nor he about me. I've scarcely seen him since the horrible Tuesday ride. The truth [*245*]

    17 now⟨. One mustn't be a prig, yet—⟩": there

123 5† perched ← sat [*246*]

    6 murmuring ⟨apologetically⟩ that

    20 don. ⟨⟨And ugh! his little ⟨story⟩ \stories/.⟩⟩" [*247*]

       \at the whitewashed pillars ⟨the window full of⟩ the humble . . . saints/ ← perpendicular, whitewashed, puce saint in east window, saffron saint in transept

    22† Wilbraham's bonnet ← Wilbraham again

    23 Ugh [*last word, 247; at the top of 248 is a related deletion:*] ⟨during the sermon, "is quite impossible. He's worse than his father. Hopelessly sentimental and conventional." She looked over the little church. There was the rector's wife. And Mrs Wilbraham \again/. Oh God⟩!

    27 \Ugh what a hole/ ← Oh God what a religion!

    30 \though/ ← thank God

124 17 \the aunt and ⟨her⟩ the nephew/ ← the full heart of Rickie and the empty stomach of Mrs Failing collided. They [*250*]

    26 \But . . . me./ I ← Isn't he an example, Stephen! Why I

    29 \Nothing/ ← I think and hope that nothing Cambridge ⟨There are agnostics⟩ If \a few/

    32 Agnes ← This was a little rude, and Agnes

    35 \either/." ⟨Stephen rubbed his hands together. ¶"Agnes has a sense of religion."⟩

    38 \Why . . . position?/ ← Is it that you cannot understand me, or that you will not? [*251*]

    39† I . . . won't. ← \Or is it that you won't?/

125 10 \culprit/ ← victim [*252*]

    12 \pave . . . apology/ ← try and arrange things

    19† than . . . boot boy. ← than ⟨—than that⟩ \the footman or the/ Wonham boy.

    29† Roman crossing ← ⟨Roman⟩ \railway/ Crossing [*253*]

    36† The Rings ← He was ignorant of archaeology, and the Rings

126 2† view. ⟨⟨ ⟨The visitor⟩ \Rickie/ had to crane \his neck/ and expect no longer.⟩⟩ The

    19† hence. . . . shrine. [*not in MS; fragmented deletions at the gap between 254 and 255 show drafts:*] {Their fibres are knit} ⟨greeted the ramparts of Dover or⟩ [*255:*] ⟨think for a [. . .] and love it, if he condescends to love the soil.⟩

    27 \reverenced/ ← worshipped [*255*]

127 8 a little⟨—well a little⟩ inhumane⟨⟨, in spite of ⟨all⟩ its ⟨humanity⟩ \humanism/⟩⟩. [*256*]

    24 retreat [*257*] ← fly [*487v, otherwise nearly identical to 257 from* shillings *to* nonchalent way; *in its continuation 487v, crossed through, includes a passage bracketed by Forster for possible deletion:*] way. *⟨Distance is a curious thing. Those tiny figures, though they filled him with love or repulsion, did not seem like the figures of real people. He was half inclined to neglect them

and fly after all. But as they grew, their power grew. They were no longer emblems, moving upon the face of Nature, but human beings, to whom all Nature was a background.⟩* They wished him to stop, and he obeyed. In time he heard their voices, and saw, some way behind them, a third figure, walking,—the figure of Stephen Wonham.

"Isn't it lovely!" called Agnes. "Isn't it perfectly lovely."

He raised his cap, and helped them to dismount. His aunt's manner, though quiet, was fairly pleasant. \She seemed to have forgiven him/ "This is to do instead of Stone Henge" she said. "We wanted ⟨to⟩ an antidote to the morning service, and The Rings is as good as any."

"Pang⟨!⟩." said the church bell suddenly. "Pang. Pang." They all laughed ⟨a⟩\,/ and Agnes, with a glance that said as clearly as [*end 487v; the deletion continues on 258:*] anything "Apologise", darted away, to explore the entrenchment by herself.

29† \by some hurdles/ [*257*]
  † went ← hurried
30† \He . . . nervous./
32 \disquieting/ ← strange wrinkled
33 \a little immense?/ ← wonderful?
38† said ⟨as clearly as anything⟩ 'apologise
128 9 the ⟨refreshing⟩ hardness [*258*]
  19 centre. ⟨⟨But don't tread on my ⟨turnips"⟩ \crops"/⟩⟩"
  31 \uppish/ ← casual [*259*]
  33 Rickie. ⟨I don't mind it."⟩ And
129 10 middle, ⟨and whistles,⟩ especially [*260*]
  20† friendly. ⟨He was anxious to apologise, but could not think how to begin.⟩ Agnes [*261*]
  21† "Soldiers . . . sentimental." ¶"But ← [*The undeleted passage on 262 is entirely different:*]
  "How's your foot?" she asked⟨.⟩ suddenly.
  "It gets better."
  "Mine did. Now it gets worse. I sometimes think of our family lameness as a curse."
  "So used I. I used to be ashamed. Now I'm ashamed of being ashamed. I don't believe in family curses."
  She laughed. "I sometimes think of your brother as \a possible/ Orestes."
  ⟨"Who—as what?"⟩ \As——a what?"/
  "As Orestes. He's freed from the curse⟨, and perhaps⟩\. Perhaps/ he will free his ⟨relatives⟩ relative!"
  "But
  34† glanced ← looked
130 3 tree. [*262 is depeditated through the next line:*] "Don't let me go!" she [. . .]
  7† a ← the [*263, showing a torn-through line at the end of the paragraph:*] the horror ⟨leapt at him again. There were shouts⟩
  12† he . . . possible." The ← he questioned her about the Rings. Then the [*264*]
  13† again, and he ← at him and ⟨broke him down⟩ he
  19† \for your younger brother/
  21† \which . . . recently,/
  25† among the dead ← there
    † He ⟨struck at his head and⟩ started

26† on the inner barrier ← in the earth
29† Elliot⟨! You slackster⟩, wake
30† he had dreaded lay ← was
39 \them further/ ← Miss Pembroke [*266; a slightly different version of the surrounding lines survives on the decapitated 495v, which shows three words at the
tear:*] Then he heard [. . .] Agnes, after a moment's bewilderment, had
hurried from her post ⟨of⟩ on the margin⟨: to[?] enfold⟩\, and, as if
understanding, enfolded/ him in her arms.
⟨"He's frightened" was Stephen's verdict. He⟩ Stephen had offered to
help, but as he seemed to make things \worse,/ ⟨had⟩ retired to the
central tree, and patted it curiously. The whole ⟨camp⟩ \field/, with its
⟨strange⟩ concentric circles, was visible, ⟨and reminded him of a board
for some complicated game of skill⟩ \and the broad leaves of the turnips
rustled in the gathering wind/. Miss Pembroke and Elliot were ⟨hurrying⟩
\moving/ towards the Cadover entrance. Mrs Failing⟨,⟩ stood watching
in her turn, on the opposite [. . .]

CHAPTER 14

Of the nineteen pages of XIV (*267–285*) six are late insertions written in the late
scratchy black ink of XII and XIII: *271* (134:1–7 Rickie had); *274* (134:28 He–35);
278 (136:8–24); *281* (137:14 things–18); *283–4* (137:29 Ask her kindly–138:18). Two
of these show unplaceable verso fragments: *278v*, "his brother was a knight errant,";
and *284v*, "a glimmer of hope". More revealing are *277v* and *458v*, both written in
the distinctive rusty ink of the Harold chapter and both described below. The
latter, now on an early sheet in Chapter 26, holds a version of the end of XIV and
indicates that the remaining thirteen pages of the chapter, all in the fluent gray-
brown ink of the intermediate levels in XII and XIII, recopied a complete earlier
draft; XIV too must have been revised as Chapters 25 and 26 were reshaped.
Another verso, *285v*, described at 137:29 below, shows the gray-brown ink but gives
Agnes a speech unlike any now in the text. And one gray-brown sheet, *282*, originally the bottom of *280*, shows pencilled fragments of *Where Angels Fear to Tread*,
inverted, on both recto and verso. These are perhaps drafts of Mrs Herriton's letter
to Harriet, quoted only in part at the beginning of Chapter 6 (Abinger Edition,
vol. 1, p. 74). Inverted at the bottom of *282* is the single sentence (without quotation
marks), "Caroline Abbott is helping me." The same sentence opens the passage on
282v, which then continues:

It is no concern of either of us, but we are getting to feel that the horrible man
must not have it all his own way \with the child/. It is unfair to little Irma:
after all the baby is her half brother. No: we have come to nothing definite."

132 3† why he had fainted ← what had happened [*267*]
6 exclaimed ⟨in agony⟩ "Will
13 mind. ⟨⟨They watch us ⟨togeth⟩ for ever.⟩⟩"
14† the train ← a train
29 face them, and face the world. ⟨⟨The thing could never ⟨never⟩ be
tidied up.⟩⟩ She [*268*]
32 \\did not . . . who ⟨asked Agnes⟩ \enquired after/ Rickie//. She ← Stephen
kept in his seat and took it back to the stables. With his back turned to
⟨her⟩ \Agnes/ he asked how Rickie was, and she
133 10† \—"do you . . . Rickie?"/

11 \"I do know."/ ← "Yes, Mrs Failing.⟨"⟩ I know." [*269*]

16 tears. ⟨But whatever had happened?⟩

19† his ghosts . . . afternoon?" ← sometime."

22 \That is not so. You did it to hurt him./

23† was rude . . . church. ← answered you back this morning.

30† Nothing . . . brothers. ← \No harm was done if they were not ⟨brothers after all.⟩ really brothers./ ← There was hope⟨. What if, after all, it was a lie?⟩, if it was a lie.

36 \I am not so/ childish ← This is really too childish [*270*]

134 4† \neither before nor now/ [*271*]

6† Rickie ← Her nephew [*271, which replaces deleted words still visible at the tear of 270/272:*] ¶"What about him? Do you suppose I have been twice a fool? I have not told him a single word."

"Oh?

There was a long silence. Mrs Failing had had her fun. ⟨⟨She was in fact ⟨extremely⟩ \quite/ alarmed.⟩⟩ \Mrs Failing was in an awkward position./ Her nephew

11† delicacy ← shame [*272*]

13 taste. ⟨He had even frightened her on the drive down by his chance remarks.⟩ After all

22 \Life . . . involved. But . . . were./ [*273*]

29 \doesn't care/ ← scarcely cares [*274, which replaces deleted words still visible at the tear of 273/275:*] Aunt Emily, I wish I had not been so rude to you." Mrs Failing had not disliked ⟨⟨her for ⟨it⟩ ⟩⟩ \her courage/. "My dear, don't mind. Sit down again."

135 1 \future/ ← possible [*275*]

14† off. ⟨⟨How would he get ⟨to it?⟩ there?⟩⟩ [*276*]

16† word ← \grunt/ ← cry

25† pretended . . . longer. ← had never pretended to be emancipated.

28 unfeigned, ⟨for she would have to sacrifice nothing,⟩ and [*276; 277v, decapitated at an angle, shows part of a draft of this paragraph and half the next:*] been very [. . .] ⟨condemn⟩ \censure/ them. Yet most ⟨respec⟩ [. . .] same. Why should ⟨Agnes⟩ ⟨a young⟩ a girl suffer a [stain to] appear upon her future family, if she can whiten it over? Why should ⟨not⟩ a matron not repair the consequences of her petulance? And what does a grown up man want with a grown up brother? ⟨⟨Let us have things ⟨normal⟩ \comme il faut/. Let us not be afraid of acting for the best.⟩⟩ [*277v is then nearly identical to 276 through the quotation (135:33) but ends by attributing it directly to Ansell,* a notoriously unpractical person. *277 introduces Mr Failing.*]

39† am. ⟨Just a series of chances.⟩ All [*277*]

136 2† \, in case you let it out/

10† senses. ⟨She is frank!⟩" [*278*]

11† \to people/

19 ground⟨."⟩\—but . . . prevent me."/

25 \We tell him?/ ← Tell him now? [*279*]

27 arranged? ⟨I think you must be mad.⟩"

35 \accepted/ ← paid homage to

137 6 \Doing . . . right."/¶"I ← But [*280:*] I want to do what is right." ¶"Since you asked me—I

8 \since you ask me/ ← all the same

9 \dear Rickie/

11† my father ← the dead
12 \love/ ← pity
13 his ⟨martyred⟩ mother
14 things. [*281 as a whole replaces deleted words at the tear of 280/282:*] things. And—quite another point—I don't feel I can meet him and keep silence. ⟨Suddenly I shall⟩\"/
15 \acknowledge each/ ← each living [*281*]
  † \accurately/
29 tomorrow⟨. She will tell you."⟩ if [*282; 285v, originally the top of a page, appears to have been a precursor of 280/282:*] me she says 'They are not brothers'. What is one to do?"

"I blame myself" said Rickie, trying to rouse himself from his gloom. "I ought to have spoken to him. Now she has sent him to ⟨see⟩\the/ sea, and I shall not have the opportunity."

She exclaimed in horror. "Speak? What should you speak about? He's either no one or\else he's/ worse than ⟨nothing⟩ no one. It isn't as if you even liked him—you know he's a coarse ungrateful cad. If you \did/ speak, he'ld roar with laughter, and make jokes." Her horror was perfectly genuine and so was her pity when she added "Poor fellow: I must try to be more charitable to him." In her eyes, Stephen was tainted [*Apparently the end of the paragraph, though no stop is visible.*]

138 2 He ⟨cheated himself by⟩ pretended [*283*]
4 \acknowledge him/ ← do his duty
14† nothing serious ← probably a fit [*284*]
23 Still holding her fast [*285*] ← ¶He sighed, and still holding her [*458v opens with these words.*]
26 paused. ⟨Stewart had never replied to him.⟩ "I [*285*] ← [*458v shows a deleted sentence following an undeleted* Stewart had never replied to him.*:*] ⟨And yet—surely—reply should not have been difficult?⟩ "I
32 tore the letter up. [*285*] ← [*458v:*] tore ⟨up⟩ the letter ⟨⟨that he had ⟨started⟩ begun to his friend.⟩⟩ \up./

CHAPTER 15

The eleven sheets of XV (*286–296*) suggest that Forster found the chapter relatively easy to write. The first two pages, in the fluent gray-brown ink of XIV, are neat enough to be copies and lead to the only truncated sheet, *288*, decapitated to open with a deleted "attic" (140:15). More heavily corrected pages, similar to *288* in their variable gray-black inks but not easily distinguishable from the gray-brown, then follow until *294* (143:12 though–35), which is identifiable as a revision chiefly because its verso shows a draft of the conclusion of the next chapter.

139 16† unsavoury details ← story [*286*]
17 garden⟨, amidst apple trees and dahlias⟩.
23† \The comedy is finished./ [*287*]
30† \'Nice . . . shocked!'/
140 18 \strange/ ← curious [*288*]
21 grey. ⟨Had the goddess come to this?⟩ Leighton
31 smudged. ⟨⟨ ⟨We do not like to find our manuscripts in gutters.⟩ \Next morning they left Cadover for ⟨Sawston, and the tone of this story changes.⟩ the London district, and the atmosphere ⟨of this story⟩ changes./ ⟩⟩ [*289*]
35† hoped they ← ⟨they thought that⟩ \hoped that/ if they were printed

large on thick paper ⟨that⟩ they

36† *Pan Pipes* ← 'In Touch With Nature' [*see* 283:32]

38 found . . . people ← took such keen pleasure in men

141 4 \'Andante Pastorale'/ ← "Admetus in England"

† too ← ⟨to⟩

9 \shifted its position/ ← been brushed away [*290*]

19† artificial ← unnatural

22 \Uncle Willie/ ← My sister

25 \quite another thing and/

26 \ideas/ ← things to say

\express/ ← say [*twice*]

28 'you see'⟨ ⟨⟨, nor ⟨it⟩ is it possible⟩⟩ He knew that⟨, in any artistic enterprise,⟩ idea and ⟨presentation⟩ \expression/ [*291:*] are inextricably linked—separate perhaps, but not separable⟩.

30 again. ⟨¶"I lo[?]⟩ He looked

31 felt⟨, as he had always felt,⟩ that

32 \Actual . . . real/ ← Perhaps ⟨⟨her grip on life was so ⟨constant⟩ ⟨com⟩ strong⟩⟩ \she found ⟨daily life so real⟩ flesh and blood so real/

33 \the union/ ← ⟨that⟩ {the} \that/ mixture

\shadow/ ← shadows

142 1 \she was incomparable./ ← ⟨there was⟩ \it held/ no one to match \her/. (The restaurant was ⟨⟨not absolutely respectable, but that was ⟨not⟩ the kind of thing he ⟨ever⟩ \never/ found out⟩⟩ \in Soho/.)

17 \\on account of the faux pas ⟨in⟩ \he had made last June/ // ← because of ⟨the⟩ \his/ horse-whipping speech [*292*]

29 purse ⟨⟨and ⟨was⟩ ⟨never left with⟩ never had the tips ready⟩⟩.

31 present.⟨" ¶"Good luck to you!" said Miss Pembroke. He was trying [*293:*] for the English Home Civil. ¶"But later on I⟩ [*292:*] \But later on I/

33 \edification/ ← benefit [*293*]

143 2† \I've heard nothing since June./

4 people in⟨—older as well⟩. He'ld have

12 liked ⟨and admired⟩ her ⟨exceedingly⟩ \very much/, [*294:*] though

19 Agnes \put/ ← The offices of 'The Holborn' were not unnaturally in St James's Street, and Agnes saw

24† slow of soul ← cautious in manner

144 12 please.' ⟨⟨My kindest regards to Mrs Failing when you write ⟨next.⟩"⟩⟩ \"/ He [*295*]

14 it's not been \so alarming/ ← it's . . . such an alarming interview

21 \fashionable/ ← respectable [*296*]

\on the wing/ ← of Paradise

24 \but . . . hidden/ ← and yet the world was incomplete

28 \—known it and/ forgotten ← and forgotten it—⟨forf⟩ forgotten

CHAPTER 16

The thirteen sheets of XVI (*298–310; 297* bears the part-title, "Sawston") represent much recopying, for two neat sequences, *298–301* (ends 149:16 a) and *302–308* (ends 152:15), finish in leaves depeditated to remove blank space. *305* (150:25–39 school) is a later insert distinguished by a scratchy black ink. The decapitated *309* (ends 152:32 thereby) is the earliest sheet, showing heavier revision; it led first to *294v*, now placed in XV but so similar to *310* in both content and appearance that immediate revision is suggested. The deleted name of the headmaster, Dr Browning, occasionally appears in this and the next two chapters.

147 15† almost . . . buildings. ← about five minutes' run from the school, in a healthy, airy position. [*298*]

17† with ⟨cheap⟩ creepers

148 7† \that mysterious asset/ [*299*]

19 \When . . . gritted/ ← If they were noisy [*300*]

149 6 "⟨That is \a/ ⟩ \A/ most . . . Pembroke ⟨hotly⟩. [*301*]

7 "⟨Exactly.⟩ To my mind \also/

18 and \his prudence should have/ ← and he ought to have [*302*]

23† been eaten by the rats. ← died.

33† the ⟨dim⟩ recesses† ← ⟨dimly⟩ in the \dim/ recesses

150 6 \and they . . . acquaintances./ ← She was rather unconventional, but so well established in Sawston society that it did not matter. She had two pretty daughters, but he hoped⟨, by judicious⟩ to persuade her to send them \away/ to school at Cheltenham. And ⟨fri⟩ she had been friends— close friends—with him for years. [*303*]

10 \passed . . . tears/ ← was shaken by a disgust that turned to tears

15 Sawston⟨, and he did not know any body outside⟩.

18† a disease called roseola; ← measles,

20† push Rickie's fortunes; and, ← see Rickie. And

24 the voice . . . ⟨was heard⟩ \arose/ prophesying ← Mrs Jackson prophesied [*304*]

27† them ⟨strangely⟩ when [*305*]

32† more genuine ← \really/ genuine \(which his love had not been)/ ← more genuine than his love

33 \hurrying into a/ ← entering the

34 reverenced ⟨⟨when he was ⟨feeling⟩ hot and flustered⟩⟩.

151 7 \held that position/ ← was above all [*306*]

19 the \great/ drawing room⟨—a most extreme measure—⟩, and [*307*]

28 Agnes⟨, who often talked in a way that seemed disconnected, but in reality was not⟩. "You

34 \now . . . her/ ← every day confirmed her

152 21 \For it was/ ← \\ was/ ← ¶"⟨And⟩\—and/ boys," she ⟨continued⟩ \was saying/ "are in some ways delightful creatures, don't you think?" ¶He felt [*309*]

29 good\; one . . . that."/ ← good." The woman he loved was speaking to him.

32 art⟨—let us even give up love—if we can make oth⟩ \if/

† thereby ← by so doing

33† \The woman . . . good!/† [*310 and 294v are identical from* we can *to* "I'll do it." *294v then continues:*] The ⟨world⟩ \room/ grew brighter, and it seemed to him that people would again be vivid, as they had been six months \before/. Then he was at Cambridge, idling in the hemlock meadows: now he was at Sawston, ⟨about⟩ ⟨arming for the battle. Perhaps—he asked for no reward—but perhaps after victory⟩ preparing to ⟨enter a great and vigourous machine⟩ {enter} \work a/ vigourous and beneficent machine. He ⟨entered⟩ {came} ⟨to⟩ \would/ work ⟨ye⟩. Yet he trusted that to him also benefits might accrue: that ⟨in time⟩ his ⟨him⟩ ⟨would⟩ wound might heal as he laboured and his eyes ⟨see life.⟩ recapture the Holy Grail.

346

CHAPTER 17

The opening leaf or leaves of this chapter are missing; the first of the remaining thirty-six sheets (*311–346*) begins with "the best" (154:21). The chapter is a patchwork of insertions; there are no verso passages but only twelve sheets are still full quartos. The earlier pages are *311* (ends 154:30) and *315* (156:1 up–13 then), once joined but torn through to admit the intervening pages; *320*(157:16 made–33 mouth); *324* (158:17 Mr–32); *326–7* (159:18 How–37); *332* (161:19–26 Flaccus); *335* (162:23 attracted–31); *338–9* (163:24–164:13 or); and *341* (164:24 learnt–165:3 kindly). *335, 338* and *339* show an inserted "Varden" (*335* at its depeditation), which replaces "Burton", a change also visible throughout XVIII but not later, and not in the other pages of XVII. The latest pages, in a scratchier black ink, are *318* (157:8 Rickie–11), *322* (157:39 and–158:10 lay), *330–1* (begins 160:30), *336* (ends 163:6), and *343* (165:9 to–12 nature). Throughout, the additions serve to increase Rickie's role, giving him more to say and feel.

154 21 \the best/ ← extraordinarily impressive [*311*]
29† laughed⟨, and they parted better friends than they had been for years⟩. The
30 began. [*311* still shows most of the deleted sentence replaced by *312–14:*] ⟨¶It was a nervous moment for Rickie when he first con-[*315:*]fronted the assembled house.⟩
31 Sawston . . . [*312; 316* shows a deletion, inverted at the bottom of the page, which could have been an abortive start of this passage:] ⟨It is a strange feeling, to come as an official to a place that one⟩
155 4 \These shops . . . out./ ← The shops in the high street were out of bounds [*312*]
6 \its rival,/ Cedar view. ← ⟨Evergreens⟩ \Cedar View⟨, its⟩/
12 bust of the Hermes ⟨⟨ ⟨of Praxiteles⟩, a palm—(the Shelthorpe palm repotted)—⟩⟩, and
13 \holding out a salver/ ← proffering a plate
22 \Percival/ ← Galahad [*313; see* 8:31]
156 25† their private ← the [*316*]
28† said . . . right. ← thought they ⟨really⟩ might.
35 him." ⟨So it was that Rickie stopped, with a little sob of pain, on the threshold of his new life.⟩ "You [*317*]
157 2 order. ⟨⟨¶The preparation room had ⟨that⟩ \the/ peculiar smell that ⟨seems to haunt⟩ can only be called 'educational'. It cannot be analysed. It is as subtle as a smell in Italy, though not so insanitary, and not so charming.⟩⟩
8 \So impressed . . . attended./ [*The last three words of 317 and all of 318 replace a deleted passage:*] There was nothing [*317/319:*] inside. He had expected nothing. The gesture was purely mechanical. ⟨But it⟩ \This/ arrested the boys' attention. They stopped ⟨wh⟩ talking and fixed their eyes on the two masters, and the two masters fixed their eyes on them.
21 \an inferior brand/ ← inferior creatures [*320*]
22 beyond⟨. Their demeanour was less nonchalent⟩\,/ and
† many. ⟨⟨Rickie counted the turned up collars, which told him ⟨how many were⟩ \who was/ over sixteen. As for the faces they⟩⟩ The faces
24† inclined to cry ← crying \quietly/
27 remark⟨, and confounded 'miniature' with 'immature'⟩. It
32 flowed \like . . . fugue/ ← flowed, in this order,
35† that . . . *the* ← this was *the* [*321*]
158 15† \the broader patriotism of/ [*323*]
16† anthem⟨—a ditty all blood and treacle⟩, recently

    † organist ← chaplain

17 Words . . . was [*323*] ← [*deleted on 324:*] ⟨⟨song was only ⟨three⟩ \two/ months old, and it was⟩⟩ only

24 do. ⟨Fancy not knowing your own anthem! This⟩ We [*324*]

159 1 diffident. ⟨⟨ ⟨This⟩ \That/ will never do.⟩ You [*325*]

    9† past.⟨" ¶Herbert frowned. ¶"⟩Of . . . off ← past." ¶⟨"Sawston has a past" said⟩ Herbert \frowned/. ¶⟨But not a past of⟩ \Of . . . of/

13† \he concluded nervously./

14 \A very great deal./ ← was Herbert's retort.

23 \stopping/ ← running [*327*]

24† parents! ⟨Oh the letters from the parents!⟩ 'Why

27 mission.' ⟨'I am an atheist and do not wish my boy to attend chapel.'⟩ 'Can

29† tried ⟨hard⟩ to

33† my \own/ way

39 now⟨, and all the lights out⟩. [*328*]

160 6 impressed. ⟨It seemed so wonderful.⟩ In

29 him. [*329, with a following line deleted at the depedivation:*] ⟨¶"What's that?" said a dreamy voice. They turned⟩

32 teacher. ⟨There's not such a thing as a teacher in the world.⟩ If [*330*]

161 20 \makes/ ← believes in making [*332*]

26 Flaccus.⟨" ¶Mr Elliot has studied education" said Herbert, and⟩ [*332/333:*]—⟨whatever⟩ \Whatever/

27 \snapped/ ← said

38 \festivities/ ← such treats

162 1† My brother-in-law ← Mr Elliot

16† smile ← laugh [*334*]

24 \pleasantly/ ← so strongly [*335*]

31† ask me ← tell me

32† You found ← There is [*336*]

    † called ← named

34† Drop ← You must drop

163 1 Orr's⟨, an unauthorised person⟩,

11 \for the second time/ ← He never calls a meeting or if he does only says 'Well I'm sure I don't know what we're all here for. Now I should think we'ld better go home.' And they *do* ⟨come⟩ go home. What house could go on on such lines? [*337*]

24 \By . . . out./ ← Because you're the boy's form master. First of all you must find out. Well— [*338, where the deletion includes previous lines recopied on 337, from* never sanction *to* fingers.]

34 \not . . . ailments/ ← suffered from nothing infectious [*338*]

164 4† naturally, more or less ← \more or less naturally/ [*339*]

28† highly; but you ← highly. But he found that you [*341*]

34 \intact/ ← like a father confessor

37 \at Cambridge/ ← a year ago

165 6† subjects ← questions [*342, which was once joined to 344*]

7 \became/ ← was somewhat of

15 unruly. ⟨But he never cared for the Georgics again.⟩ But [*344*]

17 \overshadow him so heavily/ ← modify him so greatly

18† had ⟨always⟩ known

22 others. ⟨He was moreover diligent and conscientious, and his heart was in his⟩ Certainly

166 1 \Rickie's intellect was not remarkable/ ← Rickie had not got much of a brain [*345*]

CHAPTER 18

The eleven leaves of XVIII (*347–357*), unlike those of the previous chapter, are remarkably coherent, all in a variable gray-black ink except for two brief, blacker additions, *349* (168:5 you–13) and the conclusion, *357* (*begins* 172:13 to teasing). The early pages are essentially those of the first draft; only *357* shows "Varden" unchanged from "Burton", and the two verso passages, *352v* and *356v*, noted below, were each abandoned halfway down leaves that were inverted and reused almost immediately.

167 1 \a husband . . . before. By the end of the term he/ had been \a husband/ three months. The ← married. The errors of Herbert and his own failures were unimportant beside this. By March he had been married three months. The [*347*]

25 \gave orders/ ← spoke kindly [*348*]

31 \made the effort/ ← did speak

168 3 \crocuses/ ← snowdrops

10 not want ⟨⟨to own her⟨.⟩, nor⟩⟩ ⟨He knew and had always known⟩ her . . . life. ⟨He desired not⟩ His [*349*]

12† to a love so pure ← to such a man† [*Part of an earlier version of the paragraph survives on 356v, unevenly decapitated in the depeditation of its recto:*] your thoughts and all your world. [. . .] "Once I would have told you that was wrong.", and after all they ⟨spoke⟩ never mentioned Gerald's name. But he hoped it was still \dear/ to her, for⟨, in a love as great as hers, it was no shame to him⟩ \\there was something in Rickie that made it ⟨not⟩ seem \not/ shameful// to ⟨come⟩ \be/ second. [that made it seem not shameful *is also still visible at the decapitation of 350*]

14 \He valued/ ← Rickie loved [*350*]

26† this ⟨reluctance, this⟩ aversion [*351*]

29 her ⟨it would leave him⟩ \no mystic influence remained/ . . . that ⟨this was wedded life.⟩ \God had united them for ever./ [*A contorted draft of this passage appears on 352v:*] Did she bless . . . reluctant, and ⟨spoke⟩ turned his thoughts to the living. And perhaps it was {this} reluctancy {to speak}, this aversion to \speak of/ the dead, ⟨⟨who ⟨have⟩ \are/ alone unchangeable,⟩⟩ \whose/ images alone have immortality, that made ⟨his wife appear a hazy, transient thing, and made him forget, from time to time, in the press of his duties, that he had entered on the full heritage of man⟩ \her own image somewhat transient,/ so that he ⟨would⟩ {could} ⟨forget \it/⟩ \forgot/, in the routine of his ⟨work⟩ \duties/, ⟨⟨that God had \ever/ joined ⟨him to her, and made them one flesh.⟩ them together to be one flesh⟩⟩ that he ⟨was leading a newer wider⟩ had entered on the full heritage of man.

32 \\They conversed \⟨intimately⟩ without restraint/ //\on other topics/ ← Their conversation was chiefly on passing topics. [*351*]

169 1 \bewilderment/ ← confusion

5 \I can't . . . ashamed./

8 \planned it/ ← captured him

9 \attempted to set up a/ ← tried to underbid the

13 \\But . . . ⟨wretched⟩ \officious/ . . . upset ⟨everything⟩ the headmaster// ← ⟨Mr Jackson had approved, and then⟩ \Then/ there came this

wretched ⟨little new master⟩ \Limpet/, and upset ⟨everything.⟩ ⟨Dr Browning⟩ \the headmaster/, [*352*]

25 \We/ are ← Most certainly we are

39 \"Physical pain doesn't/ ← "Black eyes don't

170 15† hit at her ← stroked her [*353*]

16 \I approve . . . But/

22† Silence⟨!⟩\, madam./

24 \Isn't it building/ ← It is organising

29 corps⟨, of which we hear so much,⟩ are [*354*]

30 \all very well/ ← splendid things
\a little/ ← —even Herbert—

33 \\and boys... ⟨until they love⟩\when ⟨the⟩ they hate/each other.//

171 5 if ⟨⟨ ⟨this⟩ \the noise/ jarred him, or if ⟨that⟩ \the/ cog ⟨wheel⟩ \wheels/ pinched him here and there⟩⟩ he was pinched now and then⟨, so long as he did good and attained his own salvation.⟩ \by the elaborate wheels./

39 \weedy/ ← pimply [*356, twice*]

172 3 \He/ ← Between them they

16† sixty ← seventy ← sixty [*357*]
\their hotel./ ← Dunwood House.

CHAPTER 19

The eleven leaves of XIX (*358–368*) are again a patchwork, written in pencil and four different inks. The earliest pages are the decapitated *360* (173:32–174:8 would) and *363–5* (174:19–175:30 But); *364* (174:38–175:15 a) and *365* are both depeditated, *363* decapitated. These pages are all corrected in a pencil which succeeded the ink of *358* in the midst of *359* (*at* 173:27 he) and was also used for *361* (*ends* 174:12 squalor) and *366–7* (*ends* 176:24). The pencilled sheets are corrected in the dark scratchy black of *362*, and the last paragraph of the chapter, standing alone on *368*, appears to have been added even later, in yet another gray-black ink. *367* was neatly depeditated with a one-line space remaining, so that it is difficult to know whether *368* was purely an addition. Pencil effected the change to Ilfracombe from Eastbourne on the early pages (174:2, 175:15), a change also made, in ink, in the next chapter (179:15).

173 7† at a reduction ← cheaply [*358*]

26 \zeal/ ← skill [*359*]

174 2 \Winter Garden/ ← Parade [*360*]

9 \a man . . . great./ ← one's relatives were great. But [*361*]

26 He and . . . Varden. [*362, which recopies lines still undeleted on 363 and nearly identical from* 174:19 *to* 174:28 know *except for this sentence, originally two:*] He was ⟨extremely⟩ unwilling to give up his intercourse with ⟨Mr Jackson⟩ \Widdrington's cousin/. \They had drifted apart in the term./ [*363*]

30 \sentimental books/ ← novels and sparkling repartees

32 \He tries . . . journalese."/ ← 'I can' he said 'express . . . journalese'."

175 5 poems. ⟨What do you mean?"⟩ {I don't understand."}\"/ [*364*]

13 \and he . . . Widdrington/

15 \Ilfracombe/ ← Eastbourne

20 was ⟨lonely and⟩ unhappy [*365; 364 is depeditated through a line of which the opening words are lost:*] ⟨[. . .] lonely. He needed a man of his own age. The⟩

23 letters ⟨into the paper basket⟩\,/ and

30† refused ← not accepted [*366*]

39 \his visit to Cadover/ ← last September
176 11 full of ⟨mills and thatched cottages.⟩ \men./
22 counties ⟨that he loved, she always⟩ \she/ [*367*]

CHAPTER 20

The first of the sixteen leaves of Chapter 20 (*369–384*) opens the problem of the numbering of this decade of chapters. The figure XX, sketched in darkly, stands beside a deleted figure which was probably XIX but might possibly have been XXIX. The latter is attractive because *436v*, on a leaf in Chapter 25 but transcribed below under Chapter 28, shows that Widdrington and Ansell once talked in the British Museum after Rickie had learned that Stephen was his mother's son. *436v* also provides a draft of the passage about "marble goddesses and gods" on the decapitated *382* (181:39 comfort–182:10), which is one of the earlier pages in Chapter 20; it still shows Tilliard's name as "Tillyard" in the two deleted lines which Forster recopied on *383* with "Tilliard". And the opening sentence of *369* at first read "Ansell was back in his old haunt—", implying an earlier scene in the museum. *369* is otherwise uncorrected and looks like a neat copy, though it is depeditated after the end of the first paragraph through a lost line that ended "sobbed and". Its ink is not helpful, being one of the general gray-blacks common at earlier and intermediate levels throughout Chapters 18 to 28; *436v* shows a bluer tone, as does *382*.

To complicate the problem, there is no manuscript chapter numbered XXI. Chapter 21 is clearly labelled XXII, Chapter 22, less clearly, XXIII, a third X having been deleted. Unfortunately Chapter 23 is also clearly headed XXII, but, while Chapter 24, opening with a late leaf, is unambiguously XXIV, Chapter 25 too was once headed XXIV, and has had the I of its XXIV deleted to make its XXV. Thereafter the numbers are unambiguous; that is, XXVI and XXVIII are clear, as is the XXIX of the discarded chapter of letters, so the missing XXVII was presumably also clear. Probably Chapters 21 and 22 were originally one chapter, XXI, and wrongly numbered XXII and XXIII when they were split. When Forster returned to a revision of Chapter 24 he could simply have counted the chapters to find the new number, not bothering to correct the headings of Chapters 21–23. Still, the deleted top line of the decapitated *390*, now the second leaf in Chapter 22, originally opened the second paragraph (185:6) with ⟨The sick boy, to whom Widdrington had alluded, was Varden.⟩ If more had happened in Sawston before or during Widdrington's visit, just possibly Chapter 20 might have replaced two chapters, numbered XX and XXI, though no trace of another Sawston scene remains and the number XIX would still have been an error. Throughout this decade of chapters the remnants of a consistent change in the calendar of events, moving a November or December revelation of Stephen's ancestry to the following June, perhaps reflect a scheme in which Widdrington's report to Ansell and Varden's letter to Stephen precipitated their converging visits to Dunwood House.

In any case, Chapter 20 is much revised and even its earlier leaves may be relatively late, since one of them, *382*, draws on an abandoned draft of a much later chapter. The easily distinguished latest sheets, written with a finely pointed pen, are *370–1* (177:17–178:21 University), *380* (181:12–19), and *383* (182:11–27 monuments of). Indistinguishable gray-blacks dominate the other levels, where the order of insertions is not wholly clear. *372* (*ends* 178:28) is depeditated so neatly that it could have been either the top of a full page or an insert. *373* (*ends* 179:3) was decapitated as neatly and may or may not have lost words, but it was obviously inserted to fit the decapitated *374* (*ends* 179:18 inside), which still shows words recopied on *373*. *374* also shows the change from Eastbourne to Ilfracombe (179:15), and leads naturally to the depeditated *375* (*ends* 179:37). The depeditated *376* (*ends* 180:8 friends. He) has clearly lost words, as has the decapitated *377* (*ends* 180:17 Pembroke), which opens a sequence interrupted by *380* and concluded by *381*, where the last line has been adjusted to fit the decapitated, early *382*. *384*, holding the last four lines of the chapter, is both decapitated and depeditated, so there is no way of telling how much was replaced by the full quarto of *383*.

178 21 \keep your place/ ← *stop* one [*372*]

25 intellect ⟨and his wife has a little money⟩.

32 "My cousin thinks Mrs ← "I'm inclined to think that Mrs [*373*]

179 15 doubt it.⟨" His voice was perfectly serious. "⟩I [*374*]

34 \So I gathered./ ← \I ⟨did not think⟩ cannot understand you./ ← I know. ⟨I found out that he⟩ \He/ minds. [*375*]

180 8 \He is so odd too/ [*spanning 376/377, this replaces* His *on 376 and two deleted sentences on 377:*] ⟨⟨¶"What were you saying about Rickie?" ¶"Oh yes.⟩⟩

10† cousin⟨, tooth and nail⟩.

11 \It . . . dine./ ← ⟨I mea⟩ I mean, it was an enormous sensation when we were ⟨all⟩ asked to ⟨dinner.⟩ \dine/ at Dunwood House.

16† even altering ← quite altered

17† that wife ← the wife [*378*]

23 \again November/ ← January

† Then . . . books. ← One of them went out and the woman next them cried "It's fused!" Then the cold violet radiance returned, and he lowered his eyes to the books.

26† talk to them. ← speak to them ⟨about happiness or sorrow⟩.

29 \we . . . brutes/ ← it is a cold icy business

31 him. ⟨Some row.⟩ That

34 youths \repining in/ ← youths⟨⟨! How ⟨ridiculous⟩ Mrs ⟨Pembroke⟩ Elliot would laugh at us⟩⟩ in ⟨the Reading Room of⟩ [*379*]

38 \I'm . . . I/ ← I know that I shall not be ⟨when⟩ \if/ the moment comes. I

39 plough boy ⟨and my blow will tell⟩.

181 1 \\They are only . . . ⟨appease⟩ \soothe/ . . . majority.//

5 \than action . . . rightly."/ ¶"The ← A fool would have gone to stop with them—or had a row. But I knew better. ⟨I⟩ ⟨I⟩ This business ⟨wants⟩ \requires/ a lever and I won't move in it till I've got one." ¶"Like Archimedes. The

9 him ⟨by the coat⟩. "⟨Then⟩ \Please/

10† you are bound ← I expect you

11 me.\"/ ← me. There's no mystery: I havn't the shadow of [*379/381:*] a plan in my head. I'm just watching." ¶"What for?"

17 his ⟨family⟩ history [*380*]

18 \I'm just watching./ ← I can only watch.

19† But what for? ← \Watching! What for?/ ← Watch! What for?

28† anywhere ← when it comes [*381*] \and . . . rightly/ ← and to use it as a lever

30 Widdrington⟨, never very industrious,⟩ then

37† a respectable woman? ← her⟨, or⟩? ← her?

182 4 sea. ⟨Into this artificial light and heat, Beauty, leaving the sun, had departed, and the Spirit of Life, headless and mutilated, was arranged into schools.⟩ ¶"Let us [*382; see also 436v,* p. 366]

15† bewildered ⟨and afraid⟩. [*383*]

18† Well, after all, I ← No: I'm the same. I
26† dissertation ← work
27 the Parthenon . . . monuments of [*383*] ← splendours of the Parthenon . . .
    monuments of [*deleted at the top of 384*]
29† Honest ⟨to his soul⟩, [*384*]

CHAPTER 21

The first of the four leaves of Chapter 21 (*385–388*), wrongly headed XXII, is a full
quarto written in a fine black ink like that used to open Chapter 22. The second,
386 (183:17 Within–30), is decapitated and more heavily corrected than the last
two, but all three show the intermediate gray-black inks, as does one verso, *412v*,
now in Chapter 24; deleted, inverted, and then depeditated in the decapitation of
its recto, *412v* indicates how Chapters 21 and 22 might once have been conjoined
and is shown below as the last variant of Chapter 21. One inserted leaf in Chapter
22, *392*, looks like the last two pages here. The implication is that the chapters were
separated quite soon, before a wholly different ink or pen was used, and that the
openings of both were adapted again at a later stage.

183 3† who . . . him, ← who had never really loved him [*385*]
      15 \In . . . square./ [*added to 385 in a scratchier gray ink, this corresponds to the
          deleted top line of 386:*] ⟨meaning in the universe, a fresh circle within the
          square.⟩
      18 a circle ⟨a⟩ ⟨Yes.⟩ \\within . . . the ⟨vision is baffled⟩ \visual . . .
          baffled./ // [*386*]
      19† \His mother . . . him./
      23 \a woman's tenderness./ ← ⟨a⟩ feminine tenderness and tact. This term
          they were swayed by the latter impulse.
      26 trouble. ⟨⟨They made no noise near the house. They were cleanly, quiet,
          and kind to each⟨, and⟩ other.⟩⟩ ⟨⟨He loved to ⟨watch them.⟩ \be
          near them./⟩⟩
184 1† Our boy? ← And \—our boy?/ ← And \the boy?/ ← And the child—
          he—? [*387*]
      11 \It's something/ ← Oh its something dreadful, and
      13 \mind/ ← be surprised
      17† this. Come ← this—⟨don't cry⟩—come [*388*]
      26† But . . . now; ← But he had learnt his lesson—the lesson he had learnt so
          glibly once at Cambridge, and had forgotten:
[*There is space for a chapter number at the top of 412v:*]
    At first their great sorrow drew them ⟨closer together than they had ever been
before.⟩\close together/and they would sit hand in hand without speaking, without
looking at each other, in intimate communion. There ⟨was⟩ \seemed/ nothing to
do but to ⟨comfort each other⟩ \exchange comfort/, and then bravely to return to
life. But soon the man perceived that ⟨it⟩ they could not exchange comfort,
because his sorrow was far more terrible, far more complex⟨.⟩ than hers, and she
would never understand it. He dare not phrase it even to himself, [. . .]

CHAPTER 22

The seven leaves of Chapter 22 (*389–395*) show a consistent gray-black ink except
for the first sheet, *389*, written in fine black ink and wrongly headed XXIII, and
392 (186:7 In–12 course), an insertion resembling the earlier pages of Chapter 21.
390 (185:6 His–24 pure) was decapitated and *391* depeditated to allow the additions.

The top of *390* shows the remnants of the word "square", apparently the end of a paragraph, as well as the deleted sentence which mentions Widdrington, quoted above under Chapter 20 and replaced on *389* by "Varden . . . months." (185:6) The depeditation of *395* just below Stephen's letter removed further text, but all that remains are the tops of words and symbols, certainly including a question mark, quotes, and Rickie's name.

185 1† That same term ← Soon afterwards [*389*]

      8 \during the ⟨Xmas⟩ {summer} summer holidays/ ← early in the New Year [*390*]

    11 \Soon . . . child/ ← In the ⟨lent⟩ \Lent/ term, ⟨one of those waves of hostility⟩

    26 \He . . . admit/ ← Rickie was silent and gloomy, knowing in his heart [*391*]

    31 \Comment . . . imperilled/ ← The boys were mournful, partly ⟨through⟩ \in/ anger at such unhealthiness, partly in genuine pity and remorse. The masters ⟨also⟩ {too} \also/ ⟨mourned⟩ realised the tragedy, and ⟨also⟩ felt \besides/ that if the boy was to die it would be a terrible thing for the school.

186 3 cubicle." ⟨⟨Meanwhile Mrs Varden came to stop with Mrs Orr, and the two ladies penetrated daily into Dunwood House. Agnes ⟨had⟩ found it difficult to keep her temper, for they criticised freely. Rickie, standing by, was astonished at the level to which he and all of them could sink.⟩⟩ The boy

    4† The boy . . . return. ← The boy did not die⟨⟨, but he underwent a ⟨long⟩ dreary convalescence before he could be moved⟩⟩\./

    9 \He . . . battle./ ← Little enough could he do: he could not exhort from the heights, for he had lost them himself. But he had been ⟨there⟩ \on them/. He \ just/ remembered. And others might be ⟨there⟩ \on them/ again. [*392*]

    33† \silly/ [*393*]

    35 sympathy. ⟨Herbert had been much annoyed, for the scandal had \thus/ penetrated into quite unnec-[*394:*]essary quarters.⟩

    39 \that a/ ← the full extent of ⟨them⟩ the mischief. One [*394*]

187 17 writers ⟨commended his charity and⟩ declared

    20 \majestically/ ← unctuously [*395*]

    29† April ← March

    34† might ← will

    35† \I have been otter-hunting./

CHAPTER 23

Eleven of the fifteen leaves of Chapter 23 (*396–410*), wrongly headed XXII, show the intermediate gray-blacks of the preceding chapters, a darker tone being succeeded by a lighter one. Of these the earlier are the decapitated *403* (190:24–191:5), the decapitated and depeditated *407* (192:17 final–26 Rickie), the decapitated *409* (192:34 the–193:8 brother), and probably the battered last sheet, *410*. One change on *403*, showing that Agnes originally looked "at the ground" rather than "aside" (190:24), suggests an early change in setting. The lighter sequence runs from *396* to the depeditated *404* (ends 191:11), adapting to *403* and to the later insertion of *399* (189:14–18). The finer ink of *399* is similar to that of the latest sheets, *406* (*begins* 191:37) and *408*. *405* is slightly bluer and more similar to a number of adjustments made on the earlier but not on the latest sheets, including the addition of the last paragraph in the chapter. There are two versos, both in the intermediate gray-blacks. *409v* shows one deleted line, the remnant of a draft abandoned partway down a page and lost in the decapitation of *409*: ⟨"Don't go to Cadover. Have nothing to do with them.⟩ *413v*, now in Chapter 24 and still a full quarto, shows an undeleted and inverted passage so different from the finished chapter that it opens the notes here:

[*413v:*] They never spoke of Stephen. He was classed among the disturbing dead. But Rickie felt bound to allude to their escape. Agnes surprised him by exclaiming "Where did he write from?"

"Cadover I suppose."

"Now are you sure? Did you see the address? What was the postmark?"

"I'm not sure. ⟨I presume⟩ \One presumes/ it was Cadover."

"I wish you ⟨had noticed."⟩ noticed things, instead of living in the clouds."

"I can go back, if it is of any interest to you. He is always glad to show the letters."

"Interest? My dear boy why should I care? I was only wondering whether Aunt Emily was alone or not."

"Why should you wonder? Was she alone at Christmas?"

Agnes kept up what she called 'the family connection'. She had been twice to Cadover since her marriage. Her husband would neither accompany her nor enquire about her visit. And she corresponded a little with Mrs Failing.

"She was alone at Christmas, and so charming. Oh Rickie, I do so wish you would come and see her. She is getting old, you know."

"We are ⟨g⟩ all getting old, my dear. In fact I am catching her up."

188 10† seldom ← never [*396*]
    15 \that ⟨we⟩ Varden . . . Orr. ⟨The whole thing is my fault.⟩"/ ← ⟨he cried inconsequently⟩ "I had never set eyes on Varden. It is all my fault." [my fault *not actually deleted*]
    19† \, living . . . Codford/. . . . \It is all explained./
    30 \she said uneasily./ ← And her voice filled with horror. [*397*]
    31 \disastrous/ ← awful, how perfectly awful
189 3 already." ⟨And to himself he said bitterly 'A person as charming and as successful as I am, can afford to despise these little blemishes!'⟩
    4 \displeased./ ← more angry than he had ever known her.
    † You need ← \You must/ ← I wish you would
    † cynical ← irresponsible
    10† once alone ← once ⟨of⟩ or twice [*398*]
    12† \But, . . . re-opened./ [*398, once joined to 400; 399 replaces one deleted question on 400:*] ¶"When she did mention it, what did she say?"
190 3 cried⟨: and then despised himself.⟩ \\with ⟨the⟩ a lapse ⟨of taste⟩ \of tone/ that was now characteristic in him//. [*401*]
    7 \\her ⟨other⟩ \favourite/ nephew// ← my dear brother
    8 cheeks. ⟨⟨But she was enough mistress of herself to shut the ⟨drawing⟩ \dining/ room door in case the servants were listening.⟩⟩ "What
    10† for a walk ← to bed
    11† He also flushed ← He flushed as red as she ⟨did⟩ was [*402*]
    16 \"I . . . dropped./ ← Her eyes dropped. She could not look him in the face.
    17† \: she was legacy-hunting/.
    18 \with passing tenderness/ ← tenderly
    24 looking ⟨at the ground.⟩ aside. [*403*]
    30 her. ⟨⟨But he had dreamt of ⟨another world⟩ other things.⟩⟩ She

35† As . . . goes, we ← ⟨And⟩ We

191 4† \\"I'll put it in prose."/
    \lived with/ ← stood

  5 for it. ⟨⟨This may be poetry, but it is business⟨."⟩ as well."⟩⟩\\"

  10 to him⟨, and though he was the obvious heir⟩ \at last/, he would not ⟨⟨pay \his aunt/ a little visit (⟨Stephen⟩ \the Wonham person/ was often away) or⟩⟩ even write ⟨her⟩ \his aunt/ a little note. {She rebuked him, angrily.} [*404*]

  14† \to our room/ [*405*]

  18 afternoon. ⟨By all that's holy, why⟩ Why

  † \he's my . . . mystery?"/

  23† rubbish⟨.⟩\! Give me . . . should know./"

  32 \then, and ⟨that⟩ this . . . gives us/ ← and ⟨I feel⟩ we are given

  33 \I took quite all the blame/ ← I didn't

192 2 before. ⟨His tolerance and her indifference had combined to keep the peace.⟩ In [*406*]

  5† the person ← him ⟨now⟩

  17† final insult ← final curse [*407; the opening words of the decapitated line preceding final are:*] quite square with the

  20 of ⟨superior⟩ cynical ploughboy

  25 moment. \And Stephen . . . Rickie,/

  27† \unknown/ [*408*]

  34† words, ⟨and Tilliard—or was it James?—had laughed at them:⟩ her

  † change ← poverty [*409*]

  39† \of Stephen/

193 2 wishes. ⟨Though a sincere Churchman, he severed his religion from his earthly desires. It⟩ \Religion/

  3 \good/ ← the infinite

  6 \endure the faces/ ← soften the hated features

  7 \the gloom/ ← front of him

  8† his brother. ← Stephen.

  9 awoke, ⟨screaming,⟩ having [*410*]

  10 pardon⟨.⟩\, and for ⟨sleep.⟩ rest./

CHAPTER 24

The twelve leaves of Chapter 24 (*411–422*) ought to be at least thirteen, since there is a gap between the fine black of *411* (*ends* 194:18 make) and the intermediate gray-black of the decapitated *412* (195:3–10). Probably *411* shows the correct chapter number partly by chance and partly because it is a late revision, matching the latest pages of Chapter 23 as well as each of the openings of Chapters 21 and 22. However, *412v* and *413v*, described above with Chapters 21 and 23, respectively, suggest that the division into Chapters 21–22 and the major revisions of Chapter 23 had been effected by the time Chapter 24 was first drafted. That is, the sequence of pages introduced by *412* and running through to *419* (*ends* 197:39) is the earliest extant series, interrupted only by *415* (195:37 arrived–196:12), which is a depedi-tated sheet, written in a blue-gray ink and obviously added to replace the bottom of the depeditated *414*. The only major verso, *491v*, now placed in Chapter 30 and decapitated in the depeditation of its recto, shows the intermediate gray-black ink of this early sequence and indicates that the missing sheet or sheets replaced a passage which showed Mrs Silt's visit to Dunwood House; this verso introduces the notes below. The last three pages of the chapter, *420–2*, are again in an intermediate black and, though slightly neater, could be part of the early sequence. But they must have been written after Forster decided to have Ansell visit the Jacksons rather than accept Rickie's invitation, which the surviving versos related to Chapter 27 show that he once did. Perhaps an earlier form of Chapter 24 was entirely recopied at a time when Forster was short of paper; *416* (*ends* 196:27 room,) shows, inverted at its bottom, a few deleted words which can be linked to Rickie's action in reaching for his aunt's letter in the next chapter (203:11): ⟨⟨bent ⟨towards this⟩ \swiftly/{toward} down to her⟩⟩. *417* (*ends* 197:7 he's) shows on its verso, inverted, a few lines related to the end of Chapter 6 in *A Room with a View* (vol. 3, Abinger Edition, pp. 67 and 214); only the first line was deleted:

⟨thing that has happened today.⟩
abruptly to the left. "Eccolo li!" he cried.
There he was: but \he was/ one good man, not two, and he not the right one.

[*491v:*] "We are not accustomed to carriages, Agnes, in our little house. I was only too thankful that the horse stood still. There I sat, in the dirty street, awaiting my gentleman's pleasure. He came out with two labourers, and again I waited ⟨⟨ ⟨till⟩ while they shook hands⟩⟩. He missed the step of the dog cart and scraped his shin to the knee."

"Hooray!"

"You would not say hooray if you had ⟨bee⟩ heard him —— ⟨⟨" And the poor little lady ⟨nearly cried⟩ \flushed/. "⟩⟩When he got in I said, rather unwisely, 'Well Mr Wonham, is this your idea of a 'sec'!' He grunted 'Do same few' I said 'I am not likely \ever/ to require the ⟨n[?]⟩ \attention/. Fancy if it had bolted!', and he said 'Fancy if it bolts now' and gave a lash and I didnt even dare to scream."

"What did Aunt Emily say?"

"As a matter of fact I never told her" said Mrs Silt, [. . .]

194 15   \to find/ ← and found to their dismay [*411*]
195 6   love ⟨(which he doubted—)⟩. [*412*]
    7   \(if . . . learn)/
  12† ⟨ever⟩ be published? [*413*]
  16 They ⟨⟨ ⟨put her trunk⟩ sent her trunk ⟨off⟩ to Sawston by Carter Paterson, and then⟩⟩ got into ⟨a Westminster⟩ \an/ omnibus
  22 Nature⟨—just your style⟩. He \agrees with you:/
  25 writing." ⟨⟨¶He did not contradict her. She quoted fragments of the Essays as they went up ⟨and down⟩ in the Stores lift⟨s⟩. ⟩⟩\She quoted fragments of the Essays [*414:*] as . . . lift./
  30† amid ladies ← amid people [*414*]
  32 \joints of meat/ ← meat on a spit
  34 belonged. ⟨He had always loathed the Stores.⟩
  36 \Herbert/ [*end 414; three deleted words of the new paragraph that followed* Widdrington." *survive at the tear:*] every evening writing:
196 6   personality⟨: perhaps we will show that corner to some one else.⟩. She [*415*]
  12 wife." [*end 415; deleted at the top of 416:*] ⟨⟨-ment seized her by both hands. "Sit down here: ⟨my w⟩ \this is/ my wife."⟩⟩ {us! he cried;}
  15 shrill ⟨piercing⟩ pleasant
  35 \He will never be a don. Never live in Cambridge, as we had hoped./[*417*]
197 3   \succeed?/ ← come out top?
  10 \Windsor/ ← Strand [*418*]
  18 \smile./ ← laugh. "I don't know a word about philosophy, Miss Ansell,

but I do know that the college is very badly off for scientists, and that the petal-counter is a good man."

19   I wish ⟨he⟩ \Stewart/ ⟨had gone to⟩ \had tried/ Oxford⟨.⟩ instead. ⟨That's all I know."⟩"

28† \will have none of us/ ← refuses [*419*]

35† How . . . compare? ← "Have you tried the ⟨draperies⟩ \Drapery department*?* said Agnes ⟨cheap⟩ sweetly.

198 1 \It was naughty . . . help it./ [*420*]

7 \glanced at him, but/ ← had no inclination to quarrel ⟨to-day⟩, and therefore tones. ⟨"How sorry I am for him!⟩ "Do

21 in all ways . . . self. ← offensive, patronising, tasteless⟨.⟩\, in all . . . self./ [*421*]

36† \, more dictatorial/ \she would think/ ← here her religion assisted her.

199 3 \a 'jollier man'./ ← another man. She had loved once, and once only. [*422*]

6 once only⟨, that gives all it has to one man, one woman, and can never give again. Les amours qui suivr⟩.

7 \it sprang . . . he/ ← he drew it out, and

12 that \hitherto/ ← that, throughout this story,

13 has ⟨departed.⟩ been withdrawn.

CHAPTER 25

The sixteen leaves of the much revised Chapter 25 (*423–438*) again show versos from both earlier and later chapters, but here the intermediate gray-blacks of the preceding chapters appear on only seven sheets: *423, 427, 432, 434, 436–8. 423* (*ends* 200:7), which shows **XXIV** changed to **XXV**, and *427* (201:27–33 my), both depeditated, preserve Harold versos from Chapter 13. *432* (203:27 lamb–32) and *434* (204:16 have–32 his), also depeditated and in a similar gray-black ink, are probably of the same early level. The three last leaves, *436–8* (*begins* 205:14 did), resemble the majority of those making up Chapter 24 and also show versos drawn from later chapters. *436v* preserves a page shown with Chapter 28 below, and *437v* a conclusion of Chapter 27. Both *438v* and its recto show half-sentences from Chapter 29, and *438v* also bears some bluish spelling trials of "chief". As in Chapter 24 it is difficult to know how much of an earlier draft of Chapter 25 might have been recopied on these leaves discarded from later chapters.

The remaining nine pages fall into three groups of three. A very fine-pointed gray-blue ink marks the next level, corrected in two other, later inks; these three pages are the depeditated *428* (*ends* 202:11), *433* (*begins* 203:33), and *435*, the last retaining space for another line or two. *424–6*, written in the bluish ink of *415* in the preceding chapter, are corrected in the fine gray-brown of *429–31*, which is also the ink of the latest pages in Chapter 26. *429* (*ends* 202:27), depeditated as an insert, appears to begin in blue and end in brown, indicating that the last two stages may have been one.

200 1 had ⟨just⟩ received \in the morning/ [*423*]

4† the June . . . Sawston. ← half way through the summer term.

8† talking of Stephen— ← mentioning ⟨a certain⟩ \Stephen—/ [*424*]

10† \last year/

13 \did not like/ ← greatly disliked

21† Drink. ← He drinks.

22† Dear! Really! ← Dear, dear

201 18 \alter a/ ← undertake [*426*]

21 \anything/ ← it all

22 \supposed them a/ ← taken them for a kindly

sorry \both/ for Mrs Failing ⟨but did not intend to be too hard on the beggar—⟩ and

27 \fellow/ ← person [*427*]

37† the formal ← an ordinary [*428*]

38 \will be there. Why we asked him here!/ ← is stopping there.

202 4 \As Agnes . . . to us./ ← I have been too rude to Jackson.

5† \I cannot put myself out for him./

8 \pay . . . term,/ ← come and stop,

14 opened ⟨the⟩ Mrs Silt's letter. ⟨His face turned white, and he gave something like a sob.⟩ [*429*]

31† formal invitation ← invitation⟨.⟩ to supper. [*430*]

32 It's you. ⟨No: no lies.⟩ It's you

34 \collapsed/ ← fizzled out

35† Why . . . excited? ← Why had he lost his temper?

38† like a ⟨little⟩ boy

203 1† \It's a libel./

9 \bully/ ← bewilder

35 \Only . . . thwarted by ⟨farce⟩ an interlude of farce./ [*433*]

38 \If you . . . you/ ← Have you quite

204 2† dreamt— ? ← \had a dream?/ ← \dreamt?/ ← fell asleep—?

3 \The ride where you/ ← You

7 \stray/ ← common

11† scale. ⟨But his anger against his wife blazed higher.⟩

14† He sighed. ← He shuddered violently.

\Had he ruined his ⟨only⟩ brother?/ ← Was he ⟨to blame or not?⟩ to blame for his brother's expulsion?

19 \of this deplorable affair/ ← and I agree with my sister [*434*]

20† most criminal ← \criminal/ ← arrant

22† \a person . . . on her,/

35 \was withering up/ ← simply did not care [*435*]

38 House⟨. He moved irresolutely towards the door. "And why have I never been⟩ ⟨, and his⟩\. His/ first remark was⟩\./ "Why ⟨why⟩ have . . . told?" \was . . . remark./

205 8 \businesslike statement to/ ← clean breast of the whole affair to

† \of the position/

13 \would be/ ← was [*435; deleted at the top of 436 is a variant:*] ⟨⟨ ⟨was⟩ \would be/ as loathsome as to be rich himself. If the money ever⟩⟩

15 \troubled himself/ ← meddled ← withdrew from affairs

22 \her treachery/ ← the ⟨letter⟩ poem

27† \and had never asked to know/

32 \halo/ ← radiance

206 4 \had accustomed herself to it./ ← was used to it. [*437*]

5 hear. ⟨I know, in your kind way⟩ I have tried

7 \She wants . . . Elliot name./

8 \She only told/ ← She let it loose on

13 \again with a sigh/ ← by the window⟨.⟩, still a very beautiful woman

14 \orderly mind/

15† She is . . . no more." ← \She is always laughing.⟨"⟩/\She actually finds
    our ignorance amusing."/ ← ⟨How can she find anything to laugh at?"⟩
    \She can/ laugh [*order obscure here*]

19 kissed her. ⟨She thanked him.⟩ ¶⟨⟨"Thank you, boy. ⟨That's the kind
    of thing that helps me to go on.⟩\"/⟩⟩ \She thanked him./ [*438*]

22 it⟨, as it were,⟩ with averted

25 \seraph/ ← spirit

26 \who touches/ ← ⟨whatever it may be, compelling⟩ \who/ compels

27 \seraph/ ← spirit ← proc

29 fail ⟨to be them again.⟩ in

  † function ← duty

CHAPTER 26

The twenty-five leaves of Chapter 26 (*439–463*) break off before the end of the
chapter; no manuscript exists for the passages after 216:8. Only a few pages, two of
them versos, show the earlier gray-blacks. The early rectos are *441* (207:22 old
fashioned–208:5), decapitated and depeditated, *460* (214:29 is–215:1 whose) and
462 (215:17 When–29), both depeditated; they reflect the earlier calendar, showing
a deleted "leafless" and football replaced by cricket. The early versos are *459v* and
463v, each inverted and undeleted; they open the notes below. Each of their rectos,
459 (214:13 to say–29 what) and *463* (*ends* 216:8), is an insert, *463* showing space
for another line or two and *459* having been depeditated to remove blank space.
Their ink is much bluer, and *458* (*begins* 213:38), decapitated and matching *459*,
shows on its verso a fragment of the Harold version of Chapter 14. The similar
bluish ink of *444–5* (208:39 the–209:11) and *447* (209:15 star–27 intervals), all three
of which bear Harold versos from Chapter 13, indicates that Forster had written a
wintry version of Chapter 26, in the gray-black ink of its earliest pages, before he
changed Harold to Stephen; *453* (211:39–212:16) and the depeditated *455* (212:35–
213:5 hedge) are perhaps bluish enough to join this level of revision. The other
pages are written in finer-pointed ink, sometimes blacker or bluer but not easily
distinguishable except for the fine gray-brown of the latest inserts, *452* (*begins* 211:16)
and *456–7*, similar to the latest pages in Chapter 25.

    The layers of revision in Chapter 26 can be illustrated by the development of the
paragraph opening deleted at the top of the decapitated *441*. It reads:

    ⟨⟨Ansell sat in the ⟨leafless⟩ garden, reading the ⟨essays⟩ \Essays/ of
Anthony Eustace Failing, which had at last appeared. The thought⟩⟩\⟨*Want*'⟩
⟨was rather interesting. It bore the Tols⟩ As for the Essays, they were rather
interesting. The thought/ was somewhat

Want looks older in its ink than the rest of the insertion, where the ink suggests that
Forster broke off at "Tols" and rewrote as he realized that he could give knowledge of
Mr Failing's preferred title to Stephen. Then he moved to a one-sentence opening in a
relatively black ink: "As for the book." This stands alone on *448v*, undeleted but
inverted. It reappears, augmented, at the bottom of *439* (*ends* 207:17), added when the
"was somewhat" of *441* had not yet been deleted: "As for the book. The thought".
Later *440* was added, together with *442* (*ends* 208:17); both show the pen and ink
of *443* but expand two lines deleted at its top:

    "Morning!" said a voice behind him.

He saw no reason to reply to this.

443 shares some content with *459v*, the first of the early versos, which opens at a torn-through line of which only the first two words are decipherable; the other early verso, *463v*, approximates *453*.

[*459v:*] administered inside [. . .] that afternoon, and regarded his visit as sheer waste of time. All the inmates had laboured—evidently in concert—to 'make the visit go'. They had never left him alone, nor in silence, for one moment. Agnes had displayed a brisk pity that made him wish to wring her neck. Mr Pembroke pat-ronised with ⟨large round eyes and⟩ \a sorrowful voice and/ large round eyes. Till he had met these people he had never been told that his life was a failure. But apparently they thought so: they would not have ⟨had⟩ \asked/ him to stop if it was a success.

He was honestly indifferent to their opinion, but not to their influence over the opinions of Rickie. They had not merely ⟨captured⟩ \silenced/ him: they were winning over him a spiritual victory. One evening, during a brief hour that they were alone together, Ansell had tried, very tentatively, to introduce sincerity into their intercourse. Rickie had taken alarm at once: he could not even bear allusion to their Cambridge days, and he had taken care that they should not be ⟨left⟩ alone again. In many ways Ansell was conceited, but he was never proud of being right: he had foreseen this state of things ⟨of⟩ from the [. . .]

[*463v:*]"Are you stopping here⟨?"⟩, like myself?"

"Now you're asking!" he said smiling, and kept the smile rigid on his face, as if he meditated thus. He ran a ⟨thumb⟩ \finger/ up his bristly cheek and murmured ⟨"wanted⟩ \"Wanted/ shaving."

"Mrs Elliot must be in soon. \It is very unusual for her to leave one alone./ She has gone out to see about something for the Waifs and Strays."

This information appeared to amuse him.

"Mr Pembroke, Elliot, and forty \ravenous/ boys arrive at a quarter to one."

"Do you know Elliot?"

Ansell nearly answered 'Not at all' but restrained himself and spoke as follows: "I knew him very well at Cambridge, but I havn't seen any thing of him for over two years."

"Then you aren't what you may call a friend."

"I'm what I should call a friend."

⟨⟨For a long time they kept silence. Ansell began to think that the man, in spite of his blatant healthiness, was nice. He was the kind of person one could live with⟨.⟩—absolutely flawless as far as he went.⟩⟩

"Do you know Mrs Elliot?"

"A little."

"What exactly is Elliot like?"

This was too much, and Ansell ⟨told him to⟩ \hinted that he must/ find out for himself.

⟨"You might tell a fellow."⟩

⟨"Why do you want to know?"⟩

207 1† was actually sitting ← sat [*439*]
 19† \superfluous/ [*440*]
208 6† repeated the voice ← the voice repeated [*442*]
 19† \felt bound to speak. He/ [*443*]
 21† indignantly, . . . deep in ← ⟨to see a young man pacing⟩ \indignantly, . . . rudeness. A young man was pacing/ the gravel path with his hands in
 29† neck. Maud had not exaggerated. ← neck, while

39 \vineyards/ ← \waters/ ← heart [*444*]
209 1 \many facts to/ ← deal to
   2 \a suitable quantity/ ← a very great deal
  11 \⟨firs⟩ first confronted with the ⟨great⟩ world/ ← confronted with the
     ⟨modern⟩ {'practical'} \great/ ⟨world.⟩ {idea} \world:/ Woe to the
     practical man who fails! It were better for [*end 445*]
  15 Solitude [*end 446*] ← [*deleted on 447:*] ¶Returning to the book, he read
     ⟨the⟩ \The/ Essay on Gaps. It was a curious ⟨thing⟩ \production/, not
     without literary charm. Solitude
     \pacing the fields of England/ ← and majestic
  19 profani'. ⟨⟨ ⟨All life, whether sacred or profane, obeys him. I am⟩ \Now
     ⟨I am⟩ my soul is/alone!" he cries. But ⟨he⟩ \it/is not, for he is ⟨thinking
     of⟩ \always comparing it to the souls of/ the people whom he has
     excluded. "How much better I am! How much nearer to Nature⟩⟩ But
  20 \enjoy himself/ ← admire his ⟨possessions⟩ \scenery/
  21 \the absent Profane:/ ← those whom he has excluded from it:
  31† the ⟨young⟩ man [*448*]
  32† \youth and/ impudence
  37† admiration ← thought [*449*]
210 7† little brute ← \brute/ ← young man
   8 a ⟨merciless⟩ blow
  10 philosopher's ⟨oblong⟩ {oval} skull
  20 awkwardly. ⟨⟨Behind them ⟨rose⟩ the lobelia pie⟨, now⟩ \was/ a hash.⟩⟩
     With [*450*]
  32 said Ansell ⟨somewhat puzzled⟩.
  35 \you've heard of him./ ← you know who I mean by that.
211 3 other ⟨⟨with ⟨illera⟩ illiterate awe⟩⟩. "Same [*451*]
   4 \weighed/ ← held
     hands. ⟨⟨"And same inside ⟨naturally."⟩ ⟨I'll⟩ {of course."} \as likely
     as not."/⟩⟩
  15 me! ⟨⟨I've been alone in fields as much as most ⟨chaps⟩, if you mean
     that."⟩⟩\"/
  35† says I know ← told you I knew [*452*]
  36† his . . . link. ← the Failings.
212 5 idea ⟨of one deliberately luxurious,⟩ of [*453*]
   7 bliss⟨, of a being capable of great physical happiness⟩.
   8 \surprised/ ← interested
  13 died. \I . . . money."/ ← died.⟨"⟩ I daren't buy any."
  24 ¶⟨"Hard luck."⟩ His teeth [*454*]
  37 \He/ was alarmed ← The young man was genuinely alarmed [*455*]
213 1 \could buy/ ← \bought/ ← had
   3 murmured⟨⟨, adding ⟨"W⟩ "Do you know any more?" ¶"No."⟩⟩. ¶The
   5† head of Agnes ← heads of Rickie and Agnes
   7† After . . . All the heads ← The heads [*456*]
  10† had left any message ← possessed a card
  30 thought⟨, nor god like beauty⟩. Yet [*457*]
  39 \over the farm hands/ ← about the village [*458*]
     right. ⟨Take a boy you've played with⟩" He
214 6 \young man/ ← \baby/ ← young man
  14† \mine's Wonham,/ [*459*]
  20† Mr Wonham ← the \man/ ← the \young man/ ← the \baby/ ← the
     young man

20 \should . . . nephew./ ← after his expulsion from Cadover, should have ⟨made for⟩ \run to/ Sawston.

31 more, ⟨as one does,⟩ and ⟨the end of it was she nipped me, and here I am.⟩ \in/ the end \I was nipped/ [*460*]

32 but ⟨m a⟩ ⟨football shorts⟩ \flannels/

38† a hundred ← \fifty/ ← twenty
\London/ ← Salisbury

39 \December/ ← June

215 1 \I didn't care really./ ← It was pure bluff. [*461; torn through on 460:*] ⟨⟨son I am.' I had no notion that she knew: I ⟨was only⟩ \didn't/ ⟩⟩

5† stare. ⟨⟨By this time the sun was off the country and looking ⟨at⟩ \into/ the fields I saw—" He stopped. Ansell never heard what he saw, but apparently it made him turn back to Mrs Failing and renew his command with violence. "⟩⟩Then [*461*]

6† \after all,/

7 \rolled/ ← flung

8 steps⟨⟨—it ⟨went⟩ \goes/ 'dob-dob-dob'—⟩⟩ and

9 opened ⟨it with the four of them looking on⟩ \it/

11 \comic/ ← funny

12† were both cricket teams ← was the ⟨football⟩ cricket team

14 \turned out/ ← sacked

20 them.⟨"⟩\They . . . mine."/ [*462*]

22 \rather/ ← a little

34 \taken/ ← pinched [*463*]
pouch. ⟨Don't think you'll get it again.⟩ The

35† hundred pounds ← fifty pound [*twice*]

216 3 his ⟨strong healthy⟩ body
suit⟨⟨. ⟨"Am I to read this packet of papers?" he asked. Not the baby. The man.⟩ "May I read this packet of papers?" he asked.⟩⟩—and

5† frank, proud, ← ⟨broad⟩ \clear/, ⟨strong⟩ \proud,/
and⟨, if truth is beauty,⟩ beautiful\, if truth is beauty/. ⟨All the passions and a few of the virtues looked out of it—just⟩ Of

6 tact⟨⟨, ⟨such a face knew little, but⟩ \or the suburban virtues/ or the lower dignities,⟩⟩ such

8† he said ← he asked [*end 463*]

CHAPTER 27

Only three verso fragments of Chapter 27 survive: *437v*, now in Chapter 25; *494v*, now in Chapter 30; and *A20v*, on the back of the second manuscript sheet of XXIX, which is described with Chapter 28 below. *A20v* is the latest of the three, inverted and undeleted but abandoned in mid-sentence, and written in a fine-pointed brown ink resembling that of the later sheets in Chapters 25 and 26. The other two were written in an ink similar to the intermediate gray-blacks but slightly bluer; they reflect the stage when Ansell was staying at Dunwood House rather than with the Jacksons. Both are full quartos, now inverted; *437v*, undeleted, shows the blank space of a chapter ending, while *494v* was crossed through. The two earlier drafts here follow *A20v*, in narrative order.

[*A20v:*] "No."

And Ansell, thinking he had not been told, turned angrily on Agnes, and

[*494v:*] "Did you see that man⟨?⟩" he asked, "who came to call⟨"⟩?" Rickie knew at once that the game was up. But Agnes, before he could stop her, replied "Man? What man? What was his name?"

"I don't know."

This encouraged her and she said "Oh I remember. Thank you. Yes: we did see the young fellow."

"Where ⟨he⟩ is he?"

⟨Agnes grew nervous.⟩ "He went ⟨off⟩ as soon as the [*sic*] business was finished. How did you come across him?"

"Because we sat talking together, for half an hour, in the garden."

"I am sorry." said Rickie \gravely/. "We have introduced you to the family skeleton. I must ask you not to mention it; ⟨I kno⟩ we are taking steps to prevent ⟨my⟩ Stephen Wonham from mentioning it either. I fear that you will not approve of this, but we are quiet conventional people, and have, after careful consideration, decided not to acknowledge the connection—"

"—⟨without giving⟩ \nor to give/ him lunch."

"Why should we give him lunch?"

"For one reason, Mrs Elliot, because he has had no breakfast."

[*437v:*] way."

"I think you shall, Rickie. Good bye old man——⟨it isn't any⟩ \it's no/ good."

"What do you mean——

"No good talking. We have forgotten one another's words.⟨"⟩ Don't talk—We shall only upset each other. ⟨Just give⟩ \Give/ me your hand and say good bye."

"Good bye?" cried Herbert, bustling in from his work. "But you don't go till the afternoon."

Stewart moved slowly ⟨at⟩ \to/ the door. He believed in a spiritual kingdom on earth, and ⟨knew⟩ \thought/ that his friend was \now/ excluded from it for ever.

"Good bye, old man; ⟨and there's one thing more for me to tell you. You've made a mistake.⟩ \he repeated "There's one thing more I ought to tell you—a terrible thing./ He isn't your father's son at all. He's the son of your mother."

CHAPTER 28

Grouped here with Chapter 28 are the remnants of the discarded XXIX and *436v*, which may once have followed XXIX or been part of an earlier draft of a differently developed XXVIII or XXIX. Chapter 28 is composed of two sheets, *464-5*, both depeditated. *464 (ends 227:12)* shows a fine-pointed gray-black ink, the same as that of the quickly aborted draft opening that survives on *A43v*, which is described among the sheets of Chapter 31. *465* was written very neatly in a fluent gray-brown; its final paragraph, undeleted but omitted later, stands complete before a neat depeditation with no sign of any further paragraph, but no extra space to mark the chapter end.

227   5† \to be/ [*464*]

      6 \divine/ ← outside herself

      7 \will be/ ← is

      8 \may have been/ ← seemed

    10† treasures ← things

        The face ⟨on it⟩, however ← That face, however

    12 dead. ⟨⟨ ⟨They fail⟩ \When they/ ⟩⟩ [*deleted as the last words on 464*]

    23† world? ⟨⟨¶Here is the problem for Rickie. In his poverty, which coinage ⟨will he⟩ \is he to/ choose?⟩⟩ [*465*]

[*The text of XXIX given here follows that of the two typescript leaves, A21-A22 (numbered 342 and 343 by the typist), which is identical to that of the manuscript sheets, A19-A20, except that the typescript provides more commas and advances to an unsigned fourth letter. A19 holds the manuscript of the first letter complete; the last word on A20 is the "please" of the third letter. The manuscript is very neat; the only change occurred in the third letter, when the first few words of the third sentence, "I think though that they", were deleted to allow the present second sentence to follow the first, and then recopied. The typescript shows no corrections, either by author or printer, and one error, corrected here: "did he" rather than "he did" in the third letter.]*

[*A21:*]

XXIX.

Dunwood House,
Sawston.

Sunday afternoon.

Dear Mrs Failing,

You will be sorry to hear that Rickie is extremely ill. My sister is distracted, and the task of writing to you devolves on me. I have no time for more, but beg you to send, by return of post, full details about Stephen Wonham, and his parents. Our life here has broken up very suddenly. I do not know what to do, nor how to act for the best. It is at the doctor's suggestion that I write to you for full details.

Believe me,
Yours truly,
Herbert Pembroke.

Sawston,
Sunday afternoon.

Dear Rickie,

What do you want? I think I could talk to you now, and shall call to-morrow.

Yours ever,
S. A.

[*A22:*]

Dunwood House,
Sunday evening.

Dear Stewart,

Thank you for your letter. It is wonderfully good of you. I think though that they will not want you to see me, and perhaps all had better wait till my aunt writes. I dare not think out what has happened or I should go mad. Perhaps you got the story wrong—or he did—or it is one of my aunt's jokes. I expect he is not my brother at all. There is nothing really wrong with me. Thank you again, and God bless you, but really you will hurt me less if you stop away, and please not another letter like that. I could not bear it. Everyone here is extremely kind.

Yours affectionately,
Rickie Elliot.

Sawston,
Monday morning.

Dear Rickie,

I think I could talk to you now, and shall call to-day. But what do you want?

365

[436v, on a full quarto in Chapter 25, shows an ink very similar to that of the early fragments of Chapter 27. It is inverted but undeleted as a whole, although the extended line-by-line deletions of the central section look comprehensive. The last paragraph was copied into Chapter 20 (see 181:38*). 436v:]* that anything had happened, Herbert, full of little plans and formulae, and between them Rickie, free it is true, but with the freedom of insanity. He performed his duties at the school, but that was all: his life had become a chaos of horror and remorse. In time he might become what the world calls 'definitely mad': to Ansell the change would not ⟨seem⟩ \be/ an important one.

⟨⟨"Is it true" said Widdrington, who had stolen up, "that Dunwood House is haunted?"

"Yes. Some day you will hear by what. Their secret is known by ⟨seven⟩ \six/ people\ at least/. It will leak out⟨."⟩ \in time./

"Who are they?"

"The three at Sawston, Rickie's aunt, myself, and one other."

"Who is the other?"

"The ghost.⟩⟩

He strolled out for a breath of fresh air but, as usual, he only breathed depression. The comfort of books deserted him when he paced among those marble goddesses and gods. The eye of an artist finds ⟨comfort⟩ \pleasure/ in texture and poise, but he could only think of the vanished incense and deserted temples beside an unfurrowed sea. Into this artificial light and heat, Beauty, leaving the sun, had retreated, and the Spirit of Life, headless, armless and mutilated, was arranged into schools to [. . .]

CHAPTER 29

Of the eighteen leaves in Chapter 29 (*467–484*; *466* holds the part-title, "Wiltshire"), only the first (*ends* 231:8 mistook), headed XXX, and the last (*begins* 239:28 Nothing) are late, written in the neat and fluent gray-brown of *465*. The other leaves show a fine-pointed, rusty-black, scratchy ink most similar to that of the later sheets of the Harold version of Chapters 10–14. On *483* "Harold" has been changed to "Stephen" (239:19), and Robert's surname, Wonham, has been deleted throughout; the bulk of the chapter was probably composed after the original revelation that Harold was Rickie's brother. There are three versos, *438v*, *474v*, and *479v*. *479v* was used to list the characters in four columns, bracketed into three groups. Written crosswise on the page, the columns read:

Mr Elliot ⎤	Mrs Failing	Ansell ⎤	Harold ⎤
Mrs Elliot ⎬	Mr Pembroke	His family ⎬	Rickie ⎦
Mr Failing ⎱	Miss Pembroke	Tillyard ⎦	
Robert ⎦	Gerald		

"Gerald" looks as though it was appended as an afterthought, still in the same ink. *474v* shows one deleted, inverted, unfinished, illegible word, centred as a title and beginning "Schoo" or "Schem". *438v*, now in Chapter 25, bears undeleted words recopied at the top of *481* (237:35): "perfect health . . . days." But *438v* also bears words from Chapter 29 inverted on its recto, *438*. These closed the sentence at the foot of *479* before it was revised; see 237:12 below. Then the sequence becomes puzzling, because the deleted words which once opened *481* appear to be a clean copy of those now opening *480*. Apparently Forster abandoned the half-sentence now inverted on *438* and took a new sheet, now *480* (237:13 try–237:34 that more than), and wrote the rest of the paragraph to suit the revision of the sentence ending *479*. Then he seems to have copied the same passage, as revised, at the top of another new sheet, now *481*, there continuing with Mrs Failing's reaction to the letter (237:37). Deciding then to add Whitman's lines from "Song of Myself", he used *480* to do this, running over onto what is now *438v* to finish the passage. But then he copied the brief run-over onto the top of *481*, above the now deleted end-of-paragraph there. Or he may have attempted to redraft these deleted lines in copying them to *480* in the addition of the Whitman passage and found that he preferred to restore the deleted readings; the differences in the lines are listed under *480* below. Presumably the partly used sheet that became *438* lingered with Chapter 29 until Forster took it for the revision of Chapter 25. In any case all the inks are well within the range of the scratchy, rusty-black majority of the chapter, and are unlike those on the leaves in the surrounding chapters. Two other leaves are inserts, in a particularly fine-pointed version of the rusty-black but again well within its range: *469* (231:28 The–232:5 spoke) replaces the decapitated top of *470*, and *477* (236:9–14) replaces the bottom of *476* and top of *478*.

231   8   mistook [*467*] ← [*deleted on 468:*] ⟨⟨¶A young farmer fell in love with Mrs Elliot on the occasion of her bridal visit to Cadover. He was there on business, but ⟨was stopping⟩ \stopped/ in the house, just ⟨as if he was⟩ \like/ a gentleman, and people generally took⟩⟩

    15†   interested, ⟨questioned him effusively, and⟩ \but/

    18†   she ⟨had⟩ observed

    22   \Byron/ ← Tennyson [*twice*]

    25   \filled with/ ← shaken by

    and ⟨looked in his face and smiled.⟩ liked him.

232 12   a ⟨mystic symbol, the⟩ symbol [*470*]

    16   then." ⟨She was really talking to \the poet/ Virgil, though neither of them knew it.⟩

    17†   ¶⟨To say he 'fell' in love is wrong.⟩ He advanced into ⟨it⟩ \love/

    32   most. ⟨⟨ ⟨"Thank God⟩ \I'm glad/ you've told me. But ⟨why didn't you tell⟩ \I wish you'd have told/ me before?"⟩⟩ [*471*]

233   3†   that a chance person was ← you were

    5   \A woman of her sort/ ← She

    21†   must try ← must go away⟨⟨ ⟨.⟩—to work." He took him by both hands. "Promise me that you will⟩⟩ \and/ try [*472*]

    22†   \her/

    23   try⟨⟨ ⟨."⟩, ⟨Mr Failing."⟩ sir⟩⟩."

    26   straight. ← a straight chap, Mr Failing.

    37   wasn't. ⟨⟨As a matter of fact, he was extremely ⟨handsome, and some⟩ good looking, and something besides. Or⟨,⟩ perhaps his good looks continued within, and the ⟨strength⟩ \freshness/ and beauty of his body were also in his soul.⟩⟩ For [*473*]

    38   Wiltshire ⟨and was kind to his sisters⟩,

234   2   \and perhaps . . . crops./ ← when she came with her horrible baby.

    3†   \Mr Failing . . . sentences./

    16†   experience ← experiences

    22†   hoped . . . would ← knew . . . will [*474*]

    30†   \some time or other/

    32†   admirer. ⟨So it was, that when he was ready, and did call he found her ready to meet him.⟩

235   6†   child ← orphan [*475*]

    8   \sarcastic/ ← amusing

    11   \not even . . . polite./ ← very rude.

18 come, ⟨and by this time she loved him dearly. And⟩ \and/
24 \ July/ ← June
34† so ⟨easy and⟩ respectfully [*476*]
35† hands⟨, you'ld be in my arms and all over."⟩—" ← hands, you'ld be ⟨out of⟩ in my arms and ⟨⟨out of the house⟨.⟩ ⟨besides."⟩ as well.⟩⟩ {never never undo them.} \all over."/

236 7 \discuss Mr Elliot./ ← bring in my husband.
9 ¶⟨She declared afterwards that she swore horribly. At all events he was conquered, and turned to go.⟩ {He was conquered.} But [*477*]
15† said that he loved her. ← spoke. "⟨Because⟩ I love her. ⟨Because⟩ I want to ⟨take her with me."⟩ carry her off." [*478*]
23 error? ⟨Take her, my dear sir, take her.⟩"
28 repulsed her. {Robert hummed strangely, like a purring lion.}
30† a little ← some afternoon

237 3† had ⟨just⟩ left [*479*]
4 \all traces. At midnight/ he ← them. Wonham had planned it carefully and left not a trace behind ⟨him⟩. ⟨Mr Elliot⟩ \Having/ hunted till one in the morning, ⟨and then⟩ \he/
7 \It . . . there./ ← asking who would bring an action.
13 \or else we shall/ ← if he wants to: [*end 479; inverted on 438:*] otherwise we bring one against him.
\try/ ← bring [*480, opening words; the deleted passage on 481 (see above) opens with* bring]
15 \We are/ ← I am [*480; 481 shows* We are]
or \your wife/ ← or Mrs Failing [*480; 481 shows* and your wife]
16 \ordinary/ ← like other [*480; 481 shows* ordinary]
19 \intrigued/ ← \piqued/ ← baffled [*480*]
21† living ← for \being/ ← for long walks
23 detail \. It/ grew ← detail, ⟨but⟩ \being/ a placid rapture, if such a thing can be, ⟨embracing⟩ \which embraced/ all the universe and ⟨d⟩ ⟨growing⟩ \grew/

238 3 disgusting ⟨and intolerable⟩, and [*481*]
7 replied \her husband/ ← he replied with great solemnity
18 speaks ⟨will not be brought about by⟩"—she
23 \He . . . continued./ "I ← ¶She was ⟨startled⟩ furious. ¶"I [*482*]
26 yet⟨⟨ ⟨: she often goes away suddenly for visits⟩. Frederick has invented some story of a sick friend that holds water—⟨as⟩ a sick friend abroad by some lucky chance—and of a telegram that she has sent, explaining⟩⟩. If
29 \interrupted/ ← shouted
31† There was . . . back to him? ← ⟨When they arrived, things were simpler than he expected.⟩ \By the time they arrived,/ ⟨⟨Robert had been drowned ⟨out bathing. There was really nothing to ⟨say⟩ \do/.⟩.⟩⟩ {the situation had altered.} \Robert was dead./ It was ⟨an⟩ \as/ appalling a tragedy as one can well conceive, yet Mrs Elliot still walked majestically and her eyes were tranquil ⟨as the stars. "Why are you so unhappy?" she asked them "It is only my sorrow.⟩. "Has Frederick begun to divorce me [*483:*] yet?\" she asked. "/I hope that he will not delay." ¶"I have a message" said Mr Failing. "He will receive you back.⟨"⟩ \\⟨Before he knew what⟩ \And he did not know/ that you were alone⟨."⟩ when he sent it."//

239 14 \though . . . stipulations/
25† her lover sank . . . embrace, ← ⟨Robert⟩ \her lover/ lay ⟨⟨dead ⟨before her⟩.⟩⟩ \drowned/, the water glistening upon his outspread hands,

27† had sunk ← had died ← was dead

CHAPTER 30

The twenty-one leaves of Chapter 30 (*485–505*), labelled n - 2 as well as XXXI, resemble Chapters 25 and 26 in being a patchwork of different inks, fragmented sheets and versos. The sequence is much like that in Chapter 26. The earliest ink is an uneven gray-black which appears on the depeditated opening sheet, *485* (*ends* 241:13 world), on *493* (243:28 and–244:7 also), and on *488v*, a draft of *487* (241:18–242:5 my). Then an uneven blue appears on five pages, *487*, *488*(*ends* 242:19), *491* (243:8 He–18), *494* (*ends* 244:25 Why), and *495* (*ends* 244:30), all of which show versos. *487v* and *495v* bear fragments of Chapter 13, *491v* a part of Chapter 24, and *494v* part of Chapter 27. Two fragmented leaves of shiny, yellower paper, *501* (246:19 humbug–30) and *504* (247:20 For–28 the), show bluish ink and may date from the same level as the uneven blue, since they too are succeeded by a clear, fine-pointed gray-blue which was in its turn succeeded by the fine-pointed brown of the latest sheets, *497–8* (245:9 He–32 northwards) and *503* (247:8–20 these). These latest sheets show two undeleted passages, omitted from the novel, which were perhaps efforts to develop the idea that Stephen might become "poetical" when parted from "the things he loved" (p. 242). One further verso passage, on *A49v* (see Chapter 31 below), written in the fine blue-gray of *502*, could have been a draft of the page that *503* replaced and is shown below at 247:8. In manuscript the chapter ends at 248:2, with space remaining on *505*; the last two paragraphs were added later.

241 1 \\had one ⟨impulse⟩ \instinct/ // ← was shaken by impulses [*485*]
\\that ⟨worried⟩ {puzzled} \troubled/ him.// ← that he did not try to understand.
2 \it seemed . . . he was/ ← he wondered how he had become
7† would ⟨undress and⟩ bathe
8 run ⟨naked⟩ in the ⟨midst⟩ mist
† mist ⟨till he was warm⟩.
10† there be . . . returned? ← he be 98, while acres of stuff around him ⟨was⟩ \were/ ⟨only⟩ \down to/ 50?
13 \loveable/ ← triumphant
into a ⟨⟨delightful ⟨world⟩ but impassive⟩⟩ passive
world? ⟨⟨[*deleted at the depeditation of 485:*] ¶He had other impulses—a ⟨keen⟩ ⟨bitter sense of justice, a keen belief⟩ \a hatred of the cynicism that comes from slackness/ ⟩⟩
15 \grave injury to/ ← hurting [*486*]
17† appeased. ⟨⟨He read Haeckel, Mr Blatchford, and other specialists. They ⟨hit the point.⟩ \explained things/ ⟨in a dozen ways⟩. Then the sun went down, and it became too dark to read.⟩⟩
24† Virgil ← ⟨Aeneas⟩ \the Georgics/ [*487*]
27 doom? ⟨⟨Ah for the dust and the clamour and the dogs! Ah for the ⟨little⟩ \nests of/ pink mice!⟩⟩ But
28† a pleasant woman ← who brought chocolates
30 will⟨, trusting his wife in this; and the mother was still alive.⟩\; his wife had promised to ⟨do this⟩ see to this./
242 1 \: she had none to leave/.
[*Approximating 487 is 488v:*] In their rare but intimate conversations she asked him to watch over her son. ⟨"He cannot grow up like other men. It is⟩ He ⟨promised and said⟩ \answered/ "I will watch, but I will ⟨do nothing. Such a boy must find

out life for himself.">⟩ teach him nothing except a little Latin. Such a boy must ⟨find out⟩ \discover/ the rest of life for himself." ⟨He watched and found the child⟩ In watching, he found the only pleasure of his declining years. He saw the child grow up strong, beautiful, and prosaic, blind to the Graces, blind to ⟨t⟩ Virgil, ⟨because⟩ but clinging ⟨from the first⟩ \passionately/ to the ⟨things⟩ \facts/ that Virgil loved. ⟨⟨He saw him ⟨fail him to grasp so u⟩ spend long days with poor people⟩⟩ \He saw him as the Hope of the World, dancing on the pediment of Cadover./ He loved him dearly, but in his calm wisdom was content to receive no love in return. Some day—though he should never see it—the boy would be a man and perhaps would understand.

Chance ⟨through⟩ threw Stephen into the power of Mrs Failing. Mr Failing, in his will, had made no provision for him, ⟨since⟩ trusting his wife in this; and the boy's mother was still alive and well. Then came Mr Elliot's death, and before the new home was created, the death of Mrs Elliot followed. A grave in [. . .]

6 \meet/ ← ⟨become ac⟩ fall on each other's necks [*488*]

8† twelve ← thirteen

9 lived ⟨at Cadover, or, to be accurate,⟩ in
   Life ⟨was delightful. It⟩ had

18 negligible. ⟨Nothing but private agreement.⟩ Nothing

35 \a cloudless spirit/ ← a placid mind [*489*]

38† he knew. ⟨He was not romantic, if this alone is romance.⟩ ← he ⟨should know⟩ \knew/. He . . . romance. ⟨⟨Mrs Failing, as she grew older, began to get ⟨bored with⟩ \tired of/ him.⟩⟩ [*490*]

39 \quarrel between them/ ← crisis

243 1† his personal origin ← himself and whence he came

5 as a ⟨⟨materialist ⟨and started⟩. For a short period he preached the new gospel in the village, to the horror of the vicar and the ⟨ala⟩ delight of Mrs Failing. One night she heard him arguing with⟩⟩ materialist.

6 \tore . . . reprints,/ ← ⟨beca⟩ made the sixpenny reprints into pipe spills, \never . . . again./ ← was never so amusing again.

8 \fixed himself up/ ← took to philosophy [*The sentence replaces a passage deleted on 491:*] ⟨⟨¶Trouble gathered slowly. ⟨He⟩ \For one thing he/ ⟨began⟩ \took/ to drink. Why not?⟩⟩
   \He knew of no reason/ ← \There was no reason against it./

10 nobody. ⟨Nor was he drunk often.⟩ Here

15† conceivable ← possible

17 \as often as Agnes suggested./ ← often.

18† quarrel gathered elsewhere ← trouble ⟨lay elsewhere⟩ ⟨gathered elsewhere⟩ was social ← came from the farm

19 \Presentable/ ← ⟨⟨ ⟨She⟩ \Mrs Failing/ had been too idle to educate him ⟨properly⟩{, and it never struck her that he had educated himself and adopted}. The house and the country were large, and he grew up in either as he liked. She had no idea that ⟨he⟩ \his manhood/ would ⟨ever⟩ choose between them.⟩⟩ Prominent [*492*]

20† comes ← should come

26† the germ of ← for all the world like

27 \Mrs Failing/ ← the houses [*end 492; deleted at the top of 493:*] ⟨⟨would be fun in life always and that they, like rich people, had a right ⟨not to grow old⟩ \to keep young/. "They won't settle" said Mr Wilbraham. "They're wanting things. Out they go." Then Stephen ⟨flew at⟩ \came to/ Mrs Failing⟩⟩

32† \about So-and-so/

† Mr Wilbraham blazed up. ← ⟨But he⟩ {who} \He/ worried her even
more.

244 10† you . . . door ← no proper drainage [*494*]

14 \"I am . . . farm."/

16 memoir ⟨in peace⟩. ⟨"Democracy, you know, is that form of government
in which all power is in the hands of a single democrat. I am more bored
than you think over the farm."⟩ In ⟨a fit of⟩ \her/

19† wretch of a ← tiresome

20 \more criminal/ ← worse than it had ⟨ha⟩ ever seemed before

21 \casually/ ← reluctantly

24 \an odd/ ← a furious

29 water—." ⟨He continued to fondle the chalk.⟩ ⟨He clenched his hand on
the chalk. And a⟩ A lump [*495*]

35 \trivial/ ← shadowy [*496, twice*]

245 4 \When . . . away./ ← ⟨So⟩ \When they wronged him/ he threw up his
hands and went under.

7† horrible ← filthy

8† The air seemed stuffy. ← ⟨The weather was sultry, or he would have
walked.⟩ The weather was ⟨sultry⟩ \airless/.

9† He ⟨looked around him with a new disgust. "Drains!" he thought, and⟩
spat [*497*]

17 sort. ⟨That was all.⟩ He

† complicated ← whole

22† pay back the friends ← make money. His soul would not be his own until
he repaid the men

26† He was . . . money. ← How they will muddle things without me——
How I forget! Has the bridge [*498.*] for the London Road one arch or
two? I ought to have made certain of that bridge—— But I must ⟨go to
London for⟩ {make} \get/ money. I must pay back. Then—— The pools
upstream, how exactly do they come?⟨"⟩ I ought to have made certain."
¶He dozed, and awoke still worrying about the bridge and the pools. So
he decided he was hungry. Tying his braces round him, he stepped forth
and started to make money.

33 \tawdry/ ← smart [*499*]

34 \eyes/ ← petticoats

† afternoon ← evening

36† more villainous than ← as villainous as

38† "went up" ← 'improved' ← would 'improve'

246 1† a ⟨franker squalor, a⟩ more

5† they were ⟨polluted and⟩ made [*500*]

11† river ← stream

13 employment. ⟨His soul would not be his own until he paid back the men
who had given him money and clothes.⟩ He

17 \His companions were/ ← Every one was

22† ocean ← sea [*501*]

32† a hundred ← fifty [*502*]

37† him⟨⟨: and told him what he had⟨.⟩ done. But⟩⟩; but

247 7† free. ⟨The foreman and his mates did not see him again.⟩ ← free ⟨The
dinner hour ended.⟩ \The foreman and his mates/ ⟨never saw him
again.⟩ did not see him again. [*end 502; 503 begins with an undeleted paragraph:*] ¶During these ten days he had forgotten much. The contours of
the hills were the first to go. There followed the windings of the streams

and all the details he thought were his for ever. Wiltshire, quietest of counties, flattened ⟨itself⟩ \herself/ out and became grey, nor could he at night remind himself of ⟨the⟩ \her/ stars. In which glade of the wood had he once met sheep? But here and there a memory stood firm: it is not easy to forget such a place as the Rings.

8† A few shillings . . . pocket. ← \He still had/ a few shillings. ← There remained in his pocket a few shillings. [*An earlier version of this paragraph stands abandoned, inverted but undeleted, on A49v:*] ¶He had a couple of shillings in his pocket, and these would give him pleasure of the kind he required. Like Agnes, he lived in the present, but with a sincerity that she would have rejected as unwise. Two pence went for a ride on an electric tram.

9† towards . . . county; ← back to ⟨Cadover⟩ ⟨Cadchurch⟩ Cadover.

19† slumbering. ⟨⟨ ⟨Harnham⟩ \Cadford/, ⟨Odstock⟩ \Chitterne/, Winterslow, Imber in-the-Down—⟩⟩ Salisbury

27 \rough/ ← \vigourous/ ← innumerable [*504*]

33† lips parted ← ⟨smile grew broader⟩ \teeth glistened/ [*505*]

34† Rickie ← Agnes

35† the rounds ← up to bed

36† Herbert peered ← They ⟨hurried⟩ \peered/

† hooligan ← drunken man

37† wrecked . . . fell ← He wrecked the hall, deliberately⟨, and⟩\. Then he/ lurched up the stairs, striking at the pictures as he ⟨past⟩ passed ⟨them⟩. On the ⟨stop⟩ top step, he fell

39† \Herbert . . . police./

† who . . . landing, ← ill as he was, ⟨staggered⟩ \came/ out of his bedroom,

CHAPTER 31

The process of discerning the chronological order of the drafts transcribed below is explained in the introduction to the appendix (pp. 307–10). The transcription begins with a draft of the opening of the early, undivided chapter, numbered XXXII and preserved on two deleted verso pages (*A55v, A58v*; wholly deleted verso passages transcribed below are marked by triple angle brackets). As much as survives of the undivided chapter then follows, sometimes rather patchily (*A48–A50, A33–A34, A52–A54, A40, A56v, A55–A56, A43, A57, A44, A58, A46, A47, A59–A63*). The two-chapter version (*A23–A46*) appears last; little repetition occurs until the second chapter of the division, beginning with *A45v* and *A36*, is reached. Curiously, passages which are most like the published text of Chapter 31 are often early, surviving through successive drafts on their own strength (see *A43, A44, A46* below, and pp. 254–5). In passages on leaves which Forster moved from one draft to another the changes that were obviously made in order to connect the earlier versions with the later ones are shown only in the later draft. Similarly, early revisions appear only at their first occurrence. The manuscript numbers of the moved leaves are starred below, and page references for the repetitions appear in the following list, where descriptions of the pages are given in numerical order for ease of reference. Pages termed "normal" are full quartos written, like most of the others, in gray-black ink with a narrow nib; the earlier pages tend toward blue, the later toward a paler gray.

A23–A28: normal.
A29: depeditated to avoid blank space before

A30: decapitated; compare p. 272.

A31: normal; compare *A52*.

A32: depeditated to avoid blank space before

A33*: decapitated, once the bottom of *A50* (pp. 375, 383).

A34*: depeditated continuation of *A33*, *A50* (pp. 375, 383).

A35: decapitated before being used; has end-of-chapter space to spare.

A36–A37: normal.

A38: decapitated, once the bottom of *A45v*.

A39: depeditated to avoid blank space before

A40*: decapitated, once the bottom of *A54* (pp. 376, 384).

A41: decapitated before being used; initially the bottom of *A39*.

A42: normal.

A43*: decapitated, once the bottom of *A56* (pp. 377, 385).

A43v: inverted; a beginning of Chapter 28, numbered XXVIII but aborted after a miswritten, deleted second word ("sould").

A44*: depeditated; like *501* and *504*—shiny, yellower paper; written with darker ink and thicker nib (pp. 377, 385).

A45: decapitated before being used; see *A45v*, compare *A58*.

A45v: deleted, inverted, depeditated, once the top of *A38* (pp. 383, 384).

A46*: not quite a full quarto, ink and paper like *A44* (pp. 378, 385).

A47: decapitated, depeditated, ink and paper like *A44*.

A48–A49: normal.

A49v: an inverted, undeleted variant of the events leading to Stephen's return to Dunwood House in Chapter 30 (247:8).

A50: depeditated top of *A33*.

A51: depeditated, perhaps before use; a draft of *A27*, ending with "so much beer"; differences are starred (p. 381).

A52*: normal; compare *A31* (pp. 375, 382).

A53: decapitated.

A54: depeditated top of *A40*.

A55: normal.

A55v: inverted, deleted.

A56: depeditated top of *A43*.

A56v: deleted.

A57: depeditated with space to spare.

A58: normal but with space to spare; compare *A45* (pp. 377, 385).

A58v: inverted, deleted.

A59–A60: normal.

A60v: inverted, undeleted.

A61: normal but with space to spare.

A62–A63: normal. See also p. 386 for a variant on *507v*.

⟨⟨⟨[*A55v:*]

XXXII

Next morning, at early preparation, Agnes tapped at the door, and begged her ⟨brother to⟩ brother's attention for a moment. He came out into the passage, and she whispered "He's awake"

"Have you seen him?"

"Oh Herbert—we don't know what to do. Poor Rickie is half crazy. Last night he must have ⟨got up a second time,⟩ locked \up/ the spare room, and taken the key, so that the man can't get out. He's hammering at the door, and Rickie daren't open it himself, and won't let us. All the servants are listening.⟨"⟩ You never saw such a scene."

"Poor Rickie can't bear to look at him."

"I don't know, Herbert; I don't know anything. But last night——"

He laid his hand on her shoulder. She was trembling.

"Last night—what did exactly happen?"

"He heard the noise, staggered out of bed, and caught him."

"Yes, but⟨—"⟩ then—"

"He did kiss him." said Herbert gravely. "I cannot make out why.—Dear child: what's the matter?"

"I don't know!" she sobbed. "I feel we're on the edge of something too big for us. I've never felt like this before. ⟨And I don't li⟩"

They went through to the study, and there ⟨was⟩ \had/ another surprise. The photograph of Mrs Elliot, which Rickie had flung down that terrible [*A58v:*] Sunday, \now/ stood back in its old place.

"Whose work is this?" said Herbert, stretching out his hand. "He cannot bear to see it. He must be humoured. The doctor told us so.⟨"⟩ I shall put it back in the drawer."

She stopped him. Sorrow had made her perceptions delicate. Except at the death of Gerald, she had never felt like this before.

"Herbert!" called a voice.

"Yes, my dear boy." They both went upstairs. Rickie was clinging on to the banisters. He had dressed himself, for the first time since his illness⟩⟩⟩

[*A48:*]

XXXII

"Oh I have been a fool!" he moaned next morning, sitting up in bed. "I have put my head in it this time."

"You have indeed" said Ansell quietly.

"Do give us water."

⟨There was⟩ \"There's/ a siphon ⟨beside him⟩ \by you"/. ⟨Ansell⟩ Then ⟨Ansell⟩ \he/ ⟨struck⟩ lit an Etna, and began to prepare some tea. Stephen looked at \him/ in bewilderment.

"Who put all these things here?"

"Rickie⟨."⟩ ordered it."

"Why?"

"You'ld better ask him." He returned to his book. He still worked at philosophy, though Cambridge, the only hope for such people, had rejected him.

"⟨I s⟩ Is he going to run me in⟨?"⟩ for assault."

"You had better ask him."

"How it was—(tell him)—is that all of a sudden I thought '*He*'s turned me out of Cadover'. Not the Silts; [*A49:*] was it?"

"No; not the Silts."

"And I ⟨swore⟩ \settled/ (being drunk) that I'ld break him up. Oh ⟨God⟩, what a fool I've been.⟨"⟩ Will you stick to me?"

Ansell put a marker in the book, sat down on the bed and shook hands. "Till one of us dies" he said gravely.

"What is his wife doing? Will you ⟨back me up?"⟩ \stick to me against her."/

"His wife is now negligible."

"I don't understand" he murmured, pressing his knuckles into his eyes."

"I don't suppose you do."

⟨He poured out⟩ \They drank/ the tea in silence. Outside they heard the rain, which had set in early that morning from a dirty sky. Ansell, summoned by Rickie, had watched in the room all night.

"Where are my clothes?" he asked.

The maid was to brush them and put them ready \for you/ in the bath-room."

"Odd, all this."

[*A50:*] ⟨"Absolutely⟩ \"Simply/ extraordinary.⟨"⟩ ⟨When you're dressed, you are to see Rickie."⟩\"/

\"What's to happen next?"

"You're to dress and to see Rickie./

"No I won't!" cried Stephen, starting up. "I knew there was a catch somewhere. I won't sign⟨.⟩ it."

"Sign what?"

"That piece of paper where I promised to be quiet."

"My dear man, we are \long/ past pieces of paper. The people you've told, ⟨let alone⟩ \and/ the people I've told, have ⟨published⟩ ⟨published⟩ \together spread/ the news all over England."

"Any how I won't see him."

\He took a biscuit, and nibbled it thoughtfully. Then he [*A33*:] said/ "Stephen: I believe you [*A50:*] like me. On the strength of [*A33*:] it I am going to ask a favour. See Rickie to please me. At present there is no other reason why you should."

"I call that a woman's dodge—to say 'see him to please me'. It isn't my notion of playing the game.⟨"⟩ \I don't want to see him."/

Ansell was silent, thinking perhaps of the degradation that is inherent in all contest. He could not ⟨defeat⟩ attack Agnes without borrowing one of her weapons.

[*A34*:] ⟨⟨ ⟨"Let's compromise"⟩ \"I'll meet you half way"/⟩⟩ \"I'll do this⟨."⟩ much"/ he said at last. "I'll see him out of doors."

"In the wet?"

"I must be where I can get ⟨away from him" He shuddered. "⟩ \clear——/ Something's wrong with the drains in this house. I don't know what. They've already upset me once. One can't breathe for a certain smell that—I don't know."

"I do know. But you'll find the same smell out of doors. It isn't only the drains in the house. ⟨He⟩ \Rickie/ also has been upset by that smell. He's been laid up with it, ever [*torn*] ⟨Visit your fellow patient, Stephen. Have a⟩ [*torn; about one-third of A34 is missing. A52:*] He waited for him in the passage. Was he only a rowdy boy who smashed furniture⟨, or something incomparably greater?⟩ \?/ ⟨Were they all boys⟩ \\Was he himself \only/ a boy//, who tried to get out of life something that is ⟨not in it?⟩ ⟨only found in⟩ \confined to/ books? ⟨Or a man whom books have sharpened to detect abnormal hopes?⟩ He had always held that ⟨he⟩ we neglect the ⟨abnormal⟩ \unusual in life/, that people are less alike than we pretend, and events more extraordinary. At Cambridge he had written a paper—and a very clever paper it was—to prove that the conventions ⟨had⟩ \have/ been drifting further from the realities for about two thousand years. There was need (he said) of a great revision, or we might destroy the essence of humanity. Was all this ⟨meer⟩ \mere/ young-mannishness? ⟨The test⟩ \These questions/, he felt certain, ⟨was at hand today.⟩ would \all/ be answered today

Stephen came out, clean and shaven, but rather black in the lips and bloodshot in the eyes. "It's a pity you drink" he remarked "but I quite see how it is, and don't expect you'll ever stop yourself."

Stephen was offended. "I could stop myself any minute if I chose. But I don't choose."

Ansell smiled rather sadly, and they proceeded ⟨to Rickie's room⟩ ⟨down stairs⟩ to the study. [*A53:*] They ⟨marched⟩ \proceeded/ into Rickie's bed room. He was sitting up ⟨⟨for the first time, ⟨and his pale face was almost beautiful⟩ ⟩⟩ in a gorgeous dressing gown, and his pale ⟨wa⟩ face was almost beautiful against the crimson folds. Once more he looked ⟨what⟩ \the man/ Ansell had always known him to be—⟨a man⟩ extraordinarily civilized, capable of subtle and varied relations with his fellows.

"Here you are," he said gently, rising to greet them.

"⟨Stephen's worrying⟩ \Stephen wondered/ about the damage he did. That's all right, isn't it?"

"Of course that's all right.⟨"⟩—Don't go, Stewart."

⟨⟨ ⟨"I think I will.⟩ "I cannot help you any more." And he⟩⟩ \But Ansell could help him no more. He/ left them together. It was the first time they had met since the Rings. When the door had shut, Rickie stepped forward, put his arms round [*A54:*] his brother, and kissed him. ⟨Then he went back to his seat.⟩

There was a profound silence. The portrait of their mother looked down upon them both, with sightless eyes.

"She has risen from the dead" said Rickie. "There is nothing else to say. I've tried to think the matter out—but it lies beyond thought—beyond morality—at all events beyond my morality. ⟨One day⟩ I tried to curse her—or to forget her—or to pretend your ⟨wronged⟩ father wronged her. Dear Stephen, nothing was any good. If you understand me, she is more like the corn. She has risen from the dead."

Stephen remained motionless, his hands still in his pockets, his ⟨ha⟩ arms pressed ⟨to⟩ close to his side.

"Living in houses, as I must, we forget Nature. But at times [*A40*:*] she enters and makes her comment. She has commented on me. I daresay you have heard about my child. ⟨Then⟩ I had a dream \afterwards/ which I take now to be a vision. 'Come away!' said a voice to my mother. 'Let them die out!'—and I saw Orion. I can bear to die out now⟨, for⟩\." His voice rose prophetically. "/I have seen just a little way up and down the generations, and I know there is a purpose in the tiny corner of the world that I have touched. ⟨Though⟩ I stand with my face to the night⟨,⟩\. But/ it is not really darkness, for ⟨the⟩ \those/ I loved are handing the torches on. She has risen from ⟨⟨⟨[*A56v:*] the dead⟨. She⟩ \and she/ will rise again⟨—perhaps as long as our race⟩ exists. Perhaps great nations—no, better still, ⟨⟨in ⟨all⟩ ⟨every⟩ \⟨every⟩ ⟨all⟩/ the coming ⟨years⟩ \year/⟩⟩ \perhaps/ a few happy men ⟨⟨may exist⟨—a⟩ \and/ few happy women—hers, and like her⟩⟩ \and women will be hers and like her to/ all time. When I see this, ⟨god⟩ \God/ pardon me my own morality seems a very tiny thing, good enough for myself, but an insult to her.⟩⟩⟩ [*A55:*] the dead and she will rise again. Nothing greater could happen to me—not even a child of my own."

So Rickie gazed at the \pure/ stream to which he would never contribute, and watched the waters ⟨grow⟩ broaden towards ⟨the rising sun and⟩ the sea. And Stephen, because he had promised Ansell, listened to every word he ⟨sl⟩ said, and the time came at last when he was expected to reply. Through the window there floated large soft soots, driven in by the rain, and one of these settled on his cheek. He tried to flick it off, and his flesh was smeared. He drove his hand back into his pocket, with a slight shudder. Whatever should he say?

Rickie, now back in his arm chair, saw that the ⟨simple⟩ fellow was bewildered. "You will never find me very obvious" he said smiling. "When I try to be direct it ⟨often⟩ \usually/ ends in insincerity. I have to say in a hundred words what luckier people say in two. But as far as the present moment I can be plain enough. This is [*A56:*] your home, and all my money is yours also."

Stephen had little instinct for character, though his grip was certain in the end. It was long before he grasped that Rickie was in his right mind. Then he shuddered more violently and said "But are you asking me to live ⟨with you?"⟩ in this house?"

"On the mantel piece is a photograph. You know who I mean. She planned that we should live together, and then suddenly died."

"I can't follow—because—Didn't you know I called here last Sunday week?"

"I did know. But since then something has happened."

"What?"

It was not easy to explain.

[*A43*:*] "Last Sunday week" began Stephen, his voice rising, "I came to call on you⟨, because I heard of you as educated.⟩\. Not as this or that's son./ Not to fall on your neck. Nor to talk about torches and ⟨corn and⟩ Orion. Nor—Damn your dirty little mind! I meant to say I didn't come for money. Sorry. Sorry. I simply came. I came as I was last Sunday week and I havn't [*A57:*] altered since."

"⟨You⟩ \I/ have altered ⟨for me⟩" said Rickie, shading his eyes, though the light was greyer. "Last Sunday week, through my own ⟨weakness⟩ \cowardice/ and wickedness, I did not know who ⟨we⟩ you were. I thought you were my father's son. Mrs Failing encouraged me, because she has so few interests in the world, and it amuses her to see people going wrong. As I said before, we can't think it out. She has simply risen from the dead."

[*A44*:*] ⟨"But⟩ \"And/ where do I come in?" He bared his arm suddenly and slapped it. "*I* havn't risen from the dead. *I* havn't altered since last ⟨Monday⟩ \Sunday/ week.⟨"⟩ I'm—" He stuttered violently and ⟨black⟩ veins stood out on his temples. He could not quite explain what I am. "The man towards Andover— ⟨I end by respecting him. Those were⟩ \after all he ⟨had⟩ was having/ principles. But you've—" His voice broke. "I mind it." He was almost crying. "——I'm——*I* don't alter——blackguard one week——most wonderful angel the next——\I keep to one or the other——/you've hurt something most badly in me that I didn't know was there."

There was a profound silence, for both the young men were on the verge of tears. ⟨⟨ ⟨As Rickie said, the⟩ \The/ matter⟩⟩ \The contest between them/ lay beyond all thought and morality, far back in the arms of Nature. ⟨⟨The portrait of their mother—she ⟨too⟩ had once cried \'I am!'/ in her joy— [*A few undeleted words of the original continuation survive at the tear on A44:* them both with sightless eyes. *A58:*] was now haggard and ghostlike: the sun had fallen on her too ⟨much⟩ \strongly/ in the Cambridge ⟨room⟩ days⟩⟩

"Don't let us talk" said Rickie. "We shall only make things worse. But I want you to know I am sorry, and that in never discovering what kind of a man you were I have committed the greatest of human sins."

"*I* never asked you to talk." He waited a minute, and then tramped angrily to the door.

"Stephen——"

"I don't want your apologies. ⟨I never liked poetry.⟩ I'm going back to where I belong."

The rain tilted ⟨a⟩ slightly against the house. The wind was rising, the clouds thickening. This sluggish drizzle would turn into a storm.

"You can't go back in ⟨this⟩ \such/ weather" said Rickie, and began ⟨his⟩ a new appeal—not to pity for he was in [*A46*:] no mood to whimper. For all its pathos, ⟨this was a meeting of grown men⟩ \there was something heroic in this meeting/. "I warn you to stop here \with me/, Stephen. No one ⟨else⟩ \else/ in the world will look after you ⟨but m⟩. As far as I know, you have never been \really/ unhappy yet or suffered ⟨from your⟩, ⟨as I have,⟩ \as you should do/ from your {own} faults. You're a drunkard and last night you nearly killed yourself. Never mind why I'm willing to cure you. I am willing, and I ⟨wan⟩ warn you to give me the chance.⟨"⟩ Forgive me or not as you choose. I care ⟨more⟩ for other things \more/."

Stephen looked at him with a faint approval. The offer was ridiculous, but it came ⟨with⟩ from a man to a man.

"Let me tell you of ⟨my⟩ \a/ fault \of mine/ and how I was punished for it" continued Rickie. "Two years ago I behaved badly to you, up at the Rings. No: even a few days before that. We went for a ride, and I thought too much of other ⟨things⟩ \matters/ and did not try to understand you. Then came the Rings, ⟨⟨and I ⟨struck {at} you in the face⟩ \hated you/,⟩⟩ and in the evening when you called up to me most kindly, I would not answer. But ⟨⟨the ride was my ⟨chief⟩ \real/ fault.⟩⟩ {my punishment ⟨dates⟩ \begins/ from the ride.} \the ride ⟨began things⟩ was the beginning./ Ever since⟨,⟩\ then,/ I have taken the world at second hand. I have bothered [*end A46*]

[*A47*:] ⟨saw what a great day [*torn*] -ing sorrow.⟩ \Yet this had been a great morning, in spite of its piercing sorrow./ One by one Stephen had stripped him of his illusions, until the world was ⟨real⟩ again real. Ansell had tried, but he was sentimental, he was Cambridge, and could but evoke the reality ⟨that⟩ they had found in ⟨the⟩ \that/ beautiful past. This man belonged to the present, and showed it to him as a ruined city, destitute of grace and love, whose ⟨every fragment⟩ arches gashed an unrelenting sky. Such a city is better than a life in fog: better even than enchanted gardens.

[*torn*] is he doing now?"

[*A59*:] There was a flash of lightening. Agnes entered with the thunder and hurried to close the window⟨.⟩ \observing/ "Who would have thought it would have turned like this?" She, like her brother, was dazed. Rickie was ill and must be humoured. Ansell was strong and must be admitted. If Stephen \slept a night here and/ broke a little furniture it was nothing in the general wreck. For a week she had faced torrents of gossip, and still lived. There had been ⟨lett⟩ an article in the local paper, and enquiries from parents. One boy had been taken away. Though she never foresaw the course of her own emotions with much clearness, she began to see that she would get over the scandal in time, just as she had got over other things. Like Rickie, she might have said "Am I not withered up at last? Has not the power to suffer died in me?" Meanwhile she must fasten the windows, against this unexpected storm⟨; though she minded thunder⟩.

⟨⟨"I have asked him to live with us" he ⟨told her⟩ \gasped/, "and he will not.⟩⟩ \"He will not live with us" he told her, without looking up./

"If he ⟨would⟩ \did/, I shouldn't" she retorted sourly. "What's all that rubbish on the floor?"

[*A60v*:] it might sound strange to a third person. Stephen had never seen them together since their marriage. He was attentive and surprised. ⟨She turned to him

378

and said "I am⟩ \"Come with me!" she called to her/ husband, ⟨"⟩ and so
unkindly that the words leapt out of his mouth

[*A60:*] never seen them together since their marriage. He was attentive and surprised. It seemed that they did not agree.

"But you ⟨too⟩ \two/——" he ⟨said suddenly⟩ \exclaimed/. She stopped, attentive also, though she knew not why. Rickie lay huddled up in the chair. The air
was stifling ⟨since she had closed the windows⟩, and outside the sky was seething
downwards ⟨on the house⟩ \on Dunwood House/. The rain had ceased, except for
a few enormous drops. ⟨The trees were motionless,⟩ Most of the trees were motionless, but here and there a dozen leaves twitched violently, as though unseen mouths
were blowing upon them. Yet opposite were the well known houses, respectable,
unmoved, and ladies she knew were closing their windows or telling their servants
to close them. In the suburbs it seems impossible ⟨sho⟩ that Nature should ⟨ap-
proach⟩ arrive.

"What about us?" she asked. A wind seemed to ⟨blo⟩ come from the ground, for
the leaves of their little oak tree fluttered upwards. She glanced at it, and as she did
so Stephen stepped between her and the door, saying "I don't ⟨you⟩ think you
love each other" ⟨and the⟩\. The/ leaves fluttered back.

[*A61:*] The storm was making her nervous. Her heart leapt painfully at his
words and she could not reply to them nor rebuke his impudence. She could not
even breathe.

⟨He whispered—or was it that her ears were deaf? In the dark room she only
saw him. Was she trembling like the tree outside? Why would not the thunder roll,
and be done? Why would not the thunder discharge itself and go?⟩

"Don't you love him?" he asked. ⟨B⟩ She started forward. By accident ⟨they⟩
\their hands/ touched and she burst into tears

"What is it?" said Rickie absently. "He is not stopping \here/. You have got
your \own/ way again."

They parted, but it was too late. Life played on Agnes one of its mysterious
tricks. Something in him, in the feel of him recalled other terrors, victory, defeat—
all [*A62:*] the radiant possibilities that had perished on a suburban football field.
The woman she had wronged awoke in her, and crying "Gerald! Gerald!" she
flung herself into his arms. Ah he was Gerald for a moment! For a moment she lay
on the breast of the man she loved. For a moment of unutterable bliss ⟨his⟩ \that/
mortal spirit entered ⟨the⟩ immortal flesh, and beneath her lips lips that the grave
had ravaged were warm and strong.

Her husband did not ⟨here⟩ \hear/ the cry, so tremendous was the thunder that
shook the house. He did not see her motion for the light had dazzled him. He did
not hear Stephen's voice, sheltered by the reverberations and dying away as they
died. "Poor girl——has it been like that——don't think I shall ever tell him——
Ah poor girl——!" Then the moment passed, the spirit returned to the grave, the
lips were those of a stranger, and the memory of them an eternal shame.

Voices called. There were screams and a smell of burning. She was told that the
boys' part had been [*A63:*] struck by the storm. Without a word, she hurried into
danger.

Stephen followed her, transfixed with pity. {He understood their whole tragedy}
\Here was a tragedy he could understand/ At last he had forgotten his own wrongs.
But he turned and went back to his brother, to whom all this episode had been a
blank, in whose ears still rang the refusal of ⟨brotherhood⟩ \forgiveness/ and the
sound of a tearing photograph.

⟨"The⟩ \"Your/ house has caught, Rickie" he said kindly. "You must come my way now."

"The house has caught!" cried Ansell rushing in upon them.

"Stephen——do you mean you're stopping?"

"No one's stopping!" they ⟨g⟩ cried "Come ⟨away with us⟩ \our way/—— Come back to the thing's you've forgotten."

For a moment he ⟨struggled, murmuring⟩ \murmured/ about duty.

"But he must have a great coat!" said Stephen. \"He can't go without a great coat."/

⟨For⟩ \To/ Rickie also a mortal spirit was incarnate in immortal flesh. Last time, when that ⟨th⟩ voice had said those words, he had ⟨answered angrily⟩ \silenced it ⟨angrily⟩ fretfully/. He obeyed \it/ to day, and the three of them followed the course of the storm.

[*The first chapter of the revision into two:*]

[*A23:*]

⟨XXXII⟩ \XXXI/

Though Cambridge, the only hope for such people, had rejected Ansell, he still worked at philosophy. He and Mr Jackson were reading ⟨Hartmann⟩ \together/ when a frantic message from Dunwood House arrived. The message was ⟨followed⟩ \pursued/ by Mr Pembroke in person: it ought never to have been ⟨send⟩ \sent/: Rickie was not responsible for his actions: would they ⟨⟨kindly take no notice⟨.⟩ of it⟩⟩ \have the goodness to ignore it/.

There followed ⟨a f⟩ ⟨a familiar duel⟩ \a duel on familiar lines/. Ansell said "Rickie asks me to come and ⟨sleep⟩ \sit up/ in the man's room. I shall come." Mr Pembroke replied "I forbid you the house \for the third time during the last ten days/ and I appeal to Jackson to support me." Ansell picked up his cap and started, while his host chanted after him through the streets "I warn you sir! I have forbidden you my house! You are putting yourself in the wrong⟨."⟩, sir."

To the outside ⟨duel⟩ world their duel ⟨was⟩ \had been/ comic. Few things are funnier than men who stop taking off their hats ⟨and shaking hands, and imagine that by⟩ \to each other and ⟨om⟩ imagine that by/ ⟨so doing⟩ \this omission/ [*A24:*] ⟨the verities of life will alter⟩ \they have altered the verities of life/. Ansell had never imagined it. His mind ⟨had always travelled⟩ \was accustomed to travel/ to the ultimate ⟨facts⟩ \fact/. He thought not "will he be rude?" but "will he have locked ⟨the⟩ \Rickie's/ door?" Therefore in ⟨this duel⟩ \these duels/ he won, and poor Mr Pembroke, who had stopped him by a splendid speech in the hall would find ten minutes afterwards that he had come up the back stairs. "He's no better than a plough boy" he would exclaim. "I understood that he was an ineffective man, intellectual."

By mutual consent they were ⟨silent⟩ \civil/ in the presence of Rickie. They knew he had enough to bear already. He seemed fond of them both, and listened to ⟨Herbert with⟩ \Herbert's/ condolences with quiet eyes. Once Herbert said "Your father, dear boy. Try to look on the bright side ⟨of this⟩ \of the shield/. Your father was a much better man than we supposed." As he spoke he was suddenly pulled by Ansell, and found himself ⟨out⟩ in the passage, with the door locked. All this seemed ⟨very⟩ comic to the outer world.

This evening Agnes awaited them⟨.⟩ \\, ⟨al⟩ among the débris ⟨of⟩ \in/ the hall// "I supposed you would come" she said to Ansell coldly. "You [*A25:*] will have to sleep on the floor. I could not possibly ask the maids to put up a bed at this hour." Her manner was shattered: she seemed to have lost the power of estimating things. Stephen ⟨⟨now lay ⟨on⟩ \in/ the spare room bed,⟩⟩ \had been put to bed in the spare room. He was/ snoring heavily⟨, while⟩ \./ Rickie stood and looked at him. It was ⟨a moment⟩ \an interval/ of chaos. They none of them knew which way events would turn. "We never ⟨expecting⟩ \expected/ him back" whispered Rickie. "In all our talks we did assume he had really gone." Ansell drew him away gently. A few directions were given to the servants, and then they dispersed ⟨to their beds.⟩ for the night.

The dawn was a sordid business. Ansell⟨, saw⟩ ⟨saw⟩ \watched/ the grey light ⟨fall on⟩ \reveal/ the face of the drunkard. ⟨⟨His mind, (which his ⟨fri⟩ enemies called morbid, his friends powerful)⟩⟩ \He/ analysed that face carefully, and he knew what it would ⟨look like⟩ \become/ if Stephen got drunk often. ⟨⟨He heard a ⟨murmurs⟩ \murmur/ of "Pools——how do they ⟨come⟩ \lie/——how did the road bend—"⟩⟩ Sparrows twittered, and gradually the man woke up.

"Oh my head!" he groaned, and then sat up with a [*A26:*] sharp cry. He did not know where he was.

"It's Dunwood House" said Ansell from his shadowy corner. "I'm the man you talked to in the garden, last Sunday week. ⟨Steph⟩ Shall we have some tea?"

"Dunwood House——" For the first time in his life he ⟨looked⟩ \was/ ashamed. "I've broken things" he said guiltily. "I'm remembering. I must pay for them. Why ever did I come here?"

The sigh of rain drops was heard on the pane.

"I'ld better go⟨"⟩ without ⟨⟨ ⟨drinking⟩ \having/ any of⟩ their tea" continued Stephen. ⟨"It's all come back.⟩ \"I remember ⟨now.⟩ it all./ I've been drunk. I'ld never have come \back/ here else. You must explain to ⟨them⟩ \the Elliots/. Apologies and so on. They aren't my sort, and with beer in me, I wanted to break them up. Just at the angry time I happened to trip against the catch of their front gate. Can you explain all that without getting it wrong? I'll send money for ⟨breakages⟩ \the broken ornaments/ when I raise it. I remember a ⟨kind⟩ \sort/ of stone man, holding a baby made of two potatoes."

Ansell, who had never loved the Hermes, gave an [*A27 and A51; to read A27, include the starred insertions, copied from A51, but drop the starred deletions; the unstarred changes appear on A27:*] appreciative cackle. "I may ⟨tell it⟩ \give your message/ wrong" he said lightly "You'ld better see Rickie yourself."

"No thank 'ee." His spirits were \quickly/ improving. "It's lucky *⟨I didn't see him last time. I never hit ⟨woman⟩ women.⟩* for him ⟨we didn't meet last time⟩ \he didn't see me last time/: I never hit women. Lord, why don't I!" he added after a pause, *\and contemplated the problem of sex./* "There's another funny thing too. A woman'ld sooner hit another *⟨wow⟩* woman than she'ld hit a man. *\I've watched them choose./* *⟨⟨ ⟨What they call⟩ \What's called/ chivalry⟩⟩* What they call chivalry cuts both ways—women feel it just the same for us."

This truth, on which we will not base our lives—*⟨preferring to base them on half of it;⟩* finding them more graceful when based on half of it—was already familiar to Ansell. But it came *⟨very⟩* strangely at four o'clock in the morning, *⟨⟨ ⟨from lips⟩ \through lips that/ had swallowed so much beer. [*end A51*] ⟩⟩* through lips so recently locked by beer. It seemed the flowering time of Stephen's philosophy. As he crawled out of bed and prepared, leisurely, to quit Dunwood House for ever, he gave Ansell his opinions on the subject of marriage.

[*A28:*] "You can't own people. That's where Flea Thompson ⟨in particular goes wrong.⟩ \has gone so wrong./ And he will pretend he could never love any girl but this⟨⟨. He's changed twice already, but ⟨he⟩ doesn't like me to say so.⟩⟩\, though she's not the same one./ Those notions are all very well for ⟨poets⟩ \a poet/—but when it comes to ⟨us men!⟩ \a fellow!/ Well *I*'m certain that if I couldn't get one woman I'd get another and that a woman would feel the same if she couldn't ⟨me⟩ get me."

He plunged his head into the basin. No one is perfectly logical: he was using the ⟨Elliot's⟩ \Elliots'/ soap.

"True enough." said Ansell. "Towzled, but true."

"Towzled?"

"The whole world is a little towzled. The demiurge, before he made our planet, forgot to wash his hands"

But Stephen ⟨⟨ ⟨sailed⟩ \went/ forward⟩⟩ \proceeded/, and his voice, through the splashing of water seemed to alter and to become humble, beautiful, pure. "I know what you mean by towzled, because Mrs Failing ⟨once⟩ said \it/ of me [*A29:*] too⟨. She said no decent woman will ever touch me.⟩ \\ \ just before I left/. She pitied my wife. She trusts I'll never marry.// Yet I don't know. Mightn't I find a girl—naturally not refined—and be happy with her in my own way? I would tell \her/ straight I was nothing much—faithful of course, but that she should never have all my thoughts. Out of no disrespect to her, but because all one's thoughts can't belong to any single person."

"But you must know!" exclaimed Ansell. "You must have followed this Elliot business from the start."

"Elliot business? Where's a towel? I was talking of Mrs Failing and Flea. I was \saying/ we're not poets, and ought to go gently." And Ansell had again the sense of one who had been back, far back, to the sources of incident, to the table of the gods⟨, to Pan⟩.

[*A30:*] ⟨A great romantic⟩

Romantic love is {of course} greater than this. There are men and women—we know it from history—who have been born into the world for each other and ⟨no⟩ \for/ no one else, who have accomplished the longest journey locked in each other's arms. But romantic love is also the code of modern morals, and for this reason popular. Eternal union, eternal ownership—these are tempting baits for the average man. He swallows them, will not confess his ⟨mistakes⟩ \mistake/, and—perhaps to cover it—⟨shouts⟩ cries 'dirty cynic' at such a man as Stephen.

"There is an Elliot ⟨affair,⟩ \business,/ ⟨though.⟩ \bye the bye./ I nearly told you about it on the lawn. ⟨But⟩ I didn't want to ⟨equip⟩ \bias/ you then. I do now.⟨"⟩ I must."

But Stephen would not attend. Indeed he could not. His brain had been wiped clean of the Elliots. He strolled naked about the room, interrupting ⟨Ansell⟩ [*A31:*] with the most trivial remarks. Then he began to dress and Ansell, in gathering anxiety, referred to Rickie in every sentence that he spoke. The conviction ⟨grew⟩ \had grown/ in him that the two must ⟨meet.⟩ \talk./ For what purpose he did not know: he could not parallel ⟨the⟩ \this/ situation, either in literature or life. But he had always held that we neglect the unusual in life, that people are less alike than we pretend and events more extraordinary. At Cambridge he had written a paper— and a very clever paper it was—to prove that the conventions have been drifting from the realities for about two thousand years. There was need (he told his audi- ence) of a great revision, or we might destroy the essence of humanity. Was all this ⟨crude⟩ \mere/ young-mannishness? If Rickie and Stephen talked, he felt that ⟨the question⟩ \such questions/ might be answered to day.

"You're delightfully tame this morning⟨"⟩!"

"So'ld you be if you'ld got my head."

⟨"Is it bad?⟩ "I'm certain you wouldn't hit Rickie \now/. It isn't in you."

Stephen laughed, and pulled on a boot.

⟨"You may⟩ "You may as well see him⟨."⟩, mayn't you?"
[*A32:*] ⟨"He's asleep.⟩ ⟨"At four in the morning?"⟩ \"So early?"/
"We'll wake him up."

"I don't want to see him." He put on his cap and held out his hand. "Pleased to have met you. Give my message about the ⟨broken⟩ ornaments."

"Where are you going?"

"Back to the same sort of thing⟨."⟩, I suppose."

"Do you like it?"

He laughed, and tried to open the door. It was locked.

"Oh yes——" stammered Ansell. "As ⟨I⟩ a matter of fact the key's \in/ my pocket."

"Give it us⟨."⟩, then."

He hesitated. "The ⟨fact⟩ \truth/ is I want ⟨to⟩ you to see Rickie." He ⟨saw⟩ \observed/ ⟨the⟩ \a/ storm gathering, and was inspired to say "I believe you like me. On the strength of [*A33*:] it I am going to ask a favour. See Rickie to please me. At present there is no other reason why you should."

"I call that a woman's dodge—to say 'see him to please me'. It isn't my notion of playing the game. I don't want to see him."

Ansell was silent, thinking perhaps of the degradation that is inherent in all contest. He could not attack Agnes without borrowing one of her weapons.

[*A34*:] "I'll do this much" he said at last. "I'll see him out of doors."

"In the wet?"

"I must be where I can get clear—— Something's wrong with the drains in this house. I don't know what. They've already upset me once. One can't breathe for a certain smell that—I don't know."

"I do know. But you'll find the same smell out of doors. It isn't only the drains in the house. Rickie also has been upset by that smell. He's been laid up with it, ever [*A35:*] since you left."

"Well near out doors, at all events."

This little point was adjusted. The talk was to ⟨talk⟩ take place ⟨in⟩ downstairs, in the study. Since the study window was broken the room would be full of air.

[*The second chapter of the division, with a deleted opening:*]

⟨⟨⟨[*A45v:*]

XXXIII

"I am here" ⟨said⟩ \began/ Rickie "to offer an apology. Without attempting to justify myself, I wish to explain how it was—" But his voice broke, he forgot his fine speech. To his half awakened brain light came, and he did the only possible thing. He put his arms round Stephen and kissed him. He murmured "My brother——son of my mother——son of my mother. May God bless you." Hither the ten days had brought \him/. He could not think the matter out. It lay beyond morality, beyond thought. He only knew that his mother had risen from the dead.

Stephen, ⟨not unkindly⟩ who ⟨knew⟩ \realized/ that the man was ill, [*A38:*] ⟨⟨pushed him gently backwards into a chair. [*A45v:*] He said ⟨again⟩ [*A38:*] "It's I who ought to apologize \I suppose/.⟩⟩ ⟩⟩⟩

[*A36:*]

⟨XXXIII⟩\XXXII/

To Rickie the news came in the midst of distracting dreams. All night he had tried to think the matter out. His mother had fallen from her old pedestal, and he was left with no human ideal. Only the hand of Ansell seemed stretched ⟨out⟩ to him through the darkness ⟨and he⟩\. He/ knew that his friend was helping him, and ⟨⟨awoke at ⟨the⟩ last to the news⟩⟩ \when he woke it was to hear/ "I have left him sitting quietly in the study. I cannot help you any more."

He dressed slowly—he was barely convalescent—and tried to think what he should say. The task was difficult, for he did not know what he wanted to say. He dreaded Stephen, yet he could not let him go, and now was the time to see him, quietly, before Agnes and Herbert were up. ⟨T⟩ He groped his way down, ⟨through⟩ the silent house. The study shutters had been unbarred⟨⟨, and the grey light entered there ⟨also⟩ He saw \the room/ as though for the first time, in ⟨the⟩ \that/ cheerless morning light.⟩⟩\./ On the table a man was sitting, black against the grey. He seemed to dominate the ⟨room⟩ \study/ and to ⟨dispise⟩ despise it, and his unbrushed hair stood out like [*A37:*] a halo. ⟨Eyes⟩ Rickie was ⟨conscious of⟩ \aware of/ ⟨indignant⟩ ⟨conscio⟩ \his eyes,/ contemptuous eyes, piercing the gloom with a promise of blue. The spirit went out of him, for ⟨he had known those eyes before, bent on him⟩ \those eyes had watched him before,/ not in contempt. They had watched {over} him as a child⟨ ⟨⟨. He thought ⟨it is⟩ "It is too horrible" and the voice that dwells beyond thought, beyond morality, replied "Or is it too wonderful? ⟨⟨Is it what you ⟨pray⟩ \have prayed/ for, whenever you were lonely and alone?"⟩⟩\" He repeated "It is too horrible. I am sure."/⟩⟩ ⟩\, departing on his last walk, when he had told ⟨him⟩ his mother not to bother him./

"I am here," he began, "to offer an apology. \I have heard from Mrs Failing./" He cleared his throat. "Without attempting to justify myself I owe it to myself, if not to you, to explain how it was that—." But his voice broke, he forgot his fine speech. To his half awakened brain light came, and he did all that was possible. He put his arms round Stephen, and kissed him. ⟨⟨Hither the ten days ⟨had⟩ and the night had brought him.⟩⟩ He could not think the matter out. He only knew that his mother had risen from the dead.

Stephen, ⟨⟨who ⟨h⟩ realized⟩⟩ \realizing/ that the man was ill, did not rebuff him. He let him whisper "My brother——son of my mother——son of my mother——" Then he ⟨pushed him gently⟩ \lifted him/ into a chair saying "It's I who ought to apologize, I suppose. [*A38:*] He explained again ⟨w⟩ how he had come to the house and how, some day, he would pay for the ornaments that he had broken.

"Son of my mother——" repeated Rickie closing his eyes. "Kiss me. Forgive me."

The other now stood by the window, playing with the glass that he had broken the night before.

"I've tried to curse her——or to forget her——or to pretend your father ruined her. Dear Stephen, ⟨nothing's⟩ \nothing was/ any good. I can't get behind it. Son of my mother, kiss me; forgive me."

[*A39:*] "Forgive you?" said Stephen, uneasy at the repetition ⟨⟨of ⟨these⟩ \such/ words⟩⟩ \of these words/. ⟨In them alone did he perceive⟩ \⟨Here⟩ In them alone had he perceived/ any ⟨appeal⟩ \approach/ to sense. Woe to this man in the chair, if ⟨we⟩ he were a real man! But Rickie proceeded to say things that were without sense: these things:

"We forget Nature. We lose touch with her. But in time [*A40*:*] she enters and makes her comment. She has commented on me. I daresay you have heard about

384

my child. I had a dream afterwards which I take now to be a vision. 'Come away!'
said a voice to my mother. 'Let them die out!'—and I saw Orion. I can bear to die
out now." His voice rose prophetically. "I have seen just a little way up and down
the generations, and I know there is a purpose in the tiny corner of the world that
I have touched. I stand with my face to the night. But it is not really darkness, for
those I loved are handing the torches on. She has risen from [*A41:*] the dead and
she will rise again. ⟨All I say comes back to that.⟩ \All that I say leads back to her
resurrection./ Kiss me, forgive me. Nothing greater could happen to me—not even
a child of my own."

So Rickie gazed at the pure stream to which he would never contribute and
watched it broadening towards the sea.

"Your friend was to wait outside. Shall I call him?"

"Forgive me first."

Stephen, intent upon a grazed finger, said "Oh yes!" irritably.

"Then God bless you."

Outside the light was increasing, and with it the rain. Within, the portrait of
⟨their mother⟩ \Mrs Elliot/ looked down \upon her sons/, with sightless eyes.

[*A42:*] "You know what forgiveness means" he continued solemnly. "From you
to me it is not a little thing. It means that you will share my money: that you will
live⟨.⟩ here. You do not give me a friendly nod and ⟨get rid⟩ \then/ go. I would
not stand it."

Stephen had little instinct for character, though ⟨this⟩ his grip was sure in the
end. "Money? Life?" he said ominously. "We weren't talking of ⟨⟨things ⟨that⟩
like that.⟩⟩ \real things. I thought you were ill./ Do you—say it again.⟨"⟩ Do
⟨are⟩ you ask me to live in this bad house? ⟨I thought you were ill.⟩"

"On the mantlepiece is a ⟨photop⟩ photograph. You know who I mean. She
planned that we should live together and then suddenly died."

"I can't follow—because—Money and life?—Were you never told I called here
last Sunday week?"

"I was told. But——"

"Did your wife act without your permission⟨?"⟩ then?"

"No.⟨"⟩ But then I didn't know. I had made an unspeakable mistake. I thought
you were my father's son."

Stephen's anger and bewilderment were increasing.

"I hated my father" said Rickie. "I loved my mother." And never had the
phrases seemed so destitute of meaning.

[*A43*:*] "Last Sunday week" began Stephen, his voice rising, "I came to call on
you. Not as this or that's son. Not to fall on your neck. Nor to talk about torches
and Orion. Nor—Damn your dirty little mind! I meant to say I didn't come for
money. Sorry. Sorry. I simply came \\, as I was, and I havn't altered since."

\"Yes⟨"⟩——/ Yet our mother——she has risen from the dead⟨—I love
her⟩."//

[*The additions on A43* now lead not to A57 but directly to A44* (p. 377), which is connected
to A46* in this version by a brief passage on A45, below. An inserted "Therefore", in the ink
of A45, appears on A44* after "arms of Nature."*]

\Therefore/ [*A45:*] ⟨when they disaggreed \on it/ they⟩ \they/ could give each
other⟨,⟩ terrible inexplicable wounds.

"Don't let us talk" said Rickie. "It is all getting worse. Simply say that you
forgive me, my brother."

"No!" he shouted. "No, no," and struck furiously at the broken glass.

Then Rickie began a new appeal—not to pity, for now he was in [*see A46**,
p. 378]

CHAPTER 32

The eight leaves of Chapter 32 (*506–513*), finally headed XXXIII, show the fine-pointed, slightly grayer or slightly bluer inks of the drafts of Chapter 31. Probably a version of the chapter was complete before the division of Chapter 31, because *506–7* obviously replace *A64–A65*, which open the notes below; *508* (259:30 for–260:7 our) was once the bottom of *A65*, and *509* followed. *510* (260:28 enquiries–261:5) is an insert, as is *511*, where revisions reflect the change to Agnes's less physical response to Stephen. *512* (261:18 all–28 that) is earlier and depeditated; *513* is later, closely resembling the more hastily written *506–7*. *507v* shows an undeleted variant related to *A63*: "heard it before, saying those words." *A64* is neatly headed XXXIII:

[*A64:*] By the month of November, Dunwood House ⟨had risen⟩ \was rising/ from its ashes. The fire had not been disadvantageous to Mr Pembroke. Since the boys were at school they had not been able to make use of the patent appliances, but on the other hand, they had none of them been killed. ⟨His own part⟩ \The/ private house had been saved, and the ⟨new⟩ \other/ buildings had been insured so heavily that they could be reconstructed with even greater attention to sanitation and hygiene. Moreover the excitement distracted gossip a little from his more intimate affairs.

Technically, Agnes lived ⟨him⟩ with him no longer. Mr and Mrs Elliot had left Sawston. But ⟨S⟩ she had stayed \on/ with him as a visitor, ⟨ever since July⟩ \\ever since ⟨June⟩ \July/ //. And what he called 'the negotiations' were still in progress on this November afternoon. "Here" he told her "are all Rickie's letters, here my minutes of the interview with \old/ Mr Ansell, here is \a note from/ Stephen Wonham's ⟨present address⟩."

She only gave him half her attention, for a beautiful wreath had just arrived from the ⟨cemetary⟩ florist's. She was [*A65:*] taking it up to the cemetery: to day was the anniversary of her child's death.

"What am I to do? Rickie now asks for ⟨the⟩\these/short stories ⟨he once wrote⟩."
"Send all you can find, I suppose."
"It seems that he is writing a book."
⟨"Is he.⟩ "Ah?"
"⟨And also that he⟩ \He/ has \also/ altered his will. Fortunately he cannot alter much. But I fear that ⟨about⟩ \the/ two thousand pounds, that ⟨is⟩ \are/ not settled on you, will go."

259 1† did not receive ← never received [*506*]
2† happened⟨. To question the three men was impossible and his⟩ \when . . . His/
3† She⟨, in the full agonies of reaction, made⟩ \could make/
8 \unbalanced/ ← unhealthy
14 \then/
15† those ← the
16† his ← those
17† last month ← \last week/ ← after him
22† her child . . . year. ← was the anniversary of her child's death. [*507*]
25† what is ← \the two thousand pounds/ ← all that is
260 3 lie⟨, which a man won't pardon⟩; [*508*]
5 \which . . . pardon/ ← and at last he broke loose.
6 \classic/ ← Greek
8† Wiltshire ← Cadover [*509*]
\a thunderbolt on Sawston [and]/ ← an avalanche
10† money which . . . own ← two thousand pounds

12† 〈either〉 to learn 〈or to suffer〉 from
     \from such lessons/ ← by such facts
14† do them harm ← \be revenged/ ← wrong them back
17 \Tell . . . though./ ← Did you enquire about Stephen Wonham?
22† and . . . More ← and her lips curved to a smile. "Does he drink more
30† She smiled ← Her lips curved [510]
32† The poise . . . tired! ← 〈He followed the tracks of Gerald.〉
35† degradation. 〈His figure stood firm in the mist, disturbing her.〉 She
36† her lover; ← Gerald,
  † \with . . . understood,/

261 7† humanity? 〈Yet she had turned to him, as to Gerald.〉 It ← humanity? Yet 〈into his arms she had fallen.〉 \she had . . . Gerald./ It [511]
8 \anyone/ ← any woman
10 had 〈fallen into his arms.〉 \turned . . . truth./
14 written—〈〈 〈Mrs Failing〉 \all the family/ is on our side—don't—〉〉 Mrs
20 \prevailed/ ← grown [512]
25† Rickie. ← 〈Rickie.〉 her husband.
29† fail. 〈And—best of all!—his〉 \His/ [513]
  † away. ← to death.
30 Rickie! 〈What will be left him in a little time?〉 I
  † civil ← friendly
32 \moved/ ← walked
33† after his death ← \there/
34† she . . . renew ← no one had renewed
35† as ← like

CHAPTER 33

The twenty-six leaves of Chapter 33 (*514–539*), numbered XXXIV, show four or five levels of revision and a final scene so different from the published one that it is transcribed below; in the published text Stephen's thoughts on marriage and the paragraph on "Romantic love" (272:6, *A30*) have been salvaged from the discarded Ansell-Stephen portion of Chapter 31. Among the manuscript leaves the earlier pages are the slightly bluer *517–18* (263:16 for–264:1 trying), *522* (265:21–266:6 earth), *526–7* (267:20 because he–268:11 agreed), *534* (270:13–17 over), and perhaps *535–6* (*ends* 271:24 turned). These are succeeded by *514* (*ends* 262:9), *516* (*begins* 262:26 For) and *528* (268:11 ¶It's–24), all in a pale brown ink. Gray-black inks then follow, modulating into the scratchy black of the later pages, *515*, *529–30* (268:25–269:10 if), *533* (*begins* 269:39), and *538*, for which see below; *539*, again in a paler ink, is later still. The versos are relatively minor. At the intermediate levels *534v* provides a draft of the sentence which opens *523*, and *523v* shows two lines which were copied onto the bottom of *521* in order not to waste paper; *539v*, in the ink of *536* or *537*, shows a nearly exact draft of the last few lines of the chapter. Among the late sheets *529v* shows an abandoned draft of *515*, and *538v* shows a deleted passage related to Forster's trip to the Loire valley in October 1906:

    Last October I determined to go to the river Loire. My plan was to strike it at Orleans (the upper waters being not so interesting) 〈and then〉 to proceed down stream to Blois and stop a few days there; to go on, by Amboise, to Tours; to stop a week or more

262 5† In . . . Madingley ← Once [*514*]

     11† with his chin on ← \with his elbows on/ ← smoking over [*515; the last phrase undeleted on 529v*]

     12 also . . . sulky. [*515*] ← [*529v:*] also⟨, in spite of Mrs Failing's anger⟩. He had said, rather pathetically, that ⟨all these new places muddled him, especially London, and he could not remember⟩ he needed a country to which he was used

     15 sulky. ⟨¶"I've won this time" Rickie said to them. "But it is certainly wearing."⟩ [*515*]

     16† \He knows everything./

     24 He means . . . Good bye! ← He said he'ld have a bout this evening. Good bye!

     26† "But . . . cried. ← "Good bye! they cried. "But . . . pass." [*An earlier* they cried. *is deleted at the decapitation of 516.*]

263 11† \the poems . . . two years. ¶Then/ ← a book. As he did so [*516*]

     16† shunting, . . . sure. ← shunting, the door opened, and Stephen clambered up from the line. He was \now/ in high spirits⟨, and⟩\. He/ sat on the dusty floor of the carriage, roaring with laughter ⟨and pinching⟩ \and pinching/ his ⟨brother's⟩ {senior's} \brother's/ legs. Rickie was not ⟨equally⟩ \so/ pleased. [*517*]

     26† with . . . floor. ← too." ← to Cadover with you!" ← to Cadover." [*518*]

     28† \Get up./

     30 \settled/ ← jolly well swore

     35† Stewart's lofty brow ← ⟨Ansell⟩ \Stewart/. Then he began to sing that ⟨famous⟩ \historic/ ballad 'Old Em'ly, she limps.'

     37 I felt. ⟨⟨If I ⟨am to make friends with⟩ \visit/ my aunt—we decided by letter I ⟨ought to⟩ \might/—I've no right to drag you down ⟨upon her⟩ there on her.⟩⟩\"/

264 11† morning!" . . . station?" ← ⟨day!⟩ \morning!/ What stopped us⟨?"⟩ \getting there?" ¶"Sawston railway station, of course. No trains⟨.⟩ till six. Ugh how ill we felt! Then Stewart found us." [*519*]

     15† did what . . . alone. ← got to Wiltshire.

265 3† In that case ← Then [*521*]

     4† laughing, but quite ← pleasant but

     † \Stephen . . . spoilt him./

     14† "Oh, ← "You old woman,

     15† and ⟨then⟩ I don't

     19 \temple . . . letter/ [*521; abandoned on 523v:*] temple. ¶"So you said

     27† "I . . . sleep?" ← "Have you never been ⟨asleep⟩ \tempted to go to sleep?" [*522*]

     28 \Just . . . train/ ← Rickie was baffled. The train

     31 confused him, ⟨as Stephen had discovered,⟩ and

     33† "Do . . . life. ← "⟨It seems to me that yours⟩ \Yours/ is a ⟨most⟩ perilous attitude.

     34 \A man ⟨like you must⟩ will have other/ ← For men have other— graver—

266 1† "⟨Of course.⟩ What else

     2† Rickie . . . window. ← \Rickie sighed and gazed thoughtfully out of the window./

     4 \He observed that the/ ← The

     6† were . . . ⟨bright⟩ green . . . \under elms or/ . . . ⟨water⟩ \waters/. [*523; an abandoned draft stands inverted on 534v:*] were flowing, merging, parting a little for some green valley, where cattle stood beside translucent

14† He said ← He ⟨said crossly that this⟩ blushed and said
16† "Surely ⟨it is.⟩\!/"
18 \decently/
19† seized ⟨by the waist⟩ and
22 trick⟨, on the edge of the finest scenery in England⟩.
26† No\, no/. [524]
27† \I promise./
36† \and conceit/
37 \Stephen was ⟨easy to live with⟩ an easy . . . with./ ← ⟨and⟩ he was the easiest person to live with in the world.

267 1 apology. ⟨How else could he be equipped for life?⟩ "You
14† mountain ⟨the Bacchic torches still ascend⟩, and [525]
17 \said . . . reveller./ ← he said mournfully.
19† a ⟨very⟩ happy moment ⟨for him⟩, partly . . . must care [525; *the sentence replaces lines deleted at the top of 526:*] ⟨the capital. ¶It was a happy journey, for Rickie was now certain that his brother cared⟩
23† disentangle himself from ← leave [526]
26† though . . . come. ← there was a reward.
32 \saints robes/ ← the garments of heroines and saints
33 \who . . . watching./ ← and rather hard to manage.
38† don't ⟨at all⟩ mind

268 3 \Pious/ ← Churchy ← Religious [527]
6 'settled things' ⟨with the aid of sixpenny reprints⟩.
7 \straw/ ← damn
8 \And . . . settled/ ← It was hard indeed that one so enlightened
14† maturity⟨⟨ ⟨. It would furrow slowly⟩, and the hints grew plainer at each revolution of the carriage wheels. Were he a pilgrim, one would say he was approaching his shrine⟩⟩. "You [528]
15† the \old/ spire
22† other downs ← Marlborough downs ← Berkshire downs
25† time \for that/. [529; *undeleted lines at the foot of 528 are similar:*] ¶"I ⟨shant⟩\shouldn't/ have time. What about Cadbury Rings, if tomorrow's fine?" ¶"Tomorrow will be fine.—But I say—to touch it!"
26† Or . . . Stonehenge. ← Stonehenge is wired in, but you still \can/ see it without paying. [529]
30† kindly ← gently
33† used to them⟨: in London he had forgotten so many names, but all was coming back now. "Not the bridge for the London Road though: I can't remember whether it has one arch or two. Odd what a little thing fidgets one. I wish we⟩\. He wished they/
34† \Cadchurch/

269 3† "I do," said Rickie. ← Rickie lowered his eyes. [530]
20 \a bystander/ ← another boy [531]
24 \bystander/ ← second boy
32 \What's . . . boy?/ ← The boy's right enough. [532]
39† irritation ⟨soon⟩ passed [533]

270 5† that they ignored ← them empty and idle, ignoring
7† frothy ⟨brawling⟩ sea
12† assertive ← garrulous
16 \climbed up her slopes/ ← scrambled up the barriers [534]
21 \at . . . entrenchment/ ← ⟨towards⟩ at Cadbury Rings [535]
31† leisure. ← time⟨, and a deity⟩.

37† winter ← autumn [*536*]

271 13† The conversation . . . will you?" ← "Hold the reins, will you." said Stephen, and tried to light the lamp that was near him. The match went out. He did not try again but said "Drive ⟨on. It's easy⟩ \a little/," and folded his arms.

26 chalk. [*537; from this point until* The paper caught (272:37) *the manuscript reads:*] "Would we see the Rings in the day time?" he asked, and received the answer "We do see them.⟨High across the stream.⟩" Soon even the road vanished, and invisible water gurgled through the wheel spokes. The horse had chosen the ford.

"No hurry" whispered Stephen. "It is our stream. Let him drink."

⟨"They heard the horse drink⟩ \The horse drank/, and his sobs and tremors stole to them down the shafts. He ceased, but the tremor continued

"Are you ready?" said Rickie gently. Then he waited, while black land was united to black sky. But the sky overhead was clearer and in it twinkled the Plough and the central stars. "The horse is ready. Should we go on?"

The cart gave a little lurch and ceased to tremble. He felt the seat beside him. It was empty.

"Stephen—what's this?"

[*538:*] "Can't I get out?" said an unsteady voice. "Is there any objection?"

"No" said Rickie gravely "None."

"I got out to—to show you a kind of game."

"Are you in the water?"

"Yes."

"How is the game played?"

But he had already forgotten about the game. It was an excuse for something that he did not understand. "Matches" he said, and rattled a box in the darkness. "You may think it pretty. Mr Failing taught me. Now give me paper."

⟨"⟩Under the seat of the trap Rickie found loose papers ⟨lo⟩ and crumpled them into a ball. But Stephen had wandered to the horse's head. He patted it, while the waters ran south, bathing the ancles of them both. He kissed it. In the stillness each little noise seemed transfigured ⟨⟨ ⟨and it⟩ \. It/ seemed not night,⟩⟩ \The night was not darkness,/ but a bandage laid over the eyes. "Where are you?" said Rickie. Then a face ⟨⟨ ⟨rose⟩ \flickered/ out of the darkness.⟩⟩ [*539:*] flickered out of the gloom.

"Quite a current" ⟨and⟩ he whispered and bending down he illumined the dimpled surface of the ford "Give me your paper now."

But the face had been transfigured likewise, dear though it remained. ⟨It⟩ \In one moment it/ too had been bathed, cleansed, purged from the crudities of youth. The bar of manhood ⟨had been set on⟩ \overshadowed/ the lips, arresting the eye ⟨with⟩ \like/ a flourish of gold. Some faces are knit by beauty, or by intellect: Stephen's had waited for the touch of the years.

⟨Then the⟩ \So they played. The/ paper caught

272 37 \from the match/ [*539, where the rest of the paragraph is like the text. There are some early variants on the inverted but undeleted 539v:*]

273 4 \tunnel/ ← cavern

6† declared . . . afloat ← \said . . . afloat/ ← declared that he still saw it

7 arch, ⟨⟨where the stream ⟨turned⟩ \passed/ under a willow, burning⟩⟩ burning

CHAPTER 34

The twenty-one leaves of Chapter 34 (*540–560*) are relatively neat, perhaps because of extensive recopying; there are no versos and the few fragmented sheets do not make the precedence of the inks entirely clear. A gray sequence runs from *540* to *548* (*ends* 278:6 small), interrupted only by the insertion of *546* (277:2–22 below), a hasty gray-brown full quarto replacing the decapitated top of *547*. Uneven brown ink then runs from *549* to *552* (*ends* 279:39), but both *550* (278:23–36 penetrated) and *552* are depeditated at passages slightly different from the published text. A bolder gray then runs from *553* to *556* (281:7–22), which is depeditated as an addition and is quite different from the text. The last four sheets all show brown ink but were not originally consecutive; *557* (*ends* 281:31) is decapitated, *558* (*ends* 282:4 wife) is depeditated as an insert, *559* (*ends* 282:16) is depeditated, and *560*, a full quarto ending with plenty of extra space at 282:30, without the last paragraph of the chapter, is so neat that it must have been recopied.

274   3† somehow arrived ← was announced [*540*]

11† lumps of chalk having ← for stones had

12† For . . . Stephen. ← "Save them ⟨every one⟩" she told Leighton, and now they stood in a row on the mantlepiece, ⟨⟨so that she saw them three times ⟨every⟩ \a/ day⟩⟩ \where she could see them/. Rickie saw them too, and expected that ⟨Stephen would be⟩ their first topic ⟨of discussion⟩ would be Stephen.

16† was . . . said. ← seemed to be with them always, ⟨now in the room, now close to the window outside⟩

19 success ⟨and the sale of his other books had revived in consequence⟩. [*541*]

31 \True Patriot/ ← Two Patriots

275 12† the earth? ← her? [*542*]

14† \"Do you . . . possible."/

17 \"I think not ⟨on the whole⟩."/ ← "No, Aunt Emily. I don't think I agree."

30† \foolishly and/ [*543*]

35† cannot help interfering. ← will.

36† despises me. ← cannot help it.

276 16† with ⟨a divine⟩ pity [*544*]

19† one \little/ fact

† as . . . theory. ← of. It does go against your theory.

26 rubbish⟨—ruined arches, terrible but distinct⟩. Two [*545*]

28† room ⟨⟨and I ⟨still see⟩ \saw/ the dots of their tobacco, crossing and recrossing in the dark⟩⟩.

† What happened to ← Where are

29† They . . . good, ← I never thought much of them,

38† inconveniences ← grieves

277 7† frowned. "⟨Why?⟩ In [*546*]

21 "Go on." [*Not present in the similar passage deleted at the top of 547.*]

22† The day . . . below, ← Straight underneath us is the [*547:*] the day,

24† "You are ← In the silence he heard her fingering the stones on the mantlepiece. \"You are/ ← In . . . mantlepiece. "It is

† after a pause ← at last

\not like you at all/ ← not sympathize

25† eating \my/ biscuits

26† you? ⟨⟨Once, for my sins, I ⟨was taken a voyage round the world⟩, \circumnavigated the ⟨globe⟩ ⟨world⟩ earth/, but I came back as certain as ever that ⟨she⟩ \it/ is flat.⟩⟩ I am

29† But . . . usual. ← I should not sleep a wink if I believed you. But I shall sleep. [548]

33† with. ⟨She missed Stephen terribly.⟩ Rickie ← ⟨for⟩ \with. She . . . terribly./ Rickie

278 4† ⟨⟨ ⟨the⟩ \far/ ⟩⟩ greater \, inasmuch . . . entirely/.

8† lumps of chalk. ← stones. [549]

12† He had . . . He stood ← ⟨⟨That evening his brother had fallen in love, though not with any person, ⟨and had knelt, but⟩ \and had/ knelt, but to no visible altar, and had been baptized, but not by any human priest.⟩⟩ They had pretended it was a game, each knowing that the other pretended, and Rickie had driven away alone. ⟨"Good night! he had called. His⟩ \He/ too was content. ⟨⟨For ⟨he⟩ \a/ moment he⟩⟩ \He/ stood

16† chalk ← stone

23† preparing ← stripping [550]

27† again November. ← winter.

28 \stopped/ ← was

29 At nine ← He cleared the table quickly, and at nine

30† house, . . . zenith. ← house. ¶⟨Stars shone only⟩ \The stars were ⟨bright⟩ still only bright in the zenith⟨, becoming⟩\. They became/ fainter as they descended the sky and ⟨disappearing⟩ disappeared while the horizon was still distant.

36† It was . . . his face. ← The gravel was new and needed rolling ⟨and Rickie would have⟩ \Rickie stumbled./ [551:] ⟨he was not quarrelling with them.⟩ After the lodge gate ⟨walking was smoother⟩ \the road improved/.

39 bridge ⟨to drop cigarette ashes into the stream⟩.

279 2† had not noticed ← did not know

7 \were in Cadford/ ← reached their destination

14† "Where? Why?" ← "Gone? Where?"

21† Leighton. "⟨That will smarten them up.⟩ Why ← Leighton ⟨consoling him⟩. "That . . . Why [552]

23 \To . . . London."/ ← One to one part of London, another to another."

27 pace. ⟨He noticed the bad smells as they passed the farm.⟩ This

35† fight till he died. ← ⟨fight till he⟩ dropped. [*The deleted opening words of 553 (see* 279:39 *below) were once to take over here, but the cut was not implemented and* 552 *continues:*]

† \Stephen . . . love./

37 \Rickie caught . . . felt/ ← he ⟨showed⟩ shone as a hero, and Rickie felt

39† for such a man. ← for ⟨him.⟩ such a man. At last [553:] ⟨fight like a hero. That evening Rickie⟩ \he/ understood his brother. ⟨⟨He had a work before him, which he ⟨could⟩ \would/ worthily perform.⟩⟩ His pride and pleasure in him increased, and ⟨it⟩ a supernatural blessing seemed to descend on both of them. The spirit of the generations ⟨spoke⟩ \praised them/⟨, and its⟩\. Its/ voice was a woman's.

280 1† "The . . . Those ← "Here we are" said Leighton "The Antelope is those

3[please ask ← mind asking

7† hiding all but the legs of ← almost hiding

9† scene⟨, on the whole,⟩ was picturesque\—fairer . . . town/.

17† Rickie⟨, who was puzzled⟩. [*554*]

18† stuffy ← airless

† and . . . drinking ← though they sound cheerful enough

26† drinking?" ← drunk."

28† be. ⟨He promised me.⟩ If

32† "In ← "Nothing's left him, if he's untrue to himself. He's made that way. He isn't like ⟨us⟩ me⟨. Nothing⟩\: nothing/ could rescue [*555:*] Stephen. In

35 stamped ← mimicked

36† speak out ⟨like a man.⟩?

37† "He can't stand ← "Drunk as a tinker

281 1 \furiously/ ← severely

5† he's drunk. Tell . . . and I ← my brother is drunk. Tomorrow morning tell him that he's broken his word: that it means he'll break it again: that he's hopeless from this night forward, and I

10† ¶In the room . . . with friends. ← ¶He turned to Leighton and said quietly "Here is the end of our journey."

Leighton nodded.⟨"⟩

"⟨I am not hysterical.⟩ \It's been a mad attempt./ So little kept Stephen together. ⟨Henceforward he⟩ ⟨He⟩ \Now he/ falls to pieces⟨, and so⟩\. So/ do I. I'm ruined. ⟨So⟩ \Very/ little kept me together⟨:⟩, either: only his Will." [*end 556; 557 opens with a deleted end-of-paragraph:*] ⟨I'm ruined."⟩

"Ruined?" asked Leighton. "Why, there's nothing the matter with you⟨.⟩\, and/ Stephen's only had a drop too much. ⟨⟨We all say the worst we ⟨know⟩ \can think/ of then.⟩⟩

27† such . . . fellow ← the high strung gentleman

home. ⟨The laughter pursued them. Stephen brayed hoarsely and tried to follow. They hurried away, and⟩ \As they hurried away,/ the shoulders

32† that's wrong? ← to talk like this? [*558*]

34 that ⟨tangible⟩ people are

39† leant ← knelt

282 3 degradation! At [*Deleted at the top of 559 are related lines:*] ⟨living had gone: the conventions would claim him in the end. At⟩

4† \childish/ [*558*]

5† \He was too weak./ [*559*]

8† out, ⟨little by little,⟩ in drunkenness

10† \by a man/

† \in a man. She would not continue./

13 \turf/ ← earth

14 bather, ⟨⟨ the ⟨ro⟩ ⟨shadowy world, the sho⟩ ⟨marriage of⟩ round earth⟩⟩ the shoulders

16 dream. ⟨Let us beware of the earth—Nothing tangible [nothing human,] is real. The game⟩ [*end 559*]

18† \: I told . . . bad/. [*560*]

21† \Again nothing mattered./

23† a . . . pass ← the passing of a slow goods train

† In the glare of the engine ← Then

24† through . . . of ← remembering their appointment at

25† lay ⟨dead⟩ drunk
27† and ⟨to⟩ push
28† train went ← train, instead of killing him at once, passed
29† Cadover, ⟨absolutely hopeless,⟩ whispering

CHAPTER 35
The eleven leaves of the final chapter (*561–571*), numbered XXXVI, reach only
to the child's goodnights at the depeditation of *571* (288:34); there is no manuscript for the final three paragraphs of the novel, although parts of the next line
can be deciphered at the tear. The pages are relatively neat. The earliest appear
to be the first two, *561–2*, ending at 283:32 with a depeditation which shows a
reference to the need for an introduction to Rickie's stories, and the last two,
570–1 (*begins* 287:35 with). A sequence of full quartos runs from *563* to *569*,
interrupted only by the decapitated *565* (285:11–21), perhaps an addition.

283 1 over ⟨some sweetpeas down⟩ a ⟨sombre⟩ \sober/ [*561*]
18 \is . . . want/ ← said Mr Pembroke
21† "I don't remember." ← "No."
27 \Is . . . plain?/ ← So you understand [*562*]
  \Submit these ten/ ← Send these eight
30† four ← five
31 a ⟨most interesting book⟩ {nice} \volume/ . . . might call
32 'Pan Pipes' ← 'In Touch with Nature' [*see* 140:36]
284 1† used up ← bagged [*563*]
2† bearing ← putting up
8 \impatiently/ ← haughtily
10† furrard. ← on.
13 \proceed/ ← get on
15 \with all those details that sold/ ← that boomed
17 \penned/ ← wrote
20† leads . . . life. ← is always occupied. They entertain on a large scale.
21† \since you insist/
29† smiled ← stared [*564*]
30† child ← little girl
31† cuddling ← licking
34† It . . . harm. ← I was the same. It did me no harm.
  \up! . . . dirty/ ← up, beast! Go and clean your tongue
285 35† is ⟨very⟩ good [*566*]
36 interview.⟨⟨" ¶"I never object to a bit of business⟨."⟩ \on Sunda/⟩⟩ \Is
  it . . . plain?"/
286 2 only ⟨five?"⟩ four?" ⟨⟨¶Mr Pembroke grew red. ⟨"I was meaning——
  "⟩ He wished to retort 'I mean—', and by an unfortunate slip said "I am
  mean."⟩⟩
7† lifted . . . palm. ← began to be alarmed; Stephen stepped between him
  and the door. [*567*]
8† his voice drove ← he shouted
11 \it fetched./ ← I know a little. I see the papers, and that book's
  still selling.
12† \and tidied . . . introduction/
14† I think ← often
  † that won't comfort us. ← \that's no excuse./ ← that's because
  you're a fool.
16 \Sham/ ← Rotten [*in each case*]

394

18† snatched . . . world." ← laid both hands on him. "That was a lie. For a man can answer back in the world. He can run away \in it/. ⟨Look!⟩"

20† saw \only/ the

21† but in it a ← ⟨and the⟩ \with a/

  † would . . . sea. ← flowed towards the Avon and would in time glide past the spire of Salisbury ⟨and the tower of Christ church and⟩ \to/ be mingled in the sea.

22† even at ← at all

25† there's . . . answer ← \there's no smaller world. There's one world, Pembroke. One./ Men answer ← you can't have it any smaller. Men answer [568]

28 \a man . . . answers/ ← them that ⟨five⟩ \four/ . . . they answer

29† ⟨that⟩ you're a ⟨bloody⟩ liar

37† money ← two thousand pounds

287 1† filched ← stolen

5† "Steady . . . Take ← "Oh go" he said gently. "Go home, little boy, go home. I will give to you

10 \unclerical/ ← wrong [569]

11 \blurred over/ ← forgot

13 he never \heeded/ ← ⟨it never occurred to him⟩ he never thought of listening to

15 \was . . . magisterial/ ← paid ⟨little⟩ \small/ attention

17 \send up . . . caned/ ← give a thousand lines

28† could . . . indistinct. ← \did not regret that ⟨heart rending⟩ tragedy, already half forgotten, indistinct./ ← rejoiced that the link had snapped that might have bound him and his sister to this unsavoury man.

39 \Old vagrancies awoke/ ← \The ⟨interview⟩ \visit/ had moved him more than he knew/ ← Something stirred within him [570]

288 7 he cried. ← ⟨she⟩ he cried, and ⟨it is⟩ time that I slept out again.

8 \where I used to be/ ← \to the left/ ← between the beech copses that ⟨one⟩ you see from Cadbury Rings

15† The child ← ⟨"No."⟩ \"I wont."/ And the child [571]

18† \Don't worry . . . dreadfulnesses./

22 impertinently⟨, and the sound made her love him more than ever⟩.

26 why he{, the accident} was here

Textual Notes

The text of this edition of *The Longest Journey* is the result of comparing the seven editions published during Forster's lifetime with each other and with his manuscripts. The comparisons of the editions were computer-aided, the major work being done by the IBM 3081 of the University of Cambridge. The seven editions were "read in" by means of an optical scanner; the first "in" was freed of obvious scanning errors in order to establish a standard for comparison; a trial comparison against the second "in" revealed that the basic text needed also to be rid of such distractions as justifying hyphens; and four editions were compared to the revised standard. By then it was clear that the basic text could be edited to conform to the patterns of the Abinger Edition in order to run the last two comparisons with a double purpose, exposing errors in those two editions while confirming the editorial changes. A final comparison of the finished, fully edited text with the earlier standard produced a list of changes which accord with those made in earlier Abinger volumes except for the retention of Forster's "learnt", in this volume not changed to "learned".

In the computer comparisons there were great advantages over the alternative of gathering seven people to read the novel aloud: computers do not tire, do not make phonetic errors, and will repeat the whole exercise on demand. They turn up every iota of difference in what they are given. Collation and evaluation of the differences are as subject to human error as always, but the printouts recording the process are now housed in the King's College Library and may be consulted by anyone in pursuit of error or the minutiae of eight different editorial practices, for the end result of using the computer in this way is that, if the typesetting computers hold true to the course prescribed by the master tape, faults in the Abinger text of *The Longest Journey*, as in the surrounding editorial matter, must be attributed not to anonymous typists or compositors but to the editor herself. A further result is that a concordance to the Abinger text of the novel has been compiled by John Dawson of the Literary and Linguistic Computing Centre of Cambridge University. Copies can be consulted in the Centre and in the King's College Library; they list "key word in context" uses of all but the most common words in the novel, like "and" and "he". The accompanying word counts show such totals as these: "love" (100); "money" (64); "real" (33); "reality" (9); "realize" (10); "realized" (5); "realizes" (1); and "really" (73).

All substantive differences between this and the seven earlier editions are noted below, as are a few differences in style and spelling and punctuation, in particular the reparagraphing of the American editions. Accidentally created words have been included as a formality even when they are clearly wrong, but obvious misspellings, including most wrong plural possessives, have been omitted. (Singular possessive forms, like "Watts'" and "Aeneas's", have remained constant since the first edition and are unchanged here.) Hyphenation and spelling and punctuation of course differ from edition to edition, though not as much as they differ from manuscript to first edition; in the comparisons the most noticeable characteristic of the Abinger styling of these matters is the simplification of all double dashes and comma-dash combinations to a single unspaced dash. Otherwise the punctuation of this edition, like the substance, is essentially that of the first British edition (Blackwood, 1907; Kirkpatrick A2*a*), although, as the appendix of manuscript variants indicates, many changes from the punctuation in the manuscript, especially the reduction of sentences beginning "But" or "And" to clauses following semi-colons, must be attributed to Blackwood's editor rather than to Forster or his typist. No printers' proofs exist to show whether Forster rejected any such changes; clearly he accepted many. Blackwood was in fact more tolerant of Forster's inconsistent treatment of commas in series and his unusual colons or quotation marks than many of his later publishers, allowing him also his "bran-new" (181:34), changed to the traditional "brand-new" by his subsequent British and American editors, including this one.

Both Blackwood and Forster's typist served him well, for he was by no means a perfectionist in his proofreading, and, excluding his misspelled French (199:9), there are only eight relatively obvious errors in the first edition, caught by one or another later editor, and only twenty less obvious variants, most of which could easily have originated in a typist's misreading of the manuscript. (See Appendix C for occasional examples of what may be other minor misreadings.) Six Abinger returns to the styling or punctuation of the manuscript are also listed below; one of these (112:17) changes a speaker. The only error noted by Forster was "circling" for "ceiling" (118:5), corrected in his hand in his mother's copy of the first edition, now in the King's College Library. This error was also caught in the second British edition but not in the American editions; it is part of the evidence that Forster made no corrections for the first American edition (Knopf, 1922; Kirkpatrick A2*b*). The other evidence is that the Knopf edition was simply not well proofed and shows a number of misprints as well as more than a hundred variants. The second American edition, in a paperback range of Knopf publications (Vintage, 1962; Kirkpatrick A2*g*), corrected the misprints of the first but added more than twenty further variants, half of them simple slips in setting, like the four has/had confusions, and the other half either conscious or unconscious adaptations to American usage. About the same proportion of slips and adaptations characterizes the first Knopf printing, where only ten or twelve of the changes have more than a very minor effect. American unfamiliarity with the British use of "stop" to mean "stay for a visit", for instance, must be responsible for the substitution of "thing" for "time" (115:37), although "anything" for "any writing" (180:8) is surely a misreading. But only the American editions, with all their faults, spell Pittsburgh correctly.

The second British edition was the Uniform edition published by Edward Arnold (Arnold, 1924; Kirkpatrick A2*c*). There is again no evidence that Forster made any corrections. Although five of the obvious Blackwood errors, including "ceiling", were caught, and there were very few misprints, some sixteen variants were added and have persisted through all later British editions. Some of them, like the wrong "correction" of Cadford (279:7) and the removal of the mildly unconventional quotation marks in Stephen's goodnights (288:3), look like the work of a too-helpful editor and argue against Forster's involvement. Two uncaught compositor's errors prepared the way for further error in the second Arnold edition (Pocket Edition, 1947; Kirkpatrick A2*d*) and its revisions, where an added quotation mark (197:6) and, in the 1955 revision, an added question mark (54:16), complete two corruptions of dialogue. The Pocket Edition of 1947 was sometimes pleasingly idiosyncratic in the thirty-four variants it created; its "stormy-petrol" (194:27) and the Vintage "Interstate" (285:21) are my favorites among the inadvertencies of the various editions. The Pocket Edition was very carefully corrected in its 1955 imprint, which in two cases (67:2 and 127:23) restored manuscript readings, clearly on the basis of the editor's general knowledge, and also half-corrected Forster's miswritten French. Fourteen of the 1947 variants escaped, however, together with the wrongful quotation marks, and nearly all of these recur in the fourth and fifth British editions, both set from the 1955 Pocket Edition and published within six weeks of each other.

Of these two the earlier (Penguin, 1960; Kirkpatrick A2e) is the better. The Penguin edition adds only fifteen variants of its own and redeems its errors by its choice of the correct spellings in Forster's French and in his allusions to Mrs Bennet of *Pride and Prejudice* and to Petty Cury and the Footlights of Cambridge. I have concurred in these corrections and have also accepted one of the Penguin changes in punctuation (219:31) even though there is no manuscript evidence for it. The World's Classics edition (Oxford, 1960; Kirkpatrick A2f) also completes the correction of Forster's French and rightly rejects the plural "friends" (62:9) introduced by the Pocket Edition, but it then adds thirty minor errors of its own, one of them (59:8) a slip that also appears in the American editions. One further correction was made in the 1962 imprint of the Pocket Edition, where the wrongful quotation marks (197:5-6) have been deleted; it is tempting to think that Forster himself might have discovered the error, or perhaps been consulted by a diligent reader at Arnold, but there is no record of the reason for the change.

In the variants listed below the editions have been abbreviated: Blackwood to B; Arnold 1924 to A; Pocket Edition to PE; Penguin to Pen; Oxford to Ox; Knopf to K; Vintage to V. The most common patterns of inheritance, in descending order of occurrence, are: K, V (115); A, PE, Pen, Ox (14); PE, Pen, Ox (14); B, K, V (8). Page and line numbers locate the Abinger readings, given first; variant readings appear to the right of the vertical bar. The Abinger readings listed are in almost all cases those of the manuscript; MS, indicating that the manuscript concurs with the reading on the same side of the bar, appears only when there is a divergence from the Abinger reading or from all the other editions.

5	22	**Rhinegold"** | **Rheingold** PE, Pen, Ox (Abinger quotation marks)
30	28	**whom** | **when** K, V
31	5	**Pray** MS | **pray** editions
32	35	**left** | **felt** K
		Pembrokes | **Pembrokes'** V
34	32	**in** | **on** V
		holidays | **Holidays** PE 1947
35	1	**is** | **it** Ox
	6	**bitter** MS | **little** editions
39	17	**More** | new paragraph K, V
40	1	**They** | new paragraph K, V
	7	**The** | new paragraph K, V
	33	**would remember** MS | **could remember** editions
42	4	**woods and heather** MS | **woods and heath** B | **the woods and heath** other editions
	10	**and** | omitted K, V
	12	**middle** | omitted K, V
	19	**of** | omitted K, V

43	2	**traditions | tradition** V
	15	**Perhaps |** new paragraph K, V
	23	**Sawstonian | Sawtonian** K, V
	25	**masters' | master's** B, K, V
	35	**the boarders | boarders** K, V
45	13	**proudest | the proudest** K, V
	21	**reverence | reference** PE 1947
46	12	**attempted | attempt** V
	32	**schoolboys | the schoolboys** K, V
	33	**that |** omitted K, V
50	10	**animal | animals** PE, Pen, Ox
	24	**run** MS | **ran** editions
52	35	**Should |** new paragraph K, V
53	29	**never could | could never** K, V
54	16	**he is. | is he.** A, PE 1947 | **is he?** PE 1955, Pen, Ox
55	5	**Rickie |** new paragraph K, V
	13	**his | the** K, V
	29	**"Oh |** new paragraph K, V
56	1	**ever | even** V
	7	**life | a life** K, V
57	26	**come | comes** Ox
	28	**dolls' | doll's** B, K, V
	39	**Addenbrooke's | Addenbrookes** K, V
58	2	**substructures** MS | **substructions** editions
	21	**as easy as easy | as easy** Ox
	24	**a genius | genius** Ox
59	8	**has | had** K, V, Ox
	20	**would | should** K, V
60	18	**start and | start to** PE, Pen, Ox
61	21	**quite efficient | efficient** K, V
	30	**his | this** Pen
62	9	**friend | friends** PE, Pen
	13	**—but |** omitted Ox
	28	**Journalese | journalese** PE, Pen, Ox
63	2	**The little | The** K, V
	20	**Oh . . . difference! |** not repeated K, V
	32	**outsides | outside** K, V
65	16	**a |** omitted K, V
67	2	**Dolomites | dolomites** B, K, V, A, PE 1947
	15	**would know** MS | **knew** editions
68	23	**time, | time.** Ox
71	3	**Truth** MS | **truth** editions
	9	**That | The** K, V
	28	**a | at** Ox
	30	**round |** omitted K, V
	36	**got | got a** K
72	35	**hoped | hoped for** V
75	2	**for two | two** K, V
	14	**glazed | blazed** K
77	22	**quite | quiet** A, PE, Pen, Ox
78	1	**which | what** Ox
79	30	**a | your** PE 1947

83	6	**(she | (She** K, V
84	11	**was | were** K, V
	12	**they | he** K, V
85	9	**the shallow | shallow** K, V
	18	**Battlesden | Battleston** MS, editions
	26	**lay | would lay** K, V
	28	**on a | on the** K, V
86	32	**next | the next** K, V
87	1	**shepherds | Shepherds** K, V
	33	**a |** omitted K, V
		cleverer | clever V
88	29	**Arcady:** MS | **Arcady.** editions
		eyes: | eyes. K, V, Pen (perhaps broken in Pen)
89	3	**he | be** A
	11	**Pittsburgh | Pittsburg** MS, British editions
	28	**Eustace | Eustrace** K, V
90	19	**Mr | Mrs** Ox
93	5	**come | came** PE 1947
	11	**ago |** omitted K, V
94	26	**The |** new paragraph K, V
95	23	**Stephen! |** new paragraph A
	28	**The |** new paragraph K, V
96	2	**dealings | dealing** Pen
	3	**a |** omitted K, V
		certain MS | omitted editions
	28	**not have | have not** A, PE, Pen, Ox
97	2	**Rings | Range** K, V
	32	**superiors | superior** B, K, V
	36	**this | his** K, V
98	6	**reading-room | reading-rooms** K, V
100	6	**him." | him?"** A, PE, Pen, Ox
	8	**that |** omitted K, V, MS
	28	**that |** omitted K, V
	30	**"your | "Your** V, MS (after a full stop)
101	9	**Failing | Fielding** Ox (perhaps seeing "fielder")
102	14	**questioned | queried** K, V
	37	**delightful | delighted** Ox
103	14	**and of | and** K, V
106	14	**it. | it does.** K, V
108	34	**see— | —see** K, V
109	1	**the water | water** K, V
	14	**a | the** V
110	15	**These | Those** PE 1947
111	26	**at first |** omitted K, V
112	6	**Was** MS | **Were** editions (overwritten in MS)
		outside | outsides Pen
	17	**asking."** MS | **asking.** editions
	33	**her *you* | *her* you** Ox
114	13	**songs | song** K, V
115	18	**towards | toward** Pen
	22	**arms | hands** PE, Pen, Ox
	37	**time | thing** K, V

116	9	**carriers'** | **carrier's** Pen
117	3	**extraordinarily** | **extraordinary** B, A
	31	**new** | omitted K, V
118	5	**ceiling** | **circling** B, K, V
119	4	**acro-ter-ium** MS | **acro-terium** editions
	30	**girl?** | **girl!** Ox
123	28	**of** | omitted V
125	17	**hope** | **I hope** K, V
	22	**Cadbury** | **Cadsbury** K, V
127	23	**stacks** | **sacks** B, K, V, A, PE 1947
128	36	**moment** | **minute** K, V
129	11	**his** | **the** K, V
	37	**deferential** | **differential** K, V
130	32	**a** MS | **the** editions
	37	**had** | omitted K, V
131	2	**its** | omitted K, V
132	24	**Again** | new paragraph K, V
133	19	**sometime** | **in time** A, PE, Pen, Ox
134	8	**up on** MS | **upon** editions
	10	**out** | **came out** K, V
	12	**people** | **the people** K, V
	14	**held** MS | **had** editions
135	2	**grown-up brother** | **grown brother** K, V
	10	**step** | **steps** Ox
136	35	**cost** | **costs** K, V
	39	**repulsion, and** | **repulsion. And** A, PE, Pen, Ox
138	16	**darkness** | **the darkness** K, V
139	2	**at** | **as** K, V
	28	**Continual** | **Continued** Pen
140	39	**Mr** | **Mrs** K, V
141	9	**its** | **in** Ox
	33	**that** | omitted PE 1947
143	12	**though** | **thought** A, PE 1947
144	11	**had** | omitted K, V
147	29	**gentle man** | **gentleman** K, V, PE 1947, Pen
148	4	**of** | **of its** Pen
149	28	**Whereas** | new paragraph K, V
	29	**improved** | **had improved** K, V
150	15	**had a** | **had the** K, V
151	5	**simulate** | **stimulate** PE 1947
	8	**believed that** | **believed** K, V
	29	**and** | **and you** K, V
152	8	**of** | **from** Ox
	29	**of** | **for** K, V
155	27	**expressed** | **oppressed** PE 1947
156	29	**rabbits'** | **rabbit's** K, V
157	18	**very** | omitted K, V
	19	**in** | **in the** V
	22	**indistinguishable** | **undistinguishable** K, V
158	3	**has** | **had** V
	10	**And** | new paragraph A, PE, Pen, Ox
	35	**room full** | **roomful** V

159	30	**come | came** PE 1947
	33	**way | away** PE 1947
160	26	**He . . . spirits | He, in high spirits, met Herbert** PE 1947
162	23	**by | to** Ox
163	8	**day-boys' | day-boy's** PE, Pen, Ox
	10	**most | omitted** Ox
165	5	**working | work** Ox
166	12	**vain | in vain** K, V
167	28	**married** MS | **marriage** editions
170	1	**in | omitted** K, V
	31	**a | omitted** K, V
	38	**a flood | the flood** K, V
171	14	**can, can, can | can, can,** V
172	5	**fewer | few** A, PE, Pen, Ox
176	23	**window | windows** K, V
177	14	**sisters | sister** K, V
179	31	**all | in all** K, V
	37	**than | than to** K, V
180	8	**any writing | anything** K, V
	22	**sputtered | spluttered** A, PE, Pen, Ox
181	13	**was | omitted** K, V
	34	**brand-new | bran-new** MS, B
186	31	**this | the** Pen
187	26	**then. | then?** K, V
	37	**Yours | Your** V
189	9	**connection | connections** Pen
191	27	**a | omitted** Ox
194	3	**his | this** K, V
	5	**the fatal | a fatal** PE, Pen, Ox
	27	**stormy-petrel | stormy-petrol** PE 1947
196	15	**That | Then** V
	27	**which . . . room' | omitted** K, V
197	5	**They | "They** PE 1947-1955, Pen, Ox
	6	**all. | all."** A, PE 1947-1955, Pen, Ox
199	9	*suivent* | *suivrent* MS, B, K, V, A, PE 1947
		involontaires | *involuntaires* MS, all but Pen, Ox
	10	**warmed | warned** A, PE 1947
200	2	**satisfactorily | satisfactory** A, PE, Pen, Ox
201	4	**has | had** PE 1947
	33	**more | omitted** PE 1947
202	8	**"I** MS | **new paragraph** editions
	36	**wife. | wife?** A, PE, Pen, Ox
204	1	**he | He** PE, Pen, Ox
	2	**dreamt—?"** MS | **dreamt—"** editions. Obscure in MS, the question mark appears to have been wrongly placed after "poem", below, in TS or proof.
	4	**poem."** MS | **poem?"** editions
	6	**about** MS | **omitted** editions
205	25	**causes of | causes for** PE, Pen, Ox
	26	**dwelt, | dealt,** B, K, V
	27	**and | omitted** K, V
	32	**unacknowledged** MS | **acknowledged** editions

207	10	**anywhere | anyway** Pen
210	27	**They |** new paragraph PE 1947
		chapel | the chapel K, V
212	32	**county** MS | **country** editions
213	11	**you are** MS | **are you** editions
	24	**to | of** PE 1947
215	30	**wonder | wondered** K, V
219	31	**is. | is,** all but Pen; no MS
221	23	**his | this** Pen
	34	**meant | mean** K, V
	38	**has | had** PE, Pen, Ox
224	15	**his | this** PE, Pen, Ox
	26	**has—oh | has—of** Pen
232	20	**so |** omitted Ox
	38	**think | think of** Ox
234	22	**would | could** K, V
	28	**know", | know"** MS, British editions
236	5	**and my | and** K, V
	16	*trop | drop* PE 1947
237	8	**them | him** Ox
	20	**They |** new paragraph K, V
239	37	**and |** omitted Ox
241	27	**doom? | doom.** A, PE, Pen, Ox
242	6	**then | them** Ox
	26	**near to | near** K, V
245	5	**nor of | nor or** V
	27	**Tying | Trying** V
246	8	**ever swift, ever** MS | **even swift, even** editions
247	3	**to |** omitted PE 1947
	29	**had | has** V
249	30	**a | on a** V
252	10	**But |** new paragraph K, V
	13	**so | no** V
	20	**their | his** PE 1947
254	4	**meant | mean** Ox
	12	**he was. | it was.** PE, Pen, Ox (MS: see p. 377)
255	9	**has | had** V
	24	**idea | ideas** K, V
	36	**word | world** Pen
260	24	**his name. | him.** Ox
261	8	**It | it** Pen
	22	**stop | stopped** Pen
264	31	**of | with** K, V
	34	**noise | noise had** K, V
265	17	**called | call** A
266	6	**merging | and merging** K, V
	33	**towards | toward** V
267	15	**he | to** PE, Pen, Ox
	32	**saints' | saints** MS | **saint's** editions
268	22	**downs | towns** PE, Pen, Ox
270	16	**has | had** V
272	26	**illumined | illuminated** K, V

276 26 **a | the** A, PE, Pen, Ox
278   5 **some | the** PE 1947
279   7 **Cadford | Cadover** A, PE, Pen, Ox
280 10 **palaces | places** Pen
282 20 **we** MS | **one** editions
283   3 **Sunday | Saturday** Ox
284 14 **yes— | yes** V
285   2 **onto** MS | **on** editions
      19 **belonged** MS | **belong** editions
      21 **Intestate | Interstate** V
      30 **They've | They** K, V
286 34 **had | have** K, V
288   3 **rug." "Good | rug. Good** A, PE, Pen, Ox
       6 **till | until** K, V
      19 **dreadfulnesses | dreadfulness** K, V
      37 **here | there** Ox

General Notes

These notes often refer to the manuscripts of the novel, where revisions may illuminate a particular passage, but page references to Appendix C, "The Manuscripts of *The Longest Journey*", are given below only when the draft cannot be found easily by means of the same page number which keys the note to the text of the novel here. (In a few cases, like the spelling of "Zwieback" [p. 5], the difference is too minor to show in the appendix.) As in the Editor's Introduction, quotations from Forster's unpublished diaries and letters have here been edited for clarity and consistency, and full bibliographical details given in the opening notes to the Editor's Introduction have not been repeated here.

Page **3**: Ansell's insistence on the objective reality of the cow may bear some relation to Hegel's opinion of an overly abstract idea of the Absolute, expressed in his Preface to *Phenomenology of the Spirit*:

> Dealing with something from the perspective of the Absolute consists merely in declaring that, although one has been speaking of it just now as something definite, yet in the Absolute, the A = A, there is nothing of the kind, for there all is one. To pit this single insight, that in the Absolute everything is the same, against the full body of articulated cognition, which at least seeks and demands such fulfilment, to palm off its Absolute as the night in which, as the saying goes, all cows are black—this is cognition naively reduced to vacuity. (trans. A. V. Miller [Oxford, Clarendon Press, 1977], p. 9)

However, the tradition at King's College, Cambridge, is that Forster was drawing on an actual discussion and on actual cows, often pastured in Scholars' Piece, the college meadow by the river Cam, and visible through the trees from the college rooms Forster occupied in his second and third years as an undergraduate, before he became an Apostle. Forster's set was then W7, at the top of staircase W; H. O. Meredith "kept" across the landing, in W8, for the same two years, and had the same view. Since then Forster's cow has taken on a philosophical life of its own, at least among poets. "Is the Cow there?" is Rupert Brooke's boldly pencilled comment, almost a re-titling, at the head of Sonnet 114 in his annotated copy of Edward Dowden's 1905 edition of Shakespeare's Sonnets, now in

King's College Library. Richard Wilbur's epigrammatic "Epistemology" makes the influence trans-Atlantic:

I
Kick at the rock, Sam Johnson, break your bones.
But cloudy, cloudy is the stuff of stones.

II
We milk the cow of the world, and as we do
We whisper in her ear, "You are not true."

In his letter answering my editorial queries about the origins of "the cow of the world", Richard Wilbur writes:

It's sometimes hard to be sure what went into a poem written more than thirty years back, but I can say with certainty that the cow in my poem "Epistemology" derives from *The Longest Journey*. As an Amherst undergraduate, and at Harvard's graduate school, I shared with many a devotion to Forster's novels; it seems to me that it was then possible, without explicit reference to the novel, to express a philosophic attitude by saying, "The cow is there."

Page **5**: "Prelude to Rhinegold" is here the English title for a piano score of the first scene of Wagner's *Das Rheingold*. When Rickie recollects the music at the end of the chapter (p. 16), he quotes the accompanying song of the Rhinemaidens in the original German rather than English; the words in either language of course sound the same and evoke a full operatic performance. Both spellings are those of the manuscript, where the title replaces "a few chords". For the later description of the orchestral music, see p. 40 and its note below.

Theocritus (c. 310–250 B.C.), the Greek poet of Syracuse, in Sicily, was the subject of lectures given by Walter Headlam (1866–1908), a Fellow of King's, during Forster's first year at Cambridge. For Theocritus see also p. 112 and its note below, and for Headlam see also the note to p. 173 below.

Zwieback is in manuscript "Zweiback", the original German name for this "twice-baked" toast or rusk, sometimes sweetened and spiced.

Page **6**: "Trumpery" is made known as Agnes's malapropism for "Trumpington" when Herbert explains his wet foot; see p. 11 and its note below.

Page **8**: in the manuscript "Percival" replaces "Galahad" both here and in the later mention of the picture (p. 155). G. F. Watts painted several versions of his famous "Sir Galahad", associated with Tennyson's poem of that title. In 1897 he completed one for the chapel at Eton College, and it may have been a reproduction of this that Forster first had in mind. Unable to find any published references to a painting of Sir Percival by Watts, I thought that Forster had changed the name to that of the less perfect hero without regard to fact. However, there is a Watts painting, "Sir Perceval", in the Astley Cheetham Art Gallery, Stalybridge. It came from the collection of Charles Rickards to J. F. Cheetham in the 1880s and was presented to the Gallery in 1931. Even though the painting is so little known, it is possible that Forster may have seen or heard of it on one of his visits to Manchester.

Page **9**: Omar Khayyam's pages would be those of his *Rubaiyat*, no doubt in one of Edward FitzGerald's translations. The elements of the poet's well-known wish for wine, bread, a book of verses, "and Thou Beside me singing in the wilderness" implicitly contrast with the surrounding remains of English tea and cake. The Oswego biscuit acting as a bookmark would have been appropriately flat, dry, and narrow, almost more rectangular than oval, and also slightly sweet and crunchy. The name comes from Oswego, New York, because Oswego or "Maizena" wafers, otherwise in the range of Marie or morning coffee biscuits, were made not from wheat but from cornflour, one of the major exports of Oswego. They are not listed among Peek Frean's products after 1932, but in the manufacturer's brochure for 1900 one is centrally placed in a colour illustration of sample biscuits. As for the cake, in the manuscript it was at first a "rich sugary" one, and "chocolate" is "chocolade", again reflecting the German environment in which Forster was writing.

The "Long" is the Long Vacation, when Cambridge students can remain in residence during the summer months for extra reading. "Bedmakers" or "bedders" now do little more than their titles suggest; gyp rooms are still the places for cooking and washing up, although the college servants called "gyps" have long gone.

Page **11**: the road in front of King's College, there known as King's Parade, becomes first Trumpington Street and then Trumpington Road as it runs south. The neatly sunken, spacious gutters which border both sides of Trumpington Street are part of Hobson's Conduit, an eighteenth-century aqueduct bringing water from the south to the center of Cambridge. They cease and their occasional water goes underground outside the entrance to Pembroke College, justifying the pun of "Pem brook". Pedestrians usually find the deep curb easy to avoid.

Page **13**: the order of Herbert's list of famous British commanders reflects the perspective of his time. Arthur Wellesley, first Duke of Wellington (1769–1852), defeated Napoleon's forces in the Peninsular Wars and at Waterloo. John Churchill, first Duke of Marlborough (1650–1722), defeated the French and their allies a century earlier, in the War of the Spanish Succession. Frederick Sleigh Roberts, first Earl (1832–1914), had in 1907 conquered in India, Afghanistan, and in the Boer War in South Africa.

"Tripos", originally referring to a three-legged stool and the disputatious, jesting figure associated with it in the early days of the granting of Cambridge degrees, has become merely the name of the examinations taken for honours degrees at the University.

Page **14**: a "wide-awake" was a soft, low-crowned, broad-brimmed felt hat, punningly so called, according to the *Oxford English Dictionary*, because the felt was without a "nap". Its use was not limited to clergymen.

Page **15**: Marie Corelli (1855–1924) gained fame and fortune with such popular novels as *The Sorrows of Satan* (1895) and *The Murder of Selicia* (1896).

Page **17**: Wagner's music goes into C major. Ansell's dismissive interruption simply redefines the key of E flat and could indicate no more knowledge than a slight familiarity with the names of the black and white keys of the piano. In 1941 Forster explained his own sensitivity to key-signatures in "The C Minor of that Life", reprinted in *Two Cheers for Democracy* (pp. 119–21).

Page **18**: "this side of Madingley" is the Cambridge side; the dell, a botanic preserve belonging to the University, still survives, though it now lies between the American Military Cemetery, created after World War II, and the cut which carries the A45 motorway around to the north of Cambridge. "On Grinds", Forster's first published Cambridge essay (*Cambridge Review*, 1 February 1900, p. 185), also takes note of the dell as it describes walks ("grinds") in the vicinity of Cambridge: "a happy few find the little chalk pit this side of the village where they may wander among the firs and undergrowth, folded off from the outer world."

Procul este, profani is a Latin religious formula, an admonition to the impure to keep away from sacred venues and rituals. It was posted over the door of the summer-house in which the Countess von Arnim wrote in Nassenheide; it is best known in its occurrence as *Procul, o procul este, profani* at line 258 in Book VI of Virgil's *Aeneid*, which Forster was editing during his stay with the Countess. The words are spoken by the Sybil who guides Aeneas through the visit to Hades which culminates in the hero's meeting with his dead father, who shows him the magnificent course of his future life and the fame that will come to their descendants. Moreover, I am very much indebted to Miss Clare Scanes of King's College Library for her suggestion that this chapter may be read not only as a variant of Aeneas's descent into the underworld but also as an inversion of the Transfiguration of Christ recounted in the Synoptic Gospels (Matthew

17:1–8, Mark 9:2–8, Luke 9:28–36). Like Christ, Rickie journeys apart with his three friends, one of them also named James, but to a wilderness of dell rather than mountain, and instead of the glory of transfiguration and a cloud through which a voice speaks of "my beloved Son, in whom I am well pleased", there is only a cloud that shadows and chills the maternal earth as Rickie admits that he hates his father.

The signpost reading "This way to Heaven" recalls the opening of Forster's story, "The Celestial Omnibus", in which the placement of a sign reading "To Heaven" on a blind alley is attributed to the poet Shelley. According to Forster's diary, "The Celestial Omnibus" was written by 12 June 1907, shortly after *The Longest Journey* was published. With its references to Shelley, Keats, Dante, and Wagner, among others, the story concentrates some of the most ideal elements of the novel. The boy-hero first reaches Heaven, or Valhalla, in an enactment of the scene with which Wagner concludes *Das Rheingold*, although in Forster's story the Rhinemaidens have already regained the ring made from their treasured Rhinegold.

Page **24**: Halma is a boardgame for two or four players. The board is chequered and the corners specially marked; men are moved diagonally, characteristically in leaps over other pieces, from their home corner to the opposite one. The first player to fill in the opposite corner wins.

Page **32**: just where the Ansells live is unclear. In Chapter 9 Ansell's letters were at first written from Andover, in Hampshire, but the railway route from Andover to Salisbury, sixteen miles to the south-west, includes Porton, the stop Forster later identified as the original of "Cadchurch". See also the description of the train journey in Chapter 33.

Page **33**: the Hermes of Praxiteles was discovered in Olympia in 1877. The young god looks toward the infant Dionysus, whom he supports with his left arm. In the interview between Ansell and Stephen which was omitted from the novel Stephen remembers breaking the replica, to him "a sort of stone man, holding a baby made of two potatoes" (p. 381).

Page **37**: "went on their way rejoicing" echoes the wording of Acts 8:39.

Page **39**: the Church Defence Institution came into existence in the later nineteenth century to help protect the Church of England against the demands of the Nonconformists who wanted disestablishment. E. R. Norman writes that its "protective activity . . . did have the undesired effect of adding to the Church's appearance as an ally of the Conservative Party politics" (*Church and Society in England, 1770–1970* [Oxford, Clarendon Press, 1976], p. 190).

Page **40**: Rickie perceives Love in terms of the same music that accompanies Agnes at her first entrance (pp. 5, 16); see also the Editor's Introduction, p. xiii.

Page **42**: of the public schools compared to the fictional "Sawston School", Winchester College, which in "The Old School" Forster terms "the most bleached" of the major public schools (p. 292), was founded in 1382 by William of Wykeham, Bishop of Winchester. Eton College was founded in 1440 by King Henry VI; its sister foundation is King's College, Cambridge. Lancing College was founded in 1848 by Nathaniel Woodard for the sons of Church of England families which were not accustomed to sending their boys to public schools; it was the first of the schools established by the Woodard Foundation, which aimed for "the union of classes by a common system of education". Lancing is still intended primarily for Church of England boys, and it shares its patron saints, St Mary and St Nicholas, with Eton and King's. Wellington College was founded by public subscription in memory of the Duke of Wellington in 1853, the year after his death, for the purpose of educating sons of deceased officers. These still make up a small proportion of its numbers, as the seventy scholars of Eton funded by King Henry are still distinguished from the boys not "on the foundation".

Tonbridge School, the model for "Sawston School", was founded not in the seventeenth century but in 1553, by Sir Andrew Judde of the Skinners Company in London, which inherited its governance. As a Free Grammar School it was never intended exclusively for "the poore" or for day-boys, but by the end of the eighteenth century it was a well-established principle that local boys could receive instruction in the classics "on the foundation", and the nineteenth-century history of Tonbridge is much like that Forster gives to Sawston. There were, for instance, at least six nineteenth-century bishops educated at Tonbridge, and although none of them was Roman Catholic, one, William Alexander, became Primate of All Ireland in 1896. In 1889 local demands for a less classical curriculum were met by the opening of the Judd Commercial School. In 1890 Dr Joseph Wood became headmaster and inaugurated changes which greatly increased the number of day-boys, so that in 1893 they were organized into two "Houses", Day Boys A to K and Day Boys L to Z. Forster and his mother moved to Tonbridge so that he could become a day-boy just as the new organization came into effect; in the manuscript "a house of Day Boys" (p. 44) supersedes "Day boys I to P". The Dale Memorial Racquet Court was completed in 1897. The old chapel, built in 1859, was replaced by a temporary iron structure in 1892 and made into a museum; the new chapel was not completed until 1909. At Tonbridge, Forster immediately rose to the top of his form and was a prize-winning pupil, but P. N. Furbank gives a vivid account of his unhappiness and his lifelong "grudge against his schooldays" (*E. M. Forster: A Life*, vol. 1, pp. 40–8). Furbank also identifies "Mr Jackson" with Isaac Smedley, a Tonbridge master who moved to Westminster School in 1897. By contrast, Herbert Pembroke is an inimitable stereotype, modelled on everyone and no one, but his talent for organization and the substance of his exhortations bear some relation to qualities Forster associated with Dr Wood, who became Headmaster at Harrow in 1898. Recollections of the school anthem usually accompany Forster's severer criticisms; see p. 158 and its note below.

Page **43**: "service of perfect freedom" is taken from the Collect for Peace in the Morning Prayer of the Church of England, where it is God's service. (*The Book of Common Prayer* referred to in these notes is that of 1662, unchanged until 1928.)

Page **46**: the repetition of "prop" evokes Matthew Arnold's sonnet, "To a Friend", which opens, "Who prop, thou ask'st, in these bad days, my mind?" Arnold's "proppers" are Homer, Epictetus, and Sophocles, "Who saw life steadily, and saw it whole". Rickie Elliot's props also appear to be Greek rather than Christian, despite his allegiance to the Church of England. Plato's belief in a transcendent reality of ideal forms has of course been understood in terms of "spiritual insight" by both neoplatonists and Christian humanists. In *The Greek View of Life* (1896), G. L. Dickinson gives a useful summary of ideas that would have been familiar to Forster; Dickinson includes two sections on women, "The Greek View of Women" and "Protests against the Common View of Women", among his accounts of religion, ethics, "the individual", and art.

Herbert Spencer (1820–1903), unlike Plato, argued that one could only be agnostic about the "Unknowable" and directed his attention to a scientific, materialistic analysis of nature and society; this led to his influential advocacy of laissez-faire as a means of allowing evolutionary processes to weed out the unfit more easily. Considering Plato's famous description in the *Crito* of the philosophic death of Socrates, and Herbert Spencer's resemblance to the pragmatic schoolboys, Herbert Pembroke's expression of his belief in the opposition of religion and philosophy is either peculiarly ignorant or genuinely muddled, or both. Compare also his thoughts of Rickie on p. 287.

Page **47**: the declension of *mensa*, Latin for "table", is still one of the traditional beginning exercises in the forms of the language, but *tupto*, "I strike" or "I beat", is no longer familiar as an introduction to the conjugation of Greek verbs.

The Dikaios Logos ("Just Argument") of Aristophanes' *The Clouds* speaks this passage at lines 1002–8 of the play. In the manuscript of the novel Herbert at first failed to follow Rickie's recitation of the Greek. Forster's paraphrase is closest to the original at the end of the passage; "neglect" of legal "work" is more usually translated as an avoidance of quarrels and being haled before the bar.

A "Cleopatra with a sense of duty" would presumably not have caused her fleet to abandon Antony's at the Battle of Actium in 31 B.C.; a "kindly Medea" would perhaps not have killed her brother to enable her lover, Jason, to escape with her father's golden fleece, nor, married to Jason in Corinth and the mother of his children, would she have fed him the children as vengeance for his adultery. Both the historical and the mythical woman loved disastrously, but Medea, brought to Greece from Colchis, fits Rickie's further description better than Cleopatra does.

Page **48**: Charles Edward Mudie established his subscription lending library in 1842, and it flourished, sending its boxes of books throughout the country, until 1937. Baedeker's *London* (1908) describes Mudie's Select Library, Ltd, at 30–34 New Oxford Street, near the British Museum, as "a gigantic establishment possessing hundreds of thousands of volumes", and notes that its minimum quarterly subscription rate was then seven shillings.

Page **50**: "barley-sugar" is a forcible twisting of the wrist, so called after the twisted sticks of the hard candy.

Page **55**: the landmarks are those of the railway route from King's Cross Station in London to Cambridge; Tewin Water is just north of Welwyn Garden City. In Cambridge Forster's geography is again accurate, though he describes the excavations at the centre of town before following Rickie and Ansell in from the station, which lies to the south-east. King's Parade becomes Trinity Street as it runs north to Trinity College; south-east of the central market place, which is to the east of King's Parade, is Petty Cury ("small cookery"), to the east end of which the station tram would have taken Rickie and Ansell if the wheels hadn't fallen off. (On 24 September 1897 a wheel did come off an omnibus not far from Petty Cury, causing cuts and broken ribs rather than hearty laughter.) The trams were drawn by single horses; the lines of the station tram ran along the route Ansell and Rickie take as they walk west on Station Road and north on Hills Road, but then continued northwards toward Petty Cury past the intersection where the friends wait. The "other" tram, coming west from Barnwell, crossed Hills Road by the Roman Catholic Church and continued along Lensfield Road to Trumpington Street, where its path turned north.

Page **57**: Catiline's conspiracy to take power in Rome failed in 63 B.C., partly as a result of Cicero's speeches against him. Martin Luther inaugurated the Protestant Reformation in 1517, when he nailed his ninety-five theses to the door of the church in Wittenburg. Evolution was a much newer subject, its study intensified by the publication of Charles Darwin's *The Origin of Species* in 1859. Catullus (c. 84–54 B.C.) is celebrated as Rome's greatest lyric poet and is best known for his love poetry.

The Roman Catholic Church of Our Lady of the Assumption and the English Martyrs was built in 1887–90 in a late neo-Gothic style. The money for it was given by Mrs Lyne-Stephens of Lynford Hall, Norfolk, who was Pauline Duvernay, the French ballerina admired by Thackeray, before her marriage in 1845. When her husband died in 1860 he was reputed to be the richest commoner in England, but the Stephens money is said to have originated in the eighteenth-century Bristol trade in port wine, and there is no evidence that any of it came from doll-making. Nor does anyone appear to have "made a fortune out of movable eyes for dolls", though a number of patents for various kinds of eye movement were taken out in the later nineteenth century. Perhaps the movable eyes of the very beautiful French dolls manufactured by Jumeau in the 1880s conjoined with the French origin of Mrs Lyne-Stephens to give imaginative substance to the pun and the legend, which still persists.

Great St Mary's, the University Church at "the heart of the town", lies at the north end of King's Parade, just to the west of the market-place. The "desecrated grounds of Downing" passed by the tram on its way along Lensfield Road are those at the southern edge of the Downing College land, where red-brick villas, to be let by the college on ninety-nine year leases, had begun to be built in 1895; between 1895 and 1901 the land at the northern edge known as the "Downing Site" was also being sold to the University for laboratory buildings.

Page **58**: on the east side of Trumpington Street the "mantling canal" of what is now "Old Addenbrooke's" was a diversion of Hobson's Conduit; a parking lot now fronts the building, which was given its Italianate façade in 1865. On the west side of the street the Corinthian portico of the mid-nineteenth-century Fitzwilliam Museum still looms above many steps, and further north, on King's Parade itself, the late medieval pinnacles of King's College Chapel and the neo-Gothic screen and Porter's Lodge fronting the college still look "like nothing else in the world".

The hotel omnibus bringing the luggage would have been that of the Red Lion Hotel, in Petty Cury, now remembered by the name of the modern shopping precinct, Lion Yard, which has replaced the buildings on the southern side of the street.

Page **59**: Rickie's idealization of Agnes evokes the style of William Blake's visionary art rather than any particular example of it.

Page **60**: St John's Eve is the eve of the summer solstice, and in the manuscript the Christian name replaces "in midsummer". If Forster ever wrote such a story it has been lost; the atmosphere slightly resembles that of "The Story of the Siren", written in 1904 and rejected by editors then, but published as a Hogarth pamphlet in 1920 and reprinted in Forster's later collections. In the manuscript of the novel a deleted reference to two men in search of water also suggests the story Forster imagines in

"Malcolnia Shops", the first essay he published in the *Independent Review*, later reprinted in *Abinger Harvest*. The Latin quotation, once so well known as to be a tag, is the first line of the twenty-second of Horace's Carmine Odes (I, 22.1), in which wild beasts are said to flee from the man of integrity, who is (translations are surprisingly various) "whole in his life and free of shame".

Page **61**: Forster slightly adjusts "take the wings of the morning and dwell in the uttermost parts of the sea", words from verse 9 of Psalm 139.

Page **62**: Forster's academic honours match Rickie's, but Forster read History rather than Greek Archaeology in his fourth year, when he retired to lodgings not in Mill Lane but at 12, King's Parade, across from King's College.

In the manuscript "cow parsley" replaces "white hemlock" here and "hemlock" in its other occurrences (pp. 71, 153). The plants are both Umbelliferae and look similar, but the hemlock is poisonous, and famous for providing the drink that killed Socrates.

The "Great World" is listed as one of the "proper objects of Fear" for Cambridge academics in F. M. Cornford's satiric *Microcosmographia Academica: Being a Guide for the Young Academic Politician* (London, Bowes & Bowes, 1908, p. 13). "Females" are something else to fear, second in importance only to "Giving yourself away".

Page **63**: Peckham, now part of south-east London, would have been a suburb rather than a "sububurb" like Sawston, which seems to be further away from the city. Billingsgate lies on the Thames beneath London Bridge, and its fishmarket long ago gave its name to particularly foul and abusive language. Park Lane, at the eastern side of Hyde Park, represents wealth.

Page **64**: the story of the covenant by means of which Abram and Sarai, childless in their old age, became Abraham and Sarah and the parents of Isaac is told in Genesis 16–17. The "politics of Europe" would have been distracted as Forster wrote by the last appeal in the case of Alfred Dreyfus, the French army officer who became the object of intense anti-semitism when he was falsely accused and convicted of treason in 1894. The formal hearings of the appeal began in 1904; Dreyfus was reinstated and decorated with the Legion of Honour in July 1906. See also the note to p. 202 below.

The verses recording the love of David and Jonathan are found in the Books of Samuel, particularly I Samuel 18 and II Samuel 1:26, where David laments the death of Jonathan: "thy love to me was wonderful, passing the love of women."

Shakespeare's Sonnet 116 describes "the marriage of true minds".

The anonymous "Hall man" would have been a member of a college having "Hall" in its name, like Trinity Hall.

Page **67**: the Cambridge Union Society was founded in 1815 as a debating society and in 1866 moved into its present building, notable for its spacious parliamentary style debating chamber. The luncheon party is full of references to traditional Cambridge activities, from Rickie's mention of his walk toward Coton, a village two miles to the west which is reached most directly by a footpath across fields (and now the M11 motorway), to the suggestion of an excursion to Ely, the cathedral town fifteen miles to the north. May Week festivities of course occur in June, at the end of the Easter or "summer" term, as though May had been delayed until the end of examinations. Not everyone would climb to the roof of King's College Chapel, but most would be shown that one of the fourteen balls on the Clare College bridge has had a wedge cut out of it, reducing the total to thirteen and seven-eighths. The river Cam is so narrow that the races of the rowing shells proceed not by passing but by bumping, and the ordering of the boats is a matter of careful organization; it can take years to advance to the head of the river. And the dramatic society called the Footlights presented its first annual comic May Week revue in June 1883.

Page **68**: J. G. Buol's Restaurant Swiss, open for meals all day, was on King's Parade; it also advertised itself as "well known for Picnics and Garden Parties".

Page **70**: on the three-and-a-half-mile walk to Madingley and its Hall, where Edward VII lived during his student years at the University, Rickie's aestheticism wars with "actuality" not only in his criticism of the pictures of J. M. W. Turner (1775–1860), but perhaps also in his sense that Agnes resembles one of the heroines of George Meredith's novels. Rickie names Clara Middleton of *The Egoist* (1879) in his first letter to Ansell in Chapter 9 (p. 82); in *Aspects of the Novel* (pp. 115–16) Forster gives the double-blossomed cherry tree associated with Clara as an example of Meredith's "banners", less variable than his own "rhythms".

The Arundel Society, named after Thomas Howard, the Jacobean Earl of Arundel who was famous for his art collection, was founded in 1849 for the educational purpose of making copies of great European works of art more easily available through chromolithography. When the project was completed in 1897 the stock was purchased by the Society for Promoting Christian Knowledge.

Page **71**: Rickie's story of the Dryad resembles Forster's "Other Kingdom", written early in 1905 (see p. xlvii) but not published until 1909, when it appeared in the July issue of the *English Review*. In the novel Forster has simplified the story and adapted its setting to the Madingley dell, but in both the fictional and the "real" story one must infer the metamorphosis. The classical model is Apollo's pursuit of Daphne, who turns into a laurel tree in order to escape the god. The picture of "a man running after a maid" which Agnes sees in Rickie's room (p. 8) probably portrays the myth; Mrs Failing alludes to it directly when she expresses her dislike of laurels (p. 91). Among the discarded versions of Chapter 31 there is a deleted description of Agnes "trembling like the tree outside" (p. 379), perhaps another indication of her resemblance to Rickie's Dryad.

The Gog Magogs are hills about four miles south-east of Cambridge, large for their neighbourhood and probably named after the traditional British giants rather than the Gog and Magog of Revelations 20:8.

Page 72: a Dorcas is a women's charitable sewing society, usually affiliated with a church and named after the Dorcas of Acts 9:36–42, who made "coats and garments" for widows and was resurrected from death by Peter.

Forster's diary entries indicate that he himself had some trouble reading James's *The Wings of the Dove* (1902). On 6 July 1904, "Shall read a little Wings of the Dove" appears; on 7 August 1904, "The 'Wings of the Dove' still flag".

Page 75: apparently Rickie missed Ansell's "paper on Schopenhauer" (p. 65), the philosopher who opposed Hegel's idealism by emphasizing problems of perception and will. Schopenhauer was also known for his misogyny, another trait Ansell shares.

Page 77: a dove named Parsival suggests the conclusion of Wagner's *Parsifal*, where a white dove descends to hover over the hero's head as he takes up the chalice of the Holy Grail. By the mid-nineteenth century the Arthurian legends were thoroughly christianized, but in the manuscript Forster abandoned Mrs Lewin's explanation of the link—"We call the dove Parsival because that suggests the Bible without"—before finishing the sentence. The spelling "Parsival" rather than "Percival" brings the name closer to the form Wagner uses, but variants were common; in *The Idylls of the King* Tennyson names the knight "Percivale". It is tempting to think that the green paint suggests a false fertility, not to be aided by the redirected fish which Rickie would have liked.

Page 81: Ansell's letter introduces the quotation from Shelley's *Epipsychidion* that Rickie reads in Chapter 13 (see p. 126 and note). Ansell also appears to have been reading books like George Bernard Shaw's *Man and Superman* (1903), complete with the "Revolutionist's Handbook" that accompanies the printed play.

Page 82: Beatrice inspired Dante's *Vita Nuova*, and in the *Divina Commedia* he made her his guide through Paradise. For Clara Middleton see the note to p. 70 above. In the first scene of *Götterdämmerung* Brünnhilde sends Siegfried forth on his heroic adventures, having taught him all she knows. Goethe's words conclude his *Faust: Das Ewig-Weibliche | Zieht uns hinan.*

In reply, Ansell does not name evil women but inadequate wives who hindered their husbands: Xanthippe nagged at Socrates and became a proverbial scold; in Jane Austen's *Pride and Prejudice* Mrs Bennet's witlessness greatly tries Mr Bennet; in Wagner's *Lohengrin* Elsa, misled by the envious Ortrud (who was in manuscript Forster's first choice), distrusts her new husband enough to break her promise and ask him his name and origin, thus forcing him to return to his Grail kingdom. Ansell's colloquial paraphrase of Euripides is difficult to match to any particular line, but there is a lovely choral dance to the goddess of love in *Hippolytus* (ll. 1268–83), the play which is perhaps the best general reference for Ansell's view.

Page **83**: the old story of an ancient ship sunk in Lake Nemi, in the Alban Hills near Rome, was verified when two pleasure barges of the Roman emperor Caligula (A.D. 12–41) were salvaged in 1931, only to be destroyed in World War II. But Nemi is also the site of the grove of Diana in which the priest gained his position by killing his predecessor in single combat, to become ever-watchful against his own successor, and the problem of explaining this custom is at the heart of Sir James Frazer's *Golden Bough.* Frazer opens his work by reminding his readers that J. M. W. Turner pictures the Sibyl and the Golden Bough associated with Aeneas's journey to the underworld against the landscape of Nemi. Working from others' views, Turner painted the first of these pictures, *Aeneas and the Sibyl, Lake Avernus,* about 1798, before he visited Italy. Forster himself saw the grove in the spring of 1902 and described his visit in an undated letter to G. L. Dickinson: "I went to Nemi the other day, and got right down to the temple of Diana. The place is covered now with lilac purple and blue violets, pale blue and mauve anemones, cyclamen, and grape hyacinths. It's a glorious place."

Page **84**: Margate, on the Isle of Thanet at the easternmost end of the Thames estuary, is a popular seaside resort easily reached by Londoners; the Rhinemaidens, or Thamesmaidens, of T. S. Eliot's *The Waste Land* (1922) seem to expire there: "'On Margate Sands. / I can connect / Nothing with nothing.'"

Stonehenge is of course the ancient stone circle which lies about ten miles north of Salisbury and two miles west of the river Avon. Forster places Cadover about six miles south-east of Stonehenge as the crow flies; see p. 96 and its note.

Page **85**: for "the beginning of life" see Genesis 1:1–12.

A Battlesden car was a variety of two-wheeled road cart, horse-drawn, which originated in Battlesden, Bedfordshire; Forster wrote "Battleston", which spelling was followed in earlier editions.

Page **86**: Fleance, son to Banquo in Shakespeare's *Macbeth*, escapes the assassins sent to kill both him and his father, thus foiling Macbeth's attempt to thwart the witches' prophecy that Banquo's descendants will be kings.

Page **87**: Gilbert and Sullivan's popular comic operas would be more likely to have a chorus of agitated employees than employers. Mrs Failing is inventing one to please herself, although the title of *Utopia, Limited* (1893) might be applied to her farm.

"A thing of beauty is a joy for ever," is the opening line of John Keats's *Endymion* (1818).

Page **88**: Mrs Failing dreams of an Arcadian pastoral in the highly formal terms of John Milton's *Lycidas* (1638). In the last few lines of the elegy Milton describes the poetic shepherd, who sang his lament for his dead friend, "With eager thought warbling his Dorick lay", and then, at sunset, "rose, and twitch'd his Mantle blew: / Tomorrow to fresh Woods, and Pastures new".

Page **89**: Colonel Robert Ingersoll (1833–99) was an American lawyer and politician who championed Darwin. His very popular lectures had titles like *Some Mistakes of Moses* and *Why I Am An Agnostic*. *The Clarion*, published from 1895 to 1934, was the socialist and humanist newspaper edited in London by the self-educated Robert Blatchford (1851–1943). "Mr Blatchford" is mentioned by name in an undeleted passage at the end of the manuscript version of the first paragraph of Chapter 30 (p. 241). He is there conjoined with Ernst Heinrich Haeckel (1834–1919), the German zoologist who accepted Darwin's theories of evolution and coined the term ecology. Haeckel lectured in Cambridge in 1898, outlining twenty-six stages in man's evolution from the simplest organisms. Ernest Renan (1823–92) was the French scholar of Semitic languages who moved away from his theological training and wrote of Jesus the man; Rickie refers to one of his best-known humanist essays in Chapter 16 (see p. 152 and note). Forster's diary entry of 8 March 1904 also mentions Renan: "Reading 'what shall I do to be saved?' an atheistic pamphlet of appalling taste. What would Renan say! I wonder if all vulgarity is the same: certainly it is just now for me." Stephen's cartoon version of Job, from Pennsylvania (abbreviated Pa.), and his other pamphlets are untraceable, and it is very unlikely that anyone named Mrs Julia P. Chunk ever existed. Leonard N. Beck of the Library of Congress, having searched catalogues and the Ingersoll papers to no avail, kindly checked the telephone directories of major American cities as well, and suggests that "Chunk" is "not a name but a sound that Mr Forster thought appropriate for the context". The characteristic American pattern of full first name and middle initial adds to the illusion of reality.

Page **91**: the words of Francis Bacon (1561–1626) in his essay, "Of Atheism", read: "But the great atheists indeed are hypocrites; which are ever handling holy things, but without feeling; so as they must needs be cauterized in the end."

Page **96**: photographs of the "gray box" of Acton House, the home of his Uncle Willie that Forster used as a model for Cadover, appear in James Jamieson's *Northumberland* (1905) and Wilfrid Stone's *The Cave and the Mountain* (1966), where there is also a picture of the Figsbury Rings when they still had a tree at their centre. Acton House has no window at all in its pediment and four "lank pilasters", not five, a number which goes against the Palladian symmetry that does allow a central circular window in the triangle of the pediment. The haha, common in eighteenth-century English landscaping, is a kind of sunken ditch or fence, invisible from the house and its formal areas, which allows an unbroken vista but prevents sheep or cows from approaching too near. The term seems to have originated in the exclamation of surprise or humour suggested by Forster's provision of what sounds like a musical refrain contemporary with its development.

In his introduction Forster refers to "the valley of the Winterbourne" as he describes the location of the Figsbury Rings, east of Salisbury (see pp. lxvii and 304). There are several Winterbourne areas in Wiltshire; in this one the river Bourne runs from the north-east into the confluence of rivers that swell the Avon at Salisbury. Winterbourne Earls, Winterbourne Dauntsey, and Winterbourne Gunner all lie in the valley below the down to their south-east which is "topped" by the Figsbury Rings. Until 1968 trains would stop at Porton, a mile or so further up the valley. Forster condenses the villages slightly and places Cadover on the western side of the valley, still relatively bare of houses. Obviously the names have been changed to protect the innocent (no "Wintersbridge" exists), but Forster gleefully exploits "Cad", even squaring circles once again in the joke about the manufacturers of chocolate, Cadbury Ltd. See the note to p. 188 below for the real villages named Codford; Forster may also have known that the mound called Cadbury Castle, in Somerset, is associated with King Arthur's Camelot. The Figsbury Ring itself (singular in its formal title) was bought by the National Trust in 1930 and is described by the Trust as "an Iron Age A hill-fort, enclosing fifteen acres, univallate, with an inner quarry ditch and traces of an outer defence at the eastern entrance" (*Properties of the National Trust*, 1978, p. 162). The Roman road which Forster describes runs directly east from the Castle Hill of the ringed defences of Old Sarum, the precursor of Salisbury and probably the "Castle Rings" of the Thompsons; the Franco-German conflict they recall would have been that of 1870. The road now bridges both the Bourne and the railway before it climbs the down, and would have gone to Roman London (Londinium) by way of Winchester. It continues as a metalled road only as far as its intersection with the current London road, the A30, which runs north-east from Salisbury to Andover and London.

Page **97**: George Meredith published *An Essay on the Idea of Comedy and of the Uses of the Comic Spirit* in 1877; the Comic Muse presides over *The Egoist*.

Page **98**: "we are all much more alike than we suppose, and much better", is a comment Forster makes in a letter of 7 July 1905 to his friend Arthur Cole (*Selected Letters*, vol. 1, p. 78).

Page **101**: Dido, Queen of Carthage, loved Aeneas and killed herself when he left her to pursue his destiny in Italy. Virgil tells the story in Book IV of the *Aeneid*. In his diary entry of 22 March 1905 Forster considers Virgil's "fitful" use of the light of his interests: "For a whole book it illumines Dido: with the result that for eight books we are not interested in Aeneas." In Book VI Aeneas meets Dido's shade in the underworld, and Rickie thinks of her response in Chapter 12 (p. 109), by which time we have learned that Stephen's horse is named Aeneas.

St Chad, Bishop of Mercia, died in 672 and became the patron saint of springs.

Page **103**: "Father's boots will soon fit Willie", not so far traceable by this title, may have been a song from the music-halls, perhaps similar to "The Hobnailed Boots that Farver Wore", which was composed by R. P. Weston and Fred J. Barnes in 1907 and sung, with its Cockney sound, by Billy Williams. Or it may have been a more sentimental tune related to the death-in-the-family variety of nineteenth-century parlour poetry. Or it might be something wholly of Stephen's own making, like his poem about "Old Em'ly" (p. 112) or his song to the "stone goddess" (p. 118).

Page **104**: the Thirty-Nine Articles of the Church of England codified its doctrines in 1571, and until 1865 members of the Universities of Oxford and Cambridge as well as Anglican clergymen had to subscribe to them. They are printed in the *Book of Common Prayer*.

Page **109**: Eugen Sandow (1867–1925) was a famous strongman who advocated cold baths and body-building exercises; he is also referred to in *Nottingham Lace* (*Arctic Summer*, p. 37).

The "most beautiful spire in the world" is that of Salisbury Cathedral, the highest in England (404 ft).

Page **110**: as Cadover becomes a "perilous house" as well as a dragon's cave the elements of Arthurian romances join those of Germanic epics; experiences in Perilous Chapels test the worth of Arthurian knights, and the perilous seat at Arthur's table could be used safely only by the purest.

Page **111**: the valley of the Avon and the "skull" of the plain are noted in Forster's diary entry of 16 September 1904 (p. l).

Page **112**: the "sordid village scandal" might have been similar to that in the fourth idyll of Theocritus, in which a herdsman tells of coming upon an old farmer making love to a young woman. This and the next few idylls, which have both heterosexual and homosexual elements, provide the classical parallels to the singing contest between Stephen and the soldier.

Page **114**: the Y.M.C.A. is the Young Men's Christian Association, a lay and interdenominational organization founded in 1844 to encourage religious beliefs partly by providing healthy and sober activities as an alternative to "bad company". In Chapter 33 Stephen invokes the Y.M.C.A. when he promises not to drink (p. 266).

"Saucy Mr and Mrs Tackleton", again presumably a music-hall song, is also untraceable, and music librarians in both London and Cambridge tell me that the title sounds a bit odd to them, as though it had been made up for the occasion. Henry Carey's "Sally in Our Alley", on the other hand, has been widely known since its composition in the early eighteenth century, although the last verse is usually bowdlerized.

Page **116**: St George, the patron saint of England, traditionally conquers dragons. For a possible source of Flea's wrestling ability see p. xlvii.

Page **117**: "those woods" are in the manuscript identified as the Clarendon woods, south of Figsbury Rings.

Pan ovium custos is taken from Virgil's *Georgics* (I.17), where the poet addresses the god Pan as "guardian of the flock". See p. 160 and its note for more of the invocation, and see Forster's introduction (p. lxix) for the relationship between Stephen's memory of the sheep and the early "fantasy" chapter. In Forster's short story, "The Curate's Friend", Pan as Faun appears to the curate during an outdoor tea-party on the downs of Wiltshire, apparently not far from Figsbury Rings, but nearer to a beech copse, and saves him from what would have been a mistaken marriage to a woman named Emily. The story was first published in the October 1907 issue of *Pall Mall Magazine*, and Forster's diary entry of 31 December 1904 includes the note that "the 'Curate's Friend' . . . might be worked up and published".

Page **118**: the Demeter of Cnidus sits now in the British Museum, apparently mourning the loss of her daughter Persephone, kept by Pluto in the underworld for six months of every year; with her return comes the rejoicing of the earth mother and spring. Jane Ellen Harrison, in her *Prolegomena to the Study of Greek Religion* (Cambridge, 1903), sums up the

Athenian festival of the Thesmophoria as one in which "magical cere-
monies for the promotion of fertility [were] addressed as it would seem
directly to the earth itself" (p. 165), not only to Demeter as earth goddess.
But fasting was part of the ritual: "The women fasted sitting on the
ground, and hence arose the aetiological myth that Demeter herself, the
desolate mother, fasted sitting on the 'Smileless Stone'." (p. 127)

Page **119**: an acroterium is an ornament, sometimes a statue, decorating
and protecting the edge of a roof, usually at a gable or a corner; the
terracotta dragons of Dunwood House (p. 147) are acroteria, as well as an
indication that it too is a perilous house.

Page **123**: in the Morning Prayer of the Church of England there is a
choice between saying (or singing) the Te Deum Laudamus, which praises
God directly, and the Benedicite, which commands all the "Works of the
Lord" to "bless ye the Lord", and invokes a wonderful array of "works",
including "Showers and Dew", "Frost and Cold", "Lightnings and
Clouds", "all ye Green Things upon the earth", and "ye holy and humble
Men of Heart". By contrast the Litany, which may follow Morning Prayer
on any day, is a prayer of "miserable sinners" asking for mercy, and
freedom from a host of sorrows.

Page **124**: Ibsen's coldest-eyed heroine must be Hedda Gabler, who
brings about her own downfall in the play which bears her name; Eleonora
Duse was playing the part in London in the winter of 1903–04.

Page **126**: Rickie's reading from Shelley's *Epipsychidion* (1821) for the
most part follows the wording and punctuation of the draft of these lines
which was first published as "To ——" among the "Fragments" in Mrs
Shelley's second edition of her 1839 collection of her husband's poems,
often reprinted. Forster was perhaps using his father's copy of the 1853
edition, still among his books at the time of his death in 1970. In 1862
Richard Garnett, in his *Relics of Shelley*, re-edited the fragments. He
included these lines of the draft in a longer sequence entitled "To his
Genius" and changed "it is the code" to "'tis in the code"; later editions
of Shelley sometimes drew on Garnett's version rather than Mrs Shelley's.
Epipsychidion itself reads "it is in the code", and the other substantive
differences between the lines of the finished poem and these of the draft
are "Out of the crowd" rather than "Out of the world", "chained friend"
rather than "sad friend", and "perhaps a jealous foe" rather than "and
many a jealous foe". Of these differences Forster incorporates only the
last. The further lines that he copied into his Dante notebook (see p. xxxiii)
follow the wording but not the punctuation of *Epipsychidion*; the draft
reads quite differently.

Page **127**: the Church of England requires that the banns of marriage, which ask that anyone who knows of an impediment to the marriage declare it, be published at services on three separate Sundays before the marriage ceremony; Rickie would have heard "the second time of asking".

Jessica Thompson's Shakespearean namesake is Shylock's daughter in *The Merchant of Venice*, but "Henry Adams" is probably just a name, not an allusion to the American historian whose best-known work, *The Education of Henry Adams*, although privately printed in 1906, did not become publicly available until 1918, the year of his death.

Page **129**: in "The Curate's Friend" Forster also links Pan and the Christian figure of the Devil (Mrs Failing's "The D."). Erda is the primordial earth goddess of Norse myth who appears in Wagner's *Ring* and becomes the mother of Brünnhilde. Clearly an analogue of Demeter, she is also recognizable in Swinburne's "Hertha", in which a metaphor of the goddess as a "life-tree" develops (see also the note to p. 238). Mars is of course the Roman name for the god of war; when not reflecting the worship of a particular culture Rickie, and Forster, use the Greek names for the gods.

Bulford Camp, now Bulford Barracks, lies about six miles due north of the Figsbury Rings.

Page **135**: "The comedy is finished" broadly echoes "Our revels now are ended", Prospero's line in *The Tempest* (IV, i, 148).

Mr Failing has added "bitter" to the advice in Ecclesiastes 11:1, "Cast thy bread upon the waters: for thou shalt find it after many days".

Page **140**: in the manuscript *Pan Pipes* was at first entitled *In Touch with Nature*.

Page **141**: none of Forster's known stories is called "Andante Pastorale", a title appropriate to his use both of music and of pastoral in *The Longest Journey*, and pertinent also to Rickie's wish that literature could be more like music, expressed in his reference to Wagner's *Tristan und Isolde*.

Page **142**: the *Holborn* perhaps stands in for the *Strand*, whose offices were just off that thoroughfare. In the manuscript there is a deleted sentence, "The offices of the *Holborn* were not unnaturally in St James's Street", which plays on the way both titles are London street-names; in this case the joke emphasizes distance, and suggests that Rickie later goes westward from Cambridge Circus (at the intersection of Shaftesbury Avenue and Charing Cross Road) both to his interview and to his rooms in South Kensington. At the time Forster wrote there was no *Holborn*, although a *Holborn Review* came into existence in 1910 as the continuation

423

of *Primitive Methodist Quarterly Review*, and a *Holborn Monthly Magazine* existed earlier, briefly, from April 1903 to April 1904.

Tilliard is in manuscript "cramming" for the Civil Service examinations; he uses his French to ask for "a small amount of pheasant, if you please", and, on the next page, to think of his "social class".

Page **147**: Dunwood House bears some resemblance to Park House at Tonbridge School, which was built in 1867 as a small boarding-house, then greatly expanded in 1891 and again enlarged in 1896, but Forster has moved it to the front of the school (unless "opposite" can be taken to be generally near) and has also added the terracotta dragons. (Such dragons are by no means common, but some splendid examples survive on Lower Sloane Street in London.) Park House lay on Forster's route to school from Dryhurst, the house in the area called Dry Hill Park where he lived with his mother. Now Hilden Oaks School, it is the original of the Manchetts' house in *Nottingham Lace*.

Page **150**: Miss Herriton would appear to be Harriet, the spinster sister of Philip in *Where Angels Fear to Tread*.

Page **152**: Renan's *"Prière sur l'Acropole"* is a prayer to Athena recording the sense of revelation that came to him on the Acropolis at Athens, showing him her temple, the Parthenon, as a type of the perfect Greek harmony of beauty, wisdom, and spirituality. The revelation came to Renan in 1865, and the prayer, much admired in its time, appeared in the *Revue des Deux-Mondes* in 1876. See also p. 89 and its note above.

Page **153**: in the manuscript the "beneficent machine" replaces a metaphor of "arming for the battle"; the change decreased the heroically chivalrous element in Rickie's acceptance of the challenge of Sawston and perhaps prompted the addition of the reference to the Holy Grail. Usually the "wound" is that afflicting the Fisher King (Amfortas in Wagner's *Parsifal*) rather than the knight who comes to cure him. The "elaborate wheels" of the machine begin to "pinch" on p. 171, foreshadowing the action of the train that gives Rickie his final, fatal wound.

Page **156**: the white silk lining of Herbert's hood identifies him as a Cambridge Master of Arts rather than a mere Bachelor, like Rickie, and answers Agnes's tactful question about her brother's M.A., ignored on p. 14.

Page **157**: "the world in miniature" recurs at the end of Forster's essay, "Breaking Up" (*Spectator*, 28 July 1933, p. 119), as he concludes it by providing his own speech for the breaking-up of a school at the end of its year:

If the impossible ever happens and I am asked to help break up a school what I shall say is this: "Ladies and gentlemen, boys and bies: School was the unhappiest time of my life, and the worst trick it played on me was to pretend that it was the world in miniature. For it hindered me from discovering how lovely and delightful and kind the world can be, and how much of it is intelligible. From this platform of middle age, this throne of experience, this altar of wisdom, this scaffold of character, this beacon of hope, this threshold of decay, my last words to you are: There's a better time coming." And then that school would break up.

Page **158**: Shakespeare's words are spoken by Lancaster in *Richard II* (II, i, 43–47).

Guildford is nearly forty miles west of Tonbridge, well outside the commuting range for a day-boy.

The tone-poems of Richard Strauss (1864–1949), particularly *Ein Heldenleben* (1899), seemed to contemporary audiences discordant, even cacophonous. Forster describes similar difficulties with his school anthem in the introduction to "Literature or Life?" (*New Leader*, 2 October 1925, p. 14), where he disguises the school as "Snobston" and adds recollections of advice like that Herbert provides in Chapter 1 (pp. 14–15):

I am an old Snobstonian, and when I was at school we had an anthem, a slow, undulating ditty, almost impossible to sing in tune. The local organist had composed it, the words were by one of the masters, and the headmaster himself, in the course of a sermon, would sometimes comment on the truths it contained.

> Choose we for life's battle harp or sword or pen,
> Perish every laggard, let us all be men.
> So shall Snobston flourish, so shall England be,
> Serving King and country, ruling land and sea.

Thus the anthem ran, and, as the headmaster said, there was a great deal to be learnt from it. In the first place, we must choose a profession, and, in the second place, having chosen, we must stick. The sword is the noblest choice, because it might lead to the death of a fellow-creature; still, those boys (he always called them "bies") who felt unequal to murder had other opportunities reserved to them. Only, "bies" must stick. They must stick even if it was a case of harps. How depressed I used to feel! The pen was perhaps the best of the three evils presented, but I always imagined it as a quill, to whose squeaks I should be chained eternally. One was clearly going to be a prisoner throughout life's battle—unless, indeed, one had the courage to become a laggard or that equally contemptible creature the "bi" who didn't know his own mind.

425

Page **160**: Maenala (or Maenalus) is an Arcadian mountain range not far from Tegea, so that these lines read, roughly, "Pan, guardian of the sheep, as you love your own countryside, come, O Tegean, favouring". See also p. 117 and note.

Page **161**: the "pinchbeck mean", falsely golden, would be some hypocritical version of Aristotle's concept of a careful balance between excess and deficiency.

"Broad Church" was a term used especially in the later nineteenth century for members of the Church of England who interpreted Anglican doctrines liberally, or "broadly", so that studies like Renan's and Darwin's, for instance, could be considered despite their effect on literal interpretations of scripture.

Valerius Flaccus was a first-century Roman whose only surviving work is an *Argonautica*, incomplete. Ctesiphon, however, although defended by Demosthenes in 336 B.C. for having illegally proposed that Demosthenes himself be given a crown, is not known for any writings.

Page **163**: see p. xlvii for Forster's diary note of the anecdote about "a boy with protruding ears".

Page **165**: according to Matthew 25:31–46, on the Day of Judgement not the Spirit of Humanity but "the Son of man" in his glory will separate the sheep from the goats.

Page **171**: the Authorized Version of the Bible (the King James version of 1611, quoted here throughout) may suggest that the knowledge of good and evil which came with the disobedience of eating the forbidden fruit (Genesis 3) is the "Primal Curse", but it never uses the term; Shakespeare does, however, applying it to Cain's murder of Abel: "It hath the primal eldest curse upon't, A brother's murder." (*Hamlet*, III, iii, 36) See also p. 207, where Mr Failing regards vulgarity as the "primal curse".

Page **173**: Capstone Hill, a rocky prominence some 150 feet high, juts into the Bristol Channel at the centre of Ilfracombe, in North Devon. Its south side slopes down to the Victoria Pavilion, which then had domed glass conservatories on both its east and west sides, "Winter Gardens" famous for flowers throughout the year. The original setting of the holiday was Eastbourne, on the English Channel thirty miles directly south of Tonbridge, and in the manuscript the second use of "Winter Garden" replaces a reference to Eastbourne's Marine Parade.

The Fragments of Sophocles were to have been edited by Walter Headlam (see the note to p. 5) after the death of R. C. Jebb, but Headlam also died soon after he took over the project, which was completed by A. C. Pearson in 1917. The last of the three plays mentioned by Forster is properly called *Philoctetes at Troy*. *Philoctetes* itself is one of the seven plays which survive in full; more than a hundred have been lost.

The value of growing potatoes is also mentioned in Forster's letter to his mother of 2 July 1905, from Nassenheide, when he quotes the Count von Arnim's objection to conversations about literary earnings: "I never talk of my potatoes, though they are ten times as interesting and valuable." (*Selected Letters*, vol. 1, p. 76)

Page **176**: Morthoe or Mortehoe, four miles west of Ilfracombe, is the village nearest to Morte Point, which runs westward into the sea at the north end of Morte Bay and Woolacombe Sands.

The counties between Devon and Kent are Somerset, Wiltshire, Hampshire, and Surrey, variously pastoral.

Page **178**: according to the Supplement to the *Oxford English Dictionary*, "beak", in its meaning of "magistrate" or "justice of the peace", developed into schoolboy slang for "schoolmaster" relatively late in the nineteenth century.

Sight of the Gorgon Medusa's ugly head turned viewers into stone; Perseus used a reflecting shield to approach and decapitate her, then used the head as a weapon. Native of a land far from Greece, Medusa would be doubly out of place in pastoral Arcadia. Mr Jackson's reference to her introduces a series of counterpoints between stoniness and life which develops to include statuary when Widdrington and Ansell move to the Elgin Room of the British Museum (p. 182), where the sculptures brought to England from the Parthenon by Lord Elgin are preserved. The handsome torso of the river god Ilissus, or Ilissos, is part of the group from the West Pediment; Forster describes it more fully in an early story, "Simply the Human Form" (*Arctic Summer*, p. 239). Ansell's route back to the reading-room accords with the plan of the Museum at the time Forster wrote; the Ephesus Room and the small Greek Ante-Room in which the Demeter of Cnidus was placed lay to the south of the sculptures honouring Athena.

Page **183**: the epic shields of Homer's Achilles and Virgil's Aeneas are engraved on one side only; Forster has adapted their complexity to the proverbial concept of a shield coloured differently on either side, so that one must see "the other side of the shield" to take in the whole.

Page **186**: revivalistic literature is evangelical and fervent in its faith in Christ, whose words of forgiveness even for crucifixion are found in Luke 23:34.

Page **188**: the Church Army is an Anglican organization founded in 1882 on the model of the Salvation Army. Codford St Mary and Codford

St Peter are villages in the Wylye Valley west of Salisbury, with Codford Circle and Codford Down to their north; the name could easily have contributed to the invention of "Cadford".

Page **193**: Forster's diary entry of 11 January 1908 gives his own response to the constellation Orion, seen on a moonlit, windless night: "Orion a ghost, but the sight of him gives physical joy, as if a man of the kind I care for was in heaven." The constellation also appears, unnamed, in Forster's story of the future, "The Machine Stops", first published in 1909. And in his story of Hell, "The Point of It", published in 1911, the overcivilized hero remembers "the stars that drove me almost mad at night once": "It would be appalling, would it not, to see Orion again, the central star of whose sword is not a star but a nebula, the golden seed of worlds to be. How I dreaded the autumn on earth when Orion rises, for he recalled adventure and my youth." The soul lying next to the hero then remembers the constellation of the Twins and its associated myth: "Castor and Pollux were brothers, one human, the other divine; and Castor died. But Pollux went down to Hell that he might be with him."

Page **195**: Waterloo Station is the London terminus for trains coming from Salisbury (and Ilfracombe) on what was then the South Western Railway. To meet Agnes, Rickie might have found a connection from the south-east that would have taken him to Waterloo Junction, across the road from Waterloo Station. In the manuscript Agnes's trunk is sent down to Sawston by way of Carter, Paterson & Co., a delivery and removal firm now remembered only by older generations, and the omnibus which takes Rickie and Agnes across the river to the "Stores" of the Army and Navy Co-operative Society is perhaps unnecessarily identified as a Westminster one. Rickie and Agnes probably returned to Sawston from Victoria Station, not far from the "Stores", which were until 1922 open only to subscribers; the catalogue for 1907, with illustrations of both store and goods, has been republished as *Yesterday's Shopping* (London, David & Co., 1969).

Page **197**: glossy and slightly larger than *Mind*, which is still being published, *The Windsor Magazine*, "An Illustrated Monthly for Men and Women", cost sixpence and contained articles on contemporary painters and on social and technical matters, like railway engineering, as well as stories and serials by writers like Anthony Hope, Rudyard Kipling, and E. Phillips Oppenheimer.

Page **199**: "The loves which follow are less involuntary" is part of one of the aphorisms of Jean de La Bruyère (1645–96). His belief that one loves well and truly only the first time is expressed in the eleventh of his comments on the heart, "Du Cœur", in *Les Caractères: "L'on n'aime bien*

qu'une seule fois: c'est la première; les amours qui suivent sont moins involontaires."
At the end of 1927 Forster added his own wisdom to La Bruyère's: "love always seems a new experience, however often it recurs, and no one ever said of himself during even his thousandth affair, *'Les amours qui suivent sont moins involontaires'.* He said it afterwards, or of others." (*Commonplace Book,* p. 46) In the manuscript as in the *Commonplace Book* Forster has misspelled *involontaires;* see the Textual Notes.

Page **200**: a "beggar on horseback" misuses his good fortune. There are various forms of the proverb: *Brewer's Dictionary of Phrase and Fable* shows "Set a beggar on horseback and he'll ride to the de'il"; *The Oxford Dictionary of English Proverbs* gives first place to another ending, "and he'll ride a gallop"; Shakespeare provides "beggars mounted run their horse to death" (3 Henry VI, I, iv, 127).

Page **202**: Rickie's "I accuse" probably echoes *"J'accuse",* the opening words of the famous letter published in January 1898 by Emile Zola (1838–1902) in defense of Dreyfus. The French novelist denounced the conspiracy against Dreyfus with such power that he succeeded in being tried for libel, thus bringing wide public attention to the case.

Page **207**: "vulgarity" was discussed by Forster and his friends at Cambridge late in 1903; see p. xxxviii and also the note to p. 89 above.

Page **209**: "the holiness of the heart's imagination" is an adaptation of the well-known passage from John Keats's letter of 22 November 1817 to Benjamin Bailey: "I am certain of nothing but of the holiness of the Heart's affections, and the truth of Imagination. What the Imagination seizes as Beauty must be truth—whether it existed before or not,—for I have the same idea of all our passions as of Love: they are all, in their sublime, creative of essential Beauty." Forster was reading Keats's letters at Nassenheide, and in his diary entry of 20 July 1905 he paraphrases the first sentence above, quoting it as: "I believe in two things: Imagination, and the holiness of the Heart's affections."

Page **210**: "Fight the good fight with all thy might" is the first line of the hymn by J. S. B. Monsell (1811–75), inspired by the words of Paul in I Timothy 6:12. Forster's punctuation indicates that the hymn was being sung to the tune of "Duke Street", by J. Hatton (d. 1793).

Leo Tolstoy (1828–1910) expressed his concern for humanity not only in his novels but also, like Mr Failing, in his efforts as a landlord and in essays. These are translated from the Russian as *What Men Live By, What I Believe, What is Art?, What is Religion?,* and *What Then Must We Do?* Mrs Failing presumably objected both to Tolstoyan intensity and to alliterative titles.

Page **218**: *Benedictus benedicat* is a common grace at academic dining tables. It means "May the Blessed One bless", and the closing prayer which matches it, *Benedicto benedicatur* (p. 226), is translated "May the Blessed One be blessed".

"All the world's a stage, And all the men and women merely players" opens the famous speech of the melancholic clown, Jaques, in Shakespeare's *As You Like It* (II, vii, 139).

Page **227**: Forster reverses the terms of Christ's question, recorded in Matthew 16:26: "For what is a man profited, if he shall gain the whole world, and lose his own soul?" Lytton Strachey makes the same reversal when he too comments on the limitations of mysticism in a review of Blake's poetry first published in the *Independent Review* in May 1906. (*Literary Essays* [1948], p. 147.)

Page **231**: in the manuscript Robert's surname, like Stephen's, is Wonham, a name Forster would have met at Abinger Hammer, in Surrey, where his Aunt Laura lived in the house he inherited from her in 1924.

In the manuscript Byron (1788–1824), not so fashionable a poet in the 1870s as he had been in his lifetime, replaces Tennyson (1809–92), who became Poet Laureate in 1850. Byron is much the more passionate and iconoclastic figure.

Page **232**: Robert's knowledge of contemporary scientific farming probably derives from Count von Arnim's, but in the manuscript he is also identified with "the poet Virgil", whose *Georgics* deal with just such matters, particularly in Book I. The use of chemical fertilizer on the chalk land of Wiltshire has in fact changed the pastoral landscape that Forster knew to one more dedicated to farming. Also, since much of Salisbury Plain is now reserved for military training, walking tours over some of the routes Forster took are no longer possible. He particularly regretted the evacuation of Imber-in-the-Down; see "Little Imber", in *Arctic Summer*.

Page **234**: stones given in place of bread are mentioned toward the end of Christ's Sermon on the Mount, in Matthew 7:9: "Or what man is there of you, whom if his son ask bread, will he give him a stone?"

Page **236**: Mr Elliot resembles Tilliard in his use of French phrases; *de trop* means "superfluous" or "in the way". And his sense of French comedy leads him to quote, apparently with no awareness of irony, from Molière's *Le Medécin Malgré Lui* (1666). There Sganarelle, the "doctor in spite of himself", assures his employer, who wonders how the "doctor" can say that the heart is on the right and the liver on the left, that "we have changed all that": "*mais nous avons changé tout cela, et nous faisons maintenant la medécine d'une méthode tout nouvelle.*" (II, iv)

Page **237**: The long lines of poetry open Section 31 of Walt Whitman's "Song of Myself", published in the first edition of *Leaves of Grass* (1855). In 1868 W. M. Rossetti omitted "Song of Myself" from the carefully inoffensive selection with which he introduced the British public to the work of the American poet.

Page **238**: Swinburne (1837–1909) replaces God with "love, the beloved Republic, that feeds upon freedom and lives", in "Hertha", published with other poems honouring revolution in *Songs Before Sunrise* (1871). Forster refers to the "Beloved Republic" in his own later essays, particularly in *What I Believe* (1938), where he writes that "Love the Beloved Republic" deserves three cheers rather than the two he allots to democracy, and where he concludes a brief political interpretation of Wagner's *Ring* by emphasizing love: "Brünnhilde's last song hymns the recurrence of love, and since it is the privilege of art to exaggerate she goes even further, and proclaims the love which is eternally triumphant, and feeds upon freedom and lives." (*Two Cheers for Democracy*, p. 68) Mr Failing also appears to be thinking of the difficulties of democratic republics in his reference to the Declaration of Independence signed by England's American colonists on 4 July 1776.

Page **244**: Forster's diary entry of 3 December 1905 quotes a poor woman's account of a house "'where you could put plates under the door'". He met her when he opened a train door for her at March, in the Fens of East Anglia, and added the detail of the door to the novel only in typescript or proof. The work on the allotments would be private gardening on land "allotted" for that purpose by the landlord, who might charge for its use.

Page **246**: the river, although likened implicitly to the Styx of Hades, is of course the Thames, which originates in the Cotswolds and cuts its valley through the chalk of the Berkshire downs and the Chiltern hills before reaching London. Hindhead is to the south-west of London, and the river Wey flows north from the Hindhead area to join the Thames above Weybridge, where Forster lived from 1904 to 1924.

The sovereign is a pound, or twenty shillings, and in those days even one shilling would have been a generous tip; one of the farm workers loans Stephen a "bob", or shilling, from the nine he earns each week (p. 215).

Page **247**: Forster's diary entry of 12 July 1904 notes details used here: "My faculty for noticing things certainly gets better: I see . . . that enormous gas lamps hang from public-houses . . . that conductors say 'two pence' not 'tuppence'. But I don't know whether I read people better."

In the manuscript Salisbury is a "Gothic upstart" beside named villages, and two of them, Cadford and Chitterne, replace Harnham, the suburb of Salisbury after which Forster and his mother named their house in Weybridge, and Odstock, a village not far south of Harnham; the changes expanded the geographical range of the references. See the note to p. 270 below for Salisbury's "Gothic" origin.

Page **249**: "Ansell came to the house daily" replaces a complex series of scenes; see pp. 372–85 for earlier versions of Chapter 31. On the first page of the wholly discarded chapter (p. 380), Ansell was at first reading "Hartmann", probably Karl Robert Edouard Von Hartmann (1842–1906), best known for *The Philosophy of the Unconscious*, published in 1869 and translated from the German in 1884.

Page **250**: "the gray torrent of life" recalls G. L. Dickinson's dream at the conclusion of *The Meaning of Good*, where he beholds souls dipping in and out of the river of Time, and feels himself in the midst of "an emotional effect similar to that of twilight, cold, gray, and formless as night itself" ([London, J. M. Dent, 1907], p. 211). Only when he steps into "Turris Scientiae", the Tower of Knowledge, does the scene gain colour and beauty. But Dickinson is adapting other mystic visions, like Dante's at the conclusion of the *Divina Commedia*, and Forster recurs to the concept of rivers as bearers of life throughout the novel.

Page **259**: Cain slew Abel, "And the Lord said unto Cain, Where is Abel thy brother? And he said, I know not: Am I my brother's keeper?" (Genesis 4:9)

Page **261**: the idea that "the sins of the parents are visited on the children" develops from God's commandment that other gods shall not be worshipped: "Thou shalt not bow down thyself to them, nor serve them: for I the Lord thy God am a jealous God, visiting the iniquity of the fathers upon the children unto the third and fourth generation of them that hate me; And shewing mercy unto thousands of them that love me, and keep my commandments." (Exodus 20:5–6)

Page **263**: "And if a house be divided against itself, that house cannot stand" is part of Christ's answer to the scribes who say that he must be a devil to cast out devils. (Mark 3:22–30)
"One nips or is nipped" is a quotation from Stephen, stemming from his wrestling match (p. 117).

Page **265**: in the Bible, Paul advises Christians to avoid sins against the body, particularly fornication, for, "know ye not that your body is the temple of the Holy Ghost which is in you, which ye have of God, and ye are not your own?" (I Corinthians 6:19) The classical Greek respect for the body rests on very different reasoning; in *The Greek View of Life* Dickinson summarizes thus: "to them a good body was the necessary correlative

432

of a good soul. Balance was what they aimed at, balance and harmony; and they could scarcely believe in the beauty of the spirit, unless it were reflected in the beauty of the flesh." ([London, Methuen, 1896], p. 130)

Page **267**: Cithaeron is the mountain range west of Athens where the mystic rites of Dionysus were celebrated. In *The Bacchae* Euripides shows the dangers that await those who approach them without understanding their power.

Page **268**: the prehistoric path called the Ridgeway or Ridge Way to which Stephen refers (there are others) runs north-east from Imber-in-the-Down and then east along the northern escarpment of Salisbury Plain. It reaches a high point (713 ft) at Urchfont Hill, seventeen miles north-north-west of Salisbury, with no higher point intervening. Devizes is four miles north of Urchfont Hill, Bath eighteen miles to the north-west, and Marlborough twelve miles to the north-east across the Vale of Pewsey, and the Marlborough Downs rise to the north again. The Salisbury Avon gathers its waters from east and west in the Vale of Pewsey and cuts south from Upavon through the Plain. Beacon Hill, south-east of Bulford Camp, rises to a height of 668 feet just south of the Camp. In the manuscript Stephen remarks that Stonehenge is "wired in", but still visible "without paying". Reconstruction of Stonehenge was undertaken shortly after one of the stones fell in 1899, and the owners of the site decided to fence it both to save it from vandalism and to reroute the road which then ran through it. The *Wiltshire Archaeological Magazine* for these years gives fascinating illustrated accounts of the works.

Page **270**: "the city" moved from Old Sarum, called by the Romans Sorbiodunum and by the Saxons Sarobyrig, to New Sarum, or Salisbury, early in the thirteenth century, long after the death of William Rufus in 1100. William was killed by an arrow in mysterious circumstances in the New Forest, south-east of Salisbury, which may account for Forster's condensation of the dates. And there was a cathedral built in Old Sarum after William the Conqueror's victory; it was finished in 1092, hit by lightning five days after its consecration and then rebuilt, but in the course of the following century the clergy and the military defenders of the hill clashed. Eventually the clergy moved to the fertile land to the south of the dry and windy hill, and began to build the present Salisbury Cathedral, early Gothic in style, in 1220. As for the city buildings on the slopes, when Forster visited Salisbury he stayed with his family friend, Mrs Aylward, in her house, "Holmleigh", on Milford Hill, east of the centre of the city; in *Marianne Thornton* he describes it as "a tall sun-drenched house balanced high above Salisbury". It is now Douglas House, part of the Godolphin School.

Page **276**: a March Past is usually a military review rather than a matter of memory, as it seems to be here.

Page **278**: "a sky that was still only bright in the zenith" replaces a passage in the manuscript which makes it clear that it is the highest stars that are making the sky bright. Forster's diary entry for 14 April 1904, written at Acton House, comments on this phenomenon and perhaps marks the inauguration of his study of the stars: "Star light followed: my supreme ignorance of the constellations is a comment on the march of knowledge. For a couple of feet above the horizon—I don't know why a couple of feet—they do not appear, and they increase in brightness till they are overhead."

The "bubbles of air" also draw on an observation Forster recorded much earlier, in *Nottingham Lace*, where Edgar feels "the tiny puffs of wind, which seemed to have travelled like little bubbles through miles and miles of cool air to break themselves upon his face" (*Arctic Summer*, p. 38).

Page **279**: an inn called The Antelope is placed at Upavon in one of Forster's unpublished early essays, "Pagus Quidam". The nameless "certain village", where the narrator has trouble finding a place to stay, is perhaps Chitterne or Imber.

Page **283**: in the "fantasy" chapter it is the stock doves "who go to bed early" (p. 336).

Page **289**: Rickie's and Stephen's mother is named "Lucy" once in the manuscript, on a very early page of Chapter 10 (p. 93). Forster implies the almost magical power of personal names when Harold remembers his own at the sight of the Rings (p. 336) and when Agnes calls Rickie's name from the dell (p. 73) and in the Rings, when he is about to acknowledge Stephen as his brother (p. 130). The namelessness of the mother, which is a lack of a Christian name, links her more directly to the ancient powers of the earth.